DENMARK STRAIT

BREIDAFIORD
SNAEFELLNESS

REYKJANESS

ICELAND

VATNA
GLACIER

WEST GREENLAND CURRENT

IRMINGER CURRENT

GREENLAND SEA

The Norsemen's Voyages
of discovery
to North America

——— Erik the Red

··········· Bjarni Herjolfsson

ᴏᴏᴏᴏᴏ Leif Eriksson

——— Thorstein and
Erik the Red

·━·━·━· Thorvald and
Karlsefni

CWM

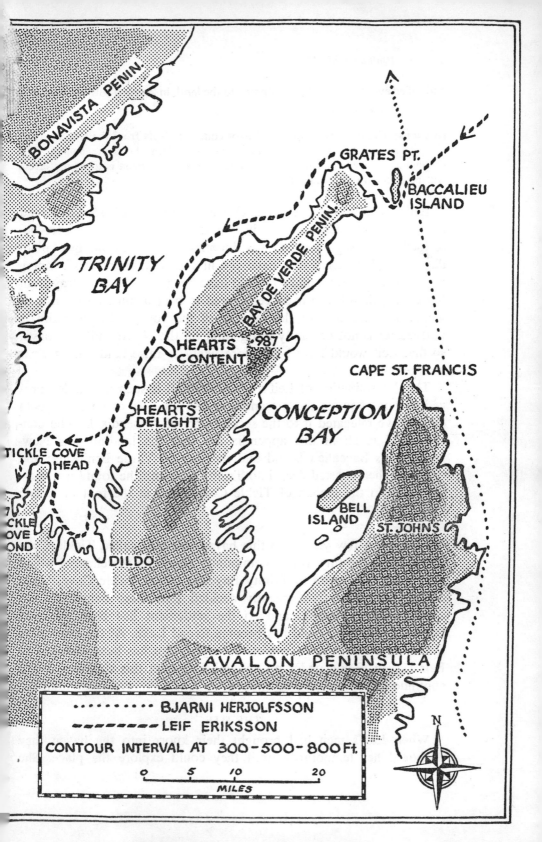

The approaches to Leif Eriksson's Vinland

and sailed away. And Leif gave a name to the land, in keeping with its products, and called it Vinland.

[SOURCES: The first paragraph consists of edited excerpts from the Greenlanders Story. The balance is an unaltered quotation from the same source. The original text, together with the reasons why an edited version is to be preferred, will be found in Appendix L.]

Leif's deep-sea passage from Greenland to Bjarni's southern land seems to have been comparatively uneventful. The northeaster described in the saga account was doubtless one of the famous "nine-day winds," which would have meant that the knorr was running free most of the way, and so would have been less likely to stray from her course than if she had been forced to beat against headwinds. It would also account for the rapidity of the voyage. Furthermore, a northeaster is not generally a fog wind on the Newfoundland coasts, so that Leif would have been more likely to raise land during clear weather.

The determination of Leif's actual landfall is such a complex procedure and requires the presentation and analysis of so much data that I have relegated it to the second part of Appendix L. The conclusions I reach in this appendix are that the landfall was Newfoundland's Baccalieu Island and the Bay de Verde Peninsula; and that Leif then coasted deep into Trinity Bay until he found a wintering place in the lagoon of Tickle Cove Pond at the foot of Tickle Cove Bay.

Up until a few years ago this haven was still called Tickle Cove Pond, while the tiny fishing community alongside the channel which connected the lagoon to Trinity Bay was called Tickle Cove. Some doltish bureaucrat has recently decided that these names do not carry sufficient dignity, and so the settlement has been renamed Bellevue, while the pond has become Broad Lake. At the same time the name of the nearby hamlet of Famish Gut has been changed to Fair Haven. Being under no obligation to abet this stupidity, I will continue to use the original names.

THE SITE

When Leif's men had brought their knorr into the haven they anchored her temporarily until they could explore the place. She

westviking

THE ANCIENT NORSE IN GREENLAND
AND NORTH AMERICA

/\

by Farley Mowat

MAPS AND DRAWINGS BY
CLAIRE WHEELER

c. 1

An Atlantic Monthly Press Book

LITTLE, BROWN AND COMPANY · BOSTON · TORONTO

The author wishes to thank Munksgaard A.S. for permission to re-
produce the Sigurdur Stefansson Map of 1570 from their volume
Islands Kortlaegning: en historisk fremstilling, by N. E. Norlund,
Copenhagen, 1944

ATLANTIC-LITTLE, BROWN BOOKS
ARE PUBLISHED BY
LITTLE, BROWN AND COMPANY
IN ASSOCIATION WITH
THE ATLANTIC MONTHLY PRESS

Published in Canada
by McClelland and Stewart, Limited

PRINTED IN THE UNITED STATES OF AMERICA

For Claire

/V.VV.\

ONE

ΛΛΛ

the westward thrust

GREENLAND
AS THE NORSE KNEW IT
and
THE EXPLORATIONS
OF ERIK THE RED
Legend
▲ dorset eskimo sites
▣ possible norse ruins
⊕ key mountains
▬▬▬ explorations of erik
the red 981-984 a.d.
▭▭▭▭ later norse routes
•••••••• search for skraelings
circa 1260 a.d.

ALTI
HAFSBOTNINN
MELVILLE BAY

SNÆ-
FELLS

NORTHERN
OBYGDIR

GREENLAND

HRAFNS FIRTH
BAFFIN BAY

NORDR-
SETTUR

BAFFIN
ISLAND

DISCO I.

WESTERN
OBYGDIR

CUMB-
ERLAND
PENIN.
7100'

KARLBUDA
CAPE DYER

HRAFNSGNIPA
7300'

BLASERK
11,000'
MT. FOREL

GUNNBJORN'S LAND

VESTRI OBYGD ROUTE

EASTERN
OBYGDIR

GUNNBJORNS
SKERRIES

CUMBERLAND
SOUND

BJARNEY
HVARFSGNIPA

N
W   E
S

VESTRI
BYGD

ICELAND ROUTE

SKUGGIFIORD
UNGAVA BAY

CAPE CHIDLEY

THE
NORSE
SETTLE-
MENTS

MID
BYGD

HVARF I
NORWAY ROUTE

HELLU-
LAND

MARKLAND ROUTE

HVARF II

OSTRI
BYGD

HVITSERK JOKUL
HAFVERF

ERIKSFIORD
HERJOLFSNESS

CAPE
FAREWELL

1

ΛΛΛΛ
.v.v.v.

the ROAD to GReenland

The Saga Tale (c. 963–981)

There was a man called Thorvald. He was the son of Asvald, son of Leif, son of Oxen-Thori. Accompanied by his son Erik, Thorvald fled from the Jaeder [a district in Norway] to Iceland because he had committed man-slaughters. Iceland was heavily colonized at that time. They settled at Drangar [Highrocks] on Hornstrandir.

Here Thorvald died. Erik then married Thorhild, the daughter of Jorund Atlisson and of Thorbjorg Ship-Bosom who was now married to Thorbjorn the Haukadaler.

Erik now left the north and took his abode at Eriksstadir near Vatnshorn in Haukadale. Erik and Thorhild had a son who was called Leif.

Then Erik's thralls caused a landslide to overwhelm Valthiofsstadir, the home of Valthiof. Eyjolf the Foul, one of Valthiof's kinsmen, slew Erik's thralls near Skeidsbrekkur above Vatnshorn.

In revenge for this, Erik then killed Eyjolf the Foul as well as Duel-Fighting Hrafn, near Leikskalar. Eyjolf's kinsmen, Geirstein and Odd of Jorvi, instituted an action against Erik at the Thing for the slaying of their kinsman, and Erik was consequently outlawed from Haukadale.

Erik then took possession of Brokney and Oxney [islands] but dwelt at Tradir on Sudrey the first winter [after being banished]. At this time [when he left Haukadale] he lent Thorgest [of Breidabolstad] his dais-posts.

After [wintering at Tradir] Erik went to Oxney and dwelt there [again calling his home] Eriksstadir. He demanded the return of his dais-posts but did not get them. He then went to Breidabolstad and carried away the dais-posts, and Thorgest gave chase. They came to blows a short distance from the farmhouse at Drangar and there two of Thorgest's sons, as well as certain other men, were killed.

From this time on each of them retained a large body of armed men with him at his home. Styr Thorgrimsson, and Eyjolf from Sviney, together with the sons of Thorbrand of Alptafirth and Thorbjorn Vifilsson, took Erik's side. The Thorgesters were backed by the sons of Thord Bellower; Thorgeir of Hitardal; Aslak of Langadal and his son Illugi.

Erik and his followers were outlawed at the Thorsness Thing.

A ship was made ready by [or for] Erik in Eriksvag; but Erik himself was concealed by Eyjolf at Dimunarvag while Thorgest and his supporters were searching for him amongst the islands.

[SOURCES: Erik the Red Saga, Karlsefni Saga and the Short Saga] *

ERIK THE RED AT DRANGAR

One foreign outlaw who chose Iceland as his sanctuary was a Norwegian named Thorvald Asvaldsson, who made a hasty exit from the Jaedir district near modern Stavanger about the year 963, "on account," as the saga primly puts it, "of manslaughters." We know little about Thorvald except that the sagas accord him the kind of sonorous genealogy which was reserved for important members of the aristocracy. We do not know the details of his crime either, but since it resulted in national outlawry we can assume it was a satisfactorily bloody one, and no such minor peccadillo as a simple case of murder.

Thorvald seems to have brought along his daughter and a red-headed son of about fourteen years of age named Erik. Other members of the family, about whom nothing has survived in history, may have accompanied the trio, together with a few of the indispensable thralls or slaves.

Thorvald was a late-comer to Iceland. Well before the time of his arrival all the good land had been taken up, leaving little except the lava deserts of the interior and the bleak and forbidding stretches of rocky land along the northern shores. He was forced to settle at a place called Highrocks on the barren and desolate coast of the northwestern tip of the island.

We are told nothing of the life the Thorvalders lived under the

---

* These sagas are identified and discussed in Appendix A. Explanations included by the author are enclosed in brackets.

ƒOREWORD
ʌᴠᴠᴧ

Most of my books have been accidental, in the sense that they
have never followed the carefully calculated course I planned at
their inception. But this book is more accidental than most. It took
its genesis from a desire to write the story of the sea-girt, cod-redolent
island of Newfoundland. I made the island my home and, after
some years there, decided I was ready. I began my story at the
beginning — with the appearance of a handful of Greenland Norse
men in the gray waters off the northern coast.

I intended to give the Norse one chapter at the most. But they
ended up by pirating the entire book right out from under me —
an act which is perfectly consistent with Viking character.

As I delved deeper into the accounts of the Norse voyages across
the Western Ocean I found myself faced with hundreds of conflicting reconstructions and interpretations of the voyages. In order to
synthesize all of them I concluded I would need to spend several
years in close company with an educated computer.

The alternative was to reconstruct the entire tale myself. This
was a somewhat intimidating prospect, since I am no specialist in
the arcane field of Scandinavian scholarship. But was this such a
frightful handicap? A fresh look at the Norse story through the
lenses of diverse studies, including climatology, seamanship, anthro-
pology, zoology and many others, might prove more revealing than
the results which had been achieved by subjecting the subject to the
single-eyed scrutiny of Norse scholarship. And I possess a working knowledge of a great many fields which bear upon the problem
of reconstructing the voyages.

I am a northerner by nature and by residence if not strictly so by
birth. When I was thirteen I made my first venture into the sub-

arctic tundra and I have been back many times since then — usually as an unencumbered wanderer, and always seeking understanding of that immutable world. I have sailed no Viking ships in northern seas, but my father began teaching me seamanship when I was old enough to walk, and I have sailed (and still sail) an antique schooner in the cold waters which hunger at the shores of New-foundland. I know the sea well enough to comprehend something of its mysteries; and I know many seamen of an earlier age (my friends and neighbors in Newfoundland) well enough to lift my admiration for them to the level of a sustained affection. The sea and the north — and the men of both — move me as little else does. I have written extensively about both.

There are a number of minor facets of knowledge and experience which have helped me too. In my youth I trained as a biologist and I have studied many of the beasts whose lives closely impinged upon the lives of the Norse. I was, for ten years, a volunteer observer for the Canadian meteorological service. In the waste of war I learned about cartography and came to value the knowledge locked in maps and charts. I am an amateur anthropologist who has lived with and written books about the men who really owned the north — the Eskimos. As for the Norse, their proud and violent ghosts have haunted me since I was old enough to lift a book, or turn a page. Beyond that I possess a scepticism which is my bane, and my strength. I am constitutionally unable to accept apparent facts without an investigation of my own.

Whether these attributes have been enough to meet the need is something else. To me they seemed sufficient.

There is no point in pretending modesty about what I have attempted. I have made a reconstruction of the Norse voyages which follows no previous book (except the original saga sources) and which is at variance with most, but which I am convinced is closer to the truth than any previous attempt. In detail I believe I have resolved a number of outstanding problems, including the degree of Celtic participation in the westward thrust; the real scope of Erik the Red's explorations; the geographical concepts of the ancient Norse as these applied to the western regions; the conflict between the two main saga sources dealing with the western voyages; the identities of the several native peoples the Norse encountered; the detailed tracks followed by all the voyagers;

the identity and location of the landfalls, havens and settlements; the major factors which prompted, shaped, and sometimes doomed the efforts of the westward venturers; and many lesser matters.

In making my claims I do not pretend that I am always first in the field, for I have been anticipated on a number of points, as I acknowledge in the text. Nor do I ignore the possibility that future writers may find it possible to consign some of my answers to limbo. But if I have been able to clear away some of the deadwood of outmoded concepts which has obscured the true story of the voyages, and so assist someone else to find better answers than mine, I shall be delighted.

This book does not work in quite the usual way. Because I have had to re-examine and analyze every available piece of information connected with the voyages and wring dry, one corner at a time, many obscure bits of evidence, some academic tedium in the text became inevitable. But I wished this book to be read for the sake of the story, and so I have tried to minimize the fault by relegating as much as possible of the supporting evidence to that section of the appendices titled "Analytical." Here it can be read or left alone, depending on whether or not the reader requires to see the proof of every plum in the pudding. Also, since I did not want to slow the narrative more than was absolutely necessary, I have collected much of the relevant background material dealing with such things as ancient climate, Norse ships and navigation into a series of essays which form the "Descriptive" section of the appendices. Although it may be unorthodox, I suggest that the reader would do well to browse through these descriptive essays before starting on the text.

My prologue is a rapid gallop through the history of European voyaging to the west from prehistoric times to the beginning of the Norse venturing. The balance of the book is divided into three sections which deal minutely and chronologically with events between about 960 and 1010 A.D. Most chapters open with the relevant section of the original saga accounts. In the Epilogue I show the unbroken continuity of westward voyaging from the cessation of Norse voyages to the beginning of modern times, and suggest that there was no considerable gap and that the Cabots and Columbus were following old trails.

Footnotes have been kept to a minimum and are almost exclusively devoted to illuminating the text. There is no bibliography because I have made sparse use of other authors' commentaries. When I have drawn upon someone else's work I have acknowledged the fact in the text.

A word of explanation regarding my use of excerpts from the sagas. There are a great many English translations of the several existing saga transcripts and these vary considerably in detail. Rather than adhere slavishly to any single version I have compiled a composite translation, and where conflict between the versions exists I have based my choice on specific linguistic research, the logic of the passage, and my knowledge of the conditioning circumstances. For those who are interested in reading an independent and eminently modern translation of the whole of the relevant sagas I suggest *The Norse Atlantic Saga* (Oxford University Press, 1964) by Gwyn Jones.

ACKNOWLEDGMENTS

I am extremely grateful to the following people for much help in a variety of ways: Mr. Percy Saltzman of the Canadian meteorological service; Professor Gwyn Jones of the University of Wales; Mr. Harold Horwood, St. John's, Newfoundland; Dr. William Taylor of the Human History Branch, National Museum of Canada; Dr. Elmer Harp of Dartmouth University; Mrs. Evelyn Stefansson and the staff of the Stefansson Collection, Dartmouth University; Jane Davison, Mary Macdonald and Esther S. Yntema.

F. M.

Burgeo, Newfoundland

contents

ᐱᐱᐱ

Foreword   vii

PROLOGUE: *The Forerunners*   3

    The Celts and the Picts. The Norse Appear upon the
    Open Sea. The Viking Scourge. The Norse Reach Ice-
    land. Norse Settlement Begins. The Westmen Flee
    Again. Iceland Becomes Norse. Icelandic Society.

      PART ONE: *The Westward Thrust*

1. The Road to Greenland   25
    Erik the Red at Drangar. Erik's Career in Iceland.
    Erik's Predecessors. The Voyage of Snaebjorn Hog.
    Ari Marsson Finds Greater Ireland. What Ari's Story
    Meant for Erik.

2. Erik Goes Westviking   39
    Erik's Course to Greenland. South from Angmagssalik.

3. The Empty Lands   47
    The House at Brattalid. The House at Narssaq. The
    Abandonment of Greater Ireland. Winter on Eriksey.
    Erik Chooses a Homestead Site.

4. The Western Wilderness   58
    Erik's Search Continues. The View from the Mountain.
    The Crossing of Davis Strait. The Vestri Obygdir.

5. Return from Exile   67
    Winter at Holm. Northward Again.

6. The Land-Taking   72
    The Ocean-Whirl. Hallowing the Land.

7. Bjarni Herjolfsson   80
    Herjolfsness.

8. Beyond the Greenland Sea   86

9. America Discovered   93

10. Hiatus   105

PART TWO: *Vinland and After*

11. The Vinland Voyage   117
   The Site. The Climate. The Latitude. The Grapevines. The Prodigal Land

12. Leif's Norway Voyage   132
   Leif's Return. The Rise of Olaf Tryggvason. Thorgunna's Story. Leif's Voyage

13. The Odyssey of Thorgisl Orrabeinsfostri   143

14. Gudrid   154

15. The Cross Comes to Greenland   161

16. Thorstein the Unlucky   168
   Drift. No Directions. Failure. Homecoming.
   Thorstein and Gudrid. The Walking Corpses

PART THREE: *Land-Seeking in the West*

17. Thorfinn Karlsefni   181
   The Greenland Settlements. Karlsefni's Purpose. The
   Western Prospect. The Colonists

18. The Outward Voyage   191
   Plotting a Course. North, West and South. The Lab-
   rador Coast (Helluland and Markland). The Marvelous
   Shores

19. Straumfiord   204
   Sandwich Bay. Belle Isle (Straumey). The Campsite at Epaves Bay

20. The Search for Vinland   217
   The Choice of Epaves Bay. The Nature of the Place.
   The Hard Winter. Where Is Vinland? Thorhall's
   Search. Thorvald's Search

21. The Land of Hope   233
   The Southern Voyage. Hop (St. Paul's Bay). The
   Dorset Boats

22. The Fatal Error   248

23. Death Comes to Thorvald Eriksson   260
    Thorvald's Search for Thorhall

24. Land of the One-Footers   270
    Karlsefni's Course. The Hop at Hampden River. The
    Beothuks

25. Retreat of the Icelanders   281

26. Freydis and the Brothers   287

EPILOGUE: *The Aftermath*   296

APPENDICES

PART ONE: *Descriptive*

A. The Sources   307
   Nature of the Sources   307
   The Sagas   308
   Authenticity of the Sagas   311

B. The Ancient Weather   313

C. Ancient Sea Levels   319

D. Norse Geographical Concepts   322
   I How the Norse Saw Their World   322
   II The Evidence Upon Which the Reconstruction Is
   Based   330

E. Norse Sea-going Ships   344

F. Norse Navigation   351

G. The Ancient Map   364

H. The Vanished Dorsets   372

PART TWO: *Analytical*

I. The Westmen in Iceland and Greenland   387
   I Iceland   387
   II Greenland   390

J. The Old Church Documents   401

K. Bjarni Herjolfsson's Voyage to Newfoundland and Labrador   405

Bjarni's Landfall   405

Bjarni's Voyage Along the Coast   408

L.   Leif Eriksson's Vinland Discovery   418

    I   The Outward Voyage   418

    II   The Location of Vinland   429

M.   Sources Dealing with the Karlsefni Expedition   439

The Location of Hop   447

N.   The Epaves Bay Site (L'Anse au Meadows)   450

O.   Karlsefni and the Beothuk Indians   458

P.   The Norse in Hudson Strait and Ungava Bay   465

Chronology of the Western Voyages   473

Index   479

iLLUSTRatioNs

Fig. 1. Comparative Plans of Greenland Houses   49

Fig. 2. The Airts   359

Fig. 3. Plan of a Typical Dorset House   374

maps

Endpapers   The Norsemen's Voyages of Discovery to North
              America

1   Norse Geographical Concepts   9, 323
2   Greenland as the Norse Knew It, and the Explora-
    tions of Erik the Red   24
3   The Norse Settlements in Southwestern Greenland   46
4   The Discovery and Exploration of Vinland   98
5   The Discovery and Exploration of Helluland and
    Markland   100, 197
6   The Approaches to Leif Eriksson's Vinland   119, 431
7   Leif Eriksson's Vinland   121
8   Grosswater Bay   206
9   Straumfiord   213
10 Sacred Bay   215, 451
11 The Epaves Bay Site   221, 454
12 The Search for Vinland   229
13 St. Paul's Bay   237
14 Thorvald Eriksson at Lake Melville   267
15 The Foot of White Bay and Hop II   274
16 The Sigurd Stefansson Map of 1570   365
17 The Sigurd Stefansson Map Compared with Modern
    Map   367

WESTVIKING

*The Ancient Norse in Greenland
and North America*

ΛΛΛΛ

/.\\.\\.\\.\\

the forerunners

The beginnings of the story of man's conquest of the vast sea barrier which separates Europe from North America is lost in the fog-chilled darkness of the Western Ocean. In the nature of things, we can never know when that restless, groping and grasping unfurred mammal who is ourself first crossed the Western Ocean from east to west. He left no mark of his passing on the faceless waters of the North Atlantic, nor did he raise any beacons on the farther shore which historians could recognize as proof of his accomplishment. He is a shadow out of time, yet he is not without substance. Centuries, and perhaps millennia, after he had vanished, men who were his brothers of the Neolithic Age not only crossed the Western Ocean but spanned the abyss of time itself to land upon the shores of medieval Europe.

They came from west to east. History preserves the records of several such "discoveries" of Europe from America, and there were doubtless more now lost to knowledge. These voyagers were true Neolithic men. Some of them were Eskimos who made the crossing in skin boats called umiaks, surviving examples of which can carry forty passengers on extended voyages. Some seem to have been archaic Indians who may have crossed in immense bark canoes. Examples of these canoes, paddled by twenty to thirty Beothuk men, were still being encountered by European fishing ships far at sea off the eastern coasts of Newfoundland in the seventeenth and eighteenth centuries.

These strangers out of time and space had the assistance of the prevailing westerly winds and currents in the middle reaches of the

North Atlantic; but those who were their peers in northern Europe in dim antiquity had an advantage to offset this. They possessed a line of island stepping-stones reaching out from the British Isles by way of the Shetlands, the Faeroes, Iceland, Greenland and Baffin Island. Nowhere along this route was there an open-water crossing of more than four hundred miles, and in the higher latitudes, currents and prevailing winds favored rather than retarded west-bound voyaging.

THE CELTS AND THE PICTS

The Shetlands and Orkneys, and perhaps the Faeroes too, were reached and settled by a seagoing race of such antiquity that they were dead and gone before the Golden Age came to the Mediterranean. Of the west-voyaging of these prehistoric people we know nothing, but we must credit them with at least as much competence upon the unquiet waters of the North Atlantic as was possessed by the Eskimos and Indians who voyaged eastward in our time. At any rate we know that the Celts and Picts, who supplanted the earlier island dwellers in the north, were seamen born and bred and had long been familiar with the cold Western Ocean when what we are pleased to refer to as the "historic period" on the northern seaboard of Europe began, about the year 330 B.C.

It was then that a Greek mathematician, astronomer and geographer named Pytheas set sail from the colony of Massilia (Marseilles) to put certain geographical theories about the northern regions to the test. Pytheas's ship sailed out past the Pillars of Hercules (Gibraltar) and worked northward until she came to a Scottish port. Here Pytheas encountered local sailors who told him of a land lying six days' distance to the northward in the wilderness of ocean. With their aid Pytheas went to seek that land, and when he came to it he called it Thule. We call it Iceland now, but the name by which the Pictish mariners of twenty-three centuries ago knew it is now forever lost.

Most of the maritime history of the Picts, and of their close neighbors, the Celts of Ireland, is lost. Only tantalizing fragments remain. We know, for instance, that as early as A.D. 232 the Desi, a Celtic people from southern Ireland, were making extensive seaborne raids on the coasts of Cornwall and Wales, while during the same period the Picts of Scotland were so efficient on the seas that they were successfully challenging Rome in British waters.

It is believed that they continued to visit Thule even during the severe climatic conditions which prevailed between the fourth century B.C. and the fourth century A.D.* They probably made no permanent lodgments in Iceland during these centuries, being content to use it as a summer hunting and fishing ground, for the Icelandic climate from Pytheas's time to about A.D. 400 would have discouraged attempts at settlement. Nevertheless, third-century Romano-British silver coins which have been unearthed at two localities in eastern Iceland suggest that there were visitors from the British Isles.

Even if the Picts and Celts had made only occasional voyages to Iceland, one or more of their vessels would eventually have strayed within sight of the Greenland coast, whose range of visibility from seaward averages about sixty miles, with a maximum of nearly a hundred miles.

Written evidence exists to substantiate the view that natives of the British Isles managed to sail more than halfway across the Western Ocean early in the Christian era, or even before it began.

In the literary mélange which he called "The Face of the Moon," Plutarch, who lived between A.D. 40 and 120, describes an "island" † called Ogygian lying five days' sail to the westward of the British Isles. Plutarch goes on to add that the natives of Britain reported knowing of three other "islands," equidistant from Ogygian and from each other, lying in the direction of the setting sun. Then, in the dialogue entitled "The Silence of Oracles," he speaks more specifically of one of these western islands and this time gives his source — a Greek named Demetrius who was a government employee of the Romans in Britain during the first century A.D.

Reporting on conversations between himself and natives of the British Isles, Demetrius told Plutarch of the existence of a large "island" which lay at a considerable distance westward from Britain and which bore a native name that sounded, in Demetrius' ear, like

*For a survey of the most recent conclusions of climatologists about ancient weather conditions in the northern regions, see Appendix B.

† Until well into the seventeenth century the word "island" was interchangeable with the word "land," and did not necessarily mean a body of land surrounded by water. Eurasia was regarded as the only continent. Any land which one reached by sailing across the sea was an "island," no matter what its size.

Cronus. Demetrius was naturally familiar with the Mediterranean Cronus myth, and we can imagine his surprise and curiosity at this apparent evidence that the natives on the Atlantic seaboard shared the Cronian legend, and even believed they knew the location of the land where the Titan, Cronus, was imprisoned.

There are good grounds for the belief* that the land whose name sounded to Demetrius like Cronus was identical with Greenland. It is a fact, at any rate, that for some centuries after the time of Pliny the Elder, geographers applied the name Cronian Sea to the waters lying beyond Iceland and bounded on the west by Greenland.

During the fifth and sixth centuries A.D., coincidental with the beginning of a long-term improvement in North Atlantic weather conditions, the navigation of the Britons, Picts and Celts began to loom large in written history for the first time. According to a recently published study of shipping and commerce in Northern Europe, the ships of these peoples came to dominate the waters of the Channel, the North and Irish seas, and even more northerly waters, as far as the coasts of Norway. Furthermore, they were apparently making more or less routine voyages to Iceland, where they procured eiderdown feathers, sea-mammal products and other exotica, some of which eventually reached Mediterranean markets.†

The vessels they used were proper ships, ranging in type from the carvel-built wooden vessels favored by the Picts and Britons to the hide-covered curraghs of the Celts.‡ An example of a fourth-century Romano-British ship recovered from the bed of the Thames gives us some idea of what the wooden vessels of those times were like. She was 60 feet long, had a beam of 16 feet, and her mast was 10 inches in diameter at the butt. Her lines were those of a sea-going ship, and she was probably not much inferior to schooners of equal size which were sailing regularly between Newfoundland and Europe well into the twentieth century.

---

* See Appendices I and J.

† *The Northern Seas,* by A. R. Lewis (Princeton University Press, 1958). By A.D. 450 what amounted to a Celtic thalassocracy existed in the Irish Sea, extending from Dalriada in Ireland to Brittany and Spain. Lewis says of it: "Though this Celtic maritime empire owed much to surviving Roman tradition in West Britain, it seems to have owed more to the earlier Celtic maritime strength in the Atlantic. . . . ."

‡ Curraghs must not be confused with the tiny, skin-covered coracles used by the ancient Britons on lakes and rivers.

Nor were the Celtic curraghs inferior to the wooden vessels of the Picts and Britons. The fact that they were covered with oxhides, instead of being planked with wood, did not detract from their seaworthiness. Fifth- and sixth-century curraghs were big, sturdy, sea-kindly ships which carried crews of up to twenty men and were able to freight considerable cargoes between Ireland and the coast of Spain. As was the case with the vessels of the Picts and Britons, the curraghs were propelled by squaresails, with auxiliary oar power for calms or for navigation in narrow waters.

The use of squaresails does not imply that these vessels were unhandy and could only run before the wind. Such acknowledged experts as Alan Villiers (not to mention innumerable masters of square-rigged ships) have demonstrated that square-rig is nearly as efficient as fore-and-aft rig, and will enable a well-designed ship to go to windward quite successfully.

The sixth and seventh centuries witnessed the full flowering of Celtic and Pictish maritime activity, with regular trading voyages being made all the way from mid-Norway to Nantes in France, and with occasional voyages to points both farther north and farther south.

It was during this period that the accounts of the voyages of the Celtic priest, St. Brendan, were composed. The Brendan story suffers from the imagination of the Irish, and it has been dramatically overcolored. Nevertheless it unquestionably preserves the memory of at least some actual voyages to real places. It is particularly explicit in its description of northern landfalls, and it demonstrates a working knowledge of navigation to Iceland, Greenland, and perhaps even to Jan Mayen Island.

During this period the Picts were trading regularly to Norway and into the Baltic. They were also firmly established on the Orkneys, Shetlands and Faeroes. In the last quarter of the sixth century, Picts of the Orkneys embraced Christianity. They and the Celts may have had semipermanent hunting and fishing settlements in Iceland by this time, for the climate there was steadily growing more amiable, coincidental with a general improvement in the weather of the whole North Atlantic region. But permanent settlement by Picts or Celts was probably still at some distance in the future since Iceland, despite the phenomenal fishing and sea-hunting which it offered, was a long way off and there was as yet no shortage of land at home in either Ireland or Scotland. Nor had these countries as yet been subjected to population pressures great enough to set an emigration wave in motion.

THE NORSE APPEAR UPON THE OPEN SEA

Up until this time the Scandinavian peoples apparently did not possess either the knowledge or the ships with which to engage in deep-sea voyaging. They were, in fact, late-comers to the open sea. Although there have been a number of archeological finds of Scandinavian boats which were built earlier than the seventh century, there are no truly ocean-going ships among them, and there is nothing to show that the Norse were capable of making deep-sea voyages before the latter part of the seventh century. Prior to this date their maritime activities seem to have been limited to coasting and fishing voyages, or to short trading trips in the relatively narrow and protected waters of the Baltic. Their trade was largely land-directed toward the Germanic regions to the south, or toward the Russian regions to the east. They had little need of deep-sea seamanship and ships, and had developed neither.

But during the later part of the seventh century a rising internal turmoil was beginning to trouble the Scandinavian countries. The Northmen were developing an appetite for luxury goods and were liberating themselves from a life of hard simplicity. Celtic and Pictish trading ships from Britain not only helped to feed and to increase this appetite but, by their mere existence, must have suggested to the Norse a means by which they could burst out of their constrained northern regions and so be able to seize what they wanted from the rich aliens to the south. The sea was a path many men could travel, and for many different reasons.

There seems to be little doubt that the Northmen began their deep-sea venturing in ships patterned after the hull models of Pictish and Celtic vessels, and that they made their first major open-water voyages along the routes to Scotland, Ireland and the Outer Islands* — routes which had been pioneered by the elder seamen of the British Isles.

The Norse were quick students. Furthermore they had independently developed a type of ship construction, based on the clinker-

---

* These included the Shetlands, Orkneys and Faeroes.

NORS
GEOGRAPHICAL CONCEPTS
circa 1200 a.d.

GREENLAND AS
ENVISAGED BY
THE NORSE c1000ad

O C E A N U S

BJARMALAND
(RUSSIA)

FINNMARKEN

HAFSBOTNIN

(SPITZBERGEN)

HALOGA-
LAND

NOR-
VEGIA

(SWEDEN)

HAFSBOTNIN

NARVO

FAEROE
SHETLAND

IRLAND

ISLAND

THE WEST SEA

HAFSBOTNIN

VEST
BYGD

EAST
BYGD

HAFSBOTNIN

(BAFFIN ISLAND)

VESTRI
BYGD

GINUNGAGAP

SKUGGIFIORD

HELLULAND
(LABRADOR)

MARKLAND

VINLAND
(NEWFOUNDLAND)

M A R E

TO
AFRICA

built wherries and skiffs they had used for fishing and coasting since late Neolithic times, which lent itself admirably to the building of ocean-going ships.

The times were also on the side of the Norse. Early in the eighth century socio-economic changes in Europe brought about a rapid decline in the seafaring activities of Ireland and Scotland. Internal troubles hastened the decay so that by the end of this century the mercantile fleets of the Celts and Picts had all but vanished from the seas. At the same time as this decline and collapse, the north was boiling up with an immensely vital ferment which was to send the Viking hordes spilling out over most of Europe, eastward into the far reaches of Russia, southward to the Caspian and Mediterranean seas and, eventually, westward to America.

The population of ninth-century Norway, Sweden and Denmark was composed of two disparate elements: the aboriginal inhabitants, who were an amalgam of peoples of the long-headed Neolithic type, overwashed by many diverse waves of forgotten immigrants; and a "master" race, originally known as the Aesir or Eastmen, who conquered the entire Scandinavian region at about the time of Christ. The Aesir (whose ruthless qualities have been so much admired in modern Germany) resisted the effects of racial assimilation with such success that in the ninth century their recognizable descendants still remained the aristocracy of Scandinavia. It was these men who, in the main, comprised the true Vikings and who organized and led the seaborne raiders who terrorized the littoral peoples of Europe for three centuries.

However, even before the Viking terror began, there were already sailings south from Scandinavia as small but stout clinker-built trading vessels, modeled on Celtic ships and manned by the elder Norse, began reviving the use of those sea routes which were being abandoned by the Picts and Celts. Late in the seventh century small groups of these plebeian Norsemen had begun to arrive in the Outer Islands — in particular the Faeroes and the Shetlands — where they intermingled with Pictish inhabitants and with Irish Celts who had settled there as early as A.D. 600. During the next century this trickle developed into a steady flow which lapped at the shores of northern Ireland and Scotland, since not only were the narrow agricultural lands of Norway becoming badly overcrowded, but the depredations and aggressions of the Vikings upon each other's homelands and peoples were becoming unendurable to many ordinary folk.

These yeomen Norse were true immigrants. Besides engaging in farming they took part in and probably greatly improved upon the local fisheries in their adopted lands, since fishing was a trade at which they were unexcelled. Many of them even gave up their pagan beliefs and accepted Christianity.

The native people of the Outer Islands, the Hebrides and northern Ireland, were passionate Christians who followed a Celtic variant of the Roman faith and often lived in semireligious communities. These colonies of papas, as the Norse called them, were not comprised solely of monastic ascetics, although this is the way they have usually been represented. Because there was as yet no rule to bar men of the cloth from leading normal sexual lives, most of the clerics were married men with families. Ascetics did exist, of course, and some of these individuals chose to live the life of starving hermits on barren islets and bare rocks where they could mortify the flesh in high medieval style; but those islands which were capable of providing a decent livelihood held much more rational Christian communities, where the cry of the newborn lamb mingled with the cry of the newborn acolyte.

While the early Norse immigrants seem to have had no particular dislike of the papa societies, and to have intermingled with them on good terms, the Vikings had nothing but contempt for Christians; and Viking contempt was usually fatal to those who earned it.

THE VIKING SCOURGE

Following in the sea paths traced by the emigrant Norse, the Vikings began raiding the outlying islands early in the eighth century. The islands were easy targets, and relatively rewarding ones. The Christians tended to lavish much of their resources on church furniture of gold and silver, and Celtic, Pictish and Norwegian settlers alike possessed valuable herds of sheep and cattle. From about 750 onwards, the Outer Islands were seldom free of Viking marauders. The scope of these raids was rapidly extended until by the turn of the century coastal Ireland, the Hebrides, northern Scotland, the Orkneys, Shetlands and Faeroes had all become singularly unhealthy havens for those who cherished the quiet life and worshipped Christ.

Many of the residents of the exposed mainland coasts of Ireland

and Scotland fled for safety to the interior of their countries, although even there they were by no means secure. But the Christian Norse-Celtic-Pictish populations of the islands had no interior regions into which they could retreat. We are told that the islands were abandoned to the Vikings, who established pirate strongholds on them until new waves of pagan Norse from western Norway eventually moved in and occupied the abandoned farmsteads.

The question of what happened to the displaced islanders has seldom been posed, let alone answered. One thing is certain — they would hardly have sought refuge on mainland Scotland or Ireland, which by this time had become the main magnets for Viking attention in the west, if they had been able to find a safer sanctuary somewhere else.

And a safer refuge did exist. It lay only four or five days' sail westward from the Shetlands and Orkneys, and only two days' sail from the Faeroes.

It is hardly open to dispute that the peoples of the Outer Islands must have known for centuries of Iceland's existence, and that they knew how to reach it and had the means to do so. The climate of this era was so genial that Iceland would have offered excellent conditions for stock farming as well as for fishing and sea-hunting. It was still effectively out of reach of the Vikings, whose longships (unlike the Norse trading vessels) were notoriously unseaworthy. Furthermore, the Norse of this period did not even know of Iceland's existence.

Iceland would have been a veritable paradise for a maritime people seeking a safe refuge where they could lead quiet, pastoral lives and devote as much time as they liked to religious activities without fear of interruption or attack. And there is sufficient evidence (which is examined in the first part of Appendix I and in Appendix J) for us to conclude that some if not most of the fleeing islanders did make their way to Iceland and established permanent settlements there during the early decades of the eighth century.

By the beginning of the ninth century the Viking terror lay over most of western Europe, and was still swiftly spreading. There were few countries bordering on the North Atlantic which were not being savaged by the Norse hordes. Most of Ireland was in Viking hands, as were the northern counties of Scotland, together with the Outer Islands.

Iceland was still untouched, but its days were numbered. The secret of its existence as a Celtic sanctuary could not have been kept indefinitely from the Vikings, who by this time had penetrated deeply into the fabric of the shattered Celtic society in Ireland, and the Pictish-Scottish societies of northern Scotland. Celtic and Pictish slaves, renegades or concubines serving the new master race must frequently have let the secret slip. In all likelihood the Vikings knew about Iceland for some decades before they did anything about it. As long as there were more rewarding targets to be found along the continental coasts of Europe, the Norse raiders would not have been much tempted by the remote fishing and farming settlements in the far western island. Furthermore, it was not until early in the ninth century that the Vikings, after suffering some appalling losses due to the unseaworthiness of the longships, began to appreciate the advantages of building vessels after the models of the plebeian merchant ships in which Norse traders had been successfully sailing the open ocean routes for many generations.*

THE NORSE REACH ICELAND

The surviving Scandinavian accounts of the first Norse voyages to Iceland, which took place in the middle of the ninth century, imply that the Norse discovered the island entirely by accident of wind and weather. But this contention is highly suspect in view of the fact that all of the early Norse visitors to Iceland were professional Vikings, which is to say they were pirates and sea raiders.

One version gives the credit for the initial visit to Naddod the Viking, who was supposedly storm-driven into the Western Ocean until he encountered Iceland. According to another version, first place belongs to Floki Vilgerdarsson, "a great Viking" who apparently sailed from Shetland, but who (so we are told) *knew* where he was going. Ingolf and his foster-brother Hjorleif, both pirates, are also listed as having been early arrivals. Before settling in Iceland, Hjorleif "went harrying in Iceland . . . he harried far and wide, winning great wealth there and taking ten slaves captive. . . ."

---

* These ships are described in Appendix E.

Although the Norse sources do not admit that Iceland was first visited by Vikings who were engaged in purposeful voyages of reconnaissance, this is probably the correct explanation of how and why they first appeared off Iceland's coasts. Certainly the subsequent actions of these first Norse visitors are hardly what we would expect from mariners who had been accidentally blown off course and who would have presumably been anxious to regain their intended ports. Naddod, for instance, remained in Iceland until after the first autumnal snowfall. Gardar Svavar, a Swedish Viking (and another of those who is credited with the first "discovery"), is supposed to have been blown there while making a voyage to the Hebrides to claim his wife's inheritance. If this was true, he could have been in no hurry to collect it, for he leisurely coasted the southern part of Iceland, wintered in the west, and completed a circumnavigation of the island the next summer.

Floki Vilgerdarsson took his departure from the Faeroes, and we are told that he knew where he was going. He and his companions spent two winters in Iceland, although there is nowhere a mention that this was intended as a settlement voyage. Floki and his companions returned to Norway, and it was not until some years later (when King Harold Fairhair was making it difficult for independent-minded Vikings to remain in that country) that Floki or any other Norsemen came out to Iceland as settlers.

We will probably be close to the mark if we envisage increasing numbers of Vikings in a new kind of vessel (one which looked far more like a merchant ship than a longship) descending on the Icelandic coasts and "harrying far and wide" until they had filled their holds with stolen cattle, slaves, and whatever else they could seize from the luckless Christian settlers whose next to last sanctuary in the west this was.

In accordance with well-established Viking precedent when over-wintering in the lands of their victims, the raiders sought out remote and lonely havens which were easily defensible, where they could sit out the winter months free from the dangers of reprisal attacks. This is why men like Gardar and Ingolf deliberately eschewed the many welcoming havens Iceland offered, and which they undoubtedly saw, in favor of wintering at some of the worst places on the coasts. Karli, who accompanied Ingolf, makes the point when he grumbles, "to an evil end did we pass through goodly countrysides, that we should take up our [winter] abode on the outlying cape."

The first Vikings probably did not care to risk wintering in the "goodly countrysides" because these were still occupied by Westmen,* who outnumbered the raiders and who would have taken a sharp revenge on any Viking they could catch. Hit-and-run raids would have been the Viking order of the day, at least until the number of raiders grew large enough so that the inhabitants could be swept away by main force.

The fact that several of the first Norse arrivals overwintered suggests another common Viking practice. When a man was outlawed from Scandinavia, with everyone's hand against him, or when he fled from it to avoid blood vengeance, it was often the custom for him to spend his time of exile buccaneering.† Individual exiles who owned their own ships sometimes joined forces with other Vikings in order to take part in raids on rich but well-defended territories in mainland Europe; but often they operated independently on less well protected if less rewarding coasts, such as Iceland in the 860's would have had to offer.

There is no reason to suppose that the pattern of events in Iceland was any different from that elsewhere in the Norse-dominated area. First came isolated raids which increased in intensity as word of a new source of loot spread. Then, when the ability of the inhabitants to offer any real resistance had been destroyed, came occupation. Most histories of Iceland state that although the island was reputedly discovered by the Norse about 860, no settlement was begun until 874. This hiatus becomes explicable when we interpret it as being the raiding period during which the local population was decimated or driven out.

NORSE SETTLEMENT BEGINS

The first Norse settlers seem to have been that same Ingolf and his foster-brother Hjorleif who had made a previous voyage to the island sometime in the 860's. By about 874 these two had managed,

---

* The Norse called all the inhabitants of the British Isles by this name, but it applied more specifically to the Scots, Hebrideans and Irish.

† Sentence of exile was usually for a term of one to three years.

after committing a series of killings, to make even Norway too hot to hold them, and they were forced to look for homesteads somewhere else. Since the Outer Islands, north Scotland and Ireland were already crowded with Norse pirates and freebooters, they decided to try their luck in Iceland. Most of the other early Norse settlers were also men who, for one reason or another (usually murder), were unable to remain in Norway, or even in the Outer Islands. These seem to have been such super-Vikings that even their peers could not tolerate them. Numbers of them followed hard on Hjorleif's and Ingolf's heels.

These outlaw's outlaws were the vanguard of a great wave of Viking settlers which began to break over Iceland around 880 as a result of the attempts of one of their own number to unify all Norway under his personal rule. This man, King Harold Fairhair, had no scruples about using Viking methods on his own kind. When the local chiefs and jarls proved reluctant to accept his suzerainty, it was his summary practice to put them and theirs to the sword.

Since the Viking aristocrats were dedicated to freedom (by which they probably meant much the same thing most of us mean when we use the word today; that is, license to do what we please without interference), they reacted fiercely to the threat of any restrictions being placed upon their enterprising natures. The struggle which ensued was brought to an end when the Viking fleet was decisively defeated by Harold at the battle of Hafrsfiord in 885. After that there was nothing left for freedom-loving Norsemen but to flee the country and find new homes elsewhere. Iceland seemed just the place to go, and go they did in such numbers that within fifty years they had occupied all the land worth having.

THE WESTMEN FLEE AGAIN

The Celts and Picts in Iceland would have realized that the appearance of the first Norse ship heralded the inevitable approach of an armada of Viking raiders who would be followed by Viking land-seekers. Those Westmen with well-developed instincts for survival would have fled the island. But where could they have gone?

The Faeroes, Shetlands, Orkneys and Hebrides were ruled out because these were completely dominated, and mostly occupied, by Vikings. Most of northern Scotland was in Norse hands, or subject to constant raids. Almost all of coastal Ireland was under Norse control, and the raiders were making incursions deep into the central parts of that country. The Viking scourge was now at its worst, and there was precious little safety from it even in England or in France. But, there was still the west. There was, in particular, that land which we now call Greenland and whose existence was known to the Irish as early as the sixth century. It would have been even better known to the Westmen settlers of Iceland in the ninth, since it is unthinkable that they could have lived in Iceland for any length of time without gaining some familiarity with the neighboring land.

Possibly the earliest Westmen to make the crossing of the by then ice-free Denmark Strait had been anchorites seeking ultimate seclusion. Archeologists have found a number of small stone cells along the southeast Greenland coast which are strongly reminiscent of anchorite cells in the Orkney Islands. Some of these are sited in the most inhospitable surroundings imaginable — just the sort of places which the masochistic ascetics preferred.

At the time of the Norse invasion the Icelandic Westmen may no longer have possessed enough ocean-going ships to have enabled them to transport their people, goods and cattle on the long ocean passage to the nearest eastern lands. They would have had little need for such large craft, particularly if, as was evidently the case, they were being kept in contact with their onetime homelands by merchant ships sailing from south Irish or from British ports. However, they would have had numbers of small craft of the curragh pattern which they used for fishing and sea-hunting. These were adequate for the 260-nautical-mile crossing of the narrowest part of the Denmark Strait to Greenland.

Fleeing Westmen would hardly have chosen to resettle themselves on the barren and forbidding east Greenland coast. It offered little or no pastoral land and, besides, it was far too close to Iceland for safety. With or without advance knowledge to guide them, they would have coasted south, rounded Cape Farewell (or passed through one of the sounds separating it from the mainland) and turned north searching for an area suitable to their pastoral needs and one which also offered a reasonable degree of security against discovery by the Vikings. They would have found ample lands in southwestern Greenland at the bottom of the deep Julianehaab fiords. For reasons which are set out in the second part of Appendix I and in

Chapters 1 and 2, it seems clear that this is indeed where many of the fugitive Westmen went.

ICELAND BECOMES NORSE

The flood of Viking immigration into Iceland which began soon after the year 870 slackened only slightly after King Harold Fairhair's death, for he was succeeded by another ambitious warlord who was determined to perpetuate the concept that Norway should be a unified and single kingdom. By A.D. 900, barely thirty years after the arrival of Ingolf and Hjorleif, Iceland had a population of nearly twenty thousand people; and by 930 this had apparently increased to nearly forty thousand.

In addition to the main wave of Scandinavian Vikings there had also been a great influx of Vikings from Ireland, Scotland and even England. After being held in subjection to the Norse for generations, the native peoples of those lands were now rising against their overlords, and many Viking settlers who had long ago seized land in the British Isles (and were themselves often of mixed blood as the result of their ancestors' free intercourse with native women) were finding it hard to hang on either to lands or lives. Many of them set sail for Iceland, preferring safety and lean times there to fat times and flames at night in the lands which would not stay conquered.

In the entourage of these British Vikings were numbers of native slaves as well as upper-class Celts and Picts, and even some Britons, who for one reason or another (usually expediency) had thrown in their lots with the Northmen, and who could expect little mercy from their compatriots if they remained at home. By 950 as much as 20 percent of Icelandic blood lines may have been non-Scandinavian. It is certain that, far from being the gigantic, flaxen-haired, blue-eyed people of heroic legend, the Icelanders tended to be small in stature, at least by modern standards; and many of them were dark-haired people who were more Celtic than Nordic in appearance.

Thus there were many diverse elements in the Icelandic population to dilute the Viking strain, a blessing for which modern Icelanders have not, perhaps, given thanks enough.*

---

* The Nobel Prize–winning Icelandic author Halldor Laxness gives a devastating picture of the nature of Icelandic Vikings in his book *The Happy Warriors*, London, 1958.

ICELANDIC SOCIETY

Icelandic society was divided into three classes. There were the aristocrats — primarily composed of Viking champions — who held most of the land. Below them was a larger group of less wealthy and less powerful yeomen who held part of a chieftain's lands in fief, or else owned small properties nearby and lived under his protection. Finally there was a large class of slaves, thralls and nominal freedmen, some of whom had been taken captive on raids as far afield as the Mediterranean.

In 930, when the first Althing, or national assembly, was convened on the gloomy plains of Thingvellir in southwestern Iceland, there were about four hundred chieftains who had parceled all habitable Iceland out among themselves. They were a supremely touchy, arrogant and independent lot who were united in only one thing — their fierce determination to resist any real diminution of their individual freedoms. It was this set determination which gave birth to what has often been called, if somewhat loosely, the first western democratic republic.

Whether it was democratic or not (or even a republic) depends on the interpretation of the words. The chieftains foregathered every spring on the plains of Thingvellir and here they "legislated" the laws under which the island lived. But these laws were unwritten, frequently unenforced, and often unenforceable, since there was no law-enforcement agency of any kind. Disputes were legion, and if a chieftain was not actually engaged in bloody skirmishings with his neighbors, he was almost certain to be taking judicial action against someone. These disputes were theoretically settled at the Quarter Courts, or local Things. However, an award of damages, of compensation against an aggressor, or even a judgment of outlawry against a malefactor had to be enforced by the person who had made the claim or lodged the charge.

In many cases justice was evaded by the use of legal trickery or massive bribes, or, if that failed, the supporters of the accused could draw their weapons and either drive the accusers into the hills or so cow the assembly that proceedings would be discreetly dropped. There was little security of life, limb or property except that which could be provided and defended by force of arms. Blood feuds perpetually swept the island like brush fires. The concept of indi-

20 · *Prologue*

vidual honor had become so highly refined that a derogatory remark
could lead to the destruction of the offender and his entire household by fire.

When one searches the Landnamabok, a contemporary Icelandic
history which lists almost every man and woman of importance
who lived in Iceland during the first decades of its occupation by
the Norse, it is difficult to find references to more than a handful
of men who died natural deaths. The majority seem to have died
violently at the hands of their fellows. The accounts of murders,
ambushes, burnings, human sacrifices and general mayhem are on
such a scale that it is a little difficult to understand how the Icelandic
race survived at all. Fortunately it was fecund.

A single quotation from the Landnamabok will give the flavor
of the times.*

Thorodda married Torfi, the son of Valbrand, the son of Valthjof, the son of
Orlyg . . . Torfi slew the men of Kropp twelve of them together. He also especially promoted the slaughter of the Holesmen, and he was at Hellisfitar, with
Illugi the Black and Sturli the Godi [priest] when eighteen cave dwellers were
slain there. They also burned, in his own house, Audun the son of Smidkel
at Thorvardsted.

These cave dwellers, by the way, may have included remnants
of the Westman population who had sought refuge in the lava caves
of the interior instead of fleeing the country.

The general contempt for life if not for law was reinforced by
a steady influx of outlaws from Scandinavia, where the rudiments
of order were being forcibly imposed by a series of short-lived kings.
By 900 it had become the custom for a man outlawed from the
mainland to flee to Iceland. Manslaughter, a euphemism for murder,
was then about as common as fist-fighting is today. Nor was it
considered particularly reprehensible — except perhaps by the victim's kin. The records of the times make it clear that a man was not
thought much of unless his battle-axe, heavy sword, or two-handed

---

* The best account of these conditions is to be found in Njal's Saga, which, incidentally to its blood and smoke, gives an excellent picture of Icelandic life around
the beginning of the eleventh century.

A discussion of the Landnamabok and other Icelandic sources is to be found in
Appendix A.

javelin had let out the life of at least one human being. The victims did not need to be foreign enemies; in fact the killing of a doughty neighbor could bring more renown than the killing of an alien warrior in a distant land.

The lives of men or of prized livestock could be bought and paid for with almost equal facility. Every free man had his value depending on his rank and connections. If his killer was rich, and agreeable, compensation could be arranged in cash. But if compensation went unpaid or if the judgment of the peer court went against the murderer, a sentence of outlawry was usually mandatory.

A man who had been outlawed had to remove himself from the community, or from the country, depending on whether the sentence was one of local or national exile; otherwise anyone could split his skull without fear of having to pay compensation. However, if the outlaw could muster sufficient strength he could and often did stay home, surrounded by armed retainers, and ignore the sentence. Outlawry was not a punishment as we understand the term; it was primarily intended as a means of giving tempers time to cool, in the usually fruitless hope that a blood feud would be prevented.

This was Iceland during the final decades of the tenth century. This was the springboard; these were the people; and the west lay waiting.

cold shadow of Drangar glacier, but from what we know of conditions on the smaller holdings in Iceland during this period we can guess at what it must have been like. The farmhouse would have consisted of one rectangular room whose low, thick walls were made of layers of peat interspersed with layers of stones to give them weight and stability. There would have been a single low door at one end of the structure, and no windows at all. Light entered through a smokehole in the roof, or through skylights which were shuttered over in the wintertime. Big timber was scarce in Iceland even then, and roofs were built without large beams. Rows of posts supported an extraordinarily heavy sod thatch by means of a system of small cross-rafters. The overall appearance of such a house was somewhat similar to that of a primeval burial mound.

Two rows of posts down the center of the room divided it into three narrow naves. The center nave contained a long, open fireplace. The two outer naves were largely occupied by built-up earthen platforms. Benches and tables stood on these during the daytime. At night they were removed and the members of the household slept upon the platforms. Halfway along one platform stood the high-seat of the master of the house, flanked by ornately carved dais-posts. Opposite, on the other platform, stood a less pretentious chair for the use of the guest of honor. Members of the family, friends, freedmen and slaves sat on benches to left and right of these central chairs, their distance from them being determined by their rank and importance.

A number of small outbuildings surrounded the farmhouse. These included a kitchen, pantry, bathhouse, occasionally a privy, and the byres and stables for the half-wild sheep and goats, scraggy little cattle, pigs and ponies.

The entire economy of the farm turned on meat and dairy products, since few grain crops could be grown in Iceland even during the best years of the warm epoch. Milk formed the staple food. It was fermented to make a sour curd called skyr which, together with butter and cheese, was stored away against the winter months when the starving cattle went dry.

No one lived by farming alone. Fishing was vital to survival and so was the hunt for seals, porpoises and small whales. Bread and even gruel were luxuries, and since most grain had to be imported, there was seldom the solace of beer.

Life on small holdings such as Highrocks was not much better than a bare existence. To such exiled aristocrats as Thorvald and his son Erik it must have seemed a far cry from the relatively luxurious and well-fed life enjoyed by the well-to-do Vikings in southern Scandinavia. When in due course Thorvald died, Erik wasted no time bettering his lot. He promoted a most advantageous marriage with a girl named Thorhild Jorunsdottir whose mother bore the imposing name of Thorbjorg Ship-Bosom. The girl's stepfather seems to have been a wealthy landowner in the fertile farming district of Haukadale in the western marches of the island.

ERIK'S CAREER IN ICELAND

After the marriage Erik abandoned the miserable Highrock holding in exchange for a farm in Haukadale — a farm which was almost certainly part of his wife's dowry. Here he prospered for a while. Then one day a neighboring farmer named Valthiof was buried alive with all his family under a landslide triggered by Erik's slaves. There must have been reason to suspect that the slaves had been acting under Erik's orders. At any rate Valthiof's relatives drew this conclusion, and one of them, Eyjolf the Foul, retaliated by murdering the slaves.

Erik made no attempt to take this killing to law, a fact which strengthens the suspicion that he was the instigator of Valthiof's death. Instead he took revenge by slaughtering both Eyjolf and his companion, a champion known as Duel-Fighting Hrafn. This exploit gained Erik a champion's reputation but it also got him into serious trouble. He was cited for manslaughter and an action was started against him at the local Thorsness Thing.

Erik had stirred up a real hornet's nest, and the array of enemies against him at the Thing was strong enough to secure a conviction and a sentence of local banishment from the Haukadale district. By the rules of the game his life was now forfeit to anyone who cared to try to take it, so long as he remained in Haukadale. Erik fled in haste, doubtless suspecting that he and his family stood a good chance of being "burned in," as the saying went, in one great conflagration of house and people. He departed so hurriedly that he did not even take his dais-posts with him, but left them behind in the care of a neighbor named Thorgest.*

---

* Apart from their monetary value, which was considerable, dais-posts had a symbolic significance which made them almost priceless to their owners. They were

Erik and his family fled first to Tradir, on westward-facing Breidafiord, where they spent the winter. In the spring they moved out into the fiord to the island of Oxney — a choice which presumably owed more to the tactical value of living on an isolated island than to the good qualities of the land. Once established at Oxney, Erik made a necessarily surreptitious journey back to Haukadale to reclaim his dais-posts. Thorgest refused to part with them, perhaps because he felt that Erik was in such bad odor locally that he could not enforce his claim. But Erik had no intention of going home empty-handed. The likelihood is that he pretended to depart from the district but actually hid with his followers in the birch forests until Thorgest and the bulk of his retainers departed on some journey or another. Erik then raided the farm and seized his posts.

Erik would have anticipated a pursuit and, in time-honored Viking style, doubtless arranged an ambush and waited for the angry Thorgest to ride into it. Two of Thorgest's sons and several of his supporters were killed in the ensuing mêlée and Erik was able to proceed triumphantly homeward, his reputation much enhanced by the affair.

This new slaughter brought both the Breidafiord and Haukadale districts into the fray, and for the next year or two there must have been great skirmishings, both with weapons and words, between the opposing factions. The home farms of both principals became armed camps, while Erik and Thorgest each sought by bribery, cajolery and threats to gain the support of as many powerful men as possible.

Erik was able to muster a good deal of support — but Thorgest was able to rally even more. In the spring of 981 Thorgest's party was strong enough to force an action at the Thorsness Thing, and since Erik had not the strength either to break up the assembly or to defeat Thorgest in open battle, he could not prevent a verdict of manslaughter. This time it was more serious. He was outlawed from Iceland for three years.

What the verdict meant in fact was that Thorgest and his followers were strong enough to take summary vengeance on Erik anywhere in Iceland — if they could catch him. But Erik still had friends. He and his family hid with Eyjolf of Sviney on that worthy's island stronghold,

---

the visible symbols of his rank and were intimately linked with his honor. They were also believed to be imbued with magical attributes, particularly when they bore the head of Thor, the Hammer God.

while a ship, which Erik had probably purchased some time earlier against just this eventuality, was hurriedly made ready for sea. Haste was of the essence, since Thorgest and his men were already out among the islands of Breidafiord searching for Erik's hiding place. The Thing would have been held quite early in the spring, and we can assume that by midsummer Erik and those of his supporters who did not dare remain behind were ready to flee into exile. But exile where?

Erik had made his decision. Like his father before him, he intended to sail west.

ERIK'S PREDECESSORS
The Saga Tale (981)

When Erik was ready he said to them [his friends and supporters] that he intended to look for that land which Gunnbjorn Ulf Dragesson saw when he was driven westward across the sea and found Gunnbjorn's Islands.

[SOURCES: ERIK THE RED SAGA, KARLSEFNI SAGA AND THE SHORT SAGA]

Although most authors appear to believe that Erik was the first Norseman to visit the mainland coast of Greenland, the probabilities are overwhelmingly in favor of there having been a good many previous voyages during the century or more between Gunnbjorn's accidental voyage and Erik's intentional one.

From references in the Landnamabok it would appear that Gunnbjorn discovered some offshore islands and saw the Greenland mainland behind them, not very long after Gardar is said to have discovered Iceland — perhaps as early as 877. There are many references to Gunnbjorn's Skerries (Islands) and Gunnbjorn's Land scattered through the Icelandic sources, and from the casual manner in which they are usually mentioned, they seem to have been well known. Their exact location is not certain now, but the modern consensus is that they lay in the vicinity of Angmagssalik, almost due west from Breidafiord.

It seems certain that Gunnbjorn's discoveries had served, from a very early date, as landfalls for Icelanders bound for Greenland to take advantage of the excellent hunting to be found there. By the end of the ninth century the steadily warming climate of the North Atlantic region had brought about a pronounced northward retreat of the populations of walrus and pelagic seals off Iceland's coasts; whereas the icy waters of the polar East Greenland Current had preserved the sea mammal hunting grounds on the east Greenland coast. An abundance of polar bears, large pelagic seals, walrus and other sea beasts would have been more than sufficient incentive to ensure that enterprising Icelanders would make regular voyages to that region across the narrow Denmark Strait.*

THE VOYAGE OF SNAEBJORN HOG

Gunnbjorn's Skerries are specifically mentioned in connection with two Greenland voyages of which Erik's was the later one. The first was made by a man named Snaebjorn Hog, circa 980. What follows is a free version of the story of this voyage, taken from the Landnamabok.

A man named Hallbjorn married Tongue-Odd's daughter Hallgerd. The young couple spent the first winter of their marriage at Tongue-Odd's house and there was little love lost between them.† Snaebjorn Hog, who was a first cousin of Tongue-Odd, was also there that winter.

In late May, which was moving time in Iceland, Hallbjorn began to get ready to move out of his father-in-law's house. When Tongue-Odd saw this he hurried off to the hot spring near Reykholt where his sheep pens stood. He did not want to be around when Hallbjorn left because he suspected that his daughter Hallgerd did not want to leave home and that there would be trouble. Odd had already spent much time trying to mend matters between the couple.

When Hallbjorn had saddled the horses he went to fetch Hallgerd from where she was sitting in her bower. When he called upon her to get up and come with him, she neither said anything nor did she move. Hallbjorn called her three times without result, then he sang a snatch of a pleading song, but this did not move her either. At last he twisted her long hair in his hand and tried to drag her out of her chair, but she still would not budge. Thereupon he drew his sword and cut off her head.

When he heard about this, Odd sent a messenger to Snaebjorn Hog asking him to ride in pursuit of Hallbjorn. Snaebjorn did so, accompanied by twelve men. They caught up with Hallbjorn near some small hillocks, and three of Snaebjorn's men and both of Hallbjorn's companions were killed. Then someone sliced off Hallbjorn's foot and eventually he too was killed.

---

*The importance of the influence of climatic conditions (particularly water temperature) on sea mammal population and distribution, and on the peoples who depend on sea mammals, is discussed in Appendix B and in Appendix H.

† This would have been an arranged marriage.

In order to evade blood vengeance from Hallbjorn's kin Snaebjorn set off on a voyage in a ship of which he was half-owner. Rolf the Redsander owned the other half. They each took twelve shipmates. Snaebjorn's companions included his foster-father Thorodd and Thorodd's wife. Rolf's main companion was Styrbjorn, who after a dream sang this song:

> The bane I see
> Of we two fellows.
> Frightful are all things
> To seaward, to the northwest.
> Frost and cold
> And fearful wonders.
> Such things tell of
> Snaebjorn slaughtered.

They sailed away to find Gunnbjorn's Skerries and [after that] they reached land where Snaebjorn would not let them go ashore by night. But Styrbjorn left the ship and found valuables hidden in a grave mound. Snaebjorn hit him with an axe, and knocked them out of his hand.

They made a stone hut for themselves and they were soon snowed in. In the spring they dug themselves out.

One day while Snaebjorn was working on the ship and his foster-father Thorodd was in the hut, Styrbjorn and Rolf killed Thorodd. Then the two of them slew Snaebjorn.

They sailed away after that and reached Halgoland [in the north part of Norway], from whence they returned to Iceland, where Rolf and Styrbjorn were killed by Sveinung, who in turn was murdered by Thorbjorn.

As is the case with most of the snippets of history contained in the Landnamabok (most of which are primarily intended to illuminate what is essentially a massive genealogy of the early settlers of Iceland), mention of this voyage is incidental to an explanation of what happened to the people who were involved in it. Still, we must be grateful for what little we are told.

No reason is given why Snaebjorn should have chosen northeastern Greenland as a place to go while he waited for things to cool off at home. But except for the purpose of hunting walrus, narwhals, polar bears, white foxes and seals, it is hard to think of any reason why the party should have sailed first to Gunnbjorn's Land and then northward to a region which Styrbjorn's verse — the oldest and most reliable part of the tale, since it is a surviving snatch from the original oral tradition — tells us lay to the northwest of Iceland and was remarkable for frost and cold. They must have gone a fair distance north too. The climatic conditions they encountered suggest it, and so do the winds and currents which took them to northern Norway after their departure from Greenland.* It is not unlikely that they wintered in Scoresby Sound which as late as the nineteenth century was noted for an abundance of walrus and polar bears.

The finding of the grave mound may have taken place soon after they reached Greenland and need not have happened in the north. The grave may have been the relic of some forgotten shipwreck; but on the other hand it may have been the burial place of some earlier voyager from Iceland, either Norse or Westman.

It is inconceivable that Erik would not have heard all the details of such a gloriously bloody affair within a very short time after Rolf's return to Iceland; but it is unlikely that the news added anything to his knowledge, or had any bearing on his plans. He knew about Gunnbjorn's Land and it is clear that a voyage to that locality was no novelty for Icelanders of his time.

Early voyages to northeastern Greenland by Icelandic hunters would have been one source of information for Erik to draw upon, but there could have been another and more valuable one. By 980 Iceland was full of Irish and Scots, both slaves and freemen, together with a good many Norse immigrants from the British Isles who had Celtic or Pictish blood in their veins. These people must have had much to tell, no matter how vague their information may have been, of the lands to the west which had been visited by Celtic mariners and which were variously known to the Icelanders as Albania, Hvitramannaland, or Irland Mikkla.

There is also a strong likelihood that Erik had specific knowledge of, and interest in, one particular Celtic discovery lying to the westward of Iceland; and he may have had a decisive personal reason for setting out in search of it when he went into exile.

This was Hvitramannaland (White Man's Land) or Irland Mikkla (Greater Ireland) as it was often called.

---

* The likelihood is that they deliberately sailed for Norway, both to dispose of the products of the winter hunt and to allow time to intervene before they dared return to Iceland.

ARI MARSSON FINDS GREATER IRELAND

Ulf the Squinter, son of Hogni the White, settled the whole of Reykness between Godfiord and Goatfell. His wife was Borg, the daughter of Eyvind Esstman and the sister of Steinholf the Lowly. Their son was Mar of [Reyk] Knolls, whose wife was Thorkatla,* the daughter of Hergils Hnappraz.

Their son was Ari, who was blown over the ocean by heavy gales to Whiteman Land [Hvitramannaland], which some call Greater Ireland [Irland Mikkla] and lies off westward in the ocean adjacent to Vinland the Good; it is reported that one can sail thither from Ireland in six days. Ari could not get back from this country and there he was baptized.

The first account of this was told by Rafn Hlymerksfari [Rafn the Limerick-farer] who had spent a long time there [in Limerick?].

Thorkel Gellirsson said that Icelanders who had heard Earl Thorfinn of Orkney tell the tale, avowed that Ari had been recognized in Whiteman Land and that he was not able to get away but was held in much regard there.

[SOURCES: Landnamabok]

Although no dates exist for Ari Marsson, it is possible to obtain an approximation of them from the relevant genealogical information found in the Landnamabok and in the various versions of the Erik the Red Saga. A genealogical table drawn from these sources reveals that Ari Marsson and Erik the Red were not only contemporaries, although Ari was some years older than Erik, but were related by marriage through Erik's wife, who was Ari's first cousin.

Both men fathered three sons. One of Ari's sons, Thorgils, was a prosperous chieftain in the western districts of Iceland at the time of the Norwegian Thangbrand's missionary visit to Iceland at about 997. Thangbrand's friend and champion during this visit was Gudleif, another of Ari's sons, who had previously spent some years on the continent as a soldier of fortune. It is reasonable to conclude that both brothers were born between 960 and 970. This would suggest a date for Ari's birth of around 940, and such a date conforms with the genealogy of his wife, Thorkatla.

There is no certainty as to the date when Ari was blown off to Greater Ireland; but since it must have been after the birth of his three sons it could hardly have occurred much before 965. On the

---

* Thorkatla's detailed genealogy occurs elsewhere in the Landnamabok.

other hand, since Greater Ireland was evidently a locality in Greenland originally inhabited by Westmen,* but which had been abandoned by them before Erik made his voyage in 981, Ari, who spent some time in Greater Ireland, could not have arrived there much later than 975.

Assuming that he was westbound for Iceland at the conclusion of a trading voyage to Europe, and that a polar nor'easter struck him and disabled his ship, wind and current would then have carried him to the vicinity of Cape Farewell, from which point the Greenland Current could have swept his ship around the cape and northward up the west coast, as it does driftwood to this day. His vessel may have been wrecked on one of the off-lying islands near the Julianehaab Bight, conceivably on the same ones where an Icelandic trader named Thorer was wrecked in Erik's time. The crew may have drowned or else failed to survive prolonged exposure on the skerries. Ari may have been rescued by the local inhabitants.

Who were the people he encountered? They were a Christian people and they were certainly not Norse. They could only have been Westmen, either refugees from Iceland or immigrants who had come to Greenland direct from the British Isles.

Wherever they came from, one would expect that their fear of Norsemen would have been at least as great as their Christian capacity for forgiving their enemies; yet they spared Ari. If he was the sole survivor they may not have felt that he posed enough of a threat to necessitate murdering him. But an even more likely explanation is that Norse merchant traders were often tendered a type of immunity, even by people who were violently antagonistic toward Vikings. Ari may or may not have actually been held captive. Our version of the Landnamabok suggests that he was; but the author of an ancient Icelandic geography transcribed by Bjorn Jonsson † implies that Ari remained in Hvitramannaland without restraint, and says that he became a leading figure in the community. Ari became a Christian, perhaps married a local woman, and settled down.

The question remains of how word of his whereabouts reached Iceland; but there need be no real mystery about this. We know from the Landnamabok that there were sailings between the British Isles and Iceland during the time the Westmen held that island. There

---

* See Appendix I, Part II, where the Ari Marsson story is analyzed in detail.
† See Appendix I, Part II.

is no reason to think that communications between the Irish at home and in the west were severed because the open-sea distance had been increased from a passage of five or six days to Iceland, to one of eight or nine to Greenland. Mariners who could sail direct from southern intervening islands were held by the Norse and infested by Viking intervening islands were held by the Norse and infested by Viking pirates) would certainly have been capable of sailing on to south Greenland. Furthermore we know from the old Icelandic geography already mentioned that there *were* sailings from Ireland to Hvitramannaland, not only by Irish mariners but by Norsemen as well.

We are told that Rafn, a Norse merchant trader living in Limerick, was the first to report the news. Rafn may have obtained it from some other Norse trader working out of Ireland, or he himself may have been one of the Norse traders who visited Hvitramannaland.

The question may be asked: Why did the Westmen permit Norse traders to visit them, thereby jeopardizing the secret of the existence and whereabouts of Greater Ireland? The answer is to be found in two circumstances. First, the times were changing and the rapid decline of Viking power in Europe may have somewhat eased the terror in which Norsemen had been held by the Westmen in their homelands. Second, Norse traders living abroad in Ireland and in Great Britain seem to have been akin to many modern businessmen in that their prime allegiance belonged to that country which offered them the best opportunity of making a profit. It is a recorded fact that after the Irish drove the Vikings out of Dublin in the tenth century, they *invited* Norse traders to come to Dublin and settle there. These traders were businessmen first and patriotic Norse a very bad last. They actually assisted the Irish in waging war against their own compatriots from the north.

Nevertheless these expatriate Norsemen were probably not permitted to visit the Westman settlements in Greenland until the Viking menace was declining. It would seem from the Landnamabok account that Rafn — or his source — did not visit Hvitramannaland until Ari had been living there for some years.

The second version of Ari's story reached Iceland at third or fourth hand through Earl Thorfinn of Orkney; but that must have been a long time after the event and probably not until the tale had become well known throughout the Scandinavian world. The prime source was Rafn, the Limerick trader. It is unfortunate that we do not know when Rafn's report reached Iceland, or in what form it was delivered. It is not impossible that it was a message from Ari himself, directed to his kinsfolk. Ari may have explained his long absence by saying he was being held against his will, whereas the truth may have been that he liked Hvitramannaland, was quite contented there, and had no desire to go back to his original family or to the brawling society of his fellow Icelanders.

In whatever form the report of Ari's sojourn in Greater Ireland reached Iceland, it would have caused a sensation, particularly among Ari's kinsfolk. And Erik the Red was one of these by virtue of his marriage to Ari's first cousin.

WHAT ARI'S STORY MEANT FOR ERIK

The time came when, like Snaebjorn Hog (and for very similar reasons), Erik had to get out of Iceland. The sagas tell us that he decided to sail west for Gunnbjorn's Land, but they do not tell us why, nor do they tell us where he intended to go from there. We know he did not go north from Gunnbjorn's Land, as Snaebjorn had done, and so we can assume he was not intending to spend his time of exile as a hunter. He actually went south instead, where game was scarce. But why? Men of his time did not undertake extensive voyages unless they had a specific and usually eminently practical purpose. They simply did not sail out into the blue just to see what lay beyond the horizon.

I suggest he had a two-fold motive. In the first place he may have intended to find and rescue his kinsman, Ari; but his most compelling reason for sailing west was probably the prospect of raiding the previously untouched Westman settlements of Greater Ireland. It was still the fashion of his time for Vikings who had incurred sentence of outlawry to use their period of exile harrying wherever there might be a chance for gain. But by 981 the opportunities available to small Viking raiding parties in European waters were becoming very slim and the risks disproportionately great, a fact of which Erik would have been aware.

This explanation of his intentions does not exclude the possibility that he also intended to keep a weather eye peeled for good new lands to be had for the taking. But essentially his was a buccaneering voyage — one which was destined to be followed in due time by land-taking and settlement. The centuries-old pattern of Viking expansion was repeating itself once more.

When we envisage Erik setting out from Breidafiord we would do well to discard the stereotype image of him as a noble and lofty-minded visionary consumed with the desire to push back the frontiers of the unknown. Erik was, as his personal history clearly shows, a ruthless, capable and hard-bitten realist. He was a Viking setting out on a Viking voyage — with all that this implies. Moreover, he knew where he was going.

2

.Λ.Λ.Λ

ERIK GOES WESTVIKING

The Saga Tale (987)

Erik told his friends that he would come back if he succeeded in finding
that country.

Thorbjorn, Eyjolf and Styr accompanied Erik out beyond the islands and
they parted with the greatest friendliness. He said if they ever needed similar
support from him, and it was in his power to give it, they should have it.

Erik sailed to sea from Snaefells Jokul and found that land [Gunnbjorn's
Land] . . . He arrived at that ice-mountain [formerly] called Midjokul but
which is now called Blaserk. He went from there southward along the land
to see if there was any habitable place [in that direction].

[SOURCES: Erik the Red Saga, Karlsefni Saga and the Short Saga]

Not much after midnight dawn begins to break over the inner
reaches of Breidafiord and the red sun, which has rested for only an
hour or two, begins to lift above the northern horizon. The dark
islets, scattered like drowning behemoths about the fiord, begin to
take on shape and substance. From the high crest of one of them a
watcher sweeps the silent waters with his gaze, in search of shifting
shadows which might resolve themselves into the seeking shapes of
Thorgest's ships. When he is satisfied that nothing moves across the
ochre-colored fiord, lightly riffled now by a dawn breeze from the
northeast, he turns northward and looks the morning in the face. For
a long time he stands unmoving, then he picks up a pole-axe from
the ground beside him and makes his way down the rocky slope
toward an almost landlocked cove below.

The cove seems overcrowded. It is so small that the four vessels lying there fill it almost to its narrow mouth. These are big ships, appearing even larger in the long light of dawn. They are lovely ships with a great sweeping sheer rising at bow and stern into sweet curving lines. Their yards are lowered and swung lengthwise along each vessel's center line, leaving only the heavy mast and tracery of rigging to show that they are vessels of the wind.*

The world beyond this cove may still lie sleeping, but there is no sleep here. Now that the light is breaking, small fires are winking into life along the shore. They are carefully tended so that no plume of tell-tale smoke will lift into the yellow skies. Each is surrounded by a restless knot of men waiting for pots of gruel to cook. More men begin to emerge from tent-roofed shelters higher on the beach. They come out spitting, coughing and stretching their arms; and their voices sound thickly, as is the way with waking men.

A boat emerges from the shadows alongside one of the anchored vessels, and such is its resemblance to the parent ship that it looks as if it might just have been delivered from its mother's broad belly. It is rowed by six men. A seventh steers it, standing erect in the stern-sheets with his face turned to the wakening breeze and his nostrils twitching. Like the oarsmen, he wears no cap, and his auburn hair is rough-cut and unkempt.

This is the way it might have been on the day in the early summer of 981 when Erik the Red began his voyage. We can take it for granted that the day was fair, for good visibility was essential so that at land-leaving they would be able to set and hold a course for Gunnbjorn's Land. They undoubtedly waited for a day with a favorable wind, perhaps a quartering breeze from the northeast.

Convoyed by the ships of Erik's friends until she was safely clear of the islands and of the danger of being surprised by Thorgest's fleet, Erik's vessel sailed out along the north coast of the Snaefells Peninsula. Leeward of her the long spine of the peninsula ran westward to its outermost cape, where Snaefells Jokul, 5000 feet in height and glacier-capped, stood sentinel on the verges of the western sea. Snaefells was the ideal departure landmark, since it would have

---

* A detailed description of the Norse ships will be found in Appendix E.

served to hold the ship on course long after the rest of Iceland had dropped out of sight below the eastern horizon.*

The saga tells us nothing of the composition of Erik's crew, but we can assume that it consisted of about twenty men. Among them we can number one or more of the Thorbrandssons; perhaps Thorkell Farsark, who was Erik's nephew; and almost certainly Thorhall the Hunter, who was Erik's foreman and right-hand man. The roster of the first settlers who later went to Greenland no doubt includes the names of several other men who were members of Erik's crew, in particular a man named Hrafn, who may have been Erik's sailing master.

Except for a few head of cattle and sheep intended to provide fresh meat on the outward voyage, the ship would have carried no livestock. She would have been well stored with kegs of skyr, salted butter, cheeses and dried fish. A few bags of meal probably completed her provisions. For the rest, her people would have expected to supply themselves by fishing and hunting — and by looting.

They would have gone well armed. Each man had his sword, pole-axe, spears and perhaps a battle axe. Wooden shields covered with ox-hide would have stood ready to be slung over the bulwarks if the need arose to repel an attack on the vessel herself. Some of the men may have been armed with bows, although the Vikings did not think very highly of the bow as a warrior's weapon. They considered it more manly to engage the enemy in close combat, where brute strength rather than skill would win the victory.

The ship would have carried spare running gear in the form of coils of walrus-hide rope. A roll or two of wadmal cloth for repairing sails or clothing as required, some simple woodworking tools, and a keg or two of seal-tar would have made up the bulk of her bosun's stores. The crew probably took the barest minimum in the way of personal gear: a skin sleeping bag, and a leather bag containing a few pieces of spare clothing would have sufficed.

ERIK'S COURSE TO GREENLAND

The fact that Erik took his departure from Snaefells Jokul shows that he did not choose the shortest and most direct run to Greenland, which would have been between Horn, the northwest cape of the

---

* The principles of Norse navigation are explained in Appendix F.

island, and the Blosseville Coast of Greenland. Instead he sailed west on a course for Midjokul (the Middle Glacier) which was evidently associated with Gunnbjorn's Land.

In later years, so the saga tells us, this landmark at the western end of the run across the Denmark Strait was known as Blaserk (Blackshirt), and here we see a logical evolution in the refinement of the description of a landfall as mariners became more and more familiar with the passage. In the early stages the landfall was an undifferentiated stretch of coast of considerable extent called Gunn-bjorn's Land. But by Erik's time the landmark which one was to look for was being more explicitly described as a prominent glacier in Gunnbjorn's Land, a glacier which must itself still have been of considerable extent. Finally the prescribed landmark became a single feature of this glacier. In this case, by analogy with a mountain in Norway which bears a similar name, it was evidently an unmistakable mountain peak.

The designation of Erik's landfall as Midjokul is of particular interest, since if a middle glacier on the Greenland coast was known to mariners of his time, there must have been at least one other known glacier to the south, and another to the north. This is corroborative evidence to demonstrate that the Norse knew a considerable amount about the east Greenland coast at the time when Erik made his voyage.

The identifications of Gunnbjorn's Land, Midjokul and Blaserk do not present any great problems. The nearest part of Greenland to Snaefells is that portion of the coast about Angmagssalik. The course from Snaefells Jokul to this nearest part of Greenland is west by north, which would have involved only a small and easily acceptable northerly deviation for anyone intending to coast south once he had reached Greenland.

The coast between Angmagssalik and Gustav Holm is fronted by a range of mountains through which the gargantuan inland ice sheet thrusts several immense, corrugated tongues to lick the edge of the sea. These tongues are part of the mighty Kronprins Fredericks Glacier, which lies just behind the coastal range and which stretches from Angmagssalik north to Aggas Island, a distance of 130 miles. This must be the glacier which was known to the Norse as Midjokul. Gunnbjorn's Skerries are evidently the islands in the vicinity of Kap

Dan at Angmagssalik, and Gunnbjorn's Land would be that stretch of coast running to the north from Kap Dan, including the coast fronting the Kronprins Fredericks Glacier.

Thrusting upward through the mile-thick Greenland icecap are occasional mountain peaks called nunatakers; and the black crests of these all but buried giants are one of the weirdest and most spectacular sights in Greenland. It so happens that one of the greatest of the nunatakers — the 11,000-foot pinnacle of Mt. Forel — thrusts its peak up through the ice of Kronprins Fredericks Glacier to form a great black patch which shows up sharply against the gleaming inland ice behind it. Although Mt. Forel is fifty miles inland it can be picked up from the bridge of a vessel eighty to a hundred miles to seaward of the coast. An officer of the Royal Navy who spent some time in these waters during the last war reports that Mt. Forel was the most visible and useful landmark along the whole of the west coast of the Denmark Strait. It would have been just as visible, and far more useful, in Erik's time; and it is to be identified with Blaserk.

Assuming that he had good weather, Erik would have made the crossing to the vicinity of Angmagssalik in about three days, of which less than a day would have been out-of-sight-of-land sailing. Those authors who attempt to make an epic voyage out of this leg of his journey demean the Norse, for their ships and seamanship were of a quality which would have made the crossing of the Denmark Strait a simpler affair than a voyage from Bergen to the Shetland Isles.

It has been claimed that Erik's ship was in great danger from drift ice; but this is nonsense. At the time he made his voyage, during a particularly warm climatic era, he probably did not even see drift ice, let alone experience difficulty with it.

SOUTH FROM ANGMAGSSALIK

From Angmagssalik south the voyage would have presented no problems. There were any number of fiords into which the vessel could have put for shelter in case of storms, and — as seamen say — Erik had "bold water," which means a steep shore with deep water up to the land, so that there would have been little danger from off-lying reefs and shoals. If the weather held good Erik would have been able to make the run to the southern tip of Greenland in three or four days, assuming that he followed the usual practice of anchoring or of lying hove-to off shore during the brief period of darkness.

Some authors have asserted that he searched the east coast looking for possible sites to plant a settlement, but this is improbable. Although the saga appears to say that he was looking for "habitable places," this may also be translated as meaning places which were inhabited. The saga indicates that Erik expected to find such places to the south; but there is no reason to believe that he would have expected to find them on the forbidding and inhospitable eastern coast. One close look at this coast would have shown him the error of holding such a hope.

In all likelihood he made his way down the barren east coast as rapidly as possible. He probably rounded the southern tip of Greenland by sailing through Prins Christians Sound rather than going outside to weather the infamous Cape Farewell with its reputation as a place of storms and foul weather. In sailing through this sound he would have passed close under the face of the most prominent glacier in southern Greenland — a wall of ice which abuts on the north shore of the sound for a distance of more than fifty miles and which is one of the most spectacular features of the southern district. This is doubtless the southern glacier of the trio of which Midjokul was the central one. It was named Hvitserk (Whiteshirt), and references to it appear in a number of accounts of later voyages to the Greenland colonies.

Having passed through the sound and the maze of channels which lie beyond it, Erik's ship would have emerged into the Labrador Sea on the southern verges of the great complex of deep fiords which comprises the Julianehaab Bight, and which still contains by far the best pastoral lands to be found anywhere in Greenland.

The frigid East Greenland Current which crowds close to the eastern coasts, chilling the narrow band of ice-free lands until they are little better than a desert (from the point of view of a pastoral farmer, at any rate), does not have the same effect upon the quiet inland waters of the Julianehaab fiords. Along this short stretch of south-facing coast, the country lying between the great fiords (which penetrate as deeply as fifty miles into the land) and the ice-free mountains beyond contains broad stretches of arctic prairie even to this day. In the tenth century, when the Little Climatic Optimum was approaching its peak, this land must have had a seductive ability to fill the heart of any pastoralist, whether Norseman or Westman, with a lust to possess it for his own.

In reaching it, Erik had arrived at that "habitable" land which he was seeking; but he had arrived too late to reap a full reward.

The Norse settlements in southwestern Greenland

who had been on Viking raids in other years would again have felt
the surge of old emotions compounded of the lust for fighting, of fear
unrecognized, and of a brigand's greed. Nevertheless, they would
have proceeded cautiously. The Westmen were no cowards, and they
could put up a sharp resistance when they had a chance. One Viking ship and crew would have been too small a force to overawe
them.

The need to achieve surprise would have been paramount in Erik's
reckoning. Probably he anchored under the lee of successive islands
and sent his afterboat on ahead to scout the land before proceeding.
The tension would have grown as the long days dragged and the land
stayed empty. No smoke rose from behind distant hills. No small
dark specks on far waters resolved themselves into fishing boats or
curraghs. And yet, with each day that passed, the land grew steadily
more desirable. Picking their way cautiously into Ketilsfiord, or
Alptafiord, under the lee of great Lundey Island, or into Siglufiord or
Hrafnsfiord, the Norse would have beheld increasingly broad stretches
of sweet, well-watered meadows, and they could not have helped but
think that very soon they must find men as well. One day, perhaps,
a group of them went scouting in the afterboat, rowed cautiously
into one of the fiords near the mouth of the Julianhaab Bight and
suddenly paused on the oars and held them motionless while the
water ran off the blades and dribbled unheeded down their arms.

Perhaps they saw before them, around a bend in the fiord, and
standing silent in a yellow meadow, the eyeless bulk of a sod house
with low stone walls veined out from it to mark the shape of one or
two small fields.

THE HOUSE AT BRATTALID

During the 1920's Scandinavian archeologists excavated a building
at Brattalid on Eriksfiord. They described it as the "earliest house
known in Greenland."

It was of sod-wall construction, but the walls were enormously
thick — as much as twelve feet thick in places. It consisted of a single
room whose interior dimensions were by no means consistent with
what we know of tenth-century Norse houses. Although the room
measured just over fifty feet in length, it was only slightly more than
fourteen feet wide. It could never have contained the two broad

3

٨.٨.٨

the empty lands

The Saga Tale (981-982)

[Erik] passed that first winter at Eriksey [Erik's Island] near the middle of the Eastern Settlements. In the following spring he proceeded into Eriksfiord and selected a site there for a homestead.

[SOURCES: Erik the Red Saga, Karlsefni Saga and the Short Saga]

Before Erik's vessel cleared the islands and sounds at the southern tip of Greenland, the Norse would have begun to see lands which appeared eminently good. Deep hidden from the winds of the open ocean by ice-free mountains, even these first inner sounds held the occasional low and level plots of land where the tall grasses of midsummer mingled with tufted cotton grass to make rich pastures which lacked only men's flocks upon them to make the pastoral scene complete.

The ship probably emerged from the Farewell archipelago not far south of Herjolfsfiord, and as she turned northwestward she would have had a protected passage inside the many islands which fringe the coast. Her people would have crowded the rails, straining their own eyes while they waited for the lookout at the masthead — the keenest-sighted man aboard — to cry the electric news that he saw signs of human life ahead.

Weapons would have been ready and bright-shining, and those

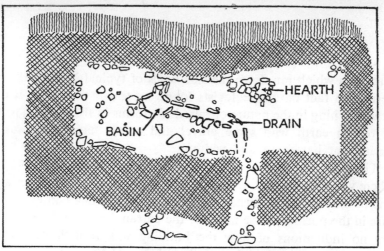

Floor plan of the ruins of the oldest habitation at
Brattalid, Eastern settlement.

Floor plan of a typical stone-and-sod-walled Norse
long house of the tenth century.

Floor plan of the Norse house at Brattalid possibly begun by Erik
the Red. The outline of what may be the original structure is shown
in heavy hachure.

Comparative plans of Greenland houses

platforms which ran down the side walls of typical Norse halls of the period. In fact the archeologists found no traces that there had ever been anything in the nature of raised platforms in the room. The floor, of beaten earth with some gravel and a few flagstones, was level throughout its length and width.

There was no sign of a central fireplace of the usual Norse type. There was only a small, rectangular floor fireplace of stone set against one of the long walls. Instead of being placed in one end of the structure in the normal Norse manner, the entrance was in the side. There are no indications of how the building was roofed, but the roof construction evidently did not follow the usual Norse design, for there were no signs of holes for the rows of posts which normally supported the broad roof span of a Norse house.

This building, which archeologists accept as having been a habitation, has no single feature about it which is diagnostically Norse. On the other hand, it possesses one peculiar feature which has not been reported from tenth-century Norse buildings in Iceland or in Scandinavia. It had running water, laid on. The water system was crude but effective. Water from a spring in a cutbank which abutted against the back wall was led through a stone-formed conduit to a stone basin set in the middle of the floor. The overflow was carried off by another conduit and disposed of under the front wall of the house.

The house is sited only a short distance from a multiroomed ruin which is identified as having been the home of the Eriker clan, and which is typically Norse in all its aspects. This large structure shows evidence of having gradually developed over a period of many years — if not centuries — from a single large skala or living hall of typical tenth-century Norse design which may well have been the original structure erected by Erik when he settled at Brattalid in 985.

The archeologists who excavated the site have refrained from offering any identification of the older structure, except to say that it "might have been the first house built by Erik, as a temporary measure, when he arrived in Greenland." This identification is not convincing. The amount of time and labor which must have gone into the raising of the tremendous sod walls of the old structure does not suggest a temporary home. Furthermore, the archeologists conclude that the house was occupied over a prolonged period of time.

Few artifacts have been recovered from this ruin, and none of these are specifically and undeniably Norse. On the other hand, floor plans of a series of tenth-century farm houses in Ireland, which are not Norse in origin, are identical with the floor plan of the building at Brattalid in all essentials, including the location of the door, fireplace and other internal structures, as well as in the ratio of length to width. One of the salient features of these Celtic structures, and a feature which continues to be characteristic of cots in Northern Ireland and Scotland, is the extreme narrowness of the buildings in proportion to their length.

THE HOUSE AT NARSSAQ

Excavations of another ancient site at Eriksfiord have recently been undertaken. This is a house ruin near Narssaq. It consists of the remains of a four-room structure of twelfth- or thirteenth-century Norse design; but it includes within its walls the remains of a much earlier building which archeologists believe must have been in existence at least as early as the turn of the tenth century. This was a single-room house which, although not as large, bears a close resemblance to the old house at Brattalid. Its internal dimensions are approximately thirty-seven feet long by fifteen feet wide, and what remains of the original turf walls average between six and seven feet in thickness. It too had a built-in water system consisting of conduits covered with stone slabs which led into, and then away from, a well-like basin in the floor.

A wide variety of artifacts have been recovered from the Narssaq site as a whole, including a rune-carved stick which has been dated to the early part of the eleventh century and which establishes Norse occupancy of the general site at that period. However, since stratification is not well established, it has not been possible to date most of the other artifacts. A number of them, including some household tools, are indistinguishable from artifacts found on Celtic sites. They can be indisputably termed Norse only if it is proved that no one but Norse settlers ever occupied this site.

The artifact collection includes a number of bone and antler weapon points. These are similar in shape to iron weapon points of the Viking period from Norway and Iceland as well as to iron points from tenth-century Celtic sites. The existence of these bone points suggests that even the very early occupants of Greenland were short of iron and were forced to use bone and antler as substitutes. But

Scandinavian historians have established the fact that the Norse settlers in Greenland did not begin to experience a serious shortage of iron (for the manufacture of weapons, at least) until the thirteenth or fourteenth centuries. It seems possible, therefore, that some or all of these bone points were fashioned by people who had been living at Narssaq for some time before the arrival of the Norse and who, due to poor communications with European sources of supply, had run out of iron.

The presence of the internal water systems at Brattalid, Narssaq, and one other similar Greenland site near Hvalsey (water systems which do not occur in Greenland Norse houses of later periods), together with the extraordinarily thick walls of these early houses, has caused some archeologists to speculate that these features may have been intended to give the houses the advantages of simple fortresses which would have been capable of withstanding an attack, or a short siege.

But if these very early structures were in fact built by the Norse, we must ask from whom it was that they had to defend themselves.

There were no Eskimos in Greenland then, and none reached the settlement areas until the thirteenth century. So far as we know, the early Norse settlers were never threatened by human enemies.

If the archeologists drew the correct conclusion in suggesting that these may have been fortress houses, the case for identifying them as being of Celtic origin is considerably strengthened. Westmen who had been driven out of Iceland would have had no reason to believe that they would be permanently secure from attack in Greenland, and it would have been common sense for them to have taken whatever measures they could to defend themselves against the eventual arrival of Viking raiders.

THE ABANDONMENT OF GREATER IRELAND

Erik may have discovered "human habitations" * in what was later to be known as Eriksfiord — but the builders themselves were gone. The shores of the fiords were devoid of any living people.

---

* In the Islendingabok it is stated that Erik found human habitations in Greenland as well as stone implements and fragments of hide-covered boats. The identity of the owners of these is discussed at length in Appendix I, Part II.

And yet the Westmen could not have abandoned Greater Ireland so very long before Erik's arrival. Perhaps Erik did not fail in his intended Viking purpose by more than a few years; but that he did fail is certain. Greater Ireland lay empty when he came upon it.

There were good reasons why its people should have left it. By the middle of the tenth century the original *raison d'être* for a Westman settlement in Greenland no longer existed. The Viking scourge had lost most of its bite. Much Viking-held territory in the British Isles had been wrested away from the Norse by the local people; in Ireland the Norse had suffered such a devastating series of defeats that the majority of them had either been forced to flee or to acknowledge the overlordship of the Celts. By the middle of this century fugitive clerics and other Celtic refugees were streaming back to Ireland in large numbers, and the country was undergoing a considerable renaissance.

Word of this happy improvement in Irish affairs would have reached Irland Mikkla with the trading ships which appear to have maintained communications, no matter how tenuous, between the two lands throughout Greater Ireland's existence. In all likelihood some of the Greenland exiles had begun returning to Ireland aboard these ships during the middle years of the tenth century. As more and more people departed to their ancestral homeland, those who were left behind would have felt less and less inclined to remain in that isolated western settlement.

We can only speculate at what life was like in Greater Ireland; but by analogy with the conditions which the Norse had to endure when they established settlements there, we can draw some conclusions. We know that it never proved practical to grow grain in Greenland, and consequently there was a perennial shortage, and often a total absence, of meal for the making of bread and beer. In later years the Norse also suffered from a severe shortage of iron and pottery, and despite the relative proximity of a friendly Iceland with its European contacts, they had to turn to stone or bone for the manufacture of tools and utensils. Within two or three decades after the establishment of the Norse settlements there was already a serious shortage of building timber, and had it not been for the early discovery and exploitation of Markland (Forest Land) in Labrador, this shortage would have become critical. The Greenland environment was, in fact, by no means as generous to European settlers as many authors have suggested.

Greater Ireland would have suffered from all these disabilities, with the addition of an even more important one — the difficulties of maintaining adequate communications with Europe. That ships made the passage is stated in the sources; nevertheless it must have been a long, hard voyage, and shipping losses must have been relatively high. The Outer Islands, Iceland and the Hebrides remained in Viking hands and so could not have been used as way-stations. Ships departing from Malin Head in northern Ireland would have had to sail about 400 nautical miles to the north-northwest in order to reach the latitude of south Greenland while at the same time avoiding the danger of encountering Viking pirates operating out of the Hebrides. They would then have had an additional 800 nautical miles to sail down a parallel of latitude — the only way they had of maintaining direction during long voyages — until they raised the Greenland landfalls.

Although the Celtic and British sailors of the times (to say nothing of the expatriate Norse traders) were undoubtedly good seamen and had good ships, such a prolonged voyage as this would hardly have been undertaken frequently. Communications must have been uncertain at best, and if Greater Ireland was in fact being progressively depopulated by emigration back to Ireland, the incentive for traders to make the long voyage would have progressively decreased.

We know that after communications between Norway and Greenland began to break down in the early fifteenth century, the Norse settlements in the far western outpost rapidly disintegrated. A similar situation must have begun to make life in Greater Ireland increasingly uncomfortable during the first half of the tenth century.

The possibility, which has been suggested by some authors, that the Westmen may have been forcibly driven out of Greenland by Erik and his followers, and that they then sailed across to the mainland of North America and established colonies there, is not borne out by any evidence. To pursue it is to pursue a most insubstantial wraith.

Whatever the facts of the matter may have been, one thing is sure. The flow of Celtic people which had trickled west from Ireland, Scotland and the Outer Isles to Iceland, Greenland and — just possibly — beyond, was at an end. This westward drift, which seems to have begun before the time of Christ and to have continued, if spasmodically, through nine or ten centuries, recedes and disappears into the darkening wastes of Ocean off forgotten Cronusland, even as the next wave rolls westward heralded by the dark-hulled ship of Erik the Red.

WINTER ON ERIKSEY

Erik and his companions probably felt sharp disappointment as the days passed and they encountered no human beings. In their imaginations, if not in actual report, Greater Ireland had doubtless appeared as a populous and comparatively wealthy land, well worth a Viking's time. But scattered and already crumbling ruins of mean sod houses, fragments of hide-covered boats, broken pots and abandoned utensils carved rudely out of stone or bone — none of these things would have smacked of a prosperous Celtic settlement.

There would have been little else for the Norse to find, for the Westmen would assuredly have taken away everything of any value. It is unlikely that there were even any half-wild cattle or sheep upon the lush green meadows. What the departing settlers were unable to take with them on the hoof, they would have slaughtered for the hides.

Frustrated, and perhaps growing somewhat apprehensive as the mystery deepened, the Norse saw the end of summer come while they were still somewhere in the extensive maze of the Julianehaab fiords. Winter was approaching and there would have been much to do in preparation for it. Their ship had to be hauled out and roofed over as a protection against ice forming inside her and spreading her planks during the bitter months ahead. Huts had to be built for the men. In lieu of Westman cattle, food in the form of fish and the fat and meat of sea mammals had to be procured and preserved. Fuel had to be gathered, and the ship's gear stowed away in safety.

And here we come upon a revealing fact. The sagas tell us that Erik chose to winter on an island near the middle of the settlement district. Although he must have examined any number of attractive mainland sites deep in the well-protected hinterland, Erik eschewed them all and chose an island. What is more, he did the same thing during his second winter in Greenland, on still another part of the coast.

Eriksey has been identified as one of the string of small and comparatively barren islands which stretches southwest from the entrance of Eriksfiord toward the open sea. These islands are not habitable now, except by Eskimos, and probably never were suitable for European habitation. Archeologists have found traces of only one small complex of Norse buildings (which apparently represents a summer fishing station) on one island, and no traces of permanent occupation on any of the others.

Considering the hospitable nature of the sheltered inner fiords, Eriksey could have had very little merit as a wintering place except for one thing: being an island it offered a high degree of security against attack. It seems obvious that Erik chose to winter in such an exposed place for the same reason that Viking raiders with small forces had always chosen similar sites when they had to winter on a coast whose inhabitants were known or presumed to be hostile. The Vikings bore the consequent physical discomforts stoically enough in exchange for the relative safety which such places offered during the season when their ships were useless to them and flight impossible.

Erik's choice of an island site was doubtless dictated by fear that the vanished people whose empty houses stood upon the shores of the fiords might return unexpectedly, or else because he believed himself close to, but not yet arrived at, that Hvitramannaland which he was seeking.

When the subarctic night drew down and the bitter winter winds blew over Eriksey, Erik and his companions must have huddled close around their fires and spent long hours discussing the summer's voyage. They probably talked at length about the fine land they had seen, for these men were raiders only by avocation — by vocation they were farmers. As the short days of the long winter slipped past, the idea of land-taking probably took root, for here was a country as good as, or better than, any they had known in Iceland; and if earlier settlers had claimed prior rights to it, they were not present to defend their claims.

One can see a dream begining to take form in Erik's mind as the talk went on through the interminable hours. It may well have been upon that wind-whipped island that the Norse Greenland settlement was first conceived.

ERIK CHOOSES A HOMESTEAD SITE

Soon after the fiord ice cleared away in the spring of 982, the knorr, recaulked, was launched into the cold waters. When she was rigged and stored and ready for a voyage, her people went aboard. Her great yard was hoisted up the mast, and as the wind filled her sail she picked up way, not toward the open sea, but toward the entry into the deep fiord which stretched inland from Eriksey.

Erik had doubtless examined this fiord the previous year, and having by then seen most of the other fiords in the district, he would have known that this one offered the best site for a homestead. So the vessel steered her course until an arm of the fiord turned north, and here, on the western side, Erik went ashore with his companions.

Around them lay a freshly verdant land rolling gently back to the foot of the mountains. Streams purled down to the salt water, and in them swam salmon and many trout. The sprouting grass gave promise of pastures which would feed scores of cattle and hundreds of sheep; and far back toward the mountains there were thickets of scrubby trees, sufficient to keep the cooking fires burning for some years to come.

It was here that Erik took his land by having some of his men march around its boundaries carrying burning brands, and lighting smoky fires at the more distant points. This was the way the Norse were used to hallowing new land unto themselves, and this was the way it would have been on that spring day.

And it may well have been that Erik stood beside a half-collapsed sod building on the higher ground, where he could overlook most of the fiord as far as its southwestern bend, and chose this as the place where he would some day raise his hall.

4

ʌ.ʌ.ʌ.

the western wilderness

The Saga Tale (982)

That summer Erik explored the Vestri Obygdir,* remaining there a long time and giving many local names there.

[SOURCES: Erik the Red Saga, Karlsefni Saga and the Short Saga]

Having selected a homestead by the side of the south Greenland fiord which was later to bear his name, Erik went aboard his vessel and sailed away to the Western Wilderness. Now if he had spent the best part of his three-year exile engaged in an evaluation of the Greenland coasts and had *then*, on the basis of his acquired knowledge of the country, selected and hallowed land in the best locality, his actions would have been in accord with the accepted theory that he undertook the Greenland venture solely to find and settle new lands.

But Erik did not do this. *He first chose a homestead site, and then went off on a voyage which was to keep him away from the selected site during the balance of his period of exile.* Those were years which could have been put to excellent use at Eriksfiord if settlement had been his original intention. Buildings could have been erected, homefields laid out and fenced, and the surrounding countryside explored in detail with a view to making the most of its potentialities. There were innumerable pioneering and preparatory tasks which a party of twenty or more men could have accomplished in advance of the ar-

---

* The Western Wilderness or uninhabitable regions.

rival of women, children and livestock. Yet nothing of the sort was undertaken. Erik sailed away instead.

Whatever signs of human habitation he might have found along the fiords of southwest Greenland would hardly have tallied with what rumor had likely described as a flourishing Celtic community which possessed sufficient wealth to attract merchant traders all the way from Ireland. And having failed to recognize the fact that he had actually found Greater Ireland, it would have been natural for Erik to conclude that the place lay still farther on — either to the west or to the southwest.

A reconnaissance party sent by Erik to scan the country from one of the 4000-foot coastal mountains in southwest Greenland would have been able to assure him that there was no more land to the southwest, but would have reported that the Greenland coast north of the Julianehaab Bight ran off in a westerly direction.

Setting out from Eriksfiord, Erik would have held his course westward along this coast in the hope that it would sooner or later lead him to the land he sought. Even after his knorr had poked her head out past Cape Desolation on the Nunnarsuit Peninsula, where the coast swings northerly, the Norse would have had no reason to guess that it would continue to run north indefinitely. They would have hoped that it would again swing westward. And there was only one way for them to find out — go and see.

Erik's progress northward was undoubtedly slow. There were innumerable fiords along the way, and he probably investigated many of them, at least until he had drawn blanks enough times to conclude that nobody could, or would, live in their desolate inner reaches. These were not like the fiords of the southwest coast. Apart from the Ivitgut fiords, their shores were terribly abrupt and almost barren; and grassy patches — when they occurred at all — were too small to have been of much use to a pastoral people.

Day after day the knorr sailed along the base of the dark mountains. Occasionally she would have passed the white wall of a seafront glacier projecting out from the inland icecap. Hopes that this coast might yet lead west and even south again to Greater Ireland might have been kept alive by the fact that the general trend of the land was well to the west of north.

Perhaps a week or ten days after leaving Julianehaab the ship would have rounded the headland of Narssaq* and entered a complicated maze of fiords wholly contained behind the wall of the coastal mountains. The Godthaab District, as it is now known, is unique in Greenland. Its maze of quiet waterways is so well protected by the encircling mountains that it has a climate all its own. A few miles to the north and south of it the fiords are barren, windswept and steep-walled slits in the face of the coast range, inimical to men. But the land lying along some of the Godthaab fiords is low and gently sloping and in many places surprisingly well covered with grass meadows.†

Although it did not hold the goal Erik was seeking, the very existence of such an "oasis" on an otherwise almost uninhabitable coast could have encouraged him to continue with the search.

A few miles past the entrance to the Godthaab fiords Erik would have found himself coasting the shore of a long bight whose northerly reaches now showed a heartening trend toward the west. He and his men would have also beheld a magnificent mountain peak lifting almost from the water's edge on the far lip of this bight. They would have seen that it rose from another of the great ice tongues thrust out by the inland glacier, and as they sailed on along the coast this towering peak would have come to dominate the whole gigantic landscape.

This was by far the finest vantage point the Norse could have encountered on the west Greenland coast, and they would have realized that from its peak the world beyond would lie revealed for a hundred miles or even more, depending on whether other highlands lay at the extreme range of vision.

THE VIEW FROM THE MOUNTAIN

This 7300-foot mountain is not only the highest on the western coast of Greenland, it is also one of the most accessible. It lies only eighteen miles east of Kangamuit Island, behind which there is a

---

* Not to be confused with the Narssaq in the Eastern Settlement.

† Godthaab could never have compared with the southern fiord district as a farming country, but it had sufficient merit so that it eventually came to be the second most important Norse colony in Greenland, although perhaps this was due more to its proximity to good hunting regions than to its pastoral qualities.

small, deep fiord running to the base of the mountain. It is not difficult to climb and has been scaled several times in recent years by people with no pretensions as mountain climbers, and without special equipment.

Erik would have been able to lay his ship so close alongside that a climbing party could have stepped off the deck onto the lower slopes. Although we do not know who these men were, there is a possibility that their leader was called Hrafn and that he was one of the more important members of Erik's party. He was perhaps the same Hrafn who accompanied Erik back to Greenland on the settlement voyage of 985, and who took up land not far away from Erik's own holdings.

At a later point in the saga of Erik the Red we come to a reference to Hrafnsgnipa (Hrafn's Mountain) as well as to a body of water lying somewhere far to the north which briefly bore the name of Hrafnsfirth. In Appendix D the possible identifications of Hrafnsgnipa and Hrafnsfirth, are examined, and we conclude that these were the respective names Erik's expedition gave to the great mountain behind Kangamiut, and to the northern part of Davis Strait.

While the Norse name of this dominating peak may be a matter of speculation, we know that Erik must have seen it and we have no need to speculate as to what he did about it. No sailor of his time, feeling his way into an unknown world, would have ignored its value as a vantage point.

Looking to the north, the climbers would have seen that the mountains lying between the coast and the inland icecap formed an increasingly broad fringe of ice-free lands — much broader than any such strip they had so far encountered anywhere in Greenland. Stretching from a point a few miles north of Kangamiut to the entrance of Disco Bay (a distance of 160 miles) this coastal strip remains ice free in our day to a depth of nearly a hundred miles. This would have been of great interest, but it would have been as nothing to what could be seen far out across the shimmering sea to the westward.

It so happens that the highest coastal mountains in east Baffin Island, reaching a height of 7100 feet, lie directly opposite to Hrafnsgnipa, and at the point where Baffin Island and Greenland are nearest to each other. Here, if anywhere, the possibility exists that the two lands may be intervisible.

The maximum intervisibility between a 7100-foot peak and a 7300-foot peak, as determined by the curvature of the earth, is 224 miles. The two peaks in question are actually 240 nautical miles distant from one another and, in order for them to be distinctly intervisible, two things are required: exceptional clarity of the atmosphere, and a mirage effect. As the *Canadian Arctic Pilot* notes: "Arctic air masses are pure, and visual range may be extremely great. Distant objects stand out with great clarity in shape and detail. . . ." Moreover, mirage effects are common phenomena in these high latitudes. The early Norse navigators found them very useful as an aid in locating far-distant landfalls, and they even had special nautical terms by which they referred to them. And mirage effects in the arctic frequently increase the intervisibility of massive objects such as mountain ranges and, in particular, of glaciers by as much as 40 per cent.

In order for the mountain massif behind Cape Dyer on Baffin Island and its attendant glaciers to be visible from Hrafnsgnipa, an increase in intervisibility, due to mirage effects, of only 10 to 15 per cent is required. However even without any mirage effect at all an observer on the crest of Hrafnsgnipa on a sunny day can see the diffraction loom of the land mass and of the glaciers on Baffin Island.*

An experienced Norse seaman would have had no hesitation in concluding that such a loom indicated the presence of a land of considerable extent.

THE CROSSING OF DAVIS STRAIT

The saga says that Erik spent a major part of this summer in the Western Wilderness, which, as we have shown in Appendix D, was part of Baffin Island. Consequently we know that at some point along the west Greenland coast Erik turned his ship's head from the land and sailed westward.

The coast close to Hrafnsgnipa would have been his logical point of departure even if none of his men had climbed the mountain or glimpsed the loom of the distant westward land, for Hrafnsgnipa had a double value in terms of Norse navigation. Not only could it have served as a vantage point; it would have served as an exception-

---

* Under exceptional conditions the mountains of east Greenland can be seen from northwestern Iceland, although the distance between these two points is more than three hundred miles.

ally useful over-the-stern steering mark which would have enabled
a vessel to be kept on course for a distance of about a hundred
miles in clear weather. This was a matter of particular importance
to Norse mariners sailing in high latitudes during the early summer.
At that season there is almost perpetual daylight to pale the skies,
and the Pole Star is no longer visible to help a mariner maintain direction. Furthermore the sun is almost useless as a direction guide
since it does not rise or set, but follows a wobbly course around the
whole horizon.

Hrafnsgnipa was thus the ideal point from which to attempt a westward probing voyage. Even if he had possessed no foreknowledge of
the existence of land to the west, and only wondered if such a land
might exist, Erik could have sailed confidently out from Cape Burnill,
and before the comforting peak of Hrafnsgnipa sank to the rim of
the horizon behind him, forcing him either to turn back or risk losing
his way, he would have raised the crest of the Cape Dyer peak ahead.

THE VESTRI OBYGDIR

As the knorr eased cautiously in from seaward the Norse would
have seen that this new land had a depressingly familiar look about
it. Here once again was a massive and deeply indented coast rising
abruptly from the sea to a high coastal mountain range behind which
stretched the inevitable fields of inland ice. Hopes of finding a gentle
and welcoming coast, which might nurture fat Westman settlements,
would soon have faded.

The similarities between the two opposing coasts are so striking
that it is little wonder that Erik and the Greenland Norse after his
day concluded that these coasts were in fact part of one and the same
land which ran north up the east side of what we now call Baffin Bay,
turned west across its northern reaches and then ran south again
down the other side.

Nevertheless there was a difference. The climate of the western
coast of Greenland is largely determined by the effect of a northward-
flowing current which, although originally of arctic origin, is tempered
by the inflow of warm waters from the Irminger Current. The Baffin
Island coast, on the other hand, is under the frigid influence of the
Canadian Current streaming directly south out of the Arctic Ocean.
Even during a mild climatic era this icy stream would have made it
impossible for anything except high arctic vegetation to survive in the

coastal regions which it dominated. Consequently Erik would have found no grassy cattle meadows, no alpine sheep pastures, and not even a trace of the scrubby forests which graced some of the south Greenland fiords. To the eyes of a Norse pastoralist this land would have seemed to be an uninhabitable wilderness, grim and forbidding and, at first glance, utterly worthless.

By the time the knorr had coasted for a few miles under the bare basalt cliffs of the Cumberland Peninsula, Erik's hopes of finding Greater Ireland in this direction would have fallen to a low ebb. But he was a stubborn and tenacious man and so he probably continued to hold his ship on a southerly course at least until he reached Cape Mercy, where he would have found the coast bending sharply off to the northwest into what we know as Cumberland Sound but which, in his disappointment with the stark country rearing black and ugly over him, he may have been glad to conclude was the southern termination of this dismal land.

However, the apparent worthlessness of this new country was an illusion. Since the Norse were an astute and observant people, they would soon have discovered that this was actually one of the richest hunting districts in the north. They would have been quick to realize that although there were no Westman settlements to offer easy riches to a raider, there was a superabundance of animal life offering equivalent wealth to a good hunter.

The Cumberland Peninsula had — and still has — a thriving population of arctic land animals; white foxes, ptarmigan, arctic hares, barrenland caribou, muskoxen and polar bears. But the sea was where the real wealth lay. The Canadian Current kept the sea temperatures low enough so that seals, walrus, narwhals, and other sea mammals whose range is restricted to very cold waters were to be found here in immense numbers. The large whales were equally abundant (they remained so well into the twentieth century, when the vicinity of Cumberland Sound was one of the best whaling grounds in the arctic); and sea birds, including eiders, murres and a dozen other species, whitened the cliffs and islets in their myriads.*

Compared to the waters of the Cumberland coast, the waters of the opposite coast of Greenland during this warm climatic era must

---

* The Norse of this period were accomplished whalers and could take even the larger species.

have been relatively devoid of game. The men of Erik's expedition may never before have seen, and probably could never have imagined, such an abundance of animal life both in the sea and out of it. Their hunting instincts would have been sharply stimulated even as their raiding instincts, thwarted by the failure to find victims, dulled into quiescence.

The saga says that Erik spent a long time in the Vestri Obygdir and that he gave many local places names there. This does not necessarily mean that he spent his time in exploration, which is the usual explanation of his long sojourn on this coast. He probably did very little actual exploring once he had established that this was not the kind of country where he might hope to find Westman settlements. In all likelihood he and his men turned energetically to the equally lucrative and almost as entertaining business of hunting sea mammals.

They may have ventured a short distance to the north beyond Cape Dyer, since this coast is, and presumably was then, an especially good walrus ground. Undoubtedly they gave names to the best hunting places, and some of these seem to have survived in the Icelandic sources. Bjarney (Bear Island) is one of them. Bjarney was apparently Leopold Island, lying just off Cape Mercy — a renowned collecting point for polar bears that have drifted south down the coast with the winter pack ice. Two capes near Bjarney were named Eider Duck Cape and Coal Cape, and these seem to have been located inside and on the north shore of Cumberland Sound. The name Karlsbuda (Karl's Booth or Camp) may also stem from Erik's time. It seems to have been the name given to the Cape Dyer end of the route across Davis Strait.

Erik and his people doubtless spent most of that summer collecting a cargo of oil, walrus hides and walrus and narwhal ivory. During a summer on this virgin hunting ground they would probably have done far better than if they had spent their time raiding the holdings of impoverished Irish settlers.

I have called the Vestri Obygdir a virgin hunting ground; but it may not have been quite that. Although very little archeological work has as yet been carried out on the Cumberland coast, it is known that the Thule culture Eskimos occupied parts of it at least as early as the thirteenth century. This was well after Erik's time, of course, but the Dorset *people also may have made use of this region, and some of the things Erik was reported to have found in "the west" may have been tools or weapons of Dorset origin which he came upon on the shores of the Cumberland Peninsula.

The discovery of the Vestri Obygdir hunting grounds was of the utmost importance in the later development of the Norse settlements in Greenland. All the sources make it clear that the Norse settlers procured most of their sea-mammal hides and oil from the obygdir, as well as the walrus ivory which was their most important export product. This ivory was the major magnet which attracted trading ships from Europe, bearing the indispensable supplies of iron and other goods which were not available in Greenland, and without which the settlements could hardly have survived as long as they did.

Hunting expeditions to the Vestri Obygdir, particularly from the Godthaab settlement area, probably continued until sometime early in the thirteenth century, when a deteriorating climate led to a huge increase in the size and duration of the Baffin Bay icepack, thereby barring off the sea route across Davis Strait. The loss was not as serious as it might have been however, since the same cold weather which brought the pack ice also brought about a southward migration of sea mammals down the west Greenland coast into regions of the Northern Obygdir which were accessible to the Norse hunters.

Erik's exploration of the Vestri Obygdir did not result in the discovery of his primary objective, but it would have been an immensely successful venture nonetheless. Doubtless he was well satisfied with the results. It is unlikely that his sense of satisfaction would have been very much increased by the knowledge that he had become the first European, of whom any record still exists, to discover what was for all but technical reasons, the continent of North America.

* A proto-Eskimo people who preceded the Thule culture. See Appendix H.

5

ᛉ.ᛉ.ᛉ

RETURN FROM EXILE

The Saga Tale (982-984)

[Erik] spent the second winter at Holm near Hrafnsgnipa. But the third summer he sailed all the way northward into Hrafnsfirth to Snaefells. He believed then that he had reached the head of Eriksfirth [Hrafnsfirth*].

He turned back then and remained the third winter at Eriksey at the mouth of Eriksfiord. The following summer he sailed to Iceland and landed in Breidafiord.

[SOURCES: Erik the Red Saga, Karlsefni Saga and the Short Saga]

Before the first autumnal storms swept down from the bleak highlands of the Cumberland Peninsula, Erik and his companions would have finished their hunting and gone in search of winter quarters.

The prospects of wintering in the Vestri Obygdir would have had no appeal to them. They would have been able to read the signs and to appreciate how bitter conditions were likely to become in winter on that bleak coast, where there would not even have been much driftwood available for their fires.

Picking a day when visibility was good and when there was a moderate westerly wind blowing, they made their return voyage across the great bay or sound (they could not have known which it

---

* This appears to represent one of the surprisingly rare occasions when a saga clerk made an error in copying a name. On the other hand it is possible that the name Eriksfirth was also applied to the Davis Strait Baffin Bay inlet during the very early period of the Norse occupancy of Greenland. See also Appendix D.

was) to the coast below Hrafnsgnipa, where the conditions governing human existence were considerably easier.

Since they had doubtless acquired a good cargo as a result of their summer's work, one might expect them to have turned south and to have continued down the coast to Eriksey; but there could have been a number of reasons why Erik was not yet ready to return to the site of his future settlement. For one thing, he had not yet found any further traces of the people who had at one time inhabited the south-western fiords. Probably he no longer expected to find Greater Ireland; but he might have been persuaded, by the great expanse of ice-free lands which observers on Hrafnsgnipa could have seen to the northward, to make one final search for the elusive Westmen in that admittedly unlikely direction.

Erik may also have wished to investigate sea-mammal hunting conditions to the northward. The remarkable hunting grounds of the Vestri Obygdir would have been a revelation. However, the Vestri Obygdir lay across a passage of two hundred miles of open water. Erik may have felt that if equally rich hunting grounds existed on the east side of the bay, at a reasonable distance to the northward of his intended southern settlement area, these might prove more convenient to exploit.

There could have been still another reason for making a voyage to the northward. Although later generations of Greenland Norse may have thought they could identify certain strange stone artifacts which had been found by Erik's party on the Baffin coasts as belonging to the Skraeling race,[*] Erik himself would not have been able to solve the mystery of their origin. He knew nothing about Skraelings, or even that such a race existed. If we assume that he found Dorset artifacts on the Cumberland coasts or elsewhere, we can be sure the discovery would have baffled him and made him uneasy. He would have had no clue to the nature of the unknown beings who had made these objects; and fear of the unknown was something to which even the Norse were not immune. Consequently Erik may have decided that it would be wise to assure himself that the coasts to the northward of his intended settlement were free of mysterious and therefore potentially dangerous people.

---

[*] This was the name by which Eskimoan people came to be known to the Norse.

WINTER AT HOLM

Erik decided to winter near Hrafnsgnipa. Again he chose an island site, one variously called Holm, Holmar and Eriksholm in the saga sources. The fact that he selected an island for the second time strengthens the deduction that he believed there were inhabitants on these long coasts.

Through some quirk of the ocean currents, relatively large quantities of driftwood, which originate from Siberian rivers, are carried right across the Arctic Ocean, south down the east Greenland coast, and finally north again up the west side, to be deposited on the shores between Kangamiut and modern Holsteinborg. Consequently Erik and his people would have had no trouble collecting fuel for winter burning, and even beams with which to roof their winter houses.

It would be fascinating to know more about the life these men led in their tiny, dark, stinking sod-and-rock shanties during the long winter months. They were a sensuous race, and they loved their drink. On Holm they presumably had no women, and they certainly had no beer. Once the winter had closed down in earnest they would not have gone out hunting, even if there had been anything much to hunt. Talk, story-telling and more talk would have occupied many of the hours. Some of them would have been fond of games (later Greenlanders were inveterate chess players). Perhaps they found emotional release in quarreling. Remembering the bloody winter spent by Rolf and Snaebjorn on the east Greenland coast, we suspect that only the exercise of an iron-fisted discipline by the expedition's leaders could have prevented mayhem.

NORTHWARD AGAIN

In the spring the knorr was launched and readied. Most of her cargo was probably left on Holm, secured in caches. Sailing empty, and taking advantage of the almost total absence of darkness at this season of the year, Erik would have driven her north at a good pace. It is unlikely that he bothered to feel his way into every fiord, for he would by now have been able to assess their potential, as havens for human beings, at a glance.

Erik would soon have discovered that the ice-free lands to the north were savagely inhospitable, being composed for the most part of range after range of precipitous mountains whose slopes were almost bare of vegetation, and whose deep, dark valleys offered pasturage suitable only to caribou and other native beasts. He would also have discovered that the sea-mammal hunting was not nearly as good as might have been expected, considering the high latitudes into which he was sailing. Perhaps he was able to arrive at the reasons why this should have been the case. He may have noted that the ice-free north-flowing current was warmer than the southbound one which lay on the western side of the body of water he apparently named Hrafnsfirth.*

Erik may have sailed into Disco Bay, and out again through the Vaigat; then into Umanak Fiord and out through Karate Fiord to round the Svartenhuk Peninsula and so leave the ice-free regions of West Greenland behind him. Ahead of him at this point lay a hundred and fifty miles of coast which consisted mainly of the peaks of drowned mountains emerging from the sea as a maze of craggy islands, while behind them the inland ice crowded hard against the shore.

It is doubtful if Erik lingered in this region, even though the sea-mammal hunting here would have been somewhat improved. Sailing steadily in continuous daylight, he probably proceeded just far enough to see that the entire east and north horizons had become a wall of ice — the greatest glacier face in all the world — and to watch in awe as gigantic icebergs, some of them as much as half a mile in length, calved from the ice face with catastrophic sound and fury, sending tidal waves roaring for miles out to sea.

This was no place for a small ship. Having seen enough to convince him that this must mark the end of Hrafnsfirth and, effectively, the end of the usable portion of this new world, Erik would have brought his ship about and headed south, leaving the blinding glitter of the interminable icefields, which he named Snaefells, thankfully astern.

This journey north would have been a disappointment in one sense, for it would have revealed no hunting grounds comparable with those of the Western Wilderness. On the other hand, Erik seems to have encountered no people either, and this may have been a relief to him. As his ship bore south again, his mind would doubtless have been engaged in plans for capitalizing on his discoveries by establishing a settlement in this new country.

---

* See also Appendix H.

Stopping briefly at Holm to pick up cargo, the ship continued south until she rounded Cape Desolation and regained the quiet waters of the Julianehaab fiords. There may have been some weeks of good weather remaining of this summer, and those members of Erik's company who intended to return to Greenland with him as settlers probably took this opportunity to choose their own homestead sites.

During the final winter of his exile, which he spent in the winter huts at Eriksey, Erik doubtless completed his plans for this new land. He did not envisage the future settlement as a small landtaking by himself and a few friends. He had come to think of it as a major colonizing venture which he would direct, and of which he would remain the leader.

In the early summer of 984 the Norse venturers loaded their vessel with the wealth they had obtained from the seas in lieu of the wealth they had hoped to obtain from the Westmen, and set sail for home. The first and in many ways one of the greatest of the Norse voyages into the far western reaches was at an end.

6

⋀⋀⋀

the land-taking

The Saga Tale (985)

The following summer Erik sailed to Iceland and landed at Breidafiord. He remained that winter with Ingolf at Holmlatr. In the spring he had a battle with Thorgest and his men, and Erik's party got the worst of it. Later, peace was arranged between them.

That summer Erik set out to colonize the land he had discovered and which he called Greenland because he said men would be more readily persuaded to go there if the land had a good name.

Wise men say that when Erik set out to settle Greenland, twenty-five ships [thirty-five in other sources] sailed out of Breidafiord and Borgarfiord, and fourteen of them reached Greenland. Some were driven back, and some foundered. This was fifteen years before Christianity was established by law in Iceland.

The following men went out with Erik and took land in Greenland: Herjolf at Herjolfsfiord, he lived at Herjolfsness; Ketil at Ketilsfiord; Hrafn at Hrafnsfiord; Solve at Solvedal; Helge Thorbrandsson at Alptafiord; Thorbjorn Glora at Siglufiord; Einar at Einarsfiord; Hafgrim at Hafgrimsfiord and Vatnehverf; Arnlog at Arnlogsfiord.

Thorkell Farserker, the son of Erik the Red's sister, took land at Hvalseyfiord and also [claimed] most places between Eriksfiord and Einarsfiord. He dwelt at Einarsfiord. From him the Hvalseyfiorders are descended. He was a man of great strength. He swam out to Whale Island after an old ox and brought it from the island on his back when he wanted to provide hospitality for his kinsman, Erik, and there was not a seaworthy vessel available.

Herjolf, the son of Bard, the son of Herjolf who was the friend of Ingolf the Settler, set about the Greenland voyage with Erik and sold his home [in Iceland]. With Herjolf on board [his] ship was a Christian man from the Hebrides who composed the Hafgerdingar Drapa [Song of the Whirling Seas]. It contains this verse:

> I begged the monk-seeker [Christ]
> To give us a good voyage.
> May the King of Heaven's Halls
> Hold his hand over me.

Erik the Red dwelt at Brattalid in Eriksfiord, which he had occupied by right of settlement. He was the man held in highest esteem, and was respected by all.

These were Erik's children: Leif, Thorvald, Thorstein and Freydis who was a bastard daughter. She was married to a man called Thorvard and they dwelt at Gardar where the Bishop's Seat now stands. Freydis was very strong-willed but Thorvard was a man of little account. She was given to him mostly for his money's sake.

The people in Greenland were heathen at that time.

[SOURCES: Erik the Red Saga, Karlsefni Saga, Short Saga, with additions from Landnamabok]

Erik's return home from his epochal voyage does not seem to have earned him a hero's reception. His old enemy, Thorgest, backed by the immensely powerful Thord Bellower, had neither forgiven nor forgotten, and Erik was once again forced to seek an island refuge — this time on Holmlatr, under the protection of his friend Ingolf. But by this time island life must have become almost second nature to him.

Although Erik was probably unable to move freely about the country for fear of Thorgest's men, people could come to visit him at Holmlatr, and they must have done so in considerable numbers as word spread of his discoveries in the west. There were a good many dissatisfied men in Iceland in those times: men who had arrived too late to take up good land, who had fallen on hard times, who were at odds with powerful chieftains, or who were simply fed up with a cheek-by-jowl existence in an overcrowded land. These men would have listened eagerly to Erik's descriptions of Greenland. It would not have been necessary for him to paint the country green in order to have gathered a good following.

Among those who decided to accompany Erik there seem to have been men of wealth and position who had no real need to go adventuring. There were probably some who looked with jaundiced eyes on the slow spread of the Christian religion, which was already becoming popular among the Icelandic women, although most men still considered that the religion of White Christ was a contemptible and lily-livered faith. The bloody worship of Thor and the phallic worship of Frey seemed more in keeping with the Viking spirit.

Excitement over the Greenland project must have become intense as winter drew along. By spring it would have reached a frenzied pitch. The value of ships — any kind of ships, whether they were seaworthy or not — must have skyrocketed as more and more people caught the fever and decided to sell out and join the west-bound colonists. The disposal of lands and homes, the driving of livestock to holding pens near the shores of Breidafiord and Borgarfiord, the arrival of pony trains laden with household goods, the repair and equipping of many vessels — all must have contributed to a hectic activity which would have kept the western settlements of Iceland in ferment.

Erik appears to have made his own personal contribution to the excitement of the hour by leaving the security of Holmlatr. Perhaps he felt that he was grown strong enough to face Thorgest's band of champions; but if so he seems to have miscalculated. We know nothing of the details of the battle which ensued, but we know a good deal from other sources about the way such battles frequently went. A score or so of stalwarts from either side would meet at a river crossing, or on some moor, and whack away at each other with their heavy, blunt-edged weapons until they were exhausted. By then a number of human extremities would have been hacked off, and a few skulls caved in. In this case the final count of detached legs and fractured skulls seems to have given Thorgest's party the victory, although neither of the principals suffered damage. This battle was followed by a reconciliation which could have been brought about only by the payment of heavy compensation to Thorgest for the deaths of his sons. Erik may have obtained the wherewithal to make such a payment from the sale of walrus hides, oil and ivory which he brought back with him from Greenland.

As spring progressed and navigation opened, the settlers' vessels would have congregated in the haven at Borgarfiord, and in the shelter of the islands in Breidafiord. It was an imposing fleet — at least twenty-five and perhaps as many as thirty-five ships of all sizes, the largest of which may have carried twenty to thirty people together with as many sheep, goats, cattle and as much household gear as could be squeezed aboard. These crowded vessels would have presented something of the appearance of small-scale arks, with their bleating, bellowing and jabbering cargoes of men and lesser animals jammed into one chaotic noisome conglomeration.

There must have been several hundred people aboard the many ships, and an exodus on such a scale from a country as small as Iceland should have made that spring a memorable one in Icelandic annals. Yet no details of the departure of the fleet are preserved in any of the sources. It is a good example of just how little of the detailed history of that period remains to us, and of how much must be interpolated on the basis of careful reconstruction.

The voyage itself, which began when the ships departed from the two fiords in the late spring of 985, also remains almost unreported. We are told only that of the ships which set sail, not more than fourteen got through to Greenland. The rest were lost or driven back by causes which are not specified in the sagas.

THE OCEAN-WHIRL

However, from references in the Landnamabok and in the King's Mirror, a Norwegian manuscript of a later date, we learn something about the catastrophe which evidently overwhelmed part of the fleet.

Accompanying the merchant Herjolf on this voyage was a skald, or saga poet, and we are told that this man composed a song called the Hafgerdingar Drapa, of which two fragments survive into our times. These seem to be no more than standard prayers for a good journey and tell us nothing; but the title of the poem tells us a great deal.

The hafgerdingar was a fearful oceanic phenomena which is described in the King's Mirror.

It is called hafgerdingar [ocean-whirl] and it has the appearance as if all the waves and storms of the ocean had been collected into three heaps out of which three great waves form. These so surround the entire sea that no openings can be seen anywhere; they are higher than lofty mountains and resemble steep overhanging cliffs. In only a few cases have men been known to escape who were upon the sea when such a thing occurred.

What the author of the King's Mirror is describing is no ordinary storm sea but a confused upheaval of the ocean which was most likely the result of a submarine earthquake or a volcanic eruption. Such upheavals have also been described in modern times, and in language not much more explicit than is used in the King's Mirror. They are terrifying, and frequently fatal, phenomena and they have resulted in the loss of large vessels even in recent years.

In nineteenth-century Scandinavian sailing directions we read that about halfway between Iceland and Cape Farewell, "the sea has been reported to break very strongly on occasion, and it is believed that submerged islands or else volcanic action is the cause." There are no submerged islands in this area, but there is a great deal of volcanic action in Icelandic waters. As this book is being written a new volcanic island is rising from the sea off the south coast of Iceland.

It seems clear that submarine volcanic activity is the explanation of the dread hafgerdingar. And since we are told in another entry in the Landnamabok that Herjolf himself "got into the ocean-whirl" when he went with Erik to settle Greenland, we conclude that the hafgerdingar was the catastrophe which overwhelmed at least part of the fleet, and that the now lost poem of the Hebridean skald commemorated that tragedy.

HALLOWING THE LAND

There was no initial shortage of land for the people who got through to Greenland. There were probably no more than a dozen chieftains in the group. Doubtless the bulk of the settlers were adherents of individual chiefs and so settled near their particular lords and on a part of their holdings.

Between them, these chieftains parceled out most of the southwestern fiord district. Twelve of them are in fact listed in the Landnamabok, and each seems to have chosen a separate fiord as his own bailiwick. This was no doubt a wise move since the only way such men could have avoided inevitable and often fatal friction with one another was by wide dispersal.

Each chieftain would have taken his land by "right of settlement" that is, by riding or walking around the bounds with a lighted torch in his hand and repeating the land-taking formula: "I take this land here for my own, for I see no inhabited dwelling hereabouts."

Uninhabited dwellings did not count. There may have been a number of such, and it can be assumed that the sites where they stood would have appealed just as strongly to this second wave of immigrants as they had to the first and now vanished occupants of Greenland. New homes doubtless rose where old ones had fallen, and in a matter of a very few years most of the traces of the elder inhabitants would have been obliterated beneath the works of the new arrivals.

Erik had taken a huge holding which embraced both sides of the northern arm of Eriksfiord, and here he established his hall at the place he named Brattalid. Here his ship and the ships of his immediate adherents came to land and unloaded. The livestock would have been no more delighted to be free of their cramped quarters and to be able to reach green pastures again than the ships' crews would have been to be rid of them. After a week or two at sea, the cattle must have made a stinking shambles out of the ships' holds.

All that summer Erik's people would have labored at the beginnings of what was to become a proper jarl's estate — one befitting Erik's exalted (and by no mean unjustified) opinion of himself. The ruins of the home of the Erikers at Brattalid * still survive and we can trace its evolution from the one-roomed skala or hall to its final form as an eight- or nine-room structure which was still standing when the Greenland Norse settlements came to their dark end.

The single-roomed skala was home to the early Norse in Greenland. Here men gathered of an evening to talk, to wait for their meals to be made ready, and after eating to listen to old saga stories or to new lays composed by local skalds, until it was time to clear away the benches and lie down to sleep. During the daytime it was the women's domain. When they were not cooking, making cheese or attending to the chores of the farm they would sit in the skala carding wool or weaving the rough cloth called wadmal out of which their clothing, ship's sails, and many other things were made.

That first summer would have passed swiftly. Many preparations had to be made, not only for the winter welfare of the people, but

* See p. 48.

for the stock as well. Not least of the heavy tasks was to cut and lay up a supply of hay. There would have been no shortage of natural hay on the pasturelands, but it must have been slow work harvesting it with only hand sickles, on such rough and uneven ground. It would have taken a man a good many hours to make much of a showing.

Fishing and hunting would have been vigorously prosecuted. Nets were probably set in the runs between the islands, and when there were a few hours to spare from other tasks, men would have rowed out over the shoal grounds to jig for fish with hand gear. While the salmon run was on, young boys and old men would have spent their time along the streams spearing or gaffing the big fish as they worked up against the current.

The women would have been as busy as the men, helping with the haying, gathering berries, drying fish, milking the cows and goats and preparing as much sour milk curd as they could get, against the long and hungry months which lay ahead.

Fuel gathering would have been a major preoccupation, for although winter came a few weeks later in Greenland then than it does today, it would have been nearly as severe as it is at present. The benevolent effects of warm cycles in arctic climates are felt during the spring, summer and autumn months, but not much during the winter.

In Greenland adequate supplies of wood for fuel were probably always hard to find. Even if we accept the unlikely assumption that the scanty local wood resources were largely untouched before the Norse arrived, the amount of available driftwood and of scrub brush which could have been cut in the dwarf copses high in the fiord valleys must have been very limited. Evidently the Norse used peat to eke out the meager wood supply; but from the earliest days of settlement it probably proved impossible to keep the houses at a comfortable temperature once winter really got a grip.

When the days grew short and the wind-filled nights brought winter to the land, it would have fallen over perhaps a score of squalid, chill, turf-built skalas scattered in terrible isolation along hundreds of miles of frozen fiords, with the great mountains hanging over them in somber silence.

It was a small enough beginning that the Norse had made, but out of it was to come a time when fully three hundred farms sheltered perhaps five thousand people in the Norse settlements of Greenland.

That was a long way in the future, but perhaps Jarl (Earl) Erik, as he had now become through his own efforts, had some intimations of it as he sat on his high seat during the long winter evenings, silent and preoccupied. The flickering light of a small fire and of a stone lamp or two played over the dirt-darkened faces of the men, women and children who composed his family, his servants and his adherents. They talked the weary hours away, played games, repaired their tools and weapons, or snored under piles of sheepskins on the platforms.

But early in the autumn of 985 one final ship had belatedly reached the new settlement in Greenland. She was a fully-laden trading vessel belonging to the son of Herjolf Bardsson. She had come from Iceland, although her course had not been direct; and therein lay a tale to stir men's imaginations through the long winter nights ahead.

7

⋀.⋀.⋀.⋀

BJARNI hERJOLfSSON

The Saga Tale

Herjolf was a kinsman and foster-brother to Ingolf the Land-taker. Ingolf granted land to the Herjolfers between Reykjaness and Vag [in Iceland]. Herjolf's son was Bard, the father of Herjolf the younger, who went to Greenland and got into the Ocean-whirl when Erik settled that land.

Herjolf [the younger] lived first at Drepstock. He was married to Thorgerd, and Bjarni was their son.

Bjarni was a most promising man. Even in his youth he loved sea-faring. Soon Bjarni owned a ship and tradegoods. He was well off [then] in wealth and stood high in men's esteem.

[SOURCES: Landnamabok and the Short Saga]

Bjarni Herjolfsson is one of the most controversial figures in the story of the Norse voyages to the west. And this seems odd, because Bjarni was apparently a peaceably inclined and work-a-day figure in a world dominated by flamboyant and sword-wielding extroverts. He was that rarest of individuals in Norse historical sources — a quiet but effective man who worked for his living.

Nevertheless he has become the unwitting cause of an impressive amount of contention, due to his having been the precursor of Leif Eriksson in reaching the mainland coast of North America. Some authors have forthrightly chosen to ignore Bjarni's existence. Others have disposed of him as being no more than the invention of some ancient saga-writer who was determined to rob Leif Eriksson of his full measure of fame and honor.

But Bjarni cannot be disposed of so easily. All of the important voyages subsequently made to North America by the Greenland Norse owe their genesis to him; and by his discovery of the great forests of Newfoundland and Labrador he helped to make it possible for the Norse Greenland colonies to survive for as long as they did. Bjarni deserves better than he has received at our hands, and for that reason we digress from the story of the voyages for a few pages in order to establish the historical legitimacy of this much neglected sailor.

About the year 870 Floki Vilgerdarsson* made one of the first Scandinavian voyages to Iceland. He carried with him three ravens which he released at intervals in order to help him locate this new land to the west; and he was accompanied by a young yeoman named Herjolf.

Herjolf was accidentally cast adrift in an afterboat somewhere near the Reykjaness Peninsula in southwest Iceland, a mishap which forced him to do a good deal of unintentional exploration in that quarter of the island before he was finally able to rejoin Floki in Borgarfiord.

At the conclusion of what was presumably a successful Viking voyage, Floki brought his vessel back to Norway, where he reported that Iceland was no fit place for a Norseman to live. However, another of his companions, Thorolf by name, was ecstatic about the place and swore that the very grass dripped butter — an exaggeration which earned him the life-long nickname of Thorolf Butter. But cautious Herjolf thought the land had both its good points and its bad ones too.

Not more than a year or two after this voyage, two foster-brothers named Hjorleif and Ingolf,* who came from the same district of Norway as Herjolf, found it expedient to spend a year or so away from home until a blood feud which they had started could cool down. They sailed, so the Landnamabok tells us, "for that land which Raven-Floki had visited." Unlike Floki, they needed no ravens to help them find their way, but if we conclude that Herjolf sailed with them as a pilot we will probably not be too far off course ourselves.

These new Viking visitors spent most of their time of exile on the south coast of Iceland, a district with which Herjolf would have been familiar, and where he could have acted as an informed guide. The

_____
* Cf. p. 13.

following spring the party returned to Norway, and although nothing is said in so many words, we have the impression that the profits from harrying Icelandic coasts were getting a little thin. Doubtless there was not much left to steal.

In any event Hjorleif went off in search of richer pastures. He spent a year harrying in Ireland, where he did very well for himself. When he returned to Norway in 873 it was to find that he and Ingolf were still unwelcome there, and in fact stood to lose their heads if they remained at home. Consequently the foster-brothers and their companions sailed away for Iceland once again, this time intending to take land and settle down.

Hjorleif was killed soon after his arrival, but Ingolf hallowed land for a considerable distance along the south coast. Then, so the Landnamabok says, he made a grant of a large piece of this land to his kinsman and foster-brother Herjolf. It was probably not by coincidence that the grant was in just that corner of the island which Herjolf had explored when he was out with Raven-Floki.

Herjolf was a yeoman, a freeman without an aristocratic pedigree; but he was evidently an energetic and capable fellow, and he seems to have become a prosperous farmer, and perhaps trader too, in this new land. He evidently did not waste his time and energy feuding with his neighbors. In a way this is unfortunate, since it meant that the saga writers did not have many words for him. The Landnamabok merely says that he had a son called Bard, who in turn fathered a son called Herjolf the younger. However, in another and later entry in connection with the history of one of the celebrated Viking families of Iceland, we are told that one Eyvind Eld was the father of Herjolf who married Thorgerd; and therein lie the clues to a success story of some proportions. This Thorgerd was the daughter of Thorstein the Red, who briefly subjugated most of northern Scotland until, as the saga indignantly puts it, "he was betrayed by the Scots and was slain in battle." Thereupon Thorgerd's widowed grandmother, Queen Aud (whose husband had made himself king of north Ireland until the Irish betrayed him too) gathered up her grandchildren and made a hasty removal to Iceland. Aud was a great lady and she and her grandchildren were of such a high degree of nobility that the family is still much revered in Iceland.

Thorgerd had been married to a man named Dalla-Koll, who seems to have died shortly after the exiles reached Iceland. It is at this point that Herjolf Eyvindsson suddenly appears upon the scene and claims the widow, thereby elevating himself to kinship rank with the first family in the land.

He is not mentioned again, but one of his children, a son named Hrut who was a sometime merchant trader and owned his own ship, managed to gain the attention of the saga tellers by becoming the lover of the Queen of Norway and then getting involved in several feuds, killings and Viking raids.

Another son, named Eyvind, achieved brief mention in Njal's Saga when he inconveniently died abroad, forcing Hrut to make a Norway voyage and so postpone his nuptials for three years. But the rest of Herjolf's offspring seem to have inherited their father's characteristics, rather than those of their mother, and their histories are obscure as a result.

There is further mention of Herjolf's son Bard in an enigmatic passage in the Short Saga which refers to Herjolf, son of Bard Herjolfsson, and his wife Thorgerd, as being the parents of Bjarni; but this passage patently confuses the Herjolf Eyvindsson and the Thorgerd who were Bard's parents, with Herjolf the younger who was Bard's son and the father of Bjarni. It is not difficult to see how such a confusion could have arisen!

In any event Bard had at least one son, called Herjolf, who lived on the family holdings near Eyrar, a small port on the southwest coast. Herjolf the younger seems to have been a merchant trader in the family tradition, and we can assume that he was a successful one, since he was evidently able to retain a skald in his personal service.

His son Bjarni, who would have been born about 950, grew up in the tradition of a seafaring family. "Even in his youth he loved to go sea-faring," and he probably began accompanying Herjolf on trading voyages when he was still a boy. Bjarni may have been skippering a vessel before he was out of his teens, even as many Newfoundlanders who are still alive today were skippering two and three-masted schooners back and forth across the Atlantic before they reached their twentieth birthdays. By 985 Bjarni would have been about thirty-five years old. His whole adult life had been spent in the merchant trading business, and it can be assumed that he was as skilled in deep-sea seamanship as any man of his times. His skill and competence are attested to by the high regard in which he was held by his contemporaries.

Seamen of all ages have much more in common across the intervening centuries than do their landsmen brothers, and we will not be
far off the mark if we envisage Bjarni in terms of the undemonstrative,
effective, hard-headed owner-skippers of nineteenth-century schooners
out of New England, Nova Scotia and Newfoundland who sailed
vessels not a great deal bigger than Bjarni's into every ocean of the
world.

The resemblance between the logs and journals of those nineteenth-
century merchant-mariners and the saga record of Bjarni's westward
voyage is uncanny. There is nothing of romance, of an overt sense of
adventure, of braggadocio in either. They are straightforward and
succinct narratives of prosaic problems met and mastered quietly —
and without heroics. Any seaman will instantly recognize in Bjarni's
story a verbatim abstract from the account of an actual voyage. It is
far too dull to have been the invention of a poet.

HERJOLFSNESS

For some years before 985, Herjolf seems to have given up voyaging and to have settled down at home in Eyrar, where he apparently
ran the shore end of the family business while Bjarni took over the
maritime part. It was customary for Icelandic merchant traders voyaging to Europe to spend the winter there selling their Icelandic wares
and buying up a cargo of goods with the proceeds. This meant that
Bjarni was able to spend only every other winter at home in Eyrar.
He was abroad during the winter which preceded Erik's settlement
voyage to Greenland.

When Erik was gathering his band of settlers for that voyage,
Herjolf decided to go along even though he must have been about
sixty years old, hardly of an age for homesteading and for the hard
life which would go with it. But homesteading was presumably not
what he had in mind.

The place in south Greenland where he established himself was
about the last location a pastoralist would have chosen. Herjolfsfiord
lay on the outer coast, not far north of Cape Farewell. It was surrounded by great, barren mountains and its shores nurtured a minimum of usable grasslands. But although it was a very poor site for
farming, it was the most logical port of entry for vessels enroute to
the Norse farming settlements. It had a good harbor and was relatively easy to make, even in foggy weather or during storms.

In contrast to almost all the other settlers, who went deeply into the fiords, Herjolf founded his little settlement adjacent to the harbor, right at the mouth of Herjolfsfiord. It seems obvious what was in his mind when he sold up his Iceland home and joined the first wave of colonists to Greenland without even waiting for the return of Bjarni from abroad. He had recognized the great trade possibilities which were inherent in the opening up of the new land, and with an astuteness which seems to have characterized members of his family, he wasted no time doing something about it. Thus Herjolfsness became the major port for the Greenland trade almost from the first days of the settlement's birth; and it retained this role through nearly five centuries until the last Norse Greenlander vanished from the land.

8

Λ.V.Λ

BeyonÒ the Greenland Sea

The Saga Tale (985)

During the summer of the year in the spring of which his father had sailed away, Bjarni and his ship arrived at Eyrar.

The news [of his father's departure from Greenland] came as a great surprise to Bjarni. He decided not to unload his vessel, whereupon his crew asked him what he intended to do.

"I intend to sail the ship to Greenland if you will accompany me," he told them. The crew agreed to accept his proposal.

"Our voyage may be thought foolish since none of us has sailed in the Greenland Sea before," Bjarni told them. Nevertheless when they had readied their vessel they put to sea.

They sailed for three days after the land was hidden by the water [lost sight of below the horizon]. Then the fair wind failed them and changed to northerly gales. There were fogs and they did not know where they were going. These conditions lasted many days.

Eventually they caught sight of the sun and could distinguish the airts.* Then they hoisted sail and sailed [all] that day before they sighted land.

[SOURCE: The Short Saga]

On one early summer's day in 984 Bjarni Herjolfsson's knorr put out from her home port of Eyrar for a foreign-going voyage. Deep laden with bolts of wadmal cloth, cheeses, dried codfish, and perhaps

---

* These were the eight octants of the horizon, as explained in Appendix F.

even a few pairs of Icelandic falcons, she was bound for a European port, most likely one in Norway.

Running east before the prevailing westerlies, she doubtless made a good passage of it, so that Bjarni and his crew may have already been engaged in selling their cargo in Norway before Erik the Red's weathered vessel reappeared in Breidafiord on her return from the Greenland exploration voyage.

Throughout the ensuing winter Bjarni carried on his business ashore. This would have entailed long trips inland with pack horses to dispose of his wares or to buy those things which would be most valued in Iceland — building timber, iron billets, honey, grain and such small wares as pottery, metal tools and weapons.

Bjarni would have been in no hurry to begin his return voyage the following year, since the prevailing westerlies, which he would have had to face, blow strongly in the spring and do not begin to slacken until July. By the time he took his westbound departure the great fleet of colonists had departed from Iceland for Greenland, an event about which Bjarni would have known nothing.

If Bjarni followed the usual route he would have sailed from the vicinity of Bergen and laid a course to clear the north tip of the Shetlands, coming just close enough to them to make a landfall and to check his position. From there he would have steered to raise the high peaks of the Faeroes to the north and would have used these as stern steering marks to set him on a course to raise the 7000-foot peak near Oraefa Jokul in southeastern Iceland, from which point he could coast the rest of the way to Eyrar. This would have been a six-or seven-day voyage for a light ship in good weather. A heavily laden merchant vessel might have taken as long as two weeks, particularly if she had to sail against headwinds. It seems reasonable to suppose that Bjarni regained his home port about the middle of July.

He must have been considerably startled by the news of the planting of a new settlement in Greenland, and of his father's decision to take part in it. However, Herjolf had doubtless left Bjarni a full explanation of his actions, together with instructions urging his son to join him in Greenland with the cargo he had brought from Norway. The first shipment of trade goods to arrive in the new colony would have commanded premium prices.

Bjarni was willing enough to follow his father, but there were problems. The ship could not be sailed without her crew, and it was therefore necessary for Bjarni to persuade his men to accompany him. Their decision to go with the ship could not have been lightly taken, since if Bjarni remained in Greenland, as he evidently intended to do, they would have had to do likewise — at least until they could find transportation back to Iceland. Perhaps Bjarni's task was made easier by the afterwash of the feverish enthusiasm for the Greenland voyage which had swept Iceland during the preceding winter. Touched by this fever, many of the members of his crew may have been happy to try their luck in Greenland.

Selling up land and gear and gathering the stores and supplies necessary to set up homes in Greenland would have taken time. The ship herself would have had to be overhauled and restored with food and water. After an absence of two summers and a winter, both Bjarni and his men would have been anxious to visit friends and relatives before setting out on a new venture from which they might not return for years, if ever. It is unlikely that Bjarni would have sailed for Greenland before early August, and he may not have got away before the middle of that month.

During his time ashore in Iceland, Bjarni would have heard full accounts of Erik's exploratory voyage; and he would also have heard the sobering story of the fleet's encounter with the hafgerdingar. Perhaps it was some survivor of the giant waves who suggested that Bjarni's voyage was a foolhardy one. But Bjarni was too experienced a mariner to have been unduly frightened by such yarns. The dangers of the sea were something he was used to and with which he could deal competently as they appeared. What would have concerned him most was the problem of finding his way to the new settlement. He would have preferred to ship a pilot — this was a standard practice of Norse mariners making a long run in unfamiliar waters — but it is unlikely that any of the men who had sailed with Erik on his first voyage were available.

In lieu of a pilot Bjarni would have needed a full set of sailing directions. These would have had to specify the proper departure landmark; the course to steer from it; the distance out of sight of land in doegr — sailing days * — to the correct landfall in Greenland, and a description of that landfall. In addition he would have needed direc-

---

* A doegr was equivalent to about 120 nautical miles. See Appendix F.

tions for the ensuing coasting voyage, including a good description of the appearance and nature of Greenland together with the relative latitude of the Eastern Settlement area.

All of this information must have been procured by Herjolf from Erik or one of Erik's men and left for Bjarni at Eyrar. There can be no doubt that when Bjarni sailed he possessed detailed instructions on how to reach the new settlement in the west. That he did reach it, in spite of having been blown many hundreds of miles off course into a totally unknown sea, is proof sufficient.

The course given to him was not the short sea crossing from Snae-fellsness to Blaserk, followed by a long coasting passage south to Cape Farewell. The saga tells us that he sailed on his initial course for three doegr out of sight of land from Iceland, with a fair wind; and this would give a total distance of about four hundred miles from shore. Since he had not sighted land at the end of this run, we know that his course must have been southwesterly, probably from Reyk-janess toward a landfall not far north of Cape Farewell. This direct route was evidently pioneered by Erik on his return voyage from Greenland to Iceland. Its use so early in the history of Iceland-to-Greenland voyaging demonstrates the confidence which Norse naviga-tors of those times had in their ability to find their way around.

From Eyrar, Bjarni coasted to the Reykjaness headland, where he took his departure on a course about west-southwest. In half a day's sailing he would have dropped the Icelandic marks out of sight astern.

That he sailed in good weather can be taken for granted. He would not have risked beginning such a voyage under any other conditions. We are told that he had a fair wind, which could mean any wind from southeast through to northeast, but it was probably closer to southeast since northeasters in Icelandic waters generally bring heavy overcast and bad visibility.

Bjarni seems to have picked his weather well, guided by the almost instinctive knowledge acquired by generations of weather-wise sea-men, and the fair wind held during the first three days of open-water sailing. By that time most of those aboard would have concluded that the worst of the passage was over and they would have been confi-dently expecting to raise the distant coast of Greenland sometime during the fourth day.

Bjarni may not have shared their optimism, for he would have been quick to notice the tell-tale signs of a break in the weather, and when late on the third day the wind began backing toward the north, he would probably have guessed what was coming.

By dawn of the fourth day the overburdened ship was apparently experiencing the full force of a polar northeaster, which in those waters is the most formidable wind a vessel can encounter. It is a hard wind, and it whips the waters of the Denmark Strait until the big seas run white-foaming to the south. The northern skies grow black with driven scud, and the spume flying from the crests of breaking waves reduces visibility to a few miles. Driven sheets of rain reduce it even further, and there are times when even the master of a big modern ship can hardly see the bows of his vessel from his protected bridge.

Wallowing in a rising sea and laboring under press of wind, Bjarni's knorr would have begun to drive off toward the south. With the wind northerly she would have been reaching, and because she had little keel and therefore not much hold on the water even when fully laden, she soon would have been making leeway at an alarming rate.

In clear weather, and as long as he could establish directions either by the sun or by the stars, Bjarni would have been able to allow for the wind drift and to compensate for it to some extent. But with a shuttered sky above, and storm smoke all around him he would have been able to maintain his direction only by observing the way the seas were running and the wind was blowing. If the wind continued to back, as a polar northeaster often does, he could easily have failed to make the necessary adjustments to his course. To complicate matters, he was running into fog. At the time the storm struck, his knorr would have been close to the junction of the warm Irminger Current and the icy East Greenland Current. This is a great breeding ground for fog, which drives southward ahead of northerly winds until it blankets thousands of square miles of the Greenland Sea.

The East Greenland Current would also have been having its invisible effect on the vessel's course and progress. One of the major Atlantic currents, it flows down the Greenland coast at rates of a knot or better. Ships crossing it from Iceland to Greenland have been set to the southward as much as fifty miles in twenty-four hours. Its effect, added to those of wind and sea, would have been to increase the knorr's southerly drift until she was not making good much more than a south by southwest course.

In a typical northeast storm the wind would soon have been blowing hard enough so that Bjarni could no longer attempt to keep his vessel heading across the running seas. Sooner or later he would have had to furl his canvas and let her ride before the wind. Being of a buoyant build she would have ridden well and easily, while her people sought what shelter they could find and waited for the gale to end.

Considering all the forces at work on her, Bjarni's knorr may have drifted southwestward at close to her own normal sailing speed of five knots. Such a drift, continuing for several days, would have carried her a long way south of Cape Farewell. No doubt Bjarni took advantage of every lull to set his sail again and try to claw up to windward and so regain some of his lost northing; but these attempts would have increased his westward progress without, perhaps, significantly affecting his southward drift.

A stiff northeaster is a rare wind in summer in the southern reaches of the Labrador Sea. It seldom occurs more than three or four times in the course of a given summer, and it is most likely to be met with in August. In Newfoundland it is known as the "nine-day wind" because, when it does blow, it tends to hold for several days with undiminished force and unchanged direction. These "nine-day winds" are, in fact, true polar northeasters such as the one Bjarni evidently encountered.

For "many days" the ship drove off into an unknown ocean under cloud-wracked skies. As she closed with the coast of North America the fog would again have engulfed her, for by then she would have been entering one of the foggiest regions in the world. In August the gray shroud stretches its opaque curtain over the approaches to the western continent from about latitude 40 degrees north, across the Grand Banks to latitude 55 degrees, a distance of 600 nautical miles.

When the "nine-day wind" died down Bjarni would have been unable to lay or steer a course as long as the fog persisted. He could have done nothing more than keep his vessel jogging aimlessly about in the murk, not knowing in which direction she was sailing. But one morning her people would have stared intently into the opalescent dome overhead as the white disc of the sun showed through the thinning pall. We can imagine smiles growing on cracked lips, and salt-caked, bearded faces wrinkling into laughter at the welcome sight.

The return of the sun would have enabled Bjarni to get his bearings, and he would also have realized, from observing that the sun stood very high in the sky at midday, that he was a long way south of the latitude of the Greenland settlement.

The sail was hoisted, and with the ship close-hauled by means of her beitass-pole,* Bjarni would have set a course as close to north as she would point, perhaps making good a northwesterly track, while men and women hustled busily about the decks, spreading clothes and gear to dry, preparing food and generally straightening up the chaos which was the aftermath of the long storm. The man with the keenest vision would have been sent aloft, for there would have been no way of telling what dangers might lurk in this unknown sea.

As the day progressed Bjarni would have noted vast concourses of birds about him. He would have seen the familiar black and white shapes of great auks slipping through the water alongside. Out of the thinning mists fulmars, jaegers, shearwaters, gannets, murres and petrels would have come skimming across the ship's wake. The presence of the myriad seabirds which haunt the Grand Banks would have warned Bjarni that land lay close aboard.

For some hours longer the ship drove on while the last remnants of the fog burned away and disappeared. Then the cry of the lookout must have brought everyone crowding to the port rail to stare into the obscure distance until they too saw the blue loom of land.

Bjarni had made a landfall — but it was not Greenland. It was the great island which we know as Newfoundland.†

---

* See Appendix E.

† The analysis of the data which establishes the identity of Bjarni's landfall as some point on the coast of eastern Newfoundland is given in Appendix K.

9

∧.∨.∧

America Discovered

The Saga Tale (985)

Then they deliberated with one another as to what country this might be; but Bjarni did not think it was Greenland. His men asked him whether or not he wished to sail close to the land [and he replied], "It is my opinion that we should close with the land."

They did so, and soon saw that the country lacked mountains but was wooded and had small hills.

They left this country to port and turned the sail toward the land. After that they sailed for two doegr before they saw another land.

The men asked Bjarni if he supposed this was Greenland yet. He replied that he no more thought this to be Greenland than the former country had been, for, he said: "Very large snow [or ice] mountains are reported to be in Greenland."

They soon approached this country and saw it to be flat and widely wooded.

Then the fair wind failed them and the men said it seemed best to them to go ashore, but Bjarni would not allow it. They pretended to lack both food and water but, "of neither of these are you unprovided," replied Bjarni; and for saying this he got some grumbling from his men.

He bade them hoist sail [when the wind came up] and they pointed the bow away from the land and sailed to sea with a southwesterly wind for three doegr, and then they saw a third land.

This land was high and mountainous with snow [or ice] mountains on it. The men asked if Bjarni wanted to lay the ship to shore here, but he said he would not: "because it appears to me that this is a useless country."

They did not lower the sail but continued on along the land until they saw it was an island. [Then] they again set the stern toward the land and held out to sea with the same fair wind.

But the wind freshened at once, and Bjarni ordered them to reef the sail and not to drive the vessel harder than ship and rigging could stand.

They now sailed for four doegr and saw land on the fourth. The men asked Bjarni whether he thought this was Greenland or not. Bjarni answered: "This most resembles what I was told about [habitable] Greenland and so we may steer to this land."

They did so, and they reached the land below a cape at ebb tide. There was a boat near the cape, and there [on the cape] dwelt Herjolf, Bjarni's father, and it is from him that the cape took its name and was afterwards called Herjolfsness.

Bjarni gave up his voyaging then and stayed with his father while his father lived; and dwelt there afterwards.

[SOURCE: The Short Saga]

Land loomed darkly through the clearing fog off the port quarter of Bjarni's knorr, and it was an unknown country on the edge of an unknown sea. "They deliberated with one another as to what country this might be," but none of the men aboard ship could have offered anything except wild conjectures.

As they came in from seaward, converging with the shore, their northern eyes, which were used to the coasts of Iceland and Norway, would have looked in vain for the familiar shapes of mountains lifting into high skies. The instructions Bjarni had been given for identifying the coast of Greenland specified high mountains; but ahead of them was a low-lying land bordered by water-worn sea cliffs pierced only by small bays and harbors. Furthermore this land was covered right to the storm-spray mark by heavy forests. Beyond the coast occasional low hills mounded green above the gently rolling contours of the country.

In our time most of the coastal forest cover of Newfoundland has disappeared as a result of four centuries of cutting and burning, so that in many regions only the rotting roots of vanished trees cling to the naked rocks from which even the soil has been scoured away by wind and water. But in Bjarni's time, as in the time of the first French and English colonists, the forests of Newfoundland were a sight to make men wonder. This was veritably a "green" land that the where the forest crowded down to the sea, they glimpsed the white boles of birches, well known to them at home.

Dusk was falling as the ship idled under the lee of Baccalieu, and Bjarni ordered her headed out to sea for the night. When she had an offing he brought her into the wind and put her to sleep, jogging gently with her head to the southerly breeze and swell. It would have been far too risky to drive on through that alien sea in darkness, with the coast of an unknown land lying off to port and, for all Bjarni knew, ahead of him as well. During the night Bjarni again took a fix with his husanotra and found that he had regained about half a doegr of his lost northing. It was something accomplished.

At dawn of the next day more land was discernible far to the north-northwest, and they laid course for it toward Cape Bonavista across the mouth of the mighty fiord we call Trinity Bay. Here too, as they closed with the land, men marveled to see hardwood forests of such a size that, had they only stood in Iceland or even in Norway, they would have represented incalculable riches.

But they stood, instead, on the edge of the world; and they had no power to tempt Bjarni Herjolfsson.

From Bonavista no more land could be seen, and Bjarni reluctantly ordered the ship headed northward into open water. Less than an hour later the lookout once more picked up a smudge of coast to the north-northwest, and once more Bjarni altered a little to close with it. This was Cape Freels, a low, forested shore guarded by innumerable reefs, at the sight of which Bjarni ordered the helm hard over so that the vessel kept her distance from the dim line of forest. Once more the day drew to an end, and again she stood off shore as darkness fell, and jogged, hove-to, until the dawn.

The new day brought overcast skies and a wind from southeasterly. Because visibility was worsening, it was not until well into the gray morning that contact with the land was regained. This was the high mound of Fogo Island lying considerably off the vessel's course, for it bore northwest instead of north-northwest as had each of the previous capes. Nevertheless Bjarni altered so that he could come close enough to make out something of its nature.

By now a pattern was emerging. It seemed to Bjarni that the coast consisted of a number of huge fiords whose headlands all trended northerly with some slight bias to the west. Taking Fogo for another in the chain, he made a departure from its northern cape in the late

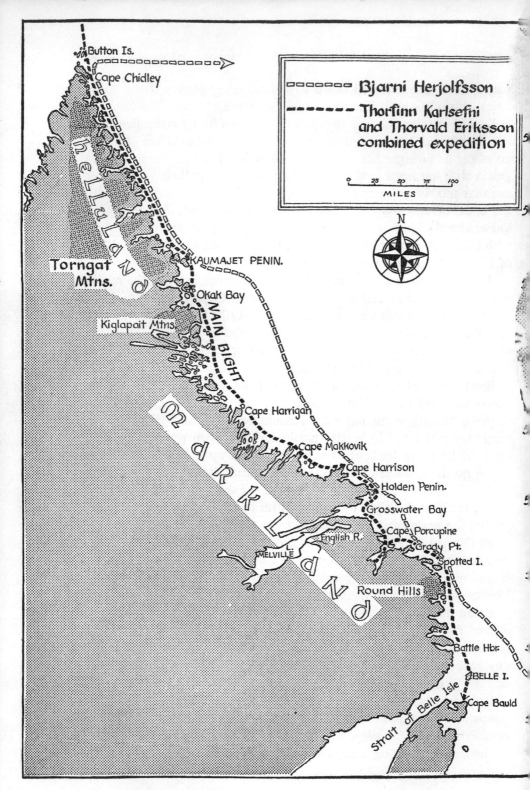

The discovery and exploration of Helluland and Markland

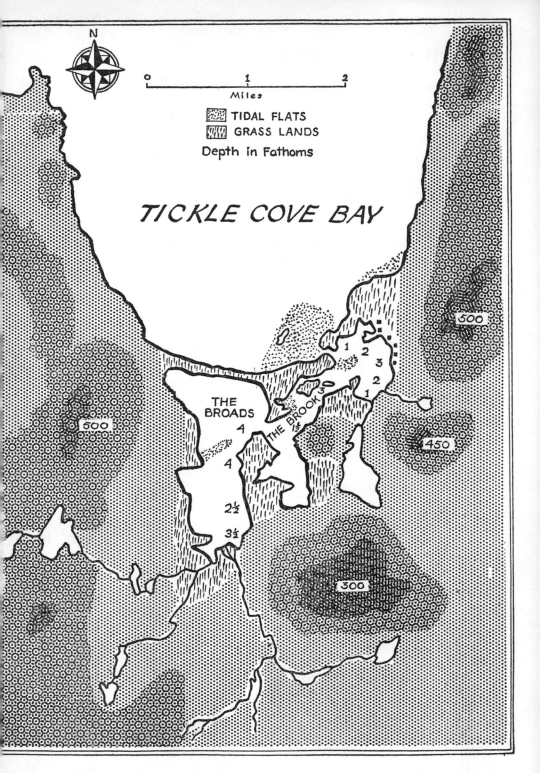

TICKLE COVE BAY

N

0   1   2
Miles

▒ TIDAL FLATS
▒ GRASS LANDS
Depth in Fathoms

600

600

THE BROADS

4

THE BROOK

1
2
3
2
1

450

4

2½

3½

300

Leif Eriksson's Vinland

may have been anchored off Tickle Cove settlement, just inside the western point of the bar, where there is a sand shoal carrying half a fathom of water at high tide, and which dries at low tide.

Almost the whole of the lagoon, or barasway as Newfoundlanders call such a place, is surrounded by flat grassland totalling something over three hundred acres in extent, where large flocks of sheep, together with horses and cows, are still pastured. This grassland appears to be natural and may have been almost as extensive in Leif's time as it is today. It consists of a light layer of soil over a deep deposit of sterile estuary sand and gravel, and it is unlikely that it ever supported any significant tree growth. There is no historical record of its having been cleared by man; no old tree roots or other indications of a vanished forest have been unearthed in the foundations, ditches and other excavations made by local people.

With such a wide expanse of open land to choose from, the Norse could have erected their temporary booths almost anywhere and still have had a long and unobstructed field of view which would have made it extremely difficult for anything or anyone to approach them unawares. That this was a matter of deep concern to them can be taken for granted. Men who themselves lived by the sword and who, moreover, were convinced of the existence of all manner of monsters and supernatural beings would hardly have been likely to pitch their camps on the shores of a new and unknown world without taking every possible precaution against being surprised. One logical place for temporary booths would have been on the seaward bar. This grass-grown sand and gravel spit would have been secure against attack except along the narrow and easily defended stretch of beach which ran west to join the mainland.

After assessing the qualities of their haven, and finding it to their taste, the Norse decided to make it their winter headquarters and so they set about building a house, or booth. This would have had to be big enough to shelter thirty-six men, and so would have been no mean structure. Finding timber with which to build it would have been no problem. The forests which then pushed up to the edge of the grassland must have been extraordinarily lush and heavy. As recently as 1920 the timber trees which could still be found and felled at the head of the various arms of Trinity Bay were among the biggest and best to be found anywhere in Newfoundland. Leif's major problem may have been to find trees small enough for easy handling.

afternoon. The lookout reported seeing no land to the west or even to the southwest, but this might have meant only that the fiord beyond Fogo was of even more majestic dimensions than those which had preceded it.

They had not yet raised a new northern cape when darkness caught them, and — feeling more secure — Bjarni kept a little way on the vessel through the dark hours, for he hated to waste a good, fair wind. Dawn came, and there was still no land in sight. As the hours passed, Bjarni began reluctantly to conclude that he had finally lost touch with the new land. For a distance of two doegr they steered as close to north as wind, current and drift would let them, and their slight set to the westward from these three factors was not apparent to them. Nevertheless it was enough to bring them to another landfall.

They picked up this land as they approached the Labrador on a course almost, but not quite, parallel to it. And the land they saw was the mammary outline of the Round Hills which lie on the otherwise featureless Labrador shore near Hawke Harbour.

Bjarni's last sight on the Guiding Star had shown him that he had regained three doegr of northing, and so he ordered the vessel's head turned toward the land, intensely curious to see if it would resemble the description he possessed of the Vestri Obygdir.

He was disappointed. Once more he beheld a low, forested country with none of the great glaciers and mountains he was hoping to see.

All the same, things were going well. He had now regained almost half his lost northing, and these new lands seemed to continue in a generally northerly direction. Again he decided to maintain contact with the coast as long as it trended the way he wished to go.

The knorr coasted, keeping a good offing, to Spotted Island, then crossed the mouth of Grosswater Bay to the Indian Islands lying off the Holden Peninsula. Here she was becalmed for a few hours, and the men, increasingly curious to set foot on shore, made a concerted effort to persuade Bjarni to launch a boat. But Bjarni would have none of it. He knew that the calm would not last long, and he was determined to take advantage of every hour of daylight and fair wind to push on north.

The breeze soon revived, this time from the southwest, a perfect sailing breeze. It brought clearing weather, and since it was off the land it roused no sea. As the ship cleared the Indian Island archipelago, the lookout reported a headland dimly seen to the northwest.

Confident that the coastal pattern of bays and capes would continue to repeat itself, Bjarni held to the north as darkness fell; but at dawn there was no land in sight. For three doegr there was nothing on the horizon, and before the end of this long run Bjarni concluded that he had lost contact with the unknown coasts for good.

His vessel had been crossing the vast Nain Bight. Under the influence of the Labrador Current, which not only set him back but also set him off a little to the west, Bjarni had not maintained a perfect course. No mariner of his times could have done so, for their navigation when they were deep-sea was very much dead reckoning.

Once more the cry came from the masthead, and again Bjarni swarmed up to have a look.

This time his heart leaped. Very distant on the northwest horizon he saw a mountain range with the gleam of ice or snow reflecting from its peaks. The ship's head was turned toward it, but the far peaks lifted over the horizon incredibly slowly, for the knorr had been a good half-day's sail offshore when her lookout sighted them.

As the ship closed with the land her people saw even greater mountains rising behind the outer ones; and these new ranges marched off to the northward, growing ever higher and carrying still more snow and ice.

Bjarni's third landfall was the outhrust Kaumajet Peninsula of northern Labrador, whose peaks stand 4000 feet high within half a mile of the coast, and which can be seen from as much as ninety miles to seaward. The Kaumajet, together with the nearby Kidlapait Range, marks the abrupt beginning of a portion of Labrador totally different from that which Bjarni had previously seen. From the Kaumajet northward, the Labrador is a steadily narrowing peninsula whose spine is the mountain massif known as the Torngat Range. The Torngats crowd seaward to produce some of the most grandiose, forbidding and violent scenery in the Western Hemisphere. Totally treeless, chilled by the Labrador Current, and crowned with perpetual snow and ice, the Torngat coast is a fearful wasteland where even Eskimos have been hard put to it to gain a foothold. It was no wonder that Bjarni believed this to be a new country, one quite distinct from those he had already seen.

Ignoring the now routine demands of his crew that he should make a landing, he held his course under the loom of the terrifying sea cliffs, and when full darkness came, he took a sight. It showed that he was now only one doegr south of the Greenland settlement.

Although the mountain coast trended somewhat west of north,* he decided to keep it in view until he had regained the last of his northing. He probably believed that it was a southward continuation of the Vestri Obygdir. As he watched the great fiords and mountains march past to the south, he felt as if he was at last re-entering the known world. It was with something of a shock that Bjarni came to the northern termination of this mountain land. It ended abruptly near Gray Strait and the Button Islands just as he was approaching his desired latitude. So Bjarni turned his back on what he now concluded must be a vast, mountainous island in the west, and set his course due east across the Labrador Sea.

It was a hard crossing. An offshore gale forced Bjarni to shorten sail and scud before it. But it was a fair wind, and so he welcomed it. Even at the height of the gale the lookout remained aloft, for no man aboard the ship could tell at what instant the land they sought might loom up out of the storm ahead.

They drove eastward for a distance of three doegr after losing sight of the Labrador. Sometime on their fourth day, land finally appeared. It loomed distant and majestic. Great, black mountains fringed the sea, and far beyond them the brilliant mass of the inland ice glittered in the autumnal sunlight. There was nothing green to be seen, and if there had been, Bjarni would have been badly worried. He had been told to look for a coast whose description fitted this ice-crowned mountain wall exactly.

So they came in toward the land they sought. They may have closed directly with Herjolfsness, although it is just as likely that they made their first landfall somewhere to the north of it and then coasted south looking for signs of human habitation. Since all the settlers except Herjolf had chosen lands well up in the deep fiords, it was only at Herjolfsness that Bjarni would have been likely to see signs of human occupation. In any event this was where he finally put in, and the great voyage ended.

---

* It must be remembered that, being without the compass and having no conception of our "compass rose" of 360 degrees and cardinal "points," the Norse did not think of directions as we do. North, to them, was not an absolute direction. It was that octant of the horizon lying between north-northwest and north-northeast. This matter is dealt with in detail in Appendix F.

And it was a great voyage, not simply because of the discovery of a new continent, but also because it represented a superb feat of seamanship.

10

⋀.⋁.⋀

hiatus

The Saga Tale (985–C. 995)

Next it is to be told that Bjarni Herjolfsson came to visit Jarl Erik and was well received. Bjarni told of his travels when he had seen these [new] lands and he was thought by many to have been lacking in enterprise since he had so little to tell of those lands. Because of this he was somewhat derided. . . .

There was now [some years later] much talk of land-seeking voyages. Leif, son of Erik the Red of Brattalid, went to visit Bjarni Herjolfsson and bought his ship from him, and manned her with thirty-five men. . . .

Leif went to the ship with his followers. There was a southern man with them called Tyrker. They made the ship ready for sea and when all was ready they sailed out to sea. . . .

[SOURCE: Edited excerpts from the Greenlanders Story.* The original version will be found in Appendix L, Part I.]

---

* Up to this point our major sources have been the three related versions of the lost Old Erik Saga; but we have now reached a stage where another of the old Icelandic manuscripts becomes important to us. This is the Greenlanders Story.

As I have explained in Appendix A, the Greenlanders Story cannot be treated as a primary source. It should be thought of as the earliest extant *reconstruction* of the story of the Norse western voyages. However, it is of inestimable value, since it contains passages drawn from sources which are no longer in existence.

What is required of anyone who wishes to make use of the Greenlanders Story is that he disentangle the fragments of original source material from the fabric into which the author of the Greenlanders Story has woven them.

In the sections of *The Saga Tale* which introduce the next several chapters I have used a number of such fragments. In each case specific references to this qualified use is made at the end of the quoted passages. An explanation of how and why these selections have been chosen will be found in Appendix L.

The sequence and timing of Leif's two major voyages, as I present them, are not

Bjarni's arrival at Herjolfsness must have been a relief to everyone concerned, but his discovery of new lands to the west does not seem to have aroused much reaction except as a curious incident in his prolonged voyage. Bjarni himself doubtless considered that his failure to raise Greenland when outward bound was an embarrassing reflection on his seamanship — a reflection which could not be entirely erased even by the consummate skill he had displayed in eventually making his proper port.

Having told the story of the voyage to his father and his father's people, Bjarni probably put the incident out of mind, for there were more important things to occupy his attention. For one thing, he and his crew would have been concerned with preparing for the winter. New houses had to be erected to accommodate his people; his ship had to be hauled out and properly secured; and the cargo of trade goods had to be stowed ashore.

When there was time for talk, Bjarni would have been far more interested in hearing Herjolf's reasons for moving to Greenland and in discussing plans for the establishment of a trading station than in talking about his own voyage.

Nevertheless there seems to have been one man at Herjolfsness that winter who saw in Bjarni's voyage an adventure worth remembering. He may well have been the Hebridean skald who had come out to Greenland in Herjolf's party and who composed the lost Hafgerdingar Drapa and who may, conceivably, also have composed a major portion of the original Old Erik Saga. In any event we credit this nameless skald with the authorship of the surviving account of Bjarni's western voyage, which forms an integral part of the Short Saga, itself a surviving fragment of the Old Erik Saga. This skald had the opportunity to hear Bjarni's story first hand, as the direct narration of a master seaman, which would go far to explaining why the account carries such an aura of credibility.

The quotations from the sagas which open this chapter are almost the only written records we possess concerning the history of Greenland during the decade following the settlement in 985. But since

---

those which are generally accepted. The reasons for believing that Leif sailed to Vinland at some time toward the middle of the last decade of the tenth century, and made his voyage to Norway a year or two later, are given in Appendix L and are further dealt with in Chapter Twelve.

the ordinary events of those formative years are of importance to an understanding of the remarkable events which followed them, we have made a partial if somewhat imaginative reconstruction of them.

During the winter of 985–986 the isolation of the settlers was intense. They were widely dispersed in little groups, and the problems of caring for their stock and for themselves through the first critical winter left them little time or energy for long journeys over the frozen fiords or across the intervening mountain ranges to visit neighbors.

With the passing of the fiord ice in the spring the isolation was not much alleviated. Although boats and vessels could have begun to move about again, there would have been little time for pleasure jaunts. The fencing of the home fields, the building of livestock shelters in distant pastures, and the urgent general need to force this land to produce the wherewithal for sustaining human life engrossed everyone's attention and energy — with a few exceptions.

Bjarni and his father were not bound to the land for their living, or at least not to the same extent that the other settlers were. The livelihood of the Herjolfers depended on trade, and in their storehouses they had the entire cargo of goods Bjarni had brought from Norway, plus whatever stock Herjolf had brought with him from Iceland. These goods had to be taken to the customers if they were to be sold.

Soon after the ice cleared, Bjarni and Herjolf had one of their vessels manned and loaded. Then they set out to visit the scattered colonists. Perhaps they were accompanied by the Hebridean skald, whose task it would have been to entertain the prospective customers when settlers and visitors alike gathered around the homestead hearth-fires in the evenings. The skald would have been called upon for many lays, including the Hafgerdingar Drapa and his Saga of Bjarni's Western Voyage.

One day the Herjolfers' vessel sailed around the northern bend in Eriksfiord and came to a mooring below the stead of Brattalid, where Erik had his home. This was something in the nature of a state visit, since Erik was the acknowledged chieftain of the new land.

Herjolf and Bjarni doubtless made lavish gifts to Erik, to his wife Thorhild and perhaps to the three half-grown sons, Leif, Thorstein and Thorvald, since gift-giving by a visiting merchant was a customary way of buying the good will of chieftains.

That night there was probably a formal feast, with Erik seated on his high chair, flanked by his famous dais-posts, while across from him sat Bjarni and Herjolf. After the meal the talk could have turned to Bjarni's voyage.

It was probably rough talk and since Bjarni and Herjolf were mere traders they would have been considered fair game for the humor of men like Thorhall the Hunter, who was the black-visaged and reputedly foul-mouthed overseer of Erik's estate in winter, and his hunter and sea-rover in the summertime. It is easy to imagine the contempt which Bjarni's cautious attitude toward his accidentally discovered new lands would have aroused among such men. The prudence of a good merchant seaman would have won no plaudits from those who made a virtue out of recklessness.

Theirs was a show of disdain which Bjarni would have had to bear stoically, for there was no recourse short of resorting to the sword and axe, and Bjarni was not a dueling man. Perhaps he took his revenge by charging exorbitant prices for his wares.

After Bjarni's departure from Brattalid there must have been intense discussion of his voyage and much speculation as to the identity and merit of the lands he had seen. But at this stage the settlers were in no position to follow up Bjarni's discoveries. They required time to establish themselves before contemplating any new adventures.

Then, too, Erik himself was probably opposed to new land-seeking voyages. Anything which threatened to deflect men's energy away from the new colony would have aroused his natural and formidable ire. Greenland and Greenland alone was the scene of his ambitions. In the scale of those times it was an independent kingdom in the making, and Erik's explorations had taught him that its resources could support a population quite big enough to satisfy his own ambitions for power and pre-eminence.

At the time of Bjarni's voyage, Leif Eriksson was about fifteen years of age. The experiences of his boyhood had naturally given him a taste for the adventurous life, and with the example of his father's exploits as a land-seeker and land-taker before him, he would not have been normal if he had not dreamed of someday accomplishing similar feats.

Bjarni's tale of lands to the west provided food for such dreams. Still, there was nothing Leif could do about it for the moment. The prohibitions against undertaking any more land-seeking voyages applied to him equally with all the others. Although he was in many ways already a man, he was still under the authority of his domineering father and still too young to seek his own destiny in the mysterious western reaches of the gray Atlantic.

During the next seven or eight years, more and more Icelanders gave up their submarginal holdings on that island and took passage for Erik's colony. As the best farmsteads were taken up, the newcomers began to push farther west to the Ivitgut fiords, which then became known as the Western Settlement.* Farming land in this new settlement was neither as extensive nor as good as in the Julianehaab district, but it was adequate for the moment.

As both the Eastern and Western settlements became better established, and as herds and flocks grew in size, the early urgency which had forced men to work with single-minded intensity from dawn until dusk began to diminish. When summer came, the well-organized farms could be left under the guiding hands of women, older children, slaves and elderly retainers. Men in the prime of life were free to take on other tasks which were more to their tastes, such as hunting and wood-gathering journeys up the west coast, excursions far out to sea after whales, and summer-long voyages to the rich hunting grounds of the Vestri Obygdir.

Later records tell us that it became the custom for each important settler to send a boatload of men to the obygdir every spring. These excursions were of vital importance, not just to supply the settlements with wild meat, hides and oil, but also to procure the barter capital with which trade goods could be purchased from Norwegian and Icelandic merchants. Walrus tusks, in particular, had become so valuable a commodity in Europe that one good summer in Greenland's obygdir could make a hunter relatively rich. These prolonged hunting and fishing voyages seem to have led to a new development in the maritime skills and techniques of the Greenlanders — or perhaps it was a reversion to ancient Norwegian techniques.

The Greenland of the Norse was a coastal country of prodigious length, and men had little need for ocean-going vessels which were too big to be handled by small crews or to be maneuvered in the remote and narrow channels of the innumerable fiords. What was

---

* Until sometime shortly after A.D. 1000 the Godthaab Fiord area was apparently not settled and the Ivitgut Fiord district bore the name Vestri Bygd. For a full explanation of this identification see Appendix D.

needed was something rather like the afterboat of a knorr, which itself was a survival of the ancient clinker-built skiffs and wherries that had been in use on the Norwegian coast since primeval times. Consequently the Greenland boats seem to have developed as large, double-ended rowing skiffs equipped with a sail. They drew almost no water and could be hauled out at need by their own crews. They were very maneuverable, ideally suited for whaling, sealing or walrus hunting.

No examples of them survive, but we can determine some further details about them from later sagas and other sources. They seem to have been six-oared, six-man boats of about three tons displacement. While they were primarily intended for coasting voyages, they were good enough sea-boats to be able to make regular crossings to the Vestri Obygdir.

There is no indication in the sagas of where the materials came from to build these Greenland skiffs. No natural hardwood was available in Greenland except what little might appear as driftwood. Nevertheless, good hardwood was essential to the construction of Scandinavian clinker-built skiffs, since these boats owed their strength, elasticity and lightness to the fact that their frames were very small, and their planking very thin.

Probably the first generations of Greenland skiffs were the result of a form of cannibalism. The ships which had brought the settlers to Greenland would have begun to deteriorate through lack of use, lack of care, and a shortage of hardwood to keep them in repair. Doubtless their owners chose to break them up before they rotted out, and to use the salvaged materials for building the smaller and more useful coasting skiffs.

This source of materials would have served for a while, but the presence of a minimum of several hundred settlers in Greenland would soon have exhausted this supply of timber, together with whatever usable hardwood had formerly existed in the driftwood wrack along the shores; while even the rough driftwood must have rapidly vanished into fireplaces along with a good part of the dwarf local "forests."

As buildings grew larger and more numerous, timber for rafters and supporting posts would have become scarcer, and its value would have soared. Greenland did not even have any natural softwoods of sufficient size to be of much use in this connection, consequently the settlers would have had to rely mostly on wood imported from Norway.

Lumber is a bulky substance not worth nearly as much, in terms of the cargo space it occupies, as such things as iron and manufactured goods. It is unlikely that many of the traders who voyaged from Norway to Greenland chose lumber as a cargo.

A dearth of timber, both soft and hard, must have been the first important scarcity the Greenlanders experienced, apart from the perennial shortage of grain, whose partial or complete absence they may have become somewhat used to in Iceland. It was inevitable that sooner or later men would recall Bjarni's description of the new lands to the west which were almost literally hidden under immense stands of virgin forest.

We do not know when the Greenlanders stopped talking about Bjarni's land and decided to go and see for themselves if its reputed forest wealth really did exist. But if we cannot know the date we can at least make an informed guess as to the identity of the man behind the proposal of a westward voyage.

As Leif grew older he must have begun to chafe at the limited opportunities which Greenland offered for the accomplishment of great and famous deeds. Early in the last decade of the century he was a fully grown man and, to a large extent, his own master. The ferment of ambition must have been growing hot within him. The Greenland of his father's dream had become a reality by then. Consequently Erik's initial resistance to new westward voyages had doubtless diminished. He too must have been concerned about the timber shortage. He may even have concluded that it was time for his eldest son to add something to the luster of the family name by undertaking a spectacular venture on his own account.

Leif's first problem seems to have been to find a suitable ship. The Erikers evidently no longer owned such a vessel. If they had done so, we can assume that Leif would have used it. By this time the shortage of seagoing vessels seems to have become acute throughout the settlements. However, the Herjolfers owned two ships; and since they had no use for more than one of these, Bjarni had doubtless hauled up his own vessel and placed her in storage. He was a good and careful seaman, and he would have taken care of her. She would have deteriorated but little during the intervening years providing she had been kept in a vessel shed and protected from the weather. No doubt Bjarni was glad enough to sell her, since he seems to have had no intention of going to sea again. The Short Saga tells us that after reaching Herjolfsness, he gave up voyaging and remained ashore even after his father died.

It can be assumed that part of the bargain between Leif and Bjarni was that the merchant skipper agreed to supply Leif with information concerning the western lands, including their position and the best route by which they might be reached. It is also likely that some of the thirty-five men Leif hired as his crew were former members of Bjarni's crew.

Having bought his ship, signed on a crew and put in hand the business of getting her seaworthy, Leif would have turned his attention to the navigational problems confronting him. To begin with, he had to decide which of the three lands was to be his destination. The northernmost land would have been quickly eliminated since, according to Bjarni's report, it was utterly worthless. The middle land offered possibilities, but Bjarni could have determined from seaward, without ever having effected a landing, that its forests consisted mostly of conifers, or softwoods. On the other hand, the forests of the southern land would have revealed the presence of deciduous trees, the valuable hardwoods which were in such short supply in Greenland.

Assuming that he made the logical choice and picked the southern land, Leif would next have had to decide how best to reach it. He had a choice between retracing Bjarni's entire route, which would have involved three separate departures, three landfalls, and a number of different courses or of steering a direct course from south Greenland to Newfoundland.

There was probably never any real doubt in Leif's mind as to which route he should follow. Apart from the difficulties inherent in retracing multiple courses and finding multiple landmarks, there was also the matter of pride to be considered. To have chosen to backtrack Bjarni would have smacked of timidity, particularly since Bjarni had been derided as an overly cautious, if not cowardly man.

For these and other reasons listed in Appendix L, I conclude that Leif chose to attempt the direct passage.

Bjarni may have discussed the matter with Leif somewhat in this vein:

"When I first reached that southernmost land I had no way of

telling how far west of the settlement I had been blown, although
the position of the Guiding Star told me how far south I was. Not
knowing my westing, I could not risk laying a direct course for
Herjolfsness. That is why I coasted until I had my northing, and could
safely sail east.

"But after I reached Herjolfsness, it was not much trouble to
work my courses and distances backward so that I could get a fair
idea of how far west of Herjolfsness that southern land must lie, and
of what the course to it should be. I estimate that it lies between the
south and the southwestern airts (south-southwest) and at a distance
of not more than six or seven doegr.

"My advice is that you should hold your course in the third portion of the southwest airt (a little west of south-southwest). It is also
my advice that you wait for a northeast wind before departing. If you
run before such a wind there will be less risk of making leeway and
of being set off your course and, too, you will complete your voyage
more swiftly.

"This also I can tell you — the mid-part of the southern land lies
five and one-half doegr south of Herjolfsness (comparative latitude);
but you will have to pass through a great fog-ocean as you approach
the land, and then it is likely you will not be able to see the Guiding
Star and so will have difficulty in determining how far south you are.

"When the fogs grow thick you must watch the birds of the ocean,
and from their kinds and numbers you will know that you are nearing
the southern land even though you do not see it."

Bjarni doubtless added a detailed description of the landfalls and
the appearance of the land; but since Leif was perhaps accompanied
by some of Bjarni's old crew, this information may not have been
quite so vital.

With his ship ready for sea Leif had only to wait for a favoring
breeze. One morning a gray, cold wind came blowing down across the
inland ice. Perhaps Bjarni and Leif stood together on the bleak slopes
of the Herjolfsness headland, their faces turned toward the northeast
and the rising breeze. Perhaps, too, the older man felt the surge of
an old desire within him — the hunger to know the sea-bride once
again.

Below him Bjarni would have been able to see the ship — *his* ship
once — lying at her moorings in the haven, her crew busy about her

decks with last-minute preparations. She was ready. The wind was fair. And the young man beside him — this arrogant son of an arrogant chieftain — was more than ready.

Bjarni may still have been watching when the knorr was rowed out past the haven entrance. Her big sail was swayed up and the slat and bang of her running gear ceased as the sail bellied out and the ship began to pick up way. A bone would have begun to show at her teeth as she ran swiftly off toward the southwest reaches of the unknown ocean. Driving fast before a rising wind, she would have diminished rapidly from Bjarni's view until she slipped from sight, hull down under a gray horizon.

And now, as the saga-men were wont to put it with a succinct finality, Bjarni Herjolfsson and his father are out of this story.

.\\.\\.\

vinland and after

11

ᴧᴠᴧ

the vinland voyage

The Saga Tale (c. 995–996)

They made their ship ready for sea and when all was ready they sailed out to sea . . . before a northeaster and were out for II [U or V?] doegr before they sighted land.

They sailed to land, reaching an island which lay to the northward of the country and they went up there and looked about them in fine weather. There was dew on the grass and they touched the dew with their hands and brought it to their mouths, and they thought they had never known anything to taste so sweet.

After that they returned to their ship and sailed through the sound which lay between the island and that cape which projected northward from the land itself. They sailed westward around the cape.

There were extensive shoals there [at the place they eventually reached after rounding the cape] at ebb tide and their ship went aground. It was a long way to look from the ship to get sight of the sea.

They were so curious to go ashore that they could not wait until high water floated their ship, but hurried to the land where a river flowed from a lake into the sea.

As soon as the tide rose under their ship they rowed back to her in their boat and took her up the river and so into the lake where they anchored.

They brought their leather bags from the ship and built booths there. Later they decided to stay for the winter and they built a large house.

There was no shortage of salmon in the river or in the lake, and these were larger salmon than they had ever seen before. The qualities of the surrounding country were so good that they believed there would be no shortage of cattle fodder in the wintertime. No frost came in winter and the grass withered only a little.

The length of day and night was more nearly equal than in Greenland or Iceland. Sunset came after Eykarstad [about 3:00 p.m.] and sunrise before Dagmalastad [about 9:00 a.m.] on the shortest day of the year.

When they had built their house Leif said to his followers: "Now I will divide the company into two parts so that the land can be explored. One half of the company shall remain at home while the other half goes exploring; but not farther away than they can return in the evening; and they are not to separate."

For a while they did as he had said and Leif alternately went out with them or stayed home at the hall. Leif was a very tall and vigorous man, a brave fellow to look at, a shrewd man and careful in all things.

One evening word came that a man was missing from one of the [exploration] parties. This was Tyrker, the southerner. Leif was much distressed by this because Tyrker had been with his father and himself a long time and had been very fond of Leif during his childhood.

Leif gave Tyrker's companions a tongue-lashing and ordered an expedition to be made in search of him by twelve men, and went along himself.

They had gone only a short way from the hall when Tyrker came to meet them and was warmly greeted. Tyrker had a big forehead, restless eyes and a freckled face. His stature was low and unprepossessing but he was a man who was foremost in all crafts.

Leif said to him: "Why were you so late foster father of mine, and [why] did you leave your comrades?"

Then Tyrker spoke for a long time in his southern tongue, and rolled his eyes a lot and made wry faces, but they did not understand what he said. Finally he explained in Norse:

"I have walked not much farther than here but I have something interesting to relate. I found vines and grapes."

"Is that true, foster father?" asked Leif.

"Of course it is true," he replied, "for I was born there [in the south] where neither vines nor grapes are scarce."

Then they all went to bed, but in the morning Leif said to his crew:

"Hereafter we shall have two tasks. Every day we will either gather grapes and cut vines, or fell timber to make a cargo for my ship."

They cut a full cargo for the ship and when spring came they made ready

The choice of a house site would have depended to some extent on whether Leif had been able to satisfy himself that there was little or no danger from local denizens — animal, human or supernatural. If he felt secure enough he might have chosen to build on the mainland under the lee of the high hill which lies just behind the present settlement of Tickle Cove. Here the Norse would have found good shelter from winter winds; the forest would have been close enough so that wood gathering would have been no problem; and there would have been an excellent source of fresh water in two small streams that even now seldom freeze in wintertime. It is a notable fact that where one set of human beings choose to build their homes is very often the place selected by the next group, and the next after that. At any rate there has been continuous human habitation of the east side of Tickle Cove Pond for at least the last three hundred years.

The lack of any reference to native peoples at Leif's haven is particularly noteworthy. At that period in history most of the Labrador coast, together with the west coast of the Great Northern Peninsula of Newfoundland, was still occupied by Dorset Eskimos. The rest of Newfoundland, except for the Avalon Peninsula, was populated by Beothuk, or proto-Beothuk, Indians. For some reason which we cannot as yet explain, but which was probably connected with their dual caribou-sea food economy, the Indians seem to have seldom crossed the narrow neck which connects the Avalon Peninsula to the main body of the island, and which also separates Trinity Bay from Placentia Bay.* At Tickle Cove Leif would have found no Dorsets, and it is unlikely that he would have encountered Beothuks, or found signs of them. On the other hand if his Vinland had been located at any of the alternative sites, such as the northeastern bays, he could hardly have avoided seeing signs of either Dorsets or Beothuks.

If Leif *had* met any natives, it is nearly certain that the saga would have mentioned the fact. Meetings with natives loom large in all subsequent accounts of Norse voyages to Newfoundland and Labrador. The absence of any mention of a native population, present or suspected, in connection with Leif's voyage provides strong corroborative evidence supporting the identification of Trinity Bay as Vinland.

---

* Although a large number of Dorset, proto-Beothuk and Beothuk sites are known from most other parts of Newfoundland, none have been found on the Avalon Peninsula, where even scattered finds of artifacts are extremely rare. There are no artifact finds at all from the foot of Trinity Bay.

THE CLIMATE

A problem which has bothered many authors and which has cast a shadow over the acceptability of any Vinland site north of Cape Hatteras is contained in the saga phrase: "No frost came in winter and the grass withered only a little."

There seem to be three possible ways of resolving this difficulty in connection with Tickle Cove Pond.

In the first place we can assume (as many others have done) that the meaning of the translation, or the text itself, is in error and that it should read: "*little* frost came in winter and the grass withered only a little." Another possible solution may be found by a comparison with a similar phrase in the descriptions of conditions at Karlsefni's Hop.* "There was no snow and all of the livestock lived by grazing." The similarity of these two descriptions suggests that the author of the Greenlanders Story may have borrowed the essence of the phrase from the original of the Erik the Red Saga.

A case can be made for the acceptance of either of these solutions; but the saga account may be perfectly accurate as it stands. Because it is situated fifty-five miles in from the northern headlands, Tickle Cove remains almost unaffected by the cold Labrador Current, which sweeps across the mouth of Trinity Bay. But it *is* influenced by the weather of Placentia Bay, which is separated from it by a neck of land only six or seven miles wide. Placentia Bay, and the whole south coast of Newfoundland, has a much milder climate than the northeastern coast, since it is open to warm southerly winds blowing in across the Gulf Stream. Tickle Cove receives almost the full benefits of these mild southerly winds while at the same time remaining largely free of the fog which usually comes with such winds and which greatly reduces the amount of sunshine in Placentia Bay and on the south coast generally. Crop-sprouting times at settlements near the bottom of Trinity Bay average two to four weeks earlier than at settlements well up the bay shores. Snow-fall is generally light at Tickle Cove, and frequent winter thaws tend to keep the ground snow-free much of the time. Winter temperatures seldom go more than a few degrees below freezing point, and during some winters there is very little frost at all.

---

* See Chapter 21.

These are the conditions which prevail now. When we consider how much better weather conditions were during the Little Climatic Optimum we see that there is a strong likelihood that the Greenlanders Story report of a frost-free winter may be a sober statement of observed fact. Even if it is not strictly accurate (the Norse had no thermometers), the degree of exaggeration need be very small.

It is a widespread misapprehension that Newfoundland has a cold, even subarctic climate. The truth is that the average winter temperatures of the southern and eastern coastal regions of the island are much higher than those of any other place in eastern Canada, and even of most parts of the New England states as far south as northern Massachusetts.

THE LATITUDE

A great deal of scholarly effort has been expended in attempts to establish a Vinland latitude from the saga statement that sunset at Vinland came after Eykarstad and sunrise came before Dagmalastad, on the shortest day of the year. These terms do not refer to clock times, since the Norse of this period had no clocks. They apparently refer to the azimuth directions of the sun at sunrise and sunset. The astronomer H. Geelmuyden (*Arkiv for Norisk Fiologri*, III, 128) determined the azimuth value of Eykarstad from an old Icelandic law book called the *Gragas*. He concluded that the direction was south 52½ degrees west. He then worked out the latitude where the sun would set in this direction on the shortest day of the year during the early eleventh century. The result was 49 degrees 55 minutes.

Many other attempts have been made along similar lines, and the results generally give a latitude between 46 and 52 degrees north latitude. The latitude of Tickle Cove Pond is 47 degrees 37 minutes.

THE GRAPEVINES

We come now to the one element in the Vinland description which has caused more dissension than anything else contained in all the sagas. This is the reference to vines and grapes. The antagonists whose arguments have raged (and continue to rage) about this point fall roughly into three camps.

In the first are those who believe that Leif did find authentic wild grapes. Because wild grapes no longer grow farther north than southern New Brunswick, these people insist that Vinland must be looked for south of New Brunswick, possibly as far south as Florida.

The second camp includes those who think that the Norse words vin and vinber (vine and vine-berries) do not refer to grapes at all, but should be identified with various kinds of wild berries from which wine could have been made, thereby greatly extending the northern limits within which Vinland can be sought.

Those in the third camp believe that the word vin as it was originally used in the sagas, had nothing to do with grapes or wine or berries, but was an ancient Norse word for pastures; hence, they say, Vinland should be translated as Pastureland.

As far as Tickle Cove Pond is concerned, the entire argument is academic.

Tickle Cove Pond possesses excellent pastures, and evidently did in Leif's time. If Vinland means Pastureland, Tickle Cove merits the name.

The whole of Newfoundland, and the Trinity Bay district in particular, abounds in wild berries of which wine can be made, including all the species which scholars have suggested might be identified as the saga wine-berries.

Finally, there were wild grapes in Newfoundland, and in quantity, until as late as the middle of the seventeenth century.

This last is a statement which will not please those who have insisted that Leif must have landed in New England, and whose best argument has always been that wild grapes could never have been present in the northeastern maritime regions of Canada. These authorities believe that Cartier's report of wild grapes on the Ile d'Orleans in the St. Lawrence River, at latitude 47 degrees, was a latter-day forgery, and that the same thing applies to records of wild grapes having been found in the Magdalen Islands in the St. Lawrence Gulf at latitude 47 degrees 30 minutes.

Evidence of the existence of wild grapes in Newfoundland comes from several sources. Foremost among these is a journal kept by a Plymouth surgeon named James Yonge who made four voyages to Newfoundland between 1662 and 1670 as a surgeon to the English fishing fleet. Yonge later became a Fellow of the Royal Society and published a large number of scientific papers and books, including three medical textbooks which were in wide use for many years after his death.

He was a keen observer of natural history, and his journal contains many notes on birds, mammals, fishes and plants — particularly those of Newfoundland. His identifications and comments have been checked by modern botanists and zoologists and have been found to be extremely accurate.

Yonge also traveled widely in the Mediterranean and was a surgeon on a ship engaged in the wine and raisin trade, so he was not likely to have been in much doubt as to what grapes looked like. In describing the animals and plants on the Avalon Peninsula, of which Trinity Bay is a part, Yonge had this to say: "Here are beaver, otter, and deer plentiful; for fruits strawberry, raspberries, whorts, and wild grapes incredible." *

Further references to the occurrence of wild grapes in Newfoundland are found in L. A. Anspach's *History of the Island of Newfoundland,* published in 1827. Anspach quotes one Patrick Gordon in a work published in London in 1772 as stating that those parts of Newfoundland held by the French (of which Placentia Bay was one of the main regions) produced wild grapevines in abundance. It is also stated that a series of severe winters in the late eighteenth century destroyed the wild grapevines in Newfoundland and that they never reappeared. This is consistent with recent climatological studies, which show that there was a period of very adverse weather in the western regions of the North Atlantic beginning about the middle of the seventeenth century.

There is therefore nothing surprising in the existence of wild grapes in Newfoundland in the tenth century. This was the period when the Little Climatic Optimum dominated the entire North Atlantic region. Climatologists have shown that between 1000 and 1200, vineyards in western Europe were being cultivated 4 to 5 degrees of latitude farther north than their present limits. This is a distance of 240-300 nautical miles. The present northern limit of wild grapes on the eastern American seaboard is about 45 degrees north latitude, or only 157 nautical miles south of Tickle Cove Pond.

One further point merits attention both in this connection and with reference to the general excellence of the Tickle Cove area. At the present time the districts at the bottom of Trinity and Bonavista bays are the only places in Newfoundland where fruit is produced

---

* *The Journal of James Yonge, Plymouth Surgeon,* edited by F. N. L. Poynter (London: Longmans, 1963).

commercially. Damsons, apples and blue plums are commonly grown. The climate of most of Newfoundland is suitable to these and other domestic fruits, but the orchards of Bonavista and Trinity bays exist because the bottomlands of both bays contain the best soil to be found in all eastern and central Newfoundland. These are the same soils which once produced the luxuriant hardwood forest which was still in its virginal condition in Leif's time.

THE PRODIGAL LAND

Tickle Cove on a summer's day in the twentieth century is as lovely a place as one could wish to see. It could have been no less attractive in the tenth century. We can imagine Leif's men rowing out on the Broad to fish for sea trout and salmon; or see them walking across the wide meadows, marveling at the tall grass swaying about their knees and thinking greedily of what they could do with land like this. As the tide fell some of them might have gone to the great curving sickle of the outer beach to gather clams, blue and brown mussels and other shellfish for roasting or boiling over great open fires. Dry firewood — a luxury in Greenland — would have been present in huge quantities, windrowed above high-tide level on the beach.

If they chose they could have taken their boats out through the tickle into the waters of the open bay, where great pods of pilot whales followed the squid and herring almost to the landwash. It would have been no trick to kill as many of these harmless mammals as they desired. The Norse of Leif's time, who are known to have been expert whalers, might have used a method familiar to their ancient ancestors. Rowing small boats, and making a great racket by shouting and water splashing, the old Norwegians used to drive panic-stricken schools of the smaller species of whales into the ends of bays where the beasts would strand themselves in scores or hundreds. If Leif's men did this at Tickle Cove they would only have been anticipating a whale fishery which still flourishes there and which still employs this ancient technique. But whether they bothered to go whaling or not, the Norse would have been impressed by the vast numbers of pilots, or potheads as they are known in Newfoundland, which crowd into the bay — a limitless supply of meat and oil waiting to be harvested.

The sea hereabouts was full of wealth, but the land was by no means niggardly. As is attested by the writings of the first arrivals in the colonial period, this part of Newfoundland was once alive with caribou. The Norse would have been familiar with the beasts, for they were found in Greenland too; but they probably had never imagined that caribou could exist in such numbers as inhabited this new land. Even today, after four centuries of continuous and heavy slaughter, it is still possible to see a thousand caribou in the course of a few days' excursion into the isolated central parts of the island.

Black bears, wolves, foxes, otters, beaver and martens would also have been abundant; and the protected waters of the Broad and of the nearby lakes would have held great flocks of ducks.

As summer waned and the berries and fruits began to ripen, Tyrker and the others would have found much more than wild grapes to amaze them with the prodigality of this land. The berry barrens on the spine of the isthmus between Trinity and Placentia bays would have been hazed with a purple wash of blueberries. Cloud-berries, those oily groundfruits beloved of all northern races, would have spread a golden glow over the surface of the muskeg bogs, interspersed with crimson bursts of cranberries. The list is almost endless: raspberries, crowberries, whortleberries, loganberries, elderberries, squashberries — all these, and more, still grow abundantly in the Trinity Bay region. And on the edge of the forests there would have been wild cherry and hazlenut trees, the fruit of both of which might have been foreign to the Norse, but most acceptable for all of that.

And the forests! Men who were used to the stunted birch thickets of Iceland and Greenland would have marveled at yellow birch trees (witch hazel, the Newfoundlanders call it) growing to heights of over a hundred feet and measuring three feet across the stump; or white birches almost as large, if somewhat less numerous. They would soon have discovered, as their axes lost their edges on the witch hazel, that here was a hardwood almost as tough as oak.

The forests were — and still are — of mixed composition. Those at the bottom of Trinity Bay include two kinds of maples as well as birch. Of conifers there are white and red pine, red, white and black spruce, balsam fir and tamarack. There was wood here to build countless ships, and the proper kind of wood for every part of a vessel: tough tamarack for ribs, witch hazel for keels and planking, and tall pines for spars and yards. There was, in fact, enough timber in this region to keep a major shipbuilding industry alive through more than three centuries of later European occupation — an industry which is not dead even now. Wooden ships are still being built at the yard in nearby Clarenville.

Each evening as the exploring parties returned to camp they would have brought reports of new and greater riches which this land held, until the day came when Leif put an end to their explorations and ordered them to get down to the serious business of turning these potential riches into usable wealth.

Felling, trimming and hewing a shipload of hardwood would have been a heavy task for these men, equipped as they were with indifferently tempered iron axes and adzes. There would have been little enough time that winter for wandering about, or for anything except hard labor. Perhaps small parties were occasionally sent off hunting for venison, but the majority of the crew must have worked like slaves at lumbering.

When the spring came the knorr must have been loaded deep with as valuable a cargo as ever set sail for Greenland from either east or west. Leif, that "shrewd and vigorous" man, would not have frittered away his opportunities.

The ship doubtless carried other articles of local produce, including dried berries and grapes, for raisins were known to the Norse. It may be that the tale of filling one of the boats with such dried fruits was no exaggeration, for a boat would have made a good enough receptacle, chocked down on deck and covered with hide tarpaulins.

Grapevines would have been of great value too, for the planks of Norse ships were not spiked to the timbers but were bound to them with withes — and wild grapevines make first-rate withes.

There is an impression implicit in the saga accounts that Leif's feelings for Vinland were peculiarly ambivalent. Although he must have valued the place as a source of wealth and also for the renown which came to him as a result of his voyage there, he never made any attempt to return to it; and it seems clear from his subsequent actions that he did not wish to see it settled. In taking this stand he may have been perpetuating Erik's assumed antipathy toward the development of new and distant lands which might have tended to drain away the Greenland settlers — for Leif was heir apparent to the chieftaincy of Greenland. Or perhaps, having discovered his personal Eldorado, he was jealously concerned to prevent anyone else from sharing its riches. He was a shrewd man, was Leif the son of Erik.

Whatever his motives may have been, Leif not only failed to return to Vinland himself but, so it appears, did nothing to help others reach it after him.

But if Leif wished to keep Vinland in limbo, it is unlikely that his men shared his feelings. As the knorr ran down the tidal river into the open waters of Trinity Bay on a morning in late spring or early summer, many of them would have looked back with hungry eyes at this place which of all the places they had ever known must have most nearly resembled a paradise on earth.

Through the years ahead their nostalgic descriptions of the land they could never possess for themselves did much to buttress the legend of that country which Leif called Vinland — but which eventually became known across the northern world as Vinland the Good.

12

/.V.\V.\

Leif's norway voyage

The Saga Tale (c. 996–997)

Now they sailed to sea and got a fair wind until they saw the mountains under the glaciers of Greenland. Then one of the men asked Leif: "Why do you steer the ship so far off the wind?"

Leif replied: "I can take care of my course [lit: I take care of my rudder]; but there is something besides that [attracting my attention]. Don't you see anything remarkable?"

The men answered that they saw nothing unusual.

"I do not know," said Leif, "if I see a ship or a reef."

Now the men saw it and said it was a reef, but Leif had sharper vision than they did so that he distinguished men on the islet.

"We will beat to windward," said Leif, "so as to approach them, if they want to be found by us and need assistance; but if they are not peaceably inclined we will have the advantage [of position] and they will not."

Then they sailed up to the reef, let fall their sail, cast anchor, and put out another small boat which they had with them.

Tyrker [who went in the boat] asked who was the leader of the [ship-wrecked] party; and the leader replied that he was called Thorer and was of Norse descent. "But what is your leader's name?" he asked.

Leif told him his name.

"Art thou the son of Erik the Red of Brattalid?"

Leif replied that he was. "And now," said Leif, "I invite you all to come aboard my ship; but bring as much of your goods as my ship will hold."

They accepted his terms. The ship was then sailed into Eriksford, to Brattalid. They unloaded the ship and Leif took Thorer, Gudrid his wife, and three of his men, to live with him; but he got other quarters for the rest of Thorer's crew as well as for his own.

Leif saved fifteen men from the islet. He was afterwards called Leif the Lucky. He was now well off both as to riches and honor.

[SOURCE: The Greenlanders Story]

When sixteen winters had passed since Erik the Red went out to take land in Greenland, Leif Eriksson went to Norway. When Leif sailed from Greenland that summer he was driven out of his course and came to the Hebrides. It was late in the season before they got fair winds again and so they remained there far into the summer.

Leif fell in love with a certain woman there whose name was Thorgunna. She was a woman of fine family and Leif believed she had supernatural wisdom.

When Leif was preparing to depart, Thorgunna begged to go with him. Leif asked her if she had the approval of her kinsmen and she replied that she did not care about that.

Leif told her he did not consider it a wise move to abduct so high-born a woman, in a foreign country, and "we so few in numbers."

"It is by no means certain that you will find yours is the best decision," warned Thorgunna.

"Nevertheless I intend to stick to it," Leif answered.

"Then," said Thorgunna," "I must tell you that I am not the only one concerned, for I am pregnant, and you are responsible. I forsee that I shall give birth to a male child, and though you are indifferent, I will rear this child and send him to you in Greenland when he is of an age to take his place with other men. And I forsee that you will get as much profit from this son as you deserve, considering the nature of our parting. Moreover, I mean to come to Greenland myself before I die."

Then Leif gave her a gold finger-ring; a Greenland wadmal cloak, and a belt of walrus ivory.

The boy later came to Greenland and his name was Thorgils. Leif acknowledged his paternity. Some men say this same Thorgils reached Iceland in the summer before the Froda-Wonders. When this Thorgils was in Greenland there seemed to be something not altogether natural about him, before the end came.

Leif and his companions now sailed away from the Hebrides and arrived at Drontheim [in Norway] in the autumn, at the time King Olaf Tryggvason came from Halgoland. Leif laid his ship up at Nidaros and went at once to visit King Olaf.

He was well received by the King, who believed he could see in Leif a man of great possibilities. The King expounded the [Christian] faith to him, as he did to all heathen men who came to visit him, and the King dealt gently with Leif. Leif and all his shipmates were then christened and they remained with the King all winter and were well treated.

[SOURCES: Erik the Red Saga, Karlsefni Saga and the Short Saga]

LEIF'S RETURN

The account of Leif's homeward passage and his rescue of Thorer not only throws light on Leif's character. It also provides further indications that he made his Vinland voyage direct from southern Greenland.

Thorer was evidently a Norwegian trader. From a later reference in the Greenlanders Story it appears that he had sailed from Norway for Greenland with a cargo which included timber. Since he still had his cargo aboard when he was wrecked we can assume that he had not yet reached the Eastern Settlements. In all probability he had rounded Cape Farewell and was beating his way up the coast when his ship was driven onto an off-lying islet or reef and wrecked.

The skerry where his ship went ashore most likely belonged to the large group of islets and reefs which runs for some fifteen miles on a line about ten miles offshore between Herjolfsness and Ketilsfiord. These, together with a smaller group off Hrafnsfiord, are the only offshore skerries near the Eastern Settlements, and the saga makes it clear that Thorer was wrecked well offshore. The Herjolfsness skerries are the ones which a ship inbound from the east would have been most likely to strike. Thorer may well have been making for the Herjolfsness haven when he came to grief.

If we combine this identification of the skerries with the saga description of Leif's approach to Greenland, "they sailed to sea and got a fair wind until they saw the mountains under the glaciers of Greenland," it seems clear that Leif made his landfall while steering northeasterly, a direct course from Vinland to south Greenland.

Considering that he was returning to his own land and to a country dominated by his own family, the caution Leif displayed in approaching the shipwreck seems curious. Either social conditions in Greenland were a good deal more disturbed than most historians have believed, or else Viking pirates had already become a threat on the Greenland coasts. Pirates from Norway and the Outer Islands are known to have been raiding Iceland about this time, and the Floamanna Saga records their presence off the Eastern Settlements of Greenland about the year 1004; so this may well be the explanation for Leif's display of prudence.

When Leif was satisfied that the wrecked mariners were bona-fide traders he offered to rescue them; but he instructed them to bring aboard as much of their goods as his already heavily laden ship could carry. He would not have been referring to Thorer's cargo of lumber, but to such things as ironware and manufactured goods. Thorer's people apparently understood this to mean that Leif would keep the goods, either as salvage or as recompense for saving their lives. This may have been one of the normal mores of the times; but on the other hand it may be an indication of how shrewd Leif was.

With the castaways on board, Leif bore up for Eriksfiord and ran down its familiar waters until he came to his moorings off the complex of buildings at Brattalid.

That would have been a proud homecoming and a memorable one. Not only had Leif reached Bjarni's fabled land but he had overwintered there successfully. He had obtained a lading of timber and other goods of great value there, and had then made a good passage home during which he had topped off his cargo with an assortment of Norwegian trade goods. It was little wonder that he received the nickname Lucky as a consequence. The voyage had been a singularly prosperous one, bringing him, in the words of the saga, "both riches and honor."

Leif was now well on his way to becoming a made man, and it is not likely that he would have been inclined to rest on his laurels. His ambitions would have been whetted by the successful Vinland voyage, but Greenland offered him little opportunity to increase his fame. The road to personal power was blocked by the unyielding figure of his father.

Erik was not yet an old man and was still exercising vigorous control over his family and over the Greenland settlements. The saga records demonstrate that Norse fathers were seldom prepared to relinquish their patriarchal powers to their sons before senility forced the issue; while their sons do not always appear to have allowed filial loyalties to stand in the way of their struggles to climb into their fathers' boots before the elder men were ready to take them off.

Erik may have been proud of Leif's exploits, but we can believe that he took a jaundiced view of Leif's ambition. The events of the next few years suggest that Leif, for his part, did what he could to unseat his father and to usurp his position.

THE RISE OF OLAF TRYGGVASON

While Leif had been making local history in the west, an illegitimate descendant of King Harold Fairhair had been making a different kind of history in the east. In 995 Olaf Tryggvason, a sea-Viking of dubious repute, deserted his brother-in-law, the King of Denmark, during an attack on England and made a sudden assault on the seaward coast of Norway, which was then under the Viceroyship of Jarl Haakon of Lade acting for the King of Denmark.

Olaf slaughtered Haakon and then busied himself with conquering the country for himself and for God. Olaf was a Christian convert, not because he had any regard for the Christian ethic but because he seems to have been one of the earliest of the north European rulers to have realized how useful Christianity could be to an autocratic monarch.

His methods of Christianizing Norway were ferocious but effective. Recalcitrant pagans of ordinary rank were summarily butchered or burned in their homes. If they were of sufficient importance to justify an effort being made to convert them, they were sometimes treated to the ordeal of the snake. The mouthpiece of a metal war-horn was forced well down the victim's gullet; a snake, usually an adder, was placed in the bell and a lid was clamped over it. The horn was then heated until the tortured snake tried to escape by crawling down the victim's throat.

Tales of the prowess of this imaginative king were quick to spread through the Scandinavian world. Skalds began singing his praises to such purpose that despite his brief reign, the Saga of Olaf Tryggvason is one of the most famous accounts of the achievements of a Norwegian king of the Viking age.

Word of King Olaf's brisk exploits doubtless reached Greenland in the summer of 996 with Thorer and his crew. The recounting of the mighty deeds of slaughter, burning and rapine which Olaf was performing would have stirred the hearts of young men of Viking character even in this far distant outpost of the Norse, and we can believe that Leif listened in jealous admiration.*

Having spent the winter as the guest of the Greenlanders, Thorer the Norwegian would have been anxious to return to Norway in the spring, but he had no ship of his own and he may not have had the wherewithal with which to purchase a vessel, even if the Greenlanders had had one to sell — which they probably did not.

But Leif was the owner of a sea-going ship. Consequently we can assume that Thorer would have used his best arguments to persuade Leif that the young man ought to make a voyage to Norway, perhaps offering to be the pilot and to supply the services of his own men as part of the crew, in exchange for a passage east. Thorer may have had an entrée into King Olaf's court, but even if he did not he could doubtless have arranged for Leif to be received there. We can readily imagine him plying Leif with stories of the glory of the court; of Olaf himself; and of the honors a brave adventurer like Leif might expect to receive from such a king.

Leif would have been easy to persuade. Now that he had become a man of wealth and substance in his own right, he would have been able to appear at Olaf's court as someone of importance, not as a

---

* In reconstructing this portion of the history of the voyages, the author of the Greenlanders Story has confused certain elements in the lives of Thorstein Eriksson and Thorer the Norseman.

To begin with, he tells us that Thorer brought his wife Gudrid with him on the Greenland trading voyage, and that this was the same Gudrid Thorbjornsdottir who later married Thorstein Eriksson and still later Thorfinn Karlsefni, and who played a leading role in the western voyages subsequent to Leif's visit to Vinland.

This is an error. The Erik the Red and Karlsefni sagas, supported by the Landnamabok, give an entirely different version of how Gudrid Thorbjornsdottir reached Greenland as an unmarried girl accompanied by her father. This version is so detailed and so well substantiated that its authenticity cannot be doubted.

Thorer *may* have had a woman called Gudrid with him, for Norse traders were in the habit of carrying women along to ease the boredom of long voyages. However, these were seldom their wives; usually they were concubines or female slaves.

The acceptable versions of the Gudrid Thorbjornsdottir story tell us that shortly after Gudrid reached Greenland she married Thorstein Eriksson and went to live with him at the Western Settlement. During the first winter of their marriage an epidemic struck that settlement, killing Thorstein. Gudrid survived to return to the Eastern Settlement, where she later married Karlsefni.

The author of the Greenlanders Story evidently knew of Gudrid's two Greenland marriages, and he had heard about an epidemic. He mistakenly concluded that it was Thorer the Norwegian trader and his crew who died of the disease, thereby freeing Thorer's wife to marry Thorstein Eriksson. He also reports that Erik died during this same epidemic, which we know was not the case, since Erik was still alive and in good health as late as 1005.

mere homespun rustic from the edge of nowhere. Moreover, he had a tale to tell of such strange adventures in the unknown Western Ocean as would have gained him a respectful hearing even among royalty.

There could also have been a hard practical purpose to goad Leif into undertaking such a voyage. He may have hoped to win acceptance as one of Olaf's liegemen, an honor which would have vastly increased both his prestige and his power in Greenland after his return.

The time was wholly propitious for such a venture since Leif not only had a well-found and well-tried ship but could count on Thorer's skill and experience as pilot and sailing master on the long and difficult voyage to Norway. Relations between Leif and his father may have already become sufficiently tense so that the idea of a Norway voyage for Leif might have seemed attractive to both of them.

So much for speculation. The fact is that Leif did make a voyage to Norway. Furthermore, almost all authorities are agreed in believing that he sailed a direct course from southern Greenland, bypassing Iceland. This in itself suggests that he was accompanied by a skilled pilot and navigator who was familiar with the route.

THORGUNNA'S STORY

The dating of this voyage has never been satisfactorily resolved, and since a knowledge of the correct date is important in establishing an intelligible chronology, I must reluctantly digress. Happily, this digression also enables me to tell the story of Leif's mistress, Thorgunna.

Although most authorities state that the voyage was made in the year 1000, the last year of King Olaf's life, I can find no convincing grounds to support such an assumption. It seems more likely that it was made about 997.

The Short Saga, which seems to be the oldest and therefore the most reliable recension of the lost Old Erik Saga, tells us that Leif arrived in Norway when King Olaf had just come down from Halgoland. Halgoland — Land of the Northern Lights — was in the northern part of Norway, and Olaf seems to have visited this district early in his reign, when he was still actively engaged in unifying his new kingdom by fire and sword. Nevertheless, the actual date of his visit to Halgoland is disputed. The Saga of Olaf Tryggvason states that it was made in the spring of the year following the death of Eyvind Cheekrift, and some scholars believe that this man died in 999. If this was the case, Olaf would have had to go to Halgoland in the year 1000, which was the year of his death when he committed suicide by jumping overboard during a naval battle with the Danes and Swedes in the Baltic.

Perhaps the matter can be settled by another quotation from the same source. The Short Saga tells us that Leif undertook his Norway voyage sixteen years * after Erik the Red went out to "settle," "take land," "go land-seeking," in Greenland (the three variants are three translations of the original by three different scholars). If the disputed word is taken to mean that Leif sailed sixteen years after Erik led the colonists to Greenland, then the year of his voyage to Norway would have had to be 1001, by which time Olaf was dead. On the other hand, if the word is to be translated as meaning that Leif sailed sixteen years after Erik first *went out* to Greenland, there is no problem, for this would date his voyage at 997.

Another event which seems to show that the voyage was made about 997 is Leif's affair with the Hebridean woman Thorgunna. Having seduced her and made her pregnant, Leif got out while the going was good.

We hear no more about Thorgunna in the sagas dealing with the western voyages. We are told only that a son was born to her and that, true to her word, she saw to it that he went to Greenland to join his father there. We are also told that this child, whose name was Thorgils, reached Iceland the summer before the Froda-Wonders. The Froda-Wonders took place during the winter of 1000-1001, which would mean that Thorgils reached Iceland by the year 1000.

The Eyrbyggja Saga tells us that a Hebridean woman named Thorgunna arrived in Iceland in the summer of 1000 aboard a ship from Dublin and went to lodge temporarily at the farmstead of Froda on the western coast. This woman was wealthy, high-born, and a most extraordinary person. She was strangely gifted with supernatural abilities. The description of her is in such close accord with what we

---

* The original vellum of the Flateyjarbok says sixteen years. However, there are several manuscript copies extant in which the figure is given as fourteen.

know of Leif's Thorgunna, and the dates involving the child Thorgils tally so exactly, that we conclude that the two Thorgunnas were one and the same woman.

Thorgunna died at Froda in the summer of 1000. She left specific instructions as to what was to be done with her possessions, including a gold ring and a scarlet cloak which sound like two of the gifts given her by Leif. The acquisitive mistress of Froda disobeyed these instructions, with macabre and catastrophic consequences.

Following the appearance of a "weird moon" the members of the household began to sicken. One by one they died; but their ghosts remained about the homestead to haunt the living. All told, eighteen members of the household died, and the grim visitation was only brought to an end when Thorgunna's last wishes were belatedly carried out. The survivors not unnaturally believed that this terrifying siege was due to Thorgunna's supernatural powers; but we can deduce that the Froda household was afflicted by an epidemic disease which was doubtless introduced by Thorgunna from Ireland, and of which she was the first to die.

According to what the Karlsefni and the Erik the Red sagas have to tell us, Thorgils was eventually sent on to join his father in Greenland; but of his subsequent history we know nothing except that he also was believed to have had something unnatural about him, something presumably inherited from his mother.

The fact that the Erik the Red and the Karlsefni sagas deliberately link the arrival of Thorgils in Iceland with the Froda-Wonders, which were brought about by Thorgunna's death, instead of saying that he arrived there in the year that Christianity was adopted in Iceland, which was the usual saga method of pinpointing the year 1000, seems to be a final confirmation of the single identification of the two Thorgunnas.

Using the combined sources, we have enough information to be able to trace Thorgunna's actions with some assurance of accuracy. To start with we know that Thorgils was conceived in the summer of Leif's visit to the Hebrides, and consequently he would have been born the following spring. Even if Thorgunna had wished to take him to Greenland as soon as possible, she would hardly have risked the life of so young a baby by attempting to take him on a long ocean voyage in an open knorr in the summer of the year during the spring of which the child was born. Since there was no winter navigation to

Iceland — and little if any between the Hebrides and Dublin — she
would have had to wait until the following summer before setting out
on her voyage.

This would indicate that Leif's visit to the Hebrides could not have
taken place later than 998, with 997 being an even more likely date.

Thorgunna must have been an indomitable and greatly courageous
person. Hers was an odyssey which few lone women would have dared
under any circumstances, let alone encumbered by a small child. If
death had not intervened she would undoubtedly have found passage
from Iceland to Greenland. One wonders what her reception would
have been at the hands of the man who had deserted her.

LEIF'S VOYAGE

If we assume that Leif heard about Olaf's usurpation of the Norwegian throne in the summer of 996 from Thorer, or even from some
other trader, the rest follows logically enough. As soon as navigation
became possible in 997 he set sail for Norway.

We have few details of the voyage except that the ship encountered
bad weather. It must have been very bad to set her so far to the south
of her intended course that she reached the Hebrides; but the summer
of 997 was remarkable for its foul weather. Much of the fishery was
a failure in Greenland that year because men could not put to sea. A
number of fishermen who tried it were lost in the attempt. Thorbjorn
Vifilsson, enroute from Iceland to Greenland, very nearly lost his
ship, which was blown helplessly about for several weeks. Another
vessel, belonging to Thorgisl Orrabeinsfostri, and engaged on the same
voyage, was blown ashore and wrecked far up the Greenland or
Baffin Island coast.

After the interlude in the Hebrides, Leif managed to make Drontheim and from there went on to visit Olaf. The record of this meeting
has many important overtones. The king, so the saga tells us, "was
gentle with Leif"; by which we are to understand that he did not use
a heated horn or a sword to bring the Christian message into Leif's
pagan heart. It may also mean that Leif was an easy convert, having
realized — as Olaf had done before him — the potentialities for the
extension and consolidation of personal power which existed in an
alliance with a strong and closely integrated religious organization.

All of the saga sources agree that Olaf treated Leif with great
consideration, and the king's motives for this are not hard to deduce.

Olaf knew that Leif was the son of the Greenland chieftain, and he doubtless guessed, if he was not told directly, that Leif's ambitions pointed impatiently at that chieftainship. He would have seen that in Leif he had at hand an instrument with which he might be able to forge a link between Norway and Greenland, a link which would eventually have had the effect of making that far-distant land subject to King Olaf Tryggvason.

So Leif wintered at the court, where he was held in high esteem, and where he gathered to himself still more of the appurtenances of power and honor with which, in due course, he could put his father's mettle to the test.

13

/.\/.\/.\

the odyssey of
thorgisl orrabeinsfostri

The exceptionally stormy weather of 997, which had driven Leif
so far off course, brought hard times to several other voyagers. One
of these was a man named Thorgisl Orrabeinsfostri (Scarleg's Foster-
son), who had received an invitation from his old friend Erik the Red
to come out from Iceland to Greenland, either for a visit or to join
the new colony there.

The storms which gave Leif so much difficulty dealt even more
harshly with Thorgisl. After a long time his ship was driven ashore
and wrecked on an unknown coast. The location of the shipwreck
has been a matter for much dispute. Most authors have claimed it was
on the northeast coast of Greenland; but if this was the case, we need
an explanation as to why the survivors spent four or five years trying
to work their way to the Eastern Settlement instead of returning to
Iceland, which would have been the simplest way out of their difficulties.

We conclude that Thorgisl missed Greenland (as so many others
did before and afterwards) and, as a climax to his efforts to reach the
Eastern Settlement, was blown north through Davis Strait, to be
ultimately wrecked somewhere on the Baffin Island coast to the northward of the Cumberland Peninsula. The evidence supporting this
conclusion is to be found in the saga text, and I have commented on
it in the various footnotes.

Apart from the fact that Thorgisl's saga deserves a place in any book dealing with the western voyages, it is also the most detailed and explicit account of the hazards of voyaging in the northwestern Atlantic during the Norse period.

What follows is a free translation of that portion of the Floamanna Saga which deals with the voyage. When the story opens Thorgisl had recently become a convert to Christianity and consequently was being plagued by his old god, Thor.

Time passes, and after the navigation season opened one spring, Erik the Red sent messages from Greenland to Iceland asking Thorgisl to join him there, and making him very good offers if he would come. At first Thorgisl was not much interested. However at that time his son Thorleif arrived home from a foreign-going voyage [perhaps a Viking raid] bringing considerable treasures with him and Thorgisl was delighted to see him. Shortly afterwards he made up his mind to make a Greenland voyage in his son's company.

Thorgisl asked his wife Thorey if she would go with him to Greenland. She replied that it was a risky business to change one's home. But Thorgisl said that Erik the Red had sent word to him to come. "You can stay home if you want to, and look after the homestead, but I intend to go," he told her. Thorey still insisted it was a mistake, but reluctantly agreed to go since he was going. This intention of Thorgisl's was widely spoken of throughout the land.

He planned to take his son Thorleif with him, together with a freeman called Col and Col's brother and sister, Starkad and Gudrun. He also took ten slaves including Snae-Col and Ozur. Thorgisl picked out big, powerful men, in case he decided to stay and settle in Greenland. He took cattle as well. There were seventeen people in Thorgisl's party. However, he also took with him another franklin, named Iostan, who was accompanied by his wife Thorgerd and his son Thorarin, and whose party totaled thirteen in all.

Thorgisl bought a ship at Leiravage and then he arranged for his estate to be looked after in his absence. He had intended to take his eight-year-old daughter Thorny with him but she became sick before they sailed and after waiting for three days for her to get better, Thorgisl decided he would sail without her.

They all got on board and waited for a fair wind. Thorgisl had a dream in which a big fellow with a red beard* warned him he was in for a hard time of it unless he changed back to his belief in Thor. But Thorgisl cried

---

* This would have been Thor himself.

out in his dream: "Begone, foul fiend!" When he woke up he told his wife about it and said that if he had had such a bad dream earlier he would have given up the voyage, but now he was determined to go on. He warned her not to tell Iostan about it. Thorey took it as a bad portent but reassured Thorgisl that he was wise to have nothing to do with Thor.

Then a fair wind came and they sailed out of Faxafiord. Iostan and his party lived in that part of the ship forward of the mast, while Thorgisl's people lived abaft the mast. When they got out of sight of land the fair wind failed and they were tossed about at sea for a long time until both meat and drink ran short.

Thorgisl had more dreams in which Thor offered help on condition that he give up the Christian religion but Thorgisl spurned these offers. The state of the people grew even more miserable. It was getting on for harvest time and still they were at sea. Some of the people were all for placating Thor, but Thorgisl said: "If I get wind of anyone sacrificing to Thor and becoming an apostate, it will go hard on him."

Another night Thor came again in a dream and promised Thorgisl that he would reach a haven in seven days if he would only do homage to him. Thorgisl replied: "Though I never get to harbor, I won't do you a favour. What's more, if you bother me again I'll do you any evil I can."

"Then," said Thor, "at least give me back my own, and what you owe me."

Thorgisl woke up and thought about this dream a long time and then he remembered that he had once dedicated a calf to Thor. He told his wife Thorey about this and said that nothing belonging to Thor should remain aboard the ship. The calf was by now grown to be an old ox, but Thorgisl and Thorey agreed to throw it overboard.

When Iostan's wife heard about this she begged for the meat of the ox since they were running out of food. Thorgisl refused, for he was bent on getting completely rid of the ox. So they threw it overboard, but they were still at sea for a long time afterwards. They had now been three months afloat, blowing about, and with seldom a fair wind.

It is told that one evening they wrecked their ship under the ice mountains of Greenland on a sandbank in a certain fiord.* The ship broke up and the stern drifted ashore to the south of where they were. All the people and livestock were saved and the afterboat came safe to shore as well. It was then early in October, a week before winter began.

Glaciers ran around the sides of the bay and the most habitable spot lay in the western part of it. Here they all labored together to build a hall

---

* It will be remembered that Greenland included both sides of Davis Strait and Baffin Bay. See Appendix D.

which they divided with a cross-partition. Thorgisl's party had one end of the hall and Iostan's party had the other. They had saved some meal from the wreck and some flotsam, and the two parties shared these things in common. Most of their cattle died [for want of fodder].

Thorgisl's men were always better at hunting and fishing than Iostan's. He made his people be temperate, and kept them quiet in the evenings and forced them to stick to the [Christian] faith. Goodwife Thorey was far gone with child at this time, and not very strong.

Iostan and his people stayed up late in the nights and had a wild time of it, engaging in mummery and gaming and one thing and another.

One time Iostan spoke to Thorgisl, saying that there seemed to be a great difference in their catches. Thorgisl told him this was because they did not work in the same way: "You keep longer at it in the evening," he said, "but we get started at it earlier in the morning." After that there was a coolness between them. Thorgisl and his people stayed quiet, but Iostan and his kept up their gaming, with lewd uproars and ribald times.

Thorey had her baby about midwinter. It was a boy and they called him Thorfinn. Thorey could not thrive on the food they had.

After Yuletime a sickness came on Iostan's company and six people died. Then Iostan himself got sick and his wife watched over him, but the sickness wore him out and he died and he and the others were buried in new-fallen snow. Then his wife died, and one after another all of Iostan's party died [in all likelihood of scurvy].

Thorarin Iostansson died last and he was buried under the wreck of the ship. There were great hauntings after that. The spirits mainly haunted the part of the hall which had been the Iostaners' in life, but they came into the other part too, and the ghost of Iostan's wife was particularly troublesome. Finally Thorgisl had all their corpses piled up and burned in a balefire, and after that there was no more trouble.

During the rest of the winter Thorgisl and his men worked at the ship [building a new one out of the wreckage]. But they could not get away that summer because the fiord ice did not clear out of the bay. They hunted all summer and built up their stock of provisions. That next winter Gudrun, Col's sister, died. Col buried her under her berth in the house.

Thorey became unable to leave her bed and she prayed to the men to find a way to get them all out of those desolate regions; but Thorgisl replied that he could see no way for them to escape.

Finally one fine day in the spring Thorgisl decided he would climb up the glaciers to see if there was any sign of the fiord ice loosening. Thorey said she did not like him going any distance away from her, and when he replied that he would only go a short distance she answered that she supposed he would have his own way this time, as always. Thorleif [and the freemen] Col and Starkad asked to go along with Thorgisl. He told them that if they did so there would be none to keep an eye on things at home, and "We should be trusting the slaves too much if we did that." Nevertheless they all took their pole-axes and went along with him. The slaves were out fishing and the overseer, a man called Thorarin, was left at the house with Thorey.

They walked and climbed most of that day, and bad weather caught them so it was late before they got back. As they approached they could see no sign of the ship. They reached the hall and went in, and all their chests of goods were gone, their supplies rummaged, and the slaves had vanished. "This is a bad lookout," Thorgisl said. They went into the dark, back part of the hall and heard a gurgling sound from Thorey's bed.

Thorgisl found that she was dead, but that the boy was sucking at her even though she was a corpse. They examined her and found that under her arm the flesh was clotted with blood and there was a little wound as if a fine knife blade had pierced her. All the bedclothes were soaked in blood.

This was the most terrible sorrow Thorgisl had ever known. They buried Thorey beside Gudrun, and Thorleif did his best to cheer his father up. The slaves had stolen all the provisions; had taken the very doors off the hinges; and all the bed coverings and blankets were gone.

All that night Thorgisl watched over his infant son and he could see that the boy would not survive unless something drastic was done. He did not intend to let him die if he could help it. Then he showed his mettle, for he took a knife and cut his own nipple. It began to bleed, and he let the baby tug at it until blood mixed with fluid came out. He did not stop until milk came out; and the boy was nursed upon that.

When Snae-Col and the other slaves went off in the ship they took the big kettle and all the tools out of the tool chest. Thorgisl and the others survived by hunting and fishing, and they tried to construct a boat, even though they had so few tools. Eventually they built a wooden-framed boat covered with hides.

So this summer passed, but they could never get enough food on hand to provision their boat for a voyage. They hauled her up in the autumn and covered her with a shed. They lived on such small game as ground squirrels and on whatever drifted ashore.*

One morning when Thorgisl came out he saw a big piece of flotsam drifting in an opening in the ice. It was some kind of sea mammal. Beside it were two giant women wearing skin clothing, and they were making up bundles of meat from the animal. Thorgisl ran up to them and slashed at one of them with his sword, which he called Earth-house-loom. He cut

---

*Ground squirrels are not native to Greenland. However, Parry's ground squirrel is locally abundant in parts of Baffin Island.

the woman's arm clean off at the shoulder. Her bundle dropped down and she ran away.*

The Norse took the flotsam for themselves and after that they were not short of provisions through the winter, but they ran short again before spring came.

Thorgisl declared that he was weary of this place and once the ice had loosened he gave the order to set out in their boat. They did not wait for the fiord ice to clear but dragged their boat along the ice-foot and, when necessary, over the floes between leads of open water.†

That summer they got south to the Seal Islands, but they had a hard time surviving on fishing alone. [This was evidently a locality well known to the Greenland Norse, and could have been a particularly good sealing place in the Vestri Obygdir; perhaps in the vicinity of Home Bay.] However, at the Seal Islands they got enough seals to last them through the succeeding winter.

At the beginning of the next summer they set out again. On one occasion they found some black-backed gull's eggs. They boiled them and the child Thorfinn ate one egg but would not eat any more. They asked him why he refused, and he replied: "You eat little enough of our food and so I will eat but little too." They spent their nights ashore and their days aboard the boat. They got only small catches of food.

---

* This reference to what are obviously natives has usually been regarded as a piece of pure invention since it is known that there were no natives on the coasts of Greenland proper at this period. However this is actually a perfectly good description of two Eskimo men dealing with a seal or walrus which they had speared at a lead in the ice. The fact that they are described as giant-sized relates them to the Tunnit, about whom there are many Eskimo legends from Labrador, Baffin Island and northwest Greenland. It is now the opinion of most archeologists that the Tunnit are to be identified with the Dorsets, who at this time were still to be found on the Baffin Island, Labrador and Newfoundland coasts, but who had apparently vanished from Greenland some centuries earlier. More detail on the Tunnit-Dorset relationship will be found in Appendix H. The Norse identification of the couple as women follows from the fact that in Eskimo cultures both sexes have long hair and dress much alike. Early European explorers also frequently mistook the men for women.

† The failure of the fiord ice to melt is important, for it should be remembered that the voyage took place near the peak of the Little Climatic Optimum. It is unlikely that this fiord could have been on the northwest Greenland coast, warmed as it was by the northward-flowing current, and in a region where in any case there are few real fiords, and none at all between Skal Island and Thule. On the other hand there are a number of very deep, very narrow fiords on the Baffin Island coast north of Cape Aston. These often remain filled with ice throughout the summer due to the chilling influence of the Canadian Current and to the fact that they are so well protected that they are not subject to much swell nor to severe wind action. These fiords also possess extensive sand and gravel beaches formed by terminal moraines from the adjacent glaciers. It is also notable that there are no fiords on the west Greenland coast which are surrounded by glaciers, while there are many such on the northeast Baffin Island coast.

One day they found the stump of an oar with these runes carved on it:

The lazy fellow had his head washed while wearily I rowed.
Often out of the cold sea, I swung the oar.
The sea gave me sore palms to my hands
While the lazy fellow had his head in the lather.*

On another occasion they dragged their boat ashore over the ice-foot and came to a cliffy place where they set up their tent.† They were almost out of food. In the morning Col walked out of the tent and found that the boat had vanished. He went back inside and lay down. He would not tell Thorgisl, thinking that he was depressed enough as things were. But after a time Thorgisl himself got up and went out and saw that the boat was gone. Then he came back and said: "Now I can't see how we can go on. Take the boy and kill him." [He meant that, since they would all soon be dead, it would be better for the boy to die quickly.]

Thorleif argued and said there was no reason to give up and kill the boy, but Thorgisl insisted that they obey orders. They took the child away and Thorleif ordered Col to kill him, because "such a deed does not befit me, as his brother, and I won't do it." Col would not do it either since, as he said, the effect of the deed on Thorgisl might have been to finish him off entirely.

They left the boy outside and went back into the tent and when Thorgisl asked if the boy was dead, they answered no. He thanked them and was greatly relieved. "I am badly upset," he told them. "But you have prevented me from committing a terrible crime." Now they all had many dreams and visions, for they were starving [details of these dreams have been omitted].

Then they heard a great deal of noise and when they went out they saw their boat was back, and there were two women near it holding onto it. These people went away at once.‡

---

* This is a most authentic touch, for it is a typical example of the use of involved simile in ancient scaldic verse. In this case the "lazy man" is the ship herself and the head washing refers to the "bone at the teeth" or the bow wave. That such a satiric verse should be carved on an oar is perfectly in keeping with what we know about the use of runes. That the incident should be preserved in the saga, where it apparently has no particular relevance, is an example of how faithful to small details the sagas could be.

† Shore-fast ice, producing a fixed ice-foot extending up to several miles offshore, is a summer feature of the northeast Baffin Island coast, but is not found, except in winter, on the west Greenland coast.

‡ Why the natives should have brought back the boat is not explained. They may not have taken it in the first place, but may have found it after it had drifted off and brought it back in the hope of establishing some sort of friendly contact with the strangers.

Some time after that the men discovered a bear struggling in an opening in the ice. It could not get out because its forepaw was broken. They ran toward it and Thorgisl hacked at it with his sword until it was dead. Then they drew it up on the ice and loaded it in their boat. The beast was frost-bitten on its forepaw, from which it can be judged how hard conditions were, when even the beasts were maimed by the cold.

Thorgisl gave a chunk of meat to every man, but they thought it was too little and grumbled among themselves, saying that he was niggardly. Thorleif spoke for the rest: "The men say you are stingy with the meat, father." Thorgisl replied: "It has to be done this way, my son, for we are starving and therefore we cannot eat too much for a while."

Next they rowed down out of a fiord [out of Home Bay?] and it took them a long time too. And then they turned toward the open sea and rowed along past many bays, taking the shortest way across the mouths of the bays [toward Cape Dyer?]. Then the ice began to open and the whole sound began to broaden out and they went straight on out [across open water — across Davis Strait]. Sometimes they dragged their boat over the ice between the leads.

They were terribly weary and even Thorgisl was half dead with thirst. There were only the five of them left now: the boy Thorfinn, Thorgisl himself, Thorleif his son and the brothers Col and Starkad. There was no drinking water near and they were almost finished for lack of a drink. Then Starkad spoke up: "I have heard tell that men have mixed together salt water and urine as a drink." So they took the bilge scoop and made water in it, and they agreed it was right to do this if men's lives depended on it. They asked Thorgisl's permission, and he replied that he would neither forbid it nor give them leave, but he himself would not drink the mixture. So they mixed it up.

Then Thorgisl asked for the scoop, saying he would give them a health. He took it, and he spoke like this: "You cowardly and evil beast [Thor] who are holding us up on our journey — you won't get your evil way and persuade me or any of the others to drink such filth!" And with that he threw the stuff overside out of the scoop.

Then he said to the rest of them, "This is a poor way for me to reward you after you saved me from committing a fearful crime when I would have had the boy killed, but the shame and abomination would always have stuck in your minds if I had let you drink. Now maybe our luck will mend."

Later that same day they were able to get drinking water from ice.*

* This whole passage is obviously concerned with a sea voyage over salt water. It could describe the crossing of Davis Strait or some part of Baffin Bay. The men were evidently away from land — where fresh water would have been readily availa-

At last they came to the mouth of a great fiord [on the other side of the sound? Possibly one of the great fiords near Holsteinsborg] and found a berth there. Later they came to a certain island and they were there three days before they discovered a linen tent. They recognized it as Thorey's tent. When they went in they found Thorarin, the slave-overseer, lying sick. They asked him how in the world he had got there. He told them that Snae-Col and the other slaves had given him the choice of going along with them or of being killed at the hall where Thorey died. He said they had spent the past winter not far from the Seal Islands.

They asked him many questions. He told them that he had been forced to take part in everything; that the slaves had taken all the goods aboard the ship; and that it was Snae-Col who had stabbed Thorey. Thorgisl told him he did not know whether he was one of the guilty or not, but in any case he would not abandon him. But before they could get Thorarin out of the tent he died, and they buried him there.

They kept on along the coast and when harvest time was drawing on again they came to a fiord where there was a boathouse. They pulled up their boat there and walked up to where they saw a small homestead.

A man was standing out of doors and he greeted them. They told him about their journey. He said his name was Herjolf, and he invited them to come and stay with him, and they gladly accepted.

The women of the house tended Thorfinn and gave him real milk to drink, whereat he said that his father's milk did not look like that.

Herjolf explained that he had been outlawed from the settlements of Greenland because he had committed manslaughter. He was very hospitable to Thorgisl and told him a ship had come that way in the summer [presumably this was the stolen ship, manned by the runaway slaves] but her people had not come ashore. He also said it was a long and a difficult journey to the Eastern Settlements, which was where Thorgisl wished to go, and so they stayed that winter with him.

In the spring Herjolf told them they could either stay on with him or take any of his boats if they wanted to continue to the settlements. Thorgisl accepted the offer of a boat and said he would do whatever he could to reward Herjolf. Herjolf replied that he expected Thorgisl would succeed in his journey, and he therefore requested that he try and get him in-lawed into the settlement. Thorgisl promised to do what he could and when they parted they blessed each other.*

---

ble — for such a long time that what they carried was used up, and they were in dire straits from thirst. By accident they seem to have discovered that it is possible to get fresh water from old sea ice or icebergs.

* It is not impossible that this may have been Herjolf Bardsson, Bjarni Herjolfsson's father. At any rate both Herjolf and Bjarni seem to have mysteriously

Now they journeyed on southward along the coast, passing Hvarf [this may have been Cape Desolation, which was at one time known as Hvarf], and they were on their way until harvest time. Early in October, when winter began, they reached Eriksfiord, which they entered. They moored their ship and set up their tent ashore . . .

Erik the Red asked Thorgisl and his men to his house at Brattalid and they accepted. Thorfinn was given a nurse but he would not drink milk before dark, and he was weaned soon after. Erik was not very gracious and the visit did not go well [perhaps because Thorgisl had become a Christian]. Thorgisl got news that his slaves were living in the country in great estate and telling very little that was true about the voyage.

That winter a [polar] bear came in among the sheep and did a lot of damage. Men from both settlements* got together and agreed to pay a bounty for the bear's death. One day when Thorgisl was in the storehouse the boy Thorfinn called out to his father, saying: "There is a beautiful white dog outside. I never saw one like it, he is so big." His father was busy and told him not to bother about it, and not to go out. However, the boy ran out anyway.

It was the bear. It had come down off the glacier. It caught the boy and he cried out. Thorgisl ran out with his sword, Earth-house-loom. The bear was toying with the boy. Thorgisl struck the bear so hard that he split its skull in two; then he took up his son, who was not badly hurt.

Thorgisl became famous for this deed and many brought him their share of the bear bounty. But Erik did not like the deed at all. Some say this was because he had an evil and heathen belief in bears.

One day when men were gathered around at Brattalid they began to talk about the relative merits of Erik and Thorgisl. One of Erik's servants claimed that Erik was a great chief, but that Thorgisl was an unimportant sort of a fellow; he wasn't even sure if he was a man or a woman. Whereupon Col snatched up a spear and ran the servant through. Erik ordered his men to seize Col, but a number of traders who were there took Col's side, and Thorgisl told Erik that it was his business to avenge his servant

---

disappeared from Herjolfsness by the time Thorbjorn Vifilsson arrived there in 997. The site of the outlawed Herjolf's stead could not have been on the east Greenland coast since there were never any farms on that coast at a distance sufficiently far north of Farewell to merit the phrase "a long and difficult journey to the Eastern Settlement." Probably the stead was on one of the lonely fiords south of Godthaab where isolated Norse farms have been discovered by archeologists. At this period the Godthaab settlement did not exist, and the name Western Settlement still referred to Ivitgut Bight, due west of the Eastern Settlement.

* These would be the Eastern and Western settlements of those times, i.e., the Ivitgut Bight and Julianehaab Bight areas. The phrase could not possibly refer to the later Western Settlement at Godthaab, since it and the Eastern Settlement were hundreds of miles distant from one another.

himself. It came close to a battle, but men made peace between them although it was hard going.

After that Thorgisl went to the Western [Ivitgut] Settlement to collect the bear money from that district. There he found Snae-Col and the other slaves. He was going to slaughter them, but he was persuaded it would make better sense to sell them for cash, and this is what he did.

Soon after that Thorgisl and his men put to sea [on the ship of Thorstan the White, a trader and a relation] and they had a hard voyage until they neared Iceland. Then they had a southerly gale and made toward the land, but for two days Thorgisl would not let them approach too close for fear of being driven ashore. They lay off for those two days, bailing to keep afloat in the heavy seas. Eight big seas swept over the ship and then a ninth came, and it was the biggest of them all. It drove Thorgisl from the bilge beam where he was bailing, and it picked Thorfinn off his knee and carried him overboard.

Then Thorgisl cried out that there was no use bailing any more since the sea which had gone over them had almost swamped the ship. But at that moment another great wave washed the boy back on deck again and he was still alive. Then they took heart and bailed for all they were worth, managing to empty the ship. But Thorfinn vomited blood, and after a while he died.

Thorgisl nearly went out of his mind with grief. He did not sleep or eat for forty-eight hours, and even after they had made land safely he would not part with the body of his son. He had to be tricked into leaving it, whereupon Col took the body to the graveyard and buried it. Thorgisl threatened to kill him for that, but later he came to his senses and they were reconciled.

Thorgisl said it was no wonder that women loved the children they had nursed at their own breasts better than they could love anyone else.

Thorgisl remarried when he was fifty-five and took over his old estate, and prospered. When he was seventy years old he challenged Helge Easterling to combat and killed him. When he was eighty-five he took ill and after a week he died, but there are many great men come from his seed and scattered far and wide over the land.

14

/\.\.\

GUÐRIÐ

Still another voyager who set to sea in that stormy year of 997 was a man named Thorbjorn Vifilsson. He was a well-known Icelandic franklin who had taken Erik's side during the troubles with Thorgest which had led to Erik's exile in the west. Probably at the same time that Erik issued his invitation to Thorgisl Orrabeinsfostri, he also sent a message to Thorbjorn Vifilsson asking him to come out and take land in Greenland. Pressed by financial troubles at home, Thorbjorn accepted. He may have set sail from Iceland in consort with Thorgisl. At any rate both ships sailed in the same year, probably from the same port, and encountered the same abominable weather.

The sections of the Erik the Red and Karlsefni sagas which tell of his experiences not only introduce us to his daughter Gudrid, who plays an important role in some of the later voyages, but also give us one of the few surviving vignettes of life in Greenland during the last decade of the tenth century. We have therefore reproduced the story in full as a free translation, interjecting such small explanations and additions from other sources as are necessary to clarify its meaning.

There was a man named Vifil, a high-born Westman who had been captured and brought to Iceland, where he gained his freedom from Queen Aud. Vifil had three sons, one of whom was named Thorbjorn.

Thorbjorn married Hallveig Einarsdottir and got with her, as a dower, the farm of Laugarbrekka. They went there to live and Thorbjorn prospered and became an important man, for he was a good farmer and his estate grew to be a fine one.

During the time when Erik the Red and Thorgest were at odds, Thorbjorn gave Erik his support and assisted him to make his escape to Greenland when he was exiled from Iceland.

Thorbjorn had a daughter named Gudrid. She was the most beautiful of women, and in every way a remarkable person. When she was still a young girl she went off to live with Orm of Arnarstapi and his wife Halldis. Orm was a great friend of Thorbjorn's. According to the customs of the times he had asked to become Gudrid's foster father, and Thorbjorn had agreed to this.

There was a man called Einar who was a handsome and well-bred man, although his father had been a slave. Einar was very fond of showy clothes. He was a foreign-going trader and he had done very well at the business. He spent his winters alternately either in Norway or in Iceland.

Now it is to be told that one autumn when he had come from Norway, Einar traveled out along the Snaefells peninsula peddling his trade goods. When he reached Arnarstapi, Orm invited him to stay for a while, since these two were friends of long standing. Einar accepted and his goods were carried into a storehouse and unpacked. He displayed them to Orm and the people of the household and asked Orm to pick out what he liked as a gift. Orm did so, commenting that Einar was a good merchant and well favored by fortune.

While they were busy looking at the goods a woman passed by the open door of the storehouse and Einar saw her.

"Who was that beautiful woman who just passed by the door?" he asked.

"That is Gudrid, my foster daughter, and the daughter of Thorbjorn Vifilsson of Laugarbrekka," Orm replied.

"She must be a good match then," Einar said. "Has she any suitors?"

"Many have courted her, my friend," Orm replied, "but she is not to be easily won, I can tell you. Both she and her father will be hard to please when it comes to the choice of a husband for her."

"No doubt that's true enough, but all the same she is the woman for me," said Einar, "And so I wish you to make an offer to her father on my behalf. Do everything you can to persuade him, and if you succeed you will have earned the full measure of my friendship. It looks to me as if Thorbjorn should regard such a match as being to our mutual benefit. Although he is a man with a great reputation and a good home and valuable possessions, I hear his fortunes are declining. Since neither my father nor I suffer from any lack of lands or money, Thorbjorn could benefit by our help if this match can be arranged."

"Much as I value your friendship," said Orm, "I am not very anxious to act for you in this matter. Thorbjorn has a haughty spirit and is jealous of his honor."

Einar replied that he expected nothing more of Orm than that he should present the suit, and so Orm reluctantly agreed.

That autumn Thorbjorn Vifilsson held a great feast, as was his custom, for he had a high position in the land. Many of Thorbjorn's friends attended, including Orm of Arnarstapi.

When Orm found an opportunity to speak to Thorbjorn alone, he told him that Einar Thorgeirsfell had paid him a visit not long since, and that he was becoming a very prosperous man. Then Orm broached the proposal of marriage between Einar and Gudrid, adding that some people might consider it an appropriate match for a variety of reasons. "This might prove to be of great benefit to you from the financial point of view," he said, "for there is a great deal of money at stake."

Thorbjorn reacted to the offer with indignation.

"I never expected to hear such talk from you suggesting that I should marry my daughter to the son of a slave in order to recoup my fortunes! If you think a match as mean as this one is suitable for her, she shall no longer remain in your keeping."

When the feast was over everyone returned home, and Orm among them. But Gudrid stayed with her father henceforward.

In the spring Thorbjorn gave another feast and a great many people attended. After the eating was over Thorbjorn called for silence and spoke to the assembled guests.

"I have lived a long time in this place," he said, "and I have had the good will of many men, and their affections too. All things considered, our relationships have been pleasant ones. But although my estate used to be thought a considerable one, I now find myself running into hard times.

"Rather than lose my honor and bring disgrace on my family I have decided to give over this farm and leave the country. I am going to put to the test the promise my friend Erik the Red made to me when we parted company in Breidafiord, he to go out to Greenland, and me to return to my own lands. It is my intention to go out to Greenland this summer and it may be that I will do better there than here."

Everyone was greatly astonished at this admission of Thorbjorn's fallen fortunes, as well as at his plans. There was much sympathy for him; for he had many friends. However, they also realized that Thorbjorn was so fixed in his purpose that nothing would dissuade him from carrying it out.

Thorbjorn gave gifts to all his guests, after which the feast came to an end and the visitors returned to their homes.

Thorbjorn then proceeded to sell his lands and such of his property as he could not take with him, after which he bought and outfitted a merchant ship which was laid up at the mouth of Hraunhofn.

Thirty persons joined him for the voyage, including Orm of Arnarstapi and his wife, for the friendship between the two men had been restored. With them went others of Thorbjorn's friends and relations who could not bear to be parted from him.

They put to sea in weather which seemed favorable for a Greenland voyage, but after they had gone beyond sight of land the fair wind failed and there came great gales and a huge sea got up. They lost their directions and drifted far off their course.*

Then illness broke out on board the ship and half their company died, including Orm and his wife.

The storms continued and they had a very long, wretched and wearisome time of it; but eventually, at the end of autumn, they made land at Herjolfsness.

Among those living near this place was a franklin named Thorkel who was a very able fellow and a good husbandman. He took in Thorbjorn and the survivors of his party and entertained them well during the winter, for which Thorbjorn and his shipmates were very grateful.

This was a year of great shortages in those parts, for the fisheries had largely failed due to the bad weather that summer, and some of the men who had gone fishing never returned.

Now there was a certain woman in the settlement whose name was Thorbiorg. She was a prophetess, and was known as the Little Seer. She had had nine sisters, all of whom were also prophetesses, but now she was the sole survivor.

During the wintertime it was Thorbiorg's custom to go about from house to house attending the winter entertainments. She was eagerly sought after by those who were curious to know their fates, or who wanted to find out what the next season would be like.

Since Thorkel was the chief franklin of the neighborhood it was considered to be his responsibility to find out when the evil times which were upon them would cease. Thorkel therefore invited the Little Seer to visit his house, and careful preparations were made to receive her, according to the customs which governed the reception of women of her kind. A High Seat had been prepared for her on which a cushion filled with poultry feathers had been placed.

Toward evening she arrived with the man who had been sent to fetch her. She was clad in a dark blue cloak, fastened with a strap and decorated with jewel-stones right down to the hem. She wore a string of glass beads around her neck, and upon her head she wore a black lambskin hood

---

* This was in the summer of 997.

lined with white catskin. In her hands she carried a staff upon which there was a knob ornamented with brass and set with jewel-stones. Around her waist she wore a girdle of touch-wood and hanging from it was a great skin pouch in which she kept the charms she used in the practice of her profession. On her feet she wore shaggy calfskin shoes with long laces, the ends of which were ornamented with brass buttons. She had catskin gloves upon her hands.

When she entered the house all of the folk felt it was their duty to offer proper greetings, and she received the salutations of each individual according to how well pleased she was with them.

Franklin Thorkel took her by the hand and led her to the seat which had been prepared for her. Then he bade her look carefully at man, and beast, and house and all therein. But the prophetess had nothing much to say.

The tables were brought forth and now it must be told what manner of food was prepared for the prophetess.

A porridge of goat's beesting * was made for her; and for meat she was given the stuffed hearts of every kind of animal which could be obtained. She had a brass spoon and a broken-pointed knife with a handle made of walrus tusk which had a double haft of brass around it.

When the tables had been removed, franklin Thorkel approached the Little Seer and asked her how she was pleased by the home and by the character of the people; and then he wished to know how soon she would have the answers to the questions he had put to her, and which the people were anxious to hear.

She replied that she could say nothing until the morrow, when she had slept in the house for a night.

Late in the following day all the necessary preparations were made for her to accomplish her soothsaying. Then the Little Seer bade them bring unto her those women who knew the incantation song which is called Warlocks, and the singing of which helped her work her spell by attracting spirits to the vicinity. But it did not seem that there were any such women about the place.

A search was made all through the house to see if anyone was familiar with this incantation, and at last Gudrid Thorbjornsdottir spoke up.

"Although I am not skilled in the Black Arts, nor yet am I a seer," she said, "yet my foster mother Halldis once taught me a spell-song which she called Warlocks."

---

* The first milk drawn from a goat after parturition.

"Then," said Thorbiorg, "you are wiser than I supposed."

"But," Gudrid added, "this is a spell for a ceremony of such a kind that I will not assist with it; for I am a Christian woman."

Thorbiorg answered: "It might still be possible to give your help to the company here and be no worse a woman than you were before. However, I leave it to Thorkel; it is up to him to provide me with my needs."

Franklin Thorkel now urged Gudrid so strongly that she felt forced to comply with his wishes. The women then made a ring around her while Thorbiorg sat up on the spell-dais where the high seat had been made ready for her.

Then Gudrid sang the song; and she did it so sweetly and so well that no one could remember ever having heard the song sung in so fair a voice.

The prophetess thanked her for the song and said: "She has indeed lured many spirits here; for those spirits which had formerly forsaken us and which had refused to submit themselves to us found this song so pleasant that they could not resist it.

"Many things are now revealed which were formerly hidden, not only from me, but from all others too. And now I am able to tell you that this period of famine will not endure much longer. Conditions will improve as spring approaches; thus the visitation of evil which has rested so long upon you will disappear sooner than you had expected.

"As for you, Gudrid, I shall reward you for the assistance which you gave us. The fate which is in store for you is now clear to me. You shall make a most worthy marriage here in Greenland, but it shall not be of long duration, for your future path leads out to Iceland, where a lineage that shall be both prosperous and famous shall spring from you; and the light shall shine over your decendants so brightly that I have not the power to describe it. And now farewell, and good health to you, my daughter."

After this the other people present crowded around the Little Seer and each of them besought her for information about whatever it was they were most curious to know. She was willing and ready with her replies, and very little that she foretold failed to be fulfilled. After this she was sent for by the people of a neighboring farm and she departed thither.

Thorbjörn Vilfilsson was then sent for. He had been absent, for he was not willing to remain in the house while such heathen rites were being practiced.

With the coming of spring the weather improved rapidly, even as the Little Seer had predicted. Then Thorbjörn fitted out his ship and sailed to Brattalid, where Erik received him with open arms and said that he had done the right thing to come thither.

Thorbjorn and Gudrid and his household lived with Erik through the following winter, but quarters for the rest were found among the neighboring farmers. In the ensuing spring Erik gave Thorbjorn land at Stokaness across the fiord from Brattalid, where he established a prosperous farmstead and where he lived thenceforward.

15

Λ.\/.\/.Λ

the cross comes to greenland

The Saga Tale (c. 997–999)

Erik was married to a woman named Thiodhild [Thorhild]* and had two [three] sons, one of whom was named Thorstein, the other Leif [and another Thorvald]. They were promising men. Thorstein stayed at home with his father and there was not another man in Greenland at the time who was thought to be as promising as he.

Leif had sailed to Norway where he was staying at the court of King Olaf Tryggvason . . . there came an occasion when the King talked to Leif and asked him: "Is it your purpose to sail to Greenland in the summer?"

"That is my intention," said Leif, "if you permit it."

"I believe this will work out well," answered the King. "You shall go there on an errand for me — to proclaim Christianity."

Leif replied that the decision was up to the King, but gave it as his opinion that it would be difficult to carry this mission to a successful conclusion in Greenland.

The King replied that he knew of no man who was better fitted for the undertaking, "and in your hands the cause will surely succeed."

"This can only happen," said Leif, "if I enjoy the support of your protection."

Leif put to sea when his ship was ready for the voyage. . . .

He landed at Eriksfiord and went home to Brattalid, where he was well received by everyone. He soon proclaimed Christianity throughout the land, and the Catholic Faith, and he relayed King Olaf Tryggvason's messages to the

---

* She seems to have changed her name when she became a Christian.

people, telling them how much excellence, and how great a glory accompanied this faith.

Erik was unwilling to forsake his old beliefs, but Thiodhild quickly embraced the new faith. She caused a church to be built at some considerable distance from the house. It was called Thiodhild's Church, and there she and those persons who had accepted Christianity — and they were many — offered up their prayers. Thiodhild would not have sexual intercourse with Erik after she received the faith, which made him extremely angry.

From this [situation] there arose the suggestion that he should explore that land which Leif had found. Thorstein Eriksson, who was a good and intelligent man and blessed with many friends, was [to be] the leader of this expedition. Erik was invited to join them, however, for everyone believed his luck and foresight would be of great assistance. Erik did not say nay when his friends besought him to go.

They thereupon outfitted the ship in which Thorbjorn Vifilsson had come out [to Greenland], and twenty men were selected for the expedition. They took little with them except weapons and provisions.

On the morning when Erik left his home he took along a little chest containing [his] gold and silver. He hid this treasure and then went his way [toward the ship]. But he had only gone a short distance when he fell off his horse and injured his arm at the shoulder joint, whereupon he cried: "Ai! ai!"

Because of this accident he sent word to his wife that she might take up the treasure he had hidden, for he attributed his misfortune to his having concealed it.

[SOURCES: Erik the Red and Thorfinn Karlsefni sagas. The section dealing with Leif's voyage to Norway is not included since we have presented it in an earlier chapter. The brief notice in this portion of the saga which attributes the discovery of Vinland to an accident of Leif's homeward voyage from Norway has been deleted for reasons given in Appendix L.]

Thorbjorn Vifilsson and his family were warmly welcomed by Erik, who showed his gratitude for Thorbjorn's aid during the "troubles" in Iceland by giving him a choice land-grant at Stokaness, directly across the fiord from Brattalid. However, the Thorbjorners did not occupy the land immediately. Instead they spent that summer and the following winter as Erik's house guests.

The difficulties Thorbjorn had experienced with the fearful weather of 997, coupled with the nonappearance of Thorgisl Orrabeinsfostri's ship, would have made a gloomy subject for discussion among the older people at Brattalid and would have led to worried conjectures about Leif's fate. But the younger people of Brattalid had more stimulating things to think about.

Women were scarce in Greenland in those early years, and marriagable young women who were blessed with good looks, good family connections and a good dowry would have been a rarity. We can believe that a number of young bucks were soon courting Gudrid; but Thorstein Eriksson seems to have taken an early lead and to have held it. He was a respected and personable young man and he was living in the same household with Gudrid. Being Erik's son he had the advantages of prestige and position, if not of wealth; and both Erik and Thorbjorn would have looked on an alliance between the two families as being to their mutual benefit. Thorstein probably would have felt secure against any rival until a day late in the summer when someone ran shouting up toward the house with the news that Leif's ship was standing up the fiord. This was news which may not have roused Thorstein to much enthusiasm. Heroes provide notoriously stiff competition when they compete with ordinary mortals for a woman's love.

There was no doubt that Leif had now become even more of a hero to many Greenlanders. He had returned home a much greater figure than he had been when he departed. Not only had he made the fabled voyage to the Fatherland, but during his stay there he had become the confidante and leigeman of a king who had treated him with such regard that he was recognized as a great man even in Norway.

All the same, it could not have been very long before the pleasure of having him safe home again began to sour — at least for some of the settlers.

Leif had brought back with him from Norway several of King Olaf's men. One of these was a priest, and others are referred to vaguely as "some holy men." They may or may not have been holy, but they were almost certainly agents of Olaf's, entrusted by him with the task of preparing the ground for the eventual inclusion of Greenland into Olaf's domains. Leif and his Norwegian companions soon began proclaiming the Christian faith on behalf of Olaf, and it can be assumed that, as was the case in Iceland, they did not hesitate to urge its adoption by the use of threats.

In the previous year, 997, Olaf had sent a delegation to Iceland nominally to convert the independent islanders. The leader was one of Olaf's nobles, a warrior named Thangbrand. His fellow "missionary" was Ari Marsson's son Gudleif, who had become a mercenary abroad and who had won a champion's reputation with the sword and battle-axe. These two roamed the island from end to end bringing Olaf's message to the Icelanders. When they encountered resistance they frequently used their swords to quiet the opposition. After they had committed several murders the island finally became too hot for them and they were forced to retire rather hastily to Norway.

Olaf was so enraged at this treatment of his emissaries that he seized every Icelander then in Norway and gave orders for them to be slaughtered. This massacre was narrowly averted when two of his prisoners undertook to persuade their countrymen at home to accept Christianity as the official religion of the nation. Olaf stayed the executioner's arm and the Icelanders bowed to the inevitable. In the summer of 1000 they passed a law at the Althing whereby theirs became officially at any rate, a Christian country.

There seems to be little doubt that having once forced the Icelanders to obey his wishes, Olaf intended to apply further pressure until he had gained political control of the island. The Icelanders were aware of his ultimate intentions and they apparently Christianized their country to buy time. Luck was with them, for Olaf died that very autumn and the immediate threat to their independence was lifted.

Olaf's plans for Greenland were doubtless identical with those for Iceland. Just as he had employed the renegade Icelander Gudleif Arisson, so he seems to have commissioned Leif Eriksson to carry out a similar treasonable task. The motives which prompted these two men to accept Olaf's orders may have differed. In Gudleif's case money may have been the incentive. But Leif was probably prepared to act as Olaf's liegeman in order to achieve power in his own country, perhaps as Jarl, ruling the land for Olaf.

Leif and his Norwegian companions wielded a double-edged weapon. On the one hand they had a message which the women were glad to listen to, for it promised a more hopeful life than they had known. On the other hand they did their proselytizing under the protection of Olaf's fierce reputation, which cast a long, black shadow. All men knew that where Norwegian trading ships could sail, Olaf's fighting ships could follow after.

Leif seems to have done well in the early stages of his campaign. Many women embraced this new faith, and not a few men must have followed suit, either to gain influence with Leif, who they may have thought was the coming man, or for the same reasons of expediency which had prompted the Icelandic Althing to its decision. Nevertheless, by no means all the Greenlanders, and apparently not even a majority of them, accepted Leif Eriksson's leadership and the new faith. The old lion was not yet dead. Erik the Red not only refused to be converted; he spoke publicly and contemptuously of the Norwegian priest as "that faker Leif brought to Greenland." Erik was not a man to give in to threats. He was well aware that Greenland was a good deal farther from Norway than Iceland was, and would have been a long reach, even for Olaf's arm.

Although the intensity of this internecine strife is only hinted at in the sagas, this should occasion no surprise. It must be remembered that when the oral sagas were first committed to vellum, the work was done by clerks (clerics) of the Holy Church and it was these clerks who recopied and preserved the sagas until well into the Middle Ages. It would be naïve of us to expect to find much forthright information espousing the heathen point of view, or reflecting adversely on the motives and actions of those who carried the Cross. However, the Icelandic records preserve a number of fragments testifying to violent and sometimes bloody resistance to the new faith in Iceland. Similar reactions indubitably took place in Greenland too.

Emotions must have burned at white heat through the winter of 998–999. While Leif and his followers visited various outsettlements seeking to persuade or browbeat the settlers into an acceptance of White Christ, Erik and his supporters would have been struggling equally hard to offset his efforts. The struggle may have stopped short of bloodshed. Considering the nature of the Norse, it would be surprising to learn that it did.

Erik's personal position was singularly unpleasant. His hold upon the little kingdom which he had founded was being undermined by his own son, and Leif's actions were not only denying Erik the patriarchal supremacy which he had amply earned, they had even been instrumental in ousting him from his own marriage bed. The consequent loss of face would have been almost intolerable.

There must have been many who were envious or resentful of Leif's meteoric rise to power and position. His two younger brothers, Thorleif and Thorvald, would have been less than human if they had not begun to feel an urgent need to win fame and fortune for themselves. Thorstein in particular would have had specific reason to envy his brother, for he was in love with Gudrid and wished to marry her, yet he had comparatively little wealth or power of his own and he had accomplished no great deeds. Leif was a towering figure in both of these regards. Moreover, he was now at least a professing Christian; and Gudrid was a Christian too. There is nothing to tell us that Leif actually did compete with Thorstein for Gudrid's hand, but remembering his seduction of Thorgunna, we can assume that Thorstein had reason to be wary of his brother. From every point of view it would seem that Thorstein had urgent need to make a mark for himself.

Knowledge that the origin of Leif's wealth lay within relatively easy reach would have ensured that someone would eventually have attempted to emulate Leif's exploit, even if there were no other factors involved. The sagas tell us that such an attempt *was* made; and the plans for it probably took shape during that first, tense winter after Leif's return from Norway.

We are told that Thorstein was the leader of the group which planned the voyage. He may indeed have instigated it, but Erik also played a major role. It was to Erik's name and personality that the venturers rallied, and he was no doubt responsible for providing the wherewithal to make the voyage possible.

A successful Vinland voyage would have refurbished Erik's reputation as a doer of great deeds, and would have demonstrated that his vigor and his courage — the two prime requisites of a Norse leader — were still unimpaired. Furthermore, it promised to enrich both Erik and Thorstein, so that the one would have the wealth to sustain his power while the other would have the means to cement an advantageous and desirable marriage.

It is significant that the sagas make no mention of Leif as having had any part in the plans. Far from being involved as a supporter of the venture, it is more likely that he opposed it. It is significant that the expedition used Thorbjorn Vifilsson's ship, the implication being that Leif would not permit his father and his brother to use his own.

A further indication of how things stood in the divided Eriker family is revealed by the description of how Erik removed a chest containing his gold and silver from his own home at Brattalid and buried it for safe-keeping during his absence. Safekeeping from whom? The only reasonable conclusion open to us is that he did not trust his wife and his eldest son. His motive in burying the money would have had to have been a strong one, since the Norse considered it extremely unlucky to bury treasure before setting out on a voyage.*

The picture of Erik riding down from Brattalid to where the expedition's vessel was berthed somewhere on the outer fiord is a moving one. He was about fifty years of age, which in those times of short, hard lives would have meant that he was past his prime. Behind him lay an estranged wife, an elder son who was doing his best to usurp his father's power, and a home which he could not even trust to call his own.

As he rode along he may have looked out over the fiord to where a score of sod buildings stood dark against green homefields with herds of sheep dotting the lower hills behind them, and he would have reflected that this had been his life's work. Now it was no longer his; or, at any rate, his control over it was threatened, and by the eldest of his own children.

Erik's determination to make this voyage was an iron one. When he fell, or was thrown from his horse, and hurt his shoulder as a result, this accident and evil omen were not enough to deter him from his purpose. With a resolution as hard as the Greenland rocks, he went aboard the ship to sail westward once again, hoping to find there the solution to many a looming problem.

---

* The Landnamabok tells the story of an Icelander named Thord who wished to make a voyage to Norway with his wife in order to claim an inheritance, and who insisted on burying the family treasures so they would be safe during his absence. His wife was so appalled at this wanton throwing down of the gauntlet to the fates that she refused to sail with him, and sure enough Thord and his ship were lost at sea.

16

.∧.∨.∧.

thorstein the unlucky

The Saga Tale (c. 999–1002)

Thereafter they sailed confidently out of Eriksfiord, for they had high hopes of their venture.

Then they were storm-tossed on the ocean for a long time and could not lay their desired course. They came in sight of Iceland and likewise saw birds from Irish waters. In truth their ship drove hither and thither all over the sea.

In the autumn they turned back worn out by hardship and exposure and exhausted by their labors. They arrived at Eriksfiord at the very beginning of winter.

Then Erik said: "We were more cheerful when we put out of the fiord in the summer; but at least we are still alive, and it might have been worse."

[SOURCES: Erik the Red Saga and Thorfinn Karlsefni Saga]

DRIFT

The saga tells us that the failure of this voyage was due to stormy weather which prevented Erik and Thorstein from steering their correct course. This is no doubt true enough as far as it goes; but it does not go far enough. An equally important reason for their failure was probably a lack of adequate sailing instructions and, specifically, a lack of knowledge of the relative latitude of Vinland.

When we examine the current and wind patterns which prevail in and over the Labrador Sea, we discover a hidden factor about which the early Norse could have known nothing. Having passed out of sight of the Greenland landmarks, a Norse ship bound for Newfoundland would have come under the influence of a current which first would set her westward, then southward and finally to the southeastward. Moreover, this current would have increased in strength as the voyage progressed and would have had its maximum effect at about the time the vessel entered the Grand Banks region. The effect would have been intensified by the eastward drift caused by the prevailing westerly and northwesterly winds of the region.

Assuming that her master steered and maintained a reasonably true course between south Greenland and Newfoundland, his actual track over the bottom would have tended to curve imperceptibly but steadily toward the south, an effect which would increase in direct proportion to the time expended in making the voyage. If he encountered any sizable delay due to unfavorable winds by the time he had run off his proper distance and was expecting to make his landfall, his real position might have been as much as 150 miles to the southeast of his calculated position. There would then have been no land anywhere in sight, nor would there have been any closer than 500 miles to the west of his position.

This is no mere theoretical calculation. Before the strong south-setting effect of the Labrador Current was recognized, scores of sailing ships bound to Newfoundland from Europe by the northern route were swept past Cape Race, missing Newfoundland entirely.

NO DIRECTIONS

The only way that an early navigator could have discovered what was happening to him, and so be able to make good his error, was by a comparison between his actual latitude and the known latitude of his hoped-for landfall. In other words, if he knew the relative latitude of the landfall, and if he was able to take sights at sea en route, he would have discovered that he had gone too far south. In order to correct the error he would then only have had to sail north until he reached the right latitude, then turn west and sail in that direction until he made the landfall he was seeking.

Knowledge of the latitude of Vinland was vital. Had Erik and Thorstein possessed it, there would have been small likelihood that Erik, a master of the arts of seafaring, would have failed so miserably where Leif, the merest tyro by comparison, had succeeded so easily.

There can be no doubt that Leif knew the Vinland latitude. Having obtained it in the first place from Bjarni Herjolfsson, he would have had ample opportunity to confirm it during his stay in the new land. Erik and Thorstein ought to have been able to obtain it either from Bjarni or from Leif. However, it looks as if Bjarni was not available at the time that Erik and Thorstein sailed. When the Christian immigrant Thorbjorn Vifilsson arrived at Herjolfsness in the autumn of 997 he was given shelter and hospitality by Thorkel, who is reported to have been the leading man in the community at that time. There is not a mention of the original landtakers and founders — the Herjolfers — in all of the long and detailed saga account of Thorbjorn's sojourn at Herjolfsness. If either Herjolf or Bjarni had still been living there, they would surely have extended their hospitality to a man of Thorbjorn's fame not only because they were the most prominent men in the area by right of settlement and so had the duty of providing hospitality for wayfarers, but also because they appear to have been Christians too.*

It is possible that Herjolf, who was born about 930, may have died around the time Bjarni sold Leif his ship in 997, in which case Bjarni might have disposed of his trading establishment and retired to Iceland to live out his days in relative luxury. On the other hand it is conceivable that the exile whom Thorgisl Orrabeinsfostri encountered while making his way down the coast to south Greenland could have been Herjolf Bardsson. Herjolf is an uncommon name in the Icelandic annals, occurring only twice in the records of the Greenland colony. If this exile *was* Herjolf Bardsson, Bjarni would probably have been living in exile with him. In any event, he would have been in no frame of mind to volunteer information to the leader of the Greenland community which had exiled his father to the obygdir.

If Bjarni was not available, Leif certainly was. And having made the voyage both ways between Vinland and Greenland, he would have been even better able to provide Thorstein and Erik with detailed and accurate sailing directions, together with the vitally important latitude observations. The question is: Did he do so? We

---

* Norse traders of this period had learned that it was advantageous to at least profess Christianity, since they often had to visit ports in Christian countries where to be both Norse and pagan would weigh doubly heavily against them.

conclude that even if Erik and Thorstein had asked for Leif's assistance he would not have given it; and pride probably kept them from asking.

Thus these new venturers to the west would have been limited to what was common knowledge about the Vinland voyage — information which was known by and obtainable from, men who had served as crew members on the previous voyages. These men would have known the general airt course, the approximate sailing distance, and the appearance of the landfall. They almost certainly would not have been privy to Leif's latitude observations.

FAILURE

Erik and Thorstein must have departed from Greenland on the direct course for Vinland, since this is the only course which is consistent with what happened to them later. Doubtless they steered south-southwest, expecting to sight Vinland in about five days. But the prevalent northwesterly weather of the Labrador Sea, combined with the effect of the currents, evidently set them considerably off course to the southward. By the end of the sixth or seventh day they may have turned westward in the hopes of picking up the coast, but by this time they would have become subject to the strongly eastward-setting Gulf Stream currents. It would have been a vain effort unless they were prepared to beat to the westward for at least five hundred miles until they reached the shores of Nova Scotia, since although no Greenlander knew it, the Vinland coast did not run on to the south but turned sharply west at Cape Race.

A few days on such a westerly course would doubtless have been enough to convince Erik and Thorstein that they were lost — or rather that Vinland was lost; and bad weather at this juncture would have made the hopelessness of the situation even more apparent. Without a latitude to guide them they would have had no means of correcting their course to Vinland short of returning to Greenland and starting over again. Storm or no storm, they had no real alternative but to accept failure and head for home.

Home would not have been so easily regained.

Although Pole Star sights would have told them how far south they were from Greenland, they would have had no way of determining how far east or west of it they were except by dead reckoning;

and dead reckoning which did not take into account the effect of the Atlantic Drift would have seriously misled them. The effect of the east-setting Gulf Stream and its subsidiary currents would have carried the knorr from ten to forty miles eastward every day that she was in their grip — and this may have amounted to several weeks in time and several hundred miles in distance. Added to this would have been the continuing effects of the prevailing westerlies. The total effect of the Atlantic Drift could have caused such a huge error in longitude dead reckoning that, in all likelihood, the voyagers were still steering northeast for Greenland when they should have been steering north*west*. It is not surprising that they eventually arrived in European waters.

This does not mean — and the saga does not say it does — that they came close to the coast of Ireland. They did see certain species of seabirds which were considered to be reliable indications that a mariner was approaching Irish waters. However, the ranges of most specifically European seabirds in the North Atlantic extend offshore to between 20 and 30 degrees west longitude. Consequently the Norse could have seen "Irish" seabirds when they were still several hundreds of miles to the west of Ireland.

Still holding to a generally northeast course, the weary mariners eventually raised the coast of Iceland and for the first time in many weeks knew where they were.

From Iceland they were at last able to lay a true course for home, and, as the saga tells us, early in the winter the ship finally came beating up into Eriksfiord at the conclusion of what was one of the longest and most harrowing voyages in recorded Norse maritime history. The spectre of death from starvation must have been a passenger on that ship for weeks; and death from thirst could have been averted only by collecting rain water. The ship herself would have been badly strained by the long weeks at sea. Doubtless she was leaking like a basket, and had to be bailed constantly to keep her afloat. It is remarkable that either ship or men survived at all.

HOMECOMING

One autumn day, just before winter began, the ship limped back to her moorings. It must have been a dreary homecoming. Thorstein's and Erik's arrival home, empty-handed and worn to shadows of themselves, would have been a great feather in Leif's cap, for it would have suggested that he was able to do what not even his father and his brother combined could equal. His sanctimonious followers doubtless shook their heads in mock piety and announced that this was White Christ's punishment upon those who still clung to Erik and the heathen gods.

Although the failure of the expedition must have weighed heavily on both Erik and Thorstein, they do not seem to have lost as much by it as might have been expected.

Christianity — and Leif's influence — presumably continued to gain ground; but it was still far from dominant. The pagans seem to have been able to hold their own and the Christians evidently failed to muster a majority in the local Thing, which was held each spring at Gardar, and consequently Greenland did not pass a Christianizing law, as Iceland had done.

As for Thorstein, his failure to find Vinland seems to have had no adverse effects on his courtship of Gudrid. Perhaps this is more revealing of Gudrid's character than of anything else; for it may be that she was the kind of woman who valued a man more for what he was than for the deeds he had done. In any event she married Thorstein in the autumn of the year after he returned, disheartened, to Eriksfiord.

Thorstein seems to have had a second string to his bow. Some time before sailing on the ill-fated Vinland voyage, he had made a partnership arrangement with a man named Thorstein the Swarthy to participate in the founding of a new settlement in the distant Godthaab fiord district. Thorstein the Swarthy sailed north first and hallowed land on Lysufiord, one of the main Godthaab fiords. We have no way of knowing if he was the inaugural land-taker in this region, but he may well have been. In any event he must have been one of the first.

In the autumn after his wedding, possibly in 1000, Thorstein Eriksson and his bride set out to help pioneer this new settlement, which was to extend the boundaries of the original Western Settlement nearly two hundred miles to the north and west.

The events of the first winter at Lysufiord are so fully dealt with in the sagas that I give the story in free translation, following the Erik the Red and the Karlsefni Saga versions. However, at the point where the corpse of Thorstein speaks, I have deleted a long passage consisting of religious propaganda and have substituted the version given in the Greenlanders Story.

THORSTEIN AND GUDRID

Now it is to be told how Thorstein Eriksson sought Gudrid Thorbjornsdottir in marriage. His offer was well received both by Gudrid and her father, and it was agreed that the marriage should take place at Brattalid that autumn.

The festivities went off very well and were attended by a great number of people.

Thorstein owned half of a stead in Lysufiord in the Western Settlement, the other half being owned by a man who was also named Thorstein, but was nicknamed the Swarthy. His wife was named Sigrid. Thorstein and Gudrid sailed up to Lysufiord in the autumn to stay with Thorstein the Swarthy. They were well received there and remained at the stead for the winter. Thorstein found lodgings for all the crew of his ship.

Now it happened that sickness appeared in their home early in the winter. Gard, who was the overseer of the farm and a man whom few liked, was the first to sicken, and he soon died.

Then one after another of the people took sick and died, including many members of Thorstein's crew. Thorstein Eriksson himself took sick, as did Thorstein the Swarthy's wife, Sigrid.

One evening Sigrid wished to go to the privy, which stood beyond the outer-door, and Gudrid accompanied her. They were seated in it facing the outer-door of the house when Sigrid uttered a loud shriek.

"We have acted foolishly in coming out," said Gudrid, "for you are in no condition to stand this cold. Let us go in again as fast as we can."

But Sigrid answered: "That we cannot do, for the corpses of all those who have died are standing between us and the door . . . and look! Among them I can see your husband Thorstein! And I see myself too! It is too dreadful to look at."

Sigrid thought she also saw the overseer, Gard, holding a whip in his hand and about to scourge the other dead people. Then the vision passed and she cried: "Let us go in quickly, Gudrid, for I no longer see the thronging dead."

So they went in; but before the morning dawned Sigrid herself was dead, and a coffin was made ready for her corpse.

Later that morning some of the men of the household went out in rowboats to fish, and Thorstein the Swarthy accompanied them to the landing place. When they came back at twilight he went down again to see their catch.

While he was there word was sent to him that he should hurry back to the house, for dreadful things were taking place there. Sigrid had tried to rise to her feet and then crawl into the bed where Thorstein Eriksson lay sick.

When Thorstein the Swarthy arrived in the room he saw that the dead woman had caught hold of the edge of Thorstein Eriksson's bed. Her husband dragged her off, and then he drove a pole-axe into her breast.

Later that night Thorstein Eriksson died. Thorstein the Swarthy bade Gudrid lie down and try to sleep, saying that he would keep watch over the bodies, and this she did.

Not long after that the corpse of Thorstein Eriksson sat up and spoke, saying he wished Gudrid to be called, for he had something to say to her.

Thorstein the Swarthy went and woke Gudrid and bade her cross herself and pray to God for help. "Your husband says that he wishes to see you," he told her, "but you must decide for yourself whether to go or not, for I cannot advise you in this."

"It may be that this is one of those strange events which shall afterwards be long remembered," Gudrid said. "I must take courage and go to my husband and hear what he has to say, for even if there is danger in this, I cannot escape my fate. Besides if I do not go to him he may well come to me."

Then Gudrid went to where Thorstein lay, and she came near to him and it seemed to her that the corpse was weeping. She bent down and he whispered a few words in her ear, but in so low a tone that no one else could hear. Then he spoke again in a louder voice so that everyone could hear what he said, and these were his words:

"Now I wish to tell Gudrid her fate so that she can better bear my death — for I am come to my final resting place. I tell you, Gudrid, that you will marry an Icelander and long shall you live with him, and many children will you bear to him, and they will be handsome, illustrious and excellent in every way. You shall go from Greenland to Iceland with him and there you shall abide for a long time, and you shall outlive your husband. After he is dead you shall make a pilgrimage to the southern lands; and when you come back you shall build a church in Iceland and live there, and you shall become a nun, and there you shall die at the end of your days.

"As for me, I wish to be buried at Eriksfiord together with all those of my people who have died here, save only Gard the overseer. Him you must burn, for he is the cause of the visitations which have afflicted us so sorely."

Then Thorstein Eriksson fell back, and they laid out his corpse.

The bodies of the dead were placed in Thorstein's ship and in the spring of the year Thorstein the Swarthy took them to Eriksfiord, where they were buried.

Thorstein the Swarthy took Gudrid and all her possessions to the home of her father, Thorbjorn. But Thorbjorn died soon after this, and all his property passed into Gudrid's possession. After that Erik took her to live at Brattalid, where he treated her as a daughter and carefully saw to all her affairs.

THE WALKING CORPSES

Some authors have concluded that the macabre descriptions of the deaths of Thorstein and Sigrid are the results of the vivid and superstition-ridden imaginations of the saga writers; but this is probably not the case. There are a number of diseases which could have produced the effects recorded in the saga. Epidemic cerebro-spinal meningitis and typhus fever are two of them. Victims of both these diseases have been known to sink into a penultimate coma which, to any observer except a trained physician, seems like death. Under the conditions of near-panic terror which the epidemic must have engendered in the people of the Lysufiord settlement, the possibility of a temporary coma being mistaken for death would have been much intensified.

The description of Sigrid's vision of the walking corpses who barred the door to the house is doubtless elaboration on the delirious babbling of a woman in the grip of a raging fever. Her grotesque attempt to crawl into the dying Thorstein's bed after she herself had been presumed to be dead, and after her corpse had been laid out, could have been the result of a final, semiconscious rally from the edge of death. The horror and revulsion which this pitiful last struggle aroused among the living is grimly testified to by the actions of her husband, who, believing she was in fact a corpse, ran her through with a pole-ax. Nor does Thorstein's brief rally from his coma smack of the supernatural, if we except only the prophecy about Gudrid's future, which was doubtless inserted into the story at some later date after Gudrid's life had run its course.

While there is not enough evidence to permit any certainty in attempting to identify the disease, the likelihood that it may have been typhus is strong. Body lice were so common as to be endemic in those times, and typhus, which is transmitted through lice, might have been brought to Greenland by a trading vessel from Norway or Iceland. Ship fever, as typhus was often called, appears to have been widespread throughout Europe during this era.

Whatever the disease may have been, that long dark winter at Lysufiord when people sickened and died in the cold, crowded and filthy sod-walled houses must have represented an eternity in hell to Gudrid and to the rest who survived it.

THREE

Land-seeking in the West

17

/\\.\\/\\

thoRfinn kaRlsefni

The Saga Tale (c. 1003–1004)

There was a man named Thorfinn Karlsefni who lived in the north of Iceland at Reyniness by Skagafirth. He was a man of fine family and was very wealthy. His mother was called Thorunn and his father was Thord Horsehead, son of Thord Bellower's daughter Thorhild Ptarmigan and Snorri, son of Thord of Hofdi and Frigerd who was the daughter of Thori the Loiterer, the son of Frigerd, daughter to Kiarval, King of the Irish. Thord of Hofdi was the son of Bjorn Chestbutter, the son of Thorvald Backbone, son of Bjorn Ironsides, son of Ragnor Shaggypants.

Thorfinn Karlsefni was a successful sea-going trader. One summer Thorfinn outfitted his ship with the intention of making a voyage to Greenland. Snorri Thorbrandsson of Alptafiord accompanied him, and there were forty other people aboard the ship with them.

At the same time Bjarni Grimolfsson from Breidafiord and Thorhall Gamlisson from the East Fiords also outfitted a ship carrying forty people, with the intention of making a voyage to Greenland.

When they were ready, Karlsefni and the others put to sea with these two ships in consort. It has not been recorded how long their voyage took them, but it is said that both ships arrived at Eriksfiord in the autumn.

Erik and other inhabitants rode down to the ships and a good trade was soon established. Erik was asked by the skippers to take such of their wares as he wished as gifts, and he responded with great generosity by inviting both crews to take up winter quarters with him at Brattalid. The merchants accepted the invitation with thanks. Their goods were then carried up to Brattalid, where there were plenty of fine large storehouses in which to keep them. There was very little shortage of anything they needed, and the merchants were well pleased with their entertainment at Erik's home during that winter.

However, as time drew on toward Yule, Erik seemed to become morose and less amiable than was his habit. One day Karlsefni spoke to him about it: "Is something bothering you, Erik? The people are saying that you are less cheerful than usual. Since you have entertained us with the greatest liberality it is only right for us to do whatever we can for you in return, so you must tell us why you are so low in spirits."

Erik replied: "You have been thoughtful and honorable guests and I am unhappy at the prospect that you may suffer as a result of our relationship. I am troubled by the thought that men in other places may say you never experienced a more wretched midwinter feast than the one at which Erik the Red was your host at Brattalid in Greenland."

"There is no need for anything like that to happen," said Karlsefni. "We have ample malt and meal and corn in our cargo, and you are welcome to take as much as you need to provide the wherewithal for as liberal an entertainment as you think fitting."

Erik accepted this offer and preparations were made for the midwinter feast, which turned out to be so magnificent that the people who attended it believed they had never before enjoyed such a superb entertainment.

Some time later Karlsefni approached Erik on the subject of his marrying Gudrid, for he assumed that Erik would have the right to bestow her hand in marriage, and Gudrid seemed to him a beautiful and accomplished woman.

Erik gave him a favorable reply, saying that by marrying Karlsefni, Gudrid would be following her fate; and he added that she was worthy of a good match and that he had heard only good reports of Karlsefni.

To cut the story short, the result was that Gudrid was betrothed to Karlsefni; a banquet was arranged; and the wedding was duly celebrated. And all of this happened at Brattalid during the course of that winter.

There was great good cheer at Brattalid that winter and there was much gaming and story telling and similar things which contributed to the entertainment of the household.

About this time there began to be much talk about the prospects of exploring Vinland the Good, for it was said that the country possessed many fine qualities. The result of the matter was that Karlsefni and Snorri outfitted their ship, intending to go in search of that country in the summer.

Bjarni Grimolfsson and Thorhall Gamlisson also joined the expedition with their ship and the people who had accompanied them.

There was a man named Thorvard who was married to Freydis, a bastard daughter of Erik the Red. He also joined the expedition, together with Thorvald Eriksson and Thorhall the Hunter.

Thorhall the Hunter had been a long time with Erik as his hunter and fisherman during the summers, and as his overseer during the winters. He was a strong and swarthy man of giant stature although getting on in years. In his manner he was overbearing. He was taciturn and usually spoke little, but when he did speak he frequently used abusive language and was always ready to stir up trouble. He paid little attention to the True Faith after it was introduced into Greenland. Thorhall was not very popular, but Erik had long been accustomed to seeking his advice. Thorhall went on the same ship with Thorvald [Eriksson] and his companions, because he had an extensive knowledge of the obygdir. They had the same ship that Thorbjorn Vifilsson had brought out [from Iceland].

All told there were one hundred and sixty people [on the expedition].

[SOURCES: Erik the Red Saga and the Thorfinn Karlsefni Saga]

That same summer when Karlsefni came from [Iceland*] there came a ship to Greenland from Norway. It was skippered by two brothers, Helge and Finnboggi, who were Icelanders from the East Firths. They stayed this winter in Greenland.

Now it is to be told that Freydis Eriksdottir made a trip from her home in Gardar to see the brothers Helge and Finnboggi. She asked them to go to Vinland with their ship and to go halves with her of all the profit they might get there. They agreed to this.

Then Freydis went to visit her brother Leif and asked him to give her the houses which he had built at Vinland. But he answered her saying he might let her use the houses, but would not give them [to her].

It was agreed between Karlsefni and Freydis that each ship [in the expedition] should carry thirty men of fighting age, and women also. But Freydis immediately broke this agreement and took five additional men and hid them.

Now they sailed out to sea having agreed beforehand that they should keep together if possible. . . .

[SOURCE: The Greenlanders Story]

---

* The text says Vinland but for reasons given in Appendix M it appears that the original must have been Iceland.

THE GREENLAND SETTLEMENTS

After Thorstein's death and Gudrid's return to the Eastern Settlement, there seems to have been a period during which the struggle between Christianity and paganism in Greenland became more or less stabilized, with Erik retaining control of the pagan part of the community while Leif was presumably the dominant man in the Christian group.

The growth of Leif's influence may have been curtailed by the news, which would have reached Greenland via Norwegian traders in the summer of 1001, that Olaf Tryggvason, the Sword of White Christ, had committed suicide in the summer or early autumn of the previous year when his ship was brought to bay by the fleet of the Danes. His inglorious death, the failure of White Christ to preserve him, and the removal of the threat which he had posed to Greenland would have heartened Erik's faction and discouraged Leif's.

Erik retained firm control of the Eriksfiord region — the most heavily populated part of Greenland — until at least as late as 1005, which is the last year in which his name is mentioned in the sagas. It is significant that during these important years there is hardly a mention of Leif in either the Erik the Red or the Karlsefni sagas.

The pagan element in Greenland may have been strengthened physically during this period. Although the Icelanders adopted Christianity as their official religion in 1000, it is clear from the saga records that many people were not prepared to abandon the old gods. Since Erik's country remained a stronghold of paganism, numbers of disgruntled heathens from Iceland may well have chosen this time to emigrate to Greenland.

The Greenland settlements were now fifteen years old, and life in them must have begun to follow established ways. Herds of sheep and cattle had multiplied. Distant pastures had been called into use. The growth of population through steady immigration had evidently spread into most of the new lands in the Godthaab Bight district. Trade with Iceland and Norway had settled into a routine exchange, and prosperity, if of a rude and tenuous nature, had apparently become fairly general.

Summertime journeys to the hunting areas absorbed the energies of the younger men. Production of walrus ivory and leather was steadily increasing, and there was a sustained demand in Europe for these two items, which became the basic foreign exchange of Greenland.

The lure of walrus ivory and hides, and of even rarer and more valuable commodities such as narwhal tusks and Greenland falcons brought traders to Greenland in considerable numbers. These traders doubtless continued to supply Greenland with badly needed timber; but the price would have remained high and the supply limited. The virgin forests of Vinland must have steadily increased in allure; but the failure of Thorstein's voyage seems to have discouraged the Greenlanders from making any fresh attempts in that direction until about 1003 — the date is arbitrary — when the arrival of two big Icelandic merchant ships, and of a man whose singular ability and energy made him the peer of Erik the Red, revived men's interest in prospects for a new Vinland voyage.

KARLSEFNI'S PURPOSE

Thorfinn Karlsefni had a most resounding genealogy and the claim that his was a famous family was no idle one. He was descended on one side from a fabled Irish king, and on the other from an almost legendary ancestor, Ragnor Shaggypants, who was claimed as a forebear by innumerable high-ranking Norwegians and Icelanders.

When Karlsefni took his place on the saga scene he would have been about twenty-five years of age. By the time he sailed for Greenland he was already a successful and wealthy sea-trader of considerable renown. What we know of his immediate background suggests a close resemblance to Bjarni Herjolfsson. The two men seem to have been very similar in outlook. They were both courageous in the best sense of the word; daring when there was a need for daring, but not reckless. Like Bjarni, Karlsefni was a seaman first and foremost, a man with a healthy regard for the safety of his ship and for the lives of his people.

The saga sources tell us almost nothing about the train of events which brought Karlsefni west from Iceland, but a good deal can be conjectured.

Following the usual trader's pattern, Karlsefni would have spent each alternate winter at home in Iceland. One winter he was presumably approached by a man named Snorri Thorbrandsson with the request that he consider making a charter voyage to Greenland during the ensuing summer.

Snorri, who was then in his fifties, was one of three sons of Thorbrand of Alptafiord (the other brothers being Thorleif-Kimbe and Helge) who had taken an active part in supporting Erik in his feud with Thorgest. When Erik sailed to Greenland to establish his colony he was accompanied by Helge Thorbrandsson, who took up land in the Eastern Settlement.

About 1002 the remaining brothers, Snorri and Thorleif-Kimbe, accompanied by several other men and their families, evidently decided to emigrate to Greenland. This may have been due to a distaste for the new religion of Iceland, but it was more likely a result of their involvement in a particularly gory feud in Alptafiord, of which another saga tells the tale. The Thorbrandssons would have required a large and well-found vessel to carry all the passengers, livestock and household goods belonging to the party; and Karlsefni's big trading knorr met their requirements.

Snorri's proposition would have been attractive to Karlsefni since it enabled him to visit Greenland on charter and at the same time to engage in private trading there. He was young and, as later events proved, adventurous. He had no doubt heard many yarns about the lands discovered by Bjarni Herjolfsson and later visited by Leif, and like any seaman he must have been curious about those new lands, new ports and new sea routes in the western reaches.

So much is conjecture, but one thing is certain: Karlsefni's voyage to Greenland was not undertaken solely as a trading venture. Even the crew of a ship engaged on the long voyage to Norway seldom numbered more than fifteen men; whereas Karlsefni's ship carried forty-two people when she sailed for Greenland. The conclusion that this was essentially an emigrant voyage is strengthened by the fact that a second vessel, carrying forty people, sailed in company with Karlsefni's knorr.

Thorhall Gamlisson from the East Fiords of Iceland was the owner-master of this second ship, and he too was a trader. Bjarni Grimolfsson appears to have been the leader of the group of emigrants aboard Thorhall's ship, even as Snorri Thorbrandsson was the leader of those traveling aboard Karlsefni's knorr. The passengers on both ships may have comprised a single party of emigrants all from the Alptafiord region.

The passage out to Greenland seems to have taken a long time, considering that the ships sailed in the summer and are not reported to have reached Eriksfiord until the autumn. However, they may not have sailed direct to Eriksfiord. Visits may have been made to the intervening fiords, either to allow Karlsefni and Thorhall to do some trading or to give the immigrants an opportunity to look for suitable lands.

By the time the ships reached Eriksfiord, the would-be settlers may already have become aware of a distressing fact. The Eastern Settlement lands were already fully occupied and the rush to the Godthaab Bight had probably left little to be looked for in the way of new lands, even in that direction.

Where then were the settlers to find satisfactory land? Although Greenland eventually supported a much larger population than that which occupied it in Karlsefni's time, this came about not through the pioneering of new homesteads so much as through the gradual splitting up of existing farms into ever smaller and less productive units in order to provide land for the new generations. The relatively few people who held most of the usable land in 1003 were probably not anxious to sell significant portions of their holdings, since money was of little value in Greenland. True value lay in land capable of supporting large enough herds to keep people in food throughout the year.

THE WESTERN PROSPECT

Eventually someone seems to have made the electrifying proposal that the would-be settlers should seek land in the new country to the west. It would not be surprising to learn that it was Erik himself who first made the proposal. Once such a fascinating project had been broached, it would have fired the imaginations not only of the Icelandic land-seekers but of a good many Greenlanders as well. Everyone would have heard stories of the unparalleled richness and goodness of Leif's Vinland, and such stories would have lost nothing over the years.

Initially the prospect of a Vinland Settlement voyage may not have been of much personal interest to Karlsefni or Thorhall Gamlisson. The two trader-skippers had successfully completed their charter voyage to Greenland, had doubtless disposed of most of their trade goods, and would have expected to complete their trading in the spring and then sail back to Iceland or perhaps on to Norway with a cargo of Greenland specialties.

But as enthusiasm for a land-taking voyage began to mount, Karlsefni and Thorhall would have been involved, since their two ships were vital to the scheme. The only locally owned sea-going vessels which might have been pressed into service seem to have been Leif's and Thorbjorn Vifilsson's. Leif did not make his ship available, and Thorbjorn's vessel had quickly been bespoken by a group of Greenlanders, headed by the last and youngest of Erik's sons, who intended to employ it themselves on the Vinland venture.

There was a third foreign-owned ship in Greenland that winter, but she was not available to the Icelandic settlers either. This ship belonged to the brothers Helge and Finnboggi, who, like Thorhall Gamlisson, were merchant-traders from the East Fiords of Iceland. They had sailed her direct to Greenland from Norway with a load of trade goods.*

The Greenlanders Story tells us that Freydis Eriksdottir made a journey from her home in Gardar to visit Helge and Finnboggi, who were wintering with local settlers on some nearby fiord. Freydis persuaded the brothers to join the general expedition and to carry her and her party to Vinland, offering them a half share of whatever profits might accrue from the voyage.

Karlsefni and Thorhall Gamlisson must have been under heavy pressure to make their vessels available to transport the Icelanders to the new lands. Likely they did not need much persuading. They too would have heard all about the fabulous cargo of lumber and other products which Leif had brought back from Vinland. The opportunity of fetching back such a cargo for themselves would have been hard to resist. In addition, Karlsefni had become emotionally involved, for he had fallen in love with Gudrid. Whether or not Gudrid was influenced by the prophecy that she would marry an Icelander, she seems to have had no objection to Karlsefni's proposal, and the marriage was celebrated with no loss of time.

---

* No mention is made of this vessel or its owners in either the Erik the Red or Karlsefni sagas; however, the Greenlanders Story speaks of them in connection with what is reputed to have been an independent voyage to Vinland conducted by Freydis, Erik's bastard daughter, and her husband Thorvald after the Karlsefni expedition had returned to Greenland. But that this voyage did not take place independently is established in Appendix M.

THE COLONISTS

The more that people talked about the projected voyage, the more irresistible it must have seemed. Indeed a much larger number of the Greenland settlers might have taken part if there had been enough ships to carry them. However, four vessels seem to have been all that were available, and these four could have carried, at the most, about one hundred and sixty adults together with their cattle, personal belongings, settlers' goods and essential supplies.

The expedition consisted of two divisions and apparently had two sets of leaders. One party consisted of the immigrant Icelanders under the overall leadership of Thorfinn Karlsefni, Snorri Thorbrandsson and Bjarni Grimolfsson; and the second included the Greenland emigrants led by Thorvald Eriksson. Freydis's party seems to have operated on its own to some extent, but perhaps it gave lip service to Thorvald's leadership.

The presence of some incipient distrust between the Greenland and Icelandic contingents even at this early stage is suggested by a statement in the Greenlanders Story to the effect that Karlsefni and Freydis (and presumably the other leaders also) agreed between them that each ship should carry only thirty men of fighting age, together with an additional and unspecified number of women. This was obviously an attempt to keep both sides as nearly equal in strength as possible; but the unscrupulous Freydis broke the agreement by smuggling an additional five Greenland men aboard the Helge and Finnboggi vessel.*

---

* Karlsefni's and Thorhall Gamlisson's ships carried approximately forty people each. According to the general agreement with the Greenlanders, it would appear that thirty of those aboard each ship were men, of whom about fifteen belonged to the permanent crew. The fifteen male colonists would have included three or four heads of families and some adult dependents and male thralls. The remaining ten people would have been women and youths — young children were probably not counted.

The composition of the group aboard the ship skippered by Thorvald Eriksson would have been a little different, since the whole party apparently planned on remaining in Vinland as settlers. This conclusion is supported by the fact that Freydis, who had no intention of settling but went along only "for honor and wealth," had to make arrangements for a ship of her own to bring back her booty. She would not have needed to do this if the plan had called for Thorvald Eriksson's ship and crew to return to Greenland after disembarking a party of colonists.

Thorvald's vessel would therefore have carried thirty Greenland men, all of whom were colonists, and a considerably larger number of women and children than did the Icelandic vessels.

The Helge and Finnboggi ship would have had a full Icelandic crew of about fif-

Because the word "exploring" occurs in reference to this voyage, it has sometimes been assumed that the expedition was primarily an exploring venture. This is clearly an error in interpretation. One hundred and sixty men and women, with their cattle and all the gear which they needed to set up a permanent settlement, all embarked on four overcrowded ships, do not comprise the elements of an exploring expedition. This was undoubtedly a colonizing venture, as indeed the Greenlanders Story specifically confirms. It was, in fact, the first recorded attempt by Europeans to establish a settlement on the North American continent.

---

teen sailors together with five women who, in accordance with the normal practice of those times, had been brought along to look after the crew's needs in a variety of ways.

Freydis and her husband Thorvald would have been accompanied by male retainers and thralls at least equal in number to the Icelandic crew, both to guarantee against treachery on the part of Helge and Finnboggi and to do the hard work involved in gathering a lading for the ship in Vinland.

18

∧∨∧

the outwarô voyage

The Saga Tale (c. 1004)

They sailed away from land to the Vestri [0] Bygd and from thence to Bear Island.

Then they sailed south beyond Bear Island for two doegr, when they discovered land and rowed to it in boats and explored that country. They found there many hellur [great stones], some of which were so large that two men could lie at full length on them, sole to sole. There were many arctic foxes there. They gave a name to this country and called it Helluland.

From thence they sailed for two doegr and bore away from the south toward the southeast until they reached a wooded country containing many animals. An island lay off to the southeast of this country and there they killed a bear so they called this Bjarney, while they called the wooded land Markland [Forest Land].

Then they sailed southward along this land and after two doegr they came to a cape [beyond which] they beat into the wind having the land to starboard. Here was a havenless coast with a long sandy beach and dunes. They rowed to the shore in boats and found upon a headland there [a hill which resembled?] the keel of a ship from which they named that headland Kialarness [Keel Point]. They called the strands there Furdustrandir [Marvelous Shore, in the sense of amazing] because they took so long to sail past them.

[SOURCES: Erik the Red Saga and Thorfinn Karlsefni Saga]

PLOTTING A COURSE

During the weeks following the decision to make the Vinland voyage, the leaders of the expedition doubtless spent long hours in

Erik's hall discussing the problems they would have to face. Chief among these would have been the question of which route to follow. The choice would have been governed by the fact that this time the ships were not to be manned solely by tough male adventurers who could withstand a great deal of hardship, but were to transport women and children whose physical endurance was limited, together with numbers of livestock which could not have survived a too prolonged deep-sea passage.

The direct route followed by Leif offered certain advantages. Not only was it the shortest way to the western lands, but a southwesterly course was in some ways the best in relation to the prevailing winds over the Labrador Sea, which in summer generally blow between north and west. Nevertheless it was unacceptable if it involved a risk of missing the landfall at the other end; and that this risk existed had been all too well established by the voyage of Thorstein and Erik. However, their unhappy experience need not have eliminated the direct route as a possibility for the new expedition, providing that Karlsefni and his fellow skippers possessed the relative latitude of Vinland.

Armed with this information, the new expedition could have departed from Greenland on a more westerly course than Thorstein and Erik had steered. When they had been out for a distance of five or six doegr they could then have altered to the southward, if they had not already sighted land, until they reached the desired latitude. After that they would only have had to beat to the west for a short distance before raising Vinland.

But the Karlsefni expedition did *not* know the latitude of Vinland. We are certain of this since although the expedition reached the Newfoundland coast, it never found Leif's Vinland because the search for it was not carried far enough to the south.

Leif appears to have withheld the secret of Vinland's position from the members of this new expedition, even as he evidently withheld it from Thorstein and Erik. The suspicion that he was distinctly uncooperative is strengthened by the fact that his name is not even mentioned in the Erik the Red and the Karlsefni saga accounts of the new voyage, except for a single casual reference. This concerns two Scots slaves originally given to Leif by King Olaf. The saga tells us that Erik and Leif loaned these slaves to Karlsefni, but it was evidently Erik, and not Leif, who made them available to the expedition.

Deprived of the benefit of Leif's information, the careful merchant skippers would have been forced to rule out the short, direct route to Vinland for fear that their voyage might become a repetition of the Thorstein voyage. They would also have had doubts about the wisdom of attempting to backtrack Bjarni's course from Greenland to Vinland. Even helped by a following wind it had taken Bjarni four days to cross the stretch of open water lying due west of the Eastern Settlements. If easterly weather was as rare in Norse times as it is now over the Labrador Sea, Karlsefni and his fellow skippers would have realized that an attempt to reverse this passage might result in their being kept at sea for many days.

There remained one other route to the new land. It was perhaps suggested by Erik, who was the first Norseman to use it. "If you sail north up the Greenland coast," he may have told the Icelandic skippers, "you will come to a great mountain on the edge of the sea, which we call Hrafnsgnipa. Take your departure from there in clear weather, and after one doegr sail westward you will raise another big mountain lying near the coast of the Vestri Obygd — the Western Wilderness. It is a short crossing and there is little danger of losing touch with the land even in stormy weather.

"Once you gain the coast of the Vestri Obygd, turn south along it. Our hunters do this when they go to Bear Island. Bear Island cannot lie far to the north of the last land Bjarni Herjolfsson found. You may even be able to coast all the way to it. In any case your course will be southward, so you will have good use of the northwesterly winds and run little risk of being swept out into the open sea as happened to Thorstein and myself. If this plan strikes you as being good, I can give you a pilot as far as Bear Island, for my factor, Thorhall the Hunter, knows the Vestri Obygd well."

Although this was a roundabout route, it offered many advantages. It was, in effect, a coasting route, and ships following it need never have been far from a supply of fresh water for the livestock, or from shelter for the ships in case of storms. Since drift ice was apparently no threat in those times, it was the safest as well as by far the shortest route across the great Labrador Sea-Baffin Bay inlet. Nor can we eliminate the possibility that, during almost two decades of Norse occupancy of Greenland, hunters in the Vestri Obygd might have penetrated some distance to the south of Bear Island — perhaps even as far as Hudson Strait.* If they had done this they would have been quick to realize, from their relative latitude vis-à-vis the Eastern Settlement, that Bjarni Herjolfsson's departure point from the last of his three western lands was on the south side of a comparatively narrow strait or sound (Hudson Strait) separating Bjarni's third land from the Vestri Obygd.

For whatever reasons, this was the route chosen by the Karlsefni expedition. Presumably led by Thorvald Eriksson's ship, carrying Thorhall the Hunter as pilot, the convoy put out from Eriksfiord one day in early summer and headed north under the towering ramparts of the west Greenland coast.†

NORTH, WEST AND SOUTH

Taking advantage of the long hours of daylight the four ships made their way up the coast to their departure landmark — the 7300-foot coastal peak near Sondre Stromfiord. They were then practically on the Arctic Circle and would have had almost twenty-four-hour daylight as they turned westward and began their crossing of Davis Strait on a day when the winds were northerly and the arctic sky was white and clear.

The lookouts would have raised the loom of the peak behind Cape Dyer only a few hours after they sank the tip of Hrafnsgnipa into the sea astern of them. Once the Cape Dyer coast was clearly in view, Thorhall the Hunter may have ordered a course alteration to the southwest, for as an experienced navigator on this coast, he would

---

* See Appendix P for details of the Norse penetration into Hudson Strait.

† Some of the extant copies of the Erik the Red and the Karlsefni sagas tell us that the ships sailed to the Vestri Bygd, which was the Western Settlement, and thence to Bear Island. However, other recensions say Vestri Obygd, the Western Wilderness. Most authors have taken the Vestri Bygd reading as the correct one, but this interpretation leads to almost insoluble difficulties. Bear Island must then be looked for on the coast of Greenland, and it has consequently been supposed that it must be identified with Disco Island. However, the sagas say that Helluland lay two doegr south of Bear Island, and in order to make Disco fill the bill the saga direction must be altered to read "southwest." This would then mean that Helluland was the Cumberland Peninsula, which leaves us with the problem of how to get the expedition to a forested country (Markland) in two more doegr on a southeasterly course, as specified in the sagas. This course and distance from Cumberland Peninsula would have taken the ships into the middle of the Labrador Sea as well as leaving them several doegr northward of timberline. Quite apart from this difficulty, the choice of Disco as Bear Island is absurd, since Disco lies nearly seven hundred miles north of Eriksfiord; and it is quite clear from all the sagas that Karlsefni was intent on finding Vinland and was not engaging in a polar expedition. A more detailed discussion of this matter will be found in Appendix D, Part II.

have felt no need to close with the land before turning south for Bear Island.

A landing was probably made at Bear Island to refill the water casks and do a little hunting and fishing in order to replenish the supplies of fresh food. The expedition may now have reached the limits of the Greenlanders' local knowledge. If so, they were facing a leap into the unknown. In any event the careful skippers would have taken advantage of this pause to make everything shipshape and secure.

The location of Bear Island — a vital element in reconstructing the rest of the journey — can be fixed with some exactness. The Greenlandiae Vetus Chorographia (a detailed analysis of which appears in Appendix D, Part II) states that Bear Island lay three days' rowing distance from Karlsbuda, which is identifiable with Cape Dyer. Karlsefni's expedition would hardly have visited Bear Island if it had lain north of Karlsbuda, so we conclude it must have lain south of that locality. Three days' rowing distance (between 90 and 105 nautical miles) southward along the coast of Cumberland Sound takes us to Leopold Island, which is at the southernmost tip of the peninsula.

Leopold Island is 2000 feet high. During the nineteenth century it was a valued landmark for whaling ships making an arrival after crossing Davis Strait or making a departure bound south for Newfoundland. Furthermore, it acts as a collecting point for polar bears which have been carried south with the polar pack during the winter. To this day it is famous among the local Eskimos as a place to hunt polar bears.

From Leopold Island the coast of the Cumberland Peninsula — the Vestri Obygd — runs sharply off to the northwest into Cumberland Sound, and to anyone unfamiliar with the inner reaches of this great inlet, Leopold Island seems to be the southern tip of a large independent landmass. Even if the Greenland hunters had explored the sound and discovered its true nature and the existence of a continuing coast to the southward, Leopold Island would still have been the obvious point of departure for Karlsefni's ships when leaving the Vestri Obygd.

The saga says that they took a departure from Bear Island and sailed "for two doegr to the south, when they discovered land." A due south course from Leopold Island runs down longitude 63 degrees 15 minutes. If it is followed without much deviation, it will bring a vessel's lookout within sight of the northern tip of Labrador after a passage out of sight of land from Leopold Island of about 250 nautical miles, or as close as need be to two doegr.

Furthermore, a ship holding to such a course will pass outside the visibility range of most of the intervening stretches of the Baffin Island coast and of Resolution Island. She might just possibly raise the loom of Cape Murchison, twenty miles to the westward of her course line, and she would probably pick up Lady Franklin Island. But Lady Franklin Island is only a few miles long and lies more than twenty miles offshore, so it might well have been ignored by the Karlsefni expedition as being unimportant. Cape Murchison could have been missed because of poor visibility in daylight, or it might have been passed during the twilight period.

It is also likely that the prevailing winds during this lap of the voyage would have been westerly to northwesterly, tending to set the ships a little to the eastward of the chosen course and farther offshore, with the consequence that the vessels would have made landfall on the Labrador slightly to the south of the Button Islands — possibly in the Cape Chidley region. Any increase in distance would have been offset, in terms of the time required for the voyage, by the influence of the southward-setting Canadian Current, which here runs at a rate of one-half to one knot.

It is significant that if Karlsefni did make his landfall on the northern tip of Labrador, he would not have seen the spectacular snow-capped mountains described by Bjarni as a feature of his third landfall. The northern tip of the peninsula has a maximum elevation of only 1700 feet. The land form rises gradually from there southward to its maximum elevation in the vicinity of Rama Bay, one hundred nautical miles south-southeast of Cape Chidley. In the saga account of Karlsefni's Helluland landfall, mountains — snow-capped or otherwise — are not mentioned for the good reason that there were none to see.

If they had made good a southerly course with a slight set to the eastward, Karlsefni's ships would have come within sight of the Labrador coast about opposite the Cape Chidley Islands in latitude 60 degrees 26 minutes. The lookouts could have raised the land off the starboard bow at a distance of up to forty miles, for these islands rise almost sheer from the sea to a height of more than a thousand feet. Directing their course to starboard, the ships would then have

□□□□□□	Bjarni Herjolfsson			
- - - - - -	Thorfinn Karlsefni and Thorvald Eriksson combined expedition			

0 25 50 75 100
MILES

N

60
59
58
57
56
55
54
53
52
51

Button Is.
Cape Chidley

Helluland

Torngat Mtns.

KAUMAJET PENIN.

Okak Bay

NAIN BIGHT

Kiglapait Mtns

MARKLAND

Cape Harrigan

Cape Makkovik

Cape Harrison

Holden Penin.

Grosswater Bay

Cape Porcupine

English R.

L. MELVILLE

Grady Pt.

Spotted I.

Round Hills

Battle Hbr.

BELLE I.

Strait of Belle Isle

Cape Bauld

The discovery and exploration of Helluland and Markland

closed with a country which Karlsefni could have tentatively identified as being Bjarni's point of departure from his third and most northerly land.

THE LABRADOR COAST (HELLULAND AND MARKLAND)

There are probably few bleaker, more barren places in the arctic regions than the granite snout of northern Labrador. Seen from seaward it appears to be completely devoid of any vegetation. The cold gray northern seas pound it unmercifully and the naked granite cliffs snarl back at the dark ocean in a grimace of perpetual ferocity. At the foot of the immense sea-cliffs, and in the steep-walled gashes which pass for coves and harbors, immense slices of frost-riven rock have slipped free of the cliffs and have come to rest in the landwash. These huge, flat slabs are as impressive now as they were to Karlsefni's people, who called them hellur (flat, or great, stones) and who named the land Helluland because of them.

Great flocks of seabirds haunt the cliffs, but there are very few land animals of any size except for arctic foxes, which prey on lemmings and such small fry or descend to the landwash to search for dead fish and other flotsam.

It can be imagined that the Norse ships did not linger long at this inhospitable landfall, but continued coasting southward as rapidly as wind and weather would allow. The two-doegr voyage southeast — a direction which the saga is careful to specify — along the mountainous coast of north Labrador would have been an exciting and a chancy one. The winds which whip down through the great valleys from the Torngat Mountains, to burst out through the narrow fiord mouths, often reach hurricane velocity even in summer, and ships under sail along that coast go warily. Still, the Greenlanders on the expedition would have been used to such conditions, even if the Icelanders were not; and they had no doubt warned their fellow voyagers of the dangers inherent in sailing close under mountain walls.

Soon after they left the Chidley region and began to see higher and higher mountains, which eventually grew so lofty that they bore snow on their peaks and glaciers in their higher valleys, they would have been confirmed in their belief that they were coasting Bjarni Herjolfsson's northern land. They would doubtless have been keeping a sharp lookout for the spectacular landmark which marked the southern end of this land, as Bjarni had defined it. When they raised the gargantuan bulk of the Kaumajet Peninsula standing off to the southeast from the land like a Gibraltar of the north, they could not have failed to recognize it.

Very likely they coasted close to this gigantic rock and were as awed as modern observers are at the sheer slopes of the Bishop's Mitre plunging four thousand feet into the sea. They may have sailed through Mugford Tickle, thereby establishing the fact that the tip of the peninsula is a 3000-foot-high island, now known as Cod Island. It seems possible that the Norse named it — in honor of its first discoverer — Bjarni Island. Later saga scribes who copied the original versions of the Erik the Red and the Karlsefni sagas, but who seem to have possessed no knowledge of Bjarni Herjolfsson's voyage, would have been responsible for interpolating the explanation that the island was called Bjarney in honor of a polar bear which Karlsefni's men found there. It is noteworthy that at an unknown point in the history of the sagas, some scribe apparently set himself the task of explaining the meaning of certain otherwise obscure names given to geographical features by the original explorers; and in at least two other cases his explanations have been shown to be interpolations.

Immediately south of Cod Island, and at a distance of two doegr from the north tip of Labrador, the voyagers would have opened Okak Bay and would have seen a dark frieze of trees stretching around its shores and covering many of its islands.* It can be taken for granted that a landing was made here. The water butts would have needed replenishing; people would have been anxious to get ashore where they could again build fires and have hot, cooked meals; and an effort would have been made to collect grass or rough forage in order to give the livestock some fresh food.

It is also probable that caribou were encountered here for the first time on the voyage. The forests at Okak were restricted to the lower and more sheltered areas, while the tundra upland plateau, which comes close to the coast in this area, must have been (it still is) excellent caribou country. The Moravians found that caribou were

---

* At the present time the line of demarcation between the almost completely barren mountain region of north Labrador and the forested coastal plains of the southern region reaches the sea just south of the Kiglapait Peninsula. In historic times it extended north to take in Okak Bay, where in the late eighteenth century Moravian missionaries still found stands of large spruce trees which were abundant enough to justify the installation of a sawmill.

numerous even on the outer islands as late as the eighteenth century.

The rugged Torngat range comes to an abrupt end at the Kiglapait Peninsula, and except for a few outlying heights, which are of relatively gentle contour and which are well wooded almost to their crests, no more real mountains are to be encountered on the coast of Labrador. South of Okak Bay the land is transformed into a rolling coastal plain rising slowly toward the interior. In Norse times it would have been so completely forested as to display the underlying rock rarely except on the most nakedly exposed islands off the coast.

This was the start of Markland — Land of Forests.

Departing from Okak Bay, the colonists probably made no attempt to follow Bjarni's course along the next leg of the journey south. They would have had nothing to gain by putting to sea, out of sight of land. Furthermore, they now knew, since they could see it for themselves, what Bjarni did not know — that the coast was continuous southward from the vicinity of the Kiglapait Peninsula. They undoubtedly chose to follow the coast since such a course would have enabled them to stay within reach of fresh water and cattle forage.

Not that proximity to this coast would have been an unmixed blessing. The great Nain Bight, which they would have entered soon after passing the Kiglapait, doubtless gave the skippers some bad attacks of nerves. It is filled with an almost unbelievable number of islands, islets, half-awash rocks and unseen reefs. In clear weather, and with a good lookout at the masthead, navigation along the seaward fringe of the bight is not too difficult. However, in thick weather, or with an onshore wind and heavy seas, it gives the most experienced seaman palpitations.

There may have been occasions (although easterly weather on this coast is uncommon in summer) when the ships had to stand off the land until the weather improved. They may also have done this at night as a routine precaution, since as they gained more southing the period of twilight would have been deepening to real darkness.

As the four ships made their cautious way to the south, the skippers would have noted that the coast — or what they could make of it beyond the chaotic mass of islands in the foreground — seemed to bend westward, then southward, and finally to swing sharply eastward once again as they passed Nain and Hopedale bights and picked up the relatively unobscured mainland coast beyond Cape Harrison.

This great, if gentle, swing to the eastward would have demonstrated to them that Bjarni's second and third lands were in fact one continuous country; but this conclusion must have become briefly suspect when they reached the extremity of the long, eastward-pointing Holton Peninsula, which lies just north of Grosswater Bay. They probably threaded their way between some of the outer Indian Islands — possibly through Cut Throat Tickle — at which point they would have discovered that they had apparently reached the end of Markland.

Looking south, they would have been able to see no more land. It is doubtful if they would even have been able to raise land to the southwest from the limited vantage point of their mastheads, particularly if the weather was at all unfavorable; and the sagas give us reason to think that they were then experiencing southeasterly weather, which would have meant poor visibility.

Under these circumstances they would doubtless have decided to stick with the land until they were sure of its trend, and to run to the westward under the northern coast of Grosswater Bay. Four or five hours on such a course would have brought them into the narrowing neck of the bay, and sooner or later they would have picked up the land lying to the south of them and would have realized with relief that they had been coasting into a deep fiord.

At this juncture they would have changed course to the southward on a long reach (if the wind was southeasterly) and crossed the bay, perhaps in the vicinity of Saddle Island. Sailing eastward now, they would have been able to reach on the other tack until they came to the massive headland abeam of George Island, whereupon they would have had to beat directly into the wind in order to round it.

The distance given in the saga for the passage from the first landing in Markland to the cape where they altered course is two doegr, which is close to the direct-line distance from Okak Bay to George Island. The distance actually sailed by the knorrir, if they coasted the fringe of islands in the Nain Bight, would have been greater; but since the ships were being helped on their way by the Labrador Current, which here flows at speeds of up to one and one-half knots, the loss from one factor would have been roughly offset by the gain from the other.

Depending on how far they ventured in Grosswater Bay, they would have had a more or less revealing glimpse of its inner reaches, which were very heavily wooded. As they sailed out of the bay they would have realized that they were sailing through a sound which ran east and west between a cape "running to the north from the land" and an "island lying to the north of the land." Someone would have been certain to comment on how closely these facts paralleled the description of the approaches to Leif's Vinland. It may even be that the suggestion was made that they should explore this fiord more fully on the chance that Vinland lay near at hand.

THE MARVELOUS SHORES

If such a suggestion *was* made, it was not acted upon. The ships continued around Pottles Cove Head and began to beat to the southward, and almost immediately they came in view of the most singular feature the voyagers had seen on the coast of Markland. Running away out of sight to starboard of them was the forty-five-mile stretch of almost perfectly straight coast, unbroken by the smallest cove or indentation and composed for the most part of a fifty-yard-wide strip of dark yellow sand backed by rippling dunes, which is now called Porcupine Strands.

The only break in this mighty beachline is a most peculiar spoon-shaped headland thrusting out from the sand beach at a point about two thirds of the way along the strands. This headland has a long, smooth spine rising from ground level near the beach, extending seaward for three miles and then falling off to sea level at the eastern extremity of the cape. Seen from some distance away it resembles nothing so much as the hull of an upturned ship lying with her keel against the sky. This headland is now called Cape Porcupine, and it is a famous landmark on that coast. Although the highest point of its spine is only 300 feet above sea level, the surrounding country is so low that it offers a superb vantage point from which the entire sweep of Porcupine Strands can be seen.

There are short stretches of sand scattered here and there on the coasts of Iceland and Greenland, but they mostly lie at the feet of bays, and none of them remotely approaches the magnitude of the Porcupine Strands of Labrador. The strands have, in fact, no rivals on the Atlantic seaboard of North America north of the New England states, and even there they are not overmatched.

The Norse were properly impressed, as is shown by the name they gave to this strange sight. They called it Furdustrandir, which means the Marvelous, or Amazing, Shores. They were also intrigued by Cape Porcupine (which is known locally as Sandy Beach Hill) and they seem to have yielded to its invitation, to have anchored their ships in its lee, and to have rowed ashore in order to scale its heights. They called this headland Kialarness which means Keel Point, and the Erik the Red and Karlsefni sagas say they did so because they found a ship's keel here. On the other hand the Greenlanders Story says that the name was bestowed on it when Thorvald Eriksson was driven on this cape during a storm, with the result that his ship's keel was damaged and had to be replaced.

Neither story is convincing. Since the local current drift is from north to south, and the general Atlantic drift is from west to east, the likelihood of Karlsefni's people having found a ship's keel here is extremely slim. As for the Thorvald Eriksson story, the account is patently apocrophal, as will appear later. There are three other Kialarnesses in Iceland and Norway, and since all of these are believed to have received their names because of their resemblances to capsized ships, we conclude that *this* Kialarness obtained its name in the same way.

19

/\.\/\.\/\.\

straumfiord

The Saga Tale (c. 1004)

Then the country became indented with bays [vagskorit] and they steered their ships into a bay.

Now when Leif was with King Olaf Tryggvason, and the King bade him proclaim Christianity in Greenland, he gave him two Scots [slaves]. The man's name was Haki and the woman's Hekia. The King advised Leif to make use of these people if he should ever stand in need of fleet runners, for they were swifter than deer. Erik and Leif had given Karlsefni the use of this couple.

When they sailed past Furdustrandir [into the bay] they put the Scots ashore and directed them to run to the southward and investigate the nature of the country. They were to return before the end of the third day. They were each clad in a garment which they called "kiafal," and which was so fashioned that it had a hood on top, was open at the sides, was sleeveless and was fastened between the legs by buttons and loops. Apart from this they were naked.

Karlsefni and his followers cast anchor during their absence, and when the Scots came back one of them carried a bunch of wine-berries and the other an ear of wild wheat. They came on board the ship, whereupon Karlsefni said they seemed to have found goodly things, and then he and his followers held on their way along a coast which was indented with fiords [fiardskorit].

They stood into a fiord with their ship. There was an island out in the mouth of this fiord about which strong currents flowed, therefore they called it Straumey [Island of Strong Currents]. There were so many eider ducks on the island that it was scarcely possible to walk between their eggs.

They sailed into the fiord and called it Straumfiord [Fiord of the Strong

Currents]. They carried their cargoes ashore from their ships and established themselves there.

[SOURCES: Erik the Red Saga and Thorfinn Karlsefni Saga]

SANDWICH BAY

When the Norse landed on Kialarness and climbed its spine they would have been able to look inland for many miles. In the foreground, just behind the beach, they would have seen a border of tall grasses, including strand-wheat, which not only makes excellent cattle fodder but which can be used as a substitute for domestic grain in the making of meal. Beyond the dunes and the verge of grasses, the country would have appeared to be one vast expanse of low-lying forest that gradually lifted to become an undulating, forest-clad highland in the far distance.

Attractive as the land was, this was no place for ships to linger. The wide-open coast offered no shelter and the sand bottom gave poor holding for the big killock anchors. Despite the anxiety of the settlers to get ashore, the skippers would have been anxious to leave this exposed place, and so the anchors were brought home and the vessels got under way.

After leaving Cape Porcupine the ships entered Trunmore Bight and probably coasted the gently curving beach at no great distance off until they rounded Sandy Point. They would then have opened a huge bay stretching away to the southwestward. The saga says, "the country became indented with bays and they steered their ships into a bay," and it is noteworthy that the specific word for bay, as opposed to fiord, is used. The reference is evidently to the two great bays, Grosswater and Sandwich, both of which are plotted in their correct latitudes on the ancient Stefansson Map (see Appendix G) so that we can be in no doubt about their correct identification.

The ships were now entering Sandwich Bay, which is one of the most attractive inlets on the Atlantic seaboard. The shores are low, and on the northwestern side they are fronted for considerable distances by sand beaches or by patches of open grassland lying between tidewater and the encroaching forests. Four large and placid rivers enter the bay through broad and shallow estuaries. They are full of salmon, have grass and marsh verges, and can be navigated for many miles by small craft.

Grosswater Bay

Liveyers, as the local residents call themselves, say that the climate is always much better in the bay than elsewhere on the Labrador, and some early visitor was sufficiently impressed with the place to name one of the major rivers Paradise.

As they worked their way past Earl Island, which almost plugs the throat of the bay, and opened the quiet reaches beyond, the Norse may again have wondered if this might not be the place they were seeking. They would have seen a large island, Huntingdon, lying off from the mouth of the bay "to the north of the land" and separated from the mainland by a sound which ran east and west. This would have fitted very well into the specific description of the approach to Vinland as it has been preserved in the saga accounts.

By the time they reached the bottom of the bay they were "a long way from the sea," and if they tried to enter the northeast arm on a falling tide they would probably have grounded on sand flats a mile or two from land. The only salient feature of Leif's Vinland which was lacking in Sandwich Bay was, and is, a barachois harbor.

That the Norse were intensely interested in the place is established by the fact that they anchored here for three days and sent the two Scots runners ashore to explore to the south "to discover the nature of the country" and probably also to look for Leif's booths. The saga does not say so, but it can be assumed that the party also launched some of their boats and sent them to explore the shoreline. When the runners came back they are said to have brought samples of vine-berries and wild wheat. The wild wheat would have been strand-wheat, and the vine-berries may have been high-bush cranberries. That they were not wild grapes seems to be established by Thorhall the Hunter's acid comment later on about the absence of grape wine, or by implication the wherewithal to make it, in that portion of the new lands which he saw.

Karlsefni seems to have been impressed by the good qualities of the country, but nevertheless to have decided to sail on. This decision may not have been a unanimous one. From what happened later it seems that at least some of the Greenlandic contingent felt that Vinland *did* lie in this neighborhood, if not even farther to the north. Thorhall the Hunter, for one, seems to have believed this, and Thorvald Eriksson may have agreed with him.

By this time there may also have been a growing feeling among the settlers that, Vinland or no Vinland, it was time to pick a site and go ashore. The summer was drawing on, and apart from being heartily sick of the crowded shipboard life, the colonists had doubtless begun to worry about their livestock, and about the vital necessity of establishing a camp and harvesting sufficient forage to see them through the coming winter. Sandwich Bay would have seemed more than satisfactory to some of the colonists, and there may have been hot-tempered disagreement when the order was given to hoist sail once more.

BELLE ISLE (STRAUMEY)

Disagreement or no, the expedition sailed on, presumably leaving Sandwich Bay through the sound to the south of Huntingdon Island, with the mainland running off ahead of them to the eastward until they cleared Grady Head and found the coast again trending southeast as far as Spotted Island.

From Spotted Island the coastline runs off almost due south and undergoes another abrupt change in character, becoming, in the words of the *Labrador Pilot,* "indented by many irregular inlets"— which is almost a paraphrase of the saga description. The hundred-mile-long stretch of coast between Spotted Island and Battle Harbour is indented by a dozen major fiords and innumerable smaller ones. However, although it is a good coast for fishermen, it has little to offer prospective farmers, for it is generally rather bleak, steep-to and rugged, although it possesses good forests. By comparison with Sandwich Bay it would have looked uninviting to the Norse, and it can be imagined that discontent and grumbling grew worse as the ships sailed on past what must have seemed like an interminable stretch of inhospitable coast. The colonists seemed to be getting no nearer to Vinland. In fact they were drawing away from the only country they had so far seen which bore any marked resemblance to Leif's fabled land.

Karlsefni and some of the other skippers must by now have become seriously concerned about their whereabouts. After leaving Cod Island, they would hardly have been able to identify any place which would have fitted what they knew of Bjarni's voyage, for they had been coasting while he had made direct sea-passages between widely isolated points along the coast. Their chances of identifying Spotted Island and the country immediately south of it as Bjarni's second land would have been small, for there are few easily recognizable features on this section of the coast. But they had committed themselves to the coast, and could go only where it led, hoping that it would eventually take them to Vinland.

When they reached Battle Harbour and rounded Cape Charles they would have been in for a severe shock. The land, which had been generally trending to the southeastward ever since they reached Helluland, now began to fall off sharply toward the southwest. South of them they would have seen what looked like open ocean (the mouth of the Strait of Belle Isle) with, far away to the southeast, the loom of an island or a distant and isolated headland.

In such a situation we can suppose that the skippers followed standard Norse practice and sent someone ashore to climb the 700-foot peak on Cape Charles in order to see what lay beyond. From this peak, or from any similar point they may have chosen in the general vicinity, an observer with ideal viewing conditions would have been able to see about thirty nautical miles. He would have had a good view of the distant land to the east and would have realized that it was in reality a big island (Belle Isle). He would have seen no

sign of land beyond it, nor to the southward. He would also have been able to confirm that the coast of Markland continued to trend southwest until it ran out of sight.

The problem of what to do next must have been a difficult one to resolve. Doubtless some of the people clamored for a return to the known advantages of Sandwich or Grosswater bays. Some may have been willing to venture a little further into the unknown, but would have preferred taking the safer course and following the coast to the southwestward, although from what could be seen of its abrupt and looming contours it could hardly have looked very prepossessing.

On the other hand the more daring and resolute men may have argued for an investigation of the distant island. They might have reminded the pessimists that on a previous occasion — at Holton Peninsula — it had looked as if Markland had come to an end, but that they had again picked up the southeast-trending coast beyond it. They may also have pointed out that the off-lying island was obviously very high and that a view from its crest would enable them to decide conclusively whether the open water was only another great inlet or was in fact open sea defining the end of Markland. Those who did not feel that the expedition had as yet reached the Vinland country probably argued strongly for one final sally to the south and in the event they won the day.

Leaving the Labrador coast at some point near Battle Harbour, the ships sailed out across the intervening eighteen or twenty miles of open water to Belle Isle. Belle Isle is a most striking plateau island, ten miles long and rising almost sheer from the sea on all sides to a tableland whose maximum altitude is just over 800 feet. It has no harbors, but there are a number of coves. The knorrir could have anchored temporarily in one of these on the leeward side of the great rock, while a few men rowed ashore and scaled the cliffs to the high tableland above.

They would probably not, as the saga says, have found "so many eider ducks on the island that it was scarcely possible to walk between their eggs." Eiders do not commonly nest on this type of large, high island; they prefer small, low lying islands close to a mainland shore. Also, the eider egg season (as well as the egg season for all other seabirds) in the Strait of Belle Isle area would likely have been over by the time the Norse arrived. What has happened here (and it has misled many commentators) is that this first island — Straumey — and some other much smaller island or islands lying near the Straumfiord Camp of the Norse have lost their separate identities and have become one island. Later references to the spring gathering of eggs seem to make this clear.*

Straumey literally means Stream Island; but in the usage of the Norse period it meant an island surrounded by especially strong currents. There are numerous applications of the word "straum" to islands, fiords, headlands and even coasts in Norway, Iceland and Greenland; and in every case the word is used to distinguish a place where the currents are particularly noteworthy.

Belle Isle stands in such a position that it receives the full force of the inshore branch of the southbound Labrador Current. It also lies full in the path of the extraordinarily powerful tidal currents flowing in and out of the Strait of Belle Isle. When the tide is ebbing through the strait, bolstered by the flow of the St. Lawrence River, it runs at an average of three knots and has been known to run as high as six knots at certain places. With a flood tide, assisted by the westbound offshoot of the Labrador Current, the stream has been known to average three and one half knots, with a maximum of seven knots.

Fishermen who use Belle Isle as a summer base report that the current flowing eastward past the island frequently reaches four knots, and when it meets the south-bound Labrador Current, maelstroms or bores occur of sufficient violence to make it impossible to keep fishing gear in the water, no matter how firmly it may be anchored.

There is no other place on the Atlantic seaboard between Cape Chidley and the Bay of Fundy where there are such strong currents covering such a broad sweep of water. It seems impossible to doubt that Straumfiord is the Strait of Belle Isle, and that Straumey is Belle Isle itself.

The argument is sometimes raised that since the Norse used the word Straum*fiord* they could not have meant the Strait of Belle Isle because it is actually a sound. However, it was not until the 1533-1536 voyage of Jacques Cartier that Europeans appear to have realized that Newfoundland was an island not connected to the mainland of Labrador at some point far to the westward of Belle

---

* Although Belle Isle probably had few nesting eiders, it was a breeding ground for vast numbers of seabirds of other species, which fact may have helped to confuse the saga scribes.

Isle. For at least fifty years before Cartier's discovery, Basque, French and English fishermen had been catching cod and whales in the northeastern arm of the Gulf of St. Lawrence, which they called the Grande Bay, under the impression that it was no more than a deep inlet opening on the sea through the Strait of Belle Isle. It is unreasonable to insist that the Norse voyagers of circa A.D. 1000 should have recognized a truth which eluded later-day voyagers for half a century.*

If it was a clear day when the men from Karlsefni's flotilla scaled Belle Isle, they would have been rewarded by a stupendous view. From the high plateau they would have been able to look down the throat of the strait as far as L'Anse Amour on the bald northern shore — a distance of nearly sixty miles. They would have seen far less of the southern shore, for it is generally low and is partly hidden behind the Cape Norman headland. Nevertheless, the impression of the strait which one gets from the crest of Belle Isle is of a very deep fiord narrowing away into the blue distance, and anyone who did not know otherwise would be convinced that the land swung eastward again from the bottom of this inlet. Consequently the Norse would logically have mistaken the tip of the Great Northern Peninsula of Newfoundland for a continuation of the Markland coast.

The most prominent feature in the foreground of this coast would have been Quirpon Head and Cape Bauld, with an elevation of five hundred feet, lying fourteen miles due south of Belle Isle. To the west of it the Norse would have seen other land, but it would have been hard to determine whether they were looking at islands or headlands, since apart from Quirpon the coastal section of the tip of the peninsula is mostly low lying and rather featureless.

They must have felt a great surge of hope as they looked south from Belle Isle. The description of the approaches to Leif's Vinland, as preserved into our time in the saga accounts, comes very close to being a description of the Belle Isle-Quirpon-Cape Norman area. It seems likely that the voyagers were convinced that they had at long last reached the portals of Vinland, and that nothing remained but to search the nearby coasts until they found Leif's harbor and his booths.

The saga tells us only that after leaving Straumey they sailed into

---

* Champlain's map of 1632 still calls the northeast section of the Gulf of St. Lawrence "La Grande Baye."

Straumfiord, went ashore, and established a wintering camp. This passage is so brief that we must assume the loss of a portion of the original account which not only explained why they went ashore, but described in some detail where they landed. As things stand we are not even told whether the camp was on the north or the south coast of the strait, nor is there any indication of what sort of harbor was chosen — an omission which could hardly have existed in the original oral saga.

THE CAMPSITE AT EPAVES BAY

We must locate the Straumfiord campsite for ourselves. We can eliminate the north shore of the strait since the voyagers would hardly have turned back from Belle Isle toward the forbidding line of thousand-foot bluffs which guard the coast from Chateau Bay to L'Anse Amour. Even if they had done so, they would have found no settlement site suitable to their needs.

The southwest coast from Cape Norman to Savage Cove can also be eliminated. It is a low limestone shore offering no reasonable shelter even for vessels of the knorr type, and it is backed by a useless morass of black spruce bogs and barrens which present almost as inhospitable a face to the sea as do the brooding highlands of the northwestern shore.

There remains only one small stretch of coast which could have been sufficiently attractive to the Norse to encourage them to establish even a temporary camp. This section encompasses the extreme northern tip of the Great Northern Peninsula of Newfoundland between Cape Bauld and Cape Norman, and includes Pistolet and Sacred bays.

From Belle Isle the flotilla would have sailed for Quirpon and Cape Bauld since this is not only the most prominent feature on the coast, it is the part of Newfoundland lying closest to Belle Isle. As they closed with Cape Bauld, the low coast to the westward of it would have begun to take form, and lookouts at every masthead would have been anxiously scanning these new shores for clues to Vinland's whereabouts. If the voyagers identified Straumey with Leif's "island lying to the north of the land," they would then have identified Quirpon with the "cape stretching to the north of the land." The fact that Quirpon is actually an island would not have been apparent to them, since it is separated from the mainland only by a very narrow

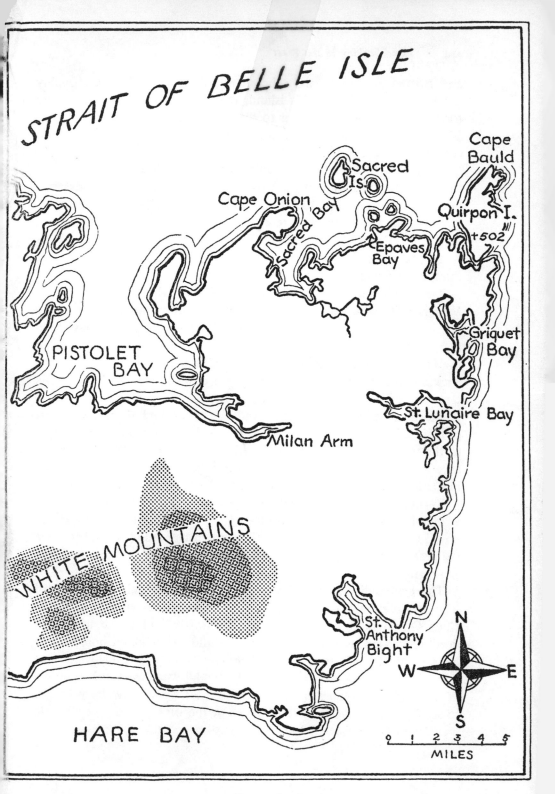

Straumfiord

and twisted gut. If, on the other hand, they felt that Straumey lay too far offshore to be Leif's island, they would have been searching for another island lying closer to the coast. In this case Great Sacred Island, lying four miles westward of Quirpon, would certainly have caught their eye.

Great Sacred Island, Cape Onion to the southwestward of it, and the sound which separates the two fit the Greenlanders Story description of the approaches to Vinland with remarkable fidelity. Consequently they bear a marked resemblance to the Baccalieu Island-Bay de Verde Peninsula-Baccalieu Tickle complex. Only the scale is wrong; for these latter features are much larger and more prominent than their Sacred Bay counterparts.

Karlsefni's problems in trying to resolve what he knew about Vinland with what he could now see of the country ahead of him may not have been so very different from those of those later-day commentators who have been attracted to the Pistolet-Sacred Bay area in the belief that it must have harbored Leif's Vinland. Apart from the Tickle Cove Pond location, there is no other place on the Atlantic seaboard of North America which so nearly (but not quite) answers to the description in the Greenlanders Story. And therein lie a set of frustrations and paradoxes which have driven a number of authors to the verge of desperation, and which have forced others to undertake heroic changes in local topography, in the sea level, or in other intractable features of the country in order to force a perfect fit.

Karlsefni and his companions were not interested in any such academic solution to the problem. They were looking for the physical reality of Vinland, and they urgently needed to find it since the time left to them for exploration must have been growing perilously short.

The probability is that they cruised west from Quirpon to Sacred Island, tentatively identifying it with Leif's island, and so rounded Cape Onion in the hope that Pistolet Bay would prove to be the fiord at whose foot lay the lagoon lake and the Vinland booths. The hope would have been tentative, because if Great Sacred Island was to be accepted as Leif's "island off the land," what were they to make of Belle Isle and Quirpon, one of which Leif would have been bound to see before raising Sacred Island? On the other hand, if Belle Isle was the indicator island, how were they to account for the excessive width of the sound — fourteen nautical miles — which separates it from the mainland cape?

Things must have looked *almost* right, but not *quite* right. And when the ships, or afterboats put off for the purpose, had descended into and explored the shallow, reef-strewn reaches of Pistolet Bay, the explorers would have found nothing to answer to the saga description of the lagoon lake, of the grassy forelands, or of the magnificent mixed forests which had made Leif rich.

Constantly fluctuating hopes and a general feeling of frustration must have plagued the leaders of the expedition almost beyond endurance. Some of them evidently continued to believe that Vinland lay somewhere close at hand, and they would have been in favor of persevering in the search. On the other hand, the colonists must have become increasingly concerned about the condition of their livestock, and of their women and children, and must have been clamoring to be put ashore, if only temporarily. Karlsefni himself may have been willing to agree to their demands for personal reasons, since Gudrid was by then at least six months pregnant.

What was needed was a temporary campsite from which further explorations could be launched while the colonists saw to the welfare of their stock. Such a place lay close at hand, and the Norse may have already glimpsed it. In sailing to the Sacred Islands they would have been able to look down into Sacred Bay and observe that there were tempting patches of grasslands between the landwash and the encroaching forests.

The decision was made, and the ships turned in to shore.

The place where they landed seems to have been in Epaves Bay, where a Norwegian author, Helge Ingstad, has excavated what may be the site of the Norse Straumfiord Camp.*

Thus on a day in the late summer of the first decade of the eleventh century, men, women and children began making their way ashore to establish what was to become the first European settlement in the New World.

---

* The Epaves Bay site is discussed in Appendix N.

20

∧∧∧

the search for vinland

The Saga Tale (c. 1004–1005)

They had brought with them all kinds of livestock.

Now they explored the country thereabouts. There were mountains in the vicinity and the land was fair to look upon. They did nothing but explore the country. There was tall grass thereabouts.

They spent the winter there but they had a hard winter and one for which they had not prepared. The fishing fell off and they grew short of food. They went out to the islands in the hope that they might find something in the way of fishing or some flotsam. Although their livestock fared well, there was little food left [for the people]. They called on God to send them food, but did not get a response as quickly as they needed it.

Then Thorhall the Hunter disappeared. They searched for him for three days and on the fourth day Karlsefni and Bjarni [Grimolfsson] found him on a clifftop.

He was lying there with eyes, mouth and nostrils gaping, and was scratching himself and muttering something. They asked him why he had come to this place and he told them not to be concerned by what he did, for he was old enough to look after himself.

Then they asked him to go home with them, and this he did.

Soon afterward a whale appeared and they got it and flensed it, but no one could tell what kind of whale it was. Karlsefni had much knowledge of whales, but he did not recognize this one. When the cooks had prepared it the people ate of it and they were all sickened by it.

Then Thorhall the Hunter approached them and said: "Did not Red Beard

[Thor] prove more helpful than your Christ? This [whale] is my reward for the verses I dedicated to Thor the Trustworthy. Seldom has he failed me."

When the people heard this none of them would eat, and they threw [the meat] into the sea and invoked God's mercy.

The weather then improved so they could row out to go fishing and they no longer lacked the necessities of life. In the spring they went out into Straumfiord and obtained provisions from both regions; hunting on the mainland, and gathering eggs and going deep-sea fishing [on the Fiord].

[SOURCES: Erik the Red Saga and Thorfinn Karlsefni Saga]

THE CHOICE OF EPAVES BAY

By the time the settlers went ashore the summer must have been almost spent, and if they had intended to remain all hands ought to have buckled down to the task of making ready for the winter. The Greenlanders, at least, were seasoned colonists who had good reason to know the vital importance of making every possible preparation. Yet, in the words of the saga, they did nothing but explore the country. This apparent fecklessness could have been due only to the fact that the colonists did not expect to have to remain at Epaves Bay.

Certainly it was not an ideal location. The Norse preferred the inner reaches of protected fiords or bays as settlement sites and seldom tried to establish pastoral settlements on exposed outer coasts unless there was no alternative. And there were a number of alternatives in the Sacred Bay region, all of them preferable to Epaves Bay.* In South Road, for example, less than six miles away, there were excellent sites at Parker Brook Bottom and at New Harbour. These offered many advantages which Epaves Bay could not boast. The grasslands at New Harbour are, and apparently always were, much more extensive than those at Epaves Bay, and in addition there was a huge adjacent stretch of bog pasture. Parker Brook is, and probably was in Norse times, an excellent salmon river; but Black Duck Brook at Epaves Bay was far too small ever to have had a significant salmon run. New Harbour and Parker Brook Bottom are well protected from the prevailing winter winds of the strait, which are northwesterlies. Epaves Bay lies wide open to these winds.

---

* The English translation is Wreck Bay, and the name is derived from the fact that the bay provides no shelter for ships, several of which have driven ashore here during northwesterly storms.

In the nineteenth century there was a settlement of twenty to thirty families at New Harbour, and these people existed primarily on what they could grow for themselves, depending on fishing only to provide money for the purchase of those few items that they could not produce. At one time there were as many as fifty head of cattle and innumerable sheep at New Harbour. In the twentieth century the New Harbour folk gradually moved out to sites on the open coast, nearer the fishing grounds, as a result of a shift from a self-sustaining economy to one dependent on the sale of dry cod. There is no record of there ever having been a pastoral — or even a fishing — community at Epaves Bay during colonial times. The bay was used, as we have noted in Appendix N, only by transient Europeans as a summer whaling base. Even the settlement at nearby L'Anse aux Meadows was always a fishing community, although some sheep and cattle were kept by the residents.

Perhaps most important is the fact that New Harbour and Parker Brook Bottom both offered good, secure winter harbors for the knorrir. The safety of their vessels to people who were venturing into an alien world would have been of paramount importance. It is hard to believe that the Norse would have deliberately chosen to risk their ships on the open strand at Epaves Bay, where no harbor of any sort existed, through the crucial winter months. The ships could have been secured at Epaves Bay only by hauling them ashore for a distance of several hundred feet beyond high-water mark, and the amount of time and effort which would have been required to accomplish such a feat would be tremendous.

I believe that Epaves Bay was originally intended to serve only as a transient camp. It was a convenient halting place where the animals could be fed back to health and where the colonists could refresh themselves after the long, crowded and uncomfortable voyage. Meanwhile the balance of the men were organized into exploring parties and sent out to search the coasts of the northern section of the Great Northern Peninsula for Leif's Vinland booths.

Karlsefni and his fellow chiefs perhaps hoped that Leif's haven might lie hidden at the foot of some fiord or bay which they had not seen from the ships, or which they had been unable to fully explore. What was needed was a detailed search of the coast both east and west, and this was a task for the ships' boats.

The afterboats belonging to the knorrir were about thirty feet long and could carry twenty people in an emergency, or eight or nine on a prolonged voyage. They were equipped with oars and sails. Being lightly built and finely fashioned, they were fast and easy to handle. Because of their shallow draft they could enter almost any body of water. The foreboat which each large knorr also carried was similar but smaller. All told the expedition probably possessed six or eight boats, and we assume that most of these were dispatched to search for Leif's booths.

"They did nothing but explore the country." This can hardly refer to overland exploration, since attempts to penetrate the dense black spruce forests which at that time covered almost all of the tip of the peninsula would have been pointless. The phrase can refer only to boat explorations. In a matter of several weeks a flotilla of six boats could have thoroughly explored the coast for some distance beyond Cape Norman to the south and west, and to Hare Bay, or beyond, to the south and east.

As the boats sailed or rowed back into Epaves Bay, and as one by one their skippers reported finding no signs of Leif's haven, the hope of locating Vinland that season would finally have failed. By then it would probably have been too late to think of seeking another site at which to spend the winter, and so Epaves Bay, where temporary booths had doubtless already been erected, would have become the location of the wintering camp, by default rather than by choice.

THE NATURE OF THE PLACE

Despite the fact that Vinland had so far eluded them, the colonists — though probably not the traders — may have been moderately well satisfied with Epaves Bay.

Apart from the shore meadow, which would have provided sufficient pasture for the limited number of cattle that the Norse could have transported in their ships, this was fine berry country; there was no shortage of firewood lying in windrows above the hightide mark and already dry and ready for use; the shore-fishery would have been excellent, and harbor seals and whales would have been relatively abundant. Late summer ducks probably abounded, and the condition of the adjacent islands would have demonstrated that these were favored breeding grounds for ducks and other seabirds.

However, although the sea was rich in food resources, the land would have proved disappointing. The black spruce forests, exposed

The Epaves Bay site

as they were to the prevailing gales and nurtured on scanty soil, would not have been very promising as a source of export timber. There were no hardwoods of any size to be found nor, as the saga later testifies, were there any grapes.*

Land animal life would have been scarce. The spruce forests do not provide caribou range,† nor are they a good habitat for arctic hares or ptarmigan. Snowshoe rabbits (varying hares), which ought to have been abundant in such a forest, did not then exist in Newfoundland but were introduced during colonial times.

It is unlikely that the people were much concerned about the food supply at first. The immediate problem was to build winter houses and to put the ships into winter quarters. With one hundred and sixty people to house and four big ships to haul out and secure, there would have been little free time left for worrying about what the winter might bring.

THE HARD WINTER

When winter came, the Norse found that life was not going to go as easily as they had hoped. The one factor which they had not considered — because they could not — was the weather. Winter weather in the Epaves Bay area today is not only cold, it is about as wild as it can be. The low coast is exposed to every wind from east through north to west, and the winds which blow over the Strait of Belle Isle in wintertime can and do blow at hurricane strength for days on end. The strength of the winter winds is alone sufficient to keep small boats from venturing out into the strait except on rare occasions; and in addition the pack ice coming south on the Labrador Current so plugs the strait and jams its shores that even big steel steamers cannot force a passage through. Consequently the strait is normally closed to all navigation, except by specially reinforced ships, from the end of October until the end of June.

Although the climate in Karlsefni's time was milder than it is now, the winds were probably just as strong; and although arctic pack ice did not close the strait for as long a period as it does at present, it

---

* Epaves Bay lies 240 nautical miles north of Tickle Cove Pond and, apart fom this increased northing, its climate is so much worse that wild grapes could probbly not have survived there.

† Deer, moose and elk were not found in Newfoundland. Moose have since been introduced.

would still have been a major problem during the midwinter months. From December to April it may well have blocked the strait, or at least denied its use to vessels as lightly built as the Norse boats were. Thus there would have been long periods when the settlers could not have launched their boats in order to go fishing. Furthermore, the ice would have raftered on the open coast, thus keeping small boats ashore for weeks or months on end.

As the storm winds blew and food grew scarce in the crude sod shanties, many people must have wished that they had given up the search for Vinland long before, and had used the extra time to make dry fish or to go whaling. They were probably not actually starving or they would have turned to the almost-last resort and begun butchering their cattle, which were doing well enough by foraging for themselves on the shore pastures, which would have been kept largely snow-free by the strong winds.

Nevertheless the people were hungry enough to call on their gods for help; and at this juncture some of the flesh of the original saga has remained more or less intact so that we have more than a skeletal account of the events which took place.

Presumably the Christians in the party (who were probably not numerous) began praying to White Christ for help; whereupon that intractable pagan, Thorhall the Hunter, decided to call on Thor. But one did not pray to Thor. The way to gain his aid was to go to some lonely place * and alternately argue, bribe, threaten, and cajole him into providing assistance — and the most efficacious cajolement was to compose a poem of praise in his honor and recite it to the wind and sky.

The clerics who were responsible for transcribing and preserving the written sagas during the Middle Ages must have been distressed by the original version of what happened, for it is quite clear that Thorhall was answered and that the Christians were not. Shortly after Thorhall followed Karlsefni and Bjarni back to camp, a whale blundered into the bay or was found dead among the ice.

Great fires were promptly lit and everyone gathered around while the cooks filled the pots with meat and hung strips of meat and blubber beside the fires to roast. The gorging which followed doubtless resulted in some stomach aches, but it is questionable whether the

---

* Thorhall may have scaled the prominent coastal cliff at nearby Cape Ardoise.

meat actually poisoned those who ate it. This could be an interjection by some righteous priest at a much later date.

It is also extremely unlikely that when Thorhall made his claim to
having been responsible for procuring the whale, with Thor's help,
the starving people rose up en masse and heaved the whale meat back
into the sea. What they almost certainly did was go right on eating
whale until the carcass was stripped and spring was approaching.
That this was in fact the case is strongly indicated in the second verse
of Thorhall's song, presented later in this chapter, which, with
a few other fragments of verse preserved in the saga, is believed by
scholars to be an unaltered fragment of the original oral saga.

With the approach of spring, the shortage of food ceased to be a
problem. As the weather improved and the pack ice disappeared, the
boats were able to get out into the open waters of the strait, where
they engaged in "deep-sea" fishing, a term which doubtless includes
whaling and perhaps sealing as well, since both whales and seals were
considered to be fish in those times and were so referred to.

It had been a long, hard winter, but one event took place which
makes this winter remarkable, from our point of view at least. At
some time in the autumn or early winter Gudrid gave birth to a son.
He was named Snorri, possibly in honor of Snorri Thorbrandsson,
who seems not only to have been Karlsefni's closest comrade but to
have also been the elder wise man of the expedition.

Snorri Thorfinnsson, who lived to become a famous man in his
own right in Iceland, was presumably the first child of white parents
to be born in North America, and in this sense he becomes the first
North American of full European descent . . . whatever that may be
worth.

Although the settlers were no longer suffering from hunger, they
seem to have remained rather discontented and there was evidently
a good deal of bickering and contention among them, bickering which
perhaps originated from differences of opinion as to what they should
do when summer released them.

A degree of dissatisfaction with the Straumfiord Camp was probably general. It had certainly not lived up to the expectations, based
on the descriptions of Vinland, which the colonists and the traders
must have had when they set out from Greenland. Apart from the
absence of wild grapes — which seem to have had the same magical

significance to these early voyagers as spices had for later ones — suitable hardwood forests and fur-bearing animals, the weather at Straumfiord must have proved to be much worse than the settlers would have been led to anticipate.

This not only affected the fishing; it seriously endangered the invaluable boats and ships. As we have noted, there was no harbor at Epaves Bay into which the ships could have been brought for safekeeping, or where the boats could have sheltered during stormy weather. In particular the open gravel beach offered no protection from the ice, which sometimes rafters forty yards inland from high-tide mark.

The shortcomings of the area may have caused the various contingents to react in different degrees. The Greenland colonists, who were particularly inured to hardship and a tough existence, would have been the least discontented, since compared with Greenland the Straumfiord area was a land of milk and honey. The Icelandic settlers would have been less inclined to accept this substitute for Vinland, not only because they were not as rough and ready as their Greenland counterparts, but also because they were subject to the influence of Karlsefni and Thorhall Gamlisson. The two shipowners were not settlers. They were traders, whose prime interest in the western lands lay in their expectations of gathering a valuable lading of local products to carry back to Greenland, Iceland or even to Norway. For them Straumfiord would have been a major disappointment, and Karlsefni seems to have been personally convinced that Vinland *could* be found and that the expedition ought to carry on a major search for it.

Some of the leaders of the Greenland contingent, and particularly Thorvald Eriksson, evidently shared this view. The trouble was that there was no agreement as to the direction in which the search should be made. In fact there appear to have been three quite divergent opinions about the matter.

WHERE IS VINLAND?

One group apparently believed the expedition had already passed Vinland during the voyage down the Markland coast — a belief which may have arisen as a result of the flotilla's brief incursion into Grosswater and Sandwich bays.

The opinions held by the other two groups were related in that both evidently rested on the belief that one of the islands near the mouth of Straumfiord was the indicator island for the mouth of Leif's fiord, and despite the failure of the local exploring parties to locate his booths, the expedition was still on the right path. This belief may have been strengthened by the discovery, during the explorations late in the preceding summer, that Quirpon was an island; for Quirpon answers moderately well not only to the saga description of the approaches to Vinland but also to a verbal description of the Baccalieu-Bay de Verde landfall.

Those who believed in the likelihood that Vinland lay somewhere at the foot of Straumfiord would therefore have been united in the conviction that they should steer to the west; but beyond this their views differed.

Perhaps because one of the westward boat expeditions of the previous year had found the south coast of the fiord beyond Cape Norman to be barren, devoid of harbors, and generally unprepossessing as far as anyone could see, some of the people may have reasoned that the search should be prosecuted along the northerly coast of the fiord. The remainder apparently felt that the southerly coast *beyond* the barren stretch offered the best prospects.

The division of opinions seems to have generally followed national lines. The Icelandic colonists together with Karlsefni and Thorhall Gamlisson, were evidently united in the belief that Vinland ought to be sought for to the southwest of Straumfiord Camp. This view was doubtless shared by Freydis and by Helge and Finnboggi. On the other hand the Greenlanders, excepting only Freydis and her band, seem to have been convinced that Vinland lay either to the north in the Grosswater Bay area, or to the west somewhere along the south coast of Labrador.

Furthermore the Icelanders apparently felt that the entire expedition should abandon Straumfiord Camp and undertake a ship-borne expedition to the southwest, while the Greenlanders appear to have felt that it would be wiser for the majority of the people, together with the cattle and the precious ships, to remain at Straumfiord Camp while long-distance boat expeditions were sent out to search for Vinland to the north and west.

In the event this divergence of opinions led to the dispatch of three separate exploring expeditions during the first summer season in the

New World. In the balance of this chapter we deal with those which the Greenlanders led.*

The Saga Tale (c. 1005)

Now they took counsel together concerning their expedition, and came to an agreement. Thorhall the Hunter wished to go northward around Furdustrandir and Kialarness and so seek Vinland, while Karlsefni wished to proceed southward off the coast, believing that the farther to the southward, the better the country would be.

Thorhall prepared for his voyage out by the islands. He had only nine men in his party. All the rest stayed with Karlsefni.

One day while Thorhall was watering his ship he took a drink and then recited this poem:

> Famous Leaders told me I would have
> The best of drink when I came hither,
> Therefore I cannot blame the land.
> But see, you Helmeted Champions,
> How instead of drinking wine
> I must raise this pail [of water]
> Which I had to stoop to fill at the spring.

Then they [Thorhall and his men] put to sea and Karlsefni accompanied them out beyond the island. Before they hoisted sail Thorhall recited another poem:

> Let us go to that quarter
> Discovered by our countrymen.†
> We will explore well
> Beyond the keel place and the sweeping sands,
> Traveling on the sea
> While these Great Warrior Chiefs
> Who think so highly of this land
> Remain behind and gorge upon
> Whale meat on this so marvelous strand.

---

* An analysis of the data on which we have based our reconstruction of the events of this first summer will be found in Appendix M, together with an explanation of how, and why, we have combined certain conflicting information from the various sources.
  † Meaning Leif's Vinland.

Then they sailed away to the northward past Furdustrandir and Kialarness, intending to cruise to the westward around the cape. But they encountered westerly gales and were [eventually] driven ashore in Ireland, where they were savagely treated and thrown into slavery. And there Thorhall was killed, according to what traders [from Ireland] have related.

[SOURCES: Erik the Red Saga and Thorfinn Karlsefni Saga]

Thorvald Eriksson gave orders to have an afterboat made ready for a voyage to the western part of the country, [intending] to make use of the summer exploring in that direction.

To [those who went on this voyage] the land seemed good. It was well wooded and it was not far from the woods to the sea, and there were white sands. There were many islands and shoals.

They found no dwellings of men or beasts but in one of the western islands they found a storage shed of wood, but no other work of man. They came back to the [Straumfiord] booths at harvest time.

[SOURCE: The Greenlanders Story]

THORHALL'S SEARCH

Thorhall put out to sea in an afterboat. Nine men would not have been a sufficient crew for a knorr, and in any case it is established that none of the knorrir were missing when the expedition finally turned back for Greenland.

Thorhall intended to head for Grosswater Bay, just north of Porcupine Strands. On the south-bound voyage the convoy had crossed this bay, and as we have noted there were enough similarities between this area and the described approaches to Leif's Vinland to suggest that Vinland might lie at the western end of the bay.

The saga is quite definite about this, for it states that Thorhall set out in search of Vinland and that once having passed Furdustrandir and Kialarness and reached the cape beyond these places, he intended to cruise to the westward. This could have taken him only into Grosswater Bay and thence, if he had persevered, into Lake Melville itself. My belief that this was what he planned is confirmed by the course followed by Thorvald Eriksson in the following summer, when he went looking for the missing party.

Luck was against Thorhall. Somewhere along his route, perhaps when the little vessel was rounding Spotted Island, he and his men

The search for Vinland

were caught by a hard westerly gale and blown offshore. Probably their small craft was dismasted, for had she kept her sailing capabilities she ought to have been able to run before the gale and still make a steady northing which would eventually have brought her to Iceland, if not to Greenland. But without her sail, or with only a makeshift jury rig, she would have been largely at the mercy of the North Atlantic.

Thorhall's afterboat may have been the first small vessel manned by Europeans to be blown from Canadian waters to Europe, but she was by no means the last. During the past century alone there have been sixteen authentic records of dories which, having been swept away from Newfoundland waters, either reached the shores of Europe at points as widely separated as Vigo in Spain and the Hebrides off Scotland, or were picked up in European waters by passing ships. Unhappily in many of these cases the two-man crew of these seventeen to nineteen-foot boats did not survive. Thorhall and his men fared better — their boat was much larger and presumably better provisioned — but their luck ran out completely when they reached Ireland. The Irish, having managed to cast off the Viking yoke, were not inclined to look kindly on Norsemen who fell into their hands; and it can be assumed that the stiff-necked and prickly-natured Thorhall would soon have given them an excuse to murder him.

Norse merchants, who, as we have noted earlier, were tolerated in Ireland as elsewhere on the continent because they were of value, heard something of the story and may even have spoken with some of Thorhall's enslaved crew, and so were able to carry word of the disaster back to Iceland.

THORVALD'S SEARCH

Some time soon after Thorhall's departure, Thorvald Eriksson launched the second part of the Greenlanders' twofold exploration plan. Another afterboat was made ready, manned by about the same number of men as had accompanied Thorhall; and this second venture may have been led by Thorvald himself. The account of the expedition states that they sailed to the western part of the country. Starting from Straumfiord, this would logically mean that they cruised westward along the north shore of the Gulf of St. Lawrence.

The genesis for this voyage was probably one of the local explorations made late in the previous summer, when a boat party reached

Cape Norman and, from the elevation behind it, looked out over the strait to the far shore, a distance of about fifteen nautical miles, and saw enough of the towering south Labrador coast to suggest to them that it might contain fiords which would answer to the Vinland descriptions.

Thorvald and his men doubtless crossed Straumfiord near Cape Norman and then coasted southwestward under the bluff and forbidding coast to Blanc Sablon, at which point the nature of the coastline changes abruptly.

From this point they would have swung nearly due west, along a far more amiable shore, and would have begun to see the deposits of shining white sand which lie at the bottoms of most of the succeeding bays and which give Blanc Sablon its name. These white sands do not form seaward beaches, as do the yellow sands at Porcupine Strand, but are found only deep inside the inlets or behind the protection of off-lying islands.

After passing Riviere St. Paul the expedition would have encountered stretches of coast which are shrouded by thousands of islands of all sizes, and which culminate in the Grand Rigolet and Mecatina regions, where for a distance of sixty nautical miles the coast is barred off by an almost uncountable number of island and reefs extending from five to ten miles out from a mainland shore where, even now, the forests crowd down to the very edge of tidewater.

The three prime elements of description given in the saga for this western expedition all fit so well with the north shore of the gulf that there is no point in laboring the identification.

There can be no conclusive answer to the question of how far west the expedition penetrated. Assuming that the boat party left Sacred Bay in late spring, and knowing — as the Greenlanders story tells us — that it did not return until harvest time, we can deduce that it was absent about three months. Theoretically the party could have gone a long way, but in fact they probably made slow progress on the outward journey, for they were exploring new country and would not have traveled by night or in bad weather. If we allow them eight weeks for the outward journey, and an average daily progress of twenty miles, they might have reached the vicinity of Sept Isles.

Nevertheless, it seems doubtful that they went so far. The chances are that they wasted days on end in the labyrinthine channels of the great island chains, and if they made anything like a thorough ex-

amination of the innumerable river mouths and inlets along the way they would have been lucky to have made good 200 miles before concluding that Vinland did not lie in this direction.

It is significant that the Norse did not meet any natives. Finds of Boreal Archaic Indian artifacts have been made along this coast, but these predate the arrival of the Dorsets, who evidently displaced the earlier Indian population here as they also seem to have done on the coasts of the Great Northern Peninsula of Newfoundland. The south Labrador Dorsets left evidence of their presence as far west as Anticosti Island, but by about the year 1000 they seem to have abandoned this region together with the shores of the Strait of Belle Isle and the east coast of the peninsula — and for the same reason * — leaving it temporarily uninhabited.

The structure which the Norse took to be a grain storage shed may have been the remnant of a Dorset house or, if they found it far enough to the west, it might have been a bark-covered meat storage shed of the type built by the Montagnais people, who reoccupied the south Labrador coast some time after the Dorsets disappeared.

When Thorvald's party arrived back at Straumfiord they would have had marvelous tales to tell of the western lands, but nothing to report about the whereabouts of Vinland. Their accounts of the western country would have been glowing ones, for the coast beyond Blanc Sablon offered any number of attractive settlement sites. The possibility of moving west may have been discussed, but nothing could have been done until Thorhall returned from searching for Vinland to the north — and Thorhall never did return.

So the second winter closed in on the Straumfiord Camp, which must by then have begun to take on the appearance of a permanent settlement. It would have been a somewhat lonely camp that winter, and one filled with dire forebodings. Not only was there no word of Thorhall and his men, but there was no word of what had happened to the ships which had sailed south that summer under the leadership of Thorfinn Karlsefni.

---

* See Appendix H.

21

.∧.∧.∧.

the land of hope

The Saga Tale (c. 1005)

Now it is to be told that Karlsefni cruised southward off the coast with Snorri and Bjarni and their people.

They journeyed a long time until they came at last to a river which flowed down from the land into a lake and thence into the sea. There were such great sandbars at the mouth of the estuary that it could only be entered at the height of flood tide. Karlsefni and his people sailed into the estuary and called it there, Hop.

They found wild wheat-fields on the low-lying land, and wherever there was woodland they found [grape] vines. Every brook was full of fish. They dug trenches on the tidal flats and when the tide fell there were flatfish in the trenches. There were a great number of wild animals of all kinds in the woods.

They remained there two weeks enjoying themselves and not keeping any watch. They had their livestock with them.

Now one morning when they looked about they saw nine skin-boats, and staves were being brandished from these boats and they were being whirled in the same direction that the sun moves, and they made a noise like flails.

Then Karlsefni asked: "What can this mean?"

Snorri Thorbrandsson answered him: "It may be that this is a peace signal, so let us display a white shield."

This they did, whereupon the strangers rowed toward them and came ashore and [the Norse] marveled at them. They were swarthy people and queer looking, and the hair of their heads was ugly. They had remarkable eyes and broad cheeks. They stayed for some time, staring curiously at the people they saw before them, then they rowed away to the southward around the point.

Karlsefni and his men had pitched their booths above the [shore of] the lake, some of their houses being at the lake [the estuary], and some farther away near the main part of the land. They remained there all that winter. No snow came and their livestock found their own food by grazing.

[SOURCES: Erik the Red Saga and the Karlsefni Saga]

The cattle went up on the land there, but it soon happened that the males became unruly and caused much trouble. They had a bull with them.

They profited by all the products of the land thereabouts; both grapes, deer, and fish and all good things.

[SOURCE: The Greenlanders Story]

While the balance of the Greenlanders remained at Straumfiord waiting for the boat expeditions to return from their search for Vinland to the west and north, the Icelandic contingent packed themselves aboard their ships and departed southward.

This south-bound squadron evidently included the Helge-Finnboggi ship, since the saga account tells us that Freydis accompanied it, and she and the Icelandic brothers would have been interested in the same things which drew Karlsefni south: grapes, furs and hardwoods.

THE SOUTHERN VOYAGE

Rounding Cape Onion, after clearing from Sacred Bay, the three ships stood across the mouth of Pistolet Bay. Cape Norman came abeam, and course was altered to follow the bleak unbroken shore which stretched away to the south-southwest.*

During the second day the shore would have begun to look more interesting, even though it was obviously not Vinland country. The ships may have entered St. Margaret Bay and perhaps explored it, but it was wooded to the shores and could not have had much of an appeal to colonists.

For one reason or another they may not have sailed close to the seaward face of the projecting Port au Choix Peninsula. Had they done so they might have had their first warning that they were not alone in this new land.

One of the most important Dorset sites so far discovered lies on the seaward face of the Port au Choix headland. It has been studied by

---

* The evidence demonstrating that this voyage was made southwestward from the Straumfiord Camp is given in Appendix M, Part II.

Dr. Elmer Harp, of Dartmouth College, over a five-year period, and the results of his work indicate that it was occupied for many centuries. The ground in and around the house ruins is so heavily carpeted with seal bones that in places they form a layer almost a foot thick. There is little evidence that much other game was taken, and most of the seal bones are from young seals.

When the harp seals are whelping on the pack ice in the Gulf of St. Lawrence, the prevailing westerly winds often set the pack tight against this section of the coast, and from an outthrust peninsula like Port au Choix it is no trick for men to go off on foot and make a great slaughter of the young seals as they lie helpless on the pans. It looks as if the Dorsets came to Port au Choix around March of each year, made a big kill of young seals, and then subsisted on stored meat and blubber until early summer, when they abandoned the sealing camp and withdrew to various rivers along the coast, where they could engage in salmon fishing.

If the Dorsets were at Port au Choix when Karlsefni's flotilla sailed past, they would have marveled at the ships; but even with good visibility it is unlikely that the Norse would have observed the low, skin-covered Dorset houses against the background of somber scrub and broken rocks of the peninsula.

From Port au Choix southward the ships sailed past a flat coastal plain which has only recently (in geological time) emerged from the sea, and which extends inland fifteen miles to end abruptly at the foot of the Long Range Mountains, which lift almost perpendicularly to heights of 2000 feet and more. This plain is a morass of spruce bogs and muskeg, with here and there a black stand of larger conifers clinging to the low back of a drowning ridge. It is a singularly depressing place, and even if there had been any cove along its coast to provide shelter for the knorrir, it is unlikely that the Norse would have bothered to go ashore.

As they sailed past this dreary coast the people on the three ships would have observed that the mountain wall was drawing closer and closer to the sea, and by the time they were abeam of Portland Creek the coastal plain had shrunk to a mere five miles in breadth.

Now they would have begun to see a change in the nature of the land. At Portland Creek they may well have been tempted to go ashore, for although there is no harbor there and the creek is too shoal and rapid to admit anything bigger than a dory, there is a cove of sorts, fringed with sandy beaches and backed by good-sized spruce standing on dry, hard ground.

Two hours' sail past Portland Creek, the Icelanders would have seen the limestone shingle of the long coast giving way to more and more stretches of yellow sands, and shortly afterward they would have entered a shallow bight across whose mouth stretched a broad gravel bar. Behind the bar lay a lagoon which could have harbored a hundred knorrir. This was Parsons Pond.

Here was a hop to delight the heart of any Norse mariner, and the broad reaches of grassy foreshore around its borders would have been equally attractive to a Norse pastoralist. But it was a hop which the Icelanders could not use. The bar across its mouth was not pierced by a deep tidal channel. The fresh waters of the lagoon drained into the sea through a shallow, winding creek to the north of the bar — a creek which would have been impassable to the ships of Karlsefni's flotilla.*

Parsons Pond must have proved a cruel disappointment to the settlers, who would have been desperately anxious to land their livestock so that the beasts could refresh themselves ashore. Nevertheless, Parsons Pond was a good omen. Although frustrated by the bar, they would have sailed on with high hopes that at long last they might be nearing — if not Vinland — at least a land of equal promise.

Only a few miles farther south they came to the twin crescentic indentations of Shallow Bay and Cow Head Harbour. These are not true harbors, being fully open to the west, but their broad sandy beaches might have been pressed into service as a place where the knorrir could have been hauled out if nothing better offered. Perhaps the ships were anchored in Cow Head Harbour while a party rowed ashore to climb the nearest elevation. This was Cow Head itself. Although it stands only 200 feet high, the surrounding country is so low and flat that from its top one can see fifteen or twenty miles up or down the coast, and inland to the foot of the mountains.

The Norse would have looked out over an apparently limitless strip of rough bog pastureland running out of sight to the north and to the south, and bounded inland by the canyoned lower slopes of the Long Range. They would have seen how those slopes and canyons were

---

* Although there is a break in the bar at Parsons Pond now, it was apparently not in existence in Karlsefni's day. See Appendix M — The Location of Hop. For a Description of the type of haven known to the Norse as a hop, see Part II of Appendix L.

St. Paul's Bay

washed dark green with heavy forest growth. But it would have been to the southward that they stared with the greatest eagerness.

HOP (ST. PAUL'S BAY)

Barely three miles from them was the sheen of a great body of water running far back into the mountains from the sea. And where it entered the sea there was a hop — bigger than the one at Parsons Pond, and even more broadly fringed with grassy meadows. Most exciting of all, the bar was cut by a broad opening.

Shortly thereafter the knorrir would have been approaching the opening into St. Paul's Bay. If the tide was rising at the time they would have been able to feel their way in across the outlying sand shoals even if they were unable to mark the narrow, winding underwater channel. Perhaps led by men in boats sounding the way, the ships would have passed through the gap and entered the estuary which lay within.

St. Paul's Bay was shoal, but there was sufficient water, even at half-tide, to have carried the knorrir along the channel which runs through the estuary and which drains the waters of St. Paul's Inlet into the bay, and thence into the sea.

The estuary or bay extends inland about a mile and a half until it is barred by a limestone ridge. This ridge is pierced by a narrow water-cut channel, a few hundred feet in length, which drains the waters of the inlet and which is known locally as "the river" because of its rapid and steady flow.

Not far inside the outer bar of the bay there is a small point with a fathom of water at its southern tip. Beyond it to the south lies a great flat which is water covered only during spring tides, and which supports a luxuriant growth of salt-water grass. The point itself and the broad foreshore to the south are covered with a rank growth of cattle grass.

As the three ships felt their way cautiously into the bay, the penned cattle on the decks would have smelled the fresh grass and raised their voices in a lugubrious chorus of desire. Nor would they have been alone in their impatience to get ashore.

Within a very few days the colonists would have concluded that Vinland or no Vinland, they had found an excellent place to plan a settlement. The amount of rough pasture immediately available around the shores of the estuary would have supported twenty times the number of animals they could have brought with them. There was sufficient hay on the flat, sandy meadows to fill any number of barns. The estuary and the lake behind it teemed with birds and with a big resident population of harbor seals. Shellfish of half a dozen species abounded, and lobsters could be had for the taking. The short river which breached the rocky dyke separating the estuary from the lake proper was full of salmon, as were the several rivers which emptied into the lake. In the shallow waters of the estuary numbers of flatfish of the sole family drifted over the gravel, and it was no trick to spear them. Later, using what was an ancient trick (it is still in use in parts of Newfoundland), the men dug trenches near the half-tide mark into which they dumped offal. When the tide rose over the pits, flatfish came in to feed, and when the tide fell again they stupidly re-mained in what seemed to them to be a safe depth of water; but the Norse would have been able to fork them out of the trenches with ease.

Some of the people would have rowed through the breach in the limestone ridge into the main lake (St. Paul's Inlet) to find a magnifi-cent sheet of water running eastward for six miles and deeply pene-trating the mountain ramparts. Within a mile of the south side of the lake the Long Range peaks rise from sea level to 2400 feet, and their lower slopes still support a dense forest. From the eastward extension of the lake two great canyons run into the heart of the mountain range, and each of them holds a big salmon river. While they were exploring the shores of the big lake the Norse would have noticed the crisscross pattern of innumerable caribou trails deeply impressed into the surface of the many open bogs and muskegs, and they prob-ably saw numbers of the animals themselves, even though at this season of the year the major part of the herds would have been out in the open barrens to the north or else high up on the mountain plateau country.

From the viewpoint of the colonists there could hardly have been a better site for a settlement. St. Paul's would have provided every-thing Vinland offered, except for stands of good mixed timber. The forests at the western foot of the Long Range seem to have always been composed for the most part of coniferous softwoods. Even the larger stands growing far back in the mountain valleys did not include much hardwood, and what there was of it would have been difficult to get out to the coast.

But if valuable export timber was scarce, wild grapes were apparently abundant. No wild grapes grow now on the west coast of Newfoundland, but as we have noted, they are reported to have been common in those parts of Newfoundland inhabited by the French as late as the seventeenth century. The St. Paul's area was part of the French coast.

St. Paul's fits every point in the saga description of Karlsefni's Hop to perfection — with one possible exception. The saga states that no snow fell, and that all winter long the livestock found their own food by grazing.

When I visited St. Paul's I mentioned this description to a local farmer. He could see nothing surprising in it. He told me that as recently as the winter of 1958 there was so little snow that the ground never did become covered. The occasional light snows, which were all that fell that winter, vanished within a few days. He also told me that, except during very unusual winters, most of the livestock was left out to forage. Several other farmers confirmed this. One of them, a man of eighty, could recall seven separate winters during which the snow had not lingered on the ground for more than a few days.

Considering that the climate was much better in Karlsefni's time, the likelihood of his having encountered what would have been in effect a snowless winter would have been much greater. Nevertheless, the saga may have been incorrectly translated on this point. What the phrase was perhaps intended to mean was that there was so *little* snow that the cattle could forage for themselves all winter.

The number of animals kept at St. Paul's has greatly diminished in recent years, not through any lack of forage but through disintegration of the human community. However, in the summer of 1963 I counted 260 sheep, 87 horses and 9 cattle all grazing on the natural meadows around the shore of the estuary. I was told that twenty years earlier I would have seen double that number of sheep and horses, and as many as fifty cattle.

An investigation into the origin of the grass meadows — as opposed to the bog pasture, which is obviously natural — could uncover no evidence that any significant portion of it had been cleared by human efforts. As is the case at Epaves Bay and Tickle Cove Pond, the meadow soil consists of a very thin coating of humus on top of deep sand which would not have encouraged forest growth. Furthermore, most of the true meadows at St. Paul's are close to the sea and exposed to strong prevailing westerlies which still inhibit any growth of forest on the coastal plain.*

I examined the whole coast of the inlet and estuary, and found the most likely site for a Norse camp on the south shore, midway between the grassy point and the river leading through the limestone dyke. This site fulfills all the requirements of the saga. It lies on a level shelf about twenty feet above high-tide mark, with a tidal grass flat on three sides of it. Fifty yards to the southeast is the beginning of an immense bog meadow. The shelf itself is part of an ancient beach and is composed of a mixture of gravels and sand, overlain by an inch or two of light soil. Unfortunately the subsoil makes excellent road fill, and in 1955 much of the site was bulldozed. Two large gravel pits now occupy about half its area.

In the cutbank along the side of one of these excavations I found a firepit which had been laid open by a bulldozer blade. An overhang of matted roots and low scrub had preserved it from serious weathering. The bottom of the pit was about 18 inches below present ground level, and in the bottom was a three-inch layer of compacted charcoal overlying a bed of well-leached gray ash. This was the only evidence of ancient occupancy which came to light during a superficial examination of the site.

An interrogation of the inhabitants of St. Paul's failed to turn up any artifacts except an iron instrument, much eroded, which appears to have been the head of a pole-axe or pike-stave and which may date to the early French colonial period. I was later told about a rock inscription at the foot of the inlet. Unfortunately I did not hear of it until I was leaving, and so I could not examine it personally. The carving consists of several letters, or letterlike marks, contained in a square or rectangle about six inches on a side and with a diagonal tail some four inches long extending out from one of the corners. This figure is incised into a large, black rock about three feet long

* I made an estimate of the amount of pasturage in the immediate vicinity of St. Paul's Bay, using aerial photographs checked against ground reconnaissance. I found that three types of pastureland were available: (1) Tide grass pasture (mud flats covered with salt water at spring tides only, and supporting a growth of salt-grass), amounting to approximately 180 acres; (2) Hay meadows (light, well drained, sandy land), approximately 450 acres; and (3) Bog pasture (wet, swampy, but well covered with tussock grasses, approximately 4000 acres.

which lies half buried in the beach near the mouth of the St. Paul's River.

One find was made on the tidal flats not far from the possible Norse site. This consisted of four roughly worked rectangular pillars of stone lying haphazardly on their broadsides just below high-water mark. The exposed faces, which were considerably water-worn, did not appear to have borne any inscriptions. I did not disturb the pillars, and it is possible that their protected undersides may be more revealing. They are approximately four feet long, 12 to 14 inches wide, and 5 to 7 inches thick. Two of them are slightly tapered. At the present time no vessel could get within half a mile of them and it would be almost impossible to ferry them in by boat, except on an unusually high tide. They do not appear to be of local rock.

Their presence was unknown to the local residents, none of whom could offer any suggestion as to their origin. They do not lie near a place which has ever been inhabited so far as the residents have any knowledge.

It is possible that they may belong to the colonial French period, but the only identification so far attempted of them (from photographs) suggests that they are prepared ballast stones. It is known that the knorrir carried ballast, and because there was very little room for it under the floors, it was usually stone slab ballast which had been roughly shaped to fit into a confined space.

THE DORSET BOATS*

The two weeks which the Norse spent "enjoying themselves" would have gone by quickly, for there was a great deal to see and do. Having anchored the ships securely under the lee of the land, the people may have pitched their temporary booths either on the point or perhaps at the site which was later to become their winter home. The cattle were turned loose on the grassy meadows with someone to keep an eye on them in case they strayed away across the great bog pasture.

No watch was kept, and no doubt it seemed unnecessary. One of the great attractions of the estuary site was that it offered almost unlimited visibility to seaward, to the south, and to the north. The view

---

* The evidence identifying the Dorsets with the people encountered by Karlsefni is to be found in Appendices H and O.

inland was obstructed by the limestone ridge, which rises to a height of about one hundred and fifty feet and was then well wooded; but a surprise attack from that direction would have seemed a remote possibility, since behind the ridge lay the open stretch of the big lake.

One morning during the third week at Hop some early riser went to the door of his booth and glanced casually out over the estuary. He must have been violently startled to see a flotilla of small boats approaching slowly across the shoal waters. His shout of alarm would have wakened the camp and brought the men pouring out all-standing, hastily buckling on their gear as they came. Since this was the first contact between North American natives and the Norse, it would have been a moment pregnant with tension — and with grim possibilities. It is doubtful whether the Norse would have felt any assurance that these unexpected visitors were even of human kind; for those were superstitious times, and mountain trolls and other weird beings still lurked in the wilderness country of Iceland and Greenland.

How the approaching Dorsets (for this is who the visitors were) must have stared at the Norse ships lying at anchor and the alien mob upon the shore. They must have felt considerable trepidation, and no doubt the Norse shared that feeling with them. Certain it is that the Norse had never before seen human beings who looked like these people, nor had they seen skin canoes similar to the ones which seemed to hover on the surface of the estuary, reflecting their owners' indecision.

At this juncture the Dorsets began doing something which seemed inexplicable to the Norse. As the saga teller describes it, the Skraelings began whirling wooden "objects" (the word is variously rendered as staves, poles, sticks, etc.) in the direction in which the sun revolves; and these objects made a noise like the sound of flails whistling through the air.

The saga description of these antics has puzzled many readers. Some have written the matter off as being an example of an imaginative adornment of the ancient saga. However, in recent years a number of authorities have leaned to the belief that what the Norse saw was Eskimoan double-bladed kayak paddles in action. In some ways this seems like a plausible explanation, but there are objections to it. It does not explain the noise; and the Norse were a sea-going people, so it is hard to believe that they would not have recognized paddles when they saw them, even if they were double-bladed. When the Skraelings landed, the Norse must have seen the paddles close at hand and could hardly have been in any doubt about their identity. Finally, most archeologists who have studied this culture do not believe the Dorsets had kayaks, or used double-bladed paddles. The kayak, which is technically one of the most sophisticated developments in the history of small craft, apparently originated with the Thule culture people who were true Eskimos and who displaced the Dorsets. Furthermore, it appears from later saga references that the skin boats of the Skraelings were not one-man craft, as kayaks are, but carried several people. They may have been similar to small umiaks of a type still used by some modern Eskimos, which are propelled by single-bladed paddles.

The mysterious whirling objects which made such a remarkable noise, and which so greatly impressed the Norse, were probably bull-roarers. These objects (also known as whizzers) are wooden instruments common to many native tribes, whose genesis goes back to Neolithic times. Modern Eskimos seldom use them now, but they were once found throughout the Eskimo cultural zone. I personally encountered them in 1947 among a primitive tribe of inland-dwelling Eskimos in Keewatin. At dusk one evening I became aware of a strange and disturbing noise. It sounded as if unseen giants were muttering in a wind-filled tunnel, and it seemed to come from all sides of me. The noise rose and fell in pitch and volume with an unearthly effect. The shaman of the band later gave me the instrument which he had used to make this noise. It consists of an elliptical spruce blade about three feet long and four inches broad at its widest part. It is less than a quarter of an inch thick and tapered to a knife edge all around. The edges are serrated with small notches. In operation the blade is whirled about one's head, either on a horizontal or a vertical plane, on the end of a sinew tether. Since one surface is slightly flatter than the other, the blade spins on its own axis at the same time that it describes rapid circles on the end of the sinew. This dual motion produces a baffling, ventriloquial sound. The visual impression is similar to an aircraft propeller turning at such speed that one sees only a glittering disc of flashing light.

Later I saw even larger bullroarers being used by the Eskimos, and these were whirled on the end of a pole which increased the centrifugal effect and consequently made a greater volume of sound.

These inland Eskimos used bullroarers primarily as a defense against supernatural beings. They believed that the weird sound would drive away, or at least hold at bay, a variety of unpleasant spirits. They may also have had other uses for the instrument, of which I remained in ignorance. Since the sound made by a bullroarer has great carrying qualities, it may have been used as a signal or as a warning device.

By analogy with known Eskimo reactions to early European contacts, we can suppose that when the Dorset band stumbled on the Norse camp they thought they had encountered a group of supernatural beings and might have begun brandishing bullroarers as a matter of prudence. On the other hand the sagas say that the flail-like objects were used on both succeeding visits of the Skraelings to Hop, which suggests that they may have had some ritual significance when two parties of strangers met.

It is doubtful whether Karlsefni's reaction to the sight and sound of his visitors was quite so phlegmatic as the saga suggests. However he and Snorri concluded that the display was meant as a sign of peace and so they responded by showing a white shield.

Eskimos are naturally a friendly people, inclined to expect the best from strangers. Once their initial surprise had eased, the Dorsets edged their boats toward shore, and when they felt secure enough, they made a landing.

The Icelanders seem to have been acute enough to treat these uncouth, fur-clad, dark-skinned and almond-eyed strangers with some degree of friendliness. After all, the visitors were obviously the occupants of this country and the Norse would have had no way of knowing how great their numbers were or how much of a threat they posed. Regardless of their individual prowess as fighting men, the settlers were a very long way from home and friends, and it behove them to walk softly.

Good relations between the two peoples seem to have been established at this first meeting, and when they parted it was in friendly style. The Norse evidently laid the basis for what they hoped would lead to lucrative trading, perhaps by giving small gifts to the Dorsets and indicating that they would appreciate furs in return. This visit of the Skraelings, as the Norse named them,* would have been

---

* The eleventh-century meaning of the name Skraeling is in doubt. Sigurd Stefansson, writing late in the sixteenth century, tells us that it meant cowardly weakling,

fraught with many possibilities, both good and bad, and we can be sure that these would have been major topics of conversation in the Norse camp during the months which followed.

Apart from its overtones of racial superiority, the account given of the visitors is a very fair description of an Eskimoan people. It is particularly valuable because it is the only surviving eyewitness description of the now vanished Dorsets.

When the Skraelings left Hop they paddled away to the south around a headland which was evidently visible from the Norse camp. This could have been Broom Point, which can be clearly seen from the slight elevation near the gravel pits.

The question of how the Dorsets happened to visit the Norse merits examination. Possibly the Norse flotilla had been seen by Dorsets as it made its way south down the coast. Awed by the sight, but intensely curious, a party of Dorsets may have followed after in hopes of getting another, and closer, look at the great sailing craft. On the other hand it is perhaps more likely that the encounter was wholly accidental and came about when a party of Dorsets who had completed the seal-hunting phase of their summer activities rowed south en route to one of the main coastal rivers to begin salmon fishing. St. Paul's may have been their actual objective; but the discovery of aliens already in possession may have led them to conclude that it would be more discrete to go elsewhere. Eventually they would have spread the news of the arrival of the Norse at least as far south as the several major encampments whose sites have been discovered on and near Bonne Bay.

The meeting with the Skraelings does not seem to have deterred the Icelanders from deciding that St. Paul's would make a fitting place to establish their settlement. They began erecting permanent houses. Some of these were built close to the shore of the estuary, while others were sited "farther away, near the main part of the land." By this we are probably to understand that some houses were built in St. Paul's Inlet, doubtless close to the mountains.

The events of the balance of that summer and of the ensuing winter have vanished from the saga record. We can assume that the set-

---

but this was a late usage. In the thirteenth century it implied a dwarfish people, but this was in reference to the Thule Eskimos and not to the Dorsets, who appear to have been singularly robust in build.

tlers were kept busy in the vicinity of the estuary with their colonizing chores. Meanwhile Karlsefni, Thorhall Gamlisson and the Helge-Finnboggi-Freydis group doubtless went into winter quarters at the foot of the inlet, where they would have engaged in cutting and preparing a cargo of spruce and pine timber in lieu of hardwoods.

All that we are told of this period is that the winter was mild and open; which must have been a matter for self-congratulation among the Icelanders, considering the miserable winter they had endured at Straumfiord.

22

⋏⋏⋏

the fatal error

When spring arrived they discovered, early one morning, a great number of skin boats rowing from the south around the headlands. They were so numerous it looked as if charcoal had been scattered on the surface of the water in front of the estuary.

From every boat, staves were being waved. Thereupon Karlsefni and his people displayed their [white] shields and when the two parties came together they began to barter with each other. The Skraelings particularly desired weapons in exchange for pelts and gray skins, but Karlsefni forbade the sale of weapons.

Karlsefni considered the matter and then he ordered the women to carry milk* outdoors to the Skraelings. As soon as they saw the milk they wanted it alone. So this was the way their trading went; that they carried off their bargains in their stomachs.

Some of the cattle were near at hand, and the bull ran out of the woods and began to roar and bellow. This terrified the Skraelings and they ran. [Some of them] turned toward Karlsefni's house and tried to enter it, but Karlsefni defended the door against them. Then the Skraelings raced to their boats and rowed away, leaving behind them their packs and their goods.

Now it is to be told that Karlsefni had a strong stockade of posts erected around the house and put everything in readiness.

"We had better take counsel," said Karlsefni, "For I think they may call

---

* More likely milk products such as cheese and skyr.

on us a third time, with many men, and not in peace. We shall follow this plan. Ten men will go out on the point and show themselves there, but another part of our company shall go into the woods and cut a path [along which] our cattle can [be driven]. When the company [attacks] from out of the woods we shall have our bull go ahead of us."

It was planned that the battle would take place with the wood on one side and the water on the other side. Everything was done which Karlsefni had proposed.

For three whole weeks nothing more was seen of them, but at the end of this time a great multitude of Skraelings was discovered coming from the south like a river of boats. This time all of the staves were being waved counter-sunwise and the Skraelings were all uttering loud cries.

Thereupon Karlsefni and his men took red shields and displayed them. The Skraelings sprang from their boats, and they met and fought together.

There was a fierce shower of missiles for the Skraelings had slings. Karlsefni and Snorri observed the Skraelings lifting up on poles large ball-shaped objects nearly the size of a sheep's belly and blueish-black in colour. They hurled these inland over Karlsefni's followers, and they made a frightening noise when they fell.

This so terrified Karlsefni and all his men that they could only think of flight and of making an escape up along the edge of the river; for it seemed to them that the crowd of Skraelings was rushing upon them from every side. They did not pause until they reached some cliffs where they [halted and] offered a stout resistance.

Freydis came out of doors and seeing that Karlsefni and the men were fleeing, she cried: "Why are you running from wretches like these? I would have thought such gallant men as you would slaughter them like cattle. If I only had a weapon I think I would put up a better fight than any of you!"

But they paid no attention to what she said and so Freydis tried to join them [in their flight] but she could not keep up, for she was pregnant. Nevertheless she followed them to the woods with the Skraelings close behind her. Now she saw a dead man in front of her. This was Thorbrand, Snorri's son, and his skull had been pierced by a flat stone [point].

His naked sword lay beside him and Freydis snatched it up and prepared to defend herself with it. The Skraelings came closer, whereupon she let fall her shift and slapped her breasts with the naked sword.

Seeing this, the Skraelings were frightened and ran down to their boats and rowed away.

Karlsefni and his companions then joined her and praised her courage. Two of Karlsefni's men and four Skraelings had been killed. Karlsefni's party had been defeated due to the superior numbers [of the enemy].

They now returned to their houses, bound up their wounds, and puzzled over who the crowd of men could have been who had seemed to attack them from the landward side. Finally they concluded that there could have been only the one party — that which came from the boats — and that the idea that there had been another crowd must have been an illusion.

[SOURCES: Composite version, assembled from Erik the Red Saga and the Thorfinn Karlsefni Saga, and from the Greenlanders Story. An explanation of why this section of the saga story has been treated in this way, and how it has been done, is given in Appendix O.]

The second visit of the Skraelings to Hop took place early in the new year, doubtless at about the time the harp seals began to whelp on the pack ice of the gulf. The saga says they appeared at Hop "When spring arrived" which can be interpreted as sometime near the end of March. This would not have been too early for journeys by skin boats, since even if the westerly winds had begun to set the pack ice in against the land, the Dorsets had only to run ashore, lift their light boats up on the beach and camp until a lane of water between ice and land opened up again.

The flotilla of boats which entered St. Paul's Bay that spring morning so many years ago probably carried an advance group of the northward-bound seal hunters, and some of the people in it had no doubt been members of the party which had visited Hop the previous summer.

The saga says there were so many boats in the flotilla that it looked as if the whole surface of the estuary had been strewn with lumps of charcoal — a graphic but probably exaggerated image. The entire Dorset population on the west coast of Newfoundland probably numbered no more than a few score families at this late stage in their history, when the Dorset culture was rapidly declining. However, the saga speaker doubtless attempted to convey the impression of vast numbers to provide an alibi for the subsequent defeat of the Norse.

A hint of this tendency to exaggerate the enemy strength can be seen in the Thorfinn Karlsefni Saga report of the arrival of the first lot of Skraelings in the previous year. "A great number of skin boats appeared in the estuary," says this saga. But the Erik the Red Saga, which often tends to be more specific, reported that there were just nine skin boats.

Once more the mysterious staves are in evidence, but that they were not connected with the propulsion of the boats seems to be firmly established by the concurrent statement that the boats were *rowed* around the point.

Trading seems to have begun as soon as the Dorset party landed, and the saga description of how Karlsefni's people handled it demonstrates that there has been little if any change in business ethics since the days of the Norse. The vignette of the shrewd Norsemen maneuvering the Dorsets into exchanging their furs and skins for dollops of whey-cheese or skyr bridges the abyss of the centuries. It is noteworthy that Karlsefni astutely forbade the selling of weapons to the Skraelings. Obviously the Norse did not wish to see the natives armed with Scandinavian weapons, which the settlers probably believed were invincible. It could never have occurred to them that the Skraelings were not only their equals but their superiors in weaponry.

While the Norse farmers and traders were busily engaged in driving their bargains with the Dorset men, some of the Skraelings seem to have been tentatively investigating their surroundings. We can imagine them staring apprehensively, but with fascination at the buildings, the ships, and all the strange things which had appeared so mysteriously upon the shores of St. Paul's Bay.

Now something took place which was of paramount importance both to the immediate fortunes of the Norse expedition and to the entire history of the Norse attempts to establish colonies in North America.

It will be remembered that the settlers had brought a bull with them to Hop, and this bull was apparently a singularly intractable and evil-natured beast, for there are two separate references in the sagas testifying to his unruliness. Nevertheless he was allowed to run free at Hop, and he apparently chose this moment to appear out of the scrub woods which bordered the bog pasture. Apparently he did not approve of the fur-clad Dorsets whom he saw before him. He bellowed, pawed the ground, and perhaps charged the nearest group.

The effect upon the Dorsets would have been shattering. They must have been tense anyway in the presence of the awe-inspiring Norsemen with their great swords and axes, their long beards, their strange clothing, and their many quite inexplicable implements and posses-sions. The sight and sound of the bull would doubtless have struck terror into their hearts and triggered a panic flight. Those nearest the boats probably fled to them. Some who had ventured farther away from the shore in among the Norse buildings bolted for the shelter of the houses in a frantic attempt to escape the bellowing behemoth which had emerged out of nowhere.

At this juncture the Norse seem to have lost their heads too. Not realizing for the moment that the bull, with which they were all too familiar, was the cause of the sudden mêleé of running, shouting natives; and being inherently suspicious by nature, they evidently jumped to the conclusion that they had been tricked, and that this was an attack.

The saga does not offer any direct proof that this is what happened, but the indirect evidence is formidable. If the Skraelings had simply fled, having suffered no physical ill effects as a consequence of the appearance of the bull, the Norse would hardly have been so con-vinced that they would soon return in battle order. If, on the other hand, the panic was general and had embraced the Norse, and if they had reacted by turning on the terrified Skraelings in the belief that this was a treachorous attack, then the inevitable bloodshed would have given the Norse good reason to fear retaliation. Karlsefni, so the saga tells us, defended the door of his house against the Skraelings, and we can be sure he did not use gentle methods.

Being thoroughly experienced in the ritual of the blood feud, the Norse would have expected the surviving Skraelings to try and even up the score. But only if the Norse had inflicted serious injuries on their visitors would they have been likely to go to the lengths de-scribed in the sagas to protect themselves from a reprisal attack, even preparing an ambush against the certainty of one.

That the sagas should neglect to explain that the Norse were responsible for what followed is not to be wondered at. A glance at most modern history books demonstrates that the tendency to blame the enemy for initiating every act of hostility is still inherent in mankind. In the case of the Skraelings the Norse would have been even less likely to admit that they had brought their troubles on them-selves, since they were soundly trounced in the ensuing battle.

That the Icelanders expected to be attacked is certain. They were so convinced of it that they committed their second major blunder, and thereby not only sealed the doom of their own colonizing venture, but made it virtually certain that no further attempts by Greenlanders or Icelanders would succeed.

After the flight of the Dorset trading party, (presumably northward to the sealing grounds, for the Dorsets still had to pursue their livelihood even if the country *was* afflicted with bloodthirsty foreign devils) the Norse picked up the abandoned packs of furs and perhaps congratulated themselves on a profitable day's work. Nevertheless they felt considerable apprehension about the consequences of the incident.

When we combine the information to be found in both saga sources, a picture emerges of energetic efforts to establish a defense. Stockades were built around some of the houses — perhaps only around those near the estuary, which commanded the beached ships. A council of war was called at which Karlsefni, and no doubt Snorri and the other leaders, worked out a complicated plan whereby the attacking Skraelings would be caught off guard.

The sagas say that the Norse chose the battleground, and that it lay between the water and the wood. It may well have been on the low sandy point at the south entrance to the estuary. Ten men were posted here with orders to expose themselves and to act as bait for the approaching Skraelings, who were expected to land and pounce on this small group before attacking the main camp. The balance of the Norse warriors were to lurk in concealment in the scrub spruce fringing the southern end of the sandy point. Paths were to be cut so that they could rush to their positions unseen as soon as the Skraelings were reported in the offing. Still other paths were cleared to the seaward edge of the woods, along which the cattle could be driven onto the beach in advance of the attacking warriors.

The sagas say that nothing happened for three weeks, at the end of which time the guard (who would have been posted on the nearest high ground) came pounding into camp with the news that a group of Skraeling boats was approaching.

What followed was a compounding of error upon error. The Norse had assumed that they would be attacked. As soon as they saw a sizable group of Skraelings approaching the camp they took it for granted that this was an attacking force and put their "strike-first" plan into action. But they could not conceivably have been able to distinguish one party of Skraelings from another, particularly at a distance, and when they themselves were keyed up to battle pitch. They could not, in other words, have distinguished between friend and foe as far as Skraelings were concerned. Moreover, it probably never even occurred to them that the second lot of Skraelings who were coming up the coast might have been quite free of hostile intentions, having heard nothing about the treatment meted out to the preceding party.

It is most unlikely that the Dorsets who had been driven from Hop after the bull episode would have returned to mount a revenge attack against the Norse. It is far more likely that they fled northward at top speed toward the sealing grounds, being not the least bit anxious to try another round with the devilish strangers who apparently wished to massacre them.

In reconstructing the encounter I envisage the next party of Dorsets appearing from the south bound for the northern sealing grounds, unaware of what had happened to the earlier party. As they cleared Broom Point and struck across the shallow bight toward the mouth of the estuary they saw a number of the aliens — about whom they had doubtless heard during the winter — appear on the sandy point and begin prancing about and waving their arms in what may have seemed to the Dorsets like an invitation to land, but which was probably a display of bravado calculated to goad the Skraelings into launching an attack.

The Dorsets turned toward these men and pulled for shore. Bullroarers aboard some of the boats may have been brought into action as a normal ceremonial indication that this was a friendly visit.

The saga's statement that the instruments were whirled *anti*-sunwise as a sign of hostility carries no conviction. Even if such a thing had been done, and even if the difference in direction had been detectable by an observer on shore, the Norse could hardly have known that this was a war sign. There may in fact have been some shouting from the Dorset boats, but this was as likely to have been intended to express friendship as hostility.

As soon as the Dorset boats grounded and the people jumped out and hauled the light vessels well up on the sand and shingle beach (for this was an open shore, exposed to the swell) the Norse attacked according to plan.

There are few coherent details of what followed. The ten men on the spit presumably snatched up their weapons and charged the

Skraelings while the main body of the Norse burst out of the forest, driving the cattle ahead of them and yelling fiercely in the best Viking style.

The Skraelings would have been momentarily paralyzed by surprise, but at the first flash of a raised sword or axe they would have recognized their danger and reacted instinctively. There was probably no time to launch their boats and get away, but they were not defenseless, for their sealing weapons were within easy reach.

We do not know exactly what these weapons were, but we can make an informed guess. The Norse sources say they included various sorts of missiles, slings, and something which looked like a blue-black sheep's belly that came hurtling through the air and frightened the Scandinavians half to death. Archeology has demonstrated that the Dorsets had an abundant supply of the most beautifully made stone points, of a wide variety of shapes and sizes. These were evidently used for arrow points and for the tips of several kinds of spears and harpoons. By analogy with what is known of later-day Eskimos we can assume the Skraelings had three kinds of missile throwers: throwing-boards, which enabled a man to fling a spear two or three times the effective distance he could achieve by hand and arm alone; slings similar to the one with which David slew Goliath, and with which some Eskimos (including the inland tribes of the Keewatin District) were very proficient; and bows and arrows. These were all hunting weapons and not primarily designed for warfare; but they could all be used just as effectively against men as against other animals.

The Norse of circa 1000 seldom made use of devices for flinging missiles. They actively disapproved of such things in warfare, considering them unmanly. Most of their fighting weapons were intended for thrusting, hacking or bludgeoning and so were most effective in close combat. Against a people who refused close combat, and who kept their distance and pelted one with sling-stones, spears and arrows, the Norse armament was practically useless. Shortly after the beginning of the battle, and before they had been able to cut down more than three or four of the Skraelings, the Norse were in full and ignominious flight.

In attempting to justify this retreat the saga makes a great deal of the strange bladderlike objects which came flying overhead. It implies that these were supernatural weapons of such potency that not even a Norseman could have been expected to stand against them. Unfortunately for Norse pride there is a simpler explanation. Part of the Skraelings' hunting equipment would have been inflated bladder floats attached to sealing harpoons. When attacked, the Dorsets simply snatched up the harpoons, bladders and all, and let fly; and what the Norse saw were these balloonlike objects whirling along in the wake of the harpoons. As to the noise they made, this can perhaps be attributed to conscious exaggeration, although a tightly inflated sealskin or seal-bladder float can make quite a satisfactory bang if it is suddenly punctured, as some of them may have been by the wildly flailing swords or spears of the unnerved Norsemen.

No bladders have been found in Dorset sites, for such materials would not have survived the intervening centuries. However, all known Eskimo peoples have used such things as a standard accessory to their hunting gear—their purpose being to prevent a harpooned sea mammal from sounding or diving to any great depth as well as to provide a surface marker which could be followed by the hunter in his boat.

The Norse warriors did not cease their panic-stricken flight until they reached a place where they could stand at bay with their backs to a rocky cliff. Such a cliff, about fifteen feet high, stands along the seaward face of the limestone ridge which separates St. Paul's Bay from the inlet, and it is less than a mile from where the battle probably began.

The rout of the Norse seems to have been so complete that they did not even halt to attempt a defense of their stockaded houses or of the women and children. Most of the noncombatants probably joined in the wild flight to the cliff; but it seems certain that if the Skraelings had vigorously pursued the fleeing Icelanders they would have had no difficulty in catching and slaughtering many defenceless fugitives. That they did not do so is confirmed by the saga, which states that the Norse lost only two people during the battle. Both of these were evidently warriors. Thorbrand Snorrisson seems to have been struck in the head by a harpoon point or by a sling-stone. He may have been able to run a considerable distance after he was struck, and the fact that his body was found by Freydis between the houses and the cliff is no sure indication that the Dorsets pursued the Norse for any distance, if indeed they pursued them at all. On the other hand, if this had been a preconceived attack with the object of wreaking vengeance, the Dorsets would have had little difficulty in pinning their enemies against the cliff and picking them off from a safe distance with their missile weapons.

The encounter with Freydis is of special interest. Being in an advanced state of pregnancy, she could not keep up with the other fugitives and was left far behind. The well-deserved and stinging rebuke which she flung at the backs of the fleeing men, and the way they single-mindedly ignored her scornful taunts and continued their panic-stricken flight, illustrate with merciless clarity the abject terror which had gripped the Norse warriors when their intended victims displayed such unexpected fighting prowess.

Freydis's personal reaction seems to have been of a different sort. Unable to keep up with her "protectors," she snatched up Thorbrand's sword and prepared to give the Skraelings a hard time of it. The business of dropping her shift, exposing her bosom and then proceeding to slap her breasts with the sword (some translators have it that she whetted the sword on her breasts) would have given anyone pause. Even a Skraeling might have retreated before such a bizarre spectacle. The story is really too good to spoil, yet there is a reasonable possibility that the incident may not have happened in quite the way it is described.

There is no other record in Scandinavian history of a woman attempting to protect herself in the face of armed attack by exposing her naked breasts. On the other hand this gesture was in general use among the Beothuk Indians of Newfoundland. There are several well-authenticated accounts of Beothuk women baring their breasts when they were in danger from the bloodthirsty early Newfoundland settlers, whose hobby it was to hunt Beothuks for the pleasure of the chase. As a method of warding off death or injury from the hands of white men, it was seldom efficacious. In two of the recorded instances the white trappers calmly raised their guns and shot the women dead. But the Beothuks had a strong taboo against killing women, and the act of baring the breast was intended to ensure that the attacker recognized his potential victim as female.

One possible explanation of Freydis's otherwise inexplicable action is that the gesture of baring the breasts was known to, and used by, both the Beothuks and the Dorsets; that the Norse observed its use during the first skirmish with the Skraelings, and that Freydis made use of it herself when she thought she was in danger. Later saga men, who would not have known why Freydis bared her breasts, may have felt compelled to invent a reason and so have added the detail of the sword-whetting or breast-beating in order to make it look like a gesture of intimidation.*

We have no proof that the Dorsets did use the gesture, or that they copied it from the Beothuks. It is perhaps more likely to have been the other way around. For we know of no North American Indians except the Beothuks who used the gesture, and since they were indubitably in contact (and probably not always friendly contact) with the Dorsets, they may have acquired it from this now extinct Eskimoan people.

The fact remains that the Skraelings did not attack Freydis after she bared her breasts. That they could easily have killed a lone woman with sling missiles, spears or arrows, despite her possession of the sword, if they had wished to do so seems obvious. That they were actually so terrified by her gesture that they all fled in panic to their boats seems patently absurd.

The final stages of the "battle," including the Freydis incident, make it clear that, far from being aggressors who had staged a premeditated attack, the Dorsets were themselves the victims of a surprise attack and were concerned only with defending themselves until they could make their escape. Although the saga makes it plain that the Norse warriors deserted the settlement (which would have included the houses, the ships, old people, small children, livestock and those women who could not run fast enough) the Dorsets took no advantage of this. They neither looted nor burned the buildings and ships, nor massacred the noncombatants — all of which they would undoubtedly have done had they come to Hop bent on getting revenge for past injuries.

While the Norse were in a state of complete confusion and so terror-stricken that they imagined Skraelings assaulting them from the landward as well as the seaward side, the Dorsets were retreating to their boats, anxious to get away from this fearful neighborhood as rapidly as possible.

The impression of the terrible capabilities of the Skraelings as

---

* See also Appendix O.

fighting men which was indelibly implanted in the Norsemen's minds as a result of this encounter was doubtless the genesis of a fearsome myth which was to haunt the imaginations of the Greenland Norse for centuries. Later records portray the Skraelings as implacable and supernaturally formidable enemies whom it was usually impossible to overpower in open battle and who could be safely attacked only if they were caught off guard, or if the Norse had overwhelming superiority of numbers.

23

.Λ.V.Λ.

death comes to
thorvald eriksson

The Saga Tale (c. 1006)

It now seemed clear to Karlsefni and his people that although this was an attractive country their lives would be filled with constant fear and turmoil because of the [danger from the] inhabitants, and so they immediately prepared to leave, desiring to return to their own country.

They sailed to the northward along the coast and found five Skraelings dressed in skin-doublets asleep near the sea. There were wooden containers beside them which contained animal marrow mixed with blood. Karlsefni and his people decided that [these people] must have been outlawed from their own country, and so they put them to death.

Later they found a cape upon which there was a great number of reindeer and this cape looked like one expanse of manure because so many reindeer had used it during the winter.

Then they arrived again at Straumfiord, where they found a great abundance of everything they needed.

Some men report that Bjarni Grimolfsson and Freydis remained behind here with a hundred people, and went no farther, while Karlsefni and Snorri proceeded to the southward with forty men, returning again that same summer after tarrying at a hop [there] for barely two months.

[SOURCES: Erik the Red Saga and the Thorfinn Karlsefni Saga]

[Meanwhile] Thorvald [Eriksson] went eastward in his knorr and then to the northward around Kialarness and then bore to the westward into the mouth of the fiord which lay there, keeping the land on the port side. The country thereabouts was forest land as far as they could see, with scarcely an open space anywhere.

When they had journeyed a considerable distance they came to a wooded headland which jutted out [into the fiord]. They made their ship fast to the land and put out their gangplank to the land. Then Thorvald and his followers went ashore.

"This is a fine place," said Thorvald, "I would not mind living here."

After that they returned aboard the ship [and continued on], and on the sands within the headland they saw three hummocks, and when they approached them they saw these were three skin boats, with three men under each of them.

They divided their party and captured them all except for one who escaped in his boat. Then they killed the eight they had captured.

[Afterwards] they came to a river which flowed down from east to west. They sailed into the mouth of this river and lay to along the southern bank. Then they went out on the [nearby] cape and looked about them. Some distance up the fiord they saw some hillocks, and they supposed that these were human habitations.

They were extremely weary and could no longer keep awake, and so they went to sleep.

Then a call from up above them woke them up.

"Wake up, Thorvald, and [wake] all the company if you want to save your lives. Get to the ship with all the men and sail off from the land as fast as possible!"

Now innumerable skin boats appeared from within the fiord and came toward them.

"Hang the shields [or war boards] over the sides of the ship and [we shall] defend ourselves as best we can," cried Thorvald, "but do not carry the fight to them."

They did as he instructed, and the Skraelings shot at them for a while and then fled away as fast as they could go.

Thorvald asked if any of his men were wounded, and they replied that none of them was.

"I have a wound under my arm," he said, "an arrow flew in between the shield [war-board] and the ship's side." He pulled out the arrow and exclaimed: "Even though there is a lot of fat around my guts this arrow will be the death of me. It seems we have found a good land, but are not likely to get much profit from it. Now I advise you to get ready and go back [to

Straumfiord] as soon as you can. But first you shall carry me to that headland which I thought was such a good place to inhabit. It seems I spoke the truth when I said I might dwell there for a while. You shall bury me there, and set up a cross at my head and at my feet and forever after call that place Krossaness."

Thorvald died and his men did all he had told them to do, and then they went away and rejoined their comrades [at Straumfiord]. They told the people there all that had happened, and they dwelt there that winter.

[SOURCES: Combined account from Erik the Red Saga and the Thorfinn Karlsefni Saga, and The Greenlanders Story. The reasons for combining this material, and an explanation of how it has been done, will be found in Appendix M.]

The shock sustained by the Norse as a result of the "battle" at Hop was tremendous. Not only was their intransigent pride demolished, but their sense of security and their belief in their own invincibility were badly shaken. They had also lost two men, one of whom, Thorbrand Snorrisson, was the son of the settlers' chief leader.

Their decision to abandon Hop was an admission of the extent of their loss of confidence, but they were not likely to have been able to leave as soon as they might have wished without incurring a serious risk of losing their ships if heavy westerly weather set the pack ice against the coast.

Meanwhile there could have been few pleasures left in life at Hop. The Norse would have believed themselves to be virtually in a state of siege, anticipating a new attack at any time. The cattle and sheep would have been rounded up and herded into pens close to or inside the house-stockades, which would themselves have been strengthened — if any one had had the courage to go out into the woods to cut the necessary logs. Men would have been unwilling to go hunting and fishing, except in large bands, or even to go gathering fodder for the beasts at any distance from the stockade. Supplies were probably scarce after the passage of the winter, and enforced confinement in and about the stockades would have prevented the food stocks from being replenished. A constant watch must have been maintained; but at night, or in foggy weather, the possibility of a surprise attack would have allowed no one any peace of mind.

By the time the leaders felt that the danger from the pack ice was largely past, nerves and tempers must have been strained to the breaking point. There was no lingering on the way north, but weather conditions would have been unsettled this early in the year and gales no doubt forced the ships to anchor occasionally. Near one of these anchorages—perhaps under the lee of an offshore island such as St. John or Flat Island — a party from the ship discovered five of the feared and hated Skraelings (perhaps the members of a single family in one of the skin-covered houses they used during the sealing season). These people were slaughtered out of hand. The excuse given in the sagas, that they were believed to be outlaws under sentence of banishment, and therefore (as in Scandinavian countries) outside the laws of humanity, is pitifully weak. This was a revenge killing pure and simple. Perhaps it made the Norse warriors feel a little better.

When they passed the Port au Choix peninsula they may have seen signs of activity at the large sealing settlement there; but if they did it can be taken for granted that they steered out to sea, giving the peninsula a good wide berth. There is no evidence that the Norse ever again — even in Greenland, centuries later, after the Thule Eskimos arrived there—dared make an assault upon an alert and numerous band of Skraelings.

The next landing appears to have been on the Ferolle Peninsula, where the Norse encountered a great herd of caribou. The description of a caribou wintering area is explicit, as anyone who has walked over one of their well-used grazing grounds can testify. The Ferolle Peninsula is, and presumably has long been, excellent winter range for the semi-migratory Newfoundland caribou which once roamed the island in tens of thousands. It is an area of low, somewhat boggy "caribou barrens" which stays almost snow-free even during heavy winters. A French account dating from the middle of the eighteenth century speaks of two large bateaux being laden with the skins of caribou killed on Ferolle in the course of a single hunt.*

So the fleeing Icelanders arrived back at Straumfiord, where they found "an abundance of everything they needed;" which can be construed to mean not only food and other supplies but also the solace and the feeling of security engendered by again being leagued with

---

* This saga passage is a further indication that Hop could not have been in a country to the south of Newfoundland since the race of woodland caribou which was found throughout the forested regions of the eastern seaboard of the mainland did not form large herds, but lived dispersed in small groups in forest cover.

others of their kind — even if these others were Greenlanders, for whom, one can safely assume, they now felt an increased measure of affection.

The return of the Icelandic ships must have been extremely welcome to the Greenlanders. There was still no sign of Thorhall the Hunter, and the forty or so Greenlanders at Straumfiord must have put in a gloomy and apprehensive winter while the conviction grew that some catastrophe had overtaken not only Thorhall but the Icelandic expedition too, leaving those at Straumfiord to face an unknown fate alone. After exchanging experiences the leaders would have called a council to decide which course they ought to follow next. Thorvald Eriksson had apparently already decided to make a ship voyage north in search of Thorhall the Hunter; but the Icelanders seem to have been divided about their future plans.*

From what the saga says of their departure from Hop, we gather that some of the colonists wished to give up the entire venture and return immediately to Greenland or even Iceland. Others may have been in favor of making one more attempt to find a suitable, and safe, site for a colony. Still others may have been willing to settle in the Straumfiord area, which although it had its drawbacks was better than anything Greenland had to offer, and which was apparently free of danger from the Skraelings.

As for the trader-skippers, the season was still young and they may still have been hopeful of acquiring a cargo of the invaluable hardwoods before turning for home. Perhaps with this in mind Karlsefni concluded that it would be worthwhile to make one last voyage in search of Vinland in the only direction which had not yet been explored — southward down the east coast of the Great Northern Peninsula.

Apparently it was decided that Karlsefni and Snorri, accompanied by a party of forty men, should voyage to the southward in one ship while the balance of the Icelanders remained at Straumfiord with those Greenlanders who did not accompany Thorvald Eriksson in his search for Thorhall.

---

* An analysis of the data justifying the reconstruction of two voyages subsequent to the return of the Hop expedition will be found in Appendix M.

THORVALD'S SEARCH FOR THORHALL

There is no difficulty in plotting Thorvald's route. In the initial stages he followed the course that Thorhall the Hunter had intended to pursue in his search for Vinland the preceding summer, and all the accounts agree that this course lay north from Straumfiord past Kialarness to the mouth of Grosswater Bay.

This was all more or less familiar ground, but once the knorr turned westward into the foot of Grosswater Bay, she would have been entering unknown waters. Coasting the south shore ("keeping the land on the port side"), Thorvald held ever westward until the north shore of Grosswater Bay came into view. It must have seemed as if the ship was approaching the foot of a typical coastal fiord, but when she came abeam of Ticorlak Head her people would have discovered that they were opening the mouth of a narrow, steep-sided strait through which the tidal current boiled at speeds of from three to five knots. The great power of this reversing current, flowing through its mile-wide channel, would have told the voyagers that the strait must lead to a large body of water still farther to the west.

Having passed through one of the two channels which embrace Henrietta Island, they would have emerged into the head of Lake Melville.

The waters over which they then sailed, or rowed, were still salt, and the Greenlanders must have suspected that they had discovered a great inland sea lying deep in the heart of the western wilderness. They would not have been far wrong, for Lake Melville, or Hamilton Inlet as it is also called, runs for ninety miles to the west-southwest from Henrietta Island, and in places it is more than twenty miles in breadth. It is both salt and tidal and therefore, properly speaking, it is an inland sea.

Once past the mid-channel guardian rock of Eskimo Island, Thorvald steered his ship south in order to retain contact with the southern shore of this mysterious sea. He continued coasting to the westward until he reached a remarkable cape. This was evidently Reed Point, a massive headland rising to 700 feet and separated from the mainland by a broad and grassy isthmus. Thorvald and his men may not have scaled the headland to its crest — they would have had to cut and thrust their way through a solid wall of forest to have done so — but they need not have climbed more than a few hundred feet to have seen that, beyond St. John's Island, the "sea" stretched out of sight to the westward, growing broader as its shores receded into the distance.

Returning to the ship, the Greenlanders cast off their lines and set their course south along the stretch of coast below Reed Point where two small and nameless points jut out to the south. Beyond the second of these, at a distance of about two miles from the great headland, there is a mile-long strip of low and level beach fringed with sand.

During historic times this beach was used as a travel camp by Hamilton Inlet Eskimos en route between the salmon rivers and caribou-hunting grounds of the interior and the seal and seabird-hunting grounds on the outer coast. Finds of Dorset artifacts have been made on the shores of Lake Melville, and as the excavations of Dr. William Taylor in Ungava have demonstrated, the Dorsets sometimes ventured as much as two hundred miles away from the sea in order to winter in interior caribou-hunting camps. These facts are of importance because some authors have denied (on the grounds that Eskimos would not have gone so far away from the open sea) that the Skraelings Thorvald encountered could have been Dorsets.

As Thorvald's knorr rounded the second of the small points, she would have opened the "sands within the headland" and her people would have been quick to spot three skin boats upturned upon the shore. Having heard firsthand of the experiences of the Icelanders at Hop, the Greenlanders knew what to do about this unexpected encounter.

We are not told that the three Skraelings who were under each of these boats were asleep, but this is the logical deduction. In any event they were so unwary that it was possible for the Norse to land and to surround the natives and capture eight of them, apparently without a struggle. Only one Dorset woke up in time, or was agile enough to escape capture and the subsequent slaughter. He managed to launch one of the boats and paddled frantically off to warn his fellows farther down the lake of the menace which had come upon them.

As for the Norse, they returned victoriously to their ship and sailed on past the sandy beach where the bloody bodies of the Skraelings lay sprawled.

The saga says that they then came to a river which flowed down from the east toward the west. At first glance this statement appears to be in error, since the rivers along the Atlantic Coast flow generally

Thorvald Eriksson at Lake Melville

from the westward toward the east. However, English River in Lake Melville fits the description perfectly.* It flows from east to west into Lake Melville within three miles of Reed Point and about half a mile to the southward of the beach where the Skraelings were murdered. According to a trapper who lived at English River for some years, the river mouth at half tide carries about a fathom of water for a distance of a quarter of a mile inland. A supply schooner engaged to bring this trapper his winter outfit used to anchor well inside the river mouth in a cove which was secure in any kind of weather.

When the knorr rounded the low point separating the south end of the sandy beach from the river, the Norse would have been delighted to see a calm and protected stretch of estuary with sand banks on either side. Carefully they felt their way into the river mouth and anchored or moored under the southern bank.

A little more than half a mile southwest of the mouth of English River a prominent hill rises to a height of seven hundred feet, jutting out to form a headland and offering an excellent vantage point from which to survey the surrounding country. After their encounter with the Skraelings we assume that the Norse would have climbed this hill, if only to assure themselves that there were no more natives in the immediate vicinity. From its crest they saw a number of "hillocks," probably in the direction of Long Point, and for reasons which are not explained they identified these as human habitations, evidently Skraelings.

Considering the earlier events of this day, one would suppose that such a sight would have sent them hurrying back to their ship with the intention of removing themselves from the vicinity of such potentially dangerous neighbors as rapidly as possible. On the other hand they may have been so overblown with confidence after their easy victory that out of sheer bravado they refused to be perturbed. In any event they pitched their tents or shelters on the shore, made themselves comfortable, and calmly went to sleep.

Nevertheless they could hardly have been so foolish as not to have posted a guard, and it was probably a sentry on the hill who saw the flotilla of Skraeling boats appear on the southeastern horizon at dawn the next day and shouted the alarm which roused the camp.

---

* According to Gwyn Jones in *The Norse Atlantic Saga* (Oxford, 1964), Jorgen Meldgaard has also reached the conclusion that this is the river that Thorvald discovered.

The Greenlanders now repented of their foolhardy decision to spend the night in such dangerous proximity to the enemy. Rushing to their ship, they hauled up the anchor or cast off the shore lines, and manned the oars. There could have been little or no wind, otherwise they would have hoisted sail and made their escape before the Skraelings reached them. As things stood they realized that they could never row the big knorr fast enough to get away, and so at Thorvald's orders they prepared to defend themselves where the ship lay drifting.

On this occasion the Skraelings, alerted by the man who had escaped the slaughter, were really hostile. In their light, speedy and easily maneuvered boats they would soon have surrounded the knorr, and coming in as close as they dared, they began letting fly with slings and bows.

Sheltered behind the oaken bulwarks of their ship, and further protected by the rows of war-boards hung over her sides, the Norse were reasonably protected against missiles. They could have been seriously threatened only by a boarding party; and the Dorsets, who probably hoped only to drive the murdering strangers away from the vicinity, made no attempt to board. After spending some time firing stones and arrows at the ship with no apparent results, the Skraelings gave it up and withdrew.

They had done better than they knew. When the crew of the knorr took stock of the results of the attack, they found that Thorvald Eriksson was mortally wounded.

He seems to have died well, which was in the Viking tradition. Being great givers of death, the Norse could accept death without demur when it came to them. He was buried according to his wishes on Krossaness, the headland which had caught his fancy. Then, giving up both the search for Vinland and the search for Thorhall the Hunter, his shipmates made hurriedly for Straumfiord. Doubtless they now thought they knew what had happened to Thorhall, even if they had found no trace of him. His disappearance would unquestionably have been laid at the door of the Skraelings.

The tale that Thorvald's men had to tell when they reached Straumfiord would have increased the people's dread of the Skraelings manyfold, and they would have wondered fearfully if there was any safety to be had from them in all this hostile land.

24

/\.\/\.\

lanò of the one-footers

The Saga Story (c. 1006)

Bjarni Grimolfsson and Freydis remained behind here [at Straumfiord] with a hundred people and went no farther; while Karlsefni and Snorri proceeded to the southward with forty men, returning again that same summer after tarrying at a hop [there] for barely two months. . . .

They traveled a long distance until they came to a well-forested land. There they sailed into the mouth of a river. . . .

It happened one morning that Karlsefni and his companions saw something in an open space in the woods above them. It seemed to gleam at them and they shouted at it. It moved and they saw it was an Einfoetingr [One-Footer] and he came limping [or hopping] down to where their ship was lying . . . Afterwards he ran away to the northward with Karlsefni's men pursuing him and catching glimpses of him from time to time. The last they saw of him he was running up a stream valley.

Then they turned back [from the chase] and one of the men recited this verse:

> We men pursued, this is the truth,
> A One-Footer who came to the shore,
> But the strange man fled,
> Running swiftly over the hills.
> This we tell you, Karlsefni.

[SOURCES: Selected from the Erik the Red Saga and the Thorfinn Karlsefni Saga. The reasons why this portion of the saga has been treated in this manner are given in Appendix O.]

[Later] they [again] became aware of natives.* A great troop of them came out from the woods. Neither side could understand the other's language.

Their packs contained gray furs and sable. They were especially desirous of procuring red cloth. They also wanted to buy swords and spears but Karlsefni and Snorri forbade this.

In exchange for perfect pelts the natives would accept a span length of red cloth which they would bind around their heads.

So the trading continued for a while until Karlsefni and his people began to grow short of cloth, whereupon they divided [what they had left] into such narrow pieces that it was not more than a finger's breadth in width; but still the natives continued to give just as much or more in exchange for it.

Gudrid remained seated inside the door of the booth beside the cradle of her son Snorri. A shadow fell through the doorway, and then a woman entered who wore a narrow black kirtle. She was rather short in stature and she had chestnut-colored hair and a band around her head. Her eyes were pale and so large that no one had ever seen such large eyes in any human skull.

She came up to where Gudrid sat and Gudrid asked: "What is your name? My name is Gudrid, [tell me] what is your name?"

"My name is Gudrid," said [parroted] the woman.

Then housewife Gudrid stretched out her hand indicating that the woman should sit down beside her, but at that moment Gudrid heard a loud noise whereat the woman vanished. [The noise was caused by] the killing of a native by one of Karlsefni's house slaves at this same time, because he seemed about to take [some of] their weapons.

One of the natives had picked up an axe. He looked at it for a while and struck at a tree with it and one after another the others tested it. It seemed to be a real treasure because it cut so well. But then one of their number seized it and struck at a stone with it and the axe broke. It seemed to him to be of little use since it would not cut stone, and so he threw it away.

Now there was a battle and many of the native host were slain. One man in the host was tall and fair and Karlsefni thought he might be the leader.

Then the natives ran away into the woods, each man for himself, and so ended their encounter.

---

* Throughout the remainder of this section of the saga story (taken from the Greenlanders Story) the word "Skraeling" is used in the original text. This usage evidently resulted from the fact that the author of the Greenlanders Story confused this second battle between the Norse and Newfoundland aborigines with the battle fought at Hop between the Norse and the Dorsets. I have therefore substituted the word "natives" in order not to perpetuate the error. This matter is fully explained in Appendix O.

Then Karlsefni and his people sailed away toward the north, believing they had seen [visited] the land of the One-Footers [Einfoetingaland] and being unwilling to risk their men's lives any longer.

They concluded that the mountains at Hop and those they had now found formed one and the same range and that they [the two places] stood directly opposite each other and were an equal distance from Straumfiord.

[SOURCES: Erik the Red Saga and the Thorfinn Karlsefni Saga]

Allowing for the loss of Thorhall the Hunter and his nine men together with the deaths at Hop, the combined expedition would by now have been reduced to between 145 and 150 people. Since Karlsefni and Snorri took forty men with them, this would have left not much over a hundred people, including the entire Greenland contingent, at Straumfiord; and the saga says that when Karlsefni sailed, Freydis* and Bjarni remained behind in the company of one hundred people. Thorvald would hardly have sailed with less than thirty men on his expedition to the north, which makes it appear that he was still at Straumfiord when Karlsefni and Snorri got under way.

It may have been as early as mid-June when Karlsefni's ship rounded Cape Bauld and turned her bows toward the south, along the east coast of the Great Northern Peninsula.

KARLSEFNI'S COURSE

From Quirpon Island to Canada Bay, Karlsefni the trader and Snorri the would-be settler would have seen little to interest either of them in this bald and forbidding coast. Beyond Canada Bay the spine of the peninsula begins to lift higher and higher as the Long Range Mountains grow in stature. The coastal cliffs become more and more formidable, in places plunging a thousand feet into the sea below. The Norse would have sailed along this unprepossessing coast as quickly as they could. Occasionally they passed the mouth of one of the steep-sided little fiords (most of them mere slits in the sheer face of the sea-cliffs), and though they may have entered some of these in search of shelter from a storm or for an anchorage at night, they would have found nothing in them of much interest either to farmers or to lumbermen. As the voyage proceeded down this uninviting coast,

---

* The adventurous Freydis did not accompany Karlsefni this time, presumably because she was in such an advanced state of pregnancy.

Karlsefni and Snorri may at least have been heartened by the fact that they encountered no Skraelings.*

Up to the time they passed Great Harbour Deep they would have been sailing along an open seaboard with nothing to the east of them except a few islands — the Gray Islands — and the wide Western Ocean. But not long after passing Great Harbour Deep the lookout must have caught the loom of land to the east. At first this loom might have been mistaken for another offshore island, but as it grew into a continuous line of highlands the Norse would have realized that they were sailing into the mouth of a big sound or fiord.

This discovery (which they doubtless confirmed by going ashore and climbing the nearest cliff) may have led to renewed hopes that they had found the great fiord which ran southward into the land to terminate at Leif's Vinland.

Assuming that they entertained this hope, they would have pushed on with all possible speed. When they reached Sops Arm they may not have stopped to explore it. If they did sail into it they would have been encouraged by what they found. Although there was no hop, there was a large, sandy river delta whose myriad islands, together with the broad lowlands to the south of them, were thickly forested — and for the first time the forests contained a fair proportion of hardwood timber.

Pressing on, they would have rounded Spear Point, sailing south into what was now obviously a fiord, and moreover one which had abruptly narrowed to only three or four miles in width.

Did Vinland and its hop lie waiting close ahead? The excitement of the Icelanders must have been intense as they ran down those last few miles into Hampden Bay, passed Miller's Island and saw the end of the fiord before them.

THE HOP AT HAMPDEN RIVER

Their hopes would have reached a climax when the ship brought up on the edge of a sand and gravel tidal flat which extended out for half a mile from the river mouth, and when the lookout at the masthead called down the news that he could see a bar, and perhaps a small lagoon behind it. A hurriedly launched boat party would have rowed through the gap in the bar and into a small expansion of the

* See Appendix H.

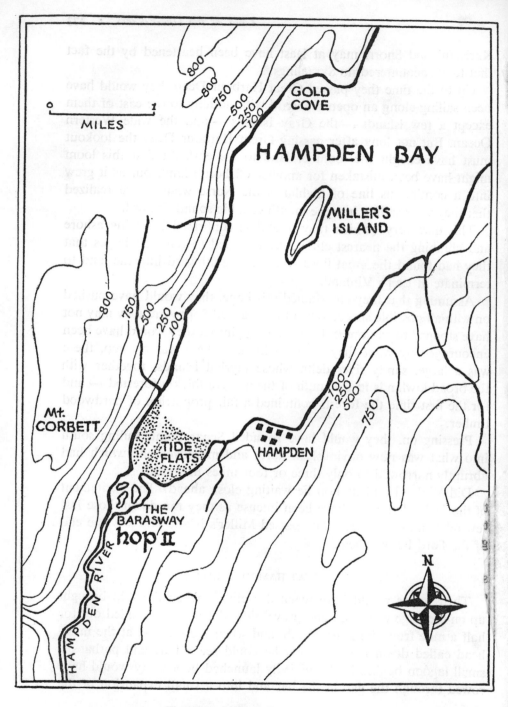

The foot of White Bay and Hop II

river mouth which formed a tiny barasway, not much more than a hundred yards in diameter, but large enough to provide a harbor for the knorr if she was eased into it at high tide.

This was a hop, although a minute one.* It could have borne no comparisons with the fabulous harbor of Leif's Vinland, nor could it have compared with the hop that Karlsefni had discovered on the west coast of the peninsula. Vinland had again eluded the Norse — but there were compensations.

The steep-walled valley of the Hampden still supports some of the finest mixed forests in Newfoundland. Ever since its rediscovery in the early years of the colonial period it has been famous for its timber, and Hampden today is a lumbering town. In the past it was not unusual for birch logs two and even three feet in diameter to be floated down the river on the spring floods, and for many generations there was a busy shipyard there. Every kind of timber, both hard and soft, needed for ship construction was available locally. In Karlsefni's day the virgin forests at the foot of the bay must have been all that he had ever hoped to find.

The low-lying floodlands at the mouth of the Hampden are not forested now, of course, and they may not have been forested in Karlsefni's time either. Finds of Beothuk artifacts at old campsites suggest that the immediate vicinity of the barachois was open land and, quite probably, it was grassland of the type found around most other Newfoundland barachoix. If this was the case, it is possible that Snorri and the colonist group aboard the ship may have had hopes that they had found a new settlement site. During the next few days they would have been busy investigating and assessing the area's potentialities. Meantime the traders' men would have lost no time beginning lumbering operations.

The location of the temporary Norse camp is not given in the saga sources, but it would logically have been on the shore of the barachois, close to where the ships were moored.

---

* There is no longer even a small barachois at the mouth of the Hampden, due to alterations in the topography made by a pulpwood company. However, British Admiralty charts show that a tiny 'hop' existed there as late as 1897. The charts also show a narrow approach channel over tidal flats through which a vessel of a knorr's draft might have been rowed. The barachois may well have been slightly larger in A.D. 1000, if we accept the hypothesis that the land has risen a few feet since then (see Appendix C). The Hampden River itself is not much more than a good-sized stream, except during periods of heavy rain. It is navigable only by canoes.

My identification of the barachois at the mouth of the Hampden with Karlsefni's second hop is dictated by two facts. First, it is the only hop-type harbor in the whole of White Bay. Second, the saga offers convincing proof that the hop must have been close to, if not actually at, the mouth of the Hampden.

They concluded that the mountains at Hop and those they had now found formed one and the same range and that they (the two places) stood directly opposite each other and were an equal distance from Straumfiord.

Since we have already determined that the western Hop was at St. Paul's Bay (or, just possibly, at nearby Parsons Pond), this statement locates the second hop in Hampden Bay. The sailing distances for a coastwise voyage from Epaves Bay to Hop and from Epaves Bay to the mouth of Hampden River are virtually identical. St. Paul's Bay lies exactly opposite to Brown's Cove, which is eight miles north of the river mouth on Hampden Bay. The Long Range Mountains fill the landscape between Hop and Hampden Bay. If there can be any objection to the use of these data to show that Hampden Bay was indeed visited by the Norse, it can only be that they are almost too exact. It may be hard for us to credit the Norse of circa 1000 with the ability to so accurately determine their position in relation to a place on the other side of the Great Northern Peninsula.

THE BEOTHUKS

If the Norse camped for any length of time in Hampden Bay during the summer months they would surely have made contact with a people they had never seen before — the Beothuk Indians. That the party did encounter these Indians is established by the account of the meeting with the One-Footer.*

The Beothuks used to leave their wintering grounds in the interior of Newfoundland in June and begin migrating to the coasts for the summer. The Icelanders may have already been established at the mouth of the Hampden before the first of those Beothuks who wintered in the area around Grand Lake and Sandy Lake began their

---

* For a detailed evaluation of the evidence supporting this conclusion, see Appendix O.

journey down the Hampden River in their birch-bark canoes. The Indians would have been heading for summer camps at Sops Arm and other inlets along both the east and west coasts of White Bay, where many Beothuk sites have been located.

The Beothuks doubtless discovered the presence of strangers at the river mouth long before the Norse knew that there were Indians about. The sounds of axes in the forest; the cries of men busy lumbering; the discovery of stumps and other signs of the felling of big trees along the river bank — all these would have served to alert the Beothuks, and they would doubtless have run their canoes ashore and hidden them while one of their number went forward to reconnoiter. This man may have climbed the steep western side of the valley and worked his way north along the crest as far as Mount Haggerty or Mount Corbett, from whose slopes he would have obtained a clear view of the bay shore and of the river mouth.

The sight of the knorr, of the Norse booths, and of strange men moving about would have amazed the Indian, but perhaps it did not frighten him unduly. Isolated as they had been for countless centuries, the Beothuks seem to have had few human enemies, and to have been a friendly and unsuspicious people. They showed no fear of the first Europeans to arrive in colonial times. On the contrary, they were so foolishly trusting that in 1501 Gaspar Cortereal had no difficulty in luring fifty or sixty of them aboard ship, preparatory to carrying them off to Spain as slaves.

There is no way of knowing whether the Beothuk scout deliberately exposed himself to the sight of the Norsemen, or whether some particularly sharp-eyed Icelander happened to spot him, perhaps through the reflection of sunlight on the numerous polished bone pendants which the Beothuks often wore around their necks and across their chests. In any event the Norse seem to have shouted at him, and the Beothuk apparently interpreted the shouting as an invitation to come down. The saga says that he limped, or hopped, down to where the ship lay, and from this we gather that he was lame, although he was still able to get along well enough.

The appearance of this lone stranger close to the ship seems to have tempted the Norse into committing an act of sheer folly. Instead of trying to make friends with him, they apparently tried to seize him. But, crippled or not, he was no easy prey. He outdistanced or outmaneuvered the Icelanders and vanished up a stream valley to the north. His winded pursuers returned to the camp, where, so the verse in the saga tells us, they made their excuses to Karlsefni for their failure.

There may have been a subsequent delay of several days before the Beothuks could make up their minds as to what to do about the Norse. Eventually they seem to have decided to confront the strangers. Since the Norse were presumably camped astride the route to the Indian summer camps, a direct confrontation could hardly have been avoided.

Meanwhile the Icelanders, with bitter memories of their encounter with the Skraelings before them, had doubtless given up their hopes of settling here and were making haste to complete their lumbering. Some of their number may have been told off to build some kind of defensive works around the booths, and every man would have gone about fully armed and alert to the dangers of a surprise attack.

When the day came that the Norse beheld a large company of Beothuks coming out of the woods toward them, they probably wished that they had departed while the going was good. There must have been some frantic scurrying for weapons and for defense positions, and the atmosphere would have been explosive as a party of stalwart Indians, their bodies glistening with a mixture of oil and red ochre, slowly advanced across the open ground.

By analogy with their known habits in a later time, we assume that the Beothuks made overtures of peace, probably by offering gifts to the strangers. These gifts could have included sable and other rich furs, the sight of which would have roused the natural cupidity of the Norse. In any event peaceful relations, if only of a tentative nature, seem to have been established. The Norse began trading, although the Beothuks may not have realized that this is what was happening. They probably thought that they were simply engaging in an exchange of gifts.

The Beothuks appear to have been greatly impressed by a piece of red woolen cloth which a Norseman offered them, and this material instantly became the thing they most desired to possess.

While the trading or gift exchanging (depending on the point of view) continued, some of the Beothuks seem to have been indulging their curiosity. One woman, bolder than the rest, dared to peek through the door of a booth where the Norse women had doubtless been told to remain until the danger of an attack was past, and saw

Gudrid, Karlsefni's wife, sitting beside the cradle of her eighteen-month-old son, Snorri. Gudrid appears to have tried to make friends with the alien woman by asking her her name, and by repeating her own. The Beothuk woman responded by trying to imitate the unfamiliar Norse syllables, whereupon Gudrid, who seems to have been a lady of parts, beckoned the strange woman to come in and join her.

One is tempted to speculate on what might have happened if the Beothuk woman and Gudrid had managed to establish some sort of rapport. The saga literature tells us of many proud Norsemen who listened meekly to the outspoken and vigorous criticisms and suggestions of their women, and sometimes even acted on their wives' advice. It is by no means impossible that if the Beothuk woman and Gudrid had become friends, the story of the Norse attempts to plant a settlement in North America might have had a different ending.

The history of later contacts between whites and Beothuks establishes the fact that these Indians wanted peaceful relations with Europeans, and went to extraordinary lengths to achieve this desire. They never succeeded, but only because of the arrant stupidity and unbelievable barbarism of the whites. No doubt it is foolish to imagine that the Norse — even the Norse women — would have been more humane and reasonable in their dealings with the Beothuks than the French, English and Portuguese of five centuries later. The fact remains that had the Norse been able to keep their sanguinary instincts in check, they would have been accepted by the Beothuks and could then have established themselves in Newfoundland without opposition from, and probably with the active cooperation of, the native people who controlled the major portion of the island.

Unfortunately, the Norse knew only one way of settling differences between themselves and alien peoples, and that was by the use of sword and axe. Even as the Beothuk woman was about to enter Gudrid's house, there was a "loud noise" and the woman vanished — not into thin air as some authors have suggested, but in flight; for blood was flowing once again in a Norse camp in the New World.

We do not know what happened. Perhaps one of the Beothuks picked up a Norse axe and began to examine it; or he may have handed it about among his friends. We are told that the Beothuks first tested the axe on a tree and then, in one version, a man is supposed to have tested it on his neighbor, who promptly fell dead. In the other version a Beothuk reputedly tried to cut a rock with it, and the axe broke. Both stories are absurd. The Beothuks were fully familiar with flint hand axes and hafted adzes. The suggestions that they would have been idiotic enough to test a Norse iron axe on each other, or to attempt to cut rocks with it, is an insult to their intelligence and to ours.

What probably happened is that the Norse reacted in a blind possessive fury when the Beothuk man picked up the axe. The saga admits that one of the natives was killed "because he seemed about to take" one of the Norse weapons. There we have it in a nutshell.

With the striking of that first blow — not accidentally, or by a Beothuk, but deliberately and by a Norseman — and the death of one of their number, panic ensued among the Indians. The saga says that in "the battle" which followed, many of the natives were slain while the rest ran wildly for the shelter of the woods. That many of the Beothuks were slaughtered can be believed. That there was a battle, in any real sense of the word, seems dubious. The saga makes no mention of any Norsemen being killed or even wounded.

It would have been immediately after this (the first but by no means the last massacre of Beothuks at the hands of Europeans) that Karlsefni and Snorri and their people got themselves back aboard their ship and hurried home to Straumfiord because, as the saga says, they were "unwilling to risk men's lives any longer" in this place. By which we are to understand that once again they were afraid of retaliation — and with the best of reasons.

25

∧∧∧

RETREAT OF THE ICELANDERS

The Saga Tale (c. 1006)

When they sailed from Vinland [Straumfiord] they had a southerly wind which took them to Markland, and there they encountered five Skraelings. One of these was bearded [meaning he was a man]; two were women and two were children. Karlsefni and his people captured the boys but the others escaped by sinking down into the ground.

They carried these lads away with them and taught them their tongue and had them baptized. The boys said their mother's name was Vaetilldi and their father was called Uvaegi. They said that kings governed their country, one of them being called Avalldamen and the other Valdidida. They stated that they had no houses [in the sense of Norse houses] and that the people lived in holes or caves.

They said too that there was a land on the other side, opposite their country, which was inhabited by people who wore white garments and who yelled loudly and carried poles before them to which cloths were attached. People believe this must have been Hvitramannaland or Ireland the Great.

And now they [Karlsefni's people] came to Greenland, where they spent the winter with Erik the Red.

But Bjarni Grimolfsson and his companions were driven out into the Greenland Sea and their ship began to sink. They did not discover until then that their ship was all worm-eaten beneath them. They hurriedly discussed what they ought to do.

They had an afterboat coated with seal-tar into which the shipworm will not bore. It was the decision of the company to transfer as many people into this boat as it would hold, but when this was done it was found that it would not take more than half the people.

Then said Bjarni: "Since the boat will not hold more than half the company it is my suggestion that those who are to go in the boat be chosen by lot; for this selection ought not to be made on the basis of rank."

This seemed to be such a manly offer that no one opposed it. They adopted the plan, and the men cast lots. It fell to Bjarni to go in the boat with half the men.

When they [who had been chosen] were in the boat a young Icelander who was still aboard the ship, and who had accompanied Bjarni from Iceland, called out: "Do you intend to forsake me here, Bjarni?"

"This is the way it must be." Bjarni answered.

"That was not what you promised my father when I left Iceland with you," he replied. "You said then that you would never desert me, and that we would share the same fate together."

"I see no other course than this one," said Bjarni. "Have you any alternative to offer?"

"I suggest we change places. You come here, and I will go there."

"So be it then," said Bjarni, "For I see you cling tenaciously to life and find it hard to die." And so they changed places.

Men say that Bjarni perished in that wormy sea together with those men who remained on the ship with him. But the boat and those who were in it went their way until they reached Iceland, where they afterwards told this tale.

[SOURCES: Erik the Red Saga and the Thorfinn Karlsefni Saga.]

By sheer good luck the Norse initially picked a settlement site at Straumfiord which had been abandoned by the waning Dorset population and not yet reoccupied by Indians. But although it was then free of natives, it had not always been so, and the Norse could hardly have avoided finding old camps or other signs that natives had once lived in the vicinity.*

Indications of prior occupancy by an unknown people might not have disturbed the Norse, secure as they were in their belief that they were a match for anyone, until Karlsefni ran into trouble with the Skraelings at Hop and discovered that they were formidable antagonists. His account of their fighting qualities must have given

---

* In 1963 the Ingstad expedition found Dorset artifacts at Epaves Bay. These predate the arrival of the Karlsefni-Thorvald party, as does a Boreal Archaic Indian site at the same locality.

rise to a good deal of uneasiness among the Straumfiord settlers, even though Hop lay a long way off to the south and west.

However, the Norse would have had no reason to feel that the settlement itself was in any jeopardy until the Thorhall search party came hurrying back from Lake Melville to report that Thorvald Eriksson had been killed by Skraelings who lived to the north of Straumfiord. This alarming news would have demonstrated to the Epaves Bay settlers that they were between two fires, one of which smoldered dangerously close to the sea-road linking Straumfiord and Greenland.

When Thorfinn Karlsefni returned from his second southern voyage toward the middle of August and nosed his ship into Epaves Bay, the stay-at-homes must have already been in an anxious frame of mind — a condition which would not have been eased by his report that not only had he again failed to find Vinland, but he had clashed with yet another native people.

The Norse had now conducted four separate exploring expeditions from Straumfiord: to the west, to the north, to the southeast, and to the southwest. They had not found Vinland, and what was even more discouraging, they found no country which was not already in the hands of natives. Karlsefni's return from White Bay seems to have put finis to the last prospects of finding Leif's Vinland. It also must have made it seem dismally clear that Straumfiord was surrounded by dangerous natives who, sooner or later, could be expected to appear at Epaves Bay. The combination of these two factors was doubtless enough to seal the fate of the colony as far as the Icelanders were concerned.

If the Icelandic colonists had needed any additional stimulus to persuade them to give up and go home, it would have been provided by the impending departure of Karlsefni and Thorhall Gamlisson. Having completed their ships' ladings, the two traders had no further interest in remaining in the New World. On the contrary, they had every reason to sail north and east as soon as possible, for summer was drawing to an end and they would have been anxious to avoid the possibility of being trapped at Straumfiord for another, and fruitless, winter.

Their departure would have left any Icelandic settlers who stayed behind dependent on Freydis Eriksdottir for ship transportation as well as subject to her erratic whims in other matters, since the Greenlanders, together with Helge and Finnboggi's men, considerably out-numbered the Icelandic settlers. The prospects of finding themselves at Freydis's mercy could hardly have been much more attractive to the Icelanders than the prospects of having to fight for their lives against the Skraelings. In the event we can be sure that when the ships of Karlsefni and Thorhall put out to sea homeward bound, they carried the whole of the Icelandic contingent with them.*

The Icelandic ships apparently did not sail for the same destinations. Skipper Thorhall appears to have taken his departure from some point not far north of Straumfiord, on course for Iceland, per-haps by way of Cape Farewell. But Karlsefni sailed for the Eastern Settlement, perhaps partly in order to sell some of his timber where it would command the highest prices, and partly to arrange for the sale of Gudrid's Greenland property, since he was intending to take his wife to live in Iceland.

The saga says that Karlsefni sailed first to Markland, and he may conceivably have retraced his outward course all the way back to Greenland. It seems more likely that he sailed north either to the un-mistakable landmark of the Kaumajet, or to Bjarni Herjolfsson's point of departure near Cape Chidley, and then turned easterly across the Labrador Sea to a landfall in southern Greenland. He may even have pioneered the route between the Kaumajet and Greenland, a route which appears to have been used in later years by Greenlanders visiting the Labrador coast for softwood timber.

The account of the capture of the two Skraeling children affords us our last glimpse of the Dorset peoples before they vanished out of time.

The children were found in Markland, which could mean any-

---

* The Erik the Red and Karlsefni sagas tell us that after the return of Karlsefni's second southern expedition, Greenlanders and Icelanders settled down together to spend a final winter at Straumfiord. The unstated corollary is that the entire flotilla sailed for Greenland as a unit in the spring of the fourth year. The Greenlanders Story, on the other hand, concludes its account of the western voyages with a description of a separate voyage by Freydis Eriksdottir to Vinland — a voyage which, as we have shown in Appendix M, could not have taken place. We are also told that the survivors of the Greenland contingent, led by Freydis, returned to Greenland the summer after Karlsefni and his Icelanders arrived there. This being the case, we need have no difficulty in resolving the conflict between the two accounts.

I conclude that the Icelanders departed toward the end of the third summer, with sufficient time in hand for a voyage back to Greenland before the autumnal gales began. But for reasons which I will discuss in the next chapter, the Greenland contingent chose to remain behind for one more winter.

where along the Labrador coast south of Okak Bay. They were doubtless members of a family group, and when the Norse surprised the family the three adults hid from their pursuers in crevices among the rocks.

The boys were carried off and eventually taught to speak Norse — no matter how imperfectly. They told their captors their parents' names and also the names of two personages whom the Norse took to be the kings of Skraeling Land. However, since no Eskimoan culture embraced the notion of any form of organized leadership, let alone a monarchy, we conclude that the Norse interpretation was faulty and that Avalldamen and Valdidida were doubtless pre-eminent supernatural entities in the Dorset religion — perhaps comparable to Kaila or Sila of recent Eskimo cultures. According to some ethnologists the four names mentioned by the boys show affinities to the Eskimo-Aleut language stock, which is what we would expect from a Dorset source.

The statement that the Dorsets did not have houses in the sense that the Norse did, fits with what we know of Dorset structures, which, while they can hardly be described as holes or caves, were in fact semi-subterranean.

One of the main points of interest in the account given by the children lies in what they had to say about a land on the other side, opposite their country, which was inhabited by an alien race. As we have suggested in the chapter dealing with Ari Marsson, the origin of this story evidently lies in an encounter between Greenland Dorsets and Westman settlers in southwestern Greenland, during which the Skraelings observed a Celtic religious celebration or procession.

So it happens that with their own final appearance in history the Dorsets shone the light of human recognition on those forgotten Europeans whose first venturings into the dark wilderness of the North Atlantic, centuries before the time of Christ, led them on to Greenland. This is our last glimpse of the people who laid the train along which the flame of Norse audacity burned westward to reach and finally to gutter out upon that ultimate shore — the fringes of a continent which other Europeans, following after, would one day take and make their own.

It is surely a strange and moving thing that in the concluding paragraphs of the last of the sagas which tells of the westward venturing of the Norse we should briefly touch the faces of three peoples — the Greenland Norse, the Dorsets, and the Greenland Celts — all of whom were doomed to vanish utterly.

Karlsefni's ship and people reached Greenland safely and the knorr sailed up into Eriksfiord. The returning venturers were welcomed by Erik the Red and spent the winter with him there.

"But Bjarni Grimolfsson and his companions were driven out into the Greenland Sea . . ." They probably encountered strong northwesterly gales which not only set them far enough south so that they missed Cape Farewell, but which severely strained their ship.

She may have been in bad shape in any case as a natural consequence of having spent two years in the relatively warm Newfoundland waters, where the shipworm abounds and is immensely destructive to the hulls of unprotected wooden vessels. In more northern waters the worm is neither so abundant nor so voracious. Even so, it was the custom in Greenland and Iceland to coat the bottoms of seagoing vessels with seal-tar, a thick and sticky substance made by evaporating seal oil until only a heavy residue remained. In Newfoundland the Norse probably did not have the materials or the opportunity to prepare sufficient quantities of this vital bottom coating.

The saga account of what ensued when the vessel began to sink requires no commentary. Bjarni Grimolfsson was lost, but Thorhall Gamlisson survived and lived on for many years in Iceland, where he became known as "The Vinlander."

The account of the loss of the ship makes a fitting period to a brave and hopeful voyage into a new world — but one which was brought to nothing as much by human stupidity as by the ill will of those implacable fates in whose existence the Norsemen had such an invincible and unshakable belief.

26

∧∨∧

fReydis and the brothers

The Saga Story (c. 1007)

They spent the third winter at Straumfiord. Then the men began to form into factions and to quarrel over the women. Those who were without women tried to seize the wives of the married men and there was serious trouble as a result.

[SOURCES: Erik the Red Saga and the Thorfinn Karlsefni Saga.]

When Freydis* came to carry her possessions into the house she found that the brothers [Helge and Finnboggi] had come ahead of her and had carried their things to the house.

Then Freydis asked: "Why did you bring your belongings in here?"

"Because we supposed," said they, "that the agreements between us would be kept."

"It is to me that Leif [Karlsefni] lent the house," said she, " and not to you!"

Then Helge said: "We brothers cannot match your wickedness."

Then the brothers took away their belongings and built themselves a house away from the sea near a lake, and put it all in order.

Meanwhile Freydis was having wood felled [as cargo] for her ship.

Now winter drew near and the brothers proposed that games should be played and entertainment set afoot [between the Icelandic crew and the Greenlanders].

---

* The short portion of the Greenlanders Story which describes the purportedly independent voyage of Freydis to Vinland has not been reproduced here. We begin the narrative with a description of a quarrel between Freydis and the brothers Helge and Finnboggi over possession of a house.

This was done and things went well for a while until the men began to quarrel with each other, and then their companionship broke up and the games ceased, and nobody visited back and forth between the houses; and so things went for most of the winter.

Before dawn one morning Freydis got out of bed and dressed and took her husband's cloak and put it on. But she did not put on her shoes. The weather was such that a heavy dew had fallen.

She went to the house of the two brothers and approached the door. One of the men had gone out a little while earlier and had only half-closed the door behind him. She opened the door and stood in the hallway a while without making any noise.

Finnboggi, who lay farthest inside the house, was awake and he asked:

"What do you want here, Freydis?"

"I wish you to get up and come outside, for I want to talk to you," she answered.

He did what she asked and they went to a log that lay close to the shelter of the house and sat down upon it.

"How do you like things here?" she asked him.

"I think the products of this land are good," he replied, "but I don't like the troubles between us, for they are no fault of mine."

"That is true enough, and I agree with you," she said. "But this is the reason I came to see you. I want to exchange ships with you brothers because you have a larger ship than mine and I want to go away [make a voyage?] from here."

"That can be arranged, if it is your pleasure," he answered.

Then she went home and Finnboggi went back to sleep.

She got into her own bed and her cold feet awoke Thorvard [her husband] and he asked her why she was so cold and wet.

She answered with great indignation: "I went to see the brothers to try and arrange to get their ship, since it is larger than ours, and they took this request so badly they assaulted me and roughed me up. But you! You coward! You won't avenge either my shame or your own, and here am I far away from home and Greenland. I swear I'll leave you unless you avenge this insult!"

Thorvard could not stand her jibes and so he called upon his men to get up at once and bring their weapons. The men did so, and then they all went to the house of the brothers and broke in. They surprised [the Icelanders] sleeping and took them all captive and then they bound them and led them out of the house one at a time. Freydis had each one killed as they were brought out.

This left the brothers' women, and nobody would kill them.

"Give me an axe!" Freydis cried.

Someone did so, and she slew the five women who were in the house and left them dead.

After this evil work was finished they went back to their own house and it was apparent that Freydis thought she had acted very cleverly. She said to her followers:

"If we manage to get back to Greenland, I will kill any man who speaks of what has happened. We shall say this: that they [the Icelanders] chose to stay behind when we went away."

Now early in the spring they loaded the [brothers'] ship with all the goods they could find and that the ship would hold. Afterwards they put to sea and had a good voyage, and came into Eriksfirth with their ship early in the summer.

Karlsefni was there, having prepared his ship to sail [to Norway] and he was only waiting for a fair wind before departing. It is said by many people that no richer ship than his ever sailed from Greenland.

Freydis now went to her house [at Gardar] which had stood untouched in her absence. She gave particularly rich gifts to all her companions and followers because she wished to conceal her misdeeds: and so she lived in her own home.

But not all her men kept their word to be silent about her wickedness, and so rumors of it came out at last. Reports of this reached Leif, her brother [Erik, her father]*, and he thought these rumors very bad indeed.

Then he took three of Freydis's men and tortured them until they all confessed what had happened and were agreed in their versions of it.

"I cannot afford," said Leif [Erik], "to punish my sister [daughter] Freydis as she deserves, but I foretell this fate for her and hers: that they [she and Thorvard] and their offspring will gain little by this act, and will not prosper as a result of it."

And so it came to pass that everyone thought ill of them from that time forth.

[SOURCE: The Greenlanders Story.]

The tangled web surrounding the slaughter of Helge and Finnboggi and their people may never be properly unraveled. In the reconstruction which follows I have attempted to make sense out of what

---

* The author of the Greenlanders Story had disposed of Erik prior to the Karlsefni-Thorvald-Freydis voyage to the western lands. Consequently he was forced to substitute Leif for Erik as head of the family when he wrote his account of what happened to Freydis after her return to Greenland. We conclude that it was Erik who discovered the true facts about what had happened at Straumfiord, and who forecast a black future for his wayward daughter.

seems like a senseless act; but, while I have taken into account all the known facts, the reconstruction necessarily remains largely speculative.

We know that Freydis came out to the new lands solely to enrich herself, as Leif had done before her, by gathering a cargo of the land's most valuable products. When Karlsefni and the Icelanders abandoned Straumfiord and sailed homeward they had ladings, but Freydis and her partners, Helge and Finnboggi, had not had the opportunity to amass a cargo of comparable value. We can believe that Karlsefni would have been willing to give Thorhall Gamlisson a share of the hardwood from Hampden Bay, but considering the hostility between the Greenlanders and the Icelanders, it is unlikely that he would have done the same for Freydis or for her allies.

With her cupidity unsatisfied (it may have been further inflamed by the wealth brought back by Karlsefni) Freydis was not yet willing to leave the new lands, nor was she willing to allow the Greenland settlers to depart even if they had wished to do so.

She was in a position to enforce her will. After Thorvald Eriksson's death, ownership of his ship had fallen to her, or she had taken it. Acting through her flaccid husband, she probably usurped the leadership of the entire Greenland contingent. It would have been difficult for the settlers to oppose her. Not only did she have the backing of her retainers, but at this stage she also would have had the support of Helge and Finnboggi and their crew. This would have given her a strength of thirty-five or forty fighting men as opposed to no more than twenty male survivors from Thorvald's group of settlers.

Freydis may well have decided to remain at Straumfiord for another winter, not because she was interested in giving the colonization plan that much longer to prove itself, but so that she could make a journey south to the land of the hardwoods early in the following spring. If this was her plan, she would have had need of the able-bodied colonists both to strengthen her fighting force and to serve as lumberjacks when she ventured into the lands of the One-Footers.

It will be remembered too that by the terms of her initial agreement with Helge and Finnboggi she was entitled to half the value of the cargo they could carry home. This agreement would no longer have satisfied Freydis now that she had her own ship. Therefore she may also have wished to keep the Greenland settlers at Straumfiord to be used, if necessary, against the Icelandic sailors and their masters.

The impression we get of her character suggests that she was quite capable of playing a double game — first making use of the Icelanders to help her enforce her will on the Greenland settlers, and later using the Greenland settlers to give her an overwhelming balance of power over the Icelanders.

After the departure of Karlsefni and Thorhall Gamlisson there were about eighty people left at Straumfiord. Men probably outnumbered the women by about three to one, which would have led to tension and trouble in any isolated community. In a Norse community of those days it would have made for a violently explosive situation. The Norse were renowned for their uninhibited concupiscence and gargantuan sexual appetites, and we can take it for granted that the brief reference in the Erik the Red and Karlsefni sagas to woman trouble is a masterly understatement.

We are told that the quarrel between the two groups, which led to the Icelanders setting up a new hall some distance away from the Greenlandic settlement grew out of a conflict over possession of Leif Eriksson's booths in Vinland. Since we know that the expedition never found Vinland, let alone Leif's booths, we recognize this as an interpolation. Perhaps what really happened is that even before the Karlsefni section of the expedition departed, Freydis had begun to develop a plan whereby she would acquire the entire wealth which was to have been shared between her and the brothers. As part of this plan she may have deliberately set about rousing hostility between the remaining Icelanders and the Greenlanders.

The "house" incident may have taken place substantially as described. Possibly it had to do with the occupancy of one of the houses abandoned by the Icelandic contingent. Helge and Finnboggi may have occupied one of these houses, only to be forced out of it by Freydis on the grounds that Karlsefni had given her the use of it.*

What is important about this incident is that Freydis was already breaking the agreements made between her and the brothers at the beginning of the voyage. The text establishes the fact that the brothers did everything in their power to avoid a clash. Their willingness

* A mile and a half west of Epaves Bay a good-sized lake lies close to the coastline. Its north end is 175 yards from the bottom of Rudder Cove, and its western side is the same distance from the bottom of Pond Cove. Pond Cove offers an excellent small harbor and it may well be that the brothers moved, with their ship, to Pond Cove and built their hall just inland from it, on the protected lake shore.

to placate Freydis, even at the cost of their pride, is by no means typical of Norse behavior and suggests that they were fully aware of the precariousness of their own position. The withdrawal of the Icelanders to a site well away from the Greenlanders drives home the point.

It is not difficult to believe that Freydis then attempted to inflame the situation to the point where the Greenlanders would spontaneously attack and massacre the Icelanders. We can imagine some of the methods she may have used. Apart from playing on the suspicion which was evidently latent between the two groups, she may also have pointed out that the Icelanders had five women for their solace, but were selfishly unwilling to share their services with the Greenlanders. There were a score of other ways by which she could have played upon the tempers of men who were unruly at the best of times, and who, after three years of isolation in an alien land, could have been all too readily incited to mayhem.

The breakdown of the brothers' efforts to establish peace between the two camps is documented in the saga. After this failure it appears that all communications between the two camps were severed. The Icelanders must have felt themselves to be living in a state of siege.

So the winter passed and spring arrived, and Freydis's plan had not yet borne fruit. The tension between the two camps had not yet errupted into outright violence, perhaps because the spineless and incompetent Thorvard, Freydis's husband, refused to act.

Time was running out and Freydis must have felt that it was now or never. So she applied the final goad.

Superficially the account of her visit to the brothers' hall appears to make little sense. However, it must be remembered that the account of what happened presumably originated with Freydis. The Icelanders were unable to give their version, for they were dead. Perhaps some of the ambiguities in the tale were deliberate attempts on Freydis's part to confuse the issue. Freydis's claim that she went to visit the Icelanders in the middle of the night, having sneaked out of her husband's bed and having foregone wearing shoes so as not to wake the household, all for the purpose of a simple little business talk, is transparent nonsense.

What happened was probably this: on the one hand she deliberately forced her husband's sword arm by setting up a situation which suggested he was being cuckolded by one of the Icelandic brothers; while on the other she made a large, and presumably fairly public, outcry to the effect that Thorvard was not man enough to avenge an assault upon her person.

That Thorvard was a dullard is suggested by an earlier reference to him in the saga sources; but he was not so supine that he could withstand this double-edged attack. Baffled and badgered, unable to cope with the cunning of his quick-witted virago of a wife, he was finally driven in blind exasperation to play the part Freydis had prepared for him.

What actually took place when Freydis visited the Icelanders, will never be known. Perhaps she did not visit them at all — we have only her word for it that she did. In any event we can be quite sure that the Icelanders would not meekly have agreed to exchange vessels with her. They would have had to be completely spineless to agree to anything of the sort. If she did visit them it may have been merely to lull their suspicions by pretending that she had undergone a change of heart or to convince them by a concrete offer of her favors that they had nothing to fear.

The surprise attack on the Icelandic camp, which was doubtless mounted just before dawn, accomplished what Freydis desired — it eliminated the Icelanders from any share in the proceeds of the expedition and put their ship, which was larger and better than Thorvald's old vessel, into her hands. Something of the pitiless resolution which motivated her can be seen in the grim aftermath, when she personally slaughtered the five Icelandic women in order to keep their mouths shut. That she had to do this herself may have been due to some vestiges of compassion on the part of the Greenland men but it was more likely due to their desire to keep the women alive for their own use.

The saga tells us that soon after the massacre Freydis and her people loaded the Icelanders' ship and sailed home to Greenland. They seem to have made the return journey early in the season, for they arrived at Eriksfiord before Karlsefni sailed for Norway. Having taken over Helge's and Finnboggi's share of the products of the new land together with their ship, Freydis may not have made any further effort to add to the ship's lading. Possibly she never intended to visit Hampden Bay but only suggested this as a means of keeping Helge and Finnboggi at Straumfiord after the Icelandic colonists departed.

The Greenlanders would have done their best to hide the evidence of their crime, for they could not have known that there would be no more voyages to Straumfiord, and they would not have cared to risk the chance of some future expedition discovering the true fate which had overtaken the brothers, their men and their women. Perhaps the old vessel which had once belonged to Thorbjorn Vifilsson, and had made two voyages out over the western waters from Greenland, made her last voyage in the Strait of Belle Isle laden with the corpses of the Icelanders, and red with flames.

Crowded into the brothers' ship, the Greenlanders made their way home; but not even Freydis's threats could stop all mouths. Eventually somebody talked, in liquor maybe, and a rumor of what had happened reached Erik. His torturing of three of Freydis's men revealed the full story, but he himself would have had to try to hush it up because if it had become public knowledge he would have been held responsible together with Freydis and her people by the relatives of the dead Icelanders.

Karlsefni, who had wintered with his good friend Erik, probably saw and talked to Freydis and her crowd when they arrived in Eriksfiord. But apparently he heard no whispers of the bloody deed with which the last members of the great expedition to the west had sealed its inglorious and final end.

Karlsefni prepared his ship and sailed out to sea and he had a good voyage and came to Norway safe and sound. He stayed there that winter and sold his wares; and both he and his wife enjoyed the friendship of the most distinguished men in Norway.

The next spring he prepared his vessel for the voyage to Iceland. One day, when she was ready and lay at the quay waiting for a fair wind, a southerner — a native of Bremen in Saxonland — came to see him. The visitor wished to buy Karlsefni's husanotra.

"I will not sell," Karlsefni told him.

"I will give you half-a-mark in gold for it," said he.

Karlsefni thought this was a good price, and so he sold it. The southerner went away with the husanotra. He did not know what sort of wood it was [made of]; but it was mazur [birch] brought from Vinland.

Karlsefni put out to sea and brought his ship to the northern part of Iceland at Skagefiord. There his ship was laid up for the winter and he and Gudrid went to his home at Reyniness.

His mother thought he had made a poor match [in Gudrid] and would not live with them that winter. Later when she became convinced that Gudrid was a very superior woman, she came home again and they all lived happily together.

In the spring Karlsefni bought Glumboland and built his house there, and live with them that winter. Later when she became convinced that Gudrid

After Karlsefni was dead, Gudrid became the trustee of the property and of Snorri, her son, who was born in Vinland.

When Snorri was married, Gudrid went abroad [on pilgrimage] and to the South [probably to Rome]. Afterwards she returned to the home of Snorri, her son, and he had a church built for her at Glumbo. Later Gudrid became a nun and an anchorite and lived there the rest of her life.

Many great people in Iceland are descended from Karlsefni and Gudrid.

God be with us all, Amen!

[SOURCES: Erik the Red Saga, the Karlsefni Saga and the Greenlanders Story]

∧∨∧

the aftermath

The subsequent history of the Norse westward venturing is sunk in obscurity. There are a few fragmentary references scattered here and there in the Icelandic literature and in other ancient sources which make it plain that the Greenlanders continued to make voyages to the Labrador for timber until at least as late as 1347; but there is no indication of any further attempt to establish settlements in North America.

There were also apparently a number of accidental visits. Approximately in the year 1025 an Icelandic merchant named Gudleif Gudlaugsson set out on a voyage from Dublin to Iceland by the direct route. He encountered heavy easterly and northeast gales and was driven far off course to the west and southwest. When the summer was nearly over, so the saga* tells us, he found land and anchored in a convenient harbor. Here he was approached by dark-complexioned natives who spoke a language the Icelanders did not understand, but which they thought bore some similarity to the Irish tongue. That it was not Irish can be taken for granted since Gudleif or some of his men would have understood it if this had been the case.

The saga gives a very circumstantial account of this incident. It describes how the Icelanders were taken prisoner, but eventually released through the good offices of an elderly white man whom they later identified as a skald named Bjorn Asbrandsson who had disappeared many years earlier while on a voyage out of Iceland, probably Greenland bound. This castaway had achieved a position of

---

* Eyrbyggja Saga.

some distinction among the natives with whom he was living and was satisfied to remain with them. Gudlief and his men managed to sail back to Iceland, where their story gained wide circulation.

Bjorn may have been bound for Erik's colony when he was lost. We know he departed from Iceland with a northeast wind, which would have been the correct wind for a voyage to southern Greenland. No doubt he was blown past Farewell and, like others before him, eventually made land to the west. There his ship seems to have been wrecked, and Bjorn was the sole survivor of the ship's complement at the time of Gudleif's visit some twenty or thirty years later. It has been suggested that Bjorn may have been the prototype of the legendary Glooscap, the mysterious god who appeared out of the sea and who lived with the Mic Mac Indians of Nova Scotia for a long time.*

We can be sure of one thing, that during the centuries following the Karlsefni voyage, Norse ships must have continued to blunder onto the northeastern coasts of the continent from time to time. Most of the people were probably killed, or if they were lucky made their way back home again; but some may have remained alive in the New World until they and their blood were lost by assimilation into one or another of the native tribes.

In 1059 there may have been a deliberate attempt to revisit Vinland — perhaps sparked by Gudleif's experiences. There is a record of a Celtic or Saxon priest named Jon, who had at one time worked in Iceland, having gone to Vinland or Vendland on a missionary voyage. He was subsequently reported to have been murdered by the natives there.

This reported voyage is of interest, for if it is authentic it suggests that all hope of making use of the new lands may not have been abandoned, and it also seems to confirm that the chief difficulty in the way of settlement was the native population. Perhaps someone

---

* There can be no doubt that Bjorn Asbrandsson actually existed. He was forced to leave Iceland because he had become the lover of Thurid, the daughter of the renowned chieftain, Snorri Godi, who was also one of Ari Thorgilsson's most reliable sources in the compilation of his famous history, the Islendingabok. Unfortunately for Bjorn, Thurid was already married and her husband took a dim view of the affair. In the ensuing mêlée Bjorn wounded the husband and killed two of his friends, for which he was exiled. Upon Bjorn's return to Iceland three years later the frightened husband persuaded the powerful Snorri Godi to prevail on Bjorn, by threats or bribes, to stay out of the country. Bjorn then seems to have set sail for Greenland.

in Iceland or Greenland concluded that if the natives could be Christianized they might become more tractable. At any rate this proved to be a very efficacious method when used by later-day Europeans in their attempts to occupy "heathen" countries, and it is not yet completely in discard.

Assuming that Jon was sent to Vinland, his death should have reinforced the belief that no settlement could be established in the New World in the face of the opposition of the natives. Yet, oddly enough, the next chronological reference to the new lands is also to a missionary expedition. This one seems to have taken place in 1121, when Erik, Bishop of Greenland, is reported to have sailed for Vinland. Nothing further is known about him except that he was succeeded by a new bishop in 1124, from which we draw the conclusion that his luck was no better than Jon's.

The Vinland referred to here was not Leif's Vinland, which was apparently never rediscovered, but was the later Vinland of the Stefansson map — the Great Northern Peninsula of Newfoundland. It is an ironic thought that if Leif's original Vinland *had* been rediscovered by Karlsefni or later voyagers (with or without Leif's aid) the Norse might very well have succeeded in establishing a settlement in the New World. At Trinity Bay they would probably never have been involved in serious conflict with a native population. As early as the last decades of the sixteenth century parts of adjacent Conception Bay were settled by the English, and these nascent lodgments, unlike those such as ill-fated Roanoke on the mainland, never suffered from a hostile native population. If the Norse had settled Trinity Bay in the eleventh century, their offspring might be there yet.

Vinland seems to have been left to its own devices after Erik's visit, having proved too tough a nut for the Norse to crack. However, the Greenlanders continued to make voyages to Labrador and to the western coasts of Baffin Bay and into Davis Strait. In 1266 an expedition was sent from the Eastern Settlements into north Baffin Bay to find out where the Skraelings (Thule Eskimos) who had recently appeared in northwest Greenland were coming from. This expedition appears to have reached Devon or Bylot Island and to have reported that this was good hunting country. By 1300 Norse hunters were wintering at least as far north as Uppernavik, where a rune stone inscribed by them was later found.

Interest in the northwestern regions seems to have burgeoned during this period, perhaps largely because exploitation and explorations of the southwestern (Vinland) regions was denied to the Norse by the presence of the relatively large and militarily effective native population.

A number of archeological finds suggest that the Greenland Norse made use of the Jones Sound district to the north of Devon Island. Beacons, cairns and eiderduck nesting shelters, all of which appear to be non-Eskimoan, have been found in some numbers in this region.

There is another ruin in this area which has not previously been mentioned in the literature dealing with the Greenland Norse. This is a stone tower which was discovered on the southern shore of Cornwallis Island by Lieutenant Sherard Osborn, R. N., during the search for Sir John Franklin in 1850–1851. Osborn describes the ruin as being a conical-shaped building, the apex of which he assumed had fallen in. It was about twenty feet in circumference and the remaining walls stood five feet six inches high. Osborn concluded that it had been constructed by someone with a good knowledge of stone masonry, and illustrated this strange building in his book.* Its similarity to certain Greenland Norse structures, particularly polar bear traps, is at once apparent.

The extent of Norse penetration westward into the North American arctic can only be conjectured, but it may have been considerable. Hudson Strait and Ungava Bay appear to have been known to the Greenlanders and there is no reason to doubt that sooner or later they ventured into Hudson Bay (see Appendix P). They were still active on the Labrador coast (presumably lumbering) as late as 1347, when a Greenland vessel with a crew of eighteen men was blown off course while en route from Markland to Greenland, and made port in Iceland.

Only a few years later, about 1360, it is believed that an expedition from Norway under the command of one Paul Knutsson was sent out to Greenland by royal command to try and bring the erring Greenlanders, who had reputedly fallen into paganism, back to a proper recognition of the Church of Rome. This expedition may also have had another and more important purpose — that of discovering what

---

* *Stray Leaves from an Arctic Journal* (London, 1852).

had happened to the inhabitants of the Western (Godthaab) Settlement, which by 1350 had apparently been abandoned without any indication of where its occupants had gone.

Although there is no documentary evidence from European sources to tell us what happened to the Knutsson expedition, there may be documentation from North America. In 1898 a stone inscribed with runic characters was found enmeshed in the roots of a tree near Kensington, Minnesota. The inscription on the stone translates as follows:

8 Goths [Swedes] and 22 Norwegians on exploration journey from [or *for*] Vinland across West. We had camp by 2 Skerries one day's journey north from this stone. We were and fished one day. After we came home found 10 men red with blood and dead. AVM [ave Maria] save from evil. Have 10 men by the sea to look after our ships 14 day's journey from this island. Year 1362.

This stone — now called the Kensington Stone — has been the center of bitter controversy between scholars ever since it came to light. Some insist that it must be a forgery; but others point out that, considering all the circumstances, it is more difficult to believe it is a forgery than to accept it as authentic.

One of the major reasons why acceptance of it has met such resistance is the location of the find, deep in the heart of the continent. Perhaps this difficulty is subject to a simple resolution.

The place where the stone was left by the Norse need not have been the place where it was found. It could have been discovered by Indians and taken away by them. Considered as a cult object, it could have remained in their hands for years or even for generations, and it may have been carried a considerable distance from its original site.

At least one parallel case is known, — that of an "inscribed stone" which was obtained by Pierre de La Verendrye in what is now North Dakota in 1738. This stone, which seems to have been used by Indians as a cult object, was taken by La Verendrye to Montreal and later sent to France, where it eventually disappeared. It is said to have been covered with writing which looked Tataric. Since Tataric and Runic alphabets bear a similarity to one another, this stone too may conceivably have been inscribed with runes.

If we admit the possibility that the Kensington Stone might have

The sanguinary nature which had enabled the Vikings to overrun so much of Europe was their prime undoing in the western continent. Instead of giving them suzerainty over Newfoundland and Labrador, the ready hand with sword and battle-axe cut them off from the prospects of occupying the magnificent new world they had discovered. Nevertheless their westward voyaging was not a sterile and bootless episode in history, as some historians would have us believe.

It was not a dead-end venture leading nowhere and to nothing. Although the Norse failed to settle the New World, they pioneered and established the sea routes to the west which were followed by later waves of European venturers in the fifteenth century.

The belief that all knowledge of the Norse routes was lost with the decay of the Greenland colonies is naïve in the extreme. Sea lore does not pass away with the death of a single society but is perpetuated and handed on through the members of that amorphous guild to which all seamen, of whatever race, automatically belong. There can be no doubt that the Bristol, Basque, Portuguese and north European merchants, fishermen, whalers and pirates who are known to have frequented both Icelandic and Greenlandic waters from at least as early as the beginning of the fifteenth century came to share some of the knowledge of the western waters which had been amassed by the Northmen. There can be equally little doubt that they made use of, and transmitted, this knowledge to others after the Greenlandic society had virtually disappeared.

Basque whalers are believed to have been fishing in the Labrador Sea as early as 1420 and it is inconceivable that they would not have heard about and visited Helluland and Markland and then coasted south to discover — if they were not actually told of its existence — the fabulous whaling grounds of the Strait of Belle Isle. It is equally inconceivable that British and French cod fishermen, as well as their Basque counterparts, had not found their way to the Vinland region — the Land of Baccaloas, or codfish — and discovered the Grand Banks many years, if not decades, before the first "official" discovery of this region was recorded by John Cabot.

There is good reason to believe that Columbus, who was a well-informed member of the maritime fraternity, knew about the old Norse sea routes into the northwest. About the year 1477 he visited Iceland, perhaps in order to obtain detailed first-hand information. It is true that he had no desire to sail to the Land of Baccaloas, but he did wish to circumvent it to the south, and for this reason he would have been anxious to know as much as possible about its shape, position and extent.

All through the fifteenth century fleets of European ships fished cod in Icelandic waters, and their crews had much intercourse with the Icelanders. The Iceland colony itself might very well have starved and disappeared during this fiercely adverse climatic period had it not been supported by supplies, obtained in exchange for dried cod, from English ships. The skippers of these ships could hardly have avoided hearing reports of the lands and routes toward the west. The information which in 1570 enabled Sigurd Stefansson to construct his amazingly accurate chart of the early Norse discoveries in Newfoundland and Labrador would surely have been available in some form or another to seamen visiting Iceland one hundred or one hundred and fifty years before his time.

Documents may not exist to prove the point, for merchant seamen are seldom thoughtful enough to bequeath convenient documents for the edification of future historians; but common sense and even a peripheral understanding of the sea and seamen should lead us to recognize the fact that the routes pioneered and developed by the Norse were never wholly abandoned and never lost to view. Even before the Greenland Norse colonies vanished, other men in other ships were already sailing those ancient sea routes, and they continued to sail them until eventually they were followed by the officially acceptable discoverers whose names now stand in the history books, and to whom alone accrues the credit which is due to many nameless and forgotten seamen.

The Norse westward ventures during the decade at the turn of the millennium cannot be written off as isolated and unimportant incidents out of the mainstream of North American history. It was the voyagers of those times who traced the track over the pathless western ocean — the track which became a great sea highway over which other men of Europe later sailed to seize and occupy a continent.

pARt I

/\.\/\.\

descRiptive

APPENDIX A

∧.∨.∧

the sources

AN INTRODUCTION TO THE ANCIENT SCANDINAVIAN DOCUMENTS
WHICH TELL THE TALE OF THE WESTWARD VENTURING

NATURE OF THE SOURCES

The sources dealing with the Norse voyages to the west fall into three general categories. Least important of these are the fragmentary references and brief notices which are found scattered through the surviving body of Icelandic literature.* These serve to confirm what we are told in the major sources as well as to extend our knowledge of the individuals concerned, and in some cases they help to clarify obscure points.

The second category includes the minor sources, foremost of which are two primitive Icelandic histories, the Islendingabok, which is a brief résumé of the early Scandinavian history of Iceland; and the Landnamabok, which is a detailed genealogy of the more important early settlers and their families, enlivened with succinct accounts of many trivial and some major events in the history of the island. The original version of the Islendingabok, which is no longer extant, was written in the early twelfth century by Ari Thorgilsson. Compilation of the Landnamabok probably began at about the same time, and in its original form it may have been partly the work of the same author. Several recensions† of it exist although the original version has been lost.

The major sources consist of a number of vellums, most of which

---

* These are identified as they are referred to in our text.
† Revisions of the original text.

seem to have had their genesis in a single oral saga, or perhaps in two very similar and closely related oral sagas.

THE SAGAS

There are many types of sagas, including mythological tales, pure romances, family chronicles, highly embellished lives of kings, and sober factual accounts of historical events. The saga, or sagas, with which we are concerned belong in the last group. They were not written as deliberate history in the sense that the Islendingabok was, yet they are historical compositions in the proper sense of the word since they record the deeds of individuals; and these deeds are what, in the long run, comprise the true histories of nations and of peoples.

The original oral accounts which detailed the history of the western voyages have long since vanished into silence. It may be that there were two such parent sagas, but since this is a question which can probably never be resolved, I have chosen to refer to the original progenitor, or progenitors, in the singular as the Old Erik Saga. I do not know when this saga was composed. It may be that a skald living at the time of the great western voyages pulled together bits and pieces of previous saga accounts leading up to the major adventures and unified them into one sequential tale. In any event it seems certain from internal evidence — not least of which is the strong feeling that the skald personally participated in the latter events of which he sang — that the Old Erik Saga must have come into existence around the beginning of the eleventh century.

Most of our knowledge of the Old Erik Saga is contained in four vellum documents,* three of which are closely related and seem to stem from a common written as well as a common oral ancestor. I refer to these three throughout the text as the Short Saga, the Erik the Red Saga, and Thorfinn Karlsefni Saga or Karlsefni Saga.

The Short Saga is a fragment of a transcript of what may have been one of the earliest written versions of the Old Erik Saga and which could date to as early as the beginning of the twelfth century. Unfortunately this fragment covers only the first part of the tale, beginning with the genealogy of Erik the Red and cutting off abruptly at the termination of Bjarni Herjolfsson's voyage. This document was

---

* Of which a number of slightly variant paper copies also exist.

found in a huge compendium of ancient Icelandic literature which was transcribed into a single massive vellum volume, now known as the Flateyjarbok, at the instance of Jon Hakonarsson during the last half of the fourteenth century.

The Thorfinn Karlsefni Saga was found in a smaller, though similar, compendium known as the Hauksbok. This collection was compiled by, or at the orders of, Hauk Erlandsson, who was a lineal descendant of Thorfinn Karlsefni, during the first half of the fourteenth century. Someone — either Hauk or his hired scribes — has apparently polished this version into finer literary form, but its contents still remain essentially the same as those of its two brethren. Internal evidence makes it clear, however, that it is copied from a later transcript than the one which fathered the Short Saga fragment.

The closely related Erik the Red Saga is contained in yet another compendium, a vellum codex numbered 577 in the Arna-Magnean Collection in Copenhagen. It is somewhat cruder and rougher in style than the Karlsefni version. Although the extant copy was evidently transcribed (by an indifferent hand) near the end of the fourteenth century, it nevertheless appears to have originated from a slightly earlier transcript than did the Karlsefni Saga. Nevertheless both of these versions appear to have shared a parent transcript of a later generation than that which was the basis for the Short Saga fragment. They are very similar in all but minor details, and they have the same shortcomings. They share a major hiatus in that they fail to record Bjarni Herjolfsson's voyage and, in effect, Leif Eriksson's as well.

Our fourth source, which I refer to as the Greenlanders Story, is a special case. Although the surviving copy of it also forms part of the Flateyjarbok collection, it was not associated with the Short Saga in the Flateyjarbok and apparently bears no relationship to it. Neither does it appear to be a lineal descendant of a single ancient oral saga, as do the other three transcripts. Instead it is apparently a compendium in its own right, a late thirteenth- or early fourteenth-century *reconstruction* of the western voyages based on, and including some substantial sections of material from a variety of sources. Its author seems to have put together the material at his disposal and, finding it inadequate, to have himself supplied the missing links in order to produce a logical sequence. In so doing he was only anticipating what several hundred scholars have attempted to do since his time.

We do not know what his sources were. He may have drawn some elements from the vellum ancestor of the Short Saga, although he was evidently not familiar with the Erik the Red Saga and the Karlsefni sagas or with their immediate common ancestor. However, he did have access to information which is not to be found in the Erik the Red and the Karlsefni sagas. His account of Leif Eriksson's expedition, contrived as it certainly is in its preliminary parts, is the only real account of that famous voyage to survive into our times. Thanks to the Greenlanders Story we are able to fill in the second of the two major lacunae in the Erik the Red and the Karlsefni sagas, the first being the story of Bjarni Herjolfsson, which is supplied by the Short Saga.

The portion of the Greenlanders Story which deals with Leif contains the one major sequence which seems to be derived more or less in toto from an ancient source. For the rest the author seems to have had only fragments, vague reports and possibly some badly corrupted remnants of oral tradition to draw upon. His account of the post-Leif voyages is sequentially impossible — nevertheless it contains a good many morsels of valuable information which are not to be found in the other sources. Almost invariably these snippets throw special light upon the part played by the Greenlanders in the western voyages, and this is particularly helpful to us since we suspect that in the Erik the Red and the Karlsefni sagas a good part of the original references to the Greenlanders may have been edited out.

These three versions all seem to suffer from bias; only the Short Saga appears to be reasonably free from it. I have examined the evidence supporting this conclusion at some length in Appendix M and have concluded that the Greenlanders Story reflects the Greenlanders' point of view in general and that of Leif Eriksson's descendants and supporters in particular; while the Erik the Red and the Karlsefni sagas do the same partisan service for the Icelanders in general, and for Thornfinn Karlsefni in particular. The Greenlanders Story may actually have been the work of a Greenlander (in which case it would be one of the very few Greenlandic works to have survived the disappearance of the Greenland settlements) as opposed to the Erik the Red and the Karlsefni sagas, which were transcribed by Icelandic scribes for Icelandic owners. It is not beyond the realm of possibility that the Icelanders of the fourteenth century may even have taken liberties with the original texts to the extent of deliberately omitting the section of the Old Erik Saga which dealt with the voyages of Bjarni and Leif.

Although the problems of coordinating the two conflicting versions are many, they can be resolved. When this has been done we find that we have a surprisingly complete account of all the western voyages from Erik the Red's first visit to Greenland, to the final return of Freydis Eriksdottir from the doomed Vinland colonizing venture.

AUTHENTICITY OF THE SAGAS

The accuracy and reliability of the saga material has been closely scrutinized by competent scholars, and they are generally in agreement that these old documents may be relied upon as being the authentic stuff of history, although errors in detail certainly do occur. Some moderns find it hard to believe that an account which originated nearly a thousand years ago could have survived into our time as anything more than a vague and much corrupted myth; but when we examine how the saga tales survived we find it easier to accept their essential authenticity.

The transcripts of the saga with which we are concerned were fixed in their existing physical form not more than three or four centuries after the events which they record took place. Consequently they have been subject to change and alteration during less than half of their total history. The active transmission period itself falls into two parts. From the date of the Old Erik Saga's composition, which was contemporary with the events described, it was preserved by professional saga tellers and transmitted orally by them for a period which would not have been much in excess of a hundred years before being committed to parchment. During this century there was, in effect, no literacy in Greenland and very little in Iceland; and the phenomenal skill of the saga men in preserving and transmitting the oral traditions and history of their people would still have been in a highly developed state. Many studies have been made of the ability of illiterate peoples to transmit oral history accurately over long periods of time, and these show that the chances of any significant corruption taking place in a century or less are very small. A hundred years could have been bridged by only two or three generations of saga men, so that there need not have been more than two or three oral transmissions of it before it was first written down on vellum.

Unlike modern printed books, ancient vellum manuscripts tended to be long lived. They were originally produced by clerks (clerics: priests) of the Church, and each hand-written transcript required a great deal of work and was most expensive to make. Consequently it was treated as a treasure in its own right, quite apart from the enormous value which the learned men of the times put upon its contents. It was usually preserved in carefully guarded church archives although in Iceland, where literacy soon became widespread among the wealthy class, private ownership of vellums became fairly common. Such family-owned parchments were thought of as priceless heirlooms and were treated accordingly.

It is probable that no more than three generations of written transcripts intervened between the writing of the first vellum version of the Old Erik Saga and the production of those vellum recensions which survive into our times. In the case of the Short Saga fragment there may have been only a single intervening transcript generation.

When we consider these matters it should not surprise us to find that the sagas which recount the Norse western voyages are of a very high standard of accuracy.

APPENDIX B

/\.\/\.\/\.\/\

the ancient weather

CLIMATIC CONDITIONS IN THE NORTH ATLANTIC REGION
DURING THE PERIOD OF THE NORSE VOYAGES.

Prior to 3000 B.C. the whole of the region in which we are interested was under the influence of a great warming trend known as the period of Climatic Optimum. This was a time of warm, moist weather which saw the treeline advancing far to the north out over the now treeless tundra barrens of the Arctic, and which probably saw the summer disappearance of ice from the entire surface of the Arctic Ocean. From about 3000 B.C. until early in the Christian era there was a continuous overall deterioration in the weather, and it appears that about 500 B.C. there was a sudden sharp worsening of conditions which must have been almost catastrophic.

By the time Pytheas sailed north in 330 B.C. the arctic ice pack extended considerably farther south than it does today; thus there would have been nothing odd about his reported encounter with the polar pack only a day's sail north of Iceland. Climatic conditions continued to be very bad until the fifth century A.D., with major cyclonic disturbances and cold, wet weather which would have hindered distant deep-sea voyaging during these centuries. However, during the fifth century the long-term adverse variation seems to have ended and an upswing toward a better climate began. By the beginning of the ninth century the improvement had become so marked that there was again little drift ice in the northern seas. Apart from being much warmer, the climate was also drier; there were fewer cyclonic storms, and there was a shrinkage of glaciers in Iceland and Greenland and on the Canadian Arctic Islands.

Once again there may have been little permanent ice in the Arctic Ocean; a condition which would have permitted exploratory (or accidental) voyages to proceed far to the north and which may have given rise to the persistent belief of later centuries in an ice-free Arctic Ocean which could be crossed en route to Cathay and the East. This belief motivated many arctic explorers, including Henry Hudson, and was not finally laid to rest until the failure of the Hayes Expedition in 1861.

This favorable long-term variation continued to produce an overall improvement in the northern climate until an optimum was reached at about the beginning of the eleventh century. This period has been named the Little Climatic Optimum and it lasted until the early thirteenth century.

Some of the characteristics of this period were described by the English meteorologists H. H. Lamb at the UNESCO Symposium on Climate Change held in Rome in 1961:

> The arctic pack ice had melted so far back that the appearance of drift ice in waters near Iceland and Greenland south of 70 degrees north latitude was rare in the 800's and 900's A.D. and apparently unknown between 1020 and 1200 when a rapid increase in frequency began. . . . the annual mean temperatures [in southern Greenland] must have been 2 to 4 degrees C. above present values. It seems probable that sea temperatures in the northernmost Atlantic were up by a similar amount.

While an annual mean increase in temperature of only 2 to 4 degrees does not seem like much, it is more than sufficient to produce a major change in climatic conditions.

The Little Climatic Optimum with its relatively warm, storm-free weather and moderate precipitation was brought to an end by the beginning of an adverse variation which was destined to continue for five centuries and which brought about a severe deterioration in the north Atlantic climate. This deterioration was most pronounced between the mid-thirteenth and mid-fifteenth centuries. During this period the sea-water temperatures fell as much as 3 degrees C. below those of the Little Climatic Optimum. Thereafter, until about the mid-seventeenth century, there was a slight warming followed by another severe variation characterized by extremely cold winters, fierce cyclonic storms and heavy ice conditions which lasted until near the middle of the nineteenth century. Since then the north Atlantic region had been experiencing another warming trend.

It must be remembered that we have mentioned only the variations, or major cycles. But during the entire period under discussion there were innumerable short-term fluctuations, some of which climatologists have been able to pinpoint. For instance it is believed that there was a brief period around A.D. 1000 when stormy conditions prevailed. It is interesting to note that just prior to 1000 the sagas record a period during which there were such heavy gales that many voyages undertaken during those times came to grief.

Although the existence of the Little Climatic Optimum has been established, and the general conditions which it brought about are known, it is not so easy to describe in detail what the climate was actually like in Greenland and northeastern Canada during this period. In his book *Climate Through the Ages* (London, 1949), C. E. Brooks has drawn together most of the available information on Greenland's climate during the period of the Norse occupancy. In his summing up he says:

When the country was colonized in the tenth century its climate was much more favourable than at present. . . . There was less ice than at present in the East Greenland Current and it is even possible that at first there was no ice at all: Baffin Bay seems to have been largely free of ice. . . . Toward the close of the twelfth century deterioration again set in and the ice conditions rapidly became very bad. The summer thaw became shorter and shorter and, about A.D. 1400, the ground became permanently frozen.

The archeological work of Dr. Paul Norlund in Greenland has produced some rather macabre evidence which demonstrates that the climate did deteriorate — in a very marked manner. Norlund excavated the Norse graveyard at Herjolfsness in 1921. At that time the ground of the graveyard thawed only to a depth of a few inches during the summer. But Norlund's work showed that the level of the permafrost — ground which never thaws throughout the year — must have been steadily rising for a century or more before the Herjolfsness graveyard ceased to be used. He found the earliest coffins at a considerable depth, while the later ones were laid in increasingly shallow graves. The clothes found in many of the deep burials had been so well preserved by permafrost that they could almost have been put back into use. The fact that these graves had not been dug in permafrost in the first place was proved by the presence in the coffins of plant roots which could not have penetrated into frozen soil.

Norlund's work proved conclusively that the South Greenland climate must have started to get colder after about 1200, and that the ground which at the time of the first burials could not have been frozen at all during the summer, gradually became permanently frozen to within a few inches of the surface.

Pollen research carried out by Knud Jessen in the vicinity of Gardar has revealed that certain species of small trees which became rare in Greenland in the later period of the Norse occupancy were much more abundant during the early period. Bog analysis in the Western Settlement by Dr. Johs. Iverson has revealed that there was an abrupt change in the character of the vegetation toward the end of the occupancy of that settlement (about 1325) consistent with what would have been expected from a period of colder weather. A zoologist, Dr. Degerbol, who examined extensive middens of animal bones at the Western Settlement, found the skeletal remains of a number of species of sea mammals, including the ca'ing whale and the white-beaked dolphin, whose range is restricted to much warmer waters than those which are presently to be found off Greenland. Geographers have shown that the outer edges of the Greenland Ice Cap have advanced closer to the coast than they were in the early period of the Norse occupancy, and archeologists have confirmed that a number of the ancient Norse farm-sites would not have been habitable if the glacial ice conditions of modern times had prevailed at the period when they were settled.

The sagas themselves make no mention of ice as a navigation hazard until late in the thirteenth century, after which there are frequent references to pack ice being encountered in northern waters. It has been argued that the voyage of Thorgisl Orrabeinsfostri, which took place about 997, came to grief because of pack ice encountered on the east Greenland coast. However, a careful reading of the saga makes it plain that this was not the case.*

The detailed changes in climate in Labrador and Newfoundland are not so well documented because there has been little field work done in these regions as yet. But there is clear evidence that forest

* See Chapter 13.

growth in southern Labrador, and in all regions of Newfoundland, has changed dramatically both in kind and in quantity over the past eight centuries. Pollen analysis from Labrador bogs and from points on the periphery of the region reveal that during the Little Climatic Optimum the range of many species of trees extended well to the north of their present limits. Hardwoods such as oak, which in eastern Canada are now largely restricted to southern Ontario, were found in relative abundance north to the Gulf of St. Lawrence in New Brunswick and Nova Scotia. The limit of several coniferous species entended a hundred to several hundred miles farther north than it does at present. The northern range of hemlock, for example, was about two hundred miles to the north of its present limits.

Studies of the treeline in Ungava and in other parts of the Canadian eastern Arctic show marked evidence of a retreat which has allowed the open tundra to push southward during the last few centuries by more than a hundred miles in many places.

Historical records of Newfoundland climatic conditions may be properly said to have begun with the saga accounts of the Norse voyages to the west. From these it appears that the Newfoundland climate at about 1000 A.D. was more temperate than it is now, which is in accord with the Greenland findings. Records from the early colonial period show that the climate then was still considerably better than now. A letter from John Guy, who established a settlement in Conception Bay in 1610, says in part: "the doubt that have been made of the extremity of the winter season in these parts of Newfoundland are found by our experience causless; and that not only may men safely inhabit here without the need of stove, but navigation may be made to and fro from England to these parts at any time of the year."

Captain Winne, or Wyn, writing in 1622, says: "The winter in Newfoundland is short and tolerable, continuing only in January, February and part of March . . . neither was it so cold here the last winter as in England the year before; I remember but three several days of hard weather indeed, and they not extreme neither; for I have known greater frosts and far greater snows in our own country [England]."

Examples of places which at the present time have climates comparable to those of Greenland and Newfoundland in the tenth century are difficult to choose, because the local climate of any area is conditioned by too many specific influences such as the duration of daylight, the effect of prevailing winds, relation of exposed sea coasts to interior zones, and the effect of ocean currents. However, we can probably obtain a workable mental image of what weather conditions were like in southwest Greenland in 1000 A.D. if we think of it as having had a climate rather similar to that of the present-day Bergen coastal districts of Norway, but with a lighter rainfall and snowfall; while the climate of Newfoundland in the tenth century was probably much like that of west coastal Scotland, although with a greater amount of summer sunshine.

The intervening oceanic waters were much warmer than now, and the incidence of drift ice much reduced. In fact drift ice probably consisted of no more than seasonal fiord and channel ice formed in the high Arctic each winter, and more or less completely melted before summer was very old. The polar vortex of air circulation was apparently much reduced from its present size, and there were fewer big storms as a result, so that there would have been a higher incidence of clear weather and of the good visibility which was so important to Norse navigation.

APPENDIX C

(.V.·.V.·.)

ancient sea levels

HARBOR SEA LEVELS AND COASTLINES, IN NORSE TIMES, AS THESE
RELATE TO THE WESTWARD VOYAGES

The question of whether there has been any important change in
sea levels between the tenth century and the present has loomed large
in many commentaries dealing with the saga voyages. A number of
authors who have been unable to locate suitable harbors for the Norse
explorers in the areas they believed to be identifiable with Vinland
and Straumfiord have explained this difficulty by assuming that the
sea level has changed so radically that the harbors no longer exist.

Variations in apparent sea level are due to one of two factors, or
to a combination of both. The land itself may have been rising or
sinking, or the amount of free water in the oceans may have been
changing due to the enlargement or shrinkage of great areas of glacial
ice. Since the end of the last major glaciation and the retreat and disappearance of most of the continental glaciers, there has been little
change in the volume of free water in the oceans, but there have been
major changes in the level of some of those lands which were once
covered by glacial ice.

Under the weight of the vast overburden of ice most of the glaciated lands were depressed, or "sank," well below their preglacial
levels. When the ice burden was removed, these lands began to rebound. The rebound process was, and is, an extremely complex one
that is still taking place. The amount of rebound which has so far
occurred varies from several hundred feet in some parts of the central arctic regions, to as little as a foot or two in areas along the southern fringe of the once glaciated region. Furthermore, the amount of

rebound varies according to the landforms, so that some mountainous areas which were not so thickly covered by the ice show less rebound than do some low, plains areas. In other cases this situation is reversed. The *rate* of rebound also fluctuates without apparent rhyme or reason. The land appears to lift in stages and at erratic intervals. Relatively sudden uplifts of from several to as much as a hundred feet appear to have taken place followed by long periods when there was little or no rebound.

Because there are so many factors involved, and because the rate and degree of uplift is never constant even in one area, let alone between different areas, it is impossible to do as some authors have done and postulate a standard rate of change in sea level over many hundreds, or even thousands of years. Tectonic experts have concluded that while there was some rebound on the northeastern seaboard of the United States and in Nova Scotia and New Brunswick, much of this was offset by the eustatic effect of the increase in the volume of free water following upon the melt of the major glaciers; thus they conclude that *there has been no significant change in sea levels in these regions during the past thousand years.*

The coasts of Newfoundland show a mild degree of rebound during the past millennium, but there is no agreement among the experts as to how much this amounts to. One fact is indisputable; the emergence of the Newfoundland coast has been highly erratic — a series of upward jerks followed by long pauses.

To complicate matters there is evidence that "tipping" of parts of Newfoundland has occurred in conjunction with the general rebound, so that some areas have actually been depressed slightly, bringing about a local *rise* in sea level. This effect is particularly noticeable in the Trinity and Conception Bay regions, where there is evidence that postglacial drowning has taken place. On the whole, however, it is thought that sea levels in this part of Newfoundland have undergone no important change during the past thousand years.

The Great Northern Peninsula shows evidence of a very strong degree of emergence. In the region of Hare Bay the land has lifted as much as two hundred feet, but most of this rebound evidently took place soon after the disappearance of the ice overburden and there is no evidence that there has been much change during the last millennium. Geologists have not as yet been able to obtain much exact data about the changes which have taken place in this region since

Norse times, but there is another source from which we can obtain a comparison between sea levels then and now.

The examination of a number of Dorset sites which are known to have been occupied prior to A.D. 1000, and probably not much earlier than 400 B.C., demonstrates that there cannot have been any very marked change in sea levels during the past two thousand years along the coasts of the great Northern Peninsula.

A number of these sites, including Englee on the east coast and Parsons Pond on the west coast, lie between ten and twenty feet above present high-tide levels. They are often on exposed and open coasts and are therefore subject to the effects of abnormal storm seas. In the case of one of the Englee sites, houses were built and occupied at a height of only seven feet above present spring high-tide levels on a shelving beach wide open to the eastward.

These sites could not have been occupied if the sea level at the time of occupancy had been much above present levels. Most other Dorset sites which have been examined, including the Port au Choix site, also suggest by their location and orientation that when they were established and occupied the sea levels could not have been notably higher than they are at present.

On the other hand there is evidence, both from folk sources and from finds of French artifacts on beaches, that there *has* been an uplift of from one to two feet in the St. Anthony-Quirpon region during the past two hundred years. But it appears that this has been the result of a relatively abrupt local "jump" and there are no grounds for assuming that this uplift ought to be interpreted as meaning that the rebound has been taking place at the steady rate of a foot every century since A.D. 1000.

Although the data are certainly incomplete, it seems safe to conclude that any sea-level changes which may have taken place along those portions of the Newfoundland coast visited by the Northmen are not significant in terms of the harbors and havens which the Norse may have used, and which still exist into our times.

APPENDIX D

.∧.∨.∧.

nORSE GEOGRAPhICAL CONCEPTS

In order to make sense out of the surviving fragments of the history of the Norse voyages to the west, we must be able to visualize the northwestern regions as the Norse saw them.

Our present concept of those regions has developed through many centuries of exploration culminating in a century or more of increasingly sophisticated scientific techniques which have given us what we believe to be a correct idea of the shape and position of the northern lands and seas. It should be obvious that our ideas of how this part of the world looks, as we have described it on charts and maps and globes, would be totally foreign to an eleventh-century Norseman; but it is surprising how many authors, in their attempts to reconstruct the Norse voyages, have persisted in viewing the ancient world through modern eyes.

In Part I of this appendix I present a picture of the northern regions as I believe the Norse saw them. In Part II, I examine the evidence which substantiates the reconstruction.

I: HOW THE NORSE SAW THEIR WORLD: A RECONSTRUCTION OF
HOW THE ATLANTIC WORLD LOOKED TO THE NORSE VOYAGERS.

To begin with, the Norse never did envisage Greenland as an island, nor even as the separate geographical entity which we know it to be. This should not make us feel superior, since it was not until the beginning of the twentieth century that we were able to establish the fact that Greenland really was an island.

Neither did the Norse think of Greenland or of the more westerly countries adjacent to it as huge land masses. Their contact with all the western lands was peripheral in the strict meaning of the word.

Godthaab fiords comprised the inhabited region, or the Greenland Settlements. But Greenland itself continued northward a long way beyond Godthaab, to swing west again past Melville Bay then south down the west side of Baffin Bay to reach its southwest termination on the shores of Hudson Strait.

The Norse seem to have realized that Hudson Strait was not just another fiord. The tremendous tidal currents which are to be met with at the mouth of the strait — they run as high as seven knots — would have been evidence enough to convince any sea-going people that some huge body of water must lie to the westward. The Norse evidently concluded that this unknown sea must be Mare Oceanum and that Hudson Strait was ginungagap — a sound through which the Western Ocean communicated with the Outer Ocean.

South of this ginungagap, which made a natural boundary for southwest Greenland, lay a different country which included Helluland, Markland and Vinland. During the sixteenth century reports evidently reached Iceland that Newfoundland (Vinland to the Norse) was separated from America by a great strait (the Cabot Strait). Speculation then arose as to the possibility that this might be another ginungagap — but this all happened long after the period with which we are concerned.

The northern and northeastern Newfoundland regions seem to have been as far as Norse practical knowledge of the western lands extended. Icelandic theorists supposed that the Vinland coast continued south, then east, until eventually it linked up with the southwest coast of Africa, thus completing the enclosure of the Western Ocean from the south.

To sum up, the Norse conception of Greenland at about the end of the tenth century was of a narrow band of coastal lands fronting on the Western Ocean, and running from some indeterminate point well north of Iceland south, then north, then west, then south again down the east Baffin Island coast. This was the Norse Greenland; and this is how we must think of it if we are to understand the story of their western voyages.

We must also understand the Norse topographical nomenclature, which was largely based on whether or not a certain area was habitable. Thus the whole of Greenland, in their view, consisted of two primary divisions: the habitable parts, which they called bygdir, and the uninhabitable parts, called obygdir (ubygdir).

The Greenland bygdir eventually occupied the stretch of coast from just north of Cape Farewell to the Godthaab Bight. In later years this region was heavily populated at its two extremities. These were then known respectively as the Eastern Settlement and the Western Settlement (Ostri Bygd and Vestri Bygd). However, shortly before about 1000 Godthaab Bight seems not to have been settled at all although a Vestri Bygd did exist at that time. From evidence found in the Floamanna Saga account of the voyage of Thorgisl Orrabeinsfostri about 997, it is apparent that the name Vestri Bygd then belonged to the settlement on the group of fiords which make up the Ivitgut Bight and which lie due west of the Eastern Settlement and adjacent to it. As colonization pushed on to the north and west from Ivitgut, the name Vestri Bygd continued in use but came to include the Godthaab Bight. Eventually it seems to have referred exclusively to the Godthaab region, and the old Ivitgut settlement became known as the Mid Bygd, or Middle Settlement.

We learn from the Erik the Red and the Karlsefni sagas that when Thorstein Eriksson married Gudrid, he went to take up residence on a farm at Lysufiord in the Western Settlement. Lysufiord was in the Godthaab Bight, and it looks as if this was the time when settlement of that region began, and as if Thorstein was one of the early settlers there. This would have been about the year 1000.

All the rest of Greenland consisted of obygdir; but the obygdir were themselves subdivided. There were deserts in the obygdir by which the Norse meant areas that were of no use to them for hunting, fuel-gathering, farming or any other purpose. There were also jokuls, which usually denoted glaciers but which also described snow-covered or ice-covered mountains. The obygdir also included the best hunting regions known to the Norse.

Greenland had three obygdir, all of them oriented from the settled area. The Ostri Obygd (eastern wilderness) encompassed most if not all of the east Greenland coast. The Nord Obygd (northern wilderness) extended northward from the settlements on the west Greenland coast at least as far as Uppernavik and may have come to include certain regions at the foot of Baffin Bay on Jones Sound and Ellesmere Island. The Vestri Obygd (western wilderness) originally seems to have meant only the coast of the Cumberland Peninsula, but the name may eventually have referred to most of the east Baffin Island coast.

It is important to note that few of the topographical names and geographical divisions were fixed in their final form at the time they were first bestowed. The scope and meaning of these names changed with the centuries. Some were replaced by other names, and some were lost. The Vestri Obygd is a particular case in point. Initially it seems to have been well known and to have served as a major sea-mammal hunting ground for the Greenland Norse; but as the centuries passed, knowledge of it began to dim.

Consequent upon the deterioration of climatic conditions which began early in the thirteenth century, the incidence of pack ice in Baffin Bay and Davis Strait increased to the point where direct voyages between Greenland and Baffin Island become extremely hazardous. Eventually the Baffin Pack dominated Davis Strait for much of the summer season, as it did again during the eighteenth and the nineteenth centuries. At about the same period that drift ice was increasing, the cooling conditions would have begun to bring the sea-mammals southward down the west coast of Greenland and so into closer proximity to the Norse settlements. For these dual reasons the summer hunting parties gradually began to abandon the Baffin Island coasts and to conduct their sealing and whaling on the coasts lying northward of the settlements — in the Nord Obygd.

After the early thirteenth century there are no further references to the Vestri Obygd. The lands lying due west of central Greenland, across Davis Strait, begin to take on a vague and even somewhat mythical character as direct knowledge of them faded. But they were never quite forgotten, and to the end of the occupation of Greenland by the Norse colonists, they were apparently considered to be an integral part of Greenland, even though they came to be known by such names as Furdustrandir and Greater Helluland.*

The loss of the name Vestri Obygd had important historical repercussions. Scribes engaged in transcribing the Icelandic records after the thirteenth century were sometimes confused by references in ancient manuscripts to a "Vestri Obygd" about which they themselves evidently had no knowledge. There seem to have been a number of occasions when these scribes undertook to correct what they presumably thought was a clerical error by deleting the letter "O" (or "U") thus changing the name to Vestri Bygd, thereby initiating a number of confusions which have baffled and misled scholars ever since.

---

* See Appendix P.

II: THE EVIDENCE UPON WHICH THE RECONSTRUCTION IS BASED

The first reference to a land lying west of modern Greenland is found in the account of the first Norse voyage west of Cape Farewell — the voyage of Erik the Red. The reference is tantalizingly brief, but then the whole of the surviving account of Erik's three-year expedition to Greenland can be set up in fifteen or twenty lines of type.

That summer [the first full summer he spent in Greenland] Erik explored the Vestri Obygdir, remaining there a long time and giving many local names there.

This is a succinct statement, but its meaning appears unmistakable. Nevertheless all but two or three of the authors who have commented on Erik's voyage have insisted that the Western Obygdir must, of necessity, be located on the west coast of modern Greenland. They have concluded that it was impossible for Erik to have anticipated his son Leif in reaching North America proper, and they have put forward many arguments to convince us that Erik could not have crossed Davis Strait.

In the first place they say that because what we now call Greenland was completely uninhabited when Erik visited it, it would have been inevitable that he should have referred to its western coast as the Western Obygdir.

In taking this stand they ignore the fact that the saga account of Erik's voyage refers to other localities he visited by names which were not established until after the Norse settled Greenland. Thus the saga says: *Erik passed the first winter at Eriksey near the middle of the Eastern Settlement.* Furthermore, the history of the name Vestri Obygd shows that it was in use after Greenland was fully settled from Cape Farewell north to Godthaab, and after the remainder of the west coast north of Godthaab had been given the general name of Nord Obygd.

It is clear from the saga accounts that Erik spent his first full summer exploring the Vestri Obygdir, from which we know that it must have been a land of some considerable extent. The saga then goes on to say that during his second summer he explored north to Snaefells, which has been satisfactorily identified as the glacier region north of Uppernavik on the west coast of modern Greenland. Thus if we are to accept a west Greenland location for the Vestri Obygdir we must believe that Erik spent two full summers exploring the west coast of Greenland. This is not impossible, but it seems improbable.

One other argument remains to be disposed of. It has to do with the confusion which has arisen because the Greenland Norse named their two major centers of habitation the Eastern Settlement and the Western Settlement. The historians and archeologists who set out during the nineteenth century to find the sites of the Norse settlements, went looking for them on the east and west coasts of present-day Greenland. When they eventually found the Eastern Settlement (Ostri Bygd) on the southwest coast, and the Western Settlement (Vestri Bygd) far to the northwest of that again, they and many who have followed them appear to have suffered from a bad case of disorientation.

One of the results was to convince some authors that when the Icelandic sources said "west" they may just as well have meant "north," and when they said "east" they may as easily have meant "south." From this they have gone on to deduce that when Erik sailed north up the Greenland coast he thought he was sailing west, and therefore the Vestri Obygd was on the west coast of Greenland.

One of the results was to convince some authors that when the Icelandic sources said "west" they may just as well have meant "north," and when they said "east" they may as easily have meant "south." From this they have gone on to deduce that when Erik sailed north up the Greenland coast he thought he was sailing west, and therefore the Vestri Obygd was on the west coast of Greenland.

The truth of the matter is that the original Vestri Bygd really *was* west of the Ostri Bygd. Proof of this is to be found in what we are told in the Floamanna Saga about Thorgisl Orrabeinsfostri's adventures (for the full account see Chapter 13). While Thorgisl was at the Eastern Settlement a polar bear appeared and caused havoc among the sheep of the *two* settlements which in approximately 997 constituted settled Greenland. The men of *both* Eastern and Western settlements got together and put up a bear bounty, which Thorgisl claimed when he had killed the bear. A little later he found some of his runaway slaves in the Western Settlement when he went there to collect the bounty. It is obvious that these two settlements must have been adjacent, and that one polar bear could not have been harrying the flocks at Godthaab and in the Julianehaab region at the same time. Since the Ivitgut settlement was adjacent to the Eastern Settlement, and lay due west of it, we have no hesitation in identifying it as the original Vestri Bygd. Furthermore there is no evidence of any sort to show that the Godthaab Vestri Bygd was in existence until about 1000.

The Ivitgut settlement has always posed something of a puzzle to Greenland historians. Aage Roussel, writing in the *Arctic Encyclopedia,* suggests that it might have been the first Norse refuge in Greenland since it has no church ruins and the farm ruins are small and crude. They show few of the architectural developments which took place over a period of several centuries in both the Godthaab and Julianehaab Bight settlements.

The solution to this problem would seem to be that the Ivitgut area, which was very poor pastoral country compared with the Julianehaab or Godthaab regions, *was* settled at an early date — before Christianity had taken hold — but that it was settled by second-wave immigrants who could not find land in the Julianehaab district. They moved west, perforce, and settled the Ivitgut region. When, at about A.D. 1000, a band of colonists decided to make the long voyage north to settle the Godthaab fiords, they were doubtless joined by many of the Ivitgut settlers. For a while the name Vestri Bygd continued to describe all the settlement sites west of the Eastern Settlement, but in the course of time the name came to identify only the major center of population, which was in the Godthaab region. When that happened, the more or less abandoned Ivigut region became known as the Mid Bygd, or Middle Settlement.

If Erik's Vestri Obygd was not on the west coast of modern Greenland, where could it have been? It could have been, and I believe it could *only* have been, on the west side of Davis Strait.

That it did not include Labrador is established by the saga accounts of the Vinland voyages which show that this was unknown territory until it was glimpsed by Bjarni Herjolfsson in 985, and later explored and named Helluland by other voyagers.

This leaves Baffin Island; but Baffin Island has an eastern coastline almost 1000 miles long and we must narrow the field a little. The most likely location of Erik's Vestri Obygd would seem to have been that portion of Baffin Island which lies closest to Greenland, and this is the Cumberland Peninsula.

This identification is strongly supported by certain passages in the saga accounts of the Vinland voyages, notably the description of the outbound journey of Thorfinn Karlsefni, where it is stated that the Vinland voyagers sailed from the Eastern Settlement to the Vestri Bygd (Obygd) and from there to Bjarney (Bear Island). From Bjarney they sailed south for two days and sighted Helluland (Labrador).

In some of the recensions of the Erik the Red and the Thorfinn Karlsefni sagas, the reading is *Vestri Bygd*. But in at least two versions, one of which is thought to be directly derived from the narrative verse of the ancient oral saga, the reading is *Vestri Obygd*. Thus, according to the *Gronlands Historiske Mindesmaerker,* the line runs: *Sigdlu peir sidan undan landi i obygdir vestri [Sailed they thereupon from land to the western uninhabited country].* A second version reads: *Thereupon they sailed from land to the western uninhabited country.*

There appears to be no acceptable reason why the saga narrator should have bothered to note that Karlsefni sailed from Eriksfiord to the Western Settlement at Ivitgut (or even Godthaab) as part of the sailing directions for the route to Vinland. Since no other sailing instructions are given for the voyage between Eriksfiord and Bjarney Island, I deduce that this must have been a well-established route. I also note that *all* the sources state that Karlsefni sailed "from land" to reach the Vestri Bygd (Obygd), and this describes an open-water passage, not a coasting voyage, which a journey to either Ivitgut or Godthaab would have been.

If the reading of Vestri Bygd is accepted it then becomes necessary to place Bjarney Island somewhere on the west coast of Greenland but at a point from which one can reach Helluland by sailing south for two doegr, or about 240 nautical miles. There is actually no point from which one can do this; but some authors, assuming that the Vestri Bygd meant the Godthaab fiords, have concluded that Bjarney must have been Disco Island, which lies 700 miles *north* of Eriksfiord. A voyage to Disco seems like an extraordinary side jaunt (a total of 1400 miles) in the wrong direction for an expedition which was sailing, as Karlsefni was, to a place lying a long way *south* of Eriksfiord.

The identification of Bjarney with Disco, or with any other point on the west Greenland coast, poses an insurmountable problem of another kind. The saga says that Karlsefni sailed *south* from Bjarney for two doegr (240 nautical miles) and reached Helluland. Two doegr in the southern airt from any point between Cape Desolation and Disco would have taken Karlsefni into the middle of Davis Strait or the Labrador Sea — and nowhere else.

If, however, the correct reading is Vestri Obygd, there is no problem. Karlsefni would have crossed Davis Strait presumably at its narrowest point, which lies between Cape Burnhill in Greenland and Cape Dyer on the Cumberland Peninsula. Having arrived in the Vestri Obygd he would then have coasted south to Bjarney, which (as we shall show later) was probably Leopold Island, off Cape Mercy. From there he had only to sail for two doegr almost due south in order to reach Helluland — the northern portion of Labrador.

It is significant that when Karlsefni's expedition left Eriksfiord it was accompanied by a man named Thorhall the Hunter. The sagas say that Thorhall had been with Erik the Red for a long time, serving as his hunter during the summer and as his farm overseer in winter. It is specifically stated that Thorhall had an extensive knowledge of the obygdir. The Erik the Red Saga states that he went on the Karlsefni expedition because of this knowledge, from which we conclude that he shipped as a pilot. A knowledge on Thorhall's part of the Nord Obygdir would have been of no particular value to the expedition; but if he had possessed a knowledge of the Vestri Obygdir his presence would have been of great value. Thorhall probably did have this knowledge, having doubtless accompanied Erik on his first voyage to Greenland when, as the sagas tell us, Erik spent a summer exploring the Vestri Obygdir and presumably finding and "bestowing a name" on Bjarney.

There are a number of independent references in other sources to lands lying west of Greenland which are to be identified with Baffin Island, or the Vestri Obygdir.

In the *Historia Norwegiae,* written in the second half of the thirteenth century, we find this statement: "On the other side of the Greenlanders, to the northwest, hunters have encountered a dwarf-sized people whom they call Skraelings.

The Cumberland Peninsula lies northwest from the settled parts of Greenland, and it is known to have been occupied by Thule culture Eskimos as early as the twelfth century.

In the archives of the Royal Danish Library in Copenhagen there is a manuscript known as AM 770c. It is a copy of an ancient Icelandic geography dating to the early fourteenth century. In part it reads:

On the west side of the great ocean [the Western Ocean] which reaches from Spain and which . . . spreads among the lands, are named in a northward direction first Vinland the Good; next Markland is named still to the northward; then are obygdir where the Skraelings live; then there are still obygdir as far as Greenland; and then there are two bygds, the West Bygd and the East Bygd. Beyond that there are hafsbotnar [sea-bottom-bays], jokuls and obygdir which turn toward Halgoland.

In this account we can easily trace the westward lands north from Vinland to Skraeling Land, which was a name applied to Helluland in the twelfth century, then "still obygdir as far as Greenland," which would mean inhabited Greenland and include the Vestri Bygd and the Ostri Bygd. The concluding section of the account deals with the Eastern Obygdir and the land-ribbon running across the top of the Norwegian Sea to connect eventually with Norway.

The Gripla Geography gives much the same description but in reverse and with some variations:

North of Norway lies Finnmarken. Then the land turns northeast to Bjarmaland . . . from Bjarmaland there are obygdir lying across the north to Greenland. In front of these lie sea-bottom-bays. Then the land turns southwest and there are glaciers [on it]; and both fiords and islands lie in front of these glaciers [here the four glaciers which we have already mentioned are located on the east Greenland coast] the last is nearest the Settlements and is called Hvitserk. Then the land turns north [here follows a description of some of the settled fiords and an enumeration of Greenland churches]. Now is to be told what lies over opposite [settled] Greenland. That land is called furdustrandir. There the cold is so intense that it is not habitable as far as men know. South of it lies Helluland which is called Skraelingarland. Thence it is but a short distance to Vinland the Good, which some suppose is a projection from Africa. Between Vinland and Greenland is Ginungapap* which comes out of the sea which is called Mare Oceanum and which surrounds the world.

The Gripla account, which was written after deteriorating climatic conditions had resulted in the isolation of most of Baffin Island from Greenland, does not mention the Vestri Obygdir by name, but speaks

---

* Hudson Strait, separating southwest Greenland from America. See also Appendix P.

instead of furdustrandir. This word simply means remarkable coasts, and in this particular usage it may have been intended to emphasize the remarkable climatic differences which then existed between the Baffin Island and west Greenland coasts.

Four short fragments, evidently drawn from some common source, are also worth noting. These are AM 736, AM 764, AM 192 and AM 194. Two of them will serve to represent the group.

[AM 192] From Bjarmaland extend obygdir northward until the beginning of Groenland. South of Groenland is Helluland, then is Markland; thence it is not far to Vinland the Good. . . .

[AM 194] South of Groenland is Helluland, then is Markland; thence it is not far to Vinland the Good.

These fragments establish the fact that the three western lands, Helluland, Markland and Vinland, lay south of Greenland. Since none of them lie south of modern Greenland it is to be concluded that the Norse Greenland included the east coast of Baffin Island.

One other major source remains to be mentioned. This is a transcript made by the Icelander Bjorn Jonsson in the mid-seventeenth century, from an ancient (perhaps twelfth-century) Icelandic vellum which was a fragment of a larger document, since lost. The parchment fragment was evidently much damaged and difficult to decipher when Jonsson copied it. It is known as the Graenlandia Vetus Chorographia and it has received scant attention from most scholars since it cannot be made to fit the theory that the Greenland of the early Norse was essentially the same as the land we now call Greenland. However, when it is analyzed on the assumption that eastern Baffin Island was a part of Greenland, it ceases to present any real difficulties. Since it bears largely on several aspects of our subject I reproduce it here in full with a line-by-line analysis.

Greenland turns toward the southwest. The first part of the standard description of the lands stretching westward from Europe is missing, and the text begins where Greenland turns southwest from about the latitude of Iceland.

Most southerly is Herjolfsness and next to the west Hvarfsgnipa. The most southerly district in what is now modern Greenland is Herjolfsness. The most southerly place on the west side of Davis

Straits is Hvarfsgnipa (Hvarf Mountain). The word Hvarf itself seems to have meant the "turning place." There were several hvarfs in ancient Greenland, including one on the east Greenland coast not far north of Cape Farewell, which was the landfall for ships inbound from Norway and perhaps from Iceland. Another was apparently Cape Desolation, where ships turned north en route to the Godthaab district. Hvarfgnipa is to be looked for as a mountain where ships turn away from land. It is perhaps identifiable with the 3800-foot peak which stands just behind Cape Mercy at the south tip of the Cumberland Peninsula. Or, possibly, with a peak on the Cape Dyer headland.

There went Erik the Red the farthest and is then said to have gone to the bottom of Eriksfiord. Hvarfsgnipa was the farthest west reached by Erik during the summer he spent exploring the Vestri Obygdir. After he had completed that exploration he returned to the east coast of Davis Strait, where he wintered before sailing north to what he believed to be the bottom of the inlet we call Baffin Bay. The Davis Strait–Baffin Bay inlet seems also to have been called Hrafnsfirth at one time. However, both these names were eventually transferred to the two fiords in the Julianehaab Bight which were settled by Erik and Hrafn respectively.

On the east side where the land is called Hafverf is Star then is Spalsund, then Drangey. On the east side of the bay, (Eriksfiord–Davis Strait) opposite the land where Hvarfsgnipa lies, is a place called Hafverf, which means "sea distance." Hafverf is apparently a point near Cape Farewell from which sailing distances to Iceland and to Europe were calculated. Star is a homestead at the junction of five fiord arms just north of Cape Farewell. Spalsund is probably Prins Christians Sound, which connects with Star and through which ships bypassed the difficult and dangerous rounding of Cape Farewell. Drangey is an unidentified homestead or island in the southern archipelago.

Then is Solvedal. It is built farther east. Then Tolafiord, then Melrackness. Solvedal may be a farmstead the ruins of which were found at the present site of Igdlorssuit. Tolafiord is one of the several fiords east and south of Herjolfsness. Melrackness is a cape in that area. Beginning with Hafverf, the author has now dealt with the geography lying south of Herjolfsness.

Then is Herjolfsfiord church, then Hellisey and Helliseyarfiord.

Then Ketilsfiord, two churches, then Hrakbjarney, Lundey, Syllenda of Eriksfiord, then Alptafiord, Suglufiord church, Hrafnsfiord. These are all known localities (most of which have been identified by archeologists) between Herjolfsfiord and Hrafnsfiord, which lies on the south edge of the main settlement area in the Julianehaab Bight. Syllenda of Eriksfiord appears to be a reference to the old name for Baffin Bay-Davis Strait, since it can have no connection with the later-day Eriksfiord lying deep inside the Julianehaab Bight. Thus this Syllenda may have been named during Erik's exploratory voyage and is sited on the original Hrafnsfiord-Eriksfiord inlet (Davis Strait-Baffin Bay) as opposed to some other place of the same name which was located elsewhere, perhaps in Iceland.

The Sliettufiord goes out of Hrafnsfiord; Hornafiord, Ofundfiord, then there is Bishop's seat, then comes one to the end of Eriksfiord, then Eriksfiord church; from it goes Austkarsfiord church, Halfgrimsfiord, Hvalseyarfiord. H . . . F H . . . F H . . . F from Dryness, then Isafiord, thence goes Utibliksfiord, then Strandafiord. The author has here enumerated most of the fiords of the Julianehaab Bight; from south to north, with a mention of the Bishop's seat which was at Gardar, and of Eriksfiord and the church built there by Erik's wife. The names of three of the fiords seem to have been indecipherable on the original vellum, and Bjorn represented them by H . . . F. Isafiord appears to have been the last fiord actually in the bight. Utibliksfiord and Strandafiord probably lie under the lee of the Nunnarsuit Peninsula, whose westerly point is Cape Desolation.

Then the Midfiords are built nearest. Then one is called Kellufiord, another Dyrafiord, then Thorvaldsfiord, Steinsfiord, Bergthorsfiord. The Midfiords lie in the Ivitgut Bight, north of Cape Desolation, and separated by it from the Eastern Settlement. The author again lists the main fiords from south to north.

Then there is six days' rowing in a six-oared boat with six men to Vestri Bygd. From the north limits of the Midfiords to the mouth of the Gothaab Bight, which contained most of the later-day Western Settlement homesteads, is about 180 nautical miles. The distance which could be covered by a six-oared boat in a day was a standard distance measurement representing between 30 and 35 of our nautical miles. Thus six such days represents a distance of 180–210 nautical miles or very nearly the correct distance between the Mid Bygd and the Vestri Bygd.

(*Here are enumerated the fiords.*) This is an interjection by Bjorn, who evidently found that the next section of the vellum was indecipherable. We know the names of some of these fiords (including Lysufiord) from other sources, but we do not know how far north the Western Settlement region extended. The author of the Chorography probably gave us this information, but damage to the ancient vellum has now deprived us of it. The text again becomes intelligible with the following phrase: *Then is the Vestri Bygd from Lysufiord six days' rowing.* Up to this point there has been no difficulty in following the Chorography. But here, as a result of the loss of that section of the original which Bjorn Jonsson could not read, we come to what appears to be an insurmountable stumbling block. At any rate it has been so considered by most scholars.

Either Bjorn was able to decipher enough of the missing section to lead him to suspect that it was a list of the fiords of the Western Settlement or, which is more likely, he naturally assumed this was the case because this was how the author had treated the Eastern and Middle settlements. There is no reason to find fault with his judgment. But what are we to make of the statement that to the Western Settlement from Lysufiord, which itself lay in the center of the Godthaab Western Settlement, and was the most important and heavily settled of the fiords, is a distance of six days' rowing, or between 180 and 210 nautical miles.

Did the author of the Chorography suddenly become nonsensical at this juncture? Or did Bjorn Jonsson miss more than just a list of the fiords of the Western Settlement? And, if he did miss something else, what was it?

To accuse the original author of having suddenly gone off the rails is ridiculous since up to this point he has demonstrated his ability to present a concise and accurate description of Greenland — a description which is quite unmatched for detail in any other source which we possess. The most reasonable conclusion open to us is that the indecipherable portion of the vellum contained something in addition to a list of the Western Settlement fiords.

What appears to be missing is an explanatory phrase, or word, preceding "Vestri Bygd" which either in its own right or by reference to a part of the indecipherable description of the Western Settlement, identified a locality which marked the limit of the Vestri Bygd district. Applying this as a working hypothesis, we read the phrase:

Then is the [limit of the] Vestri Bygd from Lysufiord six days' rowing. By analogy with the author's mention of Hafverf in the south and Hvarfsgnipa to the west of Greenland, we deduce that our hypothetical landmark would have been a prominent and easily recognizable feature which would have served as a good reference point from which directions could be given to other localities.

All we are actually told about this supposed landmark is that it lies six days' rowing distance from Lysufiord. However, we know that it must lie toward the north. The author of the Chorography has already described the coast from Hafverf north to Godthaab Bight, and he would hardly refer back to a locality lying six days south of Lysufiord, which would take us back to the Mid Bygd. It could not lie west of Lysufiord, since a distance of even 210 nautical miles to seaward comes nowhere near the opposite land of Baffin Island, the nearest point of which lies 320 sea miles from the mouth of the Godthaab Bight.

A distance of 140 nautical miles in a direct line north from Lysufiord (or 175 nautical miles following the coast) brings us to the most prominent feature on the west coast of Greenland south of Disco Island. This is the Cape Burnill headland and the mountain behind it. The headland is in itself not spectacularly impressive, but just behind it a tongue of the inland ice cap thrusts out almost to the sea, and near its seaward tip looms a 7300-foot rock peak — the highest on the west Greenland coast.

From the crest of this mountain it is possible in clear weather, to see the land loom of a sister peak rising to a height of 7100 feet from behind Cape Dyer at the eastern extremity of Baffin Island. With the assistance of mirage effects — and mirages are common in these latitudes — modern observers have been able to see, with the naked eye, the loom of the glaciers which lie far behind Cape Dyer.

Can this be the lost locality which lies six days' rowing distance from Lysufiord? It is so prominent a landmark that it must have been well known to the Greenlanders and the author of the Chorography would have been unlikely to omit it in his description of the Western Settlement district. It must certainly have had a name, and the name may still exist in the Icelandic sources.

In the oldest surviving version of the Old Erik Saga, the Short Saga, we are told that when Erik finished his exploration of the Vestri Obygdir he wintered at Holm, an island near Hrafnsgnipa (Hrafn's

Mountain). The following summer he sailed north from Holm "into Hrafnsfirth"* until he thought he had reached the bottom of what was evidently Baffin Bay, near Snaefells. As we have shown in Chapter Five this account refers to a voyage up the west coast of Greenland from the general vicinity of the Western Settlement, perhaps as far as Melville Bay.

Hrafn's Mountain and the great peak behind Cape Burnill may well be one and the same place. We know from other sources that it was standard practice for Norsemen on voyages into unknown seas to take advantage of coastal mountains in order to gain an idea of what lay ahead of them. When Erik first sailed north from what was to become the Eastern Settlement, he would almost certainly have paused below the Cape Burnill peak in order to send some of his party to scale its crest. It is a made-to-order lookout and it is surprisingly accessible. From the crest on a clear day — and we assume they chose such a day — the observers would not only have been able to detect the presence of a glacier-capped land far to the west of them. They would also have been able to see that the coast they were following continued into the north for an indeterminate distance.

The man who climbed the mountain and who provided the information which suggested that Baffin Bay might be a great inlet could have been the same Hrafn who returned with Erik to Greenland in the settlement year of 985 and who took up residence near Erik at the fiord which came to bear his name. But before the settlement was made, and during the exploration voyage, it seems possible that the name Hrafnsfiord was bestowed by Erik on the sea-bottom-bay which was presumably discovered from the peak of Hrafnsgnipa.

Thence is six days' rowing to Karlbuda, then three days' rowing to Bjarney. Karlbuda means Karl's Booth or Shelter, and can be taken as referring to a hunting camp as distinct from a permanent place of habitation. It probably belonged to one of the summer hunters who went off from the settlements each year in search of walrus, narwhals and other sea mammals which were not sufficiently numerous on the settlement coast. Bjarney means Bear Island, or an island where polar bears — the only kind present in these latitudes — were hunted.

---

* Eriksfiord in the Erik the Red and the Karlsefni sagas.

Wherever Karlbuda was located, it could not, as we have already shown, have been six days from Lysufiord. It must therefore have lain six days from somewhere in the vicinity of the place we have identified as Hrafnsgnipa, either to the north or to the west.

If it was to the north it would have had to be in the vicinity of Disco Island, and Bjarney must then have lain three days farther north, or somewhere near the Umanak Peninsula. But we have already established, through our examination of the Erik the Red and the Karlsefni sagas, that Bjarney could not have been in the vicinity of Disco, but was almost certainly in the Vestri Obydgir of Baffin Island.

Let us now look west from Hrafnsgnipa. We find that it is 185 nautical miles, or six days' rowing distance, from Cape Burnill to Cape Dyer on a crossing which enables voyagers to keep sight of land, either astern or ahead of them, throughout most of the passage if the weather is clear.

Cape Dyer is on the Cumberland Peninsula which for reasons enumerated elsewhere would have been a better hunting ground for the Norse of the tenth century than any part of the west Greenland coast south of Uppernavik. It seems clear that Karlbuda is to be looked for near Cape Dyer.

Bjarney lay three days from Karlbuda. It could not have lain to the north for this would make nonsense out of its use as a way-station during Karlsefni's voyage for Vinland. Three days' rowing south of Cape Dyer (105 nautical miles) takes us to Cape Mercy, the southeast termination of the Cumberland Peninsula, off which lies Leopold Island. Both Leopold Island and the whole eastern coast of the Cumberland Peninsula are still good polar bear country. Leopold Island meets all requirements for Bjarney and in addition provides a 2000-foot departure landmark for any vessel, such as Karlsefni's, proceeding farther to the south.

Twelve days' rowing around ——ey Eisunes Adanes on the north side. With this mutilated sentence the surviving fragment of the Chorography comes to an end. But, imperfect as it is, we can perhaps make something out of this final passage. The missing word which ends in "ey" is the name of an island, and it may be Bjarney, although not necessarily so. Eisunes means Coal Point, and Adanes means Eider Duck Point. The twelve days' rowing around may refer to Cumberland Sound, since the length of its coastline from headland to headland is roughly 380 nautical miles. To row around the sound and return to Leopold Island would consume about twelve days.

There are many capes on the north side of Cumberland Sound, and eider ducks nest on a number of them as well as on the islets lying nearby. There are also numerous deposits of soft coal on Baffin Island, and at least three have been reported from Cumberland Sound.

This is about all the Graenlandia Vetus Chorographia can tell us. We cannot complain, for it has told us a great deal.

Considering the quantity and quality of the evidence, it is hard to understand why so many commentators have resolutely closed their eyes to the likelihood that the Greenland Norse reached and explored part of Baffin Island very early in their history.

There is nothing particularly remarkable in such a feat. Men who could and did sail confidently from Norway to Iceland and Greenland would hardly have found the 185-mile-wide Davis Strait much of a barrier. Just as it was inevitable that the Europeans who reached Iceland should soon have found Greenland, so it was equally inevitable that the Greenlanders would soon have found Baffin Island.

That Erik the Red should have been the first to do so is a tribute to his daring and his energy; but there is nothing about such an exploit to place any strain on our credulity.

norse sea-going ships

THE CONSTRUCTION AND CHARACTERISTICS OF THE SHIPS
WHICH CROSSED THE WESTERN OCEAN

The ships used by the western voyagers were trading vessels — knorrir as the type was called throughout the Scandinavian world. The knorr was a plebian relative of the aristocratic Viking longship, for both sprang from a common ancestry in the little clinker-built skiffs of the northern fiords whose origins are lost in the mute aeons of the stone ages. But while the longship developed as a swift and fearsome blade with which the raiding Vikings could let the blood of the coastal peoples of Europe, the knorr developed out of the need for a staunch, cargo-carrying ship which could endure the northern seas.

Longships were fit to terrify entire populations of landsmen, and their dragon-beaks could be thrust into the most protected bays, and even far up rivers running into the very heart of alien lands. But they were quite unfit to face the violence of the open sea where the only terror they could engender was in the hearts of their own passengers and crews. Countless Hollywood films, historical novels and even staid histories of the Viking era nothwithstanding, the longship was a seafaring man's abomination and was seldom voluntarily hazarded far from the comforting shelter of land except under conditions of dire necessity. Inordinately long and narrow and with almost no freeboard, the longship either broke her back or swamped if she met really heavy weather. Furthermore, longships' crews were often composed of men who were better butchers than seamen. The Viking

crews and their longships were well wed; both were shaped for and
devoted to the arts of destruction; and had but little other purpose.

It was quite different with the knorr. She was a working ship, and
her people were working men. They were sailors, perhaps the best
sailors of their times, and their ships could hold their own with any
sailing vessels of comparable size that have ever gone to sea.

Like the longship, the knorr was clinker built, usually of thin oak
planks lashed with withes to naturally curved timbers, and fastened
to each other with soft iron rivets. She was double-ended, had
a single mast and single square sail, and was steered by a side steering
oar. There the resemblance ended. The knorrir which plied between
Norway and Iceland, on to Greenland and finally to the coasts of
North America had a much greater displacement than did the longships. Some were more than a hundred feet overall, and as much as
ninety feet on the waterline. They were shallow built, but very beamy
and with a good freeboard. They had cutwaters fore and aft and a
long, if somewhat shallow keel which improved their sailing qualities
when on the wind. They ranged between forty and eighty tons displacement, and could carry from twenty to forty tons of cargo on an
ocean passage.

They were utilitarian ships, but they were still lovely to look at for
their lines curved sweetly aft from the high stem post to the equally
high afterpost; and they had about them a delicacy of appearance
which today is found only in yachts. But they were by no means
fragile. Their unique construction was designed to give them strength
through suppleness rather than through a massive and rigid construction. Because the planks were only lashed to the frames, and
because planks and timbers were made of thin and pliant wood, the
knorr could "work", as seamen say, which means that when she was
under extreme stress she could twist and writhe like a living thing,
easing out from under the sea's hammer blows and giving when the
strain grew unbearable. She was resilient, and very, very tough. Because she was shallow draft, light for her size, and with a broad beam,
she kept the surface of the ocean like some great sea-fowl instead of
driving through it as would a modern deep-hulled ship.

She was steered by means of a side rudder called the steer-board
which was mounted on what has ever since been called the starboard
side of the vessel. The tiller was brought in over the after gunwale at

right angles to the center line of the ship so that it passed athwartship, enabling the steersman to push forward on it, or to haul back with the full power of both arms. This was an advantage which was lost when the stern rudder became popular. The side rudder had yet another advantage. It was pivoted at its mounting on the side of the ship so that a very deep, thin and therefore efficient blade could be used which, when the ship entered shallow waters, could be tilted up to clear the bottom. As a result of this arrangement knorrir could operate in as little as five feet of water and could enter almost any small cove or harbor, or they could be run right up on the shore, if it was sand or mud, with no danger of damaging the vital rudder.

Internally the hull was one big open hold with a small foredeck and afterdeck. A bailing well was provided abaft the mast, and another forward. Pumps were unknown then, and bailing was done by a man who stood in the well to fill a wooden bucket which his mate then swung up and overboard by means of a lever arrangement.

The single mast was placed just forward of midship and was very strongly stepped in a huge wooden fish. On big knorrir this mast was sixty feet long and stout in proportion. A wooden platform at the masthead was sometimes provided for the lookout.

The ship's gear was simple, and mostly made of wood. A drum windlass was mounted just forward of the afterdeck and was used for hauling up the sail, by means of a halyard passing through a hole near the top of the mast; for bringing home the anchors; and — when set up taut — to turn the halyard into a backstay. Anchors were usually of the type known as kiliks, a framework of supple rods encasing a long, heavy stone and fitted with four wooden flukes. It is an intriguing fact that kiliks dating to 1200 B.C., excavated from a Danish peat bog, are identical in design and construction with kiliks in general use today in Newfoundland, Norway and other northern maritime countries.

Blocks for the running rigging were made of hardwood and were not fitted with sheaves but had smooth holes worked in them to allow the passage of the ropes, which in most cases were made of walrus hide, which is almost frictionless when wet or oiled.

Knorrir normally carried two ship's boats. On deep-sea passages these were lashed upside down in a fore-and-aft position on top of the cargo, one forward of the mast and one abaft of it. The afterboat was generally a six-oared, clinker-built, scaled-down version of the parent ship twenty to thirty feet long. It could be rowed or sailed.

Since there was no decked-over hold, cargo was placed on the flooring and covered with tarpaulins made of hides. These were water-proofed with seal-tar (seal oil evaporated to the consistancy of thin, black treacle) or sometimes with butter. They were stretched over the ship's boats, whose keels supported them in the same way a ridgepole supports a tent, and were lashed down in the scuppers on both sides of the vessel, leaving just room enough for a man to pass along close to the gunwales. The scupper holes which carried away the water that fell on the tarpaulins did not open out through the sides of the vessel but drained through the flooring into the bilges, from which the water had to be removed by bailing. Bailing was the bane of life aboard these ships, for they took a lot of spray, and some-times solid seas as well.

The single immense squaresail was made of coarse woolen cloth to which strips of walrus or seal hide were stitched diagonally to hold it in shape. One or several rows of reef points were fitted and the sail could be reefed either by making the reef points fast to the yard or by lowering the yard and putting a reef into the loose-footed bottom of the sail. The foot of the sail was clewed down to pin-rails set between the projecting upper sections of the ship's timbers; and the two sheets from the yardends were belayed to cleats on the afterdeck. Standing rigging consisted of one or more pairs of stays made fast below the gunwales with deadeyes. Parrels were used to hold both yard and sail to the mast.

The most unusual piece of sailing gear was the beitass. This was a removable pole which functioned rather like a spinnaker boom. Its heavy end was seated in a socket on the deck abeam of the mast, and the lighter end was fitted to the forward leech of the sail in order to keep it stretched and drawing when the ship was sailing on the wind. This point of sailing was called beita, from which modern sailors de-rive the term "beating" to windward.

It is an almost universal misconception that with their single big squaresail, Norse vessels could only run off before the wind. In fact they could and did sail to within five or six points of the wind, largely due to the employment of the beitass. Nor is this mere speculation. Twice during modern times replicas of early Norse ships have crossed the Atlantic. The first of these was a replica of the Gokstad ship — a tenth-century vessel found in a ship grave in Norway. She was of the type known as a karv, an intermediate form partway between the longship and the knorr, but not as seaworthy as the latter. Nevertheless this replica, built of similar materials and of the same construction as the original, sailed from Bergen on April 30, 1893 and reached Newfoundland safely on May 27. During the passage she encountered several severe storms and most of the passage was made against headwinds; but when she was reaching, with a favoring breeze, she was occasionally able to log a speed of 11 knots.

The other crossing was made in 1932 by a replica of a small knorr, 60 feet overall, with a 16-foot beam and a 3-foot draft. This little vessel, the Roald Amundsen, made her westward passage along one of the routes followed by Columbus, but she improved on Columbus's best time by something over 30 per cent. Not content with this remarkable passage, her skipper, Captain Folgar, then sailed her back to Norway by way of Newfoundland. Using the beitass pole Folgar experienced no difficulty in sailing her within five points of the wind.

The skippers of both vessels — and they were men of wide experience in sailing ships — were full of praise for the seagoing qualities of the karv and knorr, and it is clear from an analysis of their logs that the replicas performed better than any known sailing vessels designed before the beginning of the nineteenth century, and of many which were designed after that date. Compared to the knorr, the lumbering, top-heavy monstrosities which carried Columbus, Cabot, Cartier and the Cortereals over the Western Ocean were seagoing death traps, as indeed the records prove they were for the roster of these later-day ships which were lost on the Atlantic passage is legion.

Of course the knorr would not go to weather with the efficiency of a modern fore-and-after. Apart from the fact that she would not point so high, she tended to make more leeway, for despite her deep steering oar, which acted like a leeboard, she had little hold on the water. Nevertheless when running free, or reaching, a knorr could have held her own with some of the most famous of our latter-day banking schooners.

Knorrir even had auxiliary power in the form of heavy sweeps, usually three pairs forward and two or three pairs aft. With a man standing to each sweep the ship could be propelled at two or three knots in calm waters, and this speed could be increased by using the afterboat to tow the parent ship.

If these vessels had any major defect, it lay in their accommodations. They were not built for comfort. There was no galley, and no way of cooking, except on rare occasions when calm weather made it possible to light an open fire on a hearth of stones rigged just forward of the afterdeck. For the most part passengers and crew subsisted on cold rations. If they were lucky they quenched their thirst with beer.

The accommodations were limited to the unlighted dog-kennels under the two decks. These dark, triangular spaces were only ten or twelve feet long and not more than twelve feet broad at the widest part. They were rarely as much as five feet high, so that they offered no headroom.

The crews were surprisingly large considering the size of the ships — usually fifteen to twenty men. This was in part due to the need for much muscle to man the bailing tubs and to supply auxiliary rowing power; but it was also due to the ever-present possibility of battle, particularly on the European approaches, where Viking pirates lurked. Even in Iceland and Greenland big crews were useful, for though the knorrir were trading ships, and usually came in peace that peace could often be maintained only by a show of force. Both Icelanders and Greenlanders, as well as most Europeans, had a way of taking what they fancied from the cargo of a trader and paying for it only if it appeared certain that the trader could enforce his claims.

The captain of a knorr was generally its owner, and was officially its helmsman. On long passages he would be relieved by trusted subordinates — usually relatives of his. It seemed to be an almost invariable rule that only freemen were shipped as seamen aboard the trading vessels, possibly because the temptation toward, and opportunity for, rebellion was strong aboard such ships.

The carrying capacity of the knorrir seems phenomenal to us, for there were occasions when a knorr would ship her own crew, plus twenty or more human passengers, half a dozen small northern cattle, a flock of sheep and goats, and tons of miscellaneous cargo including sufficient forage to keep the animals alive for two or three weeks. The cattle, and probably most of the human beings, lived under tarpaulins stretched over the hold while the rest of the people, including women and children, must have been packed into the tiny cabins like worms in a can. Nevertheless the passengers at least enjoyed plenty of fresh air, which was a good deal more than could be said for those who traveled in the noisome deep holds of the immigrant ships which plied the Atlantic well into the nineteenth century.

Sailing a knorr in good weather must have been a magnificent experience. As the cutwater snored through the long Atlantic swells, the bone in the vessel's teeth would have foamed up high and white. The motion must have been light and easy, with none of the heavy lurching and stomach-heaving pitching of the deep-hulled vessels of our day. Even when running fast before a brisk breeze, she must have been a joy to handle, for the deep rudder, pivoting on its own axis, would have required only a light touch on the tiller in order to make the vessel answer smartly to the steersman's wishes. Under favorable conditions the knorr would have been an ocean-yachtsman's dream, and in fact in northern Norway they still build and sail pleasure yachts which are essentially only scaled-down versions of this ancient ship.

/\\.\\.\\

norse navigation

HOW THE NORSE FOUND THEIR WAY ABOUT THE OCEANIC WORLD

One of the major obstacles to an understanding of the Norse ocean voyages lies in the general belief that the arts of deep-sea navigation are of relatively recent origin.

This belief has no basis in reality. We know, for instance, that the prehistoric peoples of the Pacific were highly accomplished oceanic navigators. Using accurate star charts in conjunction with a delicate instrument made out of a coconut shell and designed for measuring stellar altitudes, Polynesian sailors of ancient times were able to get about in their vast ocean, only remotely dusted with islands, with a facility which modern men were not able to surpass until well into the eighteenth century.

The Pacific peoples were not unique in this regard. We know that as far back as 300 B.C., Pytheas, the Massilian Green mathematician, was able to determine latitudes. We know that the astrolabe was in use by Hipparchus around 150 B.C. It is true that during the Dark Ages much esoteric knowledge from ancient times was lost, but it is also true that most of the practical knowledge garnered by the ancients survived. The navigational arts were of an intensely practical nature, and what had been learned about them by the Cretans, Phoenicians, Egyptians, Greeks and Romans would have been maintained in being, since the continuity of man's use of the sea and ships never suffered a serious interruption. Unlike land lore, valid sea lore is not subject to loss with the death of its parent society, for it is of universal import and becomes the common property of seamen everywhere.

During the period when the Western Mediterranean area was plunged into chaos and decay, a functioning knowledge of seamanship and navigation was preserved, if not improved upon, by Arab sailors. As southern Europe returned to a semblance of civilized organization, this knowledge was redistributed to various western peoples. The Basques, who were among the modern world's most competent seamen, appear to have learned the ancient navigational arts, including the ability to determine relative latitude, from the Arabs before the end of the ninth century. By the year 912 their ships were voyaging as far north as the Faeroe Islands, where Basque sailors must inevitably have made contact with Norse seamen, with a consequent interchange of seafaring knowledge.

The Norse were themselves in direct contact with the Arab world at about this same time, and they displayed a keen interest in some aspects of Arab learning. One early Norse king even imported an Arab mathematician to his court to instruct the Northmen in this science — a science which we may believe would have included information on methods of locating a position on the surface of the earth through the use of stellar, or even of solar sights.

That the Norse *could* determine latitudes, and that they did make use of this knowledge on their long western voyages, is apparent from the historical records. However, their concept of latitude was not the same as ours. They never devised a linear grid calibrated in degrees and stretching from the poles to the equator. What we think of as latitude was, to them, the difference in altitude of a celestial object as this difference was observed between two points. The navigator would know that the North Star stood at a certain altitude when viewed from his home port. If he voyaged north of his home port the altitude of the North Star would increase, and if he voyaged south it would decrease. By measuring the amount of altitude variation he was able to determine how far south or north he had voyaged. Such a measurement gave him his latitude relative to his reference point, in terms of units which could have been completely arbitrary so long as the observer knew what distance was represented by one of the chosen units.

The North Star, or Guiding Star, as the Norse called it, is, for all practical purposes, a fixed point in the heavens. It neither rises, sets nor circles. It does not alter its position with the seasons. It appears to change position in the sky only when the observer changes his latitude. The North Star rises as one goes north until, at the pole, it stands straight overhead. As one goes south it sinks until it reaches the horizon at the equator. For purposes of latitude determination it is at its most useful when it stands between 20 and 80 degrees above the horizon, since within these limits its altitude can be most easily and accurately measured.

A rough latitude (accurate to within four or five degrees) can be obtained by anyone observing the North Star with the naked eye. With practice such a visual observation can result in a "fix" accurate within two or three degrees. However, a really accurate latitude can be obtained by using an instrument of such a simple nature that it could be conceived of and constructed by any illiterate savage, providing he had the need for such an instrument to spur him on.

All that is required is a straight stick about three feet long which has been marked with equidistant notches. If the notches are cut one-half inch apart, the "instrument" can be made to measure latitudes to within half a degree, or thirty miles.

Such an instrument is simplicity itself to use. The stick is held vertically at a standard distance from the eye, with the bottom of it on the line of the horizon and with the North Star appearing against the notched edge. The number of notches between the bottom and the star is then the star's altitude in arbitrary units. Assuming that the user has previously established, by trail methods, the distance which is represented by a difference in altitude of one notch, he can immediately determine how far to the south or north of a known reference point he is, or in other words his latitude relative to the reference point.

If instead of a stick the observer fashions a flat piece of wood into the form of a quarter-circle and marks off degrees on the arc he can, by holding the instrument so that the flat base is along the horizon and the North Star appears to touch the edge of the arc, read off his actual latitude in degrees. Such a home-made device enables the observer to obtain latitudes accurate to within a quarter of a degree, or fifteen miles.

An instrument of either type can be readily used at sea. With such an instrument it would have been comparatively easy for the Norse to make long ocean crossings by a method which was still in use as late as the early twentieth century, and which consisted of sailing along a parallel of latitude. There is considerable evidence in the sagas to show that the Norse used this method — particularly on such routes as the direct passage between Norway and Greenland. which was one frequently followed. This is an open-water passage in excess of 1000 nautical miles from last sight of land at the Faeroes to first sight of Greenland's east coast. It was imperative that an accurate course be followed on this passage since any serious southerly deviation would result in the mariner missing Greenland entirely. Direction could not have been maintained by the use of lodestone or compass for the Norse did not possess these instruments. Neither could it have been maintained over such a long passage by any form of dead reckoning or by observing winds and seas. Such a course could have been maintained only if the mariners involved were able to determine their relative latitude at reasonably frequent intervals. In effect, they had to keep the North Star at the same altitude from day to day, in order to steer a true west course and make their desired landfall.

Although the form of the instrument used by the Norse is lost to us, we do know its name. In a fifteenth-century reference to the Norse voyages, a reference which is apparently drawn from a twelfth-century source, we find this statement: "It is told that Karlsefni [Thorfinn Karlsefni, who made the most important of the New World voyages about A.D. 1004] made a husanotra of wood and then went to seek Vinland the Good." In the Greenlanders Story there is another reference to a husanotra — one again in a context which makes it appear that it was an important piece of equipment for anyone undertaking a distant voyage.

Attempts to identify the husanotra have entertained many scholars. The old Norse word has been minutely dissected and analyzed, and the most highly qualified linguistic authorities have concluded that it meant such widely diverse things as "a house-neat timber," "a wooden ornament associated with the castle abaft the mast," "a weathervane or other instrument at the point of a gable of a house, or on a ship," "an ornament on a ship's bow or stern," and even "a wooden broom." These explanations were obtained by attempting to make literal sense out of the root meanings of the composite word.

Modern scholars have obviously lost touch with the tenth-century meaning of the word; but older scholars evidently knew what husanotra meant, in the common usage of Norse times. Saxo Grammaticus, a famous clerk of the Middle Ages, translated the Norse Saga of

Arrow-Odd into Latin, and when he came to the word husanotra he translated it as *gubernaculum*. During the sixteenth-century, *gubernaculum* meant a device for assisting in steering a vessel or controlling her course. Moreover, in its original Latin sense it meant a device for governing or controlling an action.

Torfaeus, in his *Historia Vinlandiae,* translates husanotra as *cornis*. Modern scholars do not seem to have understood what he meant by this word either, although its derivation from Latin and Greek makes it clear that Torfaeus was referring to a device, or instrument, having a curved edge, which would be a partial description of a simple astrolabe.

Werlauff, in *Symbolae ad Geographiam Medii Aevi ex Monumentis Islandicas,* translated the word as *scopae* — another word which is no longer in use, but whose Greek root means to aim or to look out; and which in medieval use meant a sighting device.

If these older translations, which were a good deal closer in time to the original than any current efforts, are not enough to show that a husanotra was some sort of navigational instrument, the context in which the word is used in the sagas would seem to establish the fact. The saga tellers considered the husanotra to be an object of such value and importance that it merited attention even in their condensed accounts of the great western voyages. It was a device which was associated with the success of protracted voyages into strange waters. They would hardly have bothered to mention it if it had been something as trivial as an ornament, or a mere weathervane.

Finally, the conclusion that early Norse sailors could and did determine relative latitudes with remarkable exactness is convincingly supported by an analysis of the Sigurd Stefansson map of Helluland, Markland and Vinland.*

While the ability to determine relative latitude was of immense importance to the Norse western voyagers, it had its limitations. Much of their sailing was done in high northern latitudes, where in summer the period of darkness during which the North Star could be seen was of short duration or nonexistent. Consequently we are not surprised to find that major oceanic voyages were usually undertaken as early as possible in the spring, or as late as possible in the summer, when too much daylight would have been less of a problem. Too

* See Appendix G.

much daylight not only made it difficult to obtain latitude fixes from the North Star, it also deprived the navigators of the use of the sun as an aid to maintaining direction, since in very high latitudes the sun tends to circle the horizon instead of rising approximately in the east and setting in the west.

Nevertheless there were times when open-ocean voyages had to be made during a period of continuous daylight, or when the sun and stars were obscured by clouds. It such cases the Norse navigators relied on alternative methods of maintaining course.

Foremost among these was the use of landmarks. It was the almost invariable custom for a Norse skipper bound deep-sea to take his departure from the most prominent landmark on the home coast and to shape his course toward the most visible landmark on the desired foreign coast. In our day, when compasses are commonplace, we have forgotten just how useful such a procedure can be; nevertheless the landmark system of sailing is still in vogue in some remote areas and among peoples who do not have the compass. It is surprisingly effective if the landmarks are prominent enough; and on the mountainous coasts of Norway, Iceland, Greenland and Labrador prominent landmarks are to be found in abundance.

Under conditions of good visibility a lookout at the top of a fifty-foot mast can see the peak of a 7000-foot mountain from a distance of 110 miles. Given perfect visibility, he can see the "loom" of such a peak from as much as 125 miles distant. Helped by a mirage — and mirages are commonplace in high latitudes — the range of visibility may be increased by as much as an additional 40 per cent.

Although viewing conditions may seldom have been ideal, they probably were on the average fairly good over the waters sailed by the Norse during the generally good weather which prevailed throughout the tenth century. In any event we know that one of the major conditions which governed the departure of a knorr on a deep-sea voyage was clear weather which would enable her navigator to maintain his direction "over the stern" for as great a distance as possible.

The value of this method of navigating can be grasped if we consider that, assuming near-perfect conditions of visibility, it would have been, and still is, possible to sail from Norway to North America by way of the Shetlands, the Faeroes, Iceland, Greenland and Baffin Island without ever being out of sight of land for more than two hundred miles, or thirty-six hours at the average speed of a knorr. Even under moderate viewing conditions such a voyage could have been made without the navigator's being forced to rely on dead reckoning for more than a few days at a time.

The method of steering a knorr may itself have had a direct connection with the ingrained habit of using landmarks. Knorrir were steered with side rudders rather than with stern rudders. This meant that instead of pointing along the ship's longitudinal axis, the tiller was athwartship. Thus the helmsman could stand facing astern or ahead with equal ease. When making a departure he could face the stern and so maintain course until the chosen landmark sank below the horizon. When an arrival landmark was picked up ahead of him, he could as readily face forward and so direct his course toward the new mark.

One other important aspect in connection with landmark sailing was that it became customary to refer to open-sea distances between two places as being measured from *last sight* of the departure landmark to *first sight* of the arrival landmark. Consequently Norse sea distances were out-of-sight-of-land distances and could be as much as three hundred miles short of actual shore-to-shore distances.

The use of landmarks and relative latitudes did not by any means exhaust the Norse navigator's repertoire. He also made extensive use of what we shall call "sea marks." These were of particular importance to him during stormy weather when neither landmarks nor the sun and stars could be relied upon.

Under such conditions a helmsman could hold his course by reference to the direction of the wind. If the wind veered or hauled he would be made aware of the change by the divergence between the wind, and the sea or swell, and so could make the necessary corrections which would enable him to maintain his original course. Although this may sound like a very imprecise method, a practiced seaman of today can still hold his course by watching wind and water, and do so with almost as high a degree of accuracy as if he were steering by a compass.

Many other kinds of sea mark were also used. In one set of sailing instructions for the direct course between Norway and Greenland it is specifically stated that the navigator should hold far enough to the north so that he would encounter the numerous pods of whales which "lie half a day south of Iceland." Even now sadly depleted pods are to be found in this region, where they gather to feed on rich beds of krill.

Seabirds were invaluable sea marks. Many species of oceanic birds tend to maintain rather definite range limits over the open waters of the Atlantic, a fact well known both to ornithologists and to modern seamen of the Atlantic fishing fleets. Furthermore their abundance in any given area is usually an indication of good fishing grounds, which in turn mean shoal waters or undersea banks that usually lie adjacent to mainland shores. Up until the middle of the eighteenth century navigators sailing from England for Newfoundland kept a sharp lookout for the first appearance of noddies, whose presence in any numbers was an infallible indication that the ship had arrived over the Grand Banks. That the Norse made similar use of birds is indicated in the saga account of Thorstein Eriksson's voyage, during which he was blown east until he reported encountering sea birds of those species which were to be found off the coastal waters of Ireland.

The usefulness of celestial objects was not limited to the determination of latitude alone. The North Star was a fair indicator of true north — the only north the Vikings knew, since magnetic north came into use only with the compass — from which the other directions could be ascertained.* The sun, when the latitude was not too high, was also helpful in establishing directions. It is a known fact that peoples who do not use the compass, such as the Chipeweyan Indians of northern Canada, can so develop their sense of direction that a brief glance at the sun *at any time of the day* will enable them to orient themselves with amazing accuracy. The Norse deep-sea navigators would unquestionably have developed a similar aptitude.

Since they had no compass, the Norse thought of directions rather differently than we do. They used the whole horizon as their rose, and divided it into eight cardinal segments called airts. Each airt could itself be divided into three parts, each being equal to 15 of our degrees. However, for the most part the courses recorded in the sagas

---

* The North Star does not indicate true north. At present it appears to describe a circle around true north or 2 degrees 30 minutes diameter. In the year 1000 A.D. this circle was of the order of 10 degrees, so that north, by the North Star, would have been subject to a 5-degree error, either east or west. This must be borne in mind when we interpret the directions recorded in the sagas.

released a raven, which circled a few times and then struck off on the vessel's back track, toward the Faeroes. On the second day another raven circled for a long time high in the pale sky, and finally returned to perch upon the vessel's mast. But on the next day, the raven climbed to a great height and then flew purposefully off toward the west. Following it with their eyes until it vanished, the Norsemen set their course by that of the bird and in due time raised the coast of Iceland.

Some people deride this account as being apocryphal. There is no reason to think that it is anything of the sort. On the contrary, the use of ravens by the sailor who later came to be called Raven-Floki was no more than what one might have expected from a seafaring people who were very closely attuned to the world in which they lived.

APPENDIX G

/\.\V.\/\
.\V.\V.\

the ancient map

A DISCUSSION OF THE SIGURD STEFANSSON MAP SHOWING NORSE
DISCOVERIES IN AMERICA

The archives of the Royal Library in Denmark contain a remarkable map known as the Stefansson Map. It is a copy of an original
drawn by an Icelandic cartographer named Sigurdur Stefansson in
the year 1570.*

The Stefansson Map shows the eastern and western coasts of the
North Atlantic north of about latitude 50 degrees. What makes it of
prime importance is that it accurately pinpoints the locations of Helluland, Markland and the Vinland of the Karlsefni expedition. This
map has been a thorn in the flesh of those who have tried to place
Vinland in New England, since it unequivocally locates Vinland on
the Great Northern Peninsula of Newfoundland.

The original source of Stefansson's information is not known, but
in 1607 a Dane named Hans Poulson Resen apparently made use of
the original Stefansson Map (not the copy which we possess) in con-
structing a map of his own showing the Norse discoveries in the west,
in whose legend he incorporated the information that the original
source was an ancient chart, rudely delineated, and made some centuries earlier. Resen's map deals only with the western coast of the
North Atlantic and he has grossly distorted the Helluland-Vinland
section, perhaps in order to rationalize it with the most imperfect
knowledge of this area which existed among contemporary European
cartographers. In one respect, however, it is in almost perfect agree-

---

* Some scholars mistakenly claim 1590, but the point is unimportant.

The Sigurd Stefansson Map of 1570

ment with the Stefansson Map, and this is in its delineation of Greenland.

That the centuries-old original to which Resen refers cannot be Stefansson's 1570 map is obvious. Resen must therefore have been referring to a common source of great antiquity which he probably never saw himself, since he worked in Europe, but which he knew to have been the basis for Stefansson's map. Stefansson worked at the monastery at Skaholt in Iceland, and it is known that at that time the archives of the monastery contained a great many very early Icelandic documents which have since been lost. It follows that the basis of at least the western portion of the Stefansson Map was an ancient chart or charts preserved in these archives.

There seems to be no other rational way to explain the origin of this map. Consequently we conclude that the Norse navigators of the period of the western voyages were able to draw charts, and in fact did so; and that these charts were no haphazard scrawls but represented the Canadian coast with an accuracy which was not approached by the cartographers of mainland Europe until well into the seventeenth century.

The section of Stefansson's map which deals with the early Norse discoveries (as distinct from the portion representing the European coast, and which he presumably drew from contemporary sources) is most startling in the accuracy of the relative latitudes given to prominent landmarks. The latitude grid on the existing map was imposed by Stefansson or the later copyist and is modern; nevertheless whoever imposed it must have had an original frame of relative latitudes at his disposal on the original source map, from which he was able to convert to the modern grid.

All of the latitudes of North American localities on the original map appear to have been relative to Cape Farewell on the south tip of Greenland. When Stefansson or the copyist set out to convert these to the modern latitude grid, he evidently did not have an accurate latitude for Cape Farewell, since he places it 3 degrees 5 minutes too far north. But all the plots for landmarks on Labrador and Newfoundland (with one exception which we will deal with later) also show approximately a 3-degree displacement to the north according to the modern grid. This means that relative to Cape Farewell the landmarks are positioned with an astonishing accuracy, ad

The Sigurd Stefansson Map compared with modern map

The lefthand panel shows a section of the Stefansson Map. The axis of the Vinland Promontorium has been swung on the pivot of Chateau Bay in order to bring it into correct orientation with the Labrador Atlantic Coast. The latitudes have been corrected by subtracting 3 degrees, which is the actual error recorded on the original for Cape Farewell in Greenland, which was evidently the control point from which Stefansson calculated the latitudes for Labrador and Newfoundland. The remarkably close agreement of his corrected latitudes with those shown on the section of a modern map on the right will be apparent.

one moreover that few if any maps or charts of this part of North America prior to about 1680 could begin to match.

It is indisputable that whoever made the voyages from which the original data for Stefansson's map was drawn, must have been capable of obtaining relative latitudes with a precision which would have been considered extraordinary in the seventeenth century. Since there is no record of any European of Stefansson's period, or before it, having made a voyage from Cape Farewell to Cape Chidley and then along the entire Labrador coast, concluding with an exploration of the northern peninsula of Newfoundland, there seems to be no alternative but to give the credit for this superb example of position fixing to ancient Norse seamen. Since it is also evident from the inscriptions on the map itself that the voyages must have been contemporary, or nearly so, with those recorded in the Erik the Red and Karlsefni sagas and the Greenlanders Story, there seems to be no escaping the conclusion that the Stefansson Map records the discoveries made on those early voyages and, in particular, on the Karlsefni expedition.

Karlsefni himself, after his return to Iceland, might well have drawn a chart of his explorations — a chart which eventually found its way into the archives of Skaholt. At some later time this chart might have been combined with a chart of Greenland and eventually this combined chart could have been incorporated by Stefansson into his map of the northern reaches of the Atlantic.

The Stefansson Map certainly appears to be composed of three separate sections. From Iceland eastward the latitudes are roughly accurate on the modern grid, and the delineation of the British Isles, the northern islands, and Iceland is in agreement with what is shown on other maps of circa 1570.

Greenland is represented in considerable detail, including, off its eastern coast, the island of Jan Mayen, which does not appear to have been discovered by the Norse until the twelfth or thirteenth centuries. Considering also the inaccuracy (in terms of modern latitude) of the Cape Farewell latitude, we conclude that Stefansson's source for this portion of his map was probably a chart dating from shortly after the beginning of the thirteenth century.

The Labrador-Newfoundland segment is in such close accord with the saga accounts of the Karlsefni voyage that it can be assumed to have been derived from the explorations of the early eleventh century.

There is, however, one gap in the composite map and this lies in the delineation of the Vestri Obygd, or the Cumberland Peninsula area of Baffin Island. Baffin Bay itself is shown much shrunken, and its west coast is shown as a straight line, from which we deduce that ?tefansson had no detailed map of this area from which to work and ?erefore simply connected up the foot of Baffin Bay with the north-?rn tip of Labrador by means of a piece of undifferentiated coast. His ?ailure to treat of this area suggests that the western exploration chart ?howed only *new* lands. If this chart indeed originated with Karlsefni, ?e would not expect him to have concerned himself with known ?nds, including his Greenland departure coast, or the Vestri Obygd.

This failure to delineate the Baffin Island coast has misled some scholars into assuming that the bulge marked "G" (Helluland) on the Stefansson Map is intended to represent the Cumberland Peninsula. However, the latitudes of the north and south terminations of this bulge are those of Cape Chidley and the Kaumajet Peninsula, re-spectively; while the position of the bulge relative to Greenland con-firms its identification as the mountainous section of the Labrador coast lying between Cape Chidley and the Nain Bight, as does the delineation of Ungava Bay behind the bulge.

The large bight on the Stefansson Map lying south of Helluland represents Nain Bight. Its north and south extent is accurately shown, but the depth of the bight is exaggerated. This is readily understand-able since it would have been nearly impossible for any early voy-ager to obtain an accurate idea of how deep it was. The entire bight is so choked with islands as to confuse even modern navigators, and the low-lying mainland shore behind these islands strengthens the im-pression that the bight is far deeper than it actually is.

The second bight on the Labrador Coast, shown just below Mark-land, is the Grosswater Bay-Sandwich Bay bight, and is accurately outlined as well as being very nearly correct as to scale.

The projecting peninsula marked *Promontorium Winlandiae* is the Great Northern Peninsula of Newfoundland. Its axis is incorrect since it is shown to run almost due south while in reality it runs off south-southwest by west. As a consequence of this distortion, the relative latitude of Cape Bauld is not correct either, but is in error by a degree and a half. It is most unlikely that this distortion existed on the orig-inal chart. What seems to have happened is that Stefansson, or a copyist before his time, tried to rationalize this southernmost portion of the map into agreement with a belief which was current before the fourteenth century that the Vinland Promontorium was connected with Africa by a coast of unknown length which ran far to the south and then swerved eastward to become part of the African coast. The commentary on the Stefansson Map itself suggests this: "Our people were of the belief that this [Vinland Promontorium] closed the ocean off from the south: but I gather from the reports of more recent [travelers] that either the sea, or a gulf, separates it from America."

That the orientation of the peninsula has in fact been distorted is demonstrated by the results achieved when one restores the peninsula to its correct axis. When we swing it (as I have done on the accompanying map) so that it runs off to the south-southwest by west, we find that the relative latitude of Cape Bauld becomes correct. This is the way it must have appeared on the original chart, for if there was one place at which the Norse voyagers had ample time and opportunity to check and recheck their latitude it was at their Straumfiord Camp, a few miles from Cape Bauld.

The general legend on the map, which is presumably Stefansson's own work, requires comment.

A. These lands, which the Angles reached, have the name of parched and dry, from the dryness of the sun or the burning of the cold.

B. The nearest of these [lands] is Vinland, which they call "the good" because of the fertility of the soil and the fruitful growth of usable materials. Our people were of the opinion that this closed the ocean off from the south. But I gather from the reports of more recent [travelers] that either the sea or a gulf separates it from America.

C. A rocky region, of which there is frequent mention in history.

The land the Angles or English reached is southeastern Labrador, but exactly to whom Stefansson is referring is unknown. Perhaps he is referring to one or other of the Cabots, who seem to have visited southeastern Labrador between 1497 and 1499.

The reference to Vinland the Good is a clear indication that Stefansson was drawing on data belonging to the Vinland exploration period. Stefansson himself was not too sure of the actual geography in the vicinity of Vinland, and this is understandable since he was exposed to three conflicting ideas about it. The original saga accounts (and presumably the voyage charts) indicated that the Strait of Belle Isle (Straumfiord) was a closed fiord, and gave no idea of how far south Vinland itself extended. The medieval geographers concluded that Vinland had to be connected with Africa since they thought of the entire Atlantic as an enclosed sea. Stefansson himself seems to have been aware of the fact, which was widely known by 1500, that there was a strait (Cabot Strait) to the south of Newfoundland.

The comment on the "rocky region," or Helluland, is interesting, for it confirms what we know from other sources — that this area remained well known to the Icelanders and Greenlanders for a considerable period after the original exploration voyages.

For the rest, the Stefansson Map speaks for itself, confirming in every important particular the fact that the Norse explored the eastern Labrador and northern Newfoundland coasts, and establishing the locations of Helluland, Markland and the Vinland of the Karlsefni expedition.

APPENDIX H

.Λ.V.Λ.

the vanished dorsets

A DESCRIPTION OF THE DORSET ESKIMOAN CULTURE AND OF THE
PEOPLE THE NORSE CALLED SKRAELING

In 1925 Dr. D. Jenness of the National Museum of Canada examined a number of ancient artifacts which had been collected near Cape Dorset in southwestern Baffin Island. Dr. Jenness demonstrated that these relics belonged to a hitherto unknown culture to which he gave the name Cape Dorset.

Since then a great many Dorset sites have been discovered, and a number have been excavated so that it is now possible to draw some conclusions about this mysterious people who at one time occupied most of the eastern arctic regions of North America.

Although I have consulted most of the available sources dealing with the subject, much of the synthesis which follows is based on the recent evaluations of Dorset culture by Dr. William Taylor of the National Museum of Canada, and on information obtained from Dr. Elmer Harp of Dartmouth College. However, neither Dr. Taylor nor Dr. Harp can be held responsible for my interpretations.

The Dorset culture appears to have developed *in situ* in the Foxe Basin-Hudson Strait area of the eastern Canadian Arctic and to have originated from a Siberian neolithic people who were the first human beings to reoccupy the Arctic after the passing of the last glaciation. These ancient people, who are conventionally referred to as Pre-Dorset, had reached Cape Denbigh in Alaska by 3500 B.C., and sites occupied by their descendants and dating to about 2000 B.C. have been found in northeastern Greenland. Little is known about them as yet, but some time around 800 B.C. they seem to have been gestating a new and largely indigenous culture which by about 600 B.C. had become recognizable as Dorset.

Dorset began to spread rather rapidly, obliterating its parent culture in the process. It spread westward back along the old migration routes (which had brought the Pre-Dorset people into the eastern Arctic), as far as Bernard Harbour. It spread northward to occupy some of the most remote of the high arctic lands, including Melville and Ellesmere islands. From Ellesmere it crossed to Greenland and worked southward down both coasts at least as far as Disco on the west and Angmagssalik on the east. It also spread southward from its Foxe Basin cradle to Ungava and then down the Labrador coast to the Strait of Belle Isle. From there it worked westward perhaps as far as Anticosti Island. It also crossed the strait and worked down both coasts of the Great Northern Peninsula of Newfoundland.

Considering the truly vast area that it came to occupy, we can conclude that the Dorset culture was not only a most vigorous but also a highly effective cultural complex. Until quite recently many authorities believed that Dorset was either an Indian or a composite Indian-Eskimo culture; however this view can no longer be sustained. The Dorsets were neither Eskimo nor Indian as we understand these terms. The most likely theory of their origin is that their Pre-Dorset ancestors stemmed from the same basic stock which eventually gave rise to the Eskimo peoples. Thus the Dorsets are related to the Eskimos, but they were not necessarily Eskimos themselves. Dr. Taylor believes that they spoke a variant of the Eskimo-Aleut language. They almost certainly wore a form of the tailored fur garments which are distinctive of Eskimoan and related cultures throughout the circumpolar regions. They used skin-covered boats. They may have built snow-houses, and they certainly built semi-subterranean houses which belong to the Asiatic neolithic tradition. Finally, they were a littoral folk and hunters of sea-mammals rather than inland dwellers.

From the evidence of archeology, and in particular as a result of the five-year excavation program which Dr. Elmer Harp has recently completed at the Dorset site of Port au Choix in Newfoundland, a good deal can be deduced about their way of life. Port au Choix seems to have been occupied by Dorsets, at least seasonally, for nearly a millennium, and they built more or less permanent houses there. These were rectangular structures, sometimes with a rounded back portion, from twenty to thirty feet in length and fifteen to twenty feet in width.

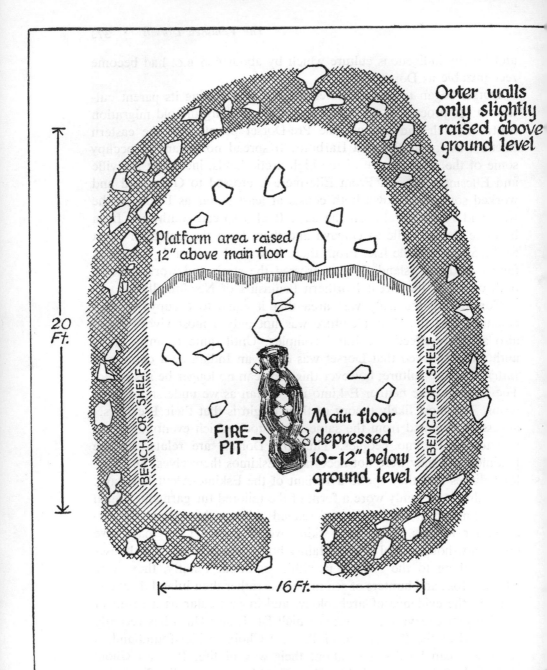

Plan of a typical Dorset house

The main floor space was excavated to a depth of a foot or two below the surrounding ground level, and low walls of turf and stones were raised outside this excavation, perhaps to an additional maximum height of two or three feet. No evidence remains as to how these large houses were roofed, but it was probably by some system of wooden or whalebone rafters covered with hides and turf. The rear of the house was raised above the general floor level to provide a large bench where people presumably slept in one communal bed. There seems to have been a central hearth and there may have been earth benches along the side walls facing the hearth. Seen from some distance away the houses must have resembled low earth mounds or hillocks; but they would have been roomy, warm and comfortable dwellings for all that external appearances were against them.

We know little about the Dorsets' physical appearance. The Norse, who encountered them in Newfoundland and Labrador shortly after A.D. 1000, have not left very clear descriptions except to say that they were swarthy and, by Norse standards, ill-looking; and that they had remarkable eyes and broad cheeks. What *is* notable about these first Norse contacts with Dorsets is that no mention is made of their having been small of stature. Apart from the meetings in Newfoundland and Labrador during the first decade of the eleventh century, the Norse sources contain only one other account of contact with a people who could have been Dorsets. This is found in the Floamanna Saga in connection with the story of Thorgisl Orrabeinsfostri, who was shipwrecked far to the north of the Greenland settlements, apparently on Baffin Island, about 997. Thorgisl met natives who are described as giants or, more accurately, as very large people. These could only have been Dorsets, since the succeeding native race — the Thule Eskimo — did not occupy these regions until the twelfth century had begun.

The latter-day Norse had a great many contacts with Thule Eskimos. There are numerous references to them in the sagas and in other sources, and the Thule people are almost invariably described as being dwarfish, or pygmylike. This is most significant in view of the fact that the Thule people preserved and handed down to their descendants of modern times many stories of their own contacts with the Dorsets, whom they called Tunnit. In every case these stories speak of the Tunnit as being larger and stronger than the Thule authors of the tales. In many cases these Eskimo folk tales specifically describe the Tunnit as having been giants. Skeletal material of undeniably Dorset origin is very scarce, but what little has been recovered seems to support the belief that the Dorsets were an Eskimo-like people of larger stature and more robust build than contemporary Ekimos.

The idea, which has been proposed and maintained by some recent authors, that the Dorsets were a pygmy race seems to have originated in part from the small size and delicate nature of their artifacts. The Dorsets were among the world's most talented workers in stone, and the majority of their points and edge tools are indeed small. This was not because they were a race of midgets; it was due to the fact that they and their forebears had developed such a high degree of technical proficiency in the manufacture of stone implements that they were able to reduce the unwieldy stone tools and points used by less accomplished cultures to smaller, lighter and more efficient proportions.

In addition to possessing a truly remarkable skill as workers in that intractable material, flint, the Dorsets were marvelous artists. A considerable number of their bone and stone carvings have been found, and not only are these the earliest examples of true art so far discovered in the North American arctic regions; they are good enough to hold their own with any native sculpture produced in the Arctic since their time.

Because the Dorsets occupied such a huge portion of the north for so long, local variants in their culture undoubtedly developed here and there. However the Dorsets with whom we are particularly concerned — those who lived in Greenland, along the western shores of Baffin Bay, Davis Strait and the Labrador Sea, and in Newfoundland — seem to have been pre-eminently a seal-hunting people.

Whereas later Eskimo peoples hunted all types of northern sea mammals, including both great and small whales, seals and walrus, it seems that the Dorsets in the areas with which we are most concerned concentrated on seals. Of course they made use of many other kinds of animals, including fishes, birds and land mammals, when the opportunity offered. Nevertheless, the seal remained the core of their culture, and according to the evidence of extensive bone middens in Greenland and Newfoundland they displayed a marked predilection for one particular species of seal — the pelagic and migratory harp seal, which is by far the most abundant member of its family in the northern waters of the Atlantic.

Wherever seals were to be found in sufficient numbers, there the Dorsets built their houses or pitched their skin tents. Fanning out from the rich sealing waters of Foxe Basin and Hudson Strait, they followed where the seals led. Their westward movement does not concern us, but the northward and eastward movements do. The Dorsets seem to have appeared in Greenland while their culture was still in a formative stage. An early Dorset variant known as the Sarqaq culture was in existence there by about the seventh century before Christ, but well before the beginning of the Christian era true Dorset had taken over and was established at least as far south as Angmagssalik and Disco.

The pelagic seals went where they could find their chosen food-fishes. These fishes in turn went where they could find *their* food, and so on down to the ultimate link in this food chain, the ocean plankton. But the optimum range of plankton, and consequently the range limits of many species of fishes upon which the pelagic seals depend, is largely determined by climatic conditions, of which water temperature is the most important single element. When it rises much of the plankton, together with the fishes which feed on it directly or indirectly, and the seals, who feed on the fishes, move to colder waters, and vice versa. Thus the seal populations shift as the general oceanic climate shifts; and as the seals shift their range so also must those peoples who depend upon them for a livelihood.

Between the mid-seventeenth and mid-eighteenth centuries there was a period of severe climatic regression in North Atlantic regions, one of whose results was a pronounced southerly extension of the ranges of many arctic sea mammals. Walrus were breeding in the Gulf of St. Lawrence while harp seals were being killed in large numbers off the coasts of New England.

Climatologists have demonstrated that between 500 B.C. and A.D. 500, the North Atlantic regions suffered from an even more severe regression, which became most intense between about 180 and 350 A.D. During this period the southward extension of the ranges of arctic sea mammals must have been very marked, and it was during this period that the Dorsets ventured farthest to the south.

However, during the sixth century A.D. the period of cold weather came to a close, and the climate began to grow steadily more genial. By the eleventh century the water temperatures in the vicinity of Greenland had risen by as much as three degrees Centigrade, which must have resulted in a tremendous change in the biotic conditions in the sea, and which would have been more than sufficient to bring about a drastic northward shift in the range of the pelagic seals and many other sea mammals.

If the sea mammals went north, the Dorsets would have followed; and this is probably the explanation of why Erik the Red met no natives in Greenland when between 981 and 983 he explored the coasts from Angmagssalik on the east around Cape Farewell and north up the west coast probably as far as Melville Bay.

There are excellent modern analogies for this postulated northward withdrawal of the Dorsets. Toward the middle of the nineteenth century a minor warming trend began to affect the North Atlantic regions. By the early 1920's the seal population on Greenland's west coast had thinned out to the point where the Eskimos could no longer make a living by seal hunting unless they went north at least as far as Uppernavik. The Danish authorities had no desire to see a mass migration of the Eskimos to the north, and the Eskimos themselves did not wish to move, so a compromise solution was found by starting a fishery for cod — a species of fish which until that time had been rare in Greenland waters, but which in its turn was moving north.

On the east Greenland coast the evidence of a northward withdrawal of the seal population and a consequent drastic reduction in the size of the Eskimos population was even more apparent. Prior to 1828 the east coast Eskimos had little or no contact with European civilization, and in fact were almost unknown even to the Danes who administered the island. During the years 1828-1830 an expedition was sent north up the east coast and this party found fairly large numbers of Eskimos.

In 1884 another expedition went north, this time reaching Angmagssalik. It discovered that during the years since 1830 the Eskimo population of the coast between Cape Farewell and Angmagssalik had declined by about 50 per cent, and there were clear indications of a rapidly decaying culture. The answer to the riddle of what had happened to these people was not hard to find. They themselves explained it to the Danes. The seals were going, they said. The pack ice in the East Greenland Current was diminishing, and the seals were going.

If the Danes had not arrived when they did and if they had not provided a substitute economy for these Eskimos, the East Greenland coast south of Scoresby Sound would have been devoid of Eskimo inhabitants within a few more years.

Something similar seems to have happened to the Dorsets in the Baffin Bay-Davis Strait-Labrador Sea regions when the Little Ice Age came to an end and the climate began to grow warmer again. However the northward withdrawal of seals and Dorsets would not have taken place at the same rate on both sides of this great sea inlet. This is because the west coast of Greenland is washed by a northward-flowing current which is warmed by the waters of the Irminger Current; while the opposite coasts are washed by a southward-flowing polar current running directly out of the Arctic Ocean. Its waters would have remained very cold until the warming trend had become well established.

The Dorsets who occupied Newfoundland are believed to have reached the Strait of Belle Isle well before the start of the Christian era, and recent carbon-14 dates from Port au Choix seem to confirm that this site was first occupied almost 2400 years ago. At one time or another the Dorsets occupied the whole west coast as far south as Cape Ray on the Cabot Strait, and the east coast of the Great Northern Peninsula, probably as far south as Little Harbour Deep. They may also have occupied the Baie Verte Peninsula and Horse and Grey islands. Pack ice conditions in the waters off these localities would have favored them as major breeding grounds and concentration areas for the vast harp seal herds.

Early in the autumn the harp seals migrate southward from their summer range among the arctic islands, following the Canadian and Labrador currents down the west side of Baffin Bay and Davis Strait. In late February and March they congregate among the pack ice of the Gulf of St. Lawrence and off the northeastern coasts of Newfoundland, where the females climb up on their chosen pans and whelp. The pups remain on the ice until they are old enough to swim, a matter of two to three weeks, and during this period they and their mothers are very vulnerable. This is the time when the great kills are made by sealers — kills which even recently have run as high as half a million animals in a single season. Often an onshore wind sets the pack tight to the coast, and when this happens shore-sealers walk out across the pans from land and kill large numbers. If the ice remains off the coast, shore-sealers sometimes row out to it in small boats.

The whole west coast of Newfoundland and the east coast of the Great Northern Peninsula must have been a veritable sealer's paradise during the very cold epoch which saw the arrival of the Dorsets.

The Newfoundland Dorsets did not come to an uninhabited land. They encountered people of an ancient Indian culture which Dr. Harp calls Boreal Archaic and which was the precursor of the Beothuk culture. The Dorsets displaced these early residents from the coastal regions and, over the succeeding centuries, the newcomers prospered and became a numerous and relatively settled race. Although many sections of the coasts they occupied have not as yet been studied by archeologists, more than twenty habitation sites have already been discovered. Most of these have the appearance of considerable age and permanence; a natural consequence of the fact that the Dorsets did not have to go looking for the seals — the seals came to them, and in such numbers that they were doubtless able to obtain most of their annual requirements of fat and oil, and much of their meat, during the months that the great herds were near their coasts.

At the Dorset site at Port au Choix the accumulation of seal bones has to be seen to be believed. It covers several acres and in places it is almost a foot deep. Nor is it unique. Some Dorset sites on the east coast of the peninsula have been turned into gardens by local families, and they plant their turnips in soil which is still so rich and black with the remains of seals that it is actually greasy to the touch. Although some of these gardens have been worked for a century, it is still an annual spring chore to pick out and cart away barrowloads of ancient seal bones.

It appears that in February or March of every year the Dorsets congregated at the best sealing stations along both coasts. Using skin boats when necessary, or walking out over the pack ice when possible, they made huge kills of young harp seals. They probably smoked or dried large quantities of meat, and stored still more of it in deep pits where it would keep for a surprisingly long time. Blubber was no doubt rendered down and stored in skin or bladder bags.

The Newfoundland Dorsets were not, however, entirely dependent on seals. They also made extensive use of the excellent salmon rivers which abound on the peninsula, and they probably hunted caribou in winter. The west-coast Dorsets would have been particularly well off in this regard, for the great barrens and flats of the west coast once harbored one of the largest herds of caribou in Newfoundland — a herd which probably numbered in the tens of thousands.

As long as the cold climate continued to bring multitudes of harp seals to the coasts each spring, the Newfoundland Dorsets would have remained a numerous and vigorous people. They must have had some contact with the Boreal Archaic or proto-Beothuk Indians, but there is no evidence that there was much conflict. The Dorsets depended primarily on hunting seals off the coasts; while the Indians depended on caribou hunting in the interior of the main part of the island. Their lives seem to have been almost devoid of the influence of war, and they appear to have developed as peaceful peoples.

However, when the climate began to warm toward the Little Climatic Optimum, things changed for the Newfoundland Dorsets. Over a period of several centuries the seals became steadily less abundant and harder to reach from shore. As long as the polar current — locally the Labrador Current — continued to bring an adequate quantity of winter ice south to form the whelping pack off the Newfoundland coasts, the seals would have continued to breed there and to carry on their age-old pattern of migration. But as the Labrador Current grew warmer the pack would have diminished in size and would have tended to remain farther off shore, away from the eastern coasts. Something similar would also have been happening in the gulf, but there, under the influence of the prevailing westerly winds, the remaining pack would still have tended to drive against the west coast of the Great Northern Peninsula, even as it shrank in size from year to year.

Within the past half century there has been a noticeable decrease in the size of the Atlantic sealing pack coincidental with a warming trend in the weather. Sealing skippers of long experience say that the area of the main pack — the "front" as they call it — has shrunk by at least 50 per cent during the last forty or fifty years. *This shrinkage has now resulted in an almost total cessation of the shore-sealing activities which were once carried on along most of the northeastern coasts of Newfoundland.* There is now little or no shore-sealing from the north and east coasts of the Great Northern Peninsula. However, shore-sealing is still carried on from the west coast, and reasonably large kills are made there even though they are not comparable to the kills of fifty years ago.

By analogy, and from the various data at our disposal, we can reconstruct what probably happened to the Newfoundland Dorsets as the Little Climatic Optimum approached its peak. Sealing in the Strait and on the east coast would have been the first to suffer. Perhaps as early as the sixth or seventh century A.D. it would have been difficult for the north- and east-coast Dorsets to make an adequate living from the sea. Nor did they have broad coastal barrens full of caribou to fall back upon, since on the east coast the Long Range Mountains border the sea and fall into it in abrupt cliffs.

Some of the east-coast Dorsets may have crossed over to join their relatives on the west coast, but here too the sealing would have been falling off. Perhaps the remainder drifted north, seeking waters where the seals still lived in quantity, or perhaps they simply died out and disappeared.

By about A.D. 1000, when the climate was approaching its warmest period, the remaining west-coast Dorsets must have been having a hard time getting enough seals. In fact their sealing had probably fallen off to the point where it alone would not support them. They could have survived only by relying more and more heavily on caribou, and probably they did so. But even so their numbers had evidently declined to the point where only a vestigial population still remained in Newfoundland.

These survivors were the Skraelings whom the Norse encountered on their Vinland voyages. It is an ironic fact that the Dorsets seem to have vanished from Newfoundland within a century after the Norse had abandoned hope of settling the country — a decision which was forced upon them by their conflicts with a people who were about to disappear not only from Newfoundland, but from time itself.

Shortly after the Norse encountered them in Newfoundland, the Dorset people as a whole came under a much more formidable pressure from another race. The Thule Eskimos, whose culture seems to have originated in Alaska, had begun to sweep eastward. Although they may not have been the physical equals of the Dorsets, they had a far more sophisticated and adaptable hunting culture. They used kayaks, had dogs (which the Dorsets apparently never owned), and dog sleds, and hunted every kind of sea mammal from the great baleen whales down to the smallest seals.

The Thule people, who were the forbears of modern Canadian and Greenland Eskimos, were aggressive as well as able. Within a century or so of their arrival in the eastern Dorset area they had obliterated the Dorset culture. We do not know if this was brought about through a process of annihilation or absorption. Perhaps some Dorsets were absorbed into the Thule society, but from the surviving tales of conflict between Thule and Tunnit peoples we conclude that most of the Dorsets, who seem to have been generally a rather tractable and unwarlike people, were either killed or driven to areas where they could not support themselves, and so went down into oblivion. At about the end of the eleventh century the last of them appear to have vanished and to have been supplanted by Eskimos. It is possible that some remnant groups survived for a little longer in such remote places as the northeastern tip of Greenland; but of this we have no certain knowledge.

The Dorsets were a primitive people in the historical sense, but they nevertheless possessed a highly developed culture. They were apparently peaceful and contented specialists who had found an ideal niche for themselves, but who lacked the will or the strength to defend it against aggressive interlopers. In all likelihood they were a more civilized people — in the most meaningful sense of the word — than the Norse, who thought of them, and treated them — as semi-human savages.

PART 2

/\./\./\

analytical

APPENDIX I

/\\.\\/\\

the westmen
in iceland and greenland

SOME OF THE EVIDENCE DEMONSTRATING A CELTIC OCCUPATION OF
GREENLAND AND ICELAND BEFORE THE ARRIVAL OF THE NORSE

I: ICELAND

Some of the most convincing testimony to the fact that Westmen — a term used by the Norse to describe inhabitants of the British Isles in general — were settled in Iceland when that island was first visited by the Norse is to be found in the Norse historical records themselves.

This testimony is of particular interest since it occurs in two works which were not written until the middle of the twelfth century, long after Iceland had become a Christian community; while the records from the actual period of the Norse "discovery" of Iceland, when the Norse were still pagans, make no mention at all of Celtic occupancy; and in some cases they state categorically that the island was uninhabited. The reticence of the early chroniclers is what one would expect, for they were undoubtedly as narrowly chauvinistic as we still are today.

The silence was eventually broken by two Icelandic historians who were prominent Christians and whose religious loyalties had presumably modified their racial patriotism to the point where they felt compelled to make at least peripheral mention in their written works of the unhappy Celtic Christians who had been supplanted in Iceland by the Norse.

One of these works is the Islendingabok, composed by Ari Thorgilsson, circa 1120. The other is the Landnamabok, one of whose recensions seems to have been a joint effort by Ari Thorgilsson and Sturla Thordarsson, and which dates from a little later in the same century.

The Islendingabok tells us that at the time Norse settlement began:

Iceland was covered with forests between mountains and the seashore. Then Christian men whom Norsemen called Papas were here; but afterwards they went away because they did not wish to live here together with heathen men, and they left behind them Irish books, bells and croziers. From this could be seen that they were Westmen.

The Landnamabok version differs only in details:

Before Iceland was settled from Norway there were here people called Papas. They were Christians. . . . There have been found remains of them [such] as Irish books, bells, croziers and other things which show that they were Westmen. These were found in the east at Papii and Papylia. Moreover it is stated in English books that at this time there was trafficking between the two countries.

The Landnamabok contains two other references, one of which is an incidental aside in a lengthy genealogy. It deals with the landtaking in Iceland of a Norseman called Ketil the Foolish:

Ketil . . . settled land between Geirland's River and Firth River above Newcome. Ketil dwelt at Kirkby [Place of the Church], there the Papar had formerly had their abode.

The other Landnamabok reference is an account of the first successful attempt at settlement by the Norse, when Ingolf and Hjorlief established themselves on the south coast of Iceland about the year 874. This account contains a peculiar story which is intended to explain how the Westman Islands, which lie just off the southern shore, got their name.* According to the Landnamabok explanation, some of Hjorleif's Irish slaves murdered him and then fled to the Westman Islands, where the avenging Ingolf tracked them down, slaughtered some and drove the rest to destruction over the high cliffs. This tale is full of clumsy inventions. It is much easier to believe that while there may indeed have been a slaughter of Celts, those unfortunates were in fact settlers who had been in occupation of the islands for some time, or else they were refugees driven from the mainland of Iceland; and that the name commemorates the Celtic occupation rather than the dubious deeds of a handful of slaves.

Sturla Thordarsson's comment that according to "English" books there

---

* A respectable number of surviving place names in Iceland, including the Westman Islands, are of Celtic origin.

was trafficking between Iceland and the British Isles prior to the arrival of the Norse requires more consideration than it has usually been given. The "English" books of which he speaks no longer exist, but the suggestion seems to be implicit that they referred to regular voyages, and there would have had to be a reasonably large Celtic population in Iceland to have made such long voyages worthwhile.

There is, however, one book extant which does speak of a Celtic voyage to Iceland long before the Norse got there. It is called *De Mensura Orbis Terrae* (On the Measurement of the Earth) and it was written by an Irish cleric called Dicuil, at the court of King Louis the Pious in France. Dicuil may have written his book as late as 835 or as early as 800. In it he has some curious things to say of Iceland:

It is now the thirtieth year since some clerics who dwelt upon that Island [Iceland: he calls it Thule] from February to August told me that not only during the summer solstice but also during the days near that time, toward evening, the setting sun hides itself as if behind a small hill so that there is no darkness for even a small time.* A man may do whatever he wishes, even to picking lice from his shirt just as well as if it was by the light of the sun . . . therefore it is evident that those are in error who have written that the sea around Thule is frozen . . . [since] these clerics who sailed there did so during a time of the year when naturally it would be at its coldest, and landed on this island, and dwelt there . . . but they found that one day's sail from it toward the north, the sea was frozen.

This tells us that a group of clerics, who were perhaps passengers on a merchant ship, landed on Iceland in February — a time of the year which no sane man would have picked for a voyage to that island unless he was sure of some sort of prepared reception awaiting him. Significantly, these clerics noted that earlier descriptions of Iceland, which had stressed the coldness of its climate, were no longer applicable — as indeed they would not have been in the eighth century after three hundred years of steadily improving weather. The fact that they commented on this at all is an indication that Iceland had been visited during the cold climatic era preceding the fifth century.

Dicuil does not quote the clerics as saying anything about settlements; but there is no reason why he should have done so. He was writing a scientific treatise dealing with mathematical and geographical matters, and he draws upon information from the clerics — who were the only relatively educated men in those times — only in order to obtain data with which to support his own thesis.

---

* An accurate description of the sun's motion in the north of Iceland at this season of the year.

The Celtic occupancy of Iceland appears to be confirmed by recent archeological work during which seventh- and eighth-century Celtic religious and art objects have been uncovered at a number of Icelandic sites. An interesting fact about these sites is that some of them have been known for a long time, but it has always previously been assumed that they were Scandinavian. It is not difficult to understand how such an error could have arisen; Norse farm buildings, tools and household equipment of this period are difficult to distinguish from their Celtic counterparts in general and are almost indistinguishable from the structures and materials used by mixed Norse, Celtic and Pictish settlers in the Outer Islands and the Hebrides.

This is a point to be kept in mind; for it has a bearing on the problem of determining what happened to the Westmen who fled from Iceland when the Viking invasion of that island began in earnest.

II. GREENLAND

There is as yet no indisputable archeological evidence to support the contention that Westman fugitives from Iceland settled in Greenland. No exclusively Celtic artifacts or undeniably Celtic sites have been reported. The possibility has not been publicly entertained that some of the very early Greenland sites, which have all been assigned to the Norse settlement period by the Scandinavian archeologists who excavated them, might have been originally occupied by Westmen.

Such prior occupation is difficult to demonstrate due to the resemblances which existed between Norse and Westman buildings and artifacts of this period. The problem is further complicated by the likelihood that Norse immigrants to Greenland would have occupied the very sites used by earlier settlers, and may even have taken over the abandoned buildings themselves.*

However, if there is no indisputable archeological material to show that the Westmen fled to Greenland, there is testimony of other kinds which demonstrates that this must have been what happened. There is, for instance, the Landnamabok story of Ari Marsson, who about 970 was storm-driven west from Iceland to a land named Irland Mikkla or Greater Ireland. Here Ari encountered a Christian community which could not have been anything else except Celtic (Irish), and was baptized.†

In order to dispose of Celtic claims to the discovery of Greenland, many writers have preferred to ignore the story of Ari Marsson or have chosen to label it as fiction. They have had to do this over the most serious ob-

---

* This problem is dealt with in more detail in Chapter Three.
† The full text of the Landnamabok account will be found in Chapter One.

jections, since the personal history of Ari is among the best documented of any of the early Icelandic voyagers. The Landnamabok traces Ari Marsson's ancestry back to some of the original Norse settlers in Iceland, and it does the same for his wife, who was directly descended from Aud the Deep Minded, one of the most prominent of the early settlers. The salient fact that Ari was a real person cannot be questioned.

The author of the Landnamabok quotes two separate sources as providing the basis for his account of Ari's voyage. One of these was Earl Thorfinn of Orkney, who was a famous historical figure. His version of Ari Marsson's tribulations was transmitted through a man called Thorkel Gellirsson, or Gellisson. This Thorkel Gellirsson was the grandson of Ari Marsson. He was also the uncle of Ari Thorgilsson, the first Icelandic historian, whose Islendingabok is considered to be the very cornerstone of Icelandic historical sources. It is conceded by many scholars that the author of the extant recensions of the Landnamabok drew much of it from the works of this same Ari Thorgilsson; and, in fact, the original version of the Landnamabok may well have been largely written by Ari Thorgilsson himself.

Thorkel Gellirsson was a widely traveled man and he provided Ari Thorgilsson with much information about family matters — which would have included Ari Marsson's story — as well as about early times in general, including the Islendingabok and Landnamabok accounts of the settlement of Greenland by Erik the Red. It would therefore follow that if one insists on dismissing the Ari Marsson story, one has little choice but to concede the logic of also dismissing the Islendingabok and Landnamabok accounts of Erik's settlement in Greenland, since both accounts derived from Thorkel Gellirsson. But these have been accepted by all authorities as being unquestionably true.

The problem of locating Ari's landfall has seldom been tackled in an unemotional way. Most authors who have dealt with Ari have boldly held to the contention that he landed on the mainland of the continent, somewhere on the New England coast. In their anxiety to shake the conventional insistence of those historians who believe that the Westmen never got beyond Iceland, Ari's supporters have generally tended to make outrageous claims which have served only to give their opponents an excuse to consign the whole matter to limbo.

The Landnamabok tells us that:

Greater Ireland . . . lies off westward in the ocean adjacent to Vinland the Good; it is reported that one can sail thither from Ireland in six days.

That Greater Ireland could not have been on the coast of North

America ought to be self-evident both from the distances involved and from the fact that the prevailing winds and currents between the British Isles and the American seaboard set so strongly to the east that an accidental drift on such a course, and for such a distance, becomes impossible.

It is 2650 nautical miles from Ireland to Cape Cod, and 1710 miles between the closest point in North America (eastern Newfoundland) and the westernmost part of Ireland. If, in the face of the Gulf Stream and the prevailing westerlies, a ship of the period *wished* to sail to America, and somehow managed to keep up a daily average of 120 nautical miles, it would have taken her fourteen days to sail from Ireland to Newfoundland, and twenty-two days from Ireland to Cape Cod. This is the theoretical minimum time needed, but the skippers of the fast and able Newfoundland schooners which made the Atlantic run for many decades used to consider themselves lucky if they could cross from Ireland to Newfoundland in twenty days.

Where then was Greater Ireland? Unless some since vanished island existed in mid-Atlantic in Norse times, it could only have been in Greenland.

It is reported to have lain six days' sail west of Ireland. Here we are not given a specified distance as part of a set of sailing directions. Instead we are told only how far it was *reputed* to lie from Ireland. Nevertheless the direct out-of-sight-of-land distance, in terms of Norse sailing days or doegr (a doegr equals 120 nautical miles) between Erris Head in Ireland and Cape Farewell in Greenland is just over eight days. As for the direction, west in Norse parlance meant in the western airt, or between west-southwest and west-northwest. The course from Erris Head to Cape Farewell is west-northwest.

Considering the prevailing winds and currents in the North Atlantic it is apparent that if a vessel approaching Iceland from Ireland or southern Norway was to be caught in one of the polar northeasters which are the prevalent winds in the region north of 62 degrees, she would not only make leeway to the westward as a result of the wind, but would also be carried in that direction by the Irminger Current. The most likely landfall for her, assuming she could not sail her desired course, would then be southern Greenland, which lies adjacent to Vinland (Newfoundland) in relation either to Iceland or to Ireland.

Additional documentary evidence to help us locate Greater Ireland exists in a little known — or, it may be, largely ignored — work written by an Arab named Idrisi who lived at the court of Roger of Sicily about the middle of the twelfth century. Roger was a Norseman, and many fellow Norsemen came to visit him in Sicily and were employed by him as mercenaries. Idrisi undoubtedly obtained his information about the North Atlantic regions from these expatriates.

Among other things Idrisi gives a set of sailing distances for the northern regions:

Between the extremity of Ireland and the extremity of Scotland, two days' sail are reckoned.
From the northern extremity of Scotland to Reslanda [Iceland] three days.
From the extremity of Reslanda to Greater Ireland, one day.

When we examine the chart we find that it is a 240-nautical-mile voyage from Malin Head, the northern point of Ireland, to Cape Wrath, the northwestern extremity of Scotland. Two days' sail, by the Norse standard measure, was 240 nautical miles.

From Cape Wrath in Scotland to the nearest point in Iceland, Hofn (which lies under the lee of the 7000-foot Vatna Glacier) is approximately 300 nautical miles out of sight of land.* Three days sail by Norse measurement is 360 miles.

From the Vatneyri Peninsula in western Iceland to the nearest point on the Greenland coast is 155 miles out of sight of land.

It will be noted that the route from Ireland to Greater Ireland, as outlined by Idrisi, entails only six days of open-water sailing, which suggests that the reported distance given in the Landnamabok derives from the same source used by Idrisi, and refers to the same indirect route described by the Arab chronicler.

In any event, Idrisi's data seem to establish beyond any reasonable doubt what was already self-evident, that "Greater Ireland" was in fact a part of Greenland.

If we are to take Idrisi's location literally, we must assume that Greater Ireland included the east coast of Greenland. The supposition that Greater Ireland extended south down the east coast from a point opposite Iceland to Cape Farewell, and some short distance up the western coast to include the pastoral lands of the Julianehaab and Ivitgut bights, is not unreasonable. The place was, after all, called Greater Ireland presumably in a direct size comparison between it and Ireland.

There are two other references to Greater Ireland in the Norse literature. One of them is in a paper copy of an old parchment which was transcribed

---

* Norse deep-sea sailing distances appear to have always been given from the last sight of land astern to the first loom of land ahead. For a discussion of the Norse measurement of nautical distances and general navigational procedures, see Appendix F.

by Bjorn Jonsson in Iceland in the seventeenth century. The original
document, now lost, appears to have been a geographical description of
the northern regions dating from the late fourteenth or early fifteenth
century:

> Now there is, as stated, south of that part of Greenland which has settle-
> ments, deserts, unsettled areas and snow-mountains, then Skraelings, then
> Markland, then Vinland the Good. Next to it, and a little back, lies Albania,
> that is Hvitramannaland; thither formerly were sailings from Ireland. Irishmen
> and Icelanders recognized here Are [Ari], son of Mar and Kotla from
> Reykjaness, who had not been heard of for a long time and who had become
> a chieftain in the land.

This passage is the one usually quoted as proof that Greater Ireland
was on the continent of North America. But by the time this geographical
description was written, two or three centuries had elapsed since Greater
Ireland had been supplanted by the Greenland colonies established by
Erik the Red. It appears that the author's knowledge of Ari and of Greater
Ireland (by whatever name) was obtained from an early recension of the
Landnamabok. We know that there were earlier and perhaps more detailed
versions than those we now possess. The Landnamabok would have told
him, as it still tells us, that Albania (Hvitramannaland or Irland Mikkla)
lay somewhere to the west adjacent to "Vinland the Good." It probably
would not have occurred to him that it might have been located in Greenland, which, so far as he would have been able to tell from the available
records, had been uninhabited before Erik's time.*

His quandary was probably not so very different from those of more
recent authors. Faced with the problem of where to locate Greater Ireland,
the author of this passage gave it a vague position in the direction of
Vinland. But the phrase "next to it, and a little back" may not mean back
from *Vinland* as most authors have assumed, but back from (settled)
Greenland. Since no inhabitable lands lay between the Greenland settlements and Iceland, this would be further proof of a failure to identify the
location of Greater Ireland with the Greenland settlement area.

If the author of this geography does not help us to locate the exact
whereabouts of Greater Ireland, he does give us one important piece of
information which we would not otherwise possess. He states that both
Irishmen and Icelanders recognized Ari Marsson there; and this is evidence
not only that there was sea-borne intercourse between Ireland and Greater
Ireland, but also that Norse traders had personal knowledge of the place.

---

* Erik failed to locate Irland Mikkla in Greenland through his failure to correctly
identify the abandoned settlement there. See Chapters Two to Four.

The other reference is contained in the Saga of Erik the Red and has to do with an incident which took place during the homeward voyage of the Icelander, Thorfinn Karlsefni, from Newfoundland to Greenland about 1006. Somewhere on the coast of Labrador the Norse encountered some Skraelings and captured two young boys, whom they carried off.* The children were taught to speak Norse.

They said too that there was a land on the other side, opposite their country, which was inhabited by people who wore white garments and who yelled loudly and carried poles before them to which cloths were attached. People believed this must have been Hvitramannaland or Ireland the Great.

These Skraelings were Dorsets, and the Dorsets once inhabited the coasts of Greenland at least as far south as Disco and Angmagssalik. They abandoned Greenland due to a dearth of seals consequent upon the warming climate, sometime after the seventh century but well before the arrival of Erik the Red in the tenth century.†

At first glance it seems far-fetched to suggest that a roving party of Dorsets might have encountered a Westman settlement on the southwest coast of Greenland, observed a religious celebration or procession, and have been so impressed by this fantastic (to their way of thinking) performance that the story became one of their folk-tales and was passed on from generation to generation through several centuries. However, it is a well-documented fact that primitive people who possess no written language frequently display a remarkable ability to retain a folk memory of things which occurred in the far distant past. Apart from the circumstantial stories concerning the Greenland Norse which Eskimos were still telling to white men in the twentieth century, about four hundred years after the Greenland Norse had become extinct, a particularly relevant example of the enduring folk memory of the Eskimos is to be found in the experiences of C. F. Hall.‡

Hall was an American explorer who lived with the Eskimos of southern Baffin Island during 1861-1862. He became conversant with their language and eventually they led him to where, so they said, white men had built a house a "long time ago." The site turned out to belong to the Frobisher expeditions which had sailed west from England in the middle of the sixteenth century. Although Europe had forgotten the location of Frobisher's discoveries — in Hall's time it was believed that Frobisher had landed on

---

* See Chapter 25 for details of this encounter.
† See Appendix H for details of Dorset migration and distribution.
‡ Charles Francis Hall, *Arctic Researches and Life Among the Esquimaux* (New York, 1865).

the southern tip of Greenland — the Eskimos had preserved a folk memory of the event which was nothing short of phenomenal. They gave Hall the most detailed and circumstantial account of what their ancestors had observed about the appearance and activities of the white men and the sailing ships which had appeared off the south Baffin Coast three hundred years earlier. These accounts were so detailed that Hall immediately realized that the people and ships described could have belonged only to the Frobisher expedition. These conclusions have since been fully authenticated.

It is a somewhat humiliating thought that Frobisher's geographical discoveries, which had faded to an almost mythical status even in the written records of Europeans, should have been restored to their rightful place through the tenacious folk memory of a stone-age people.

When we consider this example of how retentive the Eskimoan mind can be, it no longer seems beyond the bounds of possibility that the Dorset children were speaking of an actual encounter between their ancestors and Westmen in south Greenland two centuries earlier.

It is difficult, if not impossible, to find an adequate alternative identification for the people described by the Skraelings. The Celtic clergy wore white robes; they engaged in processions during which there was much singing and chanting, which the bewildered Dorsets would doubtless have described as "yelling"; and they carried staves to which religious banners were attached. It has been suggested that the people seen by the Dorsets might have been Nauscopie or Montagnais Indians from the interior of Labrador, but anyone familiar with the ethnology of these forest people will find this explanation impossible to accept.

The location of this country, which the Norse of about 1000 *themselves* identified as Hvitramannaland, can hardly be anywhere other than Greenland. It lay "on the other side, opposite their country," which surely means the other side of Davis Strait or the Labrador Sea, opposite to Labrador.

A number of ancient Church documents also exist which refer to Greenland, under the names Gronland and Cronland, as having been a Christian country about A.D. 830, or approximately 130 years before the Norse colonists in Greenland accepted Christianity. If Greenland was occupied by Christians at this time, they would almost certainly have been Westmen.

Some scholars have claimed that these documents must be forgeries, on the grounds that it is an established fact that no Europeans did precede the Norse to Greenland. For those who may be interested in drawing their own conclusions we present a brief summary of the history and contents of these papers as Appendix J.

There is another documentary source, this time Norse in origin, which seems to bear on the problem of what happened to the Westmen from Iceland. It is found in Ari Thorgilsson's Islendingabok account of the exploration of Greenland by Erik the Red in the years 981 to 984:

The Country which was called Gronland was discovered and settled from Iceland. Erik the Red was the name of the man from Breidafiord who went there and took possession of the land at the place since called Eriksfiord. He called the country Gronland, saying people would desire to go there if the country had a good name. Both east and west in the country they found human habitations, fragments of skin boats and stone implements, from which it was evident that the same kind of people had been there as inhabited Vinland and whom the Gronlanders called Skraelings.

Ari Thorgilsson's explanation of how Greenland got its name, written about a century and a half after the event, may be correct. On the other hand it may be an interpolation made by a man who was puzzled (as we still are today) why anyone would call a country which was six-tenths glaciers, about three-tenths barren rock and mountains, and about one-tenth arctic prairie, a *green* land.

If Erik actually did christen the country with this name because he had the inborn instincts of a modern real-estate promoter, as Ari Thorgilsson suggests, then he must have been rather short-sighted. It is one thing to practice a flagrant piece of deception on someone you will never see again. It would have been quite something else to have duped several hundred fiery Norsemen with whom Erik was not only going to have to live in close contact, but whom he also expected to follow his leadership. The story does not seem very plausible.

Furthermore, we possess accurate information as to how Erik, or his followers on the initial exploration venture, really did describe Greenland. Late in the summer of the year when Erik's colonization fleet departed from Iceland for Greenland, the son of one of the settlers arrived home in Iceland from a Norway voyage to find his father gone with Erik. The son, Bjarni Herjolfsson, was a trader who owned his own ship. He decided to follow his father and to this end provided himself with sailing directions — he had never been in the Greenland Sea before — and a description of the new country. This information could have originated only from Erik or from one of those who accompanied him on his exploratory voyage.

Bjarni was blown off course, and the first land he saw was an abundantly wooded country. He at once realized, and said so, that this truly green land was not what he was looking for. Two days later he raised the green forested coasts of another land. When his men asked him if this was

Greenland he replied *that he no more thought this to be Greenland than the former country had been, for, he said: "Very large snow [or ice] mountains are reported to be in Greenland."*

Bjarni continued his voyage, crossed the Labrador Sea to the eastward, and finally raised the five-thousand-foot coastal mountains, backed by an immense inland ice sheet, of the land he sought: *When he was still a considerable distance out to sea, and could have seen nothing green at all, he remarked: "This most resembles what I was told about Greenland and so we may steer to this land.**

By a considerable stretch of the imagination it might be possible for us to accept the name Greenland as being applicable to the relatively minuscule section of the country where the first Norse settlement was established. However, the Norse not only used the name for the whole of the island we now call Greenland. They also used it to include the opposite western coasts of Baffin Island.† *Green*land is such an obvious misnomer for this vast expanse of arctic and subarctic territory (most of which Erik saw during his exploratory voyage) that Ari's supposition as to the origin of the name becomes even more dubious.

Erik probably did not coin the name at all. He probably knew it before he left Iceland, for there were many people there, both Celtic slaves and Norsemen, whose ancestors had lived either in Ireland or on the Outer Islands for generations, and who could have known about Cronusland, or Cronland. It seems to be a remarkable coincidence that the native name which Demetrius, the Romanized Greek civil servant of the first century, thought sounded like Cronus, or Cronusland, should bear such a startling resemblance to the name Gronland. The coincidence becomes even more striking when we remember that in at least two of the early ninth-century references to Gronland in the Hanoverian church documents, the name is spelled with a C, as Cronland.

The Norse records do not tell us that Erik might have found Celtic settlements in Greenland. On the other hand, the remainder of the quoted passage from the Islendingabok comes close to fitting the pattern established by that self-same source in connection with Iceland, by admitting, in a backhanded sort of way, that the Norse were not the first discoverers.

Erik found human habitations, skin boats, and implements of stone instead of Irish books, bells and croziers.

The defenders of the generally accepted thesis that the Norse were first in Greenland have dismissed the possibility that this passage may indicate the earlier presence of Europeans, by insisting it must refer to relics left

---

* Bjarni's story is told in Chapters 7 to 9.
† See Appendix D.

behind by natives, even as the Islendingabok specifies. It is not impossible that they are right; nevertheless the matter merits investigation.

The first thing which strikes us is that Erik found these things between 981 and 983; but no Norseman encountered a Skraeling — the name used by the Norse for all Eskimoan people — until the time of Karlsefni's expedition to Newfoundland about 1004. It is apparent that Erik himself could not have identified the things he found as being of Skraeling origin.

Archeological studies have established that people of several Eskimoan cultures once inhabited the land we now call Greenland. The first of these were people of the Pre-Dorset culture who, according to carbon-14 dating, were in north Greenland by about 2000 B.C. The second culture is known as Dorset.* Sites belonging to this people, and dating from as early as 600 B.C., have been found as far south as Disco on the west coast and Angmagssalik on the east. However, none of the known Dorset sites in Greenland appear to have been occupied later than the ninth century A.D., and the Dorsets had entirely vanished from Greenland well before the Norse arrived there late in the tenth century.

The next Eskimo people to appear were of the Thule culture, but they did not reach Greenland earlier than the twelfth century. Thus there was a hiatus of about three hundred years in the Eskimoan occupation of the area we now call Greenland.† This hiatus began well before Erik the Red's time and continued until long after his death.

Yet Erik found recognizable human habitations, and fragments of skin boats. Ruins of ancient Eskimo houses are difficult to detect, and even when detected convey very little of their original purpose to the eye of anyone who is not skilled in their identification. If Erik actually did recognize that some low, grass-grown mounds, typical of old Dorset house ruins, had once been human habitations, he was demonstrating an acumen which professional archeologists of the twentieth century will admiringly applaud. But it must be remembered that Erik presumably did not even know that Eskimos existed.

The fragments of skin boats pose another problem. Rawhide is not a durable substance when exposed to weathering; neither would the light wooden or bone framing of Dorset boats have remained recognizable as such for more than a few decades after abandonment. If the fragments found by Erik were indeed of Dorset origin it would mean that these

---

* The story of the Dorsets is given in Appendix H.

† With the possible exception of extreme northeastern Greenland. A remnant Dorset population may have survived the rest of the race in the ice-free "oasis" north of latitude 80 degrees, perhaps into the twelfth century. However, Erik made no explorations to this exceedingly remote district.

people must have been on the coasts "both east and west" shortly before 981. And this, so archeologists say, could not have been the case.

On the other hand we know that the Westmen used skin boats — skin-covered curraghs. Any habitations that they might have built in Greenland would still have been recognizable as such when Erik arrived, and what is more they would have presented a familiar appearance to him so that he would have been in no doubt that they had been built and occupied by human beings.

At first glance the reference to "stone implements" seems to point directly to a native people. These "implements" may indeed have been of Dorset origin, but the Greenland Norse themselves made wide use of stone implements, due to a shortage of iron. Not only did they make weapon points, hammers and in some cases even axe heads of stone, but many of their pots and similar utensils were carved out of soapstone. Westmen in Greenland would have made use of the same materials for the same reason. There is also a difference of opinion among scholars as to the correct translation of the Old Norse phrase which we have rendered here as "stone implements." It has been suggested that the phrase should be rendered as meaning something like a stone anvil; and stone anvils were used by both the Westmen and the Norse, but never by Eskimoan people.

To complicate the problem, Erik explored portions of the western region of the land the Norse called Greenland, especially the east coast of the Cumberland Peninsula. This coast is probably what is meant by the word "west" in the Islendingabok account; and on the Cumberland Peninsula he might have found relatively recent remains of Dorset culture. However, the Islendingabok specifies that he found the remains "*both* east and west," which would include the present western coast of Greenland. The ultimate explanation may be that he found Dorset relics on Baffin Island, and evidence of Westmen settlements on the east coast of Davis Strait in what is now thought of as Greenland proper.

APPENDIX J

⁄\.\/.\/.\

the old church documents

These records consist of a number of church documents some of which are preserved in the Hanoverian archives, others being held in the Vatican archives.

The first and most important of them is an early copy * of a decree issued by Lewis, or Louis, the Pious, Emperor of the New Roman Empire, at a General Diet convened at Aix-la-Chapelle in the year 834. It is concerned with the missionary activities of two Benedictine monks, Witmar and Ansgar, who for several years prior to 831 had been preaching the gospel in the northern regions. Both of these men were present at the Aix-la-Chapelle Diet to deliver a report on their work.

Lewis the Pious was so impressed by their activities that with the consent of the diet and subject to later confirmation by the pope, he appointed Ansgar to be archbishop of all the northern countries and in particular of Denmark, Sweden, Norway, the Faeroes, *Cronland*, Helsingoland, *Island* and Scritfinnland (Finnland).

Copies of the decree were then dispatched to Rome, whither Ansgar journeyed to present himself to Pope Gregory IV. Gregory confirmed Ansgar in his appointment by the issuance of a papal bull dated 835. This bull reads in part: "We appoint our son himself, the above mentioned Ansgar, and his successors as our delegates to all the surrounding nations: to the Danes, the Swedes, the Norwegians, the Funelanders, the Gronlanders, the Helsingers, the Iselanders."

Although the existence of these two documents has been known for at least a century, little mention of them is to be found in most of the books which have been written about the discovery and settlement of Iceland

---

* Evidently not later than the eleventh century.

and Greenland. The deduction which must be made from them, that these two islands were known to, and probably settled by, Christian Europeans long before the arrival on the scene of the Norse, has not been accepted by the followers of the Nordic school who insist that Greenland and Iceland were not settled and were virtually unknown before their discovery by the Northmen. On the rare occasions when these two documents have been mentioned, it has usually been with the assurance that they must be forgeries, or at the least that the references to Greenland and Iceland must be later interpolations. The basic argument which is advanced to discredit the documents is that since it is "established" that Greenland and Iceland were not settled prior to the Norse arrival, the documents cannot be valid.

One of the few authors who have presented a detailed examination of these documents is P. De Root. In *The History of America Before Columbus* (Philadelphia, 1900) he faithfully gives all the arguments which have been advanced against acceptance of the parchments, after which he shows that there is no indication of forgery nor any credible motive why either forgeries or interpolations should have been attempted. He then produces a considerable weight of corroborative evidence testifying to the authenticity of the documents.

For these two parchments do not stand alone. In April of 846, Pope Sergius II issued a bull confirming Ansgar's archbishopric; while in May of 858 Pope Nicholas did likewise, expressly including Greenland and Iceland. During the succeeding sixty years four other bulls or imperial diplomas were issued from Rome confirming Ansgar's successors as archbishops of the northern regions, including Iceland and Greenland. During the next two and a half centuries a further series of bulls were issued to confirm the continuing validity of the initial bull issued by Pope Gregory IV, and in almost all of these the names of Greenland and Iceland appear, although there are some changes in spelling so that Cronland and Gronland are rendered Groenland, or Greenland.

Additional evidence supporting the authenticity of the original bull of Gregory IV is to be found in the Life of St. Rembert, who was the second metropolitan of Hamburg, which See at one time held the administration of Greenland. St. Rembert's life was written by a contemporary of his about the end of the ninth century. In the first chapter of this biography is the statement: "Lewis, King of the Franks, established in the northern part of the Saxon province an archiepiscopal see from which the preaching of the word of God should extend to the neighboring nations of the Swedes, Danes, Norwegians, Funelanders, Greenlanders, Icelanders, Scritfinns and Slavonians."

Evidence supporting the general authenticity of these documents is also found in the writing of the Irish priest Dicuil,* who lived and worked at the court of Lewis the Pious and who, about 835 or even earlier, wrote a famous book called *De Mensura Orbis Terrae* (*On the Measurement of the Earth*). Dicuil's book was a scientific treatise, but it includes mention of a visit to Iceland by Christian clerics late in the eighth century. These people spent some time on the island, and may have been visiting a settlement or community there, although Dicuil's only mention of them, or interest in them, is concerned with what they could tell him about the geographical features of the place. Nevertheless, the fact that this reference exists at all should leave us with no grounds for surprise at finding Iceland referred to as a Christian country in the various documents stemming from Ansgar's appearance at the Diet of Lewis the Pious.

To declare this whole complex of sources to be spurious, or to have been tampered with, is surely stretching scholarly suspicion beyond reasonable limits. To allow such a blanket condemnation would provide a precedent whereby anyone could arbitrarily invalidate any ancient document which was at odds with his desired conclusions.

These documents not only indicate that Christian communities already existed in both Greenland and Iceland as early as A.D. 830. They also show that the *names* of both islands antedate their "discovery" by the Norse and so must be presumed to have originated with the Celts or Picts. Thus we find that the predecessor of the Norse name of Groenland, or Greenland, was Cronland or Gronland, which is in accord with what Plutarch and other ancient writers tell us about Cronusland, and the Cronian Sea, as Greenland and the Greenland Sea were apparently known in Britain early in the Christian era. The name Iceland would seem to derive from the observations made of that island by men who visited it during the adverse climatic period, which roughly spanned the centuries from 500 B.C. to A.D. 500, and during which, as both geologists and climatologists agree, almost all of the island except for a narrow coastal strip was covered with glaciers, of which only a few remained by the time the Norse arrived to settle a land whose climate had become at least as genial as that of central Norway.

One other document deserves mention in this connection. In the Vatican archives there is a letter from Pope Nicholas V, dated 1448, in which Nicholas refers to Greenland as having been a Christian country for about six centuries prior to that date, which brings us back to the time of the issuance of Gregory's bull. Nicholas goes on to add that the residents of Greenland (in his time) had received their faith through the preachings "of their glorious evangelist, the blessed Saint Olaf." This reference to Olaf as the founder of Christianity in Greenland has been used by the

* See pp. 389.

proponents of the Nordic school as proof that either Nicholas V made an error, or his scribes did, and wrote six instead of four centuries and a half, which was the duration of the Norse Christian occupation of Greenland prior to 1448. However, as De Root points out, it is quite logical to explain the mention of Olaf as being no more than a politic act of acknowledgment of that Nordic saint, considering that at the time Nicholas wrote his letter Greenland was in the possesssion of the Norse, and the original Celtic occupation of that island was no more than a tenuous memory.

/\\./\\./\\.\

BJARNI HERJOLFSSON'S VOYAGE
TO NEWFOUNDLAND AND LABRADOR

A DETAILED RECONSTRUCTION OF BJARNI'S ROUTES AND LANDFALLS,
AND THE EVIDENCE SUPPORTING IT

BJARNI'S LANDFALL

There are two schools of thought as to where Bjarni made his landfall. One believes that it was at some point on the New England coast, preferably near Cape Cod; while the other believes that it must have been on the southeast coast of Labrador or on the east-facing shore of Newfoundland.

The pattern of prevailing surface winds and ocean currents is what governs the movements of sailing ships now, and is what would have governed them in Bjarni's time. Current patterns in the North Atlantic are believed to have remained generally unaffected by the cyclic changes in general climate over the past thousand years. The atmospheric circulation system may have undergone a southerly shift since the time of the Little Climatic Optimum, but this would not have made a significant change in wind patterns in the part of the Atlantic where Bjarni made his unpremeditated voyage.

The prevailing July and August winds in the region between Iceland and Newfoundland are mainly westerlies, although there is a sufficiently high incidence of northeasterlies to make it possible for a ship to be blown southwesterly across the intervening waters. In this section of the Atlantic the currents would also favor, rather than retard, a vessel drifting or sailing on such a course.

However, when we look at that portion of the Western Ocean lying south of Newfoundland, and generally south of latitudes 45 to 50 degrees, we find an entirely different picture. Here the prevailing winds, and particularly those of summer and early autumn, are overwhelmingly southwesterlies. Oceanic northeasters are almost unknown during these seasons, and are never of long duration. Moreover, if a ship driving down from the northeast did blow south of Newfoundland, she would then meet and be carried back to the eastward by the Gulf Stream, which pours up along the American coast toward the northeast until it meets the Labrador Current just south of Newfoundland, at which point it is deflected sharply eastward.

Throughout the history of sail in the Western Ocean it has always been a recognized fact that a vessel would have to fight her way west if she attempted to make a direct passage from northern Europe, including the British Isles, to the New England coast. Wise skippers usually chose one of two round-about routes instead. They either sailed south to the Azores region, where they crossed the Atlantic with the Northeast Trades and then coasted north; or they laid their courses into high northern waters, crossed to the Grand Banks of Newfoundland, to make Cape Race, and then beat west and south to their destinations through North American coastal waters.

There are many reports of sailing vessels that were trying to sail the direct course having been delayed by head seas, head winds, and a head current for as much as two months and finally giving up the attempt. The assumption that Bjarni's vessel, whose crew was doing all that could be done to prevent their ship from making any southwesterly progress, was blown or drifted from southeast or eastern Greenland waters to the New England coast, requires us to ignore the very nature of the North Atlantic and the conditions which prevail upon it. It is easy enough to draw a line on a map from southeast Greenland waters to Cape Cod, and a hypothetical ship can then be made to drift the necessary distance of 1700 or 1800 nautical miles along that line. In practice it is an impossibility.

To drive a final spike into the heart of the New England landfall theory, there is the unassailable fact that Bjarni could never have regained the Eastern Settlement of Greenland from any place south of Newfoundland in the time, or on the courses, which are recorded in the saga.

There are two ways by which we can locate the landfall. In the first place we can attempt to reconstruct Bjarni's course from the area where his drift began, using the data given to us in conjunction with a detailed study of the currents and of the prevailing weather conditions which he would have been likely to encounter. Unfortunately we cannot apply this method in a properly analytical way since Bjarni himself did not know where he was at any given time and was unable to keep track of his course by dead reckoning. There is, however, a way of reconstructing the drift in a different manner, which we will come to in a moment.

The second approach to the problem involves backtracking Bjarni from his final landfall in the Eastern Settlement. Happily the saga sailing directions from the point of first landfall in North America to the final landfall in Greenland are so complete that we can reverse them with little possibility of error.

If we apply both methods, and if the backtrack gives us a landfall in the area suggested by a reconstruction of the outbound voyage, we can feel confident that we have found the place where Bjarni first saw the coast of North America.

Since it was not feasible (nor, from my point of view, desirable) for me to repeat Bjarni's drift, I dragooned several master mariners who had spent much of their lives skippering sailing vessels in North Atlantic waters into assisting me. One of these men commanded a whaler in Greenland waters for fifteen years. Three of them skippered Newfoundland schooners employed in the transatlantic salt-cod trade. One was captain of a square-rigged ship, and another spent thirty-two years aboard sealing vessels out of St. John's. Another was master of a deep-sea salvage tug in the North Atlantic for twenty years and knew as much about the drift as any man alive.

I asked each of these men to assume that he was in command of a sailing vessel of a knorr's size and capabilities in the area where Bjarni's drift began. I gave them all the details recorded in the saga as to Bjarni's intended course and the conditions he is reported to have encountered, and asked them to predict the landfall.

All of them replied that in such a ship, rigged as she was, they would not have expected to see North America at all unless the vessel was caught in a really sustained nor'easter — a "nine day wind"— in which case they thought she might have fetched the coast of Newfoundland or Labrador somewhere between Cape Race and Spotted Island. They were emphatic and, in the case of the tugboat skipper, profane about the impossibility of ever seeing any land on this side of the Atlantic if they happened to be blown so far south that they missed Newfoundland entirely. Three of them were prepared to add that the most likely landfall, in their opinions, would have been one of the headlands of the northeastern Newfoundland coast.

Using only the data available for the outbound voyage, we can narrow down the probable area of the landfall a little more. The saga description of it —*"the country lacked mountains but was wooded and had small hills"* — fits (or would have fitted before most sections of the shore were denuded of forests by colonial settlers) the coast from Cape Race to Spotted Island, with some conspicuous exceptions.

The whole of the Great Northern Peninsula of Newfoundland must be eliminated since the Long Range Mountains, which form its spine, cannot possibly be described as "small hills." This exclusion carries with it the automatic elimination of the great bight between Fogo Island and Cape Bauld, because if Bjarni had made his landfall anywhere within this bight, he could hardly have avoided seeing the Long Range Mountains. Furthermore, it is stated that after leaving the first landfall the ship sailed for two doegr before land was again sighted. It Bjarni had made his first landfall within the bight he would have coasted the land to the northeastward as far as Cape Bauld, at which point he would have been within sight of Labrador and would have continued coasting it.

These exclusions leave two widely separated stretches of coast still to be examined: the Labrador shore from the Strait of Belle Isle to Spotted Island; and the Newfoundland coast between Cape Race and Fogo Island.

When we now apply the second method — that of backtracking Bjarni's course — we find that the Labrador stretch must be eliminated for several reasons. The distances and times involved become too foreshortened, and the descriptions of the last two American lands which Bjarni saw cannot be made to fit the actual terrain. Furthermore, there are not enough, or large enough, coastal indentations to account for the sequence of open-water passages. A complete reconstruction of the reverse course from the Eastern Settlements leads naturally to one part of coastal Newfoundland and one only — that section lying between Fogo Island and Cape Race.

The topography and the forest cover prior to the colonial period at almost any point along this stretch of coast fit the saga description perfectly. However, it can be assumed that Bjarni's landfall would have been on a coast with a seaward exposure, rather than deep within one of the several great bays between Cape Race and Fogo, and so we can further reduce the possibilities to the east coast of the Avalon Peninsula, or to one of the headlands of the Bay de Verde, Bonavista or Cape Freels peninsulas, or to Fogo Island itself.

If any of these seems to have a slight edge over the others it is the straight, eighty-mile length of the Avalon Coast, which runs north-northeast from Cape Race to Cape St. Francis. This is not only the most easterly portion of North America, it is so oriented as to have been the most natural landfall for Bjarni's ship, considering her probable position at the termination of her drift, and the actions taken by her crew when the fog finally cleared.

BJARNI'S VOYAGE ALONG THE COAST

Regardless of the exact point of the landfall, Bjarni's subsequent actions would have been part of a single pattern. He would have sailed northward in order to regain his lost latitude, keeping the land in sight as long as it continued to run in the direction he desired to go.

If his landfall was Cape Ray or the east coast of the Peninsula he would then have coasted north to Cape St. Francis, from where he would have raised Baccalieu Island and the headland of the Bay de Verde Peninsula. Crossing the mouth of Conception Bay, he would have passed Baccalieu, raised the Bonavista Peninsula and sailed northward to it across the mouth of Trinity Bay. Soon after leaving Bonavista on a northerly course he would have raised the Cape Freels headlands. A course line across these four headlands runs only slightly west of north, and so far Bjarni would have been going in the desired direction.

As he approached Cape Freels he would have found an extremely low-lying coast, for the flat, barely undulating and forest-clad interior runs almost imperceptibly into the sea along the twenty-five-mile stretch of shore. Perhaps lured by the illusion of a land more distant than it really was, Bjarni may have sailed in closer than usual. If he did he would have found himself in a hideous maze of sunkers, reefs, islets and shoals. This mariner's nightmare extends for eight miles off the Cape Freels shore and has been a great ship-killer in its time. It would have given Bjarni, that careful navigator, a case of the horrors and he would have clawed off again as fast as possible.

Even holding so far offshore that the land was barely in sight, Bjarni would have begun to realize that this new stretch of coast was trending more to the west, but before he could have become too concerned about it he would have raised the abrupt contours of Fogo Island standing to the north.

The bold shores of this island — he would not have recognized it as an island, since to an observer crossing the mouth of Hamilton Sound the opening appears to be a landlocked bay — may have tempted him to come in closer to the land once again. Consequently when he passed the northeast headland of Fogo he would have had a clear view westward and would have seen no sign of any further land in that direction. He would have had the impression that the main land mass was actually falling away to the southwest, as indeed it does into Notre Dame Bay.

If there was one thing Bjarni would not have done under any circumstances it would have been to take a course which increased his southing. He may now have concluded that the series of headlands he had been coasting belonged to a large island, and that since he had evidently reached its northern end, there was nothing for it but to set a course northward into the open sea.

Accepting the inevitable, he trimmed his sail for the new course and steered northward away from the "first" land.

They left this country to port and turned the sail towards the land. After that they sailed for two doegr before they saw another land.

I interpret this as meaning that they left Fogo and the Notre Dame Bay coast (what they could see of it) behind them over the port after quarter. The sail was trimmed so that the yard was swung to the port side of the ship with the yard pointing aft over the port quarter in the direction of the land. This would have meant that they had a wind from between east and east-southeast. Since they referred to the wind which brought them to the second land as being a fair wind, the likelihood is that it was east-southeast — a quartering breeze.

With the wind from easterly, Bjarni's knorr would have made leeway to the westward. In addition she would have been set westward by the Labrador Current. This current sweeps southerly along the Labrador coast to the Strait of Belle Isle, where one limb turns west into the Gulf of St. Lawrence and another turns southwestward to pour down into the great northeastern bight of Newfoundland. The westerly set to which Bjarni's knorr would have been subjected would have amounted to about twenty-four miles in two days on the course he was steering. To this we must add at least another ten miles for two days' leeway.*

If he had actually maintained a course due north from Fogo he would have gone sailing straight up through Davis Strait and would not have seen land again until he got to Disco, some 1200 nautical miles to the north. But we know that he did see land in two doegrs' distance. This land could only have been some portion of the Labrador coast. However, in order to have made a landfall on the Labrador, he would have had to sail a course over-the-bottom of the order of north twelve degrees west. This twelve-degree westward set is almost exactly accounted for by the combined effects of the current and his leeway.

Every year during the century and a half which ended with the beginning of the Second World War, large fleets of Newfoundland schooners used to put out from Trinity, Conception and Bonavista bays bound for the summer cod fishery on the Labrador. Few masters of these vessels had charts or even knew how to use them. But the skippers who had compasses knew the course they had to steer from Fogo, their departure point, in order to raise a certain landmark called the Round Hills on the Labrador between Hawke Harbour and Domino (Spotted Island) — the turning point where the Labrador coast bends sharply westward into Sandwich Bay. This course had been established by purely empirical means over many genera-

---

* Because the position of the North Star, about A.D. 1000, did not indicate *true* north, course setting by means of the North Star could entail an error of up to 5 degrees. See Appendix F.

tions, and it was 10 degrees east of the actual magnetic course. This was an allowance for the effect of the Labrador Current.

Bjarni, sailing north without making any allowance for the current, about whose existence he could have known nothing, would have followed an over-the-bottom track which in two doegr would have taken him to a point off the Labrador where he would have raised the Round Hills. Furthermore, he could not have raised any other land en route on such a course except, just possibly, Belle Isle. But if he saw Belle Isle at all he would have seen it from a considerable distance and would doubtless have evaluated it as a small isolated island off in the sea by itself.

A mariner approaching the Labrador coast between Hawke Harbour and Domino sees what appears to be a level and almost featureless land forming a monotonous, slowly rising plain which becomes part of the Labrador Plateau at a distance inland of twenty to thirty miles. In Bjarni's time it was forested to the edge of the mainland shore, and most of the innumerable off-lying islands were also timbered, as is shown by the relic forests still found on their barren slopes.

The only useful landmarks on the whole of this long stretch of coast are the domes of the Round Hills which reach heights of between 600 and 800 feet. They are important landmarks only because the rest of the country is so completely featureless. The most easterly of them, on Venison Island, is 680 feet high and has a seaward visibility of about 30 nautical miles. It is the first land seen by ships approaching this coast.

They soon approached this country and saw it to be flat and widely wooded.

His people asked Bjarni if he thought this second land might be Greenland, and he replied that it was no more like Greenland than the first had been: "For," he said, "very large snow [or ice] mountains are reported to be in Greenland."

Having unexpectedly encountered land again, and moreover a land which bore strong resemblances to the one he had left behind him, Bjarni may have begun to doubt that the first land was an island after all. He would have remembered that up until the time he abandoned the first land he had been making his way from headland to headland across a series of increasingly large bays, but always on a steady north-by-northwest course. The possibility may now have occurred to him that instead of passing from one separate island to another, he had only crossed a particularly large bay.

As he coasted north past Domino and Spotted Island he would have seen a now familiar pattern repeating itself as the coast again began to run off to the westward.

Considering the way the coast of this new world seemed to behave, Bjarni was perhaps tempted to follow it for a short distance to see if it might veer north again. If he went only as far as Grady Island he would have been rewarded by seeing the distant land horizon curving north. If he then took a northward departure from Grady Island he would still have had the comforting presence of land to the west of him — although a long way to the west — as he crossed the mouth of the Grosswater Bay–Sandwich Bay bight.

His next close approach to shore would have been to the outer islands of the eastward-thrusting Holton Peninsula. Perhaps it was here that the "fair wind failed" and the men wished to go ashore. By "failing" the saga means that the wind fell out, leaving the vessel becalmed, perhaps near some of the islands of the Indian Harbour archipelago, where the men might have felt it was safe to risk a landing.

They may have thought so, but Bjarni disagreed. He seems to have been determined to take no avoidable risks. He kept his people on board ship, and at the first whisper of the breeze making-up he ordered the sail hoisted.

After passing through or around the White Bear Island complex off Indian Harbour, he would again have found the coast running away to the west-northwest. At this juncture Bjarni might reasonably have concluded that the entire coast consisted of many great northward-trending bays, and that if he did more or less what he had done at Fogo Island he might hope to cross the next bight and rejoin the coast again where it swung easterly at its northern termination. Such a conclusion might even have encouraged him to hope that these new lands connected with the east-facing portion of Greenland known as the Vestri Obygdir. He may therefore have decided that it would be wise to make a greater effort to keep track of the coast.

He may have deliberately chosen a course somewhat west of north in order to decrease the chances of losing touch with the land; or because of the possibility of error latent in the use of the North Star (see preceding footnote) he may have steered a somewhat westerly course by accident. We do not know what the course was, but if we assume it to have been about north-northwest we would be close to the mark.

If we lay out such a course on the chart we get a shock. The course line crosses the Nain Bight and then runs more or less parallel to north Labrador, but about fifty miles offshore. At first glance it looks as if this would be a sufficient distance from the coast to ensure that Bjarni and his people would see nothing but salt water until they arrived at Hall Peninsula on Baffin Island, which lies 560 nautical miles from the White Bear Islands but which, considering the adverse effects of the Labrador and Canadian currents, would have taken Bjarni about seven days to reach.

However, the sea chart does not tell us everything. Before jumping to conclusions we must look at the land forms along the route Bjarni seems to have followed.

Between the White Bear Islands and the Kaumajet Peninsula far up the Labrador, the coast is indented by the immense Nain Bight. On the map this bight appears to be rather shallow; but that is only because it makes such a vast sweep from south to north. If we draw a line from the White Bear Islands to Cape Mugford on the Kaumajet, we find that the bight is of the order of fifty miles in depth. And due to the fact that the land forms behind it are generally very low, it appears to run off even farther to the westward than it actually does.

The northeasterly termination of this great bight coincides with a metamorphosis in the nature of the Labrador. Beginning at the Kiglapait Mountains just south of the Kaumajet Peninsula, the flat, mostly formless, and heavily forested topography which characterizes the southern two thirds of Labrador undergoes an abrupt transformation. Barren and immensely rugged mountains suddenly leap skyward. The coastal forests vanish. The line of demarcation between these two totally different types of country is knife sharp. The Kaumajet Peninsula marks the beginning of the subarctic Torngat Mountain range, which dominates — and in fact is — the north Labrador Peninsula.

The seaward visibility of the land south of Kiglapait is seldom greater than twenty miles. However, to the north of Kiglapait the land can be seen from seaward for an average distance of sixty miles; and the Kaumajet can be, and frequently is, seen from ninety miles to seaward.

This seaward visibility limit is the working coast for coastwise navigators. It is of far greater importance than the actual coastline, except when a ship must put in to land. Consequently in any reconstruction of a coasting voyage, this visibility coast is what we must bear foremost in our minds. In tracing Bjarni thus far we have been relying heavily on the characteristics of the visibility coast, but this is the point at which we can best illustrate its importance.

The Kaumajet is the most spectacular landmark on the eastern continental shores of North America. It is a fingerlike peninsula thirty miles in length which juts out into the sea in a southeasterly direction from the upper lip of the Nain Bight. It is a mountain range in its own right, and its highest peaks rise more than 4000 feet within half a mile of the sea. It is actually the southern bastion of the ensuing stretch of mountainous coast which runs north to the end of Labrador, and which is practically indistinguishable from the southwest Greenland coast except that it is even more barren. It has no proper glaciers as modern geographers define the word, but many of the peaks of the Torngats, which reach altitudes of 5300 feet, remain snow-covered throughout the year, even during the hottest summers. There are also numerous glacierettes, which are local accumulations of snow that have been compressed to form an approximation of glacial ice.

Bjarni's visibility coast while he was crossing the Nain Bight would have lain far out of sight to port. By the time he had made a three-doegr passage without raising any further sign of the western lands, he may have assumed that this time he really had lost touch with them for good, perhaps through not putting enough westing in his course. No doubt he accepted this loss phlegmatically and determined to hold on to the north in the open sea until he reached the proper latitude, could turn east along it, and so eventually come to the settled area of Greenland.

He would have been startled when, at the end of the third day, or at the beginning of the fourth, the lookout at the masthead reported seeing land off the port quarter. Bjarni would then have altered course toward it, perhaps wryly cursing himself for his lack of faith in his own earlier conclusions about the nature of the coast.

He would have expected to close with the land fairly quickly, at first assuming it to be a continuation of the low and featureless coasts he had by now come to know rather well. But as the hours passed and the landfall lifted only very slowly over the horizon, he would have guessed that this was something different. Finally when mountain peaks and the white gleam of snow became unmistakably recognizable, he would have realized that he had reached a new land and he may have felt the leaping hope that it might be a southward extension of that part of Greenland lying northwest from the settlement area.

We leave the knorr closing with the mountain coast, and look back to the beginning of this passage.

The chart distance from the White Bear Islands along a north-northwest course to its intersection with the visibility coast of the Kaumajet is 230 nautical miles. However, the saga tells us that Bjarni covered three doegr, which would be about 360 nautical miles, between departure and landfall. It therefore looks as if the Kaumajet could not have been his third landfall after all. But once again appearances are deceptive.

On this leg of his voyage Bjarni would have been sailing squarely into the teeth of the south-flowing Labrador Current. Although its rate of flow varies considerably, on the average the Labrador Current runs southward between the Kaumajet and Indian Harbour at a speed of between one and one-half and two knots, at a distance off shore of between eight to thirty miles.

This represents a speed of 36 to 48 nautical miles per day. If we take the mean of 42 miles and subtract this from the distance Bjarni's knorr would normally have run in a day, his actual distance covered over-the-bottom falls to 78 miles. Since Bjarni would have had no way of knowing about this current, he may not have realized that his three-doegr passage was foreshortened. In this case three doegr would have represented a distance of about 224 nautical miles.

We therefore conclude that the Kaumajet, whose Eskimo name means White Mountains and is derived from the fact that the peaks are usually snow covered throughout the year, was Bjarni's third landfall. The Bishop's Mitre peaks are frequently seen from ninety miles at sea. This is an almost fog-free coast in summer, and excellent visibility is the rule except during easterly weather, which is rare. The saga description of the land is brief but exact:

This land was high and mountainous with snow [or ice] mountains on it. The men asked if Bjarni wanted to lay the ship to shore here, but he said he would not: "because it appears to me that this is a useless country."

As Bjarni closed with the Kaumajet he would have seen the white spine of the still higher main range of the Torngats running away into the north. Even if, in this period of a warm climatic cycle, the Kaumajets were snow free, the great peaks to the north would probably have still borne snow-fields. There is a further description of this land in the Greenlanders Story, where it is attributed to Leif Eriksson's voyage. In describing Helluland, Bjarni's third land, it says: "Like one stony cliff was all from the snow-mountains to the sea." It would be hard to better this description as it applies to the Torngat coast. At Kaumajet itself there is a face on the Bishop's Mitre which falls 2000 feet sheer into the sea, and to the north the coast is one long sequence of great sea cliffs.

It was certainly a useless land. It always has been, and no doubt always will be. Its coastal waters are cold enough to inhibit plant growth ashore, but not cold enough to encourage a big sea-mammal population. Not even Eskimos have ever been able to make much use of it. Its cliff-sided fiords, bare of all except the hardiest arctic vegetation; its towering coastal cliffs; and the fantastic jumble of crags and peaks in the interior all combine to give it an air of forbidding desolation which knows no relief. The coast of the Cumberland Peninsula on Baffin Island seems almost hospitable by comparison.

Some authors have claimed that Bjarni's third land had to be either Resolution Island or the south part of Baffin Island. This suggests a lack of knowledge of these areas. There is nothing north of the Torngat coast which is even vaguely comparable to it until the Cumberland Peninsula is reached. But the Cumberland Peninsula lies more than 300 nautical miles north of the latitude of the Eastern Settlement in Greenland, and we can rest assured that Bjarni would have turned east when he reached the correct latitude as, indeed, the saga makes it plain he did.

They did not lower the sail but continued on along the land until they saw it was an island. [Then] they again set the stern toward the land and held out to sea with the same fair wind.

Whatever opinion he may finally have held about the relationships the other two lands bore to each other, Bjarni was sure that this one was a separate island. He had every reason to think so. It was totally different in appearance from the previous two lands. It would have seemed to him to have an abrupt southern beginning near the Kaumajet. He discovered for himself, as he coasted northward, that it had a very definite northern end, for he would have reached his desired latitude coincidental with the termination of this third land at Gray Strait, just north of Cape Chidley. From Bjarni's point of view nothing short of an attempted circumnavigation of it could have given him any reason to think that the Torngat Peninsula was not in fact an island.

The balance of the saga account tells us how he took his departure from this "island" and sailed for four doegr to the eastward (he still had the fair southwesterly wind) and fetched up very close to Herjolfsness in southern Greenland. Four doegr is the correct distance for the crossing out of sight of land between Cape Chidley and Herjolfsness. The course is almost due east, between north latitudes 60 degrees 10 minutes and 60 degrees 20 minutes.

This final leg of Bjarni's journey requires some further comment, since a number of authors have dealt harshly with the whole account of the voyage because of it. Having habituated themselves to thinking of ancient navigators as semisavages who fumbled their way around the seas in haphazard fashion, they cannot bring themselves to believe that Bjarni's eventual recovery of Greenland could have been anything but accidental. Then they argue that the saga statement which tells us that he completed his final, four-doegr passage by making a landfall near Herjolfsness is quite incredible on any accidental basis. From this they deduce that it did not happen, but was the invention of some imaginative saga-man. Their final conclusion is that since this much was invented, the whole account of Bjarni's voyage must be an invention too.

This leaves the way clear for Leif Eriksson to discover America, but it does as much injustice to our intelligence as it does to the seafaring abilities of Bjarni Herjolfsson. The reader who has borne with this necessarily somewhat tedious reconstruction of Bjarni's voyage is invited to draw his own conclusions as to whether the saga account is an invention, or whether it is the simple, direct and accurate account of a very competent piece of navigation on the part of the first European of whom we have any certain knowledge to have reached the mainland of the North American continent.

APPENDIX L

·/\·/\·/\·

Leif Eriksson's Vinland Discovery

I. THE OUTWARD VOYAGE

The evidence supporting the assumption that Leif made a direct voyage
from Southwest Greenland to Newfoundland

Next it is to be told that Bjarni Herjolfsson came to visit Jarl Erik and was well received. Bjarni told of his travels when he had seen these [new] lands and he was thought by many to have been lacking in enterprise since he had so little to tell of those lands. Because of this he was somewhat derided. Bjarni became an adherent of the Jarl's and went out to Greenland the following summer.

"There was now [some years later] much talk [in Greenland] of landseeking voyages. Leif, son of Erik the Red of Brattalid, went to visit Bjarni Herjolfsson and bought his ship from him . . ."

Thus does the Greenlanders Story open on a note of large confusion. If this version of Bjarni's activities is to be taken at face value it would mean that he went from Greenland to Norway not earlier than the summer of 1001, at which date Jarl Erik Hakonarsson became Danish viceroy for part of the coastal regions of Norway, following upon the death of King Olaf Tryggvason in the autumn of 1000. It would also mean that Bjarni could not have returned to Greenland earlier than 1002, whereupon there was talk among the Greenlanders of seeking out those lands Bjarni had discovered in 985. Leif then became interested and bought Bjarni's ship, and, according to this chronology, he could not have sailed for Vinland before the spring of 1003, since there would not have been time for him to outfit and to get away in what remained of the 1002 sailing season.

Apart from the fact that it is ridiculous to believe that it required a visit by Bjarni to Erik Hakonarsson in order to rouse the Greenlanders to an interest in exploring the lands Bjarni had sighted seventeen years earlier, all sources agree that Leif's Vinland voyage took place before King Olaf's death in the year 1000. It probably took place before Leif even visited Olaf — a visit which had to be made at some time between 995 and 1000, the duration of Olaf's reign.

Because of its impossible chronology this paragraph from the Greenlanders Story poses an apparently insoluble problem. Nevertheless there is a simple solution to it.

The author has apparently confused two Eriks. A Jarl Erik was undoubtedly mentioned in the old source he drew upon, and he assumed that this had to be Erik Hakonarsson. Acting on this assumption he found it necessary to postulate a voyage by Bjarni to visit Erik in Norway — a voyage which could not have been made prior to 1001. The mistake made by the author was that he confused Erik Hakonarsson with Erik the Red. I conclude it was Erik the Red, not Erik Hakonarsson, whom Bjarni visited, and the visit took place soon after Bjarni's arrival in Greenland in 985.

Such an error could readily have arisen out of the use of the title jarl in the ancient sources. At the time the Greenlanders Story was written, this word meant earl in the sense of a title bestowed by a king or inherited through aristocratic lineage. However in tenth-century usage it had a much broader meaning. In those times it was frequently an honorific title attached to the name of a prominent chieftain — and sometimes even self-bestowed. Thus the Erik who was the undisputed chieftain of the Greenland settlements would have been likely to acquire or to adopt the title jarl, and to have been so referred to by his supporters and retainers. The skald or skalds who composed the lay which later formed the basis of the Greenlanders Story may well have referred to Erik by such a title, since it was almost *de rigeur* for skalds to heap compliments upon the subjects of their sagas.

The probability that such a confusion did take place, combined with the unequivocal statement in the Short Saga to the effect that Bjarni never again went on distant voyages after he reached Herjolfsness in 985, adequately disposes of the problem.

Leif begged his father to be the leader of the expedition. Erik excused himself, saying he was too old and that he could not endure the hardships of the sea as before. Leif said that, with good luck, he might still be the family leader and then Erik yielded to Leif and rode from home when they were ready, and they had not far to go to the ship.

The horse which Erik rode stumbled and he fell off its back and hurt his foot. Then said Erik: "It is not fated for me to find more lands than this one where we dwell, and so we can no longer travel together." Erik went home to Brattalid and Leif went to the ship with his followers, numbering thirty men.

There was a southern man with them called Tyrker. They made the ship ready for sea and went to sea when they had finished, and found that country which Bjarni found last. They sailed to land there and cast anchor and put out the boat and went ashore and saw no grass there. Large snow-mountains [alternatively: snow fields] were seen far away, but like one stony cliff was all from the snow-mountains to the sea and it seemed to them that this land was good for nothing.

Then quoth Leif: "It has not happened to us as it did to Bjarni with this country, that we have not landed on it. Now I will give a name to the country and call it Helluland."

Afterwards they went to the ship and then sailed on the sea and found another country. They sailed again to land and cast anchor, then put out the boat and got ashore. This land was level and wood-covered and [there were] wide white sands wherever they went and [it] was not steep at the shore.

Then said Leif: "After its quality shall this country have a name, and be called Markland." They went after that to the ship as fast as possible.

They sailed out to sea before a northeaster and were out for 11 doegr before they saw land. They sailed to this land.

The account of Erik's abortive participation in this voyage is an example of the transpositions of incidents with which the Greenlanders Story is replete. This particular incident has been transposed, with some modifications, from its proper place in the later voyage of Thorstein Eriksson which is described in great detail in both the Erik the Red and the Thorfinn Karlsefni sagas. In these versions nothing is said of Erik's being inhibited from fresh adventuring by old age. Since Leif's voyage took place (as we shall show) about 995, when Erik was probably no more than forty-five years old, the plea of old age would seem to be a literary invention. In this connection it is noteworthy that the author of the Greenlanders Story kills Erik off shortly after Leif's voyage, but before Christianity is said to have come to Greenland; while it is established from independent sources that Erik was alive and hale as late as the year 1005, and that Leif brought Christianity to Greenland prior to the death of Olaf Tryggvason in 1000.

The account of Leif's outward journey seems to contain elements from the records of three separate voyages: Bjarni's, Leif's, and the combined voyages led by Thorvald Eriksson and Thorfinn Karlsefni. From the phrase *went to sea when they had finished* to *now they sailed from thence before a northeaster* the account is a mélange concocted from elements of the Bjarni voyage and from the Thorvald-Karlsefni voyage.

While the reports of the Bjarni and Karlsefni voyages, as given in the Short Saga and the Erik the Red and Karlsefni sagas, include such detailed sailing directions that the routes can be accurately followed even today, no such instructions are to be found in the initial stages of the Greenlanders Story version of Leif's voyage. After the entertaining but spurious description of Erik's tribulations, the author wafts Leif directly to Bjarni's northernmost land and then describes this land in terms which are almost identical with those which appear in the Short Saga account of Bjarni's voyage, and in the Erik the Red and Karlsefni sagas. The combined description from these three sources reads:

This land was high and mountainous with snow-mountains [alternatively: snow fields] on it . . . it appeared that this was a useless country . . . they [launched a boat] and explored that country. They found there many great stones [hellur] . . . there were many arctic foxes there . . . they gave a name to this country and called it Helluland.

The Greenlanders Story adds only that there was no grass, a fact which could easily have been inferred from, if indeed it was not actually mentioned in, the original account of Bjarni's voyage. Apart from this the Greenlanders Story version fleshes out the tale with some braggadocio attributed to Leif, which makes it more interesting but not more plausible.

For the next leg of the exploration — to the second land — the Short Saga and the Eric the Red and Karlsefni sagas again supply specific distances and directions in accord with normal saga convention, while the Greenlanders Story is hopelessly vague. This time the actual description of the second land seems to be derived from the accounts of the Thorvald-Karlsefni voyage, but it is much briefer and far more general that in the Erik the Red and the Karlsefni sagas, where Markland is described in the following terms:

From thence [Helluland] they sailed two doegr and bore away from the south toward the southeast until they reached a wooded country containing many animals. An island lay off to the southeast of this country and there they killed a bear so they called this Bjarney [Bear Island], while they called this wooded land Markland [Forest Land].

Then they sailed southward along this land [Markland] and after two doegr they came to a cape. . . . Here was a havenless coast with a long sandy beach and dunes. They rowed to the shore in boats and found upon a headland there [a hill which resembled?] the keel of a ship from which they named that headland Kialarness [Keel Point]. They called the strands there Furdust-randir [Marvelous Shore, in the sense of amazing] because they took so long to sail past them.

Now let us look again at the account of Leif's supposed visit to this same land:

This land was level and wood-covered and [there were] wide white sands wherever they went and [it] was not steep at the shore.

There is only one truly remarkable stretch of sand beach on the eastern seaboard of Labrador or Newfoundland. This is Porcupine Strand, lying north of Sandwich Bay, and the description of it given in connection with the Thorvald-Karlsefni voyage, including the singular feature of Kialarness (Cape Porcupine), establishes its identity beyond question. If Leif had actually seen Furdustrandir himself the account of his voyage would surely have dealt with such a spectacular piece of country and prominent land-mark at considerable length. But the author of the Greenlanders Story does not mention the salient feature of Kialarness in connection with Leif's voyage since he required the description of Kialarness to embellish a later, chronologically impossible, and supposedly independant voyage by Thor-vald Eriksson.

The crux of the argument which we are developing, to the effect that Leif never did sail down the Labrador coast at all, is contained in the next phrase in the Greenlanders Story version:

They sailed out to sea before a northeaster and were out for II doegr before they saw land. They sailed to this land. . . .

In saga and sailing parlance the phrase *they sailed before a northeaster* means that they were running *before* the wind, and that their course therefore was southwesterly. But it would have been impossible for Leif to sail southwest from Markland and the vicinity of Furdurstrandir unless he sailed either overland or down into Sandwich Bay, which as we show later in our text was certainly not Vinland even if it had been two doegr deep.

In order to reach Newfoundland, or any other territory south of Labra-dor, Leif would have been forced to sail *southeasterly* from Furdustrandir to Domino, then south at least as far as Belle Isle. But according to the

Greenlanders Story his course was southwesterly, and moreover, he maintained it out of sight of land for a distance of II doegr.

I have already demonstrated that Bjarni's southernmost land was the east coast of Newfoundland. If we now project Leif's final, and only stated, course back in a northeasterly direction from that southern land for two doegr out of sight of land, we find that his point of departure would have had to be near the middle of the Labrador Sea on a line connecting eastern Newfoundland with southwestern Greenland. This is an obvious absurdity, but if we project the course backward for a total distance of *five* doegr we get a departure point on the Greenland coast between Cape Farewell and the Eastern Settlement.

The discrepancy between the stated and the actual distances can be resolved in one of two ways. In the first place it is possible that a change from five to two doegr was deliberately made by the Greenlanders Story's author in order to make his text conform with the distance between Bjarni's southern and middle lands — Vinland and Markland — which is given as two doegr in the Short Saga.

On the other hand it would have been easy enough for some previous scribe to have misread a V, often written as U, in the original account as II; in which case the author of the Greenlanders Story would only have been perpetuating the error.* If this is what happened, it might help explain why he routed Leif down the Labrador coast, for he would have known (whatever else he failed to realize) that II doegr was far less than the direct distance from Greenland to Vinland, and since it was exactly the distance between Bjarni's first and second land, he might have been led to conclude that Leif must have retraced Bjarni's route.

Assuming that he reached such an erroneous conclusion he would then have been faced with the fact that no details of such a voyage existed. This need not have been an obstacle, since he could have reconstructed the "lost" section of the voyage by using the Short Saga or the Erik the Red and Thorfinn Karlsefni sagas (or one of their ancestral recensions) to supply him with the requisite information about Helluland and Markland. Of course if he used the voyage material in this way, he would have been unable to make use of the details of the Bjarni and Thorvald-Karlsefni voyage in their proper places. This seems to be exactly what he did, since he tells us nothing about Bjarni's voyage except that it took place, and when he deals with the Thorvald-Karlsefni voyage he says only that the ships put to sea from Greenland and came safely to Leif's booths in Vinland.

---

* Similar errors in the transcription of Roman numerals occur in other sagas.

I have noted how, in connection with Leif's voyage, the Greenlanders Story seems to ignore the usual saga convention of giving sailing directions. But this is more an apparent failure than a real one. It does give one set of partial instructions — from Greenland to Newfoundland direct. These instructions are brief, but this is partly because they deal with a single uncomplicated course over the open ocean. Furthermore, when the Greenlanders Story finally gets Leif to Vinland it gives us a detailed and very accurate description of that country and of its approaches — a description which is fully in accord with what we would have expected if the Vinland landfall was indeed Leif's first landfall in the New World. The contrast between this description and the perfunctory and generalized descriptions of Markland and Helluland is a telling one.

My conclusion is that the author of the Greenlanders Story had at hand a transcript of the original saga account which read approximately like this. "Now they readied their ship [in Greenland] and went to sea when they had finished. They sailed from thence on the sea before a northeaster and were out for U doegr before they saw land . . ." (followed by the account of the approach to, and description of Vinland).

Perhaps as a consequence of honest ignorance, or of a misleading error in the text, as I have already suggested; or perhaps in a deliberate effort to glorify Leif and the Greenlanders at the particular expense of Karlsefni and his Icelanders (and at the incidental expense of Bjarni Herjolfsson*) the author of the Greenlanders Story inserted a fictional prelude into his account in which he made Leif retrace Bjarni's entire route, thereby making him the discoverer of Helluland and Markland as well as of Vinland.

There remains the question of whether it is reasonable to suppose that Leif would have attempted to reach Bjarni's southernmost land by sailing directly to it from southern Greenland.

Leif would have had no conceivable reason for exploring Bjarni's northern land, since as Bjarni noted it was of no use to anybody. It was the southerly lands, with their abundance of timber, which would have attracted him, and if he had been confident of being able to lay and sail a course to one of these he would hardly have been inclined to backtrack Bjarni.

Could he have felt confident in attempting a direct passage? I believe that Bjarni — from whom he bought his ships — would have been able to provide him with all the information necessary to make such a voyage, while carrying it out successfully would have called for no more than ordinary Norse seafaring ability.

---

* See Appendix M for a discussion of apparent bias in the sources.

Bjarni himself had been unable to sail directly to south Greenland from his original North American landfall only because the Norse had no way of determining relative longitude — the amount of westering, in this case. However, by the time he reached Herjolfsness he would have amassed enough data to enable him to estimate the approximate longitude, or westering, of his southern land. He had sailed consistently north-northwest from his first landfall until he reached the latitude of the Eastern Settlement, whereupon he had sailed due east until he reached Herjolfsness. He knew approximately the lengths (in terms of doegr) of both the north-northwestern and the eastern legs of the triangle, of which the third side was the direct course from south Greenland to what became Leif's Vinland. Without possessing any knowledge of mathematics, Bjarni could have worked out the course for this direct passage by means of a rough sketch, drawn on the ground if necessary. The course he arrived at, by whatever empirical method he chose to use, would not have been dead accurate, but it would have served. Furthermore, he would undoubtedly have been able to provide Leif with the relative latitude of the southern land so that if Leif had found that he was unable to maintain the suggested course, or if it had proved to be inaccurate, he could still have made the correct landfall simply by sailing south to the proper latitude and then running down it to the west.

There would have been no special risk involved in such a passage. On the other hand the difficulties inherent in an attempt to retrace the whole of Bjarni's route, with its many courses, landfalls and distances, would have been considerable; not to mention the fact that this backtrack course would have been nearly twice as long as the direct route.

A direct voyage by Leif would have had both a precedent and a closely related antecedent. It will be remembered that Erik the Red's outbound route in 981 entailed following a dog-leg course from Iceland west to the vicinity of Angmagssalik, then a long southward coasting voyage to the south tip of Greenland. But on his homeward voyage to Iceland in 984 he must have plotted and sailed a direct course from south Greenland to Iceland — a course which Bjarni, acting on instructions which could only have come from Erik, attempted in reverse in 985. This was an open-ocean passage of about the same length as the direct passage from south Greenland to Vinland. Furthermore, it is apparent that when Leif's brother Thorstein and their father Erik attempted to reach Vinland a year or two after Leif's return from there, they sailed a direct course. That they were unsuccessful seems to have been due to the fact that they did not possess as much relevant information as was available to Leif when he set sail from Greenland.*

---

* See Chapter 16.

One point remains to be mentioned. When Leif left Vinland for home, the Greenlanders Story tells us that "Now they sailed to sea and got a fair wind until they saw the mountains under the glaciers of Greenland. . . ." This is a straightforward description of a direct passage, and while it is not conclusive evidence in itself, it shows us that there could have been no serious impediment to the passage having been direct both ways.

The Erik the Red and the Thorfinn Karlsefni Sagas offer an entirely different account of Leif's Vinland voyage and one which flatly contradicts the Greenlanders Story version.

This account is preceded by a very full chronicling of Leif's voyage from Greenland to Norway, during which he spent some time on the Hebrides, where he fathered a bastard child. His subsequent arrival in Norway and his dealings with King Olaf Tryggvason, who baptized Leif and persuaded him to become his agent in Greenland, is recorded in considerable detail. However, the account of the return voyage to Greenland is truncated, and in the middle of it there appears a remarkably brief — considering the importance of the matter — notice which purports to tell the story of the discovery of Vinland.

Leif put to sea [from Norway] when his ship was ready. For a long time he was tossed about on the ocean and came upon lands of which he had no previous knowledge. Self-sown wheatfields and vines were growing there. There were also those trees which are called masur* and of all these they took samples. Some of the timber was big enough to use for building purposes. Leif found men on a wreck [as he neared the Greenland coast] and took them with him and procured quarters for them [in Greenland] that winter . . . he was well received by everyone and he soon proclaimed Christianity throughout the land. . . .

According to this notice (it is hardly more than that), Leif discovered Vinland by accident when he was blown to the coast of North America while homeward bound from Norway to Greenland. He is supposed to have lingered in the new land only briefly and to have hastened on to Greenland that same season. Most authors have agreed that the divergencies between this account and the Greenlanders Story version cannot be reconciled. They have therefore usually tried to resolve the conflict by accepting one of the two versions and rejecting the other. Those who have chosen the Erik the Red and the Karlsefni sagas version have tried

---

* Probably birch.

to give it greater force by quoting some nine additional — and even briefer — references to the accidental-discovery story culled from a number of Icelandic sagas and related sources. The three which we quote are fully representative of all the rest.

Leif the Lucky found Vinland and then found merchants in distress at sea and by God's mercy saved their lives; and he introduced Christianity into Greenland. [From AM 194, a fourteenth-century manuscript]

King Olaf Tryggvason . . . sent Leif Eriksson to Greenland to proclaim the faith there. Then Leif found Vinland the Good. He also found men on a wreck at sea, wherefore he was called Leif The Lucky. [From a thirteenth-century recension of the Kristni-Saga]

Olaf sent Leif to Greenland . . . and he departed at once. He found men on a shipwreck in the sea and saved them. Then he found Vinland the Good. [From the thirteenth-century Heimskringla recension of the Saga of Olaf Tryggvason]

An examination of these brief notices, all of which date from several hundred years after Leif's time, with their disordered references to the three salient events in Leif's life, makes it obvious that they were originally derived either from the quoted passage in the Erik the Red and the Karlsefni sagas or from a source common to them all. They are thus no more than repetitions of the original notice, and as such they do nothing to confirm the authenticity of the initial statement.

If we are to accept this version we must not only abandon the Greenlanders Story version in toto but we must also discard the story of Bjarni Herjolfsson, which is perhaps the most convincing of all the accounts of the Western voyages. Having done this we are in effect left with nothing to show that Leif ever made a Vinland voyage at all except for the one brief notice. It is apparent that this notice does not provide sufficient evidence upon which to base a secure claim that Leif discovered anything.

I contend that either through accident or design this notice is in error and is an interpolation in the original saga account of Leif's journey to and from Norway. A careful reading of the account of the return voyage certainly gives the impression that the notice is an interjection, and one which has the effect of stuffing an already dramatic story to the bursting point by the addition of an event of great magnitude about which we are given totally inadequate information.

The insertion of this notice may have been brought about in one of two ways. The clerks who transcribed one of the ancestral versions of the Erik the Red and the Karlsefni sagas may have worked from a partial copy of an older recension from which the account of Leif's Vinland voyage and of Bjarni's earlier voyage were missing. However, a full account of the Norway voyage survived, and since the copyists would have been aware that Leif had made a Vinland voyage — a fact which would have endured in no matter how imperfect a form as part of the general historical background of the Icelanders — it would have been natural for them to insert a notice of it in what seemed to be the most logical place in the existing saga. As for Bjarni Herjolfsson's voyage, the copyists might never have heard of it at all, or if they did have some vague knowledge of it, they may have been at a loss to know how to relate it to the story of Leif and so either ignored it or else blended it into the account of Leif's discovery of Vinland.

Some echo of Barni's voyage does seem to have survived in the Erik the Red–Karlsefni notice, which opens with the sentence:

For a long time he was tossed about on the ocean and came upon lands of which he had no previous knowledge.

This sounds suspiciously like a condensed description of Bjarni's voyage to North America. The possibility that the section of the Old Erik Saga which dealt with Bjarni's and Leif's New World voyages may have been lost before the Erik the Red and Karlsefni recensions were made is strengthened by an examination of the Short Saga. This fragment is from the same original source as the other two, and up to a certain point it is very similar to them. However, the Short Saga includes a full and detailed story of Bjarni Herjolfsson's voyage, beginning at a point in the narrative where there is a notable gap in the chronology as it is recorded in the Erik the Red and the Karlsefni sagas.

The alternative explanation is that the original accounts of Bjarni's and Leif's voyages, as they were preserved in the Old Erik Saga, were deliberately suppressed by the copyists of the Erik the Red-Karlsefni recensions. Since these two recensions were prepared in Iceland by Icelanders it is possible that the feud with which I deal at length in the body of the text and in Appendix M, between the Greenlandic and Icelandic explorers in the west may have been perpetuated here. It is perhaps significant that the Karlsefni Saga, which antedates its sister version, the Erik the Red Saga, is believed to have been prepared by, or at the order of, Hauk Erlendsson, who was a direct descendant of Thorfinn Karlsefni.

But no matter how partisan Erlendsson may have been, neither he nor any other Icelandic scribe of the period could have entirely ignored

Leif's voyage, since, as I have noted, knowledge that it had taken place must have been wide-spread. But an account of the exploit could have been and actually was reduced to a single brusque reference placed out of its correct context, and the importance of the voyage was downgraded to that of a mere accident.

I conclude that Leif made two separate and distinct voyages of major importance. One of these — and it would most logically have been the earlier — was a direct voyage from Greenland to Vinland following up the original discovery of the new lands by Bjarni Herjolfsson.

The second major voyage, which probably took place some years later, was to Norway, where Leif became a Christian and the chief tool of King Olaf Tryggvason in his attempt to gain control over the distant Greenland settlements.

Either deliberately or unwittingly the copyists responsible for the Erik the Red and the Karlsefni sagas combined these two voyages into one.

II: THE LOCATION OF VINLAND

They made their ship ready for sea and when all was ready they sailed out to sea before a northeaster and were out for II [U] doegr before they sighted land.

They sailed to land, reaching an island which lay to the northward of the country, and they went up there and looked about them in fine weather. There was dew on the grass and they touched the dew with their hands and brought it to their mouths, and they thought they had never known anything to taste so sweet.*

After that they returned to their ship and sailed through the sound which lay between the island and that cape which projected northward from the land itself. They sailed westward around the cape.

There were extensive shoals there [at the place they eventually reached after rounding the cape] at ebb tide and their ship went aground. It was a long look from the ship to get sight of the sea.

They were so curious to go ashore that they could not wait until high water floated their ship, but hurried to the land, where a river flowed from a lake into the sea.

---

* The significance of this remark has puzzled many authors. I suggest that it refers to "sun-dew" or, as it is less elegantly called by children, "frog-spit." This is a frothy exudation made by a small insect which is kin to the aphids, which draws sap from a hole in the grass stem and foams it. As with the aphids, this excretion is very sweet (the aphid excretion is called "honeydew"). The insect which produces "sun-dew" is apparently unknown in Greenland and Iceland but is common in North America, including Newfoundland.

As soon as the tide rose under their ship they rowed back to her in thei boat and took her up the river and so into the lake where they anchored.

Ensuing Norse expeditions made extensive but fruitless searches fc Leif's Vinland along the southern and eastern coasts of Labrador ar along the east and west coasts of the Great Northern Peninsula of Nev foundland*. The failure of these expeditions to locate Vinland confirm the statement in the Greenlanders Story to the effect that Leif's Vinlanc was in Bjarni's southern land.

For reasons which I have detailed in connection with the story of Bjarni's voyage, as well as for others which will appear later, the hypothesis that Leif landed anywhere to the south of Newfoundland is untenable. The first set of data with which we have to deal if we are to pinpoint the location of the landfall are the sailing directions from Greenland to Vinland. We do this by scaling off the arc composed of courses in the southwest airt originating from the Eastern Settlement region of Greenland. These courses limit us to a landfall between Cape St. John and Cape St. Francis, at an average distance of five doegr out of sight of land from Herjolfsness. Since we know that Leif approached the land from the northeast and in good weather, which implies conditions of good visibility, our next step is to determine the configuration of this section of coast as it appears from seaward. When we have done this we see that Leif's first sight of land would have had to be one of the six major headlands beginning with Cape St. John and including Fogo Island, Cape Freels, Cape Bonavista, Bay de Verde Peninsula, and Cape St. Francis.

After this first sighting, *they sailed to land,* according to the Greenlanders Story, which is to be understood as meaning the nearest part of the land, *reaching an island which lay to the northward of the country, and they went up there.*

This island must have been fairly high, for the implication is that they climbed it, which is what we would expect them to do in order to see what the surrounding country looked like and to get their bearings o' it.

They then returned to their ship and sailed through the sound whic' lay between the island and *that cape which projected northward from the land itself.*

From the tenor of this statement we understand that by *the land itself* the narrator was referring to the main body of the country which therefore would have lain southward *both of the island and of the cape.*

---

* See the text dealing with the Thorvald Eriksson-Thorfinn Karlsefni expeditions, Chapters 17 to 26.

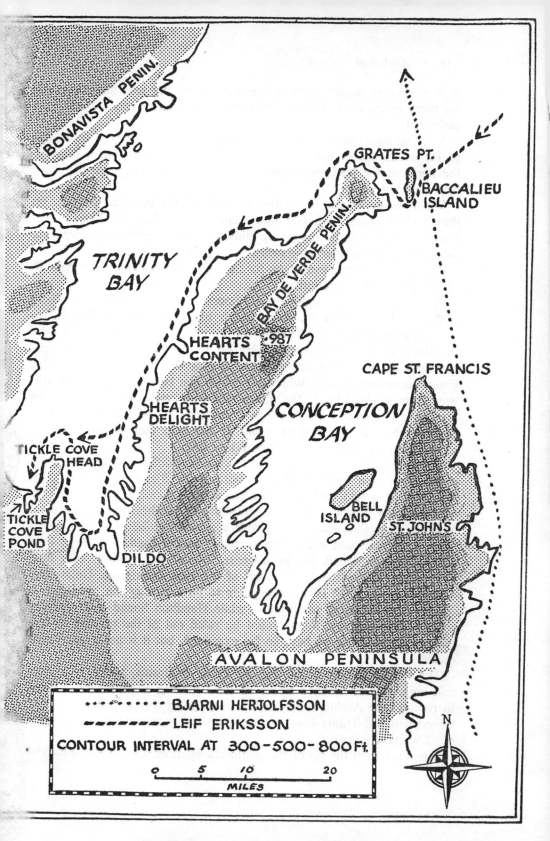

The approaches to Leif Eriksson's Vinland

It is particulary important to realize that we are not told that the island lay north of the cape. This is a misconception which many authors have embraced.

What we have here is a description of an amorphous body of land lying to the southward of the approaching ship. There is an island lying to the north of the landmass, separated from a northward-projecting cape by a sound or strait.

When we apply this description to each of the possible landfalls on the "visibility coast" we find that Cape Freels, Cape St. Francis and Cape Bonavista can be summarily eliminated from further consideration, since none of them offer appropriate islands or sounds.

The remaining three candidates for the initial landfall can all be made to fit this part of the description.

A vessel sailing on a southwesterly course into the East Newfoundland Bight could raise Cape St. John, which has a seaward visibility of 30 nautical miles, as her first landfall. As she closed with it she would raise the Horse or St. Barbe Islands lying off to the west and north of the mainland. If she then sailed to these islands she would raise Partridge Point, the eastern cape of White Bay which can be said to project northward from the land itself. The fifteen-mile-wide stretch of water between the Horse Islands and the Partridge Point-Cape St. John landmass might be thought of as a sound or strait. If the ship then sailed westward through this sound she would enter White Bay.

Fogo, the second possibility, is of a somewhat different character. Even as it served as a logical point of departure for Bjarni when he left his first land, it would and does provide a good landfall for vessels approaching the central part of Newfoundland's northeastern seaboard. It is a big island, fifteen miles long, with a seaward visibility of 24 nautical miles. Lying between it and the mainland to the south is a large inlet called Hamilton Sound. But in this case "island" and "sound" bear little relationship to the island and sound of the saga description. Unless one circumnavigates Fogo Island it appears to be a part of the mainland — an eastward-projecting peninsula — while Hamilton Sound itself appears to be a dead-end bay. Fogo cannot be ruled out of the running on the basis of the evidence we have so far examined, but it is not a good candidate.

The third possibilty is the Bay de Verde Peninsula, which is a fifty-mile-long, slightly crooked finger of land running north-northeast from its roots in the Avalon Peninsula, and separating the two great fiords of Conception and Trinity bays. Its outer tip has a seaward visibility range of 28 nautical miles.

Separated from the tip of the peninsula by Baccalieu Tickle, which is

two to four miles wide and about four miles long, lies Baccalieu Island.
Baccalieu lies eastward of the extreme northern tip of the peninsula, but
lies due north of the looming mass of Cape St. Francis and the main
body of the Avalon Peninsula. If a vessel enters the southeastern end of
Baccalieu Tickle and sails through it to the westward, she will round Grates
Point, the most northerly point of the peninsula, and then have Trinity
Bay open ahead of her to the southwest.

Baccalieu is a small but impressive island. It has an average height of
400 feet and is largely surrounded by sheer cliffs where seabirds nest in
myriads. There are several boat landings along its seaward side from any
one of which it is relatively easy to gain the high grassy crest; from where
in clear weather one can see to the foot of Conception Bay, while the Cape
St. Francis Peninsula to the southward is seen to broaden out into one
great landmass which dominates the entire scene. Twenty-five miles away
to the northwest the Horse Chops coast of the Bonavista Peninsula shows
as a dark wash on the horizon, suggesting that the intervening stretch of
water must be the mouth of a fiord of even greater size than Conception
Bay itself.

The Bay de Verde–Baccalieu–Cape St. Francis area fits the saga requirements better than any other locality on the North American coast,
but there is still another set of criteria to apply before it, or any other place,
can be accorded even tentative acceptance as the site of Leif's landfall.

The saga tells us that after Leif sailed westward through the sound he
came to a haven where he secured his ship for the winter. This haven is
described in such detail, and the Old Norse words used in the description
are so specific, that we can identify it with certainty as being of a special
type known as a hop (pronounced hope).

A hop was a body of salt water barred off from the open sea by a
natural breakwater, and connected by a channel which had the character
of a river entrance. The French call such harbors barachoix, and in English
we usually refer to them as lagoons, although in Newfoundland they are
known as barasways. They are invariably tidal and usually shallow.
Extensive shoals, sand bars and tidal flats often extend seaward for a considerable distance from their outlets. They are almost always found at the
foot of a coastal indentation where low lands abut upon the sea, thereby
making it possible for wave and current action to build up an offshore bar
which eventually comes to stand above high-tide level and so cuts off a
portion of the sea behind it, which then becomes a harbor. When such
bars form at the bottom of bays into which large streams or rivers empty,
and they often do, the opening through the breakwater becomes a true river
mouth.

There are a few hops in Greenland, a number in Iceland, and a great many on those parts of the mainland European coast which came within the sphere of Viking activity. They were highly valued as ship harbors by the Norse, and as a consequence many of the European ones still bear a local language variant of the name hop. Thus of the more than one hundred of these havens which are to be found on the shores of Great Britain, the majority still bear the suffix "hop."

Because most of them are very shallow, hops are of little use to modern vessels; but they were peculiarly well suited to Norse ships, which were shallow-draft and had flat keels running their full length so that, when they were dried out by a falling tide, they rested almost upright and without any great strain being brought to bear on the structure of the vessel. Rather than leave their ships moored off at anchor when they were not in use, the Norse preferred to bring them into shoal water, where they could either be hauled out or laid-up afloat. A hop was the perfect place either for hauling out or for laying-up afloat, since it usually had a gently sloping sand or shingle shore and was protected from both surge and heavy seas.

Here is what the saga has to say about Leif's haven: They came to a place where it was so shoal that their ship went aground some distance from shore at low tide. At this place they were a long way from the open sea, or to put it another way, they were near the foot of a deep fiord or bay. At the place where they went ashore they found a "river" draining into the sea from a "lake." When the tide refloated their ship they brought her into the lake, where they anchored her for the time being while they explored the place.

Philological studies of the Old Norse language indicate that the Norse words used at this point in the manuscript of the Greenlanders Story should not be rendered in translation as "river" and "lake" in their accepted modern sense. These words evidently had a much more specific meaning in tenth- and eleventh-century usage, and it is suggested that they should be more properly translated as "channel" and "lagoon"; or, in other words, as the description of a hop.

The saga goes on to add that both "river" and "lake" were full of salmon, and that grasslands providing natural cattle pastures surrounded the "lake." Extensive grassy flats are one of the usual characteristics of hops. It is apparent that both the "river" and the "lake" were tidal, and that the ship could have been brought into the "lake" only at high tide.

Most authors have insisted on applying the modern meaning to the original words of the saga, and such a translation has its advantages. It enables the commentator to transport Leif up any navigable river as far as is desired, even if this involves tens or hundreds of miles before the lake of the commentator's choice is reached. The inherent improbability of such an interpretation is obvious. No master of a Norse ship on the coasts of an unknown land would have deliberately hazarded her at any greater distance from the open sea — his escape route — than was absolutely necessary to provide her with a protected harbor. There would have been no conceivable advantage to Leif in ascending a river into the interior, while the risks, both real and imagined, he would have courted in doing so would have been unacceptable to any prudent man.

That Leif found and occupied a haven of the hop type is convincingly established by the saga itself. If further proof of the correctness of this conclusion is needed, it is to be found in the story of Thorfinn Karlsefni. Karlsefni made a voyage in search of Vinland some years after Leif, and although he never succeeded in locating Leif's Vinland he did attempt to plant a colony at a site whose description is nearly identical with that of Leif's haven. The Karlsefni Saga specifies that this place was a hop and calls it by that name. The same words which have been translated as "river" and "lake" from the Greenlanders Story, are used in the Karlsefni Saga to describe a channel through a bar, and a lagoon behind the bar comprising the main features of Karlsefni's Hop.

We conclude that a hop-type haven must have existed in the vicinity of Leif's landfall, and our next step is to search for one.

If Cape St. John and the Horse Islands had been Leif's landfall he would then have sailed west past Partridge Point and into White Bay. The shores of White Bay are almost uniformly precipitous, rising in many places to 800 or 1000 feet and there is no place along its coasts which can be made to fit the description of Leif's haven, except for the mouth of the Hampden River at the very head of the bay.

There is no barachois at the mouth of the Hampden now, but according to Admiralty surveys of the late nineteenth century a small and marshy lagoon once existed there. It later disappeared as a result of changes brought about by large-scale pulpwood operations on the Hampden. It consisted of a widening in the channel of the river, fronted by the sand-bars and mudbanks of the open estuary. The contours of the land are such that it could not have been much larger than a hundred yards in diameter. Nevertheless it could be identified with Leif's haven on the basis of the data we have so far examined. However, there are a number of other factors still to be mentioned in connection with Vinland which rule out the possibility that Leif's hop was in fact situated at the mouth of the Hampden. Furthermore, the Hampden was later visited by Karlsefni without being identified by him as Leif's Vinland, for which he was searching.

Hamilton Sound and the general vicinity of Fogo Island do not offer anything resembling a hop-type haven, nor do they even offer an alternative site which would be compatible with the modern usage of the words "river" and "lake."

Hops are not uncommon in Newfoundland. About fifty barachoix of sufficient size to admit and shelter a vessel of a knorr's dimensions are shown on the charts, but most of these are concentrated on the south and west coasts of the island. There are only five suitable ones on the northeastern coast. Three of these are found at the head of Trinity Bay, and it is in Trinity Bay that we must look for Leif's haven if the Baccalieu-Bay de Verde area was where he made his initial landfall.

Assuming for the moment that Baccalieu is the island of the saga description, Leif would have sailed through Baccalieu Tickle westward around Grates Point until he opened Trinity Bay to the southward. At this juncture there is an evident lacuna in the saga account, for the next thing we are told is that the knorr ran aground somewhere a long distance from the open sea. We must conclude that she had coasted deep into some bay or fiord after rounding the cape which projected northward from the land.

From Grates Point, Leif's logical course would have been to sail southward into Trinity Bay, coasting the eastern shore. If he did this he would have found no sheltered harbors of any sort until he reached Hants Head, at which point the bay constricts to a width of about twelve miles. All along this high shore Leif would have found the forests running down to the highwater mark and he would have noticed that the farther he went into what he would by then have recognized as a great fiord, the higher the trees grew and the greater was their variety.

Beyond Hants Head he would have begun to find coves and sheltered anchorages, including the excellent harbors of New Perlican, Hearts Content, Hearts Desire and Hearts Delight. However, these are all deepwater harbors with steep-to shores which in Leif's time would have been heavily forested. There would have been few places where a knorr could have been hauled out for the winter, and no clear stretches of land where the Norse could have established themselves free of the danger of being surprised by whatever denizens, human or bestial, might have inhabited these somber forests.

After passing Long Point, below Hearts Desire, the Norse would have begun to see indications that they were nearing the bottom of the fiord. Far off to the west-southwest they would have raised the 400-foot spine of Tickle Cove Peninsula. Leif may have altered course toward it, but on the other hand he may have held on down the east coast until he reached the head of east Trinity Bay, where it divides into Dildo Arm, Spread Eagle Bay, Chapel Arm and Collier Bay.

The bottoms of all these arms would have seemed singularly attractive to the Norse, for here the forests were at their most luxuriant and the conifers which had dominated the seaward portions of the coast gave way to great stands of massive white and yellow birches intermingled with alders, maples and other broad-leaved trees. The richness of these forests would have been only one of the attractions, for at the bottom of several of these arms Leif would have found small hops. These hops would have tantalized Leif, since they were all either very small or, as is the case with the Spread Eagle barasway, there was no break in the gravel breakwater so that the lagoon was landlocked and inaccessible to any kind of boat.

But the summer was still young and Leif would have had time on hand for explorations, since unlike later expeditions he had no cattle with him and therefore had no need to worry about setting up his base ashore in time to procure a winter's supply of forage. Perhaps lured on by the discovery that there were hops in the vicinity, and by the possibility of finding a more suitable one, he would have sailed out around the Tickle Cove Peninsula.

He could not have done much more than clear that bold headland before he would have begun to think that the gods were with him. Four or five miles away to the south he would have seen a grass-green line barring off the end of a broad bay, and he would soon have been able to recognize this as a sand and gravel bar topped with grass and about two miles in length, behind which lay the gleam of quiet waters extending a long way back into the land along a gently sloping and thickly wooded valley.

Guided by a lookout at the masthead, Leif would have steered his ship toward the bar with growing hopes that this might prove to be just such a haven as he was seeking. Before long the lookout would have been able to distinguish a break in the barrier near its eastern extremity — an opening which was actually the mouth of a narrow channel leading into a big lagoon fringed by gravel and sand beaches and surrounded by wide expanses of open grasslands.

If the tide was low the knorr, drawing between four and five feet, could not have sailed much closer than half a mile to that channel entrance before she took the ground; but her people would not have cared. Tumbling into the afterboat, or leaping over the side and wading through the shallows, they would have made their way to shore to find themselves standing on the barrier breakwater of as fine a hop as any Norse mariner could ever have expected to find.

The entrance to Tickle Cove Pond is protected by an off-lying shoal of mud and gravel which extends seaward for about half a mile. At low tide the shoal area dries out completely except for a narrow, winding channel carrying less than a fathom of water. The summer tidal range varies between three and four feet here, so that if Leif's ship grounded on the edge of this shoal with a falling tide, she might have dried out sufficiently to allow her people to go ashore almost dryshod. One translation of the saga, which says that they "ran" ashore from the ship, suggests that this may have been exactly what they did.

As they crossed the wide tide flats they would have noted the channel and taken sights on shore "marks" so they could find and follow it when the tide came full.

The ship grounded at a point from which it was a long way to look to the sea, or to see from the sea. This passage has been translated in a score of different ways, never with quite the same meaning. It was probably a colloquial expression, and therefore not susceptible to a verbatim translation. Assuming that "the sea" refers to the open sea beyond the mouth of Trinity Bay, the description is an understatement, for the distance is about fifty-five miles. If "the sea" referred to is the open water beyond Tickle Cove Head, the distance is about four miles, or about as far as one can see from deck level.

When the tide refloated the knorr the Norse took her up the "river" and into the "lake." At Tickle Cove this would have meant rowing or towing her through the intricate offshore channel to the opening in the natural breakwater. She could have been brought through this gap only at slack water or on a rising tide — not because there would not have been enough water to float her but because of the current. With a falling tide the waters of the Broad pour out through the gap at rates of up to seven knots. On a rising tide the current flows in through the gap at rates of up to six knots. Leif's men would have had only to keep steerage way on their vessel with the sweeps, or by means of the afterboat towing from ahead, and the rising tide would have done the rest.

Inside the gap lies the basin of Tickle Cove itself, but the channel continues through this basin and westward through a narrows until it loses itself in the main body of the Broad. The total length of this reversing tidal stream is just under one and one-half miles. It is known locally as the Brook. No matter which interpretation we may choose to put on the Norse word for "river" in the saga, this channel, run or brook still fills the bill.

At high tide vessels drawing a fathom to a fathom and a half can pass all the way along the Brook and find anchorage on sand and mud in the Broad with a maximum depth of four fathoms. Tickle Cove basin offers anchorage in up to three fathoms. At low tide there is a wide strip of exposed sand and mud flats around the whole circumference of Tickle Cove and the Broad, and a vessel of a knorr's draft can be dried out or hauled up almost anywhere. Both sections of the haven are protected from all except northerly winds, and they are completely protected against surge or seas.

Tickle Cove Pond and its environs fulfill the saga requirements for Leif's haven with an exactness which cannot be approached by any other locality on any of the coasts where Leif might conceivably have made his Vinland landfall. Since we have already established that one of the most likely spots, if not the most likely one, for the initial landfall was the Baccalieu–Bay de Verde–Cape St. Francis region, I conclude that Tickle Cove was Leif's Vinland.

APPENDIX M

/\.\/\.\

sources dealing with the karlsefni expedition

CORRELATION OF THE VARIOUS CONFLICTING SAGA ACCOUNTS OF THE
POST—LEIF ERIKSSON VOYAGES TO AMERICA

The difficulties in coordinating the two main sources which recount the history of the far western voyages become particularly complex in relation to those voyages which took place after Leif's discovery of Vinland.

The Erik the Red and the Thorfinn Karlsefni versions of the lost Old Erik Saga record only two further voyages after Leif's: (1) the unsuccessful voyage of Thorstein Eriksson, and (2) a combined expedition consisting of a Greenland contingent led by Thorvald Eriksson — and including Freydis Eriksdottir — and an Icelandic contingent led by Thorfinn Karlsefni.

However, the Greenlanders Story records four separate voyages, spanning at least a decade: (1) a Vinland expedition of two years' duration by Thorvald Eriksson; (2) the unsuccessful voyage of Thorstein Eriksson; (3) an expedition of two years' duration to Vinland by Thorfinn Karlsefni; and (4) a Vinland voyage by Freydis Eriksdottir and the Icelandic brothers Helge and Finnboggi.

Obviously both versions cannot be right, and the first part of the problem is to decide which of the two is to be considered substantially correct.

We can simplify things somewhat by noting that as far as the Thorstein Eriksson voyage is concerned, both versions agree in general substance. With regard to the three remaining voyages listed in the Greenlanders Story, I conclude that they actually represent three aspects of the single expedition described in the Erik the Red and the Karlsefni sagas. My reasons are as follows:

Unlike the Erik the Red and the Karlsefni sagas, which give a meticulous account of the outbound voyage, the Greenlanders Story gives no sailing directions, descriptions of routes followed, or accounts of the actual voyages in connection with any of these purportedly independent expeditions. This omission is significant because it was the custom for travel sagas to include at least some sailing instructions and some details about the conditions encountered en route, these things being of paramount interest to a seafaring people. Even in the accounts of voyages over well-known sea routes, such as those between Iceland and Europe, there is usually some descriptive detail concerning the actual passage.

It might be argued that the author of the Greenlanders Story had no need to mention such matters since it was to be assumed that all three voyages followed the route established by Leif Eriksson. However, the author himself never offers this explanation, nor does he imply that it might be valid. On the contrary, he seems to realize that the absence of details about the voyages may be considered somewhat odd, and when he speaks of Thorvald Eriksson's voyage we can almost detect a note of apology:

They put out to sea [from Greenland] and nothing is said of their voyage before they came to Vinland, to Leif's booths. The other two voyages are dealt with in equally summary fashion. Karlsefni's voyage: *They put out to sea [from Greenland] and came to Leif's booths whole and sound.* Freydis's voyage: *They put out to sea [from Greenland] and had agreed to keep together, but the two brothers got there first and carried their baggage up to Leif's booths.*

To suggest that three such voyages to Vinland should have been so totally uneventful and lacking in interest to a saga audience that all account of them could have been dispensed with, or lost during the transmissions of the story sources, stretches credulity beyond reasonable limits. The most likely explanation for the omission of all sailing instructions and voyage details is that only a single set of data existed in the first place, that which is recorded in the Erik the Red and the Karlsefni sagas for the combined Vinland voyage of the Icelanders and Greenlanders. Since the author of the Greenlanders Story had already mistakenly appropriated the highlights of this account in order to explain how Leif Eriksson reached Vinland,* he was left with no further voyage material upon which to draw.

If, as I believe was the case, the author of the Greenlanders Story dissected a single voyage into three parts, we would expect to find a number of inconsistencies in the finished product. There are many of these. In the single brief paragraph with which the author attempts to establish the fact that Thorvald made an independent voyage, we are told that he *came to Vinland, to Leif's booths.* However, in the ensuing passages, which are abstracted from a bonafide account of the combined Karlsefni-Thorvald

---

* See Appendix L.

voyage, the Greenlanders Story version naively makes it clear that Thorvald never *did* find either the booths or Vinland, although he spent two years searching for them.

The account of Thorvald's meeting with the Skraelings reveals another discrepancy. The Greenlanders Story would have us believe that this was the first contact between Norse and Skraelings and that Thorvald immediately launched an unprovoked attack upon these unknown people and slaughtered eight of them. Yet surely not even a Viking berserker would have been so feckless as to gratuitously open hostilities upon first contact with the inhabitants and presumed masters of a remote and alien land. Thorvald's action is intelligible only on the assumption that he had prior reason to hate the Skraelings, which would necessarily mean that there had been an earlier contact between the two races. In fact the Erik the Red and Karlsefni sagas make it clear that Thorvald's fatal encounter with the natives took place shortly after a battle had been fought between Karlsefni's Icelanders and a party of Skraelings at Hop, during which two Norsemen were killed.

The Greenlanders Story goes on to tell us that when Karlsefni made his reputedly independent voyage to Vinland after Thorvald, *his* first contact with the Skraelings was perfectly amicable. Karlsefni and his people, who would have known about Thorvald's feud with, and death at the hands of, the Skraelings if this had taken place before they arrived in the land, showed no awareness that they considered the Skraelings to be dangerous and displayed no animosity toward them, which they would surely have done if the natives had murdered Thorvald.

These initially friendly relations between Karlsefni's people and the Skraelings eventually broke down. Thereafter, but not until this point was reached, the Norse slaughtered almost every Skraeling they could lay hands on.

Among the other miscellaneous confusions in the Greenlanders Story is the statement that Thorvald's voyage was undertaken after Christianity had been introduced into Greenland, but that Erik the Red had died prior to its introduction. Since independent sources establish the fact that Erik was still hale and hearty as late as 1005, and that Christianity was introduced into Greenland no later than 1001 and probably as early as 998, this statement makes nonsense of the chronology which the author of the Greenlanders Story tells us is the correct one.

The author of the Greenlanders Story has sometimes attempted to cover up the inconsistencies in his reconstruction by inventions. One of these concerns the voyages of Thorstein Eriksson. According to the Greenlanders Story, Thorstein made his voyage to Vinland to bring back the body of his brother Thorvald, who had been killed by the Skraelings.

But the practice of carrying home the bodies of men who died or were killed in distant places was not followed in Scandinavian countries until late in the fourteenth century.* In the beginning of the eleventh century, when Thorvald was killed, it was the Norse custom to bury or cremate a warrior where he fell. If it had been customary to bring home the bodies of the dead for burial, Thorvald's own men would surely have carried home the corpse of their leader.

In chronicling the reputedly independent Freydis voyage, the author of the Greenlanders Story tells us that it took place *after* Karlsefni had returned to Greenland from Vinland, yet he refers to an agreement *between* Freydis and Karlsefni to the effect that each should carry no more than thirty men, and women besides, in their various ships during the projected Vinland voyage.

The Story version of the Freydis voyage has other revealing weaknesses. The author says that Freydis set out for Vinland the year *after* Karlsefni returned from there, but that she came back *from* Vinland in time to find Karlsefni preparing to sail from Greenland to Norway; although Karlsefni remained in Greenland only over the winter. It appears that what really happened in this case, was that Karlsefni took leave of the Greenlandic portion of the joint expedition during the third summer and returned to Greenland, en route home to Iceland, while Freydis and her people remained behind in the new lands for another winter. Thus when Freydis reached Greenland the following spring she found Karlsefni preparing to depart for Iceland or Norway with his cargo of New World produce.

A number of other reasons can be advanced to show why the number, chronology and composition of the various expeditions listed in the Greenlanders Story cannot be accepted; but no valid arguments can be presented against acceptance of these elements of the Erik the Red and the Karlsefni versions.

Nevertheless it would be folly to condemn arbitrarily the whole of the Greenlanders Story, as some have done. The Erik the Red and Karlsefni versions also have their failings, not least of these being their habit of omitting details about the Greenlanders' participation in the joint expedition — details which are preserved in the Greenlanders Story.

It may not be accident alone which has resulted in the rearrangement of the chronology and composition of the voyages in the Greenlanders Story, and in the suppression of details about the Greenlanders in the Erik the Red and the Karlsefni sagas. What we seem to be faced with here is an example of a situation which has often occurred in connection with

---

* About the time the Greenlanders Story seems to have been written. We also note that Thorvald gave orders to his men that he was to be buried where he had fallen, in keeping with the normal practice of his own times.

voyages of exploration. The Vinland expedition evidently became divided into two hostile factions, and out of the mutual recriminations, disagreements and perhaps outright hostilities between these two, and their homeland supporters and descendants, two variant versions of the expedition eventually emerged. Succeeding generations of copyists appear to have preserved these differences, and may even have enlarged upon them. The sagamen and copyists did not pretend to impartiality, as do modern scholars. They were frankly and honestly partisan, and they tended to celebrate the deeds of the group with which they were in personal sympathy.

Thus the common ancestor of the Erik the Red and the Thorfinn Karlsefni sagas may well have evolved into a form which was concerned with honoring the deeds of the Icelanders in general and of Karlsefni in particular; and we have not far to seek to understand how, and why, this might have happened. Karlsefni's Icelandic descendants embraced several illustrious members of the Roman Church, including three bishops in the three generations after his death. Acting either on instructions from their superiors or because of a sycophantic desire to please, the priestly clerks who copied the manuscripts and passed them on from one generation to the next doubtless did their best to strengthen the role played by their superiors' ancestor and the Icelanders — at the expense of the Greenlanders where necessary.

The denigration of one faction by the other would hardly have been a one-sided affair. In Greenland the saga version which evolved through the centuries would have tended to sing the praises of the Greenlanders at the expense of the Icelanders. It is not impossible that one of the sources used by the author of the Greenlanders Story may have included a saga composed on behalf of Leif Eriksson, perhaps at the order of one of his immediate descendants if not of himself. If this did happen the virtual elimination of Erik the Red from a real role in the Greenlanders Story account of the Vinland voyages would have followed as a natural consequence of the conflict between Erik and his eldest son, and as a result of the fact that Erik favored the Icelanders and did all he could to further their hopes and plans. Furthermore, the appearance of an active interest (amounting almost to direction) by Leif in the Vinland voyages which followed his own voyage, would be explained.

At some stage in the evolution of the sources of the Greenlanders Story, a Greenland partisan may also have devised a very effective means of downgrading the part played by Karlsefni and the Icelanders, by dividing the joint expedition into three parts, two of which then became entirely Greenlandic in planning and execution while the third, dealing with Karlsefni, was condensed and isolated in a narrow compass. Karlsefni's voyage may even have been eliminated in the Greenland version. The author of the Greenlanders Story, an Icelander working in Iceland after the Greenland settlements had begun to decay, implies that he obtained the portion dealing with the Karlsefni story from a descendant of Karlsefni's.

The pro-Icelandic saga versions use a somewhat more direct technique to disparage the contributions of the Greenlanders. By accident or design they reduce Leif's part in the sequence of voyages to miniscule proportions. Bjarni Herjolfsson's voyage, which is essential to an understanding of Leif's venture, is completely eliminated, leaving the story of the original discovery of the western lands in a kind of limbo. This treatment of Leif may reflect a strong degree of animosity which existed between him and the Icelanders and which was perhaps based on Leif's refusal to be of assistance to later Vinland voyagers, including his own father and brothers. It will be noted that Erik plays a respectable role in the pro-Icelandic versions and that he was himself in opposition to Leif.

When the Erik the Red and the Karlsefni sagas (and doubtless at least their immediate common ancestor) dealt with the combined expedition they undercut the Greenlanders either by omitting to detail their exploits or by assigning to the Icelanders the credit due for them. Only one Greenlandic member of the expedition receives a reasonable degree of attention in the Erik the Red and the Karlsefni sagas, and the picture presented of this man — Thorhall the Hunter — is largely derogatory. He is depicted as an uncouth, evil-tongued and barbaric pagan. It is almost as if he was deliberately selected for a detailed and unsavory portrayal as representative of the Greenlandic contingent.

Thorvald Eriksson, the leader of the Greenlanders, receives almost as short shrift as does his brother Leif. He is mentioned only twice, once when the expedition sailed, and again when he was killed at Lake Melville. No notice is taken of his westward exploration, and the credit for his exploration of Lake Melville is shorn from him and attached to Karlsefni, a matter with which we deal at length in the last part of this appendix.

Freydis Eriksdottir is also largely ignored. In the only incident in which she appears she is portrayed (perhaps with some truth) as a species of savage Amazon whose sanity seems questionable. Nothing is said of the fact that she was the leader of those Greenlanders who remained behind at Straumfiord during the third and final winter. The Erik the Red and the Karlsefni sagas abrogate even this small triumph of endurance to the credit of Karlsefni and the Icelanders.

Helge and Finnboggi, the two Icelandic traders whose ship Freydis used, are not mentioned at all. This total omission is to be explained by the fact that although they and their men were Icelanders they deliberately allied themselves with the Greenland faction.

After considering all aspects of the matter we arrive at a simple and logical solution to the problem posed at the beginning of this appendix. As far as the sequence, composition and number of the Vinland voyages is concerned, we can safely follow the Erik the Red and Karlsefni sagas; but the details of the events which occurred once the joint expedition reached the new lands must be drawn from both sources. In general when we are dealing with a phase of the story which is primarily concerned with the Greenlanders we can rely upon the Greenlanders Story for the bulk of our information, supplementing it when possible from the Erik the Red and the Karlsefni sagas. In the case of events in which the Icelanders played the leading role we must reverse the procedure. In this way we are able to reconstruct a detailed account of the expeditions which includes all the available information, and which avoids the draconian alternative whereby one version is arbitrarily chosen as being the only valid source, while the other is brusquely consigned to oblivion.

There remains one other problem in coordinating the sources. This involves an error in the interpretation of the Erik the Red and the Karlsefni sagas which has misled many authors into concluding that the return from Hop of Karlsefni's expedition was followed by only one more exploration voyage, one led by Thorfinn Karlsefni that sailed north from Straumfiord in search of Thorhall the Hunter.

In fact two separate expeditions were mounted after the return from Hop. One, led by Thorvald Eriksson, sailed north from Straumfiord to Lake Melville. The other, led by Thorfinn Karlsefni, sailed south from Straumfiord into White Bay.

The Greenlanders Story deals with Thorvald Eriksson's voyage to the north as a purely Greenlandic venture and makes no mention of Karlsefni. The sailing directions, the internal sequence of events and the geographical descriptions in this account are straightforward and unexceptionable, even though the voyage itself is placed out of context in the overall chronology of the western voyages.

On the other hand the Erik the Red and the Karlsefni sagas state that the northern expedition was conducted by Karlsefni, and the only mention made of the Greenlanders in connection with it is a brief notice dealing with the death of Thorvald.

But when we examine the sailing directions and geographical descriptions in the Erik the Red and the Karlsefni sagas, we find that they consist of two distinct sets, which are mutually contradictary. We are told that Karlsefni set off north from Straumfiord, rounded Kialarness, and sailed into what can only be Lake Melville — and thus far the description of the route is identical with that found in the Greenlanders Story account of Thorvald's voyage. But after the fight with the natives when Thorvald was killed, the Erik the Red and the Karlsefni versions tell us that the expedition sailed *north* in order to regain Straumfiord. They also tell us that the place where Thorvald was killed was directly opposite to Hop and equidistant with it from Straumfiord; and that the mountains thereabouts formed one and the same chain with those at Hop.

It is obvious that the sailing directions for the return to Straumfiord, together with the geographical description of the place where the battle with the natives took place, are nonsensical when applied to Lake Melville. But they make sense when they are applied to the foot of White Bay. One sails north from there in order to reach Straumfiord. Hop — St. Paul's Bay, on the west coast of Newfoundland — and the foot of White Bay lie directly opposite to one another. They are separated by the Long Range Mountains, which bound Hop on the east and the foot of White Bay on the west. These two places are equidistant from Straumfiord. The discrepancies in the Erik the Red and the Karlsefni accounts make it plain that we are dealing with elements of two voyages rolled into one, and there is a direct confirmation of a second, southern, voyage in the Erik the Red and the Karlsefni sagas.

Some men report that Bjarni Grimolfsson and Freydis remained behind here [at Straumfiord, after the return from Hop] with a hundred people, and went no farther, while Karlsefni and Snorri proceeded to the southward with forty men, returning again that same summer after tarrying at a hop [there] for barely two months.

The Erik the Red and the Karlsefni sagas then go on to say that Karlsefni sailed north that same summer in search of Thorhall.* While we are able to find a reasonable explanation as to why Karlsefni and Snorri should have made a voyage into White Bay (see Chapter 24) we find much more difficulty in explaining why Karlsefni should have concerned himself in a search for Thorhall the Hunter. On the other hand Thorvald Eriksson, as leader of the Greenland contingent, would have been under a heavy obligation to search for his father's factor and the nine other Greenlanders who were missing with him.

The account of the battle between the Norse and the natives during the northern trip, as told in the Greenlanders Story, is totally different from the version recounted in the Erik the Red and the Karlsefni sagas. In the

---

* Other authors have dealt with this problem on the assumption that the quoted passage is an erroneous reference to the first voyage south to Hop. Neither the context of the passage nor its contents give any grounds for suggesting such a solution.

Greenlanders Story, the Greenlanders surprised and massacred a band of Skraelings and were then attacked by a large number of Skraelings in skin boats, with the result that Thorvald Eriksson was killed. But according to the Erik the Red and the Karlsefni sagas, Karlsefni encountered a single Einfoetingr — not a Skraeling, be it noted, but a man of quite another race — who unprovoked shot one arrow at them and killed Thorvald. As we show in Appendix O, the people Karlsefni encountered were Beothuk or proto-Beothuk Indians whom he could not have met to the north of Straumfiord; but Thorvald was killed by Skraelings, which is to say Dorsets, who are known to have inhabited the shores of Lake Melville.

When all the factors have been taken into account it becomes apparent that at some point in the transmisssion of the Erik the Red and the Karlsefni sagas, the credit for Thorvald's northern voyage descended on Karlsefni, with the dual consequence that Karlsefni's own second southern voyage lost its identity and Thorvald and the Greenlanders were all but eliminated from any real role in their own expedition.

THE LOCATION OF HOP

When Karlsefni made his first voyage south from Straumfiord Camp, two routes were open to him. He could have led his little flotilla eastward around Cape Bauld, then south along the east coast of the Great Northern Peninsula into White Bay; or he could have continued southwestward through the Strait of Belle Isle — Straumfiord — and then coasted down the west coast of the peninsula.

If, as we have suggested in Chapter 20, the Icelanders confused the mouth of the strait with the mouth of the great fiord (Trinity Bay) which led to Leif's Vinland, Karlsefni's logical decision would have been to follow the southerly shore of Straumfiord into the southwest, as Leif must have done with his fiord.

In any event this is what Karlsefni chose to do, and the essence of the proof of this rests on two salient facts. In the first place, there is no harbor on the east coast of the Great Northern Peninsula (or anywhere else in White Bay) which can be equated with the description of the Hop where the first southern expedition wintered.* In the second place, and as we have already pointed out in this appendix, Karlsefni made a second southern voyage, down the east coast, the year after he discovered Hop. Since we know from the saga descriptions of the lands and peoples that this was not a repetition of his first southern voyage, we must conclude that his first southern voyage was down the west coast of the Great Northern

---

* See The Saga Tale at the beginning of Chapter 21.

Peninsula. Additional confirmation of this conclusion appears in Chapters 20 to 24.

In order to identify the actual location of Hop we must make a detailed examination of the west coast of the peninsula.

From Cape Norman south to Anchor Point the west coast of New-foundland is bald, bleak and baleful and is backed by wind-swept spruce muskegs and barren limestone ridges. There are few harbors or coves of any sort, and none that by any stretch of the imagination can be made to tally with the saga description of Hop.

From Anchor Point to Castor River the shore is low and broken, with many offshore reefs and islets offering some shelter here and there, but not much else. There are few if any natural grassy areas; instead there is a morass of spruce muskeg. The long, low Ferolle Peninsula is also covered with scrub barrens and muskeg.

From Castor River south to Eddies Cove West the shore is almost dead straight without a harbor of any sort. Then from Eddies Cove to a point five miles south of Portland Creek the land sinks into wet and desolate muskeg (the Bateau Barrens) which supports only occasional clumps of stunted spruce, and which has no harbors on its coast except an exposed one at Port au Choix and a deep-water one encompassed to the high-tide mark by coniferous forests at Hawke Bay.

Hop, as the saga describes it, cannot be anywhere on this stretch of coast.

South from Portland Creek there is a thirty-mile strip of low coast fringed with meadows and backed by vast areas of natural bog pasture. This relatively short stretch has two excellent, almost classic, barachoix harbors or hops.* To the south again, the Long Range Mountains crowd right out to the sea to form such a bold coast that apart from the steep-sided and mountainous deep-water fiords of Bonne Bay and Bay of Islands, there are no real harbors until after the Port au Port Peninsula is passed. Hop cannot be on this stretch of coast; nor can it be in Bonne Bay or Bay of Islands.

The saga account of Karlsefni's voyage down the other coast of the peninsula during the third summer helps to pinpoint the location of Hop. Karlsefni sailed south down the east coast until he reached a point opposite Hop, equidistant with it from Straumfiord camp, and separated from Hop by a range of mountains which must have been the Long Range. Since he could go only as far south as the foot of White Bay in the east, this provides conclusive evidence that Hop was not south of Bonne Bay in the west.

From the foregoing it is clear that Hop must have been located at one of the two barachoix harbors between Portland Creek and Bonne Bay —

---

* A detailed description of the type of harbor known to the Norse as a "hop" will be found in Part II of Appendix L.

had been used — probably turf on pole rafters — nothing is now visible of any of these buildings except for the shallow excavations left by the Ingstad expedition. The location of the old walls was traced by following the differing thicknesses of the sod layer. Occasional heaps of stones on the exposed, sandy floor areas probably indicated the positions of the fireplaces, ember pits and perhaps storage pits.

Mr. Ingstad has reported surprisingly few artifacts. A Dorset lamp was found in the debris of the smithy. Fragments of a pot of unspecified material and origin were described to me by Ingstad as having been found in the very large building. During "clean-up operations" in 1964, Ingstad's wife, Anne Stinne, found a soapstone spinning whorl which is similar in size and shape to those used by Norse women in Iceland and Greenland. Fragments of iron nails from the large house, a tiny piece of bronze, and some pieces of iron together with slag from the smithy complete the list of announced finds. Published reports (not by the Ingstad expedition) of the finding of buried wooden sills around the outer walls of the large house and of the small "shed" near to it during excavations made by contractors who were erecting a protective shed at the orders of the New-foundland Government have not been confirmed by the Ingstad expedition.

The most convincing evidence of Norse occupation lies in a series of carbon-14 dates obtained from charcoal fragments which came from the smithy, a nearby charcoal pit and some of the house structures. These dates show a range of from A.D. 680 plus or minus ninety years, to A.D. 1060 plus or minus seventy years, with a number of dates grouped around A.D. 1000.

The smithy is of particular interest. It contains what was apparently a large stone anvil, and it is clear that iron was worked at this site. However, since no trace of any sort of furnace has been discovered (or, at least, announced), it seems unlikely that iron was actually smelted here. The carbon dates seem to confirm that the smithy was used in the times of the Norse voyages.

With the exception of the largest structure and the small shed adjacent to it, the building ruins are in keeping with what might be expected from the Greenland Norse of circa 1000. Taken together they seem to form a rather typical homestead complex of small huts grouped around one or two large living halls. However, the largest structure is not comparable with anything known from either Greenland or Iceland of this period. It offers no diagnostic features which would indicate that it is Norse of the early eleventh century. It is sited some distance away from the rest of the complex and closer to the sea. Between it and the sea there is a large pit filled with "burned and fire-cracked" stones and pebbles, which has no parallel in Greenland of circa A.D. 1000. However, this pit closely re-

The Epaves Bay site

Legend:

1. Fire pit
2. Multi-room house
3. Smithy
4. Long house

GRASSY AREA

SCRUB and BOG, formerly forested

EPAVES BAY

0.5 FATHOM LINE

LOW TIDE LINE
HIGH TIDE LINE
STORM TIDE LINE

BLACK DUCK BROOK

sembles the tryworks fire pits used at early Basque, French, Dutch and English shore-whaling stations in northern regions. One large "wing" of the structure is fitted with a complex floor drainage system and does not shows convincing evidence that it was ever a walled room at all. It could, however, have been a blubber-cutting platform.

The Ingstad expedition claims that this great building is part of the Norse complex, but it more likely postdates Norse occupancy of Epaves Bay and may have been part of a shore-whaling establishment dating from very early colonial times. The wooden sills, which we have already mentioned, were reported from this part of the site, but the Norse did not use buried sill construction around A.D. 1000. The Ingstad expedition itself found iron nails here. Chemical analysis of the soil shows it to be highly acid, and metallurgists say that iron nails and other small agglomerations of that metal would almost certainly not have survived since A.D. 1000, but would have been completely oxidized. Buried wooden objects would have disintegrated.

Historical records show that shore-whaling establishments existed on this section of the coast at a very early date. Until recently the Strait of Belle Isle was one of the better whaling grounds in the North Atlantic region, funneling huge numbers of whales of several species through its narrow waters during their migrations to and from the Gulf of St. Lawrence. Active whaling actually survived in the strait until 1951.

We do not know with certainty when whaling began in the strait, but European fishing and whaling ships, primarily Basque, were operating in the Labrador Sea off southwestern Greenland by 1400–1420 and had evidently reached Newfoundland waters by 1436, which is the date of the earliest copy of the Andrea Del Bianca Map. This map shows the Isla de Stokafixa (stockfish: cod) far to the westward of Iceland with a given latitude and longitude which could only have belonged to Newfoundland. Newfoundland continued to be called by this name on other maps made as late as 1500, particularly by the Portuguese and Basques.

In 1534, when Jacques Cartier passed through the strait, it had long been a famous fishing and whaling ground. He sheltered briefly at Quirpon, which he spelled *Karpont*. This excellent harbor, five miles west of Epaves Bay, was and evidently had been for some time much frequented by whalers. Its name is derived from the Spanish Basque, Cap Arpón or Harpoon Cape. That it had long been in use is suggested by Cartier's failure to recognize a name which had been in existence long enough to have suffered considerable corruption. The etymology of the name can be traced from the Basque *aroi* through the Spanish *arpón* and the French *harpon* to the English *harpoon*. The present pronunciation of Quirpon is *karpoon* despite the many changes in spelling which the name has undergone over the centuries.

Cartier also found that the Grande Bay, as the strait was then known, was the regular haunt of many fishing ships. And at this point we note that in this period, and for at least three hundred years afterwards, whales were thought to be fishes and the word fishery included not only the pursuit of true fishes but of whales as well.

In 1580 an Englishman, Richard Whitbourne, reported the existence of a whaling fishery in the strait shared by Basque, French and a few English ships.* Spanish records quoted by Proust in his *History of Newfoundland* state that by far the largest fleet in Newfoundland waters between 1504 and 1580 was of French origin, and H. Horwood (*The French in Newfoundland*, St. John's, 1962) analyzed these records and demonstrated that most of these ships were Basque from the French Basque Provinces. In *Les Pêcheries de Terreneuve (Records of the Colonial Institute)* it is stated that the Basques were sending 6000 men in 200 ships to Newfoundland by 1550.

These Basque ships were almost all engaged in a dual fishery for whales and cod. It was their practice to set up shore-whaling stations when they arrived in Newfoundland in the spring. These were sited by preference at places where whales were abundant in restricted waters, as they were in the Strait of Belle Isle. Whaling was carried on by boats operating from the shore station. The tryworks were always built ashore (ship tryworks were not introduced until the end of the sixteenth century), preferably just back from gently sloping and fairly smooth beaches close to the grounds. The whales were towed in at high tide by the boats and allowed to strand as the tide fell, when the carcasses were stripped of their blubber. At the next high tide the carcasses were towed off and turned adrift so as not to foul the area, with the result that there are seldom any significant accumulations of whalebone at the sites of such stations.

The strips of blubber were hauled ashore to wooden platforms underneath which drains had been dug to carry off spilled oil, blood and gurry. Here the blubber was chopped into small pieces and then fed into the trypots. These pots were slung over deep firepits filled with small stones and

---

* "My first voyage to [Newfoundland] was about 40 years since [1580]. We were bound to the Grand Bay which lieth on the north side of that land, to kill whales etc. . . . they [the natives] live together in the north and west part [of Newfoundland] which is seldom frequented by the English; but the French and Biscaines [Basques] who resort thither yearly for the whale fishery, and also for the codfish, report them [the natives] to be an ingenious and tractable people; they are ready to assist them with great patience in killing, cutting and boiling of whales and making traine oil. . . ." Captain Richard Whitbourne, *A Discourse and Discoverie of the Newe-founde-lande.*

pebbles, which were fired with pieces of boiled-out blubber. The purpose of the stones and pebbles, which grew very hot when the fire was burning, was to provide a species of sponge or wick which would absorb and then vaporize the waste oil, allowing the gases to burn off slowly and steadily from the surface and providing a controlled heat under the pot.

After manning and refurbishing their shore stations in the spring, the Basque ships would sail off to the cod banks and spend the balance of the season fishing and making dry cod. In late summer or early autumn they returned to their shore stations, took aboard the oil and the shoremen, closed up their establishments for the winter and sailed for home.

Epaves Bay is one of the best sites on either the Newfoundland or Labrador coasts for a shore-whaling station of this type. Old occupation sites which have not yet been excavated, but which bear a striking resemblance to sections of the Epaves Bay site, have been found on Quirpon Island and at nearbye Griquet Harbour. Casual finds of fishing irons and harpoons of Basque type suggest that these too were shore-whaling stations.

No final decisions can be made about the origins of all the structures at Epaves Bay until the Ingstad expedition releases the full results of its work. At the moment there seems to be no good reason to deny the likelihood that some of the structures were built and inhabited by Norsemen of circa A.D. 1000; but it seems obvious that the large house was actually a shore-whaling establishment of the early colonial period.

Although it has not been stated as a fact, the leaders of the Ingstad expedition have strongly intimated that the Epaves Bay site was the location of Leif Eriksson's Vinland. This deduction is not consistent with the facts as I understand them and as I have set them out in this book. If we are to accept Epaves Bay as Leif's Vinland we must discard, or seriously distort, the description of Vinland given in the Greenlanders Story — and this is the only description of Vinland that we possess.

It is my belief that Epaves Bay was the site of a temporary Norse settlement established there by the combined Icelandic–Greenlandic expedition led by Thorfinn Karlsefni and Thorvald Eriksson.

.\VV.\

kaRlsefni and the Beothuk indians

AN ANALYSIS OF THE CONFLICTS BETWEEN THE NORSE AND THE NATIVE
PEOPLE OF NEWFOUNDLAND, AND THE IDENTIFICATION OF ONE GROUP OF
NATIVES AS BEOTHUKS

The combination of the accounts of two voyages (Karlsefni's second
southern voyage and Thorvald Eriksson's northern voyage in search of
Thorhall) into one produced a blend of oil and water which, as we have
seen in Appendix M, separates naturally into its component parts as soon
as it is given the chance to do so. This raises the possibility that further
details of the "lost" southern voyage may be recoverable from other
portions of the saga sources, and in particular from the conflicting accounts
of Karlsefni's encounter with the Skraelings as this is recorded in the
Greenlanders Story and in the Erik the Red and the Karlsefni sagas.

The two versions agree in some respects, but differ radically in others.
The conflict between them is usually explained as being due to corrup-
tions or additions to the original account. But the differences can be
explained more rationally on the assumption that we are dealing with the
combined accounts of two somewhat similar, but separate, encounters
between Karlsefni's party and the natives of Newfoundland — encounters
which took place during the course of two different expeditions.

When we examine the saga versions, the first thing we notice is that
they describe a battle set in two locales. The Erik the Red and the Karlsefni
sagas specify that the site was Hop, where in every instance the natives
of the area arrived from and departed to seaward in skin boats. The
Greenlanders Story claims that the action took place at Leif's Vinland,
and it makes no mention of the use of boats by the natives. On the contrary it specifies that the natives arrived out of the woods from the landward side of Karlsefni's camp, and departed in the same direction.

The accounts of the trading which preceded the battle differ materially.

The Greenlanders Story tells us that the Norse traded red cloth, and mentions no other trade goods. The Erik the Red and the Karlsefni sagas do not make any mention of red cloth but instead describe how the natives were given milk products in exchange for skins. Also, some key individuals appear in one version and not in the other. Thus we have the Freydis incident in the Erik the Red and the Karlsefni sagas, but no mention of Gudrid. On the other hand Gudrid looms large in the Greenlanders Story, while Freydis is not mentioned. Since we are told that although Freydis accompanied the Hop expedition, she did not go on the second southern expedition, we do not find her absence from the Greenlanders Story so surprising.

Even some of the incidents which appear in both versions suggest that there were two separate encounters. The account of the natives finding the Norse axe appears in both, but in the Erik the Red and the Karlsefni sagas it looks like an intrusion and is at variance with the sequence of events of the battle. The appearance of the bull is also recorded in both; but while this event seems to fit the Hop encounter, it does not ring true in the Greenlanders Story version. According to the latter, both the natives and the bull which caused such panic among them all came out of the woods, where one would suppose that the natives would have encountered the cattle, or have seen, smelled or heard evidence of them during their approach to the camp, and so have been forewarned of the presence of these unfamiliar beasts.

However the most telling indications of there having been two encounters are to be found in the evidence that the Norse battled people of two distinct races.

The natives described in the Erik the Red and the Karlsefni sagas versions of this battle are uniformly and unmistakably Eskimoan. Not only is their physical description Eskimoan, but so are the descriptions of their clothes, boats and other artifacts.

On the other hand all of the natives described in the Greenlanders Story version are distinctly un-Eskimoan. The woman who came to the door of Gudrid's hut was said to have had large, light-colored eyes and chestnut-colored hair, and to have worn something which resembled a black Norse kirtle. Eskimoan peoples have dark, almost black eyes which are not notably large (rather the reverse), and invariably have black hair if they are of pure stock.

The only authentic portraits of Beothuk Indians which we possess are of two women, Mary March (Demasduit) and Shanawdithit, who were captured and brought to St. John's in the early part of the nineteenth century. By far the most salient feature of both women according to their portraits, which were drawn from life, is their remarkably large, wide eyes.

John Guy, a seventeenth-century colonizer in Newfoundland, also noted that the Beothuks were "full eyed"; while Captain Robinson, in describing Mary March, wrote that "her eyes were larger [than those of an Eskimo]." Other first-hand descriptions of Beothuks refer to the fact that some of them had light-brown or hazel-colored eyes. As for the chestnut-colored hair, it was normal practice for the Beothuks to dress their hair with powdered red ochre mixed with oil or fat, which imparted a lustrous reddish-brown sheen to it.

The kirtle is also indicative of Beothuks. The eleventh-century Norse kirtle was a gownlike garment usually worn belted at the waist. The Beothuks wore something quite similar: a garment made from two caribou hides with the fur still on or, sometimes, from a number of otter pelts.* This was, in effect, a sleeveless fur gown and was worn belted at the waist. On the other hand there is no record of Eskimoan peoples ever having worn anything but tailored garments consisting, in essence, of a parka-like jacket and trousers of varying length. This applied to both sexes. The Norse themselves made specific note of the difference in the garb of the two peoples when they reported that the Skraelings encountered on the coast near Hop were wearing "skin doublets." Newfoundland caribou hides, incidentally, range from brown to almost black in color, while natural otter is also very dark, almost black, in appearance.

The description of a second native in the Greenland Story version is tantalizingly brief. However, this man, whom Karlsefni thought was the leader of the natives, was described as being "fair," which is an adjective that can hardly be considered applicable to an Eskimoan people. He was also referred to as being "tall." It was a historical fact that the Beothuk men were tall and well formed. The last chieftain of the race, who was murdered by white hunters on Red Indian Lake in 1819, was stretched out on the ice by his killers and measured. They reported that he was more than six feet tall.† There is also testimony to indicate that the Beothuks deliberately chose the tallest men among them to be their elected leaders.

Many Beothuks were light-complexioned, or at least appeared so to European observers. The chronicler Fabian, who saw a group of captive Beothuks at the English Court in 1498, whither they had been brought by John Cabot, noted that when they were dressed in European clothes they were indistinguishable from Englishmen. A few years later Gaspar Cortereal concluded that the Beothuks would make excellent slaves, not

---

* Pietro Pasquale, reporting on the Cortereal voyages to Newfoundland, says that the natives were dressed mostly in otter.

† The only extant adult Beothuk skeleton, which is now in the Newfoundland Provincial Museum, is of a man about six feet two inches tall.

only because of their remarkable physique but because they were the whitest-skinned "savages" known at that time. Many later diarists and travelers also commented on the Beothuks in the same vein.

We must also consider the odd incident when Freydis is reported to have displayed her naked breasts to a band of attackers who, in this case were Dorsets. This was a defense which (as we have noted in Chapter 21) was practiced by Beothuk women when they were threatened by an enemy. Since such a strange defense is not recorded as having been used by Norse women, or by any Eskimoan peoples, the suspicion arises that a demonstration of this startling gesture may have taken place during an encounter with Beothuks, and that the description of it might have been attached to the Freydis incident in order to give her actions an enhanced dramatic effect, which — no one can deny — it certainly does.

Yet another significant point is the fact that one group of natives encountered by the Norse was so passionately anxious to obtain red cloth that they gladly exchanged their possessions for tiny fragments of the material. The name Red Indian was first coined to describe the Beothuks, and only later was it applied, with considerably less validity, to all North American Indians. It came into being because the Beothuks used red ochre lavishly, not only on their clothing and the whole of their bodies including the hair, but also on their artifacts, on their skin tents and even on corpses. Red had an intense religious significance, and the Beothuk fondness for it amounted to a fixation. Red ochre pigment, as the Beothuks used it, mixed with animal oil or fat, is not bright red, being closer to the somber color of recently dried blood, as is evidenced by its appearance as a home-made paint in Newfoundland outports, where the pigment, from the same pits used by the Beothuks, is mixed with cod-liver oil. The red cloth which the Norse traded to the natives would have been singularly desirable to the Beothuks.

Another aspect of Beothuk culture may have some bearing on what the sagas tell us about the possession of furs by the natives. Eskimoan peoples use furs to keep themselves warm, and seldom use them for decorative purposes. Moreover, they tend to use such utilitarian furs as caribou and seal, both of which the Norse would have been able to get for themselves in quantity in Greenland. The Beothuks, on the other hand, made extensive use of such luxuriant furs as marten, beaver and otter. It is very unlikely that the Norse would have been able to obtain valuable furs from the Dorsets, since even latter-day Eskimos have to be extensively indoctrinated by white traders before they can be persuaded to hunt fur-bearer. However, the Norse might very well have been able to trade with the Beothuks for furs which would have been of considerable value by European standards. We are specifically told that sable was one of the furs they did obtain from the natives. Sable is another name for marten, which the Beothuks used as trimming for their clothing. Furthermore, the marten is a forest animal and is found only in the heavily wooded interior regions of Newfoundland, where the Beothuks used to winter but which were not, so far as we know, inhabited by the Dorsets.

The existence of two distinct sets of racial and cultural characteristics in the saga descriptions of the natives has been noted by most commentators. All of them, however, have chosen to resolve the paradox by insisting that the natives had to be *either* Eskimos or Indians. It seems far more reasonable to conclude that the Norse met both races, since the sagas adequately identify an Eskimoan (Dorset) and an Indian (Beothuk) culture.

This leaves us with the problem of discovering where the Norse could have encountered Beothuks. It seems certain that the Beothuks did not occupy the west coast of the Great Northern Peninsula north of Bonne Bay at the period when the Norse visited it, since the sagas make it clear that this coast was still occupied by Dorsets. The northern tip of the peninsula, in the vicinity of Straumfiord, appears (both from archeological evidence and from the negative evidence of the sage accounts) to have been free of all natives. The Indians who were then living in Labrador seem to have been Athapascan peoples belonging to what became the Montagnais and Nauscopic tribes, and who differed markedly from the Beothuks. Moreover, they seem at this period to have been restricted to the interior, while the coastal regions were still under Dorset occupation.

This leaves us with White Bay as the nearest point to Straumfiord at which Beothuks might have been met. Although this area has not been properly investigated as yet, there is archeological data to show that the Dorset occupation of the east coast of the peninsula ended well before the arrival of the Norse, due evidently to the retreat of the pelagic harp seals under the influence of the Little Climatic Optimum. At or near all the Dorset sites so far examined on this coast, artifacts have been found which belong to a late phase of Boreal Archaic culture, whose final flowering was in the Beothuks. Moreover, many of these artifacts overlie the Dorset cultural layers.

The farther south one goes in White Bay the scarcer Dorset remains become, and the more abundant are the finds of Boreal Archaic and of true Beothuk artifacts.

The Beothuks wintered in the interior of Newfoundland, living mainly on caribou and stored food during the frozen months. In the late spring or early summer they migrated to the coasts, where they lived by sealing (the resident harbor seal was the prime target), fishing and bird's-egging. One of their major wintering areas included the country around Red Indian

Lake, Deer Lake, Grand Lake and Sandy Lake. The last two of these connect by means of a short portage with the Hampden River, which drains into the foot of White Bay.

Considering the abundance of Beothuk and proto-Beothuk artifacts recovered in the vicinity of Hampden and at nearby Sops Arm, as well as at other White Bay coastal sites, it is apparent that considerable numbers of Indians used to travel to the sea at the foot of White Bay, from which point they spread northward up both coasts. There are also numerous records from colonial times detailing encounters between English fishermen and Beothuks in White Bay.*

It is almost a certainty that a Norse expedition into White Bay in summer would have encountered Beothuks. The geographical data given in the Erik the Red and the Karlsefni sagas (which is discussed in the text and in Appendix M) demonstrates that Karlsefni's ship did penetrate deeply into White Bay, and probably reached its foot. Somewhere in the bay the Norse met a strange people who were not Skraelings. This is attested to by the encounter with the One-Footer and by the subsequent reference to the country thereabouts as One-Footer Land (Einfoetingrland).

The saga seems to say that after a brief encounter the Norse immediately hurried back to Straumfiord, *being unwilling to risk their men's lives any longer.* Yet this meeting with a single stranger, whom they chased and who fled helter-skelter from them, does not seem like a sufficient reason for them to have departed in such haste and in such obvious fear of their lives. It is more reasonable to believe that the recorded meeting with the One-Footer was only the prelude to further meetings with others of his race (we remember that the expedition spent nearly two months in White Bay). Such meetings would doubtless have opened amicably (the Beothuks were an unwarlike race) with barter taking place between the two peoples. Eventually — as I envisage the probable course of events † — the Norse committed an act of outright hostility as a result of which they felt forced to flee from the prospect of reprisals; as Karlsefni fled earlier from Hop, and as Thorvald Eriksson's expedition fled from Lake Melville.

One minor problem remains to be discussed: the question of what the Norse meant by the name One-Footer. The name did not mean Unipeds, as many writers have insisted. The word may have had a special connotation in Norse usage of the period, or it may have been a figurative expression intended to express mockery or derogation of some peculiarity of

---

* W. E. Cormack, who made it his personal crusade to try and locate the last surviving Beothuks, believed that the final remnants of the race may have held out in the White Bay region. James Howley (*The Beothuks or Red Indians*, 1915) quotes a report of Beothuks having been killed at White Bay as late as 1830.

† And as the Greenlanders Story indicates.

the White Bay natives. We, for instance, do not mean it literally when we say someone is lead-footed, although perhaps some scholar of a thousand years hence may translate this, in all seriousness, as meaning a man with a foot made of lead. On the other hand the original One-Footer may have been simply that — a man who had lost a foot, or who was crippled in one leg, but who remained so remarkably agile (as he certainly was) despite his handicap that the Norse were intrigued or even admiring enough to include a reference to the fact in their name for him and his people.

In any event it is certain that the Norse were not indulging in superstitious nonsense. A fragment of verse is included in the Erik the Red and the Karlsefni sagas in which the One-Footer is specifically called a *man,* albeit a strange one. Scholars are agreed that this snatch of verse is probably a surviving fragment of the original oral saga, and its presence underlines an important fact: that the One-Footers were not only men, but were recognized by the Norse as being of a different race from the people they called Skraelings.

On the basis of the foregoing analysis I have seen fit to dissect the Greenlanders Story version and the Erik the Red and the Karlsefni version of Karlsefni's battles with the Newfoundland natives and to reconstruct them as descriptions of two separate battles with two different native peoples. In doing so I have added nothing to, nor taken anything away from, the variant versions, but have only rearranged them in what I believe to be an approximation of the form in which they existed in the original saga.

/\.\\\\\

the norse in hudson strait
and ungava bay

NEW LIGHT ON EXPLORATIONS BY THE GREENLAND NORSE INTO THE CANADIAN SUB-ARCTIC REGIONS

Over the years a considerable amount of material has been discovered, both archeological and in the written records, to indicate that the Greenland Norse explored (if they did not actually occupy as hunting grounds or for other purposes) a large area of the eastern Canadian arctic regions.

As we have shown elsewhere in this book, Greenlanders visited the southeastern coasts of Baffin Island at an early date. At a later stage in their history, when a deteriorating climate had led to the re-forming of the Baffin Bay ice pack and so closed Davis Strait and the southern portion of Baffin Bay to routine Norse navigation, the Greenlanders appear to have turned northward and to have circumnavigated the foot of Baffin Bay. The Annals of Bjorn Jonsson tell us of a ship expedition which was made to these regions in 1266, and the route is reported in sufficient detail to enable us to trace the explorers to the region of Devon or Bylot islands, and to the vicinity of the mouths of Jones and Lancaster sounds. During the past seventy years polar expeditions to this region have discovered a number of cairns and other structures, particularly in Jones Sound, which are apparently not of Eskimo origin and some of which, (specifically a series of eider-duck nesting shelters) appear to be Scandinavian. A conical stone tower which was found on Cornwallis Island,* and which bears much closer resemblances to a Norse structure than to anything known to have been built by Eskimos, suggests that the Greenland Norse may have penentrated some distance into Lancaster Sound.

To the southward there may be new archeological evidence, substantiated

---

* Details of this structure are given in the Epilogue.

by ancient documentary material, to show that the Greenlanders entered Hudson Strait and Ungava Bay. Since this evidence has not previously been presented or evaluated, I deal with it here at some length.

The first knowledge the Norse had of the existence of Hudson Strait may have been gained on Bjarni Herjolfsson's involuntary voyage of exploration up the Labrador Coast to Cape Chidley. Bjarni appears to have reached the mouth of the strait, but he probably thought it was open sea which swept west and south and so made an island out of northern Labrador, or Helluland as it came to be called.

The next Greenlanders to see the strait were the members of the Thorvald Eriksson-Thorfinn Karlsefni expedition. They crossed its mouth from south Baffin Island to the vicinity of Cape Chidley, and while there is no record of what they thought about the stretch of open water running off to the west of them, they would have suspected that it was either a strait or else an exceedingly large fiord.

The next documentary indications that the Norse continued to visit the area, and in fact came to know it rather well, are contained in a series of sagas, some of which have the character of fictionalized traditions set against an actual physical background. The first of these is the Saga of Arrow-Odd, the existing recension of which was committed to parchment in the thirteenth or fourteenth centuries, but which evidently is of considerably greater antiquity.

The story, in brief, describes the attempts of Arrow-Odd and his son Vignor to track down an enemy named Ogmund. I quote the relevant sections, with my own comments in brackets:

"I will tell you where Ogmund has gone. He has gone into that fiord which is called Skuggi. It is in Helluland's Obygdir [uninhabited regions] . . . he has gone there because he wishes to escape you. But now you may track him to his house if you wish, and see what comes of it."

Odd decided that this is what they would do. Thereupon he [and his son Vignor, in separate ships] sailed until they came into the Greenland Sea [which lay between Iceland and Greenland] when they turned south [probably at Hvarf, the turning place on the east Greenland coast] and sailed around the land [Cape Farewell] and to the West. . . . They sailed then until they came to Helluland [North Labrador, perhaps Cape Chidley] and laid their course into Skuggifiord [Hudson Strait-Ungava Bay]. . . . [After entering Skuggifiord] they saw two rocks rising out of the sea. Odd was very curious about this and they sailed between the two rocks. Toward evening they saw a large island. Odd brought his ship to its shore. Vignor asked why he did so, but Odd ordered five of his men to go ashore to look for water. Vignor said this was not necessary and did not allow any of the men from his ship to accompany the others.

Not long after Odd's men had gone ashore on the island it sank and they were all drowned. This island was covered with vegetation [some translators say heather, others say weeds, and the meaning may be synonymous with kelp or heavy sea vegetation, which is notable on the tidal islands and rocks of Ungava Bay]. They did not see it come up again. The rocks had all disappeared when they looked in that direction. . . .

When they reached the land [which they were seeking, in Skuggifiord] father and son went ashore and walked there until they saw a fortified structure, and it seemed very strongly built. . . .

The course which Odd and his son followed is the correct course from Iceland or Norway to north Labrador, or Helluland — and we are specifically told that the two men made a Helluland landfall. The events which follow, although they sound fabulous and probably appeared wonderful enough to the Norse in Odd's expedition, are not improbable.

The tidal ranges in Hudson Strait and Ungava Bay are among the greatest in the world. At the entrance to the strait, near the Button Islands, the range is of the order of 25 feet. However, inside the mouths of the strait and of Ungava Bay, the range is 40 feet, while an extreme of 52 feet has been reported from coastal points on the southwest shore of Ungava Bay. Islands of very considerable extent — some of them embracing several hundreds of acres — are periodically drowned and then exposed again by these phenomenally large tides. If Odd and his companions entered the strait during spring * tides they would have been startled and bewildered to see islands, which looked as if they should always be high and dry, rapidly disappearing beneath the fast rising waters, which in some parts of the strait flow at speeds of as much as 7 knots. While we do not need to believe that Odd's five men actually drowned on one of these disappearing islands (the saga-teller must be allowed some poetic license), it need not strain our credulity to believe that men landed to explore one of these strange, kelp-covered islands, and were forced to beat a hurried retreat to their ships when it became obvious that the whole of the island was about to disappear beneath the sea.

It should be noted that there is no other place on the east coast of North America which has such a great tidal range, with the exception of the Bay of Fundy. Furthermore, tidal ranges on the Greenland and Iceland coasts are of a very much lower order, often averaging less than three

---

* Spring tides occur directly after the new and the full moon.

feet. It is not hard to see how men who were used to such small tides would be mightily impressed by thirty- or forty-foot ones, and might in fact find it hard to believe that what they were witnessing was normal tidal action rather than some cataclysmic submergence.*

Skuggifiord is mentioned by name in one other source, the Germanic saga known as *Gunnars Saga Keldugnupsfifils*. Helluland is not mentioned, but the context of the story makes it clear that Skuggifiord had the same location in this saga as was assigned to it in Arrow-Odd's saga.

In three other sagas which are all related to one another and which also bear a relationship to the Arrow-Odd Story, Skuggifiord is not mentioned by name, but Helluland is. One of these is the Saga of Bard the Snow-fell-God, and it includes the following passages (the notes in brackets are again mine):

There was a king named Dum [literally: Fog] who ruled over those gulfs which extend north [in the northern airt] around Helluland and which are now called the Fog Seas. [king Dum was neither a person nor an entity. In typically allusive style, the saga poet is telling us that fog was king in those waters lying northward of Helluland, that is, in Hudson Strait and Ungava Bay.† Somewhat further on the saga narrator refers to another "king" who, this time, is a person.]

"I have never seen him, but I have been told by my relatives that this 'king' was called Ragnor and, from their account, I believe I recognize him. He at one time ruled over Helluland and many other countries and after he had ruled these lands a long time he caused himself to be buried alive together with five hundred men at Raknslodi. . . . It seems to me to be probable, from the reports of other people, that his burial place is in Helluland's obygdir. . . .

[A man named Gest goes in quest of this burial mound. He sails to the obygdir of Greenland — which would be south Baffin Island — where, having

---

* From the *Labrador and Hudson Bay Pilot*, 1954: "The western side of Ungava Bay is shallow for a considerable distance off shore . . ." A.P. Low describes the appearance of the northern part of this coast as "startling." The bottom was exposed for about three miles outside high water and was formed of low, rocky ridges. . . . and everywhere boulders of all sizes were strewn about . . . the tide rises (and falls) an inch a minute. . . ."

† The incidence of fog at the Cape Hopes Advance meterological station in Ungava Bay over a period of thirteen years' observations averages fifty days between June 1 and September 30. Fog conditions are even worse (in fact they are the worst in the eastern arctic) at the mouth of Hudson Strait. The average incidence of fog for June through September at Resolution Island is sixty-five days!

spent three days traversing a "lava-field" on foot he at length discovers the burial mound on an island near the sea coast.]

Some men say [adds the saga narrator] that this mound was situated to the north of Helluland. . . .

[To this we add a fragment from the Saga of Halfdan Eysteinsson.]

Ragnor brought Helluland's obygdir under his sway and destroyed all the giants there.

In these fragments we are clearly dealing with a story of great antiquity which had become somewhat mythical in its nature, but which evidently had an original basis in geographic fact at least. It is apparent that the two Ragnors of the Saga of Bard the Snow-fell-God and the saga of Halfdan Eysteinsson must be one and the same man.

At this juncture I pose the hypothesis that Ragnor was a Norseman who came out to Helluland's northern regions, perhaps as an outlaw, like Erik the Red before him, and there established himself. He did not succeed in doing so without a struggle with the natives of the area, who are significantly referred to as giants. This is the same term used in various other sources, notably the Saga of Thorgisl Orrabeinsfostri, in reference to an arctic people who were almost certainly Dorsets, rather than the smaller Thule Eskimos who themselves referred to the Dorsets as giants.

If Ragnor and his supporters settled anywhere in the Helluland region it would presumably not have been on the east coast of the north Labrador peninsula, since this area is, and we may believe always has been, a nearly "worthless land" even as it was stigmatized by the first Norse who visited it. On the other hand parts of Ungava Bay, and the west coast in particular, are still noted for their excellent sea and land hunting. Throughout the historic period a large Eskimo population has existed on the west coast of Ungava Bay and archeology has demonstrated that this area was once inhabited by a sizable population of Dorsets, whereas the northeastern Labrador coast has so far produced little evidence of Dorset occupation.

Carrying the hypothesis a step further, I suggest that the fortified building which Arrow-Odd found might be identified with Ragnor's house, or possibly even with his grave mound. The grave of Ragnor became a celebrated thing, and there seems to have been a great deal of speculation about it and several later attempts to discover it.

From the evidence of the saga sources alone it looks as if the Norse had a working knowledge of the Hudson Strait-Ungava Bay region. This assumption is supported by the independent testimony of the Stefansson

Map (see Appendix G), which clearly shows Ungava Bay in its correct relative latitude. Moreover, references in some of the ancient Icelandic geographies quoted in Appendix D show that Hudson Strait was known as ginungagap, a mighty stream which was believed to connect the Western Ocean (the North Atlantic) with Mare Oceanum.

But if Ungava Bay was the Skuggifiord of the sagas, did the Norse leave any archeological evidence of their presence there? This is a question which cannot yet be categorically answered. All that I can do is describe a recent find which may prove to be of great importance in extending our knowledge of the penetration of the Canadian Arctic by the Greenland Norse.

In July 1957 an archeological field party from the National Museum of Canada under the leadership of Dr. William Taylor was taken by an Eskimo guide to Pamiok Island in Payne Bay* on the west coast of Ungava Bay. The scientists wished to see some strange ruins which the Eskimos had reported.

The site (now named Imaha, meaning "maybe,") turned out to be a few hundred feet inland from a small harbor on the southwest part of the island. It consisted of two burial vaults, a number of collapsed Eskimoan food caches, and building ruins of two kinds. The first of these were all roughly circular tent rings of typical Eskimoan type. But the second ruin consisted of a huge rectangular stone structure measuring 85 feet long by 31 feet wide, enclosing a floor area about 75 by 18 feet, slightly depressed below ground level. An area of about 15 feet in width at each end of the enclosed space appeared to have been raised slightly above the general floor level. The walls, which were much collapsed and covered with moss, were of stones. Many massive boulders, which evidently came from the collapsed walls, had rolled into the inner floor area. The side walls were not straight in plan, but were slightly convex.

Dr. Taylor had no time to do any excavating on this extraordinary ruin. He was looking for Dorset material and in the few hours at his disposal he concentrated on one of the burial vaults. In this he found skeletal remains which he identifies as Dorset, while test excavations of some of the tent-ring houses showed them to be definitely Eskimoan and probably Dorset.

To date no archeologist has returned to this site, nor have two other sites in the vicinity which were reported to Dr. Taylor by local Eskimos been examined. One of these, consisting of "a large old rectangular house ruin with inner partitions," was said to be located on an island about six miles south-southwest of Cape Hopes Advance Station. Another,

---

* The tidal range at Payne Bay is 42 feet.

which included "two very large old rectangular house ruins," was located on a small island about three miles north of the Imaha site.*

Dr. Taylor, who had previously found Dorset caribou hunting camps in the relatively well-wooded interior on the Payne River, speculated that the big house might originally have been roofed with timber that had drifted, or been brought, down the Payne. He found that this general area provided excellent hunting of sea and land animals, and had evidently done so when the Dorsets still occupied the area, which they may have done as late as the eleventh century.

No archeologist has so far cared to speculate in public on the possible origin of the great ruin at Imaha. Nothing comparable to it is known from any aboriginal culture so far discovered in the Canadian Arctic. Both in shape, size and apparent structure (including the convex wall plan) this ruin bears a close resemblance to a singularly massive Norse longhouse of the tenth or eleventh centuries. It is not too much to say that had it been found in Greenland, Iceland or in the north of Scotland or Ireland it would have been ascribed to the early Norse — at least on the basis of what can be determined of it without excavation. It should be also noted that the structure itself is only a short distance away from a small, perfectly protected harbor which is of a depth and general nature to have made it ideal for ships of the knorr type.

No conclusions about the origin of this ruin can be made until it has been properly excavated. It is to be hoped that there will not be too great a delay in carrying this out, although up until now there seems to have been some hesitation about tackling this problem. But in the meantime, and having regard to all the evidence, it seems reasonable to conclude that the Norse were familiar with the eastern portion of Hudson Strait, and with Ungava Bay, which seems to have been known to them as Skuggifiord.

If we accept the hypothesis that they were indeed familiar with this area, the question arises as to how far west they may have penetrated into Hudson Strait. I have noted in the Epilogue that it is not farfetched to suppose that the Paul Knutsson expedition of circa 1360 passed through Hudson Strait and descended into Hudson Bay, even though this is pure speculation with no direct proof to support it. However, about a century after Knutsson there appears to have been another Scandinavian voyage into Hudson Bay. This was an expedition sent out by King Christian I

---

* Dr. Taylor's report has been published in Bulletin No. 167, National Museum of Canada, 1958.

of Denmark about 1476, under the leadership of Pining and Pothorst (both of whom were familiar with Greenland waters) and piloted by a Dane named Johannes Scolvuss.

Our information about this voyage is scanty and mostly indirect. Baron de Lahontan, Lord Lieutenant of Newfoundland and Acadia in the late seventeenth century, tells us that Labrador (by which he means northern Labrador) was discovered by the Danes and that Henry Hudson made his famous voyage into Hudson Bay as a direct result of his having seen a "memoir" of a Danish voyage into that bay.* According to Lahontan, who does not give his sources, Frederik Anschild or Anskoeld entered Hudson Strait, followed it to Hudson Bay, and wintered in the bay, where "savages" furnished him with food and skins. Lahontan seems to have thought this voyage took place about 1570–1580, but in this he is in error.

G. M. Asher, the chief authority on Henry Hudson,† is convinced that Lahontan's Anskoeld was actually Johannes Scolvuss of the 1476 Danish expedition, and this identification has been accepted by most scholars.

Adding to the weight of evidence suggesting that Hudson was forestalled is a comment by John Oldmixon in his *The British Empire in America* (London, 1708): "We know 'tis pretended [claimed, in the usage of the day] that a Dane made the discovery of this Streight [Hudson Strait] and that he called it Christiana, from the King of Denmark . . ."

Assuming that both Oldmixon and Lahontan were referring to the same Dane, and that he was Johannes Scolvuss, we are then left with the problem of determining where Scolvuss went. There is no documentary record of the voyage; but the Gemma Frisius Globe, engraved by Mercator around 1536, shows a polar continent to the westward of Greenland which bears this inscription: *Quij; the people to whom the Dane Johannes Scolvuss penetrated about the year 1476.*

So it begins to look as if Scolvuss and his companions passed through Hudson Strait, entered, explored and wintered in Hudson Bay about 1476. This was well before the disappearance of the Greenland Norse. And just as Hudson seems to have picked up news of the strait from some now lost account of the Scolvuss voyage, so we can reasonably assume that Scolvuss and Pining and Pothorst most likely heard about the great ginungagap, or sound, leading to the west, from Greenlanders who were familiar with it as Skuggifiord.

· · · · ·

---

* A Collection of Voyages and Travels Compiled from the Library of the Earl of Oxford. British Museum Collection, Cat. 456F15.
† *Henry Hudson the Navigator* (London, 1860, The Hakluyt Society).

chronology of the western voyages

A. THE EARLY PERIOD

c. 330 B.C.   Pytheas' voyages from the Mediterranean to Iceland and beyond.

c. A.D. 300   Occasional Pictish and Celtic visits to Iceland, probably to engage in summer fishing and sea-mammal hunting.

c. 450   Climatic conditions in northern waters begin to improve.

c. 500   Irish voyages to northwestern waters. Period of the St. Brendan voyages.

c. 650   Picts and Celts visiting Iceland more frequently and products of Iceland hunting expeditions finding their way to Mediterranean markets.

c. 750   Viking raids on Christian settlements in Outer Islands in full swing.

c. 770   Celtic settlements in Iceland.

c. 800   Climatic conditions much improved. Very little ice found in northern waters.

835   First papal bull referring to Christian settlements in Iceland and Greenland.

c. 860   First Viking ships appear off Iceland.

c. 870   First Scandinavian settlement in Iceland.

c. 877   Gunnbjorn Ulf Kragesson visits east coast of Greenland and discovers Gunnbjorn's Islands.

c. 880   Major Scandinavian immigration to Iceland begins.

930   Althing established in Iceland. Settlement of Iceland by Northmen completed, with little usable land remaining to be claimed.

c. 930   Herjolf Bardsson born in Iceland.

c. 940   Birth of Ari Marsson in Iceland.

c. 950   Birth of Erik Thorvaldsson (Erik the Red) in Norway, and of Bjarni Herjolfsson in Iceland.

c. 963   Erik the Red accompanies his family to Iceland, where they settle in the Hornstrandir district.

c. 970   Little Climatic Optimum established.

B. THE NORSE VOYAGES TO THE WEST

c. 970   Ari Marsson blown west from Iceland to Greenland.
              Erik the Red marries Thorhild (Thiodhild) and moves to Vatnshorn.

c. 971   Leif Eriksson born; followed by Thorstein and Thorvald Eriksson and Freydis Eriksdottir.

c. 970–977   Erik involved in a series of killings and outlawed from the Haukadale district of Iceland.

c. 975–976   Hrolf Thorbjarmarson and Snaebjorn Holsteinsson winter on the east coast of Greenland.

c. 977–978   Erik winters at Tradir. In the summer of 978 establishes a new home at Oxney.

c. 977–980   Reports of the captivity of Ari Marsson received in Iceland via Norwegian merchants in Dublin.

c. 980   Erik embroiled in a feud with Thorgest and kills Thorgest's sons.

c. 981   Erik outlawed from Iceland for a three-year term, at Thorsness Thing in the early summer. About midsummer sails for Greenland.
              First Christian missionary visits Iceland.

c. 981–982   Erik winters at Eriksey in the mouth of Eriksfiord, southwestern Greenland.

982   Erik explores the west coast of Greenland north to Cape Burnil, then crosses Davis Strait and explores the Cumberland Peninsula of Baffin Island.

982–983   Erik winters on the island of Holm near Cape Burnil.

983   Erik explores north up Greenland's west coast to the vicinity of the Steenstrups Glacier.

983–984   Erik returns south to Eriksey and again winters there.

984   Erik returns to Iceland.

985   First wave of colonists leaves Iceland for Greenland under Erik's leadership.
              In late summer Bjarni Herjolfsson sails from Iceland to join the colonists but is driven west and discovers Newfoundland and Labrador before reaching Greenland.

985–995   Early settlement period in Greenland. Eastern and Western (Ivitgut) settlements established and exploitation of the Western Obygdir in Baffin Island begun.

c. 995   Leif Eriksson determines to visit Bjarni's southernmost land, probably in order to open up a source of timber. He buys Bjarni's ship and departs in early summer, and establishes his camp in Trinity Bay, Newfoundland.

995   Olaf Tryggvason becomes King of Norway.

c. 995–996 Leif overwinters at Trinity Bay.

c. 996   Leif returns to Greenland, rescuing the trader Thorer and his men off the Greenland coast en route.

c. 996–997 Leif hears of King Olaf's exploits and determines on a visit to Norway.

c. 997   Leif sails for Norway. Visits Thorgunna in the Hebrides. In the autumn continues on to Norway. Thorbjorn Vifilsson and Thorgisl Orrabeinsfostri set out from Iceland for the Eastern Settlement. Thorbjorn arrives at Herjolfsness in the autumn. Thorgils is shipwrecked on the east coast of Baffin Island.

c. 997–998 Leif winters with King Olaf in Norway. Thorbjorn and his daughter Gudrid winter at Herjolfsness, proceeding to Eriksfiord in the spring.

c. 998   Leif returns to Greenland in late summer bringing priests and engaging in missionary activities.

c. 999   Thorstein Eriksson and Erik the Red undertake a voyage to Leif's Vinland in Thorbjorn Vifilssons's ship. Fail to reach Newfoundland and return in the autumn.

c. 1000   Thorstein marries Gudrid Thorbjornsdottir and goes to live in the new Western Settlement (Godthaab). Thorstein dies during the winter.

1000   Death of King Olaf Tryggvason in September of this year. Thorgunna and her son Thorgils Leifsson arrive in Iceland. Christianity becomes the legal religion of Iceland.

c. 1003   Thorfinn Karlsefni and Thorhall Gamlisson sail two ships from Iceland to Greenland. The Icelandic brother Helge and Finnboggi arrive in Greenland in their trading ship, having sailed thence from Norway.

c. 1003–1004 Marriage of Karlsefni to Gudrid Thorbjornsdottir. Preparations under way for a combined Greenlandic-Icelandic voyage to Vinland.

c. 1004   Four-ship expedition led by Thorfinn Karlsefni and Thorvald Eriksson sails for Vinland via Baffin Island and the Labrador Coast. Establish a wintering camp at the Strait of Belle Isle.

c. 1005   Icelandic contingent under Karlsefni sails down the west coast of Newfoundland and establishes a wintering camp at Hop in St. Paul's Bay. Meanwhile the Greenlandic contingent conducts two expeditions: a boat voyage, under Thorvald Eriksson, along the south coast of Labrador; and a second boat expedition led by Thorhall the Hunter, which was intended to explore Grosswater Bay, but which came to grief when the boat was blown offshore.

c. 1006   The Icelandic group abandons Hop and returns to Straumfiord in the spring. Part of the group, under Karlsefni, sails one ship down the east coast of the Great Northern Peninsula to the foot of White Bay, still seeking Vinland. Meanwhile Thorvald Eriksson leads a search expedition to Lake Melville looking for Thorhall the Hunter and is killed there by Skraelings. In late summer the two ships of the Icelandic contingent depart for Greenland. Karlsefni reaches Greenland and winters there but Bjarni Grimolfsson's ship is lost. The Greenlandic contingent remains for another winter at Straumfiord under the leadership of Freydis Eriksdottir.

c. 1007   The Greenlandic contingent returns to Greenland after murdering the Helge-Finnboggi crew. Thorfinn Karlsefni sails for Norway to dispose of his New World goods.

C. THE LATER PERIOD

c. 1025   The Norse trader Gudleif discovers the Icelander Bjorn Asbrandson somewhere on the coast of North America, both men having been driven there by adverse weather.

1035–1040 Frisian merchants make at least one trading voyage to Greenland.

c. 1059   An Irish or Saxon missionary priest named Jon is believed to have gone to seek Vinland and to have been murdered by the natives there.

1067   Adam of Bremen writes of the existence of Vinland.

1121   Erik, Bishop of Greenland, believed to have sailed for Vinland on a missionary expedition. Not heard of again, and replaced as Bishop of Greenland in 1124.

c. 1124   Islendingabok written.

c. 1200   Climate deteriorating at the end of the Little Climatic Optimum.

1261   Greenland accepts the suzerainty of Norwegian kings.

c. 1266   The Gardar priests from the Eastern Settlement send an expedition into northwestern Baffin Bay to reconnoiter the Skraelings.

c. 1300   A wintering party of Norse hunters carves a runestone at Kingiktorsuak, high up the west coast of Greenland.

Sea ice conditions become very bad on all the major ship routes west of Iceland.

1347   "Came ship from Greenland that had sailed to Markland, and 18 men." This ship was blown off course on her homeward voyage and landed in Iceland.

c. 1350   Ivar Bardarsson finds the Western Settlement of Greenland mysteriously deserted.

c. 1360   An expedition of the King of Norway, under Paul Knutsson, commissioned to restore Christianity to Greenland and to find out what had happened to the people of the Western Settlement.

1362   Date of the Kensington Stone, memorializing the death of a number of Northmen in the Lake Superior region.

c. 1400   Europe and the northern waters entering the Little Ice Age.

c. 1410   The Olafsson expedition makes the last recorded visit by Icelanders to the Greenland settlements. Bristol merchants fishing and trading in Iceland waters and probably trading to Greenland.

c. 1420   Basque whalers operating off the Greenland coasts and in the Labrador Sea.

c. 1476   Joint Scandinavian-Portuguese expedition to the western lands under Pining and Pothorst, accompanied by Joa Vaz Cortereal and piloted by Johannes Scolvuss.

c. 1540   Jon the Greenlander, a north European whaler, finds the corpse of the last known Greenland Norseman.

1570   Sigurd Stefansson compiles his map of Vinland, Markland, Helluland and the Northern waters.

index

ADAM OF BREMEN, 476
Aesir, 10
Africa, 327, 335, 370, 371
Aggas Island, 42
Aix-la-Chapelle Diet, 401, 403
Alaska, 372
Albania, 33, 394
Albany River, 301
Alptafiord, 48, 181, 186, 338
Althing, 19, 164, 165, 473
America, 3, 10, 243, 251, 325, 345, 356, 372, 391–392, 406, 408, 433, 467, 476; discovery, 93–104, 330, 407, 417, 428; colonization, 190; first settlement, 216, 450; first child, 224; subsequent Norse activity, 296–304; charted, 364–371. *See also* Karlsefni, Thorfinn
Anchor Point, 448
Andrea Del Bianca Map, 455
Angmagssalik, 30, 42–43, 324, 373, 377, 378, 395, 399, 425
Animals, 66, 127. *See also* individual name entries
Anschild (Anskoeld), Frederik, 472
Ansgar, 401–403
Anspach, L. A., 127
Anticosti Island, 232, 373
Arabs, 352, 392
Archeological finds, 48–52, 216, 234–235, 241–242, 299–301, 315–316, 331, 332, 337, 346, 347, 372–376, 390, 399, 450–457, 465, 470
Arctic, the, 313, 317, 318, 372–373, 376
Arctic Circle, 194
Arctic Encyclopedia, 332
Arctic Ocean, 63, 69, 313, 314, 379
Ardoise, Cape, 223n.
Ari Marsson, 34–37, 164, 285, 390–391, 394, 473–474
Ari Thorgilsson, 297n., 307, 387, 391, 397–398
Arnarstapi, 155
Arnlog, 72
Arrow-Odd, 354–355, 466–468
Asher, G. M., 472
Asia, 373
Aston, Cape, 148n.
Astrolabe, 351
Athapascan Indians, 462
Atlantic Ocean (North Atlantic; Western

Ocean), 12, 13, 76, 83, 109, 138, 203, 230, 266, 273, 325, 327, 350, 358, 362, 364, 368, 371, 377, 392, 393, 407, 455, 477; voyages, 3–4, 6–7, 144, 285, 304, 348, 349; climatic conditions, 7, 30, 43, 127, 314–315, 318, 377–378, 405; currents, 90, 405–406; drift, 172, 407. *See also* Sea levels
Aud, Queen, 82
Aud the Deep-Minded, 391
Austkarsfiord church, 338
Avalldamen, 281, 285
Avalon Peninsula, 97, 123, 127, 408, 432–433
Azores, 406

BACCALIEU BAY, 436
Baccalieu Island, 97, 120, 214, 226, 409, 433, 436, 438
Baccalieu Tickle, 214, 432, 433, 438
Baffin Bay, 63, 66, 67n., 68, 145n., 149n., 150n., 193, 298, 324, 324n., 327–329, 337, 338, 341, 369, 376, 379, 465, 477
Baffin Island, 4, 61–63, 141, 143, 147n., 148n., 325, 327, 328, 329, 332, 334–336, 340, 342, 343, 356, 369, 372, 375, 395–396, 398, 400, 412, 415, 465, 474
Baffin Pack, 329
Baie Verte Peninsula, 379
Baltic Sea, 7, 8, 139
Bard Herjolfsson, 80, 82, 83
Bard the Snow-fell-God, Saga of, 468–469
Barents Sea, 325
Basques, 211, 302, 303, 352, 455–457, 477
Bateau Barrens, 448
Battle Harbour, 208, 209, 360
Bauld, Cape, 211–212, 272, 369, 370, 408, 447
Bay de Verde Peninsula, 97, 120, 214, 226, 379, 408, 409, 430–433 *passim*, 436, 438
Bay of Islands, 448
Bear Island. *See* Bjarney (Bear Island)
Beardmore find, 301, 301n.
Bears, 31–33 *passim*, 64, 65, 129, 152, 195, 299, 326, 331, 341, 342, 418
Beaver, 127, 129

Behring Strait Eskimos, 361
Beitass, 347
Belle Isle (Straumey), 204, 207–214, 411
Belle Isle, Strait of, 208–211, 222, 232, 294, 303, 370, 373, 408, 410, 422, 447, 450, 455
Bellevue, 120
Beothuks, 3, 123, 123n., 257–258, 275–280, 381, 447, 458–464
Beothuks or Red Indians, The, by James Howley, 463n.
Bergen, 43, 87, 318, 348
Bergthorsfiord, 338
Bernard Harbour, 373
Birds, 64, 92, 113, 172, 198, 239, 358, 362–363, 376, 433
Bishop's Mitre, 199, 415
Bjarmaland (Russia), 325, 335
Bjarney (Bear Island), 65, 191, 193, 194n., 195, 199, 333, 334, 341–342, 421–424
Bjarni Grimolfsson, 181, 182, 186, 189, 217, 223, 233, 260, 270, 281–282, 286, 446, 476
Bjarni Herjolfsson, 80–81, 83–108, 111–114, 120, 135, 151n., 170, 185, 186, 193, 194, 198–201 passim, 284, 308–311 passim, 332, 362, 397–398, 405–421, 423–425 passim, 427–430 passim, 432, 473–475
Bjorn Asbrandsson, 296–297, 297n.
Bjorn Jonsson, 35, 336, 338, 339, 394, 465
Black Duck Brook, 218, 452
Blanc Sablon, 231, 232
Blaserk, 39, 42, 43, 89
Blosseville Coast, 42
Bonavista, Cape, 99, 127–128, 408, 409, 430, 432
Bonne Bay, 246, 448, 462
Boreal Archaic Indians, 232, 282n., 380, 381, 482
Borgarfiord, 72, 74, 75, 81
Brattalid, 48–52, 73, 77, 105, 107, 108, 132, 135, 159, 160, 162, 163, 166, 167, 176, 181–182, 420
Breidafiord, 29, 30, 38, 39, 67, 72, 74, 75, 87, 156, 181, 397
Bremen, 476
Brendan, St., 7, 473
Bristol ships, 302, 303, 477
British Isles and Britons (England and English), 4–8 passim, 15n., 17, 18, 35, 36, 53, 136, 211, 279, 304, 317, 358, 367, 387, 389, 392, 406, 434, 452, 455, 456, 463

Brittany, 6n.
Broad Lake, 120
Bronsted, Johannes, 301n.
Broom Point, 246, 254
Brown's Cove, 276
Bullroarers (whizzers), 244–245
Burnill, Cape, 63, 334, 340–342 passim, 474
Button Islands, 103, 467
Bygdir, 327–328
Bylot Island, 298, 465

CABOT, JOHN, 301, 303, 348, 370, 460
Cabot Strait, 327, 371, 379
Canada, 125, 126, 230, 313, 315, 317, 358, 366, 372, 383, 465–472
Canada Bay, 272
Canadian Arctic Pilot, 62
Canadian Current, 63, 64, 148n., 379, 412
Canoes, 3, 243, 275n.
Cape Cod, 392, 405, 406
Caribou, 64, 127, 129, 199, 239, 260, 263, 263n., 266, 381, 382, 460, 462
Cartier, Jacques, 126, 210–211, 348, 455–456
Caspian Sea, 10
Castor River, 448
Celts, 4–13, 16, 18, 33, 51–55, 59, 285, 286, 297, 387–390, 396, 398, 403, 404, 473
Champlain, Samuel de, 211n.
Chapel Arm, 435
Charles, Cape, 208
Chidley, Cape, 210, 284, 367–369 passim, 416, 466
Chidley region, 198
Chipeweyan Indians, 358
Chorography. See Graenlandiae Vetus Chorographia
Christian I, King of Denmark, 471
Christianity, 7, 11, 14, 35, 72, 74, 134, 136, 140, 144–146 passim, 152, 161–166, 170, 170n., 173, 183–184, 223, 298, 299, 332, 377, 379, 388, 390, 396, 403–404, 420, 426–427, 429, 441, 473–477 passim
Climate, 5, 33, 43, 44, 90, 313–318, 377–378, 405, 473, 476–477. See also Atlantic Ocean; Greenland; Iceland; Little Climatic Optimum; Newfoundland
Coal Cape, 65, 342
Cod Island, 199, 208
Col, 144, 146–147, 149–150, 152–153
Collier Bay, 435

Columbus, Christopher, 301, 303, 348
Commerce (trade), 6, 8, 53–54, 66, 83–
    87, 106, 127, 135, 137n., 181, 184–
    187, 225, 230, 251, 278, 349, 461, 473
Conception Bay, 97, 298, 317, 320, 409,
    410, 432–433
Copenhagen, 309, 335
Coracles, 6n.
Corbett, Mt., 277
Cormack, W. E., 463n.
Cornwall, 4
Cornwallis Island, 299, 465
Cortereal, Gaspar, 277, 348, 460, 460n.
Cortereal, Joa Vaz, 348, 460n., 477
Cow Head Harbour, 236
Cretans, 351
Cronian Sea, 6, 403
Cronus, 6, 398
Cronusland (Cronland), 55, 396, 401–
    403
Cumberland Peninsula, 64–67, 143,
    194n., 328, 332, 334, 337, 342, 343,
    369, 400, 415, 474
Cumberland Sound, 64, 65, 68, 195
Curraghs, 6–7, 6n., 17
Currents, ocean, 3–4, 35, 63, 70, 148n.,
    169, 171, 172, 379, 381, 405–406.
    See also names of currents
Cut Throat Tickle, 201

DAGMALASTAD, 118, 125
Dalla-Koll, 82
Dalriada, 6n.
Dark Ages, 351
Dartmouth College, 372
Davis Strait, 65, 66, 67n., 143, 145n.,
    150n., 194, 195, 298, 329, 330, 332,
    334, 337, 338, 343, 376, 379, 382, 396,
    400, 410, 465, 474
Decker, George, 452
Deer. *See* Caribou
Deer Lake, 463
Degerbol, Dr., 316
De Mensura Orbis Terrae, 389, 403
Demetrius, 5, 398
Denbigh, Cape, 372
Denmark and the Danes, 10, 136, 139,
    184, 346, 364, 378–379, 401, 402, 418,
    451, 452, 472
Denmark Strait, 17, 31, 42, 43, 90
De Root, P., 402, 404
Desi, the, 4
Desolation, Cape, 59, 71, 152, 334, 337,
    338
Devon Island, 298, 299, 465

Dicuil, 389, 403
Dildo Arm, 435
Disco Bay, 61, 70, 395, 399, 410
Disco Island, 194n., 333–334, 340, 342,
    373
*Discourse and Discoverie of the Newe-
    foundeland, A,* by Richard Whit-
    bourne, 456n.
Disease, 176–177, 302
Domino, 410, 411, 422
Dorset, Cape, 372
Dorsets (Skraelings), 66, 68, 123, 123n.,
    148n., 232, 234–235, 242–246, 248–
    264, 266–269, 271n., 273, 278, 281–
    282, 282n., 283–286, 321, 326n., 372–
    383, 395–396, 399–400, 399n., 441,
    446–447, 453–454, 458, 460–462, 464,
    469–471, 476, 477
Drangar (Highrocks), 25–28 *passim*
Drangey, 337
Drontheim, 133, 141
Dublin, 36, 139, 141, 296, 474
Ducks, 129, 204, 209–210, 210n., 220,
    343
Duel-Fighting Hrafn, 25, 28
Dutch, 302, 455
Dyer, Cape, 62–65 *passim,* 194–195,
    334, 337, 340, 342
Dyrafiord, 338
Dyrness, 338

EARL ISLAND, 206
Earl Thorfinn, 34, 36, 391
East Fiords, 181, 186, 188
East Greenland Current, 30, 44, 90, 379
Eastern Settlement (Ostri Bygd), 47,
    109, 134–135, 137n., 143, 151, 152n.,
    184, 186, 187, 193, 194, 284, 298, 302,
    328, 330–333, 338, 339, 340, 406–
    408 *passim,* 423, 425, 430, 475, 476
Eastern Wilderness (Ostri Obygd), 328,
    335
Eastmen, 10
Eddies Cove, 448
Egyptians, 351
Eider Duck Cape, 65, 342
Einar Thorgeirsfell, 155–156
Einarsfiord, 72
Ellesmere Island, 325, 328, 373
England. *See* British Isles and Britons
    (England and English)
Englee, 321
English Channel, 6
English River, 268

Epaves Bay, 216, 216*n*., 218–222, 218*n*., 222*n*., 225, 276, 282*n*., 283, 291*n*., 450–457
Erik, Bishop of Greenland, 298, 476
Erik Hakonarsson, 418–419
Erik the Red (Eric Thorvaldsson), 132–133, 192, 193, 281, 289, 289*n*., 294, 418–420 *passim*, 441, 469; saga tale, 25–26, 30, 39, 47, 58, 67, 72–73, 161, 168, 181–183, 308, 311; birth, family, childhood, 26–28, 473; appearance and character, 26, 38; marriage and children, 28, 73, 161, 474; Icelandic career and exile, 28–30, 154–155, 162, 474; voyages to Greenland, 30, 31, 33, 35, 37–55, 58–71, 87–89 *passim*, 324, 330, 334, 337, 341, 343, 378, 397, 398–399, 425, 474; Greenland settlement, 50, 56–57, 58, 61, 68, 71–80, 84, 106–111, 130, 137*n*., 139, 142–144 *passim*, 154, 156, 159–160, 163, 167, 170, 181–185, 187, 341, 391, 394, 394*n*.; conflict with Leif Eriksson, 135–136, 138, 142, 165–167, 170–171, 184, 443–444; relationship with Thorgisl Orrabeinsfostri, 152–153, 155; religion, 162, 165, 184; attempted voyage to Vinland, 162, 167–173, 192, 270, 419–420, 425, 475
Erik the Red Saga, 124, 137*n*., 140, 154, 173, 184, 188*n*., 192, 194*n*., 199, 203, 250, 284*n*., 291, 308–310, 328, 333, 334, 342, 368, 395, 420, 421, 423, 426–429 *passim*, 439–447 *passim*, 458–459, 463–464
Eriksey, 47, 55–57, 67, 68, 71, 330, 474
Eriksfiord, 47, 48, 51, 52, 55, 58, 59, 67, 72, 73, 77, 107, 135, 152, 168, 172, 173, 181, 184, 187, 194, 194*n*., 286, 293, 333, 334, 337, 338, 397, 474, 475
Eriksfirth, 67, 67*n*., 289
Eriksholm. *See* Holm
Erris Head, 392
Eskimo-Aleut language, 285, 373
Eskimo Island, 265
Eskimos, 3–4, 52, 56, 66, 68*n*., 102, 123, 148*n*., 195, 244–245, 245–246*n*., 266, 361, 373, 375–376, 378, 383, 395–396, 415, 459–461 *passim*, 470. *See also* Beothuks; Dorsets (Skraelings); Thule Eskimos
Eurasia, 5*n*.
Europe, 3–4, 6, 10, 13, 15, 35, 37, 66, 84, 87, 109, 169, 172, 176, 230, 301, 336, 344, 352, 366, 406, 434, 440, 477

Eyrbyggja Saga, 139
Eyjolf of Sviney, 26, 29, 39
Eyjolf the Foul, 25, 28
Eykarstad, 118, 125
Eyrar, 83, 84, 86, 87, 89
Eyvind, 83
Eyvind Cheekrift, 139
Eyvind Eld, 82

FABIAN (chronicler), 460
Faeroe Islands, 4, 7, 8*n*., 10–12, 14, 16, 87, 352, 356, 401. *See also* Outer Islands
Fair Haven, 120
Famish Gut, 120
Farewell, Cape (Hafhverf), 17, 35, 44, 47, 76, 84, 89, 91, 152*n*., 284, 286, 297, 324, 326, 328, 330, 337, 366–369, 378, 392, 393, 423, 466
Farming, 11, 12, 17, 27–28, 44, 56, 60*n*., 78, 109, 124, 187, 208, 239, 302
Faxafiord, 145
Ferolle Peninsula, 263, 448
Finland (Scritfinnland), 401, 402
Finnbogi, 183, 188–189, 190*n*., 226, 234, 247, 284, 287–294, 439, 444, 474, 475
Finnmarken, 325, 335
Fish; fishing, 3, 5, 7, 8, 11, 12, 17, 27, 41, 78, 109, 117–118, 126, 127, 128, 129, 141, 157, 208, 210, 211, 218, 219–220, 224, 239, 358, 376–378 *passim*, 455–457, 462, 473
Flade Isblink Glacier, 326
Flat Island, 263
Flateyjarbok, 139, 309
Floamanna Saga, 135, 144, 328, 331, 375
Floki Vilgerdarsson (Raven-Floki), 13–14, 81–82, 362–363
Florida, 126
Fog, 90–91, 96, 113, 468, 468*n*.
Fogo Island, 99–100, 408–410 *passim*, 412, 430, 432, 435
Folgar, Capt., 348
Forel, Mt., 43
Forests. *See* Timber
Foxe Basin, 372, 373, 377
Foxes, 32, 64, 129, 191, 198, 421
France and the French, 7, 17, 94, 127, 211, 240–242 *passim*, 279, 300, 449, 452, 455, 456
Franklin, Sir John, 299
Franz Joseph Land, 325
Freels, Cape, 99, 408, 409, 430, 432
French in Newfoundland, The, by H. Horwood, 456

Freydis Eriksdottir, 73, 182, 183, 188–189, 188*n.*, 189*n.*, 190*n.*, 226, 247, 249, 257–258, 260, 270, 272, 272*n.*, 283–284, 284*n.*, 287–294, 311, 439, 440, 442, 444, 446, 459, 461, 474, 476
Frisian merchants, 476
Frobisher, Sir Martin, 395–396
Froda; Froda-Wonders, 133, 139–140, 234
Fundy, Bay of, 210, 457
Funk Islands, 360
Furdustrandir (Marvelous Shores), 191, 203, 227, 228, 329, 422
Furs, 234, 248, 251, 253, 271

GARD, 174, 175
Gardar, 14, 30, 73, 183, 289, 338, 477
Geelmuyden, H., 472
Geography, Norse, 322–343
George Island, 201
Germanic regions, 8, 10
Gibraltar, 4
Ginungapap, 335
Glaciers, 148*n.*, 319–320, 326
Glooscap, 297
Glumboland, 295
Godthaab District (Vestri Obygd), 60, 60*n.*, 66, 152*n.*, 173, 184, 187, 300, 326, 328, 330–333, 337–340 *passim*
Godthaab Fiord, 109*n.*, 173, 326
Godthaab Gulf, 326
Gokstad ship, 347–348
Gordon, Patrick, 127
Grady Head, 207
Grady Island, 412
Gragas, 125
Grand Banks, 91–92, 169, 303, 358, 406
Grand Lake, 276, 463
Grand Rigolet region, 231
Grande Bay, 456, 456*n.*
Grapevines, 118, 125–128, 130, 220, 222*n.*, 224, 233, 234, 240
Grates Point, 430, 435
Gray Strait, 103, 416
Great Harbour Deep, 273
Great Northern Peninsula, 123, 211, 212, 219, 232, 264, 272, 276, 298, 320–321, 364, 369, 373, 379–381 *passim*, 407, 447, 450, 462, 476
Great Sacred Island, 214
Greater Helluland, 329
Greater Ireland (Albania; Hvitramannaland; Irland Mikkla), 33–37, 53–56, 59, 68, 281, 390–395, 396
Greeks, 4, 5, 351
Greenland, 4, 17, 118, 128–130 *passim*, 132–133, 138, 145, 145*n.*, 147*n.*, 148, 169, 171, 192, 210, 243, 297*n.*, 349, 354, 357, 423–430 *passim*, 453, 471, 476; early exploration and occupation, 5–6, 7, 30–38, 41, 48–57, 324, 345, 390–404, 474; resources, products and animal life, 30–31, 64–65, 68, 70, 74, 78, 110, 461; climate, 30–31, 60, 63, 66, 67, 78, 301, 313–318, 378, 395; voyages of Erik the Red, 39–49, 55, 58–71, 87–89 *passim*, 425, 474; topography, 43–45, 49, 57, 60, 60*n.*, 61, 63–64, 70, 103, 328, 356, 433; Norse settlement, 49–57, 58, 61, 66, 67*n.*, 68, 71–81, 84–85, 87, 106–111, 130, 134–137, 137*n.*, 139–144 *passim*, 151, 154, 156, 158, 163–167, 170, 173–177, 181–185, 187, 193, 286, 302–304, 375, 391, 394, 396, 398, 400, 404, 475, 477; living conditions, 53–54, 158; naming, 72, 397–398; religion, 73, 161–166, 173, 183–184, 390, 403–404, 420, 426–427, 429, 441, 476–477; voyage of Bjarni Herjolfsson, 79–81, 83–104, 193, 405–417, 425; natives, 148*n.*, 263, 334, 372–383, 395, 397, 399–400; trade, 184–185, 225; subsequent voyages, 296–304, 428, 465, 472; in sagas, 310–311; Norse geographical and topographical concept, 322–343; early maps, 365–369; tidal ranges, 467–468; Norwegian rule, 476. *See also* Karlsefni, Thorfinn
Greenland Current, 35
Greenland Ice Cap, 316
Greenlander-Icelander feud. *See* Karlsefni, Thorfinn
Greenlanders Story, 105–106*n.*, 120, 124, 125, 134, 137*n.*, 174, 188–190, 188*n.*, 203, 214, 284*n.*, 287*n.*, 289*n.*, 310, 354, 367, 415, 418–427 *passim*, 430, 435, 439–447 *passim*, 442*n.*, 457, 458–459 464
Greenlandiae Vetus Chorographia, 195, 336, 339, 340, 342–343
Gregory IV, Pope, 401–403 *passim*
Grey Island, 379
Gripla Geography, 326, 335
Griquet Harbour, 457
Gronland. *See* Cronusland
Grosswater Bay, 101, 201–202, 205, 209, 225–226, 228, 265, 369, 412, 476
Gudleif, 34, 164
Gudleif Gudlaugsson, 296–297
Gudrid Thorbjornsdottir, 132, 137*n.*, 154, 158–160, 163, 166, 173–177, 182,

Gudrid Thorbjornsdottir (*Cont.*)
184, 188, 216, 224, 271, 279, 284, 295, 328, 459, 475
Gudrun, 144, 146, 147
Gulf Stream, 124, 171, 172, 406
Gunnars Saga Keldugnupsfifils, 468
Gunnbjorn Ulf Kragesson, 30, 473
Gunnbjorn's Land, 30, 32, 33, 37, 39, 40, 42, 43
Gunnbjorn's Skerries (Islands), 30–32 *passim,* 42, 473
Gustav Holm, 42
Guy, John, 317, 460

HAAKON OF LADE, 136
Hafgerdingar, 75–76, 88
Hafgrim, 72
Hafhverf. *See* Cape Farewell
Hafrsfiord, Battle of, 16
Hafverf, 337, 340
Haggerty, Mt., 277
Haki (Scot), 204, 207
Halfdan Eysteinsson, 469
Halfgrimsfiord, 338
Halgoland, 32, 133, 138–139
Hall, C. F., 395–396
Hall Peninsula, 412
Halldis, 155, 157, 158
Hamburg, 402
Hamilton Inlet, 265, 431, 434
Hampden, 275
Hampden Bay, 273, 276, 290, 293
Hampden River, 273–277, 275n., 434, 463
Hanoverian church documents, 398, 401
Hants Head, 435
Happy Warriors, The, by Halldor Laxness, 18n.
Hare Bay, 220, 320
Hares, Arctic, 64
Harold Fairhair, King, 14, 16, 18, 136
Harp, Dr. Elmer, 235, 372, 373, 380
Harrison, Cape, 201
Hatteras, Cape, 124
Hauk Erlandsson, 309
Haukadale, 25, 28, 29, 474
Hauksbok, 309
Hawke Harbour, 101, 410, 411, 448
Hayes Expedition, 314
Hearts Content, 435
Hearts Delight, 435
Hearts Desire, 435
Hebrides, 11, 14, 15n., 16, 54, 76, 133, 139–141 *passim,* 230, 390, 426, 475
Heimskringla recension, 427
Hekia (Scot), 204, 207

Helge, 183, 188–189, 190n., 226, 234, 247, 284, 287–294, 439, 444, 475, 476
Helge Easterling, 153
Helge Thorbrandsson, 72, 186
Hellisey, 337
Helliseyarfiord, 337
Helluland, 194n., 198, 208, 303, 327, 332–336 *passim,* 355, 364, 369, 371, 415, 420–421, 423–424, 466–469, 477
Helsingoland, 401
Henrietta Island, 265
Henry Hudson the Navigator, by G. M. Asher, 472n.
Herjolf Bardsson, 72, 73, 75–76, 79–80, 82–85, 87, 89, 94, 103, 106–108, 151, 151–152n., 170, 473
Herjolf Eyvindsson, 80–83
Herjolfsfiord, 47, 72, 84–85, 337, 338
Herjolfsness, 72, 84–85, 94, 103, 112, 113, 134, 152n., 157, 170, 302, 315, 336–337, 416, 419, 425, 430, 475
Highrocks (Drangar), 25–28 *passim*
Hipparchus, 351
Historia Norwegiae, 334
Historia Vinlandiae, 355
History of the Island of Newfoundland, by L. A. Anspach, 127
Hjorleif Vilgerdarsson, 13, 15–16, 18, 81–82, 388
Hofn, 393
Holden Peninsula, 101
Holm, 67, 69, 71, 340, 341
Holmar. *See* Holm
Holmlatr, 72–74 *passim*
Holsteinborg, 69, 151
Holton Peninsula, 201, 209, 412
Home Bay, 148, 150
Hop camps, 233, 238–260, 262–264, 264n., 266, 271n., 272, 275–280, 282–283, 441, 445, 446–449, 458–460 *passim,* 476
Hopedale Bight, 200
Hopes Advance Station, Cape, 470
Hops, 433–436
Horn, 41
Hornafiord, 338
Hornstrandir district, 474
Horse Chops, 432
Horse Islands, 379, 431, 434
Horwood, H., 456
Howley, James, 463n.
Hrafn, 41, 61, 72, 337, 341
Hrafnsfiord, 48, 72, 134, 338
Hrafnsfirth, 61, 67, 70, 337, 341
Hrafnsgnipa, 60–63, 67–69, 193, 194, 340–341

Hrakbjarney, 338
Hraunhofn, 156
Hrolf Thorbjarmarson, 474
Hrut, 83
Hudson, Henry, 314, 472
Hudson Bay, 372
Hudson Strait, 194, 194n., 299, 301, 327, 335n., 372, 377, 466–472
Huntingdon Island, 206, 207
Husanotra, 354–355
Hvalsey, 52
Hvalseyarfiord, 338
Hvalseyfiorders, 73
Hvarf, 152, 332, 466
Hvarfsgnipa, 337, 340, 342
Hvitramannaland (White Man's Land). *See* Greater Ireland
Hvitserk (Whiteshirt), 44, 335

ICE, 149n., 151n., 225, 319, 477; drift, 43, 302, 313, 314, 318, 329; pack, 66, 222–223, 314, 316, 378–379, 465
Icebergs, 70, 151n.
Iceland (Thule), 4, 33–37 *passim*, 50, 51, 54–55 *passim*, 62n., 67, 79, 99, 111, 118, 133, 138–141 *passim*, 144, 153, 170, 175, 183, 243, 284, 286, 296–299 *passim*, 304, 325–327 *passim*, 345, 349, 371, 393, 405, 453, 455, 471, 477; exploration and settlement, 4–7, 13, 15–18, 27, 80, 82, 343, 362–363, 387–391, 397, 398, 401–404, 473; climate, 5, 7, 12, 89, 148n., 304, 313, 389, 403; resources and products, 6, 7, 27; Viking activity, 13–17, 81–82, 135, 343, 362–363, 390, 473; population, 18; society, 19–21; Eric the Red's activities, 25–26, 72–75, 154–155, 162, 425, 474; topography, 26, 76, 356, 433; sea routes, 36, 76, 87, 89, 90, 94, 140–141, 172, 303–304, 337, 440, 477; religion, 72, 74, 140, 163–165, 184, 186, 387, 402, 473–475 *passim;* trade, 84, 87, 107, 181, 184–185, 225, 304, 473, 477; emigration, 87–88, 109, 143, 186–190, 225–226, 397, 474; literature and documents, 296, 307, 312, 326, 329, 340, 366, 394, 470; in sagas, 310–311; Norse geographical concept, 325, 326, 331, 335–337 *passim;* early maps, 366–368; naming, 403; tidal ranges, 467–468. *See also* Karlsefni, Thorfinn
Idrisi, 392–393
Ile d'Orleans, 126
Imaha, 470–471

Indian Harbour, 412, 414
Indian Islands, 101, 201
Indian Ocean, 361
Indians, 3, 4, 258, 282, 297, 300, 373, 380, 381, 461, 462
Ingolf the Settler, 72, 73, 388
Ingolf Vilgerdarsson (The Land-Taker), 13–16, 18, 80–82
Ingstad, Helge, 216, 450–455
Ingstad expedition, 282n., 450–455
Iostan, 144–146
Ireland and the Irish, 4, 6n., 7, 8, 10–13, 15n., 16–18 *passim*, 33, 34, 36, 51, 53–55 *passim*, 59, 82, 140, 172, 228, 230, 296, 358, 388, 390, 392–394 *passim*, 398, 471, 473, 476
Irish Sea, 6, 6n.
Irland Mikkla. *See* Greater Ireland
Irminger Current, 63, 90, 379
Isafiord, 338
Isla de Stokafixa, 455
Islendingabok, 53n., 297n., 307, 308, 362, 387, 391, 397, 398–400 *passim*, 476
Ivar Bardarsson, 477
Iverson, Dr. J., 316
Ivitgut Bight (Mid Bygd; Vestri Bygd), 59, 109, 109n., 152n., 153, 328, 332, 333, 338, 393, 475
Ivory, 65–66, 74, 184–185

JAEDIR DISTRICT, Norway, 25, 26
James Bay, 301
Jan Mayen Island, 7, 367
Jenness, Dr. D., 372
Jessen, Knud, 316
Jon, 297–298, 476
Jon Hakonarsson, 309
Jon the Greenlander, 477
Jones, Gwyn, 268n.
Jones Sound, 299, 325, 328, 465
Journal of James Yonge, Plymouth Surgeon, 127
Julianehaab Bight, 17, 35, 44, 48, 55, 59, 60, 71, 109, 152n., 331, 332, 337, 338, 393

KAILA, 285
Kangamuit Island, 61–62, 69
Kap Dan, 43–44
Karate Fiord, 70
Karli, 14
Karlsbuda, 65, 195, 341–342
Karlsefni, Thorfinn, 297, 309; saga tale, 137n., 181–183, 191, 204, 217, 227, 233–234, 248–250, 260, 270, 281–282,

Karlsefni, Thorfinn (*Cont.*)
294–295, 310; marriage to Gudrid, 137*n.*, 182, 295, 475; background, 181, 185; character, 185; emigration to Greenland, 181–182, 185–187, 475; organizes expedition to Vinland, 182–194, 298, 399; voyages, 194–209, 264–275, 283, 333–334, 342, 354, 420–424 *passim*, 434, 447–449, 458–464, 466, 477; Straumfiord camp, 205, 210–234, 234*n.*, 247, 260, 262–265, 280, 283–284, 291, 444–448 *passim*, 450–457, 462, 463, 476; birth of son, 224, 245; Icelander-Greenlander feud, 226, 283–284, 287–294, 424, 428, 442–447, 476; Hop camps, 233, 238–260, 262–264, 275–280, 282, 445–449, 458–460 *passim*, 463, 476; return to Greenland, 284–286, 395, 476; return to Iceland, 284, 294–295, 442; voyage to Norway, 289, 293–294, 442; later years and death, 295; maps, 364, 367, 371
Karlsefni Saga, 137*n.*, 140, 154, 162, 173, 184, 188*n.*, 192, 194*n.*, 199, 203, 250, 284*n.*, 291, 308–310, 328, 333, 342, 368, 369, 420, 421, 423, 426–429 *passim*, 435, 439–447 *passim*, 458–459, 463–464
Karv, 348
Kaumajet Peninsula, 102, 199, 284, 369, 413–416
Kayaks, 243–244, 383
Keewatin, 244, 255
Kellufiord, 338
Kensington, Minn., 300–301
Kensington Stone, 300–301, 301*n.*, 477
Ketil, 72
Ketil the Foolish, 388
Ketilsfiord, 48, 72, 134, 338
Kialarness (Keel Point), 191, 203, 204, 227, 228, 260, 265, 422, 445
Kiarval, King, 181, 185
Kidlapait Range, 102
Kiglapait Peninsula, 199*n.*, 200, 413
Kiliks, 346
Kingiktorsuak, 477
King's Mirror, 75–76
Knorrir. *See* Norsemen, ships
Knutsson, Paul, 299–301, 471, 477
Kristni-Saga, 427
Kronprins Christian Land, 326
Kronprins Fredericks Glacier, 42–43, 326

LABRADOR (HELLULAND), 285, 304, 332, 334, 360, 451, 457; resources and products, 81, 207, 284; discovery, 101; Bjarni Herjolfsson's voyage, 101–103, 405–408, 410–413, 415, 423, 466, 473–475 *passim;* topography, 101–103, 199–200, 356, 422; natives, 123, 148*n.*, 232, 375, 396, 452*n.*, 462, 469; coastline, 196, 198–209, 226, 231, 361–362; Karlsefni expedition, 198–212, 395, 476–477; animal life, 198; climate, 206, 222, 224, 316–317; later Norse activity, 296, 298, 299, 303, 466–469, 472; early maps, 366–371; improbability of Leif Eriksson's visit, 422–423
Labrador Current, 102, 124, 169, 201, 210, 222, 379, 381, 406, 410–412 *passim*, 414
Labrador Pilot, 207
Labrador Sea, 44, 91, 103, 168, 171, 192, 193, 194*n.*, 284, 303, 334, 376, 379, 396, 398, 423, 455, 477
Lahontan, Baron de, 472
Lamb, H. H., 314
Lancaster Sound, 325, 465
Lancy Meadows, 450
Landnamabok, 20, 20*n.*, 30–32 *passim*, 34–36 *passim*, 73, 75, 76, 81, 82, 137*n.*, 167*n.*, 307, 387–388, 390–391, 393–394
L'Anse Amour, 211, 212
L'Anse au Meadows (L'Anse au Méduse), 219, 450
Laugarbrekka, 154–155
La Verendrye, Pierre de, 300
Laxness, Halldor, 18*n.*
Leather (hides), 184–185
Leif Eriksson, 73, 80, 163, 188, 291, 330, 416; birth, 25, 474; saga tale, 105, 117–118, 132–134, 161–162, 204, 309–311; Vinland expedition, 105, 105*n.*–106*n.*, 111–135, 169–170, 186, 188, 192, 211, 219, 290, 298, 418–440, 443–444, 447, 457, 475; early life, 107–109; character and appearance, 118, 130, 131, 135; Norway voyage, 132–134, 137–142, 162*n.*, 426–429, 475; converts to and spreads Christianity, 134, 141, 161–166, 184, 204; conflict with Erik the Red, 135–136, 138, 142, 165–167, 170–171, 184, 443–444; mistress, 133, 138–141; return from Norway, 163–167; later Vinland activity, 166, 183, 192–193, 443–444
Leiravage, 144
Leopold Island, 65, 195–196, 334, 342–343
Les Pêcheries de Terreneuve, 456

Lewis, A. R., 6n.
Limerick, 34, 36, 37
Little Climatic Optimum, 44, 125, 127, 148n., 314–315, 317, 381–382, 405, 462, 474, 476
Little Harbour Deep, 379
Little Ice Age, 477
Liveyers, 206
Long Point, 268, 435
Long Range Mts., 235–236, 239, 272, 276, 382, 407–408, 446, 448, 449
Longships. *See* Vikings, ships
Louis the Pious, King, 389, 401–403
Low, A. P., 468
Lundey Island, 48, 338
Lysufiord, 173–174, 176–177, 328, 339, 340, 342

Magdalen Islands, 126
Malin Head, 54, 393
Mallery, A. H., 451
Maps. *See* Stefansson, Sigurd
Mare Oceanum, 325, 327
Markland (Forest Land), 53, 191, 194n., 198, 200–202, 209, 211, 281, 284, 299, 303, 327, 335, 336, 355, 364, 369, 371, 394, 420–421, 477
Marseilles, 4
Marten (sable), 129, 461–462
Mary March (Demasduit), 459–460
Massachusetts, 125
Massilia, 4
Mecatina region, 231
Mediterranean Sea, 4, 6, 10, 127, 473
Meldgaard, Jorgen, 268n., 451–452
Melrackness, 337
Melville Bay, 324, 327, 341, 378
Melville Island, 373
Melville, Lake (Hamilton Inlet), 228, 265–268, 444–447 *passim*, 463, 476
Mercator, 472
Mercy, Cape, 64, 65, 334, 337, 342
Mic Mac Indians, 297
Mid Bygd, 328, 332, 338, 340
Midfiords, 338
Midjokul, 39, 42, 44, 326
Miller's Island, 273
Minnesota, 300
Montagnais Indians, 232, 396, 452n., 462
Montreal, 300
Moose, 222n.
Moravians, 199, 199n.
Mugford, Cape, 413
Mugford Tickle, 199
Munn, W. A., 450–451
Muskoxen, 64

Naddod the Viking, 13–14
Nain Bight, 102, 200, 201, 369, 412–414 *passim*
Nantes, 7
Narssaq, 60
Narssaq (Eastern Settlement), 51–52
Narwhals, 32, 64, 65, 185
National Museum of Canada, 372, 470, 471n.
Nauscopie Indians, 396, 462
Navigation, 7, 36, 41n., 41–42, 54, 62–63, 86n., 88–89, 95, 102, 103n., 112–113, 168–169, 171–172, 192–203 *passim*, 318, 351–363, 366–368, 393n., 425
Neolithic Age, 3, 10, 244, 372, 373
New Brunswick, 125–126, 317, 320
New England, 84, 125, 126, 202, 364, 377, 391, 405–406, 451
New Harbour, 218, 219
New Perlican, 436
Newfoundland, 3, 6, 83, 84, 91, 210, 286, 304, 346, 348, 358, 360–363 *passim*, 392, 418–428; resources and products, 53–54, 81, 122, 126–131, 275, 424; discovery, 92–100; animal and plant life, 92, 97, 126–127, 222, 222n., 239–240, 263, 380, 433; Bjarni Herjolfsson voyage, 93–103, 405–421, 423–425 *passim*, 427–430 *passim*, 432, 474; topography, 94, 122, 239–241, 241n., 422, 436; Leif Eriksson voyage, 112–123, 418–438, 475; climate, 120, 124, 127, 240, 316–318; natives, 123, 148n., 233–235, 242–246, 248–263, 270, 276–280, 281–282, 284–286, 298, 299, 373–383, 458–464; latitude, 125; later expeditions, 126–127, 162, 166–173, 425, 430, 439–441, 475; Vinland controversy, 120–128, 319, 327, 364, 418–438; whaling and other industry, 129–130, 381, 455–457; trade, 251; Karlsefni expedition, 181–286, 420–424, 439–464, 475–476; post-Karlsefni activity, 296–299, 303, 430; sea levels, 320–321; Norse geographical concept, 327; early maps, 365–371, 455
Newfoundland Provincial Museum, 460n.
Nicholas I, Pope, 402
Nicholas V, Pope, 403
Nidaros, 133
Nipigon, Lake, 301
Njal's Saga, 20n., 83
Nord Obygd, 328, 329, 330, 334
Norlund, Dr. Paul, 315–316

Norman, Cape, 211, 212, 220, 226, 231, 448

Norse Atlantic Saga, The, by Gwyn Jones, 268*n.*

Norsemen, 129, 286, 319, 320, 394, 424; ships, 8-10, 12, 13, 40, 40*n.*, 43, 74-75, 90-91, 110, 219-220, 286, 344-350, 356-357, 434-435; maritime activity, 8-10, 144, 392; emigration, 10-12; Viking raids, 10-15, 37-38; early Icelandic activity, 13-15, 387-390; Icelandic settlement, 13, 15-21, 390, 473; characteristics and appearance, 18-21, 166, 251, 278, 286, 291; Greenland exploration, 30-38, 42, 395; Greenland settlement, 50, 56-58, 61, 66, 67*n.*, 68, 71-81, 84-85, 87, 106-111, 130, 134-137, 137*n.*, 139-144 *passim,* 151, 154, 156-158, 161-166, 302, 400, 404, 477; sea routes, 87, 303-304; North American discovery and settlement, 93-104, 216, 330, 407, 417, 428, 450; fishing and whaling, 128, 239; superstitions, 167, 243; religion, 170*n.*, 396; weapons, 255; later western activity, 296-302, 465-472, 477; New World value and errors, 303; geographical concepts, 322-343; native contacts, 375, 382-383; burial customs, 441-442. *See also* Bjarni Herjolfsson; Commerce (trade); Erik the Red; Karlsefni, Thorfinn; Leif Eriksson; Navigation; Newfoundland

North Atlantic. *See* Atlantic Ocean

North Dakota, 300

North Sea, 6

North Star. *See* Pole Star

Northern Seas, The, by A. R. Lewis, 6*n.*

Norway and Norwegians, 6, 7, 10-12 *passim,* 14, 16, 18, 25, 32, 33, 33*n.*, 42, 51, 54, 81-83 *passim,* 87, 94, 99, 106*n.*, 107, 109-111 *passim,* 225, 289, 293, 302, 318, 325, 335, 337, 343, 345-348 *passim,* 350, 354, 356-357, 392, 397, 401-403 *passim,* 418, 419, 442, 467, 476-477; Leif Eriksson's voyage, 133-134, 137-142, 162*n.*, 163, 166, 426-429, 475; under Olaf Tryggvason, 136-139, 184

Norwegian Sea, 335

Notre Dame Bay, 409-410

Nova Scotia, 84, 171, 297, 317, 320

Novaya Zemlya, 325

Nunarsuit Peninsula, 59, 338

OBYGDIR (UBYGDIR), 327-328

Ofundfiord, 338

Ogmund, 466

Ogygian, 5

Okak Bay, 199, 199*n.*, 200, 201, 284

Olaf, St., 403-404

Olaf Tryggvason, King, 133-134, 136-139, 141-142, 161, 163-166, 184, 192, 204, 418-420 *passim,* 426-427, 429, 475

Olaf Tryggvason, Saga of, 136, 139, 427

Olafsson expedition, 477

Old Erik Saga, 105*n.*, 106, 138, 308, 311, 312, 340, 428, 439

Oldmixon, John, 472

Onion, Cape, 214, 234

Ontario, 317

Oraefa Jokul, 87

Orkney Islands, 4, 7, 8*n.*, 11-12, 16, 17, 34, 36

Orm of Arnarstapi, 155-157

Osborn, Lt. Sherard, 299

Ostri Bygd. *See* Eastern Settlement

Ostri Obygd (Eastern Wilderness), 328, 335

Otter, 127, 129, 460, 460*n.*, 461

Outer Islands, 8, 10-13, 16, 54, 55, 135, 390, 398, 473. *See also* Faeroe Islands; Orkney Islands; Shetland Isles

Oxney Island, 25, 29, 474

Ozur, 144

PACIFIC OCEAN, 351

Pamiok Island, 470

Papas, 11, 388

Papii, 388

Papylia, 388

Paradise River, 206

Parker Brook Bottom, 218, 219

Parsons Pond, 236, 236*n.*, 238, 276, 321, 449

Partridge Point, 432, 435

Pasquale, Pietro, 460*n.*

Payne Bay, 470; 470*n.*

Payne River, 471

Phoenicians, 351

Picts, 2-13, 16, 18, 33, 390, 403, 473

Pining and Pothorst expedition, 471-472, 477

Pistolet Bay, 212-215, 234, 450, 451

Placentia Bay, 123, 124, 127, 129

Plant life, 126-127, 129, 220. *See also* Grapevines

Pliny the Elder, 6

Plutarch, 5

Plymouth, 126

Pole Star (North Star), 63, 94, 101, 113,

171, 352, 355–356, 358, 358n., 359, 410n., 412
Polynesians, 351, 361
Pond Cove, 291n.
Porcupine, Cape, 202–203, 205
Porcupine Strands, 202, 228, 231, 422
Port au Choix Peninsula, 234, 235, 263, 321, 373, 379–380, 448
Port au Port Peninsula, 448
Portland Creek, 235, 448
Portuguese, 279, 301, 303, 455, 477
Pothorst. *See* Pining and Pothorst expedition
Pottles Cove Head, 202
Poynter, F. N. L., 127n.
Pre-Dorset people, 372–373, 399
Prins Christians Sound, 44, 326, 337
Proust, *History of Newfoundland,* 456
Ptarmigan, 64
Pytheas, 4, 5, 313, 351, 473

QUARTER COURTS, 19
Quirpon Head, 211, 214, 226, 321–322
Quirpon Island, 272, 452n., 455, 457

RACE, CAPE, 169, 171, 406–408
Rafn, 34, 36, 37
Ragnor, 468–469
Ragnor Shaggypants, 181, 185
Raven-Floki. *See* Floki Vilgerdarsson
Ravens, 81, 362–363
Ray, Cape, 379, 409
Red Indian Lake, 460, 462–463
Reed Point, 265, 266, 268
Rembert, St., 402
Resen, Hans Poulson, 364–366
Resolution Island, 415
Reykjaness Peninsula, 80–81, 89, 394
Reyniness, 181
Riseland, 326, 326n.
Riviere St. Paul, 231
Roanoke, 298
Robinson, Capt., 460
Roger of Sicily, 392
Rolf the Redsander, 32, 33, 69
Rome and the Romans, 5, 6n., 11, 295, 314, 351, 401, 402
Round Hills, 101, 410, 411
Roussel, Aage, 332
Royal Danish Library, 334, 364
Royal Ontario Museum of Archeology, 301
Royal Society, 126
Rudder Cove, 291n.
Runes and runic characters, 149, 300, 477
Russia, 8, 10, 325

SACRED BAY, 212, 214, 216, 218, 231, 234, 450, 451
Sacred Islands, 216
Saddle Island, 201
Sagas, 307–312. *See also* individual saga entries
St. Anthony-Quirpon region, 321
St. Barbe Islands, 431
St. Francis, Cape, 97, 408, 409, 430–433, 438
St. John, Cape, 430, 432, 435
St. John Island, 263, 266
St. John's, 450, 459
St. Lawrence Gulf, 126, 211, 211n., 230, 317, 377, 379, 410, 455
St. Lawrence River, 126, 210
St. Margaret Bay, 234
St. Paul's Bay, 238–241, 241n., 250–251, 256, 276, 446, 449, 476
St. Paul's Inlet, 238, 239, 246
St. Paul's River, 242, 246
Salmon, 78, 117–118, 128, 205, 218, 235, 239, 266, 381, 434
Sandy Beach Hill, 203
Sandy Lake, 276, 463
Sandy Point, 205
Sarqaq culture, 377
Savage Cover, 212
Saxo Grammaticus, 355
Scandinavia and Scandinavians, 8, 10, 18, 20, 28, 50, 76, 360, 473. *See also* Denmark and the Danes; Norsemen; Norway and Norwegians; Sweden and Swedes
Scolvuss, Johannes, 472
Scoresby Sound, 33, 326, 379
Scotland and Scots, 4–5, 8, 10–13, 15n., 16, 18, 33, 51, 55, 82, 192, 204, 207, 230, 318, 393, 471
Sea levels, 319–321
Seal Islands, 148, 151
Seals, 30–32 *passim,* 64, 110, 148, 148n., 224, 235, 239, 250, 263, 266, 376–382, 395, 461, 462
Sept Isles, 231
Sergius II, Pope, 402
Shallow Bay, 236
Shanawdithit, 459
Shetland Isles, 4, 7, 8n., 10–13, 16, 43, 87, 356
Ships, 6–7, 17, 53–54, 129–130, 225. *See also* Canoes; Coracles; Curraghs; Kayaks; Norsemen; Umiaks; Vikings
Short Saga, 83, 106, 112, 138, 308–310 *passim,* 312, 340, 419, 421, 423, 428
Siberia, 69, 372

Sicily, 392
Siglufiord, 49
Sigrid, 174–176
Sila, 285
Skagafirth, 181
Skaholt, 366, 368
Skal Island, 148*n.*
Skraeling Land, 335
Skraelings. *See* Dorsets
Skuggifiord, 466–468, 470–472
Sliettufiord, 338
Smith Sound, 325
Snae-Col, 144, 147, 151, 153
Snaebjorn Hog (Holsteinsson), 31–32, 37, 69, 474
Snaefells (ice fields), 67, 70
Snaefells Jokul, 40–42 *passim*
Snaefells Peninsula, 40, 89, 155, 330, 341
Snori Godi, 297*n.*
Snorri Thorbrandsson, 181, 182, 185–186, 189, 224, 233, 249, 253, 260, 264, 270–273, 446
Snorri Thorfinnsson, 224, 245, 271, 279, 295
Solve, 72
Solvedal, 72, 337
Sondre Stromfiord, 194
Sops Arms, 273, 277, 463
Spain, 6*n.*, 7, 230
Spalsund, 337
Spear Point, 273
Spitzbergen Island, 325, 326
Spotted Island, 101, 207–208, 228, 407, 408, 410
Spread Eagle Bay, 435
Star, homestead, 337
Starkad, 144, 147, 150
Stavanger, 26
Steenstrups Glacier, 474
Stefansson, Sigurd (Stefansson Map), 205, 245*n.*, 298, 304, 355, 361, 364–371, 470, 477
Steinsfiord, 338
Stinne, Anne, 453
Stokaness, 160, 162
Strandafiord, 338
Straumey. *See* Belle Isle
Straumfiord (Epaves Bay), 205, 210–234, 234*n.*, 247, 260, 262–265, 269–270, 272, 276, 280–284, 284*n.*, 287–294, 318, 369, 370, 444–448 *passim,* 450–457, 462, 463, 476
Stray Leaves from an Arctic Journal, by Lt. Sherard Osborn, 299
Sturla Thordarsson, 387, 388

Styr Thorgrimsson, 26, 39
Styrbjorn, 32
Suglufiord church, 338
Superior, Lake, 301, 477
Svartenhuk Peninsula, 70
Svavar. *See* Gardar
Sviney, 26, 29
Sweden; Swedes, 10, 14, 139, 401, 402
Syllenda, 338
Symbolae ad Geographiam Medii Aevi ex Monumentis Islandicas, 355

TANNER, DR. V., 451
Tataric characters, 300
Taylor, Dr. William, 266, 372, 373, 470–471
Thames River, 6
Thangbrand, 34, 164
Thingvellir, 19
Thiodhild. *See* Thorhild (Thiodhild) Jorunsdottir
Thor, 29*n.*, 74, 144–145, 218, 223, 224
Thorarin, 144, 146, 147, 151
Thorbiorg (Little Seer), 157–159
Thorbjorg Ship-Bosom, 25, 28
Thorbjorn Glora, 72
Thorbjorn the Haukadaler, 25, 28, 39, 72
Thorbjorn Vifilsson, 26, 141, 152*n.*, 154–160, 162–163, 166, 170, 176, 183, 188, 294, 475
Thorbrand of Alptafiord, 186
Thorbrand Snorrisson, 249, 262
Thord, 167*n.*
Thord Bellower, 26, 73, 181
Thord Horsehead, 181
Thorer, 35, 132, 134–135, 137, 137*n.*, 138, 141, 475
Thorey, 144–147, 151
Thorfinn, 146, 148–153 *passim*
Thorgerd, 80, 82, 83
Thorgest, 25–26, 28–30, 39, 40, 72–74, 154–155, 474
Thorgils (Icelandic chief), 34
Thorgils Leifsson, 133, 139–140, 475
Thorgisl Orrabeinsfostri, 141, 143–153, 154, 162, 170, 316, 328, 331, 375, 469, 475
Thorgunna, 133–141, 166, 475
Thorhall Gamlisson, 181, 182, 186–188, 189*n.*, 225, 226, 247, 283, 284, 286, 290, 291, 475
Thorhall the Hunter, 41, 108, 183, 193, 194, 207, 217, 223, 224, 227–230, 232, 264–265, 269, 272, 283, 334, 444–446 *passim,* 476

Thorhild (Thiodhild) Jorunsdottir, 25, 28, 34, 107, 161, 162, 167, 474
Thorkatla, 34, 34n.
Thorkel, 157–159, 170
Thorkel Gellirson (Gellisson), 391
Thorkell Farsark, 41, 72
Thorleif, 144, 146–147, 149, 150
Thorleif-Kimbe, 186
Thorny, 144
Thorodd, 32
Thorolf Butter, 81
Thorsness Thing, 26, 28–30 *passim,* 474
Thorstan the White, 153
Thorstein Eriksson, 73, 107, 137n., 161–166, 168–175, 184, 185, 192, 193, 328, 358, 420, 425, 439, 441, 474–475
Thorstein the Red, 82
Thorstein the Swarthy, 173–175
Thorunn, 181
Thorvald, 25–28
Thorvald Eriksson, 73, 107, 161, 166, 183, 189, 189n., 194, 203, 207, 225, 228–232, 260–262, 264–269, 272, 283, 290, 293, 421–423 *passim,* 439–442, 442n., 444–447, 457, 458, 463, 466, 474–476
Thorvaldsfiord, 338
Thorvard, 73, 182, 188n., 190n., 288, 292–293
Thule. *See* Iceland
Thule Eskimos, 66, 244, 246n., 263, 298, 302, 334, 375, 382–383, 399, 469
Thurid, 297n.
Tickle Cove Bay, 120, 437
Tickle Cove Peninsula, 435–436
Tickle Cove Pond, 120–128, 214, 222n., 436–438
Ticorlak Head, 265
Timber, 78, 81, 99, 110–112, 122, 128–130, 134, 135, 185, 199–200, 208, 239–240, 273, 275, 284, 296, 299, 317, 411, 424, 426, 435–437, 475
Tolafiord, 337
Torfaens, 355
Torngat Mts., 102, 198, 200, 413, 415, 416
Toronto, 301
Trade. *See* Commerce
Tradir, 25, 29, 474
Trees. *See* Timber
Trinity Bay, 99, 120–124 *passim,* 123n., 126–129, 131, 298, 320, 409, 410, 432–433, 436, 438, 447, 475
Trunmore Bight, 205
Tunnit, 148, 375–376, 383
Tyrker, 105, 118, 129, 132, 420

UMANAK FIORD, 70, 342
Umiaks, 3, 244
UNESCO Symposium on Climate Change, 314
Ungava, 266, 317, 373
Ungava Bay, 299, 369, 466–471
Uppernavik, 298, 328, 330, 378
Utibliksfiord, 338

VAIGAT, 70
Valdidida, 281, 285
Valthiof, 25, 28
Vatneyri Peninsula, 393
Vatnshorn, 474
Venison Island, 411
Vestri Bygd. *See* Western Settlement
Vestri Obygdir. *See* Western Wilderness
Vigo, 230
Vignor, 466–467
Vikings, 35, 74, 95, 136, 230, 433; raids, 10–13, 37–38, 52, 54, 349, 473; ships, 12–14 *passim,* 344, 348; Icelandic raids, 13–15, 81–82, 135, 473; Icelandic settlement, 15–21, 80, 473; characteristics and appearance, 16, 18, 19, 48, 56, 269; decline in power, 36–37, 53; weapons, 41, 74; New World value and errors, 303. *See also* Erik the Red; Norsemen
Villiers, Alan, 7
Vinland, 34, 106n., 137n., 311, 333, 335, 336, 355, 394, 477; Leif Eriksson's expedition, 111–123, 128–135, 162n., 475; probable location, 120, 123–128, 319, 327, 364, 367, 370–371, 418–438, 457; 475; resources, 128–131, 185, 424; Thorstein's expedition, 162, 166–173, 425, 439, 441, 474–475; Norse searches, 297–299; possible visits, 303–304, 476. *See also* Karlsefni, Thorfinn; Newfoundland

WALES, 4
Walrus, 30–33 *passim,* 64–66 *passim,* 74, 109, 110, 148n., 184–185, 376–377
Weapons, 52, 251, 301. *See also* Norsemen; Vikings
Weather. *See* Climate
Werlauff, 355
Western Ocean. *See* Atlantic Ocean
Western Settlement (Vestri Bygd), 109, 137n., 152n., 153, 173–174, 194n., 300, 302, 316, 328, 331–333, 335, 338–341, 475, 477
Western Wilderness (Vestri Obygdir), 58, 58n., 62, 63–66, 68, 70, 95, 101, 103,

Western Wilderness (*Cont.*)
109, 110, 148, 193–195, 328–335, 337, 340, 342, 369, 412, 475
Westman Islands, 388, 388*n*.
Westmen, 15–18, 20, 33, 35–37 *passim*, 45, 48, 52–55, 63–65 *passim*, 68, 285, 387–399
Whales and whaling, 64, 110, 128, 211, 217, 219, 223–224, 303, 316, 357–358, 376, 455–457, 477
Whitbourne, Richard, 456
White Bay, 276, 277, 283, 432, 435, 445–

448, 462–463, 463*n*., 464, 476
White Bear Island, 412–414 *passim*
Winds, 3–4, 87, 90–91, 120, 124, 172, 192, 222, 315, 405–406, 410
Wineland Voyages. Location of Helluland, Markland and Vinland, by W. A. Munn, 450
Winne (Wyn), Capt., 317
Witmar, 401
Wolves, 129
Wrath, Cape, 393

YONGE, JAMES, 126–127